FUNNY HA H

FUNNY HA HA

80 of the funniest stories
ever written
Selected and introduced by
Paul Merton

HEAD
of ZEUS

Typeset by Adrian McLaughlin

Printed and bound in Germany by
CPI Germany GmbH, Leck

Head of Zeus Ltd
5–8 Hardwick Street
London ECIR 4RG
WWW.HEADOFZEUS.COM

For Suki

And my grandfather James 'Jimmy' Power.
I'm sorry I never knew you.

CONTENTS

INTRODUCTION

My favourite subject in school was English. I thoroughly enjoyed writing essays – or 'compositions' as they were called when I was ten. I suppose they were short stories of a kind; peopled with strange characters and the odd joke borrowed from *The Goon Show*. Spike Milligan's scripts were my first introduction to surreal humour, and a fondness for the absurd, strange and bizarre has stayed with me since those very early days.

The first comic short stories that I remember *reading* were by Richmal Crompton, whose immortal creation Just William – aka William Brown – captivated me from the start. William, the scruffy-socked rebellious hero, was a boy to look up to. He and his gang of Outlaws had endless adventures in 1920s rural England, a time and place that seemed far removed from my own world. This is where I first experienced the pure and delightful escapism a good story can provide.

As I progressed through school, my appetite for composing fiction grew year by year. Sometimes I tested the teachers marking my efforts. One composition, featuring a budgie called Amos the Turk, was considered good enough for me to read out loud to the rest of the class. One of my first experiences of performing my own material to an appreciative audience was, however, marred by my English teacher's disdain for what I considered to be a legitimate comic ending: *I then ran out of the hotel, hailed a passing taxi, and was never seen again.* 'You can't say that!' my

teacher said, 'only other people can say "you were never seen again".' I knew he was wrong, and I refused to accept limitations being imposed on what I was beginning to look upon as my craft. My next composition finished with the words: *so there I was in the Amazon jungle surrounded by dozens of small threatening men, holding poison-tipped spears to my bare chest, when I suddenly hailed a passing taxi and was never seen again.* The teacher wrote, 'yes, alright!' in red ink at the bottom of the page, and I remember feeling a keen sense of victory as, for once, comic writing had vanquished the voice of authority.

The comic short stories I wrote during my school years were an invaluable preparation for my first experiences in showbusiness as a stand-up comedian. The first piece I performed in front of a paying audience was of a policeman giving evidence in court describing a hallucinogenic experience he had suffered after unknowingly ingesting LSD. It went really well. My love of the surreal came shining through on such lines as, *I saw Constable Parrish approaching me, disguised as a fortnight's holiday in Benidorm.* I found this type of character-driven monologue easier to write than bog-standard jokes – I was tapping into my school experience of creating fantasy worlds where a taxi could appear in a jungle, and a budgie could be named Amos the Turk. Clearly, my taste in comic writing leans heavily towards the fantastic.

Some authors in this collection are new to me. Before I began researching this book, I had never heard of Leonora Carrington. She was British born, but lived most of her life in Mexico City. She was a surrealist painter as well as a writer of short fiction and I have included two of her stories in this collection. They are prime examples of imaginative imagery combined with dazzling prose. In 'The Neutral Man', she describes the title character in one stunning sentence: *I saw a man of such neutral appearance that he struck me like a salmon with the head of a sphinx*

in the middle of a railway station. Naturally, such a description is right up my street, but I mustn't give the impression that all my selections are surreal in tone. There are many that are down to earth, although comic exaggeration always plays a part.

A word now on how the stories were selected. Firstly, most authors do not write short stories, and those that do seldom compose purely comic ones. There are very few P.G. Wodehouses out there, who delight in creating charming scenarios where nobody dies and the hero always emerges triumphant. Wodehouse is one of a handful of authors that I simply couldn't get enough of, so I have chosen three of his works for this compendium. A Jeeves and Wooster story was unavoidable, and 'Mulliners Buck-U-Uppo' has been a favourite of mine since I first read it forty years ago. But I didn't want to simply pick stories that would be familiar to the well-read reader, so my third Wodehouse choice, 'A Day with the Swattesmore,' is hopefully an obscure delight that only the most devoted of fans would have been previously aware of.

The other authors who merit a three-story selection are Saki, Joyce Grenfell, Giovanni Guareschi, S.J. Perelman, Oscar Wilde and Victoria Wood. They each create such captivating worlds that I found it very difficult to tear myself away – or to choose just one. Although Joyce Grenfell and Victoria Wood are not traditionally seen as short story writers, I have no problem stretching the definition of the form to include them here. After all, this is a book of my favourite comic writing, so it must include my favourite comic writers. Peter Cook and Dudley Moore, and the writers of 'Hancock's Half Hour' Ray Galton and Alan Simpson, are also included simply because they are too good to leave out. Ray and Alan's first entry, an extract from 'Hancock in the Police' featuring Tony Hancock and Kenneth Williams is, for my money, one of the funniest routines ever written. I urge you to listen to the actual recording of the

programme. Every line gets a huge laugh from the studio audience. The sheer density of the jokes is phenomenal and I know of no other sketch that packs so much laughter into just a few minutes. A comparison between the script as written and the final version performed live reveals the material that was added after the cast's initial read through. No doubt inspired by Kenneth Williams's sublime performance, the writers added extra lines. The performance pieces in this volume are ones that I grew up with, but they also stand up as literature on the page.

S.J. Perelman was somebody I first read when I was in my late teens, and back then I simply didn't get him. I knew he was highly regarded and that he had written a couple of Marx Brothers movies, but his prose struck me as highly mannered and simply not funny. For the purposes of this anthology, I revisited Perelman and found, much to my delight, that in the intervening years, his comic writing had improved dramatically. (I jest, because of course it was me who had changed.) I suppose I am no longer intimidated by his genius. Now, I can finally appreciate the musicality of his words as they flow effortlessly across the page.

Only one of the authors enjoying a three-story status was completely unknown to me before I began working on this tome. Giovanni Guareschi's tales of Don Camillo, the Italian priest with a hefty left hook, are absolutely delightful in their satirical swipes at human weakness in priestly form. One of the chief delights in concocting this collection has been discovering authors I might not have otherwise read. Looking down the contents list, I see that just over half the entries are by people I had never heard of a year ago.

I have listed the stories alphabetically by the author's surname, which has the effect of grouping the writers into coincidental clusters. A surreal enclave emerges around Spike Milligan, Sławomir Mrożek, B.J. Novak and Flann O'Brien, who follow one another completely accidentally and

yet so fittingly. The order could not have been bettered by design. At the end of the book, Oscar Wilde, P.G. Wodehouse and Victoria Wood make an excellent trio of dinner party guests who would, no doubt, have a lot to say to each other. In Oscar's case, although he has three titles, two of them are reviews, chosen because they give us his undisguised voice, rather than that of the dramatist hiding behind his characters. In these pieces, we hear Oscar as a dining companion sitting across the table from us, being wittily snobbish about the working-class poor. For a greater understanding of working-class culture, Victoria Woods's 'Girls Talking' is a brilliant capture of no-hope kids stuck at the bottom of the pile.

Although the authors vary wildly in background, they all share common aims. To distract, to divert. To create entertaining worlds. To melt away the misery of reality and replace it with a world of imagination, fun, excitement. A world where absurdity meets illogicality. Where animals talk to us and secret diaries become huge best-sellers beloved by millions. Having read so widely for this book, I have reaffirmed my view that comedy is particularly suited to the short story form. By its very nature the short story is a concise medium. Brevity is the soul of wit. Complicated plots are rarely funny – simplicity is often key.

You are at liberty, dear reader, to treat the following contents as if they were a box of chocolates. By all means, pick your favourites first or save them till last. There is no right order. It is my sincere wish that you will find much to delight you in the following pages and, unlike chocolate, I guarantee that none of the stories will rot your teeth.

Happy reading.

PAUL MERTON
London, 2019

THERE WAS ONCE

Margaret Atwood

Margaret Atwood (1939–) is an award-winning Canadian writer. She is the author of more than forty works of fiction, poetry and critical essays, and her books have been published in over thirty-five countries. Although she's now probably best known for her dystopian novel *The Handmaid's Tale*, this story displays brilliantly her wise wit and creative imagination.

— There was once a poor girl, as beautiful as she was good, who lived with her wicked stepmother in a house in the forest.

— Forest? *Forest* is passé, I mean, I've had it with all this wilderness stuff. It's not a right image of our society, today. Let's have some *urban* for a change.

— There was once a poor girl, as beautiful as she was good, who lived with her wicked stepmother in a house in the suburbs.

— That's better. But I have to seriously query this word *poor*.

— But she *was* poor!

— Poor is relative. She lived in a house, didn't she?

— Yes.

— Then socio-economically speaking, she was not poor.

— But none of the money was *hers*! The whole point of the story is that the wicked stepmother makes her wear old clothes and sleep in the fireplace—

— Aha! They had a *fireplace*! With *poor*, let me tell you, there's no fireplace. Come down to the park, come to the subway stations after dark, come down to where they sleep in cardboard boxes, and I'll show you *poor*!

— There was once a middle-class girl, as beautiful as she was good—

— Stop right there. I think we can cut the *beautiful*, don't you? Women these days have to deal with too many intimidating physical role models as it is, what with those bimbos in the ads. Can't you make her, well, more average?

— There was once a girl who was a little overweight and whose front teeth stuck out, who—

— I don't think it's nice to make fun of people's appearances. Plus, you're encouraging anorexia.

— I wasn't making fun! I was just describing—

— Skip the description. Description oppresses. But you can say what colour she was.

— What colour?

— You know. Black, white, red, brown, yellow. Those are the choices.

And I'm telling you right now, I've had enough of white. Dominant culture this, dominant culture that—

— I don't know what colour.

— Well, it would probably be *your* colour, wouldn't it?

— But this isn't *about* me! It's about this girl—

— Everything is about you.

— Sounds to me like you don't want to hear this story at all.

— Oh well, go on. You could make her ethnic. That might help.

— There was once a girl of indeterminate descent, as average-looking as she was good, who lived with her wicked—

— Another thing. *Good* and *wicked*. Don't you think you should transcend those puritanical judgemental moralistic epithets? I mean, so much of that is conditioning, isn't it?

— There was once a girl, as average-looking as she was well-adjusted, who lived with her stepmother, who was not a very open and loving person because she herself had been abused in childhood.

— Better. But I am so *tired* of negative female images! And stepmothers – they always get it in the neck! Change it to step*father*, why don't you? That would make more sense anyway, considering the bad behaviour you're about to describe. And throw in some whips and chains. We all know what those twisted, repressed, middle-aged men are like—

— *Hey, just a minute! I'm a middle-aged—*

— Stuff it, Mister Nosy Parker. Nobody asked you to stick in your oar, or whatever you want to call that thing. This is between the two of us. Go on.

— There was once a girl—

— How old was she?

— I don't know. She was young.

— This ends with a marriage, right?

— Well, not to blow the plot, but – yes.

— Then you can scratch the condescending paternalistic terminology. It's *woman*, pal. *Woman*.

— There was once—

— What's this *was*, *once*? Enough of the dead past. Tell me about *now*.

— There—

— So?

— So, what?

— So, why not *here*?

THE MAN WHO WALKED THROUGH WALLS

Marcel Aymé

Marcel Aymé (1902–1967) is considered one of the great French writers of the twentieth century. He first worked as a journalist, but following the huge success of his 1933 novel, *The Green Mare*, he increasingly concentrated on fiction. Aymé's ironic, disillusioned perception of the state of affairs in France following the German occupation produced a body of work as distinctive as it is readable. The story below is one of his most famous, and there is a statue of the main character, Dutilleul, in the Montmartre district of Paris.

I
n Montmartre, on the third floor of 75b Rue d'Orchampt, there lived an excellent gentleman called Dutilleul, who possessed the singular gift of passing through walls without any trouble at all. He wore pince-nez and a small black goatee, and was a lowly clerk in the Ministry of Records. In winter he would take the bus to work, and in fine weather he would make the journey on foot, in his bowler hat.

Dutilleul had just entered his forty-third year when he discovered his power. One evening, a brief electricity cut caught him in the hallway of his small bachelor's apartment. He groped for a while in the darkness and, when the lights came back on, found himself outside on the third-floor landing. Since his front door was locked from the inside, the incident gave him food for thought and, despite the objections of common sense, he decided to go back inside just as he had come out, by passing through the wall. This peculiar skill, apparently unrelated to any aspiration of his, rather disturbed him. So, the next day being Saturday, he took advantage of his English-style five-day week to visit a local doctor and explain his case. The doctor was soon persuaded that Dutilleul was telling the truth and, following a full examination, located the cause of the problem in a helicoid hardening of the strangulary wall in the thyroid gland. He prescribed sustained over-exertion and a twice-yearly dose of one powdered tetravalent pirette pill, a mixture of rice flour and centaur hormones.

Having taken the first pill, Dutilleul put the medicine away in a drawer and forgot about it. As for the intensive over-exertion, as a civil servant his rate of work was governed by practices that permitted no excess, nor did his leisure time, divided between reading the newspapers and tending his stamp collection, involve him in any excessive expenditure of energy either. A year later, therefore, his ability to walk through walls remained intact, but he never used it, apart from inadvertently, being uninterested in adventure and resistant towards the seductions of his imagination. He never even thought of entering his home by any route other than the front door and then only after having opened it by means of key and lock. Perhaps he would have grown old in the comfort of his habits, never tempted to put his gift to the test, had an extraordinary event not suddenly turned his life upside down. Being called to other duties, his deputy chief clerk Monsieur Mouron was replaced by a certain Monsieur Lécuyer, a man of abrupt speech who wore a nailbrush moustache. From his first day, the new deputy chief clerk looked unfavourably on Dutilleul's wearing of pince-nez with a chain and a black goatee, and made a show of treating him like an irritating, shabby old thing. But the worst of it was that he intended to introduce reforms of considerable scope into his department—just the thing to disturb his subordinate's peace. For twenty years now, Dutilleul had commenced his official letters with the following formula: "With reference to your esteemed communication of the nth of this month and, for the record, to all previous exchange of letters, I have the honour to inform you that…" A formula for which Monsieur Lécuyer intended to substitute another, much more American in tone: "In reply to your letter of n, I inform you that..." Dutilleul could not get used to these new epistolary fashions. In spite of himself, he would go back to his traditional ways, with a machine-like obstinacy that earned him the deputy clerk's growing hostility. The atmosphere inside the Ministry of Records became almost oppressive. In the morning he would come in to work full of apprehension, and in bed in the evenings, it often happened that he stayed awake thinking for a whole fifteen minutes before falling asleep.

Disgusted by this backward thinking that was threatening the success of his reforms, Monsieur Lécuyer had banished Dutilleul to a badly lit cubbyhole that led off his own office. It was reached by a low and narrow door in the corridor and still displayed in capital letters the inscription: BROOM CUPBOARD. Dutilleul resigned himself to accepting this unprecedented humiliation, but at home, reading a news item on some bloodthirsty crime, he found himself picturing Monsieur Lécuyer as the victim.

One day, the deputy clerk burst into Dutilleul's cubbyhole brandishing a letter and began to bellow:

"Rewrite this tripe! Rewrite this piece of unspeakable dross that brings shame on my department!"

Dutilleul tried to protest, but Monsieur Lécuyer raged on, calling him a procedure-addicted cockroach and, before storming out, crumpled the letter in his hand and threw it in Dutilleul's face. Dutilleul was modest but proud. Sitting alone in his cubbyhole, he grew rather hot under the collar and suddenly felt a flash of inspiration. Leaving his seat, he stepped into the wall that divided his office from that of the deputy clerk—but stepped carefully, in such a way that only his head emerged on the other side. Sitting at his desk, his hand still shaking, Monsieur Lécuyer was shifting a comma in an underling's draft that had been submitted for his approbation, when he heard a cough inside his office. Looking up, with an unspeakable fright, he found Dutilleul's head mounted on the wall like a hunting trophy. But the head was still alive. Through its pince-nez, the head flashed a look of hatred at him. Even better, the head began to speak.

"Sir," it said, "you are a ruffian, a boor and a scoundrel."

Gaping in horror, Monsieur Lécuyer was unable to tear his eyes from this apparition. At last, hefting himself out of his armchair, he leapt into the corridor and ran round to the cubbyhole. Dutilleul, pen in hand, was sitting in his usual place, in a peaceful, hard-working attitude. The deputy clerk gave him a long stare and then, after stammering a few words, went back to his office. Hardly had he sat down when the head reappeared on the wall.

"Sir, you are a ruffian, a boor and a scoundrel."

In the course of that day alone, the frightful head appeared on the wall twenty-three times and kept up the same frequency in the days that followed. Dutilleul, who had acquired a degree of skill in this game, was no longer satisfied with simply insulting the deputy clerk. He uttered obscure threats, exclaiming for example in a sepulchral voice, punctuated by truly demonic laughter:

"Werewolf! Werewolf! Hair of a beast!" (laughter) "A horror is lurking the owls have unleashed!" (laughter)

On hearing which, the poor deputy clerk grew even paler and even more choked, and his hair stood up quite straight on his head while down his back dribbled horrid cold sweat. On the first day he lost a pound in weight. In the following week, apart from melting away almost visibly, he began to eat his soup with a fork and to give passing policemen full military salutes. At the beginning of the second week, an ambulance came to collect him at home and took him to a mental asylum.

Delivered from Monsieur Lecuyer's tyranny, Dutilleul was free to return to his cherished formalities: "With reference to your esteemed communication of the nth of this month…" And yet, he was not satisfied. There was a craving inside him, a new, imperious urge—it was nothing less than the urge to walk through walls. Of course this was easily satisfied, for example at home, and there indeed he went ahead. But a man in possession of brilliant gifts cannot long be content to exercise them in pursuit of mediocre goals. Besides, walking through walls cannot constitute an end in itself. It is the beginning of an adventure, which calls for a sequel, for elaboration and, in the end, for some reward. Dutilleul quite understood this. He felt within him a need for expansion, a growing desire to fulfil and surpass himself, and a stab of longing, which was something like the call of what lay through the wall. Unfortunately, he lacked an objective. He looked for inspiration in the newspaper, particularly in the politics and sports sections, since he felt these were honourable activities, but finally realising that they offered no outlets for people who walk through walls, he made do with the most promising of the 'in brief' news items.

The first break-in that Dutilleul carried out was at a large credit institution on the right bank of the river. After walking through a dozen walls and partitions, he forced a number of safes, filled his pockets with banknotes and, before leaving, autographed the scene of his theft in red chalk with the pseudonym The Werewolf, with a very elegant flourish that was reproduced the next day in all the newspapers. By the end of the week, The Werewolf's name had become spectacularly famous. Public sympathy was unreservedly on the side of this superior burglar who was so cleverly mocking the police. He distinguished himself each succeeding night with the accomplishment of a new exploit, whether at the expense of a bank or a jeweller or some wealthy individual. There was not one among the dreamy type of Parisienne or country miss who did not passionately wish they belonged body and soul to the terrible Werewolf. After the theft of the famous Burdigala diamond and the burglary at the state pawnbroker's, which took place in the same week, the fervour of the masses reached the point of delirium. The Minister for the Interior was forced to resign, bringing the Minister for Records down with him. In spite of this, Dutilleul became one of the richest men in Paris, always came to work on time and was talked of as a strong candidate for the *palmes académiques*, for his contribution to French culture. In the mornings at the Ministry of Records, he enjoyed listening to colleagues discussing his exploits of the night before. "This

Werewolf," they said, "is amazing, a superman, a genius." Hearing such praise, Dutilleul blushed pink with embarrassment and, behind his pince-nez and chain, his eyes shone with warmth and gratitude.

One day, this sympathetic atmosphere won him over so completely that he felt he could not keep his secret for much longer. With some residual shyness, he considered his colleagues, gathered around a newspaper that announced his theft at the Bank of France, and declared in modest tones: "You know, I am The Werewolf." Hearty laughter greeted Dutilleul's confession and won him the mocking nickname "Werewolf". That evening, as they were leaving the Ministry, his colleagues made him the butt of endless jokes, and his life seemed less sweet.

A few days later, The Werewolf was caught by a night patrol in a jeweller's shop on the Rue de la Paix. He had added his signature to the counter and had begun to sing a drinking song while smashing various display cases with the help of a solid gold chalice. It would have been easy for him to sink into a wall and so escape the night patrol, but all the evidence suggests that he wanted to be arrested—probably solely in order to disconcert his colleagues, whose incredulity had mortified him. Indeed they were very surprised when the next day's papers ran a photograph of Dutilleul on their front pages. They bitterly regretted having misjudged their brilliant comrade and paid homage to him by all growing small goatees. Carried away by remorse and admiration, some were even tempted to try their hand at their friends' and acquaintances' wallets and heirloom watches.

It will doubtless be supposed that letting oneself get caught by the police simply in order to surprise a few colleagues shows a great deal of frivolity, unworthy of an exceptional man, but the obvious motivations count for very little with this kind of resolution. In giving up his liberty, Dutilleul believed he was giving in to an arrogant desire for revenge, while in truth he was simply slipping down the slope of his destiny. For a man who walks through walls, there can be no dazzling career if he hasn't at least once seen the inside of a prison.

When Dutilleul entered the premises of La Santé Prison, he felt that fate was spoiling him. The thickness of the walls was a veritable feast. Only a day after his incarceration, the astonished guards found that the prisoner had hammered a nail into his cell wall on which now hung a gold watch belonging to the warden. He either could not or would not reveal how this item had come into his possession. The watch was returned to its owner and, the following day, found once more at The Werewolf's bedside, along with the first volume of *The Three Musketeers* borrowed from the warden's personal library. The staff at La Santé grew very tense. Furthermore, the guards were complaining of kicks in their backsides of inexplicable provenance. It seemed that the walls no longer had ears but feet. The Werewolf's detention had lasted a week when, on entering his office one morning, the warden found the following letter on his desk:

Dear Warden, With reference to our interview of the seventeenth of this month and, for the record, to your general instructions dating from fifteenth of May of the previous year, I have the honour to inform you that I have just finished reading the second volume of *The Three Musketeers* and that I intend to escape tonight between eleven twenty-five and eleven thirty-five. I remain, dear Warden, yours respectfully, The Werewolf.

In spite of the close surveillance to which he was subjected that night, Dutilleul escaped at half-past eleven. Broadcast to the public the following morning, the news stirred deep admiration up and down the country. Nevertheless, after this latest feat, which had brought his popularity to even greater heights, Dutilleul hardly seemed concerned about secrecy and moved around Montmartre without any precautions. Three days after his escape, a little before noon, he was arrested on Rue Caulaincourt at the Café du Rêve, where he was enjoying a glass of white wine with lemon among friends.

Marched back to La Santé and triple-locked into a murky cell, The Werewolf escaped that very evening and went to sleep in the warden's own apartment, in the guest bedroom. The next morning at about nine o'clock, he called the maid for his breakfast and allowed himself to be plucked from his bed, without resisting, by belatedly alerted guards. Outraged, the warden set a guard at the door of Dutilleul's cell and put him on dry bread. Around noon, the prisoner went to lunch in a nearby restaurant and then, after his coffee, called the warden.

"Hello! Warden, sir, I'm a little embarrassed but a moment ago, as I was leaving, I forgot to take your wallet with me, so here I am stuck for cash in this restaurant. Would you be so good as to send someone to pay the bill?"

The warden rushed over himself, so furious that he overflowed with threats and oaths. Personally offended, Dutilleul escaped the next night, this time never to return. He took the precaution of shaving off his black goatee and replacing his lorgnette and chain with tortoise-shell spectacles. A sports cap and a loud checked suit with plus fours completed his transformation. He set himself up in a small apartment on Avenue Junot to which, since his first arrest, he had sent a selection of furnishings and his most prized objects. He was getting tired of the fuss over his fame and, since his stay in La Santé, he had become rather blasé about the pleasure of walking through walls. The thickest, the proudest of them now seemed to him mere Japanese screens, and he dreamt of plunging into the heart of some immense pyramid. While planning a journey to Egypt, he continued to live a very peaceful life, dividing his time between his stamp collection, the cinema and long strolls around Montmartre. His metamorphosis was so complete that, beardless and bespectacled, he could walk right past his best friends without being recognised by any of them. Only the painter Gen Paul, who picked up the least physiological change in the old denizens of the neighbourhood, at last managed to discover Dutilleul's true identity. One morning, finding himself face to face with Dutilleul at the corner of the Rue de l'Abreuvoir, he could not stop himself from saying, in his rough way:

"Well stone me, I see you've decked y'self out in fine new whistles to put the todd off the scent." (Which in common parlance means more or less: "I see you've disguised yourself as a gentleman in order to confuse the detectives.")

"Ah!" murmured Dutilleul. "You've recognised me!"

This troubled him and he decided to hasten his departure for Egypt. It was the afternoon of that very same day that he fell in love with a blonde beauty whom he bumped into twice in fifteen minutes on the Rue Lepic. Straight away he forgot his stamp collection and Egypt and the Pyramids. For her part, the blonde had looked at him with genuine interest. Nothing speaks more eloquently to the imagination of today's young woman than plus fours and a pair of tortoiseshell spectacles. She will scent her big break, and dream of cocktails and nights in California. Unfortunately, Dutilleul was informed by Gen Paul, the beauty was married to a man both brutal and jealous. This suspicious husband, who happened to have a wild and disreputable lifestyle, regularly deserted his wife between ten at night and four in the morning, double-locked in her room, with all her shutters also padlocked. During the day he kept her under close supervision, sometimes even following her through the streets of Montmartre.

"Always on the look-out, him. S'just a great bob who can't stand the thought of other Bengals fishing in his pond."

But Gen Paul's warning only fired up Dutilleul even more. Bumping into the young lady on Rue Tholozé the next day, he dared to follow her into a creamery and, while she was waiting to be served, he said that he loved her most respectfully, that he knew about everything—the dreadful husband, the locked door and the shutters, but that he would see her that very evening in her bedroom. The blonde blushed, her milk jug trembled in her hand and, her eyes moist with yearning, she sighed softly: "Alas! Monsieur, it is impossible."

On the evening of this glorious day, by around ten o'clock, Dutilleul was keeping watch in Rue Norvins, observing a robust outer wall behind which stood a small house, the only signs of which were the weather-vane and a chimney. A door in the wall opened and a man emerged who, after carefully locking the door behind him, walked off down the hill towards Avenue Junot. Dutilleul watched him vanish from view, far away at a bend in the road below, then counted to ten. Then he leapt forward, strode through the wall like an athlete and, after dashing through every obstacle, finally penetrated the bedroom belonging to the beautiful recluse. She welcomed him rapturously and they made love until late into the night.

The following morning, Dutilleul was annoyed to wake up with a nasty headache. It did not bother him badly and he wasn't going to let such a minor thing keep him from his next rendezvous. Still, when he happened to find a few pills scattered at the back of a drawer, he gulped down one that morning and one in the afternoon. By evening, his headache was bearable and in his elation he managed to forget it completely. The young woman was waiting for him with an impatience fanned by memories of the night before, and that night they made love until three o'clock in the morning.

When he was leaving, while walking through the partitions and walls of the house, Dutilleul had the unfamiliar feeling that they were rubbing on his hips and at his shoulders. Nevertheless, he thought it best not to pay much attention to this. Besides, it was only on entering the outer wall that he really met with considerable resistance. It felt as though he were moving through a substance that, while still fluid, was growing sticky and, at every effort he made, taking on greater density. Having managed to push himself right into the wall, he realised that he was no longer moving forward and, horrified, remembered the two pills he had taken during the day. Those pills, which he had thought were aspirin, in fact contained the powder of tetravalent pirette that the doctor had prescribed him the year before. The medication's effects combined with that of intensive over-exertion were now, suddenly, being realised.

Dutilleul was as if transfixed within the wall. He is still there today, incorporated into the stonework. Night-time revellers walking down Rue Norvins at an hour when the buzz of Paris dies down can hear a muffled voice that seems to reach them from beyond the tomb and which they take for the moans of the wind as it blows through the cross-roads of Montmartre. It is Werewolf Dutilleul, lamenting the end of his glorious career and the sorrows of a love cut short. On some winter nights, the painter Gen Paul may happen to take down his guitar and venture out into the sonorous solitude of Rue Norvins to console the poor prisoner with a song, and the notes of his guitar, rising from his swollen fingers, pierce to the heart of the wall like drops of moonlight.

BEER TRIP TO LLANDUDNO

Kevin Barry

Kevin Barry (1969–) is an Irish author, playwright and screenwriter. He is the author of the novels *Beatlebone* and *City of Bohane* and the story collections *Dark Lies the Island*, from which this story is taken, and *There Are Little Kingdoms*. His awards include the IMPAC Dublin Literary Award, the Goldsmiths Prize, the *Sunday Times* EFG Short Story Prize and the Lannan Foundation Literary Award.

It was a pig of a day, as hot as we'd had, and we were down to our T-shirts taking off from Lime Street. This was a sight to behold – we were all of us biggish lads. It was Real Ale Club's July outing, a Saturday, and we'd had word of several good houses to be found in Llandudno. I was double-jobbing for Ale Club that year. I was in charge of publications and outings both. Which was controversial.

'Rhyl... We'll pass Rhyl, won't we?'

This was Mo.

'We'd have come over to Rhyl as kids,' said Mo. 'Ferry and coach. I remember the rollercoasters.'

'Never past Prestatyn, me,' said Tom Neresford.

Tom N – so-called; there were three Toms in Ale Club – rubbed at his belly in a worried way. There was sympathy for that. We all knew stomach trouble for a bugger.

'Down on its luck'd be my guess,' said Everett Bell. 'All these old North Wales resorts have suffered dreadfully, haven't they? Whole mob's gone off to bloody Laos on packages. Bloody Cambodia, bucket and spade.'

Everett wasn't inclined to take the happy view of things. Billy Stroud, the ex-Marxist, had nothing to offer about Llandudno. Billy was involved with his timetables.

'Two minutes and fifty seconds late taking off,' he said, as the train skirted the Toxteth estates. 'This thing hits Llandudno for 1.55 p.m., I'm an exotic dancer.'

Aigburth station offered a clutch of young girls in their summer skimpies. Oiled flesh, unscarred tummies, and it wasn't yet noon. We groaned under our breaths. We'd taken on a crate of Marston's Old Familiar for the journey, 3.9 per cent to volume. Outside, the estuary sulked away in terrific heat and Birkenhead shimmered across the water. Which wasn't like Birkenhead. I opened my *AA Illustrated Guide to Britain's Coast* and read from its entry on Llandudno:

'A major resort of the North Wales coastline, it owes its well-planned streets and promenade to one Edward Mostyn, who, in the mid-19th century—'

'Victorian effort,' said John Mosely. 'Thought as much.' If there was a dad figure among us, it was Big John, with his know-it-all interruptions.

'Who, in the mid-19th century,' I repeated, 'laid out a new town on former marshland below...'

'They've built it on a marsh, have they?' said Everett Bell. 'TB,' said Billy Stroud. 'Marshy environment was considered healthful.'

'Says here there's water skiing available from Llandudno jetty.'

'That'll be me,' said Mo, and we all laughed.

Hot as pigs, but companionable, and the train was in Cheshire quick enough. We had dark feelings about Cheshire that summer. At the North West Beer Festival, in the spring, the Cheshire crew had come over a shade cocky. Just because they were chocka with half-beam pubs in pretty villages. Warrington lads were fine. We could take the Salford lot even. But the Cheshire boys were arrogant and we sniffed as we passed through their country.

'A bloody suburb, essentially,' said Everett.

'Chester's a regular shithole,' said Mo.

'But you'd have to allow Delamere Forest is a nice walk?' said Tom N.

Eyebrows raised at this, Tom N not being an obvious forest walker.

'You been lately, Tom? Nice walk?'

Tom nodded, all sombre.

'Was out for a Christmas tree, actually,' he said.

This brought gales of laughter. It is strange what comes over as hilarious when hangovers are general. We had the windows open to circulate what breeze there was. Billy Stroud had an earpiece in for the radio news. He winced:

'They're saying it'll hit 36.5,' he said. 'Celsius.'

We sighed. We sipped. We made Wales quick enough and we raised our Marston's to it. Better this than to be stuck in a garden listening to a missus. We meet as much as five nights of the week, more often six. There are those who'd call us a bunch of sots but we don't see ourselves like that. We see ourselves as hobbyists. The train pulled into Flint and Tom N went on the platform to fetch in some beef 'n' gravies from the Pie-O-Matic.

'Just the thing,' said Billy Stroud, as we sweated over our dripping punnets. 'Cold stuff causes the body too much work, you feel worse. But a nice hot pie goes down a treat. Perverse, I know. But they're on the curries in Bombay, aren't they?'

'Mumbai,' said Everett.

The train scooted along the fried coast. We made solid headway into the Marston's. Mo was down a testicle since the spring. We'd called in at the Royal the night of his operation. We'd stopped at the Ship and Mitre on the way – they'd a handsome bitter from Clitheroe on guest tap. We needed the fortification: when Real Ale Club boys parade down hospital wards, we tend to draw worried glances from the whitecoats. We are shaped like those chaps in the warning illustrations on cardiac charts. We gathered around Mo and breathed a nice fog of bitter over the lad and we joshed him but gently.

'Sounding a little high-pitched, Mo?'

'Other lad's going to be worked overtime.'

'Diseased bugger you'll want in a glass jar, Mo. One for the mantel-piece.'

Love is a strong word, but. We were family to Mo when he was up the Royal having the bollock out. We passed Flint Castle and Everett Bell piped up.

'Richard the Second,' he said.

We raised eyebrows. We were no philistines at Ale Club, Merseyside branch. Everett nodded, pleased.

'This is where he was backed into a corner,' he said. 'By Bolingbroke.'

'Boling who?'

'Bolingbroke, the usurper. Old Dick surrendered for a finish. At Flint Castle. Or that's how Shakespeare had it.'

'There's a contrary view, Ev?'

'Some say it was more likely Conwy but I'd be happy with the Bard's read,' he said, narrowing his eyes, the matter closed.

'We'll pass Conwy Castle in a bit, won't we?'

I consulted my *Illustrated AA*.

'We'll not,' I said. 'But we may well catch a glimpse across the estuary from Llandudno Junction.'

There was a holiday air at the stations. Families piled on, the dads with papers, the mams with lotion, the kids with phones. The beer ran out by Abergele and this was frowned upon: poor planning. We were reduced to buying train beer, Worthington's. Sourly we sipped and Everett came and had a go.

'Maybe if one man wasn't in charge of outings *and* publications,' he said, 'we wouldn't be running dry halfways to Llandudno.'

'True, Everett,' I said, calmly, though I could feel the colour rising to my cheeks. 'So if anyone cares to step up, I'll happily step aside. From either or.'

'We need you on publications, kid,' said John Mosely. 'You're the man for the computers.'

Publications lately was indeed largely web-based. I maintained our site on a regular basis, posting beer-related news and links. I was also looking into online initiatives to attract the younger drinker.

'I'm happy on publications, John,' I said. 'The debacle with the newsletter aside.'

Newsletter had been a disaster, I accepted that. The report on the Macclesfield outing had been printed upside down. Off-colour remarks had been made about a landlady in Everton, which should never have got past an editor's eye, as the lady in question kept very fine pumps. It hadn't been for want of editorial meetings. We'd had several, mostly down the Grapes of Wrath.

'So how's about outings then?' I said, as the train swept by Colwyn Bay. 'Where's our volunteer there? Who's for the step-up?'

Everett showed a palm to placate me.

'There's nothin' personal in this, lad,' he said.

'I know that, Ev.'

Ale Club outings were civilised events. They never got aggressive. Maudlin, yes, but never aggressive. Rhos-on-Sea; the Penrhyn sands. We knew Everett had been through a hard time. His old dad passed on and there'd been sticky business with the will. Ev would turn a mournful eye on us, at the bar of the Lion, in the snug of the Ship, and he'd say:

'My brother got the house, my sister got the money, I got the manic depression.'

Black as his moods could be, as sharp as his tongue, Everett was tender. Train came around Little Ormes Head and Billy Stroud went off on one about Ceaușescu.

'Longer it recedes in the mind's eye,' he said, 'the more like Romania seems the critical moment.'

'Apropos of, Bill?'

'Apropos my arse. As for Liverpool? Myth was piled upon myth, wasn't it? They said Labour sent out termination notices to council workers by taxi. Never bloody happened! It was an anti-red smear!'

'Thatcher's sick and old, Billy,' said John Mosely.

'Aye an' her spawn's all around us yet,' said Billy, and he broke into a broad smile, his humours mysteriously righted, his fun returned.

Looming, then, the shadow of Great Ormes Head, and beneath it a crescent swathe of bay, a beach, a prom, and terraces: here lay Llandudno.

'1.55 p.m.,' said Everett. 'On the nose.'

'Where's our exotic dancer?' teased Mo.

Billy Stroud sadly raised his T-shirt above his man boobs. He put his arms above his head and gyrated slowly his vast belly and danced his way off the train. We lost weight in tears as we tumbled onto the platform.

'How much for a private session, miss?' called Tom N.

'Tenner for twenty minutes,' said Billy. 'Fiver, I'll stay the full half-hour.'

We walked out of Llandudno station and plumb into a headbutt of heat.

'Blood and tar!' I cried. 'We'll be hittin' the lagers!'

'Wash your mouth out with soap and water,' said John Mosely.

Big John rubbed his hands together and led the way – Big John was first over the top. He reminded us there was business to hand.

'We're going to need a decision,' he said, 'about the National Beer Scoring System.'

Here was kerfuffle. The NBSS, by long tradition, ranked a beer from nought to five. Nought was take-backable, a crime against the name of ale. One was barely drinkable, two so-so, three an eyebrow raised in mild appreciation. A four was an ale on top form, a good beer in proud nick. A five was angel's tears but a seasoned drinker would rarely dish out a five, would over the course of a lifetime's quaffing call no more than a handful of fives. Such was the NBSS, as was. However, Real Ale Club, Merseyside branch, had for some time felt that the system lacked subtlety. And one famous night, down Rigby's, we came up with our own system – we marked from nought to ten. Finer gradations of purity were thus allowed for. The nuances of a beer were more properly considered. A certain hoppy tang, redolent of summer hedgerows, might elevate a brew from a seven to an eight. The mellow back-note born of a good oak casking might lift an ale again, and to the rare peaks of the nines. Billy Stroud had argued for decimal breakdown, for 7.5s and 8.5s – Billy would – but we had to draw a line somewhere. The national organisation responded badly. They sent stiff word down the email but we continued to forward our beer reports with markings on a nought to ten scale. There was talk now of us losing the charter. These were heady days.

'Stuff them is my view,' said Everett Bell.

'We'd lose a lot if we lost the charter,' said Mo. 'Think about the festival invites. Think about the history of the branch.'

'Think about the bloody future!' cried Tom N. 'We haven't come up with a new system to be awkward. We've done it for the ale drinkers. We've done it for the ale makers!'

I felt a lump in my throat and I daresay I wasn't alone.

'Ours is the better system,' said Everett. 'This much we know.'

'You're right,' said John Mosely, and this was the clincher, Big John's call. 'I say we score nought to ten.'

'If you lot are in, that's good enough for me,' I said.

Six stout men linked arms on a hot Llandudno pavement. We rounded the turn onto the prom and our first port of call: the Heron Inn.

Which turned out to be an anti-climax. A nice house, lately refurbished, but mostly keg rubbish on the taps. The Heron did, however, do a Phoenix Tram Driver on cask, 3.8 per cent, and we sat with six of same.

'I've had better Tram Drivers,' opened Mo.

'I've had worse,' countered Tom N.

'She has a nice delivery but I'd worry about her legs,' said Billy Stroud, shrewdly.

'You wouldn't be having more than a couple,' said John Mosely.

'*Not* a skinful beer,' I concurred.

All eyes turned to Everett Bell. He held a hand aloft, wavered it.

'A five would be generous, a six insane,' he said.

'Give her the five,' said Big John, dismissively.

I made the note. This was as smoothly as a beer was ever scored. There had been some world-historical ructions in our day. There was the time Billy Stroud and Mo hadn't talked for a month over an eight handed out to a Belhaven Bombardier.

Alewards we followed our noses. We walked by the throng of the beach – the shrieks of the sun-crazed kids made our stomachs loop. We made towards the Prom View Hotel. We'd had word of a new landlord there an ale-fancier. It was dogs-dying-in-parked-cars weather. The Prom View's ample lounge was a blessed reprieve. We had the place to ourselves, the rest of Llandudno apparently being content with summer, sea and life. John Mosely nodded towards a smashing row of hand pumps for the casks. Low whistles sounded. The landlord, hot-faced and jovial, came through from the hotel's reception.

'Another tactic,' he said, 'would be stay home and have a nice sauna.'

'Same difference,' sighed John Mosely.

'Could be looking at 37.2 now,' said the landlord, taking a flop of sweat from his brow.

Billy Stroud sensed a kindred spirit:

'Gone up again, has it?'

'And up,' said the landlord. 'My money's on a 38 before we're out.'

'Record won't go,' said Billy.

'Nobody's said record,' said the landlord. 'We're not going to see a 38.5, that's for sure.'

'Brogdale in Kent,' said Billy. 'August 10th, 2003.'

'2.05 p.m.,' said the landlord. 'I wasn't five miles distant that same day.'

Billy was beaten.

'Loading a van for a divorced sister,' said the landlord, ramming home his advantage. 'Lugging sofas in the piggin' heat. And wardrobes!'

We bowed our heads to the man.

'What'll I fetch you, gents?'

A round of Cornish Lightning was requested.

'Taking the sun?' enquired the landlord.

'Taking the ale.'

'After me own heart,' he said. "Course 'round here, it's lagers they're after mostly. Bloody Welsh.'

'Can't beat sense into them,' said John Mosely.

'If I could, I would,' said the landlord, and he danced as a young featherweight might, he raised his clammy dukes. Then he skipped and turned.

'I'll pop along on my errands, boys,' he said. 'There are rows to hoe and socks for the wash. You'd go through pair after pair this weather.'

He pinched his nostrils closed: what-a-pong.

'Soon as you're ready for more, ring that bell and my good wife will oblige. So adieu, adieu...'

He skipped away. We raised eyes. The shade of the lounge was pleasant, the Cornish Lightning in decent nick.

'Call it a six?' said Tom N.

Nervelessly we agreed. Talk was limited. We swallowed hungrily, quickly, and peered again towards the pumps.

'The Lancaster Bomber?'

'The Whitstable Mule?'

'How's about that Mangan's Organic?'

'I'd say the Lancaster, all told.'

'Ring the bell, Everett.'

He did so, and a lively blonde, familiar with her forties but nicely preserved, bounced through from reception. Our eyes went shyly down. She took a glass to shine as she waited our call. Type of lass who needs her hands occupied.

'Do you for, gents?'

Irish, her accent.

'Round of the Lancaster, wasn't it?' said Everett.

She squinted towards our table, counted the heads.

'Times six,' confirmed Everett.

The landlady squinted harder. She dropped the glass. It smashed to pieces on the floor.

'Maurice?' she said.

It was Mo that froze, stared, softened.

'B-B-Barbara?' he said.

We watched as he rose and crossed to the bar. A man in a dream was Mo. We held our breaths as Mo and Barbara took each other's hands over the counter. They were wordless for some moments, and then felt ten eyes on them, for they giggled, and Barbara set blushing to the Lancasters. She must have spilled half again down the slops gully as she poured. I joined Everett to carry the ales to our table. Mo and Barbara went into a huddle down the far end of the counter. They were rapt.

Real Ale Club would not have marked Mo for a romancer.

'The quiet ones you watch,' said Tom N. 'Maur*ice*?'

'Mo? With a piece?' whispered Everett Bell.

'Could be they're old family friends,' tried innocent Billy. 'Or relations?'

Barbara was now slowly stroking Mo's wrist.

'Four buggerin' fishwives I'm sat with,' said John Mosely. 'What are we to make of these Lancasters?'

We talked ale but were distracted. Our glances cut down the length of the bar. Mo and Barbara talked lowly, quickly, excitedly down there. She was moved by Mo, we could see that plain enough. Again and again she ran her fingers through her hair. Mo was gazing at her, all dreamy, and suddenly he'd got a thumb hooked in the belt-loop of his denims – Mr Suave. He didn't so much as touch his ale.

Next, of course, the jaunty landlord arrived back on the scene.

'Oh, Alvie!' she cried. 'You'll never guess!'

'Oh?' said the landlord, all the jauntiness instantly gone from him.

'This is *Maurice*!'

'Maurice?' he said. 'You're joking…'

It was polite handshakes then, and feigned interest in Mo on the landlord's part, and a wee fat hand he slipped around the small of his wife's back.

'We'll be suppin' up,' said John Mosely, sternly.

Mo had a last, whispered word with Barbara but her smile was fixed now and the landlord remained in close attendance. As we left, Mo looked back and raised his voice a note too loud. Desperate, he was.

'Barbara?'

We dragged him along. We'd had word of notable pork scratchings up the Mangy Otter.

'Do tell, Maur*ice*,' said Tom N.

'Leave him be,' said John Mosely.

'An ex, that's all,' said Mo.

And Llandudno was infernal. Families raged in the heat. All of the kids wept. The Otter was busyish when we sludged in. We settled on a round of St Austell Tributes from a meagre selection. Word had not been wrong on the quality of the scratchings. And the St Austell turned out to be in top form.

'I'd be thinking in terms of a seven,' said Everett Bell.

'Or a shade past that?' said John Mosely.

'You could be right on higher than sevens,' said Billy Stroud. 'But surely we're not calling it an eight?'

'Here we go,' I said.

'Now this,' said Billy Stroud, 'is where your 7.5s would come in.'

'We've heard this song, Billy,' said John Mosely.

'He may not be wrong, John,' said Everett.

'Give him a 7.5,' said John Mosely, 'and he'll be wanting his 6.3s, his 8.6s. There'd be no bloody end to it!'

'Tell you what,' said Mo. 'How about I catch up with you all a bit later? Where's next on the list?'

We stared at the carpet. It had diamonds on and crisps ground into it.

'Next up is the Crippled Ox on Burton Square,' I read from my printout. 'Then it's Henderson's on Old Parade.'

'See you at one or the other,' said Mo.

He threw back the dregs of his St Austell and was gone.

We decided on another at the Otter. There was a Whitstable Silver Star, 6.2 per cent to volume, a regular stingo to settle our nerves.

'What's the best you've ever had?' asked Tom N.

It's a conversation that comes up again and again but it was a life-saver just then: it took our minds off Mo.

'Put a gun to my head,' said Big John, 'and I don't think I could look past the draught Bass I had with me dad in Peter Kavanagh's. Sixteen years of age, Friday teatime, first wage slip in my arse pocket.'

'But was it the beer or the occasion, John?'

'How can you separate the two?' he said, and we all sighed.

'For depth? Legs? Back-note?' said Everett Bell. 'I'd do well to ever best the Swain's Anthem I downed a November Tuesday in Stockton-on-Tees: 19 and 87. 4.2 per cent to volume. I was still in haulage at that time.'

'I've had an Anthem,' said Billy Stroud of this famously hard-to-find brew, 'and I'd have to say I found it an unexceptional ale.'

Everett made a face.

'So what'd be your all-time, Billy?'

The ex-Marxist knitted his fingers atop the happy mound of his belly.

'Ridiculous question,' he said. 'There is so much wonderful ale on this island. How is a sane man to separate a Pelham High Anglican from a Warburton's Saxon Fiend? And we haven't even mentioned the great Belgian tradition. Your Duvel's hardly a dishwater. Then there's the Czechs, the Poles, the Germans...'

'Gassy pop!' cried Big John, no fan of a German brew, of a German anything.

'Nonsense,' said Billy. 'A Paulaner Weissbier is a sensational sup on its day.'

'Where'd you think Mo's headed?' Tom N cut in.

Everett groaned:

'He'll be away down the Prom View, won't he? Big ape.'

'Mo a ladykiller?' said Tom. 'There's one for breaking news.'

'No harm if it meant he smartened himself up a bit,' said John.

'He has let himself go,' said Billy. 'Since the testicle.'

'You'd plant spuds in those ears,' I said.

The Whitstables had us in fighting form. We were away up the Crippled Ox. We found there a Miner's Slattern on cask. TV news showed sardine beaches and motorway chaos. There was an internet machine on the wall, a pound for ten minutes, and Billy Stroud went to consult the meteorological satellites. The Slattern set me pensive

Strange, I thought, how I myself had wound up a Real Ale Club stalwart. 1995, October, I'd found myself in motorway services outside Ormskirk having a screaming barny with the missus. We were moving back to her folks' place in Northern Ireland. From dratted Leicester. We were heading for the ferry at Stranraer. At services, missus told me I was an idle lardarse who had made her life hell and she never wanted to see me again. We'd only stopped off to fill the tyres. She gets in, slams the door, puts her foot down. Give her ten minutes, I thought, she'll calm down and turn back for me. Two hours later, I'm sat in an empty Chinese in services, weeping, and eating Szechuan beef. I call a taxi. Taxi comes. I says where are we, exactly? Bloke looks at me. He says Ormskirk direction. I says what's the nearest city of any size? Drop you in Liverpool for twenty quid, he says. He leaves me off downtown and I look for a pub. Spot the Ship and Mitre and in I go. I find a stunning row of pumps. I call a Beaver Mild out of Devon.

'I wouldn't,' says a bloke with a beard down the bar.

'Oh?'

'Try a Marston's Old Familiar,' he says, and it turns out he's Billy Stroud.

The same Billy turned from the internet machine at the Ox in Llandudno.

'37.9,' he said. 'Bristol Airport, a shade after three. Flights delayed, tarmac melting.'

'Pig heat,' said Tom N.

'We won't suffer much longer,' said Billy. 'There's a change due.'

'Might get a night's sleep,' said Everett.

The hot nights were certainly a torment. Lying there with a sheet stuck to your belly. Thoughts coming loose, beer fumes rising, a manky arse. The city beyond the flat throbbing with summer. Usually I'd get up and have a cup of tea, watch some telly. Astrophysics on Beeb Two at four in the morning, news from the galaxies, and light already in the eastern sky. I'd dial the number in Northern Ireland and then hang up before they could answer.

Mo arrived into the Ox like the ghost of Banquo. There were terrible scratch marks down his left cheek.

'A Slattern will set you right, kid,' said John Mosely, discreetly, and he manoeuvred his big bones barwards.

Poor Mo was wordless as he stared into the ale that was put before him. Billy Stroud sneaked a time-out signal to Big John.

'We'd nearly give Henderson's a miss,' agreed John.

'As well get back to known terrain,' said Everett.

We climbed the hot streets towards the station. We stocked up with some Cumberland Pedigrees, 3.4 per cent to volume, always an easeful drop. The train was busy with daytrippers heading back. We sipped quietly. Mo looked half dead as he slumped there but now and then he'd come up for a mouthful of his Pedigree.

'How's it tasting, kiddo?' chanced Everett.

'Like a ten,' said Mo, and we all laughed.

The flicker of his old humour reassured us. The sun descended on Colwyn Bay and there was young life everywhere. I'd only spoken to her once since Ormskirk. We had details to finalise, and she was happy to let it slip about her new bloke. Some twat called Stan.

'He's emotionally spectacular,' she said.

'I'm sorry to hear it, love,' I said. 'Given you've been through the wringer with me.'

'I mean in a good way!' she barked. 'I mean in a *calm* way!'

We'd a bit of fun coming up the Dee Estuary with the Welsh place names.

'Fy… feen… no. Fiiiif… non… fyff… non… growy?'

This was Tom N.

'Foy. Nonn. Grewey?'

This was Everett's approximation.

'Ffynnongroew,' said Billy Stroud, lilting it perfectly. 'Simple. And this one coming up? Llannerch-y-mor.'

Pedigree came down my nose I laughed that hard.

'Young girl, beautiful,' said Mo. 'Turn around and she's forty bloody three.'

'Leave it, Mo,' said Big John.

But he could not.

'She's come over early in '86. She's living up top of the Central line, Theydon Bois. She's working in a pub there, live-in, and ringing me from a phone box. In Galway I'm in a phone box too – we have to arrange the times, eight o'clock on Tuesday, ten o'clock on Friday. It's physical fucking pain she's not in town any more. I'll follow in the summer is the plan and I get there, Victoria Coach Station, six in the morning, eighty quid in my pocket. And she's waiting for me there. We have an absolute dream of a month. We're lying in the park. There's a song out and we make it our song. "Oh to be in England, in the summertime, with my love, close to the edge".'

'Art of Noise,' said Billy Stroud.

'Shut up, Billy!'

'Of course the next thing the summer's over and I've a start with BT up here and she's to follow on, October is the plan. We're ringing from phone boxes again, Tuesdays and Fridays but the second Friday the phone doesn't ring. Next time I see her she's forty bloody three.'

Flint station we passed through, and then Connah's Quay.

'Built up, this,' said Tom N. 'There's an Aldi, look? And that's a new school, is it?'

'Which means you want to be keeping a good two hundred yards back,' said Big John.

We were horrified. Through a miscarriage of justice, plain as, Tom N had earlier in the year been placed on a sex register. Oh the world is mad! Tom N is a placid, placid man. We were all six of us quiet as the grave on the evening train then. It grew and built, it was horrible, the silence. It was Everett at last that broke it; we were coming in for Helsby. Fair dues to Everett.

'Not like you, John,' he said.

Big John nodded.

'I don't know where that came from, Tom,' he said. 'A bloody stupid thing to say.'

Tom N raised a palm in peace but there was no disguising the hurt that had gone in. I pulled away into myself. The turns the world takes – Tom dragged through the courts, Everett half mad, Mo all scratched up and one-balled, Big John jobless for eighteen months. Billy Stroud was content, I suppose, in Billy's own way. And there was me, shipwrecked in Liverpool. Funny, for a while, to see 'Penny Lane' flagged up on the buses, but it wears off.

And then it was before us in a haze. Terrace rows we passed, out Speke way, with cookouts on the patios. Tiny pockets of glassy laughter we heard through the open windows of the carriage. Families and what-have-you. We had the black hole of the night before us – it wanted filling. My grimmest duty as publications officer was the obits page of the newsletter. Too many had passed on at forty-four, at forty-six.

'I'm off outings,' I announced. 'And I'm off bloody publications as well.'

'You did volunteer on both counts,' reminded Big John.

'It would leave us in an unfortunate position,' said Tom N.

'For my money, it's been a very pleasant outing,' said Billy Stroud.

'We've supped some quality ale,' concurred Big John.

'We've had some cracking weather,' said Tom N.

'Llandudno is quite nice, really,' said Mo.

Around his scratch marks an angry bruising had seeped. We all looked at him with tremendous fondness.

''Tis nice,' said Everett Bell. 'If you don't run into a she-wolf.'

'If you haven't gone ten rounds with Edward bloody Scissorhands,' said John Mosely.

We came along the shabby grandeurs of the city. The look on Mo's face then couldn't be read as anything but happiness.

'Mau*rice*,' teased Big John, 'is thinking of the rather interesting day he's had.'

Mo shook his head.

'Thinking of days I had years back,' he said.

It has this effect, Liverpool. You're not back in the place five minutes and you go sentimental as a famine ship. We piled off at Lime Street. There we go: six big blokes in the evening sun.

'There's the Lion Tavern?' suggested Tom N.

'There's always the Lion,' I agreed.

'They've a couple of Manx ales guesting at Rigby's,' said Everett Bell.

'Let's hope they're an improvement on previous Manx efforts,' said Billy Stroud.

'There's the Grapes?' tried Big John.

'There's always the Grapes,' I agreed.

And alewards we went about the familiar streets. The town was in carnival: Tropic of Lancashire in a July swelter. It would not last. There was rain due in off the Irish Sea, and not for the first time.

SOME OF US HAD BEEN THREATENING OUR FRIEND COLBY

Donald Barthelme

Donald Barthelme (1931–1989) was once asked by the *Paris Review* for his biography. His response was, 'I don't think it would sustain a person's attention for a moment.' He was born in Philadelphia and raised in Houston, Texas. There he endured a normal childhood, attended the University of Houston, studied philosophy, and worked for a local newspaper. Then he was drafted, served in Korea, and returned to Houston, which he later left for New York City. There he did editorial work, especially for *Location*, and his odd short fictions made themselves known. Soon he became the most startling of the *New Yorker*'s regular contributors.

S ome of us had been threatening our friend Colby for a long time, because of the way he had been behaving. And now he'd gone too far, so we decided to hang him. Colby argued that just because he had gone too far (he did not deny that he had gone too far) did not mean that he should be subjected to hanging. Going too far, he said, was something everybody did sometimes. We didn't pay much attention to this argument. We asked him what sort of music he would like played at the hanging. He said he'd think about it but it would take him a while to decide. I pointed out that we'd have to know soon, because Howard, who is a conductor, would have to hire and rehearse the musicians and he couldn't begin until he knew what the music was going to be.

Colby said he'd always been fond of Ives' Fourth Symphony. Howard said that this was a "delaying tactic" and that everybody knew that the Ives was almost impossible to perform and would involve weeks of rehearsal, and that the size of the orchestra and chorus would put us way over the music budget. "Be reasonable," he said to Colby. Colby said he'd try to think of something a little less exacting.

Hugh was worried about the wording of the invitations. What if one of them fell into the hands of the authorities? Hanging Colby was doubtless against the law, and if the authorities learned in advance what the plan was they would very likely come in and try to mess everything up. I said that although hanging Colby was almost certainly against the law, we had a perfect *moral* right to do so because he was *our* friend, *belonged* to us in various important senses, and he had after all gone too far. We agreed that the invitations would be worded in such a way that the person invited could not know for sure what he was being invited to. We decided to refer to the event as "An Event Involving Mr. Colby Williams."

A handsome script was selected from a catalogue and we picked a cream-colored paper. Magnus said he'd see to having the invitations printed, and wondered whether we should serve drinks. Colby said he thought drinks would be nice but was worried about the expense. We told him kindly that the expense didn't matter, that we were after all his dear friends and if a group of his dear friends couldn't get together and do the thing with a little bit of *éclat*, why, what was the world coming to? Colby asked if he would be able to have drinks, too, before the event. We said, "Certainly."

The next item of business was the gibbet. None of us knew too much about gibbet design, but Tomás, who is an architect, said he'd look it up in old books and draw the plans. The important thing, as far as he recollected, was that the trapdoor function perfectly. He said that just roughly, counting labor and materials, it shouldn't run us more than four hundred dollars. "Good God!" Howard said. He said what was Tomás figuring on, rosewood? No, just a good grade of pine, Tomás said. Victor asked if unpainted pine wouldn't look kind of "raw," and

Tomás replied that he thought it could be stained a dark walnut without too much trouble.

I said that although I thought the whole thing ought to be done really well, and all, I also thought four hundred dollars for a gibbet, on top of the expense for the drinks, invitations, musicians, and everything, was a bit steep, and why didn't we just use a tree—a nice-looking oak, or something? I pointed out that since it was going to be a June hanging the trees would be in glorious leaf and that not only would a tree add a kind of "natural" feeling but it was also strictly traditional, especially in the West. Tomás, who had been sketching gibbets on the backs of envelopes, reminded us that an outdoor hanging always had to contend with the threat of rain. Victor said he liked the idea of doing it outdoors, possibly on the bank of a river, but noted that we would have to hold it some distance from the city, which presented the problem of getting the guests, musicians, etc., to the site and then back to town.

At this point everybody looked at Harry, who runs a car-and-truck-rental business. Harry said he thought he could round up enough limousines to take care of that end but that the drivers would have to be paid. The drivers, he pointed out, wouldn't be friends of Colby's and couldn't be expected to donate their services, any more than the bartender or the musicians. He said that he had about ten limousines, which he used mostly for funerals, and that he could probably obtain another dozen by calling around to friends of his in the trade. He said also that if we did it outside, in the open air, we'd better figure on a tent or awning of some kind to cover at least the principals and the orchestra, because if the hanging was being rained on he thought it would look kind of dismal. As between gibbet and tree, he said, he had no particular preferences, and he really thought that the choice ought to be left up to Colby, since it was his hanging. Colby said that everybody went too far, sometimes, and weren't we being a little draconian. Howard said rather sharply that all that had already been discussed, and which did he want, gibbet or tree? Colby asked if he could have a firing squad. No, Howard said, he could not. Howard said a firing squad would just be an ego trip for Colby, the blindfold and last-cigarette bit, and that Colby was in enough hot water already without trying to "upstage" everyone with unnecessary theatrics. Colby said he was sorry, he hadn't meant it that way, he'd take the tree. Tomás crumpled up the gibbet sketches he'd been making, in disgust.

Then the question of the hangman came up. Paul said did we really need a hangman? Because if we used a tree, the noose could be adjusted to the appropriate level and Colby could just jump off something—a chair or stool or something. Besides, Paul said, he very much doubted if there were any freelance hangmen wandering around the country, now that capital punishment has been done away with absolutely, temporarily, and that we'd probably have to fly one in from England or Spain or one of the South American countries, and even if we did that how could we know in advance that the man was a professional, a real hangman, and not just some money-hungry amateur who might bungle the job and shame us all, in front of everybody? We all agreed then that Colby should just jump off something and that a chair was not what he should jump off of, because that would look, we felt, extremely tacky—some old kitchen chair sitting out there under our beautiful tree. Tomás, who is quite modern in outlook and not afraid of innovation, proposed that Colby be standing on a large round rubber ball ten feet in diameter. This, he said, would afford a sufficient "drop" and would also roll out of the way if Colby suddenly changed his mind after jumping off. He reminded us that by not using a regular hangman we were placing an awful lot of the responsibility for the success of the affair on Colby himself, and that although he was sure Colby would perform creditably and not disgrace his friends at the last minute, still, men have been known to get a little irresolute at times like that, and the ten-foot-round rubber ball, which could probably be fabricated rather cheaply, would insure a "bang-up" production right down to the wire.

At the mention of "wire," Hank, who had been silent all this time, suddenly spoke up and said he wondered if it wouldn't be better if we used wire instead of rope—more efficient and in the end kinder to Colby, he suggested. Colby began looking a little green, and I didn't blame him, because there is something extremely distasteful in thinking about being hanged with wire instead of rope—it gives you sort of a revulsion, when you think about it. I thought it was really quite unpleasant of Hank to be sitting there talking about wire, just when we had solved the problem of what Colby was going to jump off of so neatly, with Tomás's idea about the rubber ball, so I hastily said that wire was out of the question, because it would injure the tree—cut into the branch it was tied to when Colby's full weight hit it—and that in these days of increased respect for environment, we didn't want that, did we? Colby gave me a grateful look, and the meeting broke up.

Everything went off very smoothly on the day of the event (the music Colby finally picked was standard stuff, Elgar, and it was played very well by Howard and his boys). It didn't rain, the event was well attended, and we didn't run out of Scotch, or anything. The ten-foot rubber ball had been painted a deep green and blended in well with the bucolic setting. The two things I remember best about the whole episode are the grateful look Colby gave me when I said what I said about the wire, and the fact that nobody has ever gone too far again.

"TAKE THE WITNESS!"

Robert Benchley

Robert Benchley (1889–1945) was an American humourist, critic and actor who brought his distinctive style of humour to his numerous essays and articles written for *Vanity Fair* and *The New Yorker*. He once said of his career, 'It took me fifteen years to discover that I had no talent for writing, but I couldn't give it up because by that time I was too famous.'

Newspaper accounts of trial cross-examinations always bring out the cleverest in me. They induce day dreams in which I am the witness on the stand, and if you don't know some of my imaginary comebacks to an imaginary cross-examiner (Doe vs. Benchley: 482U.S.-367-398), you have missed some of the most stimulating reading in the history of American jurisprudence.

These little reveries usually take place shortly after I have read the transcript of a trial, while I am on a long taxi ride or seated at a desk with plenty of other work to do. I like them best when I have work to do, as they deplete me mentally so that I am forced to go and lie down after a particularly sharp verbal rally. The knowledge that I have completely floored my adversary, and the imaginary congratulations of my friends (also imaginary), seem more worth while than any amount of fiddling work done.

During these cross-questionings I am always very calm. Calm in a nice way, that is—never cocky. However frantic my inquisitor may wax (and you should see his face at times—it's purple!), I just sit there, burning him up with each answer, winning the admiration of the courtroom, and, at times, even a smile from the judge himself. At the end of my examination, the judge is crazy about me.

Just what the trial is about, I never get quite clear in my mind. Sometimes the subject changes in the middle of the questioning, to allow for the insertion of an especially good crack on my part. I don't think that I am ever actually the defendant, although I don't know why I should feel that I am immune from trial by a jury of my peers—if such exist.

I am usually testifying in behalf of a friend, or perhaps as just an impersonal witness for someone whom I do not know, who, naturally, later becomes my friend for life. It is Justice that I am after—Justice and a few well-spotted laughs.

Let us whip right into the middle of my cross-examination, as I naturally wouldn't want to pull my stuff until I had been insulted by the lawyer, and you can't really get insulted simply by having your name and address asked. I am absolutely fair about these things. If the lawyer will treat me right, I'll treat him right. He has got to start it. For a decent cross-examiner, there is no more tractable witness in the world than I am.

Advancing toward me, with a sneer on his face, he points a finger at me. (I have sometimes thought of pointing my finger back at him, but have discarded that as being too fresh. I don't have to resort to clowning.)

Q—You think you're pretty funny, don't you? (*I have evidently just made some mildly humorous comeback, nothing smart-aleck, but good enough to make him look silly.*)

A—I have never given the matter much thought.

Q—Oh, you haven't given the matter much thought, eh? Well, you seem to be treating this examination as if it were a minstrel show.

A (*very quietly and nicely*)—I have merely been taking my cue from your questions. (*You will notice that all this presupposes quite a barrage of silly questions on his part, and pat answers on mine, omitted here because I haven't thought them up. At any rate, it is evident that I have already got him on the run before this reverie begins.*)

Q—Perhaps you would rather that I conducted this inquiry in baby talk?

A—If it will make it any easier for you. (*Pandemonium, which the Court feels that it has to quell, although enjoying it obviously as much as the spectators.*)

Q (*furious*)—I see. Well, here is a question that I think will be simple enough to elicit an honest answer: Just how did you happen to know that it was eleven-fifteen when you saw the defendant?

A—Because I looked at my watch.

Q—And just why did you look at your watch at this particular time?

A—To see what time it was.

Q—Are you accustomed to looking at your watch often?

A—That is one of the uses to which I often put my watch.

Q—I see. Now, it couldn't, by any chance, have been ten-fifteen instead of eleven-fifteen when you looked at your watch this time, could it?

A—Yes, sir. It could.

Q—Oh, it could have been ten-fifteen?

A—Yes, sir—if I had been in Chicago. (*Not very good, really. I'll work up something better. I move to have that answer stricken from the record.*)

When I feel myself lowering my standards by answering like that, I usually give myself a rest, and, unless something else awfully good pops into my head, I adjourn the court until next day. I can always convene it again when I hit my stride.

If possible, however, I like to drag it out until I have really given my antagonist a big final wallop which practically curls him up on the floor (I may think of one before this goes to press), and, wiping his forehead, he mutters, "Take the witness!"

As I step down from the stand, fresh as a daisy, there is a round of applause which the Court makes no attempt to silence. In fact, I have known certain judges to wink pleasantly at me as I take my seat. Judges are only human, after all.

My only fear is that, if I ever really am called upon to testify in court, I won't be asked the right questions. That *would* be a pretty kettle of fish!

ACTION WILL BE TAKEN

Heinrich Böll

Heinrich Böll (1917–1985) was one of Germany's foremost writers of the twentieth century, capturing the changing psychology of the nation through his ironic take on the travails of daily life. Conscripted into the German army, he fought on the Russian and other fronts. His wartime experiences – being wounded, deserting, becoming a prisoner of war – were central to his writing as he remembered 'the frightful fate of being a soldier and having to wish that the war might be lost.' He was awarded the Georg Büchner Prize in 1967 and the Nobel Prize for Literature in 1972.

Probably one of the strangest interludes in my life was the time I spent as an employee in Alfred Wunsiedel's factory. By nature, I am inclined more to pensiveness and inactivity than to work, but now and again prolonged financial difficulties compel me – for pensiveness is no more profitable than inactivity – to take on a so-called job. Finding myself once again at a low ebb of this kind, I put myself in the hands of the employment office and was sent with seven other fellow-sufferers to Wunsiedel's factory, where we were to undergo an aptitude test.

The exterior of the factory was enough to arouse my suspicions: the factory was built entirely of glass brick, and my aversion to well-lit buildings and well-lit rooms is as strong as my aversion to work. I became even more suspicious when we were immediately served breakfast in the well-lit, cheerful coffee shop: pretty waitresses brought us eggs, coffee and toast, orange juice was served in tastefully designed jugs, goldfish pressed their bored faces against the sides of pale-green aquariums. The waitresses were so cheerful that they appeared to be bursting with good cheer. Only a strong effort of will – so it seemed to me – restrained them from singing away all day long. They were as crammed with unsung songs as chickens with unlaid eggs.

Right away I realized something that my fellow-sufferers evidently failed to realize: that this breakfast was already part of the test; so I chewed away reverently, with the full appreciation of a person who knows he is supplying his body with valuable elements. I did something which normally no power on earth can make me do: I drank orange juice on an empty stomach, left the coffee and egg untouched, as well as most of the toast, got up, and paced up and down in the coffee shop, pregnant with action.

As a result I was the first to be ushered into the room where the questionnaires were spread out on attractive tables. The walls were done in a shade of green that would have summoned the word "delightful" to the lips of interior decoration enthusiasts. The room appeared to be empty, and yet I was so sure of being observed that I behaved as someone pregnant with action behaves when he believes himself unobserved: I ripped my pen impatiently from my pocket, unscrewed the top, sat down at the nearest table and pulled the questionnaire toward me, the way irritable customers snatch at the bill in a restaurant.

Question No. 1: Do you consider it right for a human being to possess only two arms, two legs, eyes, and ears?

Here for the first time I reaped the harvest of my pensive nature and wrote without hesitation: "Even four arms, legs and ears would not be adequate for my driving energy. Human beings are very poorly equipped."

Question No. 2: How many telephones can you handle at one time?

Here again the answer was as easy as simple arithmetic: "When there are only seven telephones," I wrote, "I get impatient; there have to be nine before I feel I am working to capacity."

Question No. 3: How do you spend your free time?

My answer: "I no longer acknowledge the term free time – on my fifteenth birthday I eliminated it from my vocabulary, for in the beginning was the act."

I got the job. Even with nine telephones I really didn't feel I was working to capacity. I shouted into the mouth-pieces: "Take immediate action!" or; "Do something! – We must have some action – Action will be taken – Action has been taken – Action should be taken." But as a rule – for I felt this was in keeping with the tone of the place – I used the imperative.

Of considerable interest were the noon-hour breaks, when we consumed nutritious foods in an atmosphere of silent good cheer. Wunsiedel's factory was swarming with people who were obsessed with telling you the story of their lives, as indeed vigorous personalities are fond of doing. The story of their lives is more important to them than their lives, you have only to press a button, and immediately it is covered with spewed-out exploits.

Wunsiedel had a right-hand man called Broschek, who had in turn made a name for himself by supporting seven children and a paralyzed wife by working night-shifts in his student days, and successfully carrying on four business agencies, besides which he had passed two examinations with honors in two years. When asked by reporters: "When do you sleep, Mr. Broschek?" he had replied: "It's a crime to sleep!"

Wunsiedel's secretary had supported a paralyzed husband and four children by knitting, at the same time graduating in psychology and German history as well as breeding shepherd dogs, and she had become famous as a night-club singer where she was known as Vamp Number Seven.

Wunsiedel himself was one of those people who every morning, as they open their eyes, make up their minds to act. "I must act," they think as they briskly tie their bathrobe belts around them. "I must act," they think as they shave, triumphantly watching their beard hairs being washed away with the lather: these hirsute vestiges are the first daily sacrifices to their driving energy. The more intimate functions also give these people a sense of satisfaction: water swishes, paper is used. Action has been taken. Bread get eaten, eggs are decapitated.

With Wunsiedel, the most trivial activity looked like action: the way he put on his hat, the way – quivering with energy – he buttoned up his overcoat, the kiss he gave his wife, everything was action.

When he arrived at his office he greeted his secretary with a cry of "Let's have some action!" And in ringing tones she would call back: "Action will be taken!" Wunsiedel then went from department to department, calling out his cheerful: "Let's have some action!" Everyone would answer: "Action will be taken!" And I would call back to him too, with a radiant smile, when he looked into my office: "Action will be taken!"

Within a week I had increased the number of telephones on my desk to eleven, within two weeks to thirteen, and every morning on the streetcar I enjoyed thinking up new imperatives, or chasing the words take action through various tenses and modulations: for two whole days I kept saying the same sentence over and over again because I thought it sounded so marvelous: "Action ought to have been taken;" for another two days it was: "Such action ought not to have been taken."

So I was really beginning to feel I was working to capacity when there actually was some action. One Tuesday morning – I had hardly settled down at my desk – Wunsiedel rushed into my office crying his "let's have some action!" But an inexplicable something in his face made me hesitate to reply, in a cheerful gay voice as the rules dictated: "Action will be taken!" I must have paused too long, for Wunsiedel, who seldom raised his voice, shouted at me: "Answer! Answer, you know the rules!" And I answered, under my breath, reluctantly, like a child who is forced to say: I am a naughty child. It was only by a great effort that I managed to bring out the sentence: "Action will be taken," and hardly had I uttered it when there really was some action: Wunsiedel dropped to the floor. As he fell he rolled over onto his side and lay right across the open doorway.

I knew at once, and I confirmed it when I went slowly around my desk and approached the body on the floor: he was dead.

Shaking my head I stepped over Wunsiedel, walked slowly along the corridor to Broschek's office, and entered without knocking. Broschek was sitting at his desk, a telephone receiver in each hand, between his teeth a ballpoint pen with which he was making notes on a writing pad, while with his bare feet he was operating a knitting machine under the desk. In this way he helps to clothe his family. "We've had some action," I said in a low voice.

Broschek spat out the ballpoint pen, put down the two receivers, reluctantly detached his toes from the knitting machine.

"What action?" he asked.

"Wunsiedel is dead," I said.

"No," said Broschek.

"Yes," I said, "come and have a look!"

"No," said Broschek, "that's impossible," but he put on his slippers and followed me along the corridor.

"No," he said, when we stood beside Wunsiedel's corpse, "no, no!" I did not contradict him. I carefully turned Wunsiedel over onto his back, closed his eyes, and looked at him pensively.

I felt something like tenderness for him, and realized for the first time that I had never hated him. On his face was that expression which one sees on children who obstinately refuse to give up their faith in Santa Claus, even though the arguments of their playmates sound so convincing.

"No," said Broschek, "no."

"We must take action," I said quietly to Broschek.

"Yes," said Broschek, "we must take action."

Action was taken: Wunsiedel was buried; and I was delegated to carry a wreath of artificial roses behind his coffin, for I am equipped with not only a penchant for pensiveness and inactivity but also a face and figure that go extremely well with dark suits. Apparently as I walked along behind Wunsiedel's coffin carrying the wreath of artificial roses I looked superb. I received an offer from a fashionable firm of funeral directors to join their staff as a professional mourner. "You are a born mourner," said the manager, "your outfit would be provided by the firm. Your face – simply superb!"

I handed in my notice to Broschek, explaining that I had never really felt I was working to capacity there; that, in spite of the thirteen telephones, some of my talents were going to waste. As soon as my first professional appearance as a mourner was over I knew: This is where I belong, this is what I am cut out for.

Pensively I stand behind the coffin in the funeral chapel, holding a simple bouquet, while the organ plays Handel's Largo, a piece that does not receive nearly the respect it deserves. The cemetery café is my regular haunt; there I spend the intervals between my professional engagements, although sometimes I walk behind coffins which I have not been engaged to follow, I pay for flowers out of my own pocket and join the welfare worker who walks behind the coffin of some homeless person. From time to time I also visit Wunsiedel's grave, for after all I owe it to him that I discovered my true vocation, a vocation in which pensiveness is essential and inactivity my duty.

It was not till much later that I realized I had never bothered to find out what was being produced in Wunsiedel's factory. I expect it was soap.

Translated by Leila Vennewitz

BOHEMIA

Mikhail Bulgakov

Mikhail Afanasievich Bulgakov (1891–1940) was a Soviet novelist and playwright. Although a native of Kiev, he wrote in Russian. Like his Ukrainian predecessor, Nikolai Gogol, he was a humourist and satirist of the first order. The object of his sharp wit was the Soviet regime and particularly the 'Homo Sovieticus', or new Soviet man, that the regime was seeking to create. Bulgakov exposed the futility of this attempt to re-engineer human souls in his novellas, like *Fatal Eggs* and *Heart of a Dog*, and in his greatest work by far (and one of the greatest novels of the twentieth century) *The Master and Margarita*.

I – How to Survive with the Aid of Literature. Astride a Play to Tiflis.

If someone asked me what I deserve, I would say in all honesty before God that I deserve hard labour.

Not because of Tiflis, however; I did not do anything wrong in Tiflis. Because of Vladikavkaz.

I was living out my last days in Vladikavkaz, and the terrible specter of hunger, (Cliché! Cliché!… "terrible specter"… However, I don't give a damn! These memoirs will never be published!) as I was saying, the terrible specter of hunger knocked at the door of my modest apartment which I had obtained with a permit. And, right after the specter, knocked Attorney Genzulaev, a pure soul with a brush mustache and an inspired face.

We talked, and here I include a stenographic record:

"What are you so down in the mouth about?" (Genzulaev)

"Apparently, I'm doomed to die of starvation in this crummy Vladi-kavkaz of yours…"

"There's no question about that. Vladikavkaz is a crummy city. I doubt there's a crummier city anywhere in the world. But why do you have to starve to death?"

"There's nothing else I can do. I've exhausted all possibilities. The Subdepartment of the Arts has no money, so they can't pay any salaries. I won't be making any more introductory speeches before plays. I had a feuilleton printed in the local Vladikavkaz newspaper for which I received 1,250 rubles and a promise that they would turn me over to the special department if another one like it ever appeared in print."

"Why?" (Genzulaev was alarmed. Understandably, if they wanted to turn me over to the special department, I must be suspect.)

"For my mocking tone."

"Oh, rubbish. They just don't understand anything about feuilletons here. I'll tell you what…"

And here is what Genzulaev did. He incited me to write a revolutionary play with him about native life. I'm slandering Genzulaev here. He pushed me and, because of my youth and inexperience, I agreed. What does Genzulaev know about the writing of plays? Nothing whatsoever, it was plain to see. Right away he openly admitted that he sincerely detests literature, and I myself hated literature, you better believe, even more than he did. But Genzulaev knows native life like the back of his hand, if, of course, you can call native life a combination of shishkebab houses, breakfasts against a backdrop of the most repulsive mountains in the world, daggers of inferior steel, sinewy horses, taverns, and disgusting music that wrenches the soul.

Therefore, I would write the play and Genzulaev would add the local colour.

"Only idiots would buy this play."

"We're the idiots if we don't manage to sell this play."

We wrote it in seven-and-a-half days, thus spending half a day more than was necessary to create the world. Despite this, it turned out even worse than the world.

I can say one thing: if there is ever a competition to see who can write the most stupid, untalented, and presumptuous play, ours will receive first prize (however, several plays from 1921–26 now come to mind, and I begin to have my doubts...), well, if not first prize, certainly second or third.

In short, after writing this play I am forever stigmatized, and naturally I can only hope that the play will molder in the bowels of the local Subdepartment of the Arts. As for the receipt, the devil take it, it can stay there. It was two hundred thousand rubles. One hundred for me. One hundred for Genzulaev. The play ran for three nights (a record), and the authors were called on stage. Genzulaev came out and took a bow, laying his hand against his clavicle. Then I came out and made faces for a long time so that I would be unrecognizable in the photograph (which was taken from below with magnesium). Due to these faces, a rumor spread throughout the town that I was brilliant but mad. It was annoying, especially because the faces were totally unnecessary, since the photographer who took our picture was requisitioned and assigned to the theater, so nothing came out on the photograph but a shotgun, the inscription, "Glory to...", and a blurred streak.

I ate up seven thousand in two days and decided to use the remaining ninety-three to leave Vladikavkaz

Why? Why Tiflis of all places? For the life of me, I do not now recall. However, I remember I was told that:

1) in Tiflis all the stores are open,
2) in Tiflis there is wine,
3) in Tiflis it is very hot and the fruit is cheap,
4) in Tiflis there are many newspapers, etc.., etc.

I decided to go. First, I packed my things. I took all my worldly possessions: a blanket, some under-clothes, and a Primus stove.

In 1921 things were not quite the same as in 1924. To be more precise, it was impossible to just pack up and go wherever you wanted! Apparently, those who were in charge of civilian travel reasoned something like this:

"If everyone started traveling, then where would we be?"

Therefore, a permit was required. I immediately submitted an application to the appropriate authorities, and where it asked, "What is the purpose of your trip?" I wrote with pride, "I am going to Tiflis for the production of my revolutionary play."

In all of Vladikavkaz there was only one person who did not know me by sight, and it happened to be the gallant young fellow with the pistol on his hip who stood as if nailed to the spot by the table where permits for travel to Tiflis were issued.

When my turn came to receive a permit and I reached out to take it, the young man started to give it to me, but then stopped and said in an authoritative, high-pitched voice, "What is the purpose of your trip?"

"The production of my revolutionary play."

Then the young man sealed the permit in an envelope and handed both me and the envelope over to someone with a rifle, saying, "Take him to the special department."

"What for?"

The young man did not answer.

A very bright sun (the only good thing in Vladikavkaz) beamed down on me as I walked along the road with the man carrying the rifle to my left. He decided to strike up a conversation with me and said, We're going to be passing through the bazaar now, but don't even think about escaping. Nothing good will come of it."

"Even if you begged me to do it, I wouldn't," I replied in all honesty.

Then I offered him a cigarette.

Smoking companionably, we arrived at the special department. As we crossed the courtyard, I fleetingly recalled all my crimes. There were three.

1) In 1907 I was given one ruble and 50 kopecks to buy Kraevich's *Physics* but spent it at the cinema.
2) In 1913 I got married against the wishes of my mother.
3) In 1921 I wrote that celebrated feuilleton.

The play? But that play could hardly be called criminal, could it? Quite the contrary.

For the information of those who have never been inside the special department, it is a large room with a rug on the floor, a huge desk of unbelievable proportions, eight telephones of different designs with green, orange, and gray cords attached, and behind the desk, a small man in military uniform with a very pleasant face.

The luxuriant crowns of the chestnut trees could be seen through the open windows. Upon seeing me, the man sitting at the desk attempted to change the pleasant expression on his face to an unfriendly and unpleasant one, but was only partially successful.

He took a photograph out of the desk drawer and began scrutinizing both it and me in turn.

"Oh, no. That's not me," I hurriedly announced.

"You could have shaved off the mustache," Mr. pleasant responded thoughtfully.

"Yes, but if you look closely," I said, "the guy in the picture has hair the color of black shoe polish and is about forty-five. I am blond and twenty-eight."

"Dye?" the small man asked with uncertainty.

"But what about the bald spot? And besides look closely at the nose. I beg you to take a good look at the nose."

The small man peered at my nose. He was overcome with despair.

"I believe you. There's no resemblance."

There was a pause, and a ray of sunlight sprang up in the inkwell.

"Are you an accountant?"

"God forbid."

Pause. The crowns of the chestnuts. The stucco ceiling. Cupids.

"What is the purpose of your trip to Tiflis? Answer immediately without thinking," the small man said in a rush.

"To stage my revolutionary play," I answered in a rush.

The small man opened his mouth, but recoiled and was completely radiated by the sun.

"You write plays?"

"Yes, I have to."

"No kidding. Was the play you wrote a good one?"

There was something in his voice that would have touched any heart but mine. I repeat, I deserve hard labor. Looking away, I said:

"Yes, a good one."

Yes. Yes. Yes. This was my fourth crime, the worst one of all. If I had wanted to remain pure before the special department, I should have answered: "No it's not a good play. It's junk. I just really want to go to Tiflis."

I looked at the toes of my worn-out boots and did not speak. I came to myself when the small man handed me a cigarette and my travel permit.

He said to the guy with the rifle, "Show the writer to the door."

The special department! I must forget about it! You see, now I have confessed. I have shed the guilt I have carried for three years. What I committed in the special department was, for me, worse than sabotage, counter-revolution or abuse of power.

But I must forget it!

II – Eternal Wanderers

People say that in 1924 it was easy to travel from Vladikavkaz to Tiflis; you simply hire a car in Vladikavkaz and drive along the remarkably scenic Georgian Military Highway. It is only two hundred and ten versts. However, in Vladikavkaz in 1921 the word "hire" sounded like a word from a foreign language.

In order to travel you had to go with your blanket and Primus stove to the station and then walk along the tracks, peering into the innumerable freight cars. Wiping the sweat from my brow on track seven, I saw a man with a fan-shaped beard standing in slippers by an open freight car. He was rinsing out a kettle and repeating the vile word, "Baku."

"Take me with you," I requested.

"No," replied the man with the beard.

"Please, so I can stage my revolutionary play," I said.

"No."

The bearded man carried the kettle up a plank and into the freight car. I sat on my blanket beside the hot rails and lit a cigarette. A stifling, intense heat filled the spaces between the freight cars, and I quenched my thirst at the faucet by the tracks. Then I sat down again and felt the scorching heat radiated by the freight car. The bearded man stuck his head out.

"What's your play about?" he asked.

"Here."

I unrolled my blanket and took out my play.

"You wrote it yourself?" the proprietor of the freight car asked dubiously.

"With Genzulaev."

"Never heard of him."

"I really need to leave."

"Well, I'm expecting two more, but if they don't show up, perhaps I'll take you. Only don't have any designs on the plank bed. Don't think that just because you wrote a play you can try anything funny. It's a long journey and, as a matter of fact, we ourselves are from the Political Education Committee."

"I won't try anything funny," I said, feeling a breath of hope in the searing heat. "I can sleep on the floor."

Sitting down on the plank bed, the beard said "Don't you have any food?"

"I have a little money."

The bearded man thought for a moment.

"I'll tell you what… you can share our food on the journey. But you'll have to help with our railway newspaper. Can you write something for our paper?"

"Anything you want," I assured him as I took possession of my ration and bit into the upper crust.

"Even feuilletons?" he asked, and the look on his face made it obvious that he thought me a liar.

"Feuilletons are my specialty."

Three faces appeared out of the shadows of the plank bed, along with some bare feet. They all looked at me.

"Fyodor! There's room for one more on the plank bed. That son-of-a-bitch Stepanov isn't coming," the feet said in a bass voice. "I'll make room for Comrade Feuilletonist."

"Okay, make room for him," bearded Fyodor said in confusion. "What feuilleton are you going to write?"

"The Eternal Wanderers."

"How will it begin?" asked a voice from the plank bed. "Come over here and have some tea with us."

"Sounds good—Eternal Wanderers," responded Fyodor, taking off his boots. "You should have said you wrote feuilletons to start with, instead of sitting on the tracks for two hours. Welcome aboard."

A vast and wondrous evening replaces the scorching day in Vladikavkaz. The evening's edge is the bluish mountains. They are shrouded in evening mist. The plain forms the bottom of the cup. And along the bottom, jolting slightly, wheels began to turn. Eternal Wanderers. Farewell forever, Genzulaev! Farewell, Vladikavkaz!

THE ROYAL SUMMONS

Leonora Carrington

Leonora Carrington (1917–2011) was a British-born Mexican artist, surrealist painter and novelist. She lived most of her adult life in Mexico City and was one of the last surviving participants in the Surrealist movement of the 1930s. Carrington was also a founding member of the Women's Liberation Movement in Mexico during the 1970s. Like her paintings, Carrington's short stories – many of which are autobiographical – contain references to strange creatures and alchemical rituals, as well as revealing a sharp eye for human absurdity.

I had received a royal summons to pay a call on the sovereigns of my country. The invitation was made of lace, framing embossed letters of gold. There were also roses and swallows.

I went to fetch my car, but my chauffeur, who has no practical sense at all, had just buried it.

'I did it to grow mushrooms,' he told me. 'There's no better way of growing mushrooms.'

'Brady,' I said to him, 'you're a complete idiot. You have ruined my car.'

Since my car was indeed completely out of action, I was obliged to hire a horse and cart.

When I arrived at the palace, I was told by an impassive servant, dressed in red and gold, 'The queen went mad yesterday. She's in her bath.'

'How terrible,' I exclaimed. 'How did it happen?'

'It's the heat.'

'May I see her all the same?' I didn't like the idea of my long journey being wasted.

'Yes,' the servant replied. 'You may see her anyway.'

We passed down corridors decorated in imitation marble, admirably done, through rooms with Greek bas-reliefs and Medici ceilings and wax fruit everywhere.

The queen was in her bath when I went in; I noticed that she was bathing in goat's milk.

'Come on in,' she said. 'You see I use only live sponges. It's healthier.'

The sponges were swimming about all over the place in the milk, and she had trouble catching them. A servant, armed with long-handled tongs, helped her from time to time.

'I'll soon be through with my bath,' the queen said. 'I have a proposal to put to you. I would like you to see the government instead of me today, I'm too tired myself. They're all idiots, so you won't find it difficult.'

'All right,' I said.

The government chamber was at the other end of the palace. The ministers were sitting at a long and very shiny table.

As the representative of the queen, I sat in the seat at the end. The prime minister rose and struck the table with a gavel. The table broke in two. Some servants came in with another table. The prime minister swapped the first gavel for another, made of rubber. He struck the table again and began to speak. 'Madam Deputy of the queen, ministers, friends. Our dearly beloved sovereign went mad yesterday, and so we need another. But first we must assassinate the old queen.'

The ministers murmured amongst themselves for a while. Presently, the oldest minister rose to his feet and addressed the assembly. 'That being the case, we must forthwith make a plan. Not only must we make a plan, but we must come to a decision. We must choose who is to be the assassin.'

All hands were immediately raised. I didn't quite know what to do as the deputy of Her Majesty.

Perplexed, the prime minister looked over the company.

'We can't all do it!' he said. 'But I've a very good idea. We'll play a game of draughts, and the winner has the right to assassinate the queen.' He turned to me and asked, 'Do you play, Miss?'

I was filled with embarrassment. I had no desire to assassinate the queen, and I foresaw that serious consequences might follow. On the other hand I had never been any good at all at draughts. So I saw no danger, and I accepted.

'I don't mind,' I said.

'So, it's understood,' said the prime minister. 'This is what the winner will do: take the queen for a stroll in the Royal Menagerie. When you reach the lions (second cage on the left), push her in. I shall tell the keeper not to feed the lions until tomorrow.'

The queen called me to her office. She was watering the flowers woven in the carpet.

'Well, did it go all right?' she asked.

'Yes, it went very well,' I answered, confused.

'Would you like some soup?'

'You're too kind,' I said.

'It's mock beef tea. I make it myself,' the queen said. 'There's nothing in it but potatoes.'

While we were eating the broth, an orchestra played popular and classical tunes. The queen loved music to distraction.

The meal over, the queen left to have a rest. I for my part went to join in the game of draughts on the terrace. I was nervous, but I've inherited sporting instincts from my father. I had given my word to be there, and so there I would be.

The enormous terrace looked impressive. In front of the garden, darkened by the twilight and the cypress trees, the ministers were assembled. There were twenty little tables. Each had two chairs, with thin, fragile legs. When he saw me arrive, the prime minister called out, 'Take your places,' and everybody rushed to the tables and began to play ferociously.

We played all night without stopping. The only sounds that interrupted the game were an occasional furious bellow from one minister or another. Towards dawn, the blast of a trumpet abruptly called an end to the game. A voice, coming from I don't know where, cried, 'She has won. She's the only person who didn't cheat.'

I was rooted to the ground with horror.

'Who? Me?' I said.

'Yes, you,' the voice replied, and I noticed that it was the tallest cypress speaking.

I'm going to escape, I thought, and began to run in the direction of the avenue. But the cypress tore itself out of the earth by the roots, scattering dirt in all directions, and began to follow me. It's so much larger than me, I thought and stopped. The cypress stopped too. All its branches were shaking horribly – it was probably quite a while since it had last run.

'I accept,' I said, and the cypress returned slowly to its hole.

I found the queen lying in her great bed.

'I want to invite you to come for a stroll in the menagerie,' I said, feeling pretty uncomfortable.

'But it's too early,' she replied. 'It isn't five o'clock yet. I never get up before ten.'

'It's lovely out,' I added.

'Oh, all right, if you insist.'

We went down into the silent garden. Dawn is the time when nothing breathes, the hour of silence. Everything is transfixed, only the light moves. I sang a bit to cheer myself up. I was chilled to the bone. The queen, in the meantime, was telling me that she fed all her horses on jam.

'It stops them from being vicious,' she said.

She ought to have given the lions some jam, I thought to myself.

A long avenue, lined on both sides with fruit trees, led to the menagerie. From time to time a heavy fruit fell to the ground, Plop.

'Head colds are easily cured, if one just has the confidence,' the queen said. 'I myself always take beef morsels marinated in olive oil. I put them in my nose. Next day the cold's gone. Or else, treated in the same way, cold noodles in liver juice, preferably calves' liver. It's a miracle how it dispels the heaviness in one's head.'

She'll never have a head cold again, I thought.

'But bronchitis is more complicated. I nearly saved my poor husband from his last attack of bronchitis by knitting him a waistcoat. But it wasn't altogether successful.'

We were drawing closer and closer to the menagerie. I could already hear the animals stirring in their morning slumbers. I would have liked to turn back, but I was afraid of the cypress and what it might be able to do with its hairy black branches. The more strongly I smelled the lion, the more loudly I sang, to give myself courage.

THE NEUTRAL MAN

Leonora Carrington

Leonora Carrington (1917–2011) was a British-born Mexican artist, surrealist painter and novelist. She lived most of her adult life in Mexico City and was one of the last surviving participants in the Surrealist movement of the 1930s. Carrington was also a founding member of the Women's Liberation Movement in Mexico during the 1970s. Like her paintings, Carrington's short stories – many of which are autobiographical – contain references to strange creatures and alchemical rituals, as well as revealing a sharp eye for human absurdity.

Although I've always promised myself to keep the secret regarding this episode, I've finished up, inevitably, by writing it down. However, since the reputations of certain well-known foreigners are involved, I'm obliged to use false names, though these constitute no real disguise: every reader who is familiar with the customs of the British in tropical countries will have no trouble recognising everyone involved.

I received an invitation asking me to come to a masked ball. Taken aback, I plastered my face thickly with electric-green phosphorescent ointment. On this foundation I scattered tiny imitation diamonds, so that I was dusted with stars like the night sky, nothing more.

Then, rather nervously, I got myself into a public vehicle which took me to the outskirts of the town, to General Epigastro Square. A splendid equestrian monument of this illustrious soldier dominated the square. The artist who had been able to resolve the peculiar problem posed by this monument had embraced a courageously archaic simplicity, limiting himself to a wonderful portrait in the form of the head of the general's horse: the Generalissimo Don Epigastro himself remains sufficiently engraved in the imagination of his devoted public.

Mr MacFrolick's mansion occupied the entire west side of General Epigastro Square. An Indian servant took me to a large reception room in the baroque style. I found myself among a hundred or so guests. The rather charged atmosphere made me realise, in the end, that I was the only person who'd taken the invitation seriously: I was the only guest in disguise.

'It was no doubt your cunning intention,' said the master of the house, Mr MacFrolick, to me, 'to impersonate a certain princess of Tibet, mistress of the king, who was dominated by the sombre rituals of the Bön, rituals fortunately now lost in the furthest recesses of time. I would hesitate to relate, in the presence of ladies, the appalling exploits of the Green Princess. Enough to say that she died in mysterious circumstances, circumstances around which various legends still circulate in the Far East. Some claim that the corpse was carried off by bees, and that they have preserved it to this day in the transparent honey of the Flowers of Venus. Others say that the painted coffin did not contain the princess at all, but the corpse of a crane with the face of a woman; yet others maintain that the princess comes back in the shape of a sow.'

Mr MacFrolick stopped abruptly and looked at me hard and with a severe expression. 'I shan't say more, Madam,' he said, 'since we are Catholics.'

Confused, I abandoned all explanation and hung my head; my feet were bathed in the rain of cold sweat that fell from my forehead. Mr MacFrolick looked at me with a lifeless expression. He had little bluish eyes and a thick, heavy, snub nose. It was difficult not to notice that this very distinguished man, devout and of impeccable morality, was the human picture of a big white pig. An enormous moustache hung over his fleshy, rather receding chin. Yes, MacFrolick resembled a pig, but a beautiful pig, a devout and distinguished pig. As these dangerous thoughts passed beneath my green face, a young man of Celtic appearance took me by the hand and said, 'Come, dear lady, don't torment yourself. We all inevitably show a resemblance to other species of animals. I'm sure you are aware of your own equine appearance. So… don't torment yourself, everything on our planet is pretty mixed up. Do you know Mr D?'

'No,' I said, very confused. 'I don't know him.'

'D is here this evening,' the young man continued. 'He is a Magus, and I am his pupil. Look, there he is, near that big blonde dressed in purple satin. Do you see him?'

I saw a man of such neutral appearance that he struck me like a salmon with the head of a sphinx in the middle of a railway station. The extraordinary neutrality of this individual gave me such a disagreeable impression that I staggered to a chair.

'Would you like to meet D?' the young man asked. 'He is a very remarkable man.'

I was just going to reply when a woman dressed in pale blue taffeta, who wore a very hard expression, took me by the shoulder and pushed me straight into the gaming room.

'We need a fourth for bridge,' she told me. 'You play bridge, of course.' I didn't at all know how, but kept quiet out of panic. I would have liked to leave, but was too timid, so much so that I began to explain that I could only play with felt cards, because of an allergy in the little finger of my left hand. Outside, the orchestra was playing a waltz which I loathed so much I didn't have the courage to say that I was hungry. A high ecclesiastical dignitary, who sat on my right, drew a pork chop from inside his rich, crimson cummerbund.

'Take it, my daughter,' he said to me. 'Charity pours forth mercy equally on cats, the poor and women with green faces.'

The chop, which had undoubtedly spent a very long time near the ecclesiastic's stomach, didn't appeal to me, but I took it, intending to bury it in the garden.

When I took the chop outside, I found myself in the darkness, weakly lit by the planet Venus. I was walking near the stagnant basin of a fountain full of stupefied bees, when I found myself face to face with the magician, the neutral man.

'So you're going for a walk,' he said in a very contemptuous tone. 'It's always the same with the expatriate English, bored to death.'

Full of shame, I admitted that I too was English, and the man gave a little sarcastic laugh.

'It's hardly your fault that you're English,' he said. 'The congenital stupidity of the inhabitants of the British Isles is so embedded in their blood that they themselves aren't conscious of it anymore. The spiritual maladies of the English have become flesh, or rather pork brawn.'

Vaguely irritated, I replied that it rained a great deal in England, but that the country had bred the greatest poets in the world. Then, to change the subject: 'I've just made the acquaintance of one of your pupils. He told me that you are a magician.'

'Actually,' said the neutral man, 'I'm an instructor in spiritual matters, an initiate if you like. But that poor boy will never get anywhere. You must know, my dear lady, that the esoteric path is hard, bristling with catastrophes. Many are called, few are chosen. I would advise you to confine yourself to your charming female nonsense and forget everything of a superior order.'

While he was speaking to me, I was trying to hide the pork chop, for it was oozing horrible blobs of grease between my fingers. I finally managed to put it into my pocket. Relieved, I realised this man would never take me seriously if he knew that I was walking about with a pork chop. And though I feared the neutral man like the plague, I still wished to make a good impression.

'I'd like to learn some of your magic, perhaps study with you. Until now…'

'There is nothing,' he told me. 'Try to understand what I'm telling you. There is nothing, absolutely nothing.'

It was at this point that I felt myself dissolving into an opaque and colourless mass. When I got my breath back, the man had disappeared. I wanted to go home, but I was lost in the garden, which was heavy with the scent of a certain shrub which people here call 'it smells at night'.

I had been walking along the paths for some time when I arrived at a tower. Through the half-open door I noticed a spiral staircase. Somebody called me from inside the tower, and I went up the stairs, thinking that after all I didn't have a great deal to lose anymore. I was much too stupid to run away like the hare with its triangular teeth.

I thought bitterly: At this moment I'm poorer than a beggar, though the bees have done all they could to warn me. Here I am, having lost a whole year's honey and Venus in the sky.

At the top of the stairs I found myself in Mr MacFrolick's private boudoir. He received me amiably, and I couldn't explain to myself this change in attitude. With a gesture full of old-fashioned courtesy, Mr MacFrolick offered me a china dish (quite fine) on which rested his own moustache. I hesitated to accept the moustache, thinking that perhaps he wanted me to eat it. He's an eccentric, I thought. I quickly made my excuses: 'Thank you very much, dear sir,' I said, 'but I'm not hungry anymore after having eaten the delicious chop the bishop so kindly offered me.'

MacFrolick seemed slightly offended.

'Madam,' he said, 'this moustache is not in any way edible. It is meant as a souvenir of this summer evening, and I thought you might perhaps keep it in a cabinet suitable for such keepsakes. I must add that this moustache has no magical power, but that its considerable size sets it apart from common objects.'

Understanding that I'd made a faux pas, I took the moustache and put it carefully in my pocket, where it immediately stuck to the disgusting pork chop. MacFrolick then pushed me onto the divan, and leaning heavily on my stomach, said in a confidential tone of voice, 'Green woman, know that there are different kinds of magic: black magic, white magic, and, worst of all, grey magic. It is absolutely essential that you know that amongst us this evening is a dangerous grey magician. His name is D. This man, the vampire of velvet words, is responsible for the murder of many souls, both human and otherwise. After several attempts, D has succeeded in infiltrating this mansion to steal our vital essence.'

I found it difficult to suppress a little smile, since for a long time I had been living with a Transylvanian vampire, and my mother-in-law had taught me all the necessary culinary secrets to satisfy the most voracious of such creatures.

MacFrolick leaned more heavily on me and hissed, 'It is absolutely crucial that I get rid of D. Unfortunately the Church forbids private assassination. I'm therefore obliged to ask you to come to my assistance. You're a Protestant, aren't you?'

'Not at all,' I replied. 'I'm not a Christian, Mr MacFrolick. Besides, I've no wish to kill D, even if I had the chance of doing so before he pulverised me ten times over.'

MacFrolick's face filled with rage.

'Leave this house immediately.' he screamed. 'I don't receive unbelievers in my house, madam. Go away!'

I left as quickly as I could on those stairs, while MacFrolick leaned against his door, insulting me in language that was pretty rich for so pious a man.

There is no proper ending to this story, which I recount here as an ordinary summer incident. There's no ending because the episode is true, because all the people are still alive, and everyone is following his destiny. Everyone, that is, except the ecclesiastic, who drowned tragically in the mansion's swimming pool: it's said he was enticed there by sirens disguised as choirboys.

Mr MacFrolick never again invited me to his mansion, but I am told that he is in good health.

THE DEATH OF A GOVERNMENT CLERK

Anton Chekhov

Anton Chekhov (1860–1904) was a Russian writer whose works, such as the stories 'The Steppe' and 'The Lady with the Dog', and plays, such as *The Seagull* and *Uncle Vanya*, emphasized the depths of human nature, the hidden significance of everyday events and the fine line between comedy and tragedy. He died of tuberculosis at the age of forty-four.

One fine evening, a no less fine government clerk called Ivan Dmitritch Tchervyakov was sitting in the second row of the stalls, gazing through an opera glass at the Cloches de Corneville. He gazed and felt at the acme of bliss. But suddenly... In stories one so often meets with this "But suddenly." The authors are right: life is so full of surprises! But suddenly his face puckered up, his eyes disappeared, his breathing was arrested... he took the opera glass from his eyes, bent over and... "Aptchee!!" he sneezed as you perceive. It is not reprehensible for anyone to sneeze anywhere. Peasants sneeze and so do police superintendents, and sometimes even privy councillors. All men sneeze. Tchervyakov was not in the least confused, he wiped his face with his handkerchief, and like a polite man, looked round to see whether he had disturbed any one by his sneezing. But then he was overcome with confusion. He saw that an old gentleman sitting in front of him in the first row of the stalls was carefully wiping his bald head and his neck with his glove and muttering something to himself. In the old gentleman, Tchervyakov recognised Brizzhalov, a civilian general serving in the Department of Transport.

"I have spattered him," thought Tchervyakov, "he is not the head of my department, but still it is awkward. I must apologise."

Tchervyakov gave a cough, bent his whole person forward, and whispered in the general's ear.

"Pardon, your Excellency, I spattered you accidentally…"

"Never mind, never mind."

"For goodness sake excuse me, I… I did not mean to."

"Oh, please, sit down! Let me listen!"

Tchervyakov was embarrassed, he smiled stupidly and fell to gazing at the stage. He gazed at it but was no longer feeling bliss. He began to be troubled by uneasiness. In the interval, he went up to Brizzhalov, walked beside him, and overcoming his shyness, muttered:

"I spattered you, your Excellency, forgive me… you see… I didn't do it to…"

"Oh, that's enough… I'd forgotten it, and you keep on about it!" said the general, moving his lower lip impatiently.

"He has forgotten, but there is a fiendish light in his eye," thought Tchervyakov, looking suspiciously at the general. "And he doesn't want to talk. I ought to explain to him… that I really didn't intend… that it is the law of nature or else he will think I meant to spit on him. He doesn't think so now, but he will think so later!"

On getting home, Tchervyakov told his wife of his breach of good manners. It struck him that his wife took too frivolous a view of the incident; she was a little frightened, but when she learned that Brizzhalov was in a different department, she was reassured.

"Still, you had better go and apologise," she said, "or he will think you don't know how to behave in public."

"That's just it! I did apologise, but he took it somehow queerly… he didn't say a word of sense. There wasn't time to talk properly."

Next day Tchervyakov put on a new uniform, had his hair cut and went to Brizzhalov's to explain; going into the general's reception room he saw there a number of petitioners and among them the general himself, who was beginning to interview them. After questioning several petitioners the general raised his eyes and looked at Tchervyakov.

"Yesterday at the Arcadia, if you recollect, your Excellency," the latter began, "I sneezed and... accidentally spattered... Exc..."

"What nonsense... It's beyond anything! What can I do for you," said the general addressing the next petitioner.

"He won't speak," thought Tchervyakov, turning pale; "that means that he is angry... No, it can't be left like this... I will explain to him."

When the general had finished his conversation with the last of the petitioners and was turning towards his inner apartments, Tchervyakov took a step towards him and muttered:

"Your Excellency! If I venture to trouble your Excellency, it is simply from a feeling I may say of regret!... It was not intentional if you will graciously believe me."

The general made a lachrymose face, and waved his hand.

"Why, you are simply making fun of me, sir," he said as he closed the door behind him.

"Where's the making fun in it?" thought Tchervyakov, "there is nothing of the sort! He is a general, but he can't understand. If that is how it is I am not going to apologise to that fanfaron any more! The devil take him. I'll write a letter to him, but I won't go. By Jove, I won't."

So thought Tchervyakov as he walked home; he did not write a letter to the general, he pondered and pondered and could not make up that letter. He had to go next day to explain in person.

"I ventured to disturb your Excellency yesterday," he muttered, when the general lifted enquiring eyes upon him, "not to make fun as you were pleased to say. I was apologising for having spattered you in sneezing... And I did not dream of making fun of you. Should I dare to make fun of you, if we should take to making fun, then there would be no respect for persons, there would be..."

"Be off!" yelled the general, turning suddenly purple, and shaking all over.

"What?" asked Tchervyakov, in a whisper turning numb with horror.

"Be off!" repeated the general, stamping.

Something seemed to give way in Tchervyakov's stomach. Seeing nothing and hearing nothing he reeled to the door, went out into the street, and went staggering along... Reaching home mechanically, without taking off his uniform, he lay down on the sofa and died.

THE TREMENDOUS ADVENTURES OF MAJOR BROWN

G.K. Chesterton

G.K. Chesterton (1874–1936) was an English critic, Catholic thinker and author of verse, essays, novels and short stories. He is best known for his novels – *The Napoleon of Notting Hill, The Man Who Was Tuesday* – as well as the Father Brown series of detective novels. A rather rotund man (weighing around 130 kg), he once suggested, 'Lying in bed would be an altogether perfect and supreme experience if only one had a coloured pencil long enough to draw on the ceiling.'

Rabelais, or his wild illustrator Gustave Doré, must have had something to do with the designing of the things called flats in England and America. There is something entirely gargantuan in the idea of economising space by piling houses on top of each other, front doors and all. And in the chaos and complexity of those perpendicular streets anything may dwell or happen, and it is in one of them, I believe, that the inquirer may find the offices of the Club of Queer Trades. It may be thought at the first glance that the name would attract and startle the passer-by, but nothing attracts or startles in these dim immense hives. The passer-by is only looking for his own melancholy destination, the Montenegro Shipping Agency or the London office of the *Rutland Sentinel*, and passes through the twilight passages as one passes through the twilight corridors of a dream. If the Thugs set up a Strangers' Assassination Company in one of the great buildings in

Norfolk Street, and sent in a mild man in spectacles to answer inquiries, no inquiries would be made. And the Club of Queer Trades reigns in a great edifice hidden like a fossil in a mighty cliff of fossils.

The nature of this society, such as we afterwards discovered it to be, is soon and simply told. It is an eccentric and Bohemian Club, of which the absolute condition of membership lies in this, that the candidate must have invented the method by which he earns his living. It must be an entirely new trade. The exact definition of this requirement is given in the two principal rules. First, it must not be a mere application or variation of an existing trade. Thus, for instance, the Club would not admit an insurance agent simply because instead of insuring men's furniture against being burnt in a fire, he insured, let us say, their trousers against being torn by a mad dog. The principle (as Sir Bradcock Burnaby-Bradcock, in the extraordinarily eloquent and soaring speech to the club on the occasion of the question being raised in the Stormby Smith affair, said wittily and keenly) is the same. Secondly, the trade must be a genuine commercial source of income, the support of its inventor. Thus the Club would not receive a man simply because he chose to pass his days collecting broken sardine tins, unless he could drive a roaring trade in them. Professor Chick made that quite clear. And when one remembers what Professor Chick's own new trade was, one doesn't know whether to laugh or cry.

The discovery of this strange society was a curiously refreshing thing; to realize that there were ten new trades in the world was like looking at the first ship or the first plough. It made a man feel what he should feel, that he was still in the childhood of the world. That I should have come at last upon so singular a body was, I may say without vanity, not altogether singular, for I have a mania for belonging to as many societies as possible: I may be said to collect clubs, and I have accumulated a vast and fantastic variety of specimens ever since, in my audacious youth, I collected the Athenaeum. At some future day, perhaps, I may tell tales of some of the other bodies to which I have belonged. I will recount the doings of the Dead Man's Shoes Society (that superficially immoral, but darkly justifiable communion); I will explain the curious origin of the Cat and Christian, the name of which has been so shamefully misinterpreted; and the world shall know at last why the Institute of Typewriters coalesced with the Red Tulip League. Of the Ten Teacups, of course I dare not say a word. The first of my revelations, at any rate, shall be concerned with the Club of Queer Trades, which, as I have said, was one of this class, one which I was almost bound to come across sooner or later, because of my singular hobby. The wild youth of the metropolis call me facetiously 'The King of Clubs'. They also call me 'The Cherub', in allusion to the roseate and youthful appearance I have presented in my declining years. I only hope the spirits in the better world have as good dinners as I have. But the finding of the Club of Queer Trades has one very curious thing about it. The most curious thing about it is that it was not discovered by me; it was discovered by my friend Basil Grant, a star-gazer, a mystic, and a man who scarcely stirred out of his attic.

Very few people knew anything of Basil; not because he was in the least unsociable, for if a man out of the street had walked into his rooms he would have kept him talking till morning. Few people knew him, because, like all poets, he could do without them; he welcomed a human face as he might welcome a sudden blend of colour in a sunset; but he no more felt the need of going out to parties than he felt the need of altering the sunset clouds. He lived in a queer and comfortable garret in the roofs of Lambeth. He was surrounded by a chaos of things that were in odd contrast to the slums around him; old fantastic books, swords, armour—the whole dust-hole of romanticism. But his face, amid all these quixotic relics, appeared curiously keen and modern—a powerful, legal face. And no one but I knew who he was.

Long ago as it is, everyone remembers the terrible and grotesque scene that occurred in—, when one of the most acute and forcible of the English judges suddenly went mad on the bench. I had my own view of that occurrence; but about the facts themselves there is no question at all. For some months, indeed for some years, people had detected something curious in the judge's conduct. He seemed to have lost interest in the law, in which he had been beyond expression brilliant and terrible as a K.C., and to be occupied in giving personal and moral advice to the people concerned. He talked more like a priest or a doctor, and a very outspoken one at that. The first thrill was probably given when he said to a man who had attempted a crime of passion: 'I sentence you to three years' imprisonment, under the firm, and solemn, and God-given conviction, that what you require is three months at the seaside.' He accused criminals from the bench, not so much of their obvious legal crimes, but of things that had never been heard of in a court of justice, monstrous egoism, lack of humour, and morbidity deliberately encouraged. Things came to a head in that celebrated diamond case in which the Prime Minister himself, that brilliant patrician, had to come forward, gracefully and reluctantly, to give evidence against his valet. After the detailed life of the household had been thoroughly exhibited, the judge requested the Premier again to step forward, which he did with quiet dignity. The judge then said, in a sudden, grating voice: 'Get a new soul. That thing's not fit for a dog. Get a new soul.' All this, of course, in the eyes of the sagacious, was premonitory of that melancholy and farcical day when his wits actually deserted him in open court. It was a libel case between two very eminent and powerful financiers, against both of whom charges of considerable defalcation were brought. The case was long and complex; the advocates were long and eloquent; but at last, after weeks of work and rhetoric, the time came for the great judge to give a summing-up; and one of his celebrated masterpieces of lucidity and pulverizing logic was eagerly looked for. He had spoken very little during the prolonged affair, and he looked sad and lowering at the end of it. He was silent for a few moments, and then burst into a stentorian song. His remarks (as reported) were as follows:

'O Rowty-owty tiddly-owty Tiddly-owty tiddly-owty Highty-ighty tiddly-ighty Tiddly-ighty ow.'

He then retired from public life and took the garret in Lambeth.

I was sitting there one evening, about six o'clock, over a glass of that gorgeous Burgundy which he kept behind a pile of black-letter folios; he was striding about the room, fingering, after a habit of his, one of the great swords in his collection; the red glare of the strong fire struck his square features and his fierce grey hair; his blue eyes were even unusually full of dreams, and he had opened his mouth to speak dreamily, when the door was flung open, and a pale, fiery man, with red hair and a huge furred overcoat, swung himself panting into the room.

'Sorry to bother you, Basil,' he gasped. 'I took a liberty—made an appointment here with a man—a client—in five minutes—I beg your pardon, sir,' and he gave me a bow of apology.

Basil smiled at me. 'You didn't know,' he said, 'that I had a practical brother. This is Rupert Grant, Esquire, who can and does all there is to be done. Just as I was a failure at one thing, he is a success at everything. I remember him as a journalist, a house-agent, a naturalist, an inventor, a publisher, a schoolmaster, a—what are you now, Rupert?'

'I am and have been for some time,' said Rupert, with some dignity, 'a private detective, and there's my client.'

A loud rap at the door had cut him short, and, on permission being given, the door was thrown sharply open and a stout, dapper man walked swiftly into the room, set his silk hat with a clap on the table, and said, 'Good evening, gentle*men*,' with a stress on the last syllable that somehow marked him out as a martinet, military, literary and social. He had a large head streaked with black and grey, and an abrupt black moustache, which gave him a look of fierceness which was contradicted by his sad sea-blue eyes.

Basil immediately said to me, 'Let us come into the next room, Gully,' and was moving towards the door, but the stranger said:

'Not at all. Friends remain. Assistance possibly.'

The moment I heard him speak I remembered who he was, a certain Major Brown I had met years before in Basil's society. I had forgotten altogether the black dandified figure and the large solemn head, but I remembered the peculiar speech, which consisted of only saying about a quarter of each sentence, and that sharply, like the crack of a gun. I do not know, it may have come from giving orders to troops.

Major Brown was a V.C., and an able and distinguished soldier, but he was anything but a warlike person. Like many among the iron men who recovered British India, he was a man with the natural beliefs and tastes of an old maid. In his dress he was dapper and yet demure; in his habits he was precise to the point of the exact adjustment of a tea-cup. One enthusiasm he had, which was of the nature of a religion—the cultivation of pansies. And when he talked about his collection, his blue eyes glittered like a child's at a new toy, the eyes that had remained untroubled when the troops were roaring victory round Roberts at Candahar.

'Well, Major,' said Rupert Grant, with a lordly heartiness, flinging himself into a chair, 'what is the matter with you?'

'Yellow pansies. Coal-cellar. P.G. Northover,' said the Major, with righteous indignation.

We glanced at each other with inquisitiveness. Basil, who had his eyes shut in his abstracted way, said simply:

'I beg your pardon.'

'Fact is. Street, you know, man, pansies. On wall. Death to me. Something. Preposterous.'

We shook our heads gently. Bit by bit, and mainly by the seemingly sleepy assistance of Basil Grant, we pieced together the Major's fragmentary, but excited narration. It would be infamous to submit the reader to what we endured; therefore I will tell the story of Major Brown in my own words. But the reader must imagine the scene. The eyes of Basil closed as in a trance, after his habit, and the eyes of Rupert and myself getting rounder and rounder as we listened to one of the most astounding stories in the world, from the lips of the little man in black, sitting bolt upright in his chair and talking like a telegram.

Major Brown was, I have said, a successful soldier, but by no means an enthusiastic one. So far from regretting his retirement on half-pay, it was with delight that he took a small neat villa, very like a doll's house, and devoted the rest of his life to pansies and weak tea. The thought that battles were over when he had once hung up his sword in the little front hall (along with two patent stew-pots and a bad water-colour), and betaken himself instead to wielding the rake in his little sunlit garden, was to him like having come into a harbour in heaven. He was Dutch-like and precise in his taste in gardening, and had, perhaps, some tendency to drill his flowers like soldiers. He was one of those men who are capable of putting four umbrellas in the stand rather than three, so that two may lean one way and two another; he saw life like a pattern in a freehand drawing-book. And assuredly he would not have believed, or even understood, any one who had told him that within a few yards of his brick paradise he was destined to be caught in a whirlpool of incredible adventure, such as he had never seen or dreamed of in the horrible jungle, or the heat of battle.

One certain bright and windy afternoon, the Major, attired in his usual faultless manner, had set out for his usual constitutional. In crossing from one great residential thoroughfare to another, he happened to pass along one of those aimless-looking lanes which lie along the back-garden walls of a row of mansions, and which in their empty and discoloured appearance give one an odd sensation as of being behind the scenes of a theatre. But mean and sulky as the scene might be in the eyes of most of us, it was not altogether so in the Major's, for along the coarse gravel footway was coming a thing which was to him what the passing of a religious procession is to a devout person. A large, heavy man, with fish-blue eyes and a ring of irradiating red beard, was pushing before him a barrow, which was ablaze with incomparable flowers. There were splendid specimens of almost every order, but the Major's own favourite pansies predominated. The Major stopped and fell into conversation, and then into bargaining. He treated the man after the manner of collectors and other mad men, that is to say, he carefully and with a sort of anguish selected the best roots from the less excellent, praised some, disparaged others, made a subtle scale ranging from a thrilling worth and rarity to a degraded insignificance, and then bought them all. The man was just pushing off his barrow when he stopped and came close to the Major.

'I'll tell you what, sir,' he said. 'If you're interested in them things, you just get on to that wall.'

'On the wall!' cried the scandalised Major, whose conventional soul quailed within him at the thought of such fantastic trespass.

'Finest show of yellow pansies in England in that there garden, sir,' hissed the tempter. 'I'll help you up, sir.'

How it happened no one will ever know but that positive enthusiasm of the Major's life triumphed over all its negative traditions, and with an easy leap and swing that showed that he was in no need of physical assistance, he stood on the wall at the end of the strange garden. The second after, the flapping of the frock-coat at his knees made him feel inexpressibly a fool. But the next instant all such trifling sentiments were swallowed up by the most appalling shock of surprise the old soldier had ever felt in all his bold and wandering existence. His eyes fell upon the garden, and there across a large bed in the centre of the lawn was a vast pattern of pansies; they were splendid flowers, but for once it was not their horticultural aspects that Major Brown beheld, for the pansies were arranged in gigantic capital letters so as to form the sentence:

DEATH TO MAJOR BROWN

A kindly looking old man, with white whiskers, was watering them. Brown looked sharply back at the road behind him; the man with the barrow had suddenly vanished. Then he looked again at the lawn with its incredible inscription. Another man might have thought he had gone mad, but Brown did not. When romantic ladies gushed over his V.C. and his military exploits, he sometimes felt himself to be a painfully prosaic person, but by the same token he knew he was incurably sane. Another man, again, might have thought himself a victim of a passing practical joke, but Brown could not easily believe this. He knew from his own quaint learning that the garden arrangement was an elaborate and expensive one; he thought it extravagantly improbable that any one would pour out money like water for a joke against him. Having no explanation whatever to offer, he admitted the fact to himself, like a clear-headed man, and waited as he would have done in the presence of a man with six legs.

At this moment the stout old man with white whiskers looked up, and the watering can fell from his hand, shooting a swirl of water down the gravel path.

'Who on earth are you?' he gasped, trembling violently.

'I am Major Brown,' said that individual, who was always cool in the hour of action.

The old man gaped helplessly like some monstrous fish. At last he stammered wildly, 'Come down—come down here!'

'At your service,' said the Major, and alighted at a bound on the grass beside him, without disarranging his silk hat.

The old man turned his broad back and set off at a sort of waddling run towards the house, followed with swift steps by the Major. His guide led him through the back passages of a gloomy, but gorgeously appointed house, until they reached the door of the front room. Then the old man turned with a face of apoplectic terror dimly showing in the twilight.

'For heaven's sake,' he said, 'don't mention jackals.'

Then he threw open the door, releasing a burst of red lamplight, and ran downstairs with a clatter.

The Major stepped into a rich, glowing room, full of red copper, and peacock and purple hangings, hat in hand. He had the finest manners in the world, and, though mystified, was not in the least embarrassed to see that the only occupant was a lady, sitting by the window, looking out.

'Madam,' he said, bowing simply, 'I am Major Brown.'

'Sit down,' said the lady; but she did not turn her head.

She was a graceful, green-clad figure, with fiery red hair and a flavour of Bedford Park. 'You have come, I suppose,' she said mournfully, 'to tax me about the hateful title-deeds.'

'I have come, madam,' he said, 'to know what is the matter. To know why my name is written across your garden. Not amicably either.'

He spoke grimly, for the thing had hit him. It is impossible to describe the effect produced on the mind by that quiet and sunny garden scene, the frame for a stunning and brutal personality. The evening air was still, and the grass was golden in the place where the little flowers he studied cried to heaven for his blood.

'You know I must not turn round,' said the lady; 'every afternoon till the stroke of six I must keep my face turned to the street.'

Some queer and unusual inspiration made the prosaic soldier resolute to accept these outrageous riddles without surprise.

'It is almost six,' he said; and even as he spoke the barbaric copper clock upon the wall clanged the first stroke of the hour. At the sixth the lady sprang up and turned on the Major one of the queerest and yet most attractive faces he had ever seen in his life; open, and yet tantalising, the face of an elf.

'That makes the third year I have waited,' she cried. 'This is an anniversary. The waiting almost makes one wish the frightful thing would happen once and for all.'

And even as she spoke, a sudden rending cry broke the stillness. From low down on the pavement of the dim street (it was already twilight) a voice cried out with a raucous and merciless distinctness:

'Major Brown, Major Brown, where does the jackal dwell?'

Brown was decisive and silent in action. He strode to the front door and looked out. There was no sign of life in the blue gloaming of the street, where one or two lamps were beginning to light their lemon sparks. On returning, he found the lady in green trembling.

'It is the end,' she cried, with shaking lips; 'it may be death for both of us. Whenever—'

But even as she spoke her speech was cloven by another hoarse proclamation from the dark street, again horribly articulate.

'Major Brown, Major Brown, how did the jackal die?'

Brown dashed out of the door and down the steps, but again he was frustrated; there was no figure in sight, and the street was far too long and empty for the shouter to have run away. Even the rational Major was a little shaken as he returned in a certain time to the drawing-room. Scarcely had he done so than the terrific voice came:

'Major Brown, Major Brown, where did—'

Brown was in the street almost at a bound, and he was in time—in time to see something which at first glance froze the blood. The cries appeared to come from a decapitated head resting on the pavement.

The next moment the pale Major understood. It was the head of a man thrust through the coal-hole in the street. The next moment, again, it had vanished, and Major Brown turned to the lady. 'Where's your coal-cellar?' he said, and stepped out into the passage.

She looked at him with wild grey eyes. 'You will not go down,' she cried, 'alone, into the dark hole, with that beast?'

'Is this the way?' replied Brown, and descended the kitchen stairs three at a time. He flung open the door of a black cavity and stepped in, feeling in his pocket for matches. As his right hand was thus occupied, a pair of great slimy hands came out of the darkness, hands clearly belonging to a man of gigantic stature, and seized him by the back of the head. They forced him down, down in the suffocating darkness, a brutal image of destiny. But the Major's head, though upside down, was perfectly clear and intellectual. He gave quietly under the pressure until he had slid down almost to his hands and knees. Then finding the knees of the invisible monster within a foot of him, he simply put out one of his long, bony, and skilful hands, and gripping the leg by a muscle pulled it off the ground and laid the huge living man, with a crash, along the floor. He strove to rise, but Brown was on top like a cat. They rolled over and over. Big as the man was, he had evidently now no desire but to escape; he made sprawls hither and thither to get past the Major to the door, but that tenacious person had him hard by the coat collar and hung with the other hand to a beam. At length there came a strain in holding back this human bull, a strain under which Brown expected his hand to rend and part from the arm. But something else rent and parted; and the dim fat figure of the giant vanished out of the cellar, leaving the torn coat in the Major's hand; the only fruit of his adventure and the only clue to the mystery. For when he went up and out at the front door, the lady, the rich hangings, and the whole equipment of the house had disappeared. It had only bare boards and whitewashed walls.

'The lady was in the conspiracy, of course,' said Rupert, nodding. Major Brown turned brick red. 'I beg your pardon,' he said, 'I think not.'

Rupert raised his eyebrows and looked at him for a moment, but said nothing. When next he spoke he asked:

'Was there anything in the pockets of the coat?'

'There was sevenpence halfpenny in coppers and a threepenny-bit,' said the Major carefully; 'there was a cigarette-holder, a piece of string, and this letter,' and he laid it on the table. It ran as follows:

Dear Mr Plover,
I am annoyed to hear that some delay has occurred in the arrangements *re* Major Brown. Please see that he is attacked as per arrangement tomorrow The coal-cellar, of course.
    Yours faithfully,
    P.G. Northover.

Rupert Grant was leaning forward listening with hawk-like eyes. He cut in:

'Is it dated from anywhere?'

'No—oh, yes!' replied Brown, glancing upon the paper; '14 Tanner's Court, North—'

Rupert sprang up and struck his hands together.

'Then why are we hanging here? Let's get along. Basil, lend me your revolver.'

Basil was staring into the embers like a man in a trance; and it was some time before he answered:

'I don't think you'll need it.'

'Perhaps not,' said Rupert, getting into his fur coat. 'One never knows. But going down a dark court to see criminals—'

'Do you think they are criminals?' asked his brother.

Rupert laughed stoutly. 'Giving orders to a subordinate to strangle a harmless stranger in a coal-cellar may strike you as a very blameless experiment, but—'

'Do you think they wanted to strangle the Major?' asked Basil, in the same distant and monotonous voice.

'My dear fellow, you've been asleep. Look at the letter.'

'I am looking at the letter,' said the mad judge calmly; though, as a matter of fact, he was looking at the fire. 'I don't think it's the sort of letter one criminal would write to another.'

'My dear boy, you are glorious,' cried Rupert, turning round, with laughter in his blue bright eyes. 'Your methods amaze me. Why, there is the letter. It is written, and it does give orders for a crime. You might as well say that the Nelson Column was not at all the sort of thing that was likely to be set up in Trafalgar Square.'

Basil Grant shook all over with a sort of silent laughter, but did not otherwise move.

'That's rather good,' he said; 'but, of course, logic like that's not what is really wanted. It's a question of spiritual atmosphere. It's not a criminal letter.'

'It is. It's a matter of fact,' cried the other in an agony of reasonableness.

'Facts,' murmured Basil, like one mentioning some strange, far-off animals, 'how facts obscure the truth. I may be silly—in fact, I'm off my head—but I never could believe in that man—what's his name, in those capital stories?—Sherlock Holmes. Every detail points to something, certainly; but generally to the wrong thing. Facts point in all directions, it seems to me, like the thousands of twigs on a tree. It's only the life of the tree that has unity and goes up—only the green blood that springs, like a fountain, at the stars.'

'But what the deuce else can the letter be but criminal?'

'We have eternity to stretch our legs in,' replied the mystic. 'It can be an infinity of things. I haven't seen any of them—I've only seen the letter. I look at that, and say it's not criminal.'

'Then what's the origin of it?'

'I haven't the vaguest idea.'

'Then why don't you accept the ordinary explanation?'

Basil continued for a little to glare at the coals, and seemed collecting his thoughts in a humble and even painful way. Then he said:

'Suppose you went out into the moonlight. Suppose you passed through silent, silvery streets and squares until you came into an open and deserted space, set with a few monuments, and you beheld one dressed as a ballet girl dancing in the argent glimmer. And suppose you looked, and saw it was a man disguised. And suppose you looked again, and saw it was Lord Kitchener. What would you think?'

He paused a moment, and went on:

'You could not adopt the ordinary explanation. The ordinary explanation of putting on singular clothes is that you look nice in them; you would not think that Lord Kitchener dressed up like a ballet girl out of ordinary personal vanity. You would think it much more likely that he inherited a dancing madness from a great grandmother; or had been hypnotised at a séance; or threatened by a secret society with death if he refused the ordeal. With Baden-Powell, say, it might be a bet—but not with Kitchener. I should know all that, because in my public days I knew him quite well. So I know that letter quite well, and criminals quite well. It's not a criminal's letter. It's all atmospheres.' And he closed his eyes and passed his hand over his forehead.

Rupert and the Major were regarding him with a mixture of respect and pity. The former said:

'Well, I'm going, anyhow, and shall continue to think—until your spiritual mystery turns up—that a man who sends a note recommending a crime, that is, actually a crime that is actually carried out, at least tentatively, is, in all probability, a little casual in his moral tastes. Can I have that revolver?'

'Certainly,' said Basil, getting up. 'But I am coming with you.' And he flung an old cape or cloak round him, and took a sword-stick from the corner.

'You!' said Rupert, with some surprise, 'you scarcely ever leave your hole to look at anything on the face of the earth.'

Basil fitted on a formidable old white hat.

'I scarcely ever,' he said, with an unconscious and colossal arrogance, 'hear of anything on the face of the earth that I do not understand at once, without going to see it.'

And he led the way out into the purple night.

We four swung along the flaring Lambeth streets, across Westminster Bridge, and along the Embankment in the direction of that part of Fleet Street which contained Tanner's Court. The erect, black figure of Major Brown, seen from behind, was a quaint contrast to the hound-like stoop and flapping mantle of young Rupert Grant, who adopted, with childlike delight, all the dramatic poses of the detective of fiction. The finest among his many fine qualities was his boyish appetite for the colour and poetry of London. Basil, who walked behind, with his face turned blindly to the stars, had the look of a somnambulist.

Rupert paused at the corner of Tanner's Court, with a quiver of delight at danger, and gripped Basil's revolver in his great-coat pocket.

'Shall we go in now?' he asked.

'Not get police?' asked Major Brown, glancing sharply up and down the street.

'I am not sure,' answered Rupert, knitting his brows. 'Of course, it's quite clear, the thing's all crooked. But there are three of us, and—'

'I shouldn't get the police,' said Basil in a queer voice. Rupert glanced at him and stared hard.

'Basil,' he cried, 'you're trembling. What's the matter—are you afraid?'

'Cold, perhaps,' said the Major, eyeing him. There was no doubt that he was shaking.

At last, after a few moments' scrutiny, Rupert broke into a curse.

'You're laughing,' he cried. 'I know that confounded, silent, shaky laugh of yours. What the deuce is the amusement, Basil? Here we are, all three of us, within a yard of a den of ruffians—'

'But I shouldn't call the police,' said Basil. 'We four heroes are quite equal to a host,' and he continued to quake with his mysterious mirth.

Rupert turned with impatience and strode swiftly down the court, the rest of us following. When he reached the door of No. 14 he turned abruptly, the revolver glittering in his hand.

'Stand close,' he said in the voice of a commander. 'The scoundrel may be attempting an escape at this moment. We must fling open the door and rush in.'

The four of us cowered instantly under the archway, rigid, except for the old judge and his convulsion of merriment.

'Now,' hissed Rupert Grant, turning his pale face and burning eyes suddenly over his shoulder, 'when I say "Four", follow me with a rush. If I say "Hold him", pin the fellows down, whoever they are. If I say "Stop", stop. I shall say that if there are more than three. If they attack us I shall empty my revolver on them. Basil, have your sword-stick ready. Now—one, two three, four!'

With the sound of the word the door burst open, and we fell into the room like an invasion, only to stop dead.

The room, which was an ordinary and neatly appointed office, appeared, at the first glance, to be empty. But on a second and more careful glance, we saw seated behind a very large desk with pigeon-holes and drawers of bewildering multiplicity, a small man with a black waxed moustache, and the air of a very average clerk, writing hard. He looked up as we came to a standstill.

'Did you knock?' he asked pleasantly. 'I am sorry if I did not hear. What can I do for you?'

There was a doubtful pause, and then, by general consent, the Major himself, the victim of the outrage, stepped forward.

The letter was in his hand, and he looked unusually grim.

'Is your name P.G. Northover?' he asked.

'That is my name,' replied the other, smiling.

'I think,' said Major Brown, with an increase in the dark glow of his face, 'that this letter was written by you.' And with a loud clap he struck open the letter on the desk with his clenched fist. The man called Northover looked at it with unaffected interest and merely nodded.

'Well, sir,' said the Major, breathing hard, 'what about that?'

'What about it, precisely,' said the man with the moustache.

'I am Major Brown,' said that gentleman sternly.

Northover bowed. 'Pleased to meet you, sir. What have you to say to me?'

'Say!' cried the Major, loosing a sudden tempest; 'why, I want this confounded thing settled. I want—'

'Certainly, sir,' said Northover, jumping up with a slight elevation of the eyebrows. 'Will you take a chair for a moment.' And he pressed an electric bell just above him, which thrilled and tinkled in a room beyond. The Major put his hand on the back of the chair offered him, but stood chafing and beating the floor with his polished boot.

The next moment an inner glass door was opened, and a fair, weedy young man, in a frock-coat, entered from within.

'Mr Hopson,' said Northover, 'this is Major Brown. Will you please finish that thing for him I gave you this morning and bring it in?'

'Yes, sir,' said Mr Hopson, and vanished like lightning.

'You will excuse me, gentlemen,' said the egregious Northover, with his radiant smile, 'if I continue to work until Mr Hopson is ready. I have some books that must be cleared up before I get away on my holiday tomorrow. And we all like a whiff of the country, don't we? Ha! ha!'

The criminal took up his pen with a childlike laugh, and a silence ensued; a placid and busy silence on the part of Mr P.G. Northover; a raging silence on the part of everybody else.

At length the scratching of Northover's pen in the stillness was mingled with a knock at the door, almost simultaneous with the turning of the handle, and Mr Hopson came in again with the same silent rapidity, placed a paper before his principal, and disappeared again.

The man at the desk pulled and twisted his spiky moustache for a few moments as he ran his eye up and down the paper presented to him. He took up his pen, with a slight, instantaneous frown, and altered something, muttering—'Careless.' Then he read it again with the same impenetrable reflectiveness, and finally handed it to the frantic Brown, whose hand was beating the devil's tattoo on the back of the chair.

'I think you will find that all right, Major,' he said briefly.

The Major looked at it; whether he found it all right or not will appear later, but he found it like this:

Major Brown to P.G. Northover.			
	£	s.	d.
January 1, to account rendered	5	6	0
May 9, to potting and embedding of zoo pansies	2	0	0
To cost of trolley with flowers	0	15	0
To hiring of man with trolley	0	5	0
To hire of house and garden for one day	1	0	0
To furnishing of room in peacock curtains, copper ornaments, etc.	3	0	0
To salary of Miss Jameson	1	0	0
To salary of Mr Plover	1	0	0
		—	
Total	£14	6	0
A Remittance will oblige.			

'What,' said Brown, after a dead pause, and with eyes that seemed slowly rising out of his head, 'What in heaven's name is this?'

'What is it?' repeated Northover, cocking his eyebrow with amusement. 'It's your account, of course.'

'My account!' The Major's ideas appeared to be in a vague stampede. 'My account! And what have I got to do with it?'

'Well,' said Northover, laughing outright, 'naturally I prefer you to pay it.'

The Major's hand was still resting on the back of the chair as the words came. He scarcely stirred otherwise, but he lifted the chair bodily into the air with one hand and hurled it at Northover's head.

The legs crashed against the desk, so that Northover only got a blow on the elbow as he sprang up with clenched fists, only to be seized by the united rush of the rest of us. The chair had fallen clattering on the empty floor.

'Let me go, you scamps,' he shouted. 'Let me—'

'Stand still,' cried Rupert authoritatively. 'Major Brown's action is excusable. The abominable crime you have attempted—'

'A customer has a perfect right,' said Northover hotly, 'to question an alleged overcharge, but, confound it all, not to throw furniture.'

'What, in God's name, do you mean by your customers and over-charges?' shrieked Major Brown, whose keen feminine nature, steady in pain or danger, became almost hysterical in the presence of a long and exasperating mystery. 'Who are you? I've never seen you or your insolent tomfool bills. I know one of your cursed brutes tried to choke me—'

'Mad,' said Northover, gazing blankly round; 'all of them mad. I didn't know they travelled in quartettes.'

'Enough of this prevarication,' said Rupert; 'your crimes are discovered. A policeman is stationed at the corner of the court. Though only a private detective myself, I will take the responsibility of telling you that anything you say—'

'Mad,' repeated Northover, with a weary air.

And at this moment, for the first time, there struck in among them the strange, sleepy voice of Basil Grant.

'Major Brown,' he said, 'may I ask you a question?'

The Major turned his head with an increased bewilderment.

'You?' he cried; 'certainly, Mr Grant.'

'Can you tell me,' said the mystic, with sunken head and lowering brow, as he traced a pattern in the dust with his sword-stick, 'can you tell me what was the name of the man who lived in your house before you?'

The unhappy Major was only faintly more disturbed by this last and futile irrelevancy, and he answered vaguely:

G.K. CHESTERTON

'Yes, I think so; a man named Gurney something—a name with a hyphen—Gurney-Brown; that was it.'

'And when did the house change hands?' said Basil, looking up sharply. His strange eyes were burning brilliantly.

'I came in last month,' said the Major.

And at the mere word the criminal Northover suddenly fell into his great office chair and shouted with a volleying laughter.

'Oh! it's too perfect—it's too exquisite,' he gasped, beating the arms with his fists. He was laughing deafeningly; Basil Grant was laughing voicelessly; and the rest of us only felt that our heads were like weather-cocks in a whirlwind.

'Confound it, Basil,' said Rupert, stamping. 'If you don't want me to go mad and blow your metaphysical brains out, tell me what all this means.'

Northover rose.

'Permit me, sir, to explain,' he said. 'And, first of all, permit me to apologize to you, Major Brown, for a most abominable and unpardonable blunder, which has caused you menace and inconvenience, in which, if you will allow me to say so, you have behaved with astonishing courage and dignity. Of course you need not trouble about the bill. We will stand the loss.' And, tearing the paper across, he flung the halves into the waste-paper basket and bowed.

Poor Brown's face was still a picture of distraction. 'But I don't even begin to understand,' he cried. 'What bill? What blunder? What loss?'

Mr P.G. Northover advanced in the centre of the room, thoughtfully, and with a great deal of unconscious dignity. On closer consideration, there were apparent about him other things beside a screwed moustache, especially a lean, sallow face, hawk-like, and not without a careworn intelligence. Then he looked up abruptly.

'Do you know where you are, Major?' he said.

'God knows I don't,' said the warrior, with fervour.

'You are standing,' replied Northover, 'in the office of the Adventure and Romance Agency, Limited.'

'And what's that?' blankly inquired Brown.

The man of business leaned over the back of the chair, and fixed his dark eyes on the other's face.

'Major,' said he, 'did you ever, as you walked along the empty street upon some idle afternoon, feel the utter hunger for something to happen—something, in the splendid words of Walt Whitman: "Something pernicious and dread; something far removed from a puny and pious life; something unproved; something in a trance; something loosed from its anchorage, and driving free." Did you ever feel that?'

'Certainly not,' said the Major shortly.

'Then I must explain with more elaboration,' said Mr Northover, with a sigh. 'The Adventure and Romance Agency has been started to meet a great modern desire. On every side, in conversation and in literature, we hear of the desire for a larger theatre of events for something to waylay us and lead us splendidly astray. Now the man who feels this desire for a varied life pays a yearly or a quarterly sum to the Adventure and Romance Agency; in return, the Adventure and Romance Agency undertakes to surround him with startling and weird events. As a man is leaving his front door, an excited sweep approaches him and assures him of a plot against his life; he gets into a cab, and is driven to an opium den; he receives a mysterious telegram or a dramatic visit, and is immediately in a vortex of incidents. A very picturesque and moving story is first written by one of the staff of distinguished novelists who are at present hard at work in the adjoining room. Yours, Major Brown (designed by our Mr Grigsby), I consider peculiarly forcible and pointed; it is almost a pity you did not see the end of it. I need scarcely explain further the monstrous mistake. Your predecessor in your present house, Mr Gurney-Brown, was a subscriber to our agency, and our foolish clerks, ignoring alike the dignity of the hyphen and the glory of military rank, positively imagined that Major Brown and Mr Gurney-Brown were the same person. Thus you were suddenly hurled into the middle of another man's story.'

'How on earth does the thing work?' asked Rupert Grant, with bright and fascinated eyes.

'We believe that we are doing a noble work,' said Northover warmly.

'It has continually struck us that there is no element in modern life that is more lamentable than the fact that the modern man has to seek all artistic existence in a sedentary state. If he wishes to float into fairyland, he reads a book; if he wishes to dash into the thick of battle, he reads a book; if he wishes to soar into heaven, he reads a book; if he wishes to slide down the banisters, he reads a book. We give him these visions, but we give him exercise at the same time, the necessity of leaping from wall to wall, of fighting strange gentlemen, of running down long streets from pursuers—all healthy and pleasant exercises. We give him a glimpse of that great morning world of Robin Hood or the Knights Errant, when one great game was played under the splendid sky. We give him back his childhood, that godlike time when we can act stories, be our own heroes, and at the same instant dance and dream.'

Basil gazed at him curiously. The most singular psychological discovery had been reserved to the end, for as the little business man ceased speaking he had the blazing eyes of a fanatic.

Major Brown received the explanation with complete simplicity and good humour.

'Of course; awfully dense, sir,' he said. 'No doubt at all, the scheme excellent. But I don't think—' He paused a moment, and looked dreamily out of the window. 'I don't think you will find me in it. Somehow, when one's seen— seen the thing itself, you know—blood and men screaming, one feels about having a little house and a little hobby; in the Bible, you know, "There remaineth a rest".'

Northover bowed. Then after a pause he said:

'Gentlemen, may I offer you my card. If any of the rest of you desire, at any time, to communicate with me, despite Major Brown's view of the matter—'

'I should be obliged for your card, sir,' said the Major, in his abrupt but courteous voice. 'Pay for chair.'

The agent of Romance and Adventure handed his card, laughing.

It ran, 'P.G. Northover, B.A., C.Q.T., Adventure and Romance Agency, 14 Tanner's Court, Fleet Street.'

'What on earth is "C.Q.T."?' asked Rupert Grant, looking over the Major's shoulder.

'Don't you know?' returned Northover. 'Haven't you ever heard of the Club of Queer Trades?'

'There seems to be a confounded lot of funny things we haven't heard of,' said the little Major reflectively. 'What's this one?'

'The Club of Queer Trades is a society consisting exclusively of people who have invented some new and curious way of making money. I was one of the earliest members.'

'You deserve to be,' said Basil, taking up his great white hat, with a smile, and speaking for the last time that evening.

When they had passed out the Adventure and Romance agent wore a queer smile, as he trod down the fire and locked up his desk. 'A fine chap, that Major; when one hasn't a touch of the poet one stands some chance of being a poem. But to think of such a clockwork little creature of all people getting into the nets of one of Grigsby's tales,' and he laughed out aloud in the silence.

Just as the laugh echoed away, there came a sharp knock at the door. An owlish head, with dark moustaches, was thrust in, with deprecating and somewhat absurd inquiry.

'What! Back again, Major?' cried Northover in surprise. 'What can I do for you?'

The Major shuffled feverishly into the room.

'It's horribly absurd,' he said. 'Something must have got started in me that I never knew before. But upon my soul I feel the most desperate desire to know the end of it all.'

'The end of it all?'

'Yes,' said the Major. '"Jackals", and the title-deeds, and "Death to Major Brown".'

The agent's face grew grave, but his eyes were amused.

'I am terribly sorry, Major,' said he, 'but what you ask is impossible. I don't know any one I would sooner oblige than you; but the rules of the agency are strict. The Adventures are confidential; you are an outsider;

I am not allowed to let you know an inch more than I can help. I do hope you understand—'

'There is no one,' said Brown, 'who understands discipline better than I do. Thank you very much. Good night.'

And the little man withdrew for the last time.

He married Miss Jameson, the lady with the red hair and the green garments. She was an actress, employed (with many others) by the Romance Agency; and her marriage with the prim old veteran caused some stir in her languid and intellectualized set. She always replied very quietly that she had met scores of men who acted splendidly in the charades provided for them by Northover, but that she had only met one man who went down into a coal-cellar when he really thought it contained a murderer.

The Major and she are living as happily as birds, in an absurd villa, and the former has taken to smoking. Otherwise he is unchanged—except, perhaps, there are moments when, alert and full of feminine unselfishness as the Major is by nature, he falls into a trance of abstraction. Then his wife recognizes with a concealed smile, by the blind look in his blue eyes, that he is wondering what were the title-deeds, and why he was not allowed to mention jackals. But, like so many old soldiers, Brown is religious, and believes that he will realize the rest of those purple adventures in a better world.

SEX

Peter Cook and Dudley Moore

Peter Cook (1937–1995) and Dudley Moore (1935–2002) are regarded as one of the greatest comic double acts the UK has ever produced. Their characters Pete and Dud first appeared in 1964. Pete is a know-it-all would-be intellectual and Dud is his put-upon sidekick, endlessly trying to impress Pete with his knowledge. Neither has any real sense. The pair developed an unorthodox method for scripting their material, using a tape recorder to tape an ad-libbed routine that they would then have transcribed and edited.

PETE. Come over here, will you please.

DUD. Here, you've been ferreting around in my sandwich box, haven't you?

PETE. I certainly have, and I found something not altogether connected with sandwiches. I refer of course to Blauberger's Encyclopaedia of Sexual Knowledge. How do you explain this?

DUD. I found it on the Heath, Pete, and I thought I better keep it in my sandwich tin to keep it dry until someone claimed it.

PETE. You're hiding it away, aren't you, because you're ashamed of it.

DUD. No I'm not. I just kept it there for safe keeping.

PETE. You shouldn't be ashamed of sex, Dud. It's no good hiding your sex away in a sandwich tin. Bring it out in the open.

DUD. It's a good book that, some good bits in it. Have you read any of it?

PETE. Yes, I've been through it up to page three thousand and one.

DUD. You've read the whole lot of it then, haven't you?

PETE. Yeah, it's quite good.

DUD. I like it because it tells you everything about sex from the word go.

PETE. It's wonderfully informative about the sexual mores throughout the ages, Dud.

DUD. And it tells you of human sexual endeavour from the time of Adam and Eve, Pete.

PETE. It certainly does, all the myths about it as well. Of course, Adam and Eve while they were in the Garden of Eden, they didn't have anything to do with sex to start with, you know. When they were in Paradise, they didn't have anything to do with sex 'cause they were wandering around naked but they didn't know they were naked.

DUD. I bet they did know. I mean, you'd soon know once you got caught up on the brambles.

PETE. They had no idea – they were remarkably stupid, as well as naked. They didn't know they were naked until up come a serpent – as some authorities have it. Up come a serpent and said, 'Here's an apple. Lay your teeth into that.' Then they laid their teeth into the apple and the serpent said, 'You're nude, you're completely nude.'

DUD. Hello nudies! Course they dashed off into the brush and covered themselves with embarrassment, didn't they?

PETE. And mulberry leaves as well. They covered themselves altogether with this primitive clothing made of leaves, and suddenly, as soon as they became completely covered, they began to get attracted to each other, and then, of course, they tore off the mulberry leaves and it all started, the whole business.

DUD. Well, I think once you've got clothes on you're more attractive to other people. Like I think Aunt Dolly's more attractive with her clothes on than off. So Uncle Bert says, anyway.

PETE. Well, Aunt Dolly is really at her most attractive when she's completely covered in wool and has a black veil over her face and, ideally, she should be in another room from you.

DUD. Who's your sort of ideal woman, Pete?

PETE. Well, above all others I covet the elfin beauty, the gazelle slim elfin beauty, very slim, very slender, but all the same, still being endowed with a certain amount of...

DUD. Busty substances.

PETE. Yes, a kind of Audrey Hepburn with Anita Ekberg overtones is what I go for. What do you like?

DUD. Me? The same sort of thing. Actually I like the sort of woman who throws herself on you and tears your clothes off with rancid sensuality.

PETE. Yes, they're quite good, aren't they? I think you're referring to 'rampant sensuality'.

DUD. Either one will do. Of course, the important thing is that they tear your clothes off.

PETE. That's the chief thing. I like a good rampant woman.

DUD. I tell you a rampant woman – or rancid – or whatever you prefer. That's Veronica Pilbrow. Do you remember her?

PETE. Do I remember her? Yeah.

DUD. She was always throwing herself on Roger Braintree, never me, though.

PETE. Well Roger Braintree at school, he always knew more than anyone else. He was always boasting about things he knew.

DUD. Old clever drawers, weren't he, eh?

PETE. You remember that time he came round behind the wooden buildings and he had, what was his name, Kenny Vare with him, and he come up and told me, 'I've discovered the most disgusting word in the world. It's so filthy that no one's allowed to see it except bishops and nobody knows what it means. It's the worst word in the world.'

DUD. What was the word?

PETE. He wouldn't tell me. I had to give him half a pound of peppermints before he let it out. Do you know what it was?

DUD. No.

PETE. 'Bastard'.

DUD. What's that mean, Pete?

PETE. Well, he wouldn't tell me. I knew it was filthy but I didn't know how to use it. So he said the only place I could see it was down at the Town Hall in the enormous dictionary they have there – an enormous one with a whole volume to each letter. You can only get in with a medical certificate. So I went down there and sneaked in, you know, very secretively, and went up and took down from the shelf this enormous great dusty 'B' and opened it out and there was the word in all its horror – 'BASTARD'.

DUD. What was the definition, Pete?

PETE. It said, 'BASTARD – Child born out of wedlock.'

DUD. Urrgh! What's a wedlock, Pete?

PETE. A wedlock, Dud, is a horrible thing. It's a mixture of a steam engine and a padlock and some children are born out of them instead of through the normal channels and it's another one of the filthiest words in the world.

DUD. Make your hair drop out if you say it. I like looking up words in the dictionary. You know, I like going round the Valence library and going to the reference library and getting out the dictionary of unconventional English and looking up 'BLOOMERS'.

PETE. Yes, it's quite a good way of spending an afternoon.

DUD. Course I tell you what, Pete, the whole business of sex is a bit of a let-down really when you compare it with the wonderful romantic tales of a novelist who can portray sexual endeavours in so much better form, Pete.

PETE. Well, he makes it all so perfect. In the hands of a skilled novelist, sex becomes something which can never be attained in real life. Have you read Nevil Shute?

DUD. Very little.

PETE. How much of Nevil Shute have you read?

DUD. Nothing.

PETE. Yes, well Nevil Shute is a master of sensuality. He has some wonderful erotic passages, like in 'A Town Like Alice' in the hardcover version, page 81. If you go down the library, it falls open at that page. It's a description set in Australia, Dud, and there's this ash-blonde girl, Tina.

DUD. [*Sings*] Tina, don't you be meaner...

PETE. Shut up. And she's there, standing on the runway, you see, of this aerodrome and it's very hot – Australian bush heat. It's very hot indeed and she's standing there waiting for her rugged Aussie pilot to come – bronzed Tim Bradley – and it's very hot. The cicadas are rubbing their legs together making that strange noise – very similar to that nasty noise which is coming from your mouth at this very moment. And it's very hot and she's covered in dust. The Australian dust is all over her. She's got dust on her knees, dust on her shoulders.

DUD. Dust on her bust, Pete.

PETE. Dust on her bust, as you so rightly point out. Dud. And it's very dusty and it's very hot – hot and dusty. And suddenly, out of nowhere, the clouds open. There's a tremendous clap of thunder and suddenly the mongoose is on her. The tropical rain storm is soaking through the frail poplin she is wearing and as the dress gets damper and damper, damper and damper, her wonderful frail form is outlined against the poplin. And then what does she hear but, in the distance, the distant buzzing of an approaching plane. She cups her ear to hear, like this.

DUD. She cups her perfectly proportioned up-thrusting ear, Pete.

PETE. She cups it, the plane comes down on the runway and comes to a halt and out comes the bronzed Aussie. But all the propellers are going very fast still. There's a tremendous rushing wind and it blows up against her and it blows the damp dress right up against her and reveals, for all the world to see, her perfectly defined...

DUD. Busty substances.

PETE. Busty substances.

DUD. What happened after that, Pete?

PETE. Well, the bronzed pilot goes up to her and they walk away, and the chapter ends in three dots.

DUD. What do those three dots mean, Pete?

PETE. Well, in Shute's hands, three dots can mean anything.

DUD. How's your father, perhaps?

PETE. When Shute uses three dots it means, 'Use your own imagination. Conjure the scene up yourself.' Whenever I see three dots I feel all funny.

DUD. That's put me in the mood to go up to the Valence library and look up 'BOSOM' again.

PETE. No, it's no good looking up 'BOSOM', it only says 'see BUST'.

DUD. But it's nice to read it all again.

PETE. It gives you something to do.

FATHER & SON

Peter Cook and Dudley Moore

Peter Cook (1937–1995) and **Dudley Moore** (1935–2002) are regarded as one of the greatest comic double acts the UK has ever produced. The pair developed an unorthodox method for scripting their material, using a tape recorder to tape an ad-libbed routine that they would then have transcribed and edited.

[*Dudley plays a working-class father. Peter plays his middle-class son.*]

DUDLEY. Is that you, Brian?

PETER. Yes, father.

DUDLEY. What time of night do you call this, then?

PETER. It's four o'clock in the morning, father.

DUDLEY. I'll four o'clock in the morning you, my boy. I've been sitting here since half past eleven wondering what's happened to you. I've been sitting here, eating my heart out. I have to get up in two hours' time.

PETER. I know, father.

DUDLEY. I have to get up at half past six. Where have you been?

PETER. Father, I'm twenty-eight years old. Surely I'm old enough to go where I like, with whom I like, at what time I like. I was out with friends.

DUDLEY. Friends? Friends? I call 'em fiends. They're nothing but a pack of whoers.

PETER. The word is whore, father.

DUDLEY. You've become a regular little rolling stone ever since you opened that stupid little shop of yours.

PETER. There's nothing stupid about the boutique, father. It happens to cater for modern trends which you may be a little out of touch with, that's all.

DUDLEY. Well, I thank the lord I've lost contact with painted ties, kinky boots and PVC underwear. What sort of a bloody job is that then, eh? Well, wash my mouth out with soap and water. What I'd like to know is, what's wrong with the drains then, eh? I've been down the drains all my life. My father before me, he's been down the drains, and my grandfather before me, been down the drains. The whole family's been down the drains for centuries. I suppose you're too big down the drains, aren't you?

PETER. Father, the mere fact that our entire family tree grew in the drains is no reason why I should spend my life in a sewer.

DUDLEY. If your mother was alive today, she'd have something to say about it. Oh, Rosie, Rosie, why did you leave me, my darling, to cope with such an ungrateful son?

PETER. Don't drag mother into it, please.

DUDLEY. I can scarcely drag your poor mother into it when she's five foot underground, can I? How did we spawn this fop? You're all la di da, ain't ya? You're too clever clever for your own father now, ain't ya? Yes, of course you're too good for the drains. I forgot. You're a bloody Marquis, aren't you? Oh, wash my mouth out with soap. Look here my boy, I tell you – the drains are too good for you. That's what it is. I've seen better things than you floating down the drains.

PETER. Father, I don't know why you go on about the drains. You know perfectly well you retired at thirty-one and you haven't been down there since.

DUDLEY. I'll haven't been down there since you, my boy. Now then, Rosie, Rosie my darling. Do you see what a popinjay we have for a son? What a strutting peacock? Did I fight in the war to hear you abuse me in such a way? Eh, did I?

PETER. I've no idea, father. If indeed you did fight in the war.

DUDLEY. If indeed I did fight? I'll if indeed I did fight you, my boy. What's this then, eh? Tell me what this is! Tell me what that is, then! Go on?

PETER. That's your navel, father.

DUDLEY. Really? That's funny. I thought I contracted that on Dunkirk, on the beach. Crawling on my hands and knees to preserve you, eh?

PETER. Father, if that's a war wound, I think you'll find I've got a similar one under my shirt.

DUDLEY. I don't want to see under your shirt. You disgust me. I've been a verger at St Thomas's, Beacontree, for forty-five years, and I've never seen you in that place. I've never seen you within two yards of its portal.

PETER. Father, I can't help being an agnostic. I wish I had faith like you.

DUDLEY. I'll I wish I had faith like you you, my boy. Now then, you come in at all hours of the morning, smelling of honey and flowers and reading your poncy magazines, and mixing your Bloody Marys. I've got a good mind to give you a good hiding. I've got a good mind to take my belt off to you.

PETER. I wouldn't do that, father. Your trousers will fall down.

DUDLEY. Very funny. Very amusing. Very witty. Oh yes. I wouldn't have had that sort of cheek from you when you were a little boy. You were such a lovely little boy. My golden-haired beauty, you were. Your mother and I, we used to go along the cliffs at Westcliff, and she used to be on one side and I used to be on the other, holding your little warm wet hands. And you used to see a ship on the horizon. You used to say 'Daddy, what's that?' I used to say 'It's a ship.' You never ask me that anymore, do you? You don't have to ask me anything.

Do you, eh? Fancy pants. All you need to do is go strutting down the Kings Road every Saturday afternoon, showing off to your fiends. Every word you say is a stab in the back. Every gesture, every look you make is a thorn in my side.

PETER. Father, there's no need for you to come down the Kings Road too. I could do perfectly well without you.

DUDLEY. I'll perfectly well without you my boy. Rosie, did we in our moment of joy, spawn this werewolf, this Beelzebub?

PETER. I don't know why you keep looking upwards when you mention mother. You know perfectly well she's living in Frinton with a sailor.

DUDLEY. That's a terrible thing to say. That's a bloody terrible thing to say. Soap and water. Do you think my wife would have left me? Do you think your mother would have left me? She loved me as I loved her. Good lord! Do you think your mother would have gone off to live with some dirty matelot in Frinton? She worshipped the ground I walked on.

PETER. She liked the ground, but she didn't care for you, father.

DUDLEY. I'll didn't care for you you, my boy. Now then, she's gone up there to the great sewer in the sky, the biggest drain of them all. All you can do is make this place into a sin cellar. Here, you're nothing but a whoer. Get out of my house. Go on. Get out of my house.

PETER. Father, it's not your house. It's my house.

DUDLEY. Oh, pardon me for living. Pardon me for having two strong sturdy legs to stand on. I'll get out of your house then, and never darken your doorstep again.

PETER. I'm going to bed, father. Why don't you have a Sydrax?

DUDLEY. Oh, Rosie, Rosie my darling, my doll, my sweetheart. Where did we go wrong? Where did we go wrong?

THE WOODEN MADONNA

Noël Coward

Noël Coward (1899–1973) was an English playwright, composer, director, actor and singer, known for his wit and flamboyance. Coward achieved huge acclaim for his plays, which include classics such as *Hay Fever*, *Private Lives* and *Blithe Spirit*, but returned again and again to the short story throughout his writing life. 'I find them fascinating to write,' he explained, 'but far from easy.'

1

Aubrey Dakers relaxed, a trifle self-consciously, in a pink cane chair outside the Café Bienvenue. He crossed one neatly creased trouser leg over the other and regarded his suede shoes whimsically for a moment and then, lighting a cigarette, gave himself up to enjoyment of the scene before him. His enjoyment was tempered with irritation. He had a slight headache from the train and the air was colder than he had anticipated, also it looked suspiciously as though it might rain during the next hour or so; however the sun was out for the time being and there was quite a lot to look at. On the other side of the water, mountains towered up into the sky, a number of small waterfalls lay on them like feathers and, in the distance, the higher peaks were still covered with snow. Little white streamers with black funnels bustled about the lake while immediately before him, beneath the blossoming chestnut trees, promenaded a series of highly characteristic types. By the newspaper kiosk for instance there was a group of young men, three of them wore bottle green capes and hats with feathers at the back, the fourth was more mundane in an ordinary Homburg and a buttoned-up mackintosh that looked quite like a cardboard box. Two artificial-looking children, dressed in red and blue respectively, galloped along the pavement bowling hoops; a gray man with an umbrella waited furtively by the ticket office at the head of the little wooden pier, obviously a secret agent. Seated at a table on Aubrey's right were two English ladies, one very grand in black, wearing several gold chains and brooches and a patrician hat mounted high on bundles of gray hair; the other, small and servile, waited on her eagerly, pouring tea, offering patisserie, wriggling a little, like a dog waiting to have a ball thrown for it. "How funny," thought Aubrey, "if the Grand one really did throw a ball and sent her scampering off yapping under people's feet!" Pleased with this fantasy he smiled and then, observing a waiter looking at him, ordered a cup of coffee rather crossly.

Aubrey Dakers at the age of twenty-seven was in the enviable position of having written a successful play and in the less enviable position of having eventually to follow it up with another. If not another play, a novel, or at least a book of short stories. His play *Animal Grab* had already run for over a year in London and showed every sign of continuing indefinitely. It had been hailed enthusiastically by the critics. He had been described as "A new star in the theatrical firmament." "A second Somerset Maugham." "A second Noël Coward." "A second Oscar Wilde" and "A new playwright of considerable promise." This last had been in *The Times* and, as was right and proper, headed the list of press comments outside the theater. The extraordinary part of the whole thing was that Aubrey had never really intended to write a play at all, nor indeed to write anything. He had been perfectly content running a little antique shop with Maurice Macgrath in Ebury Street, which had been reasonably successful for six years and they had been happy as larks together. Aubrey remembered with a pang of nostalgia those early days, before they had actually opened the shop, when the whole thing was still in the air so to speak. That fateful Easter Monday when Maurice had suddenly come up from his parents' home in Kent and broken the glorious news. "My dear!" Aubrey could still recapture the thrill in his voice, "I've got the money!—Uncle Vernon's promised it and got round father and everything and we're to start looking for premises right away—isn't it absolutely heavenly?"

Then those lovely spring days motoring over the countryside, in Maurice's sister's Talbot, ransacking every antique shop they could find and often returning long after dark with the rumble seat crammed with oddments. The bigger stuff they bought was of course impossible to convey in the Talbot so this was all sent to be stored in Norman's studio, where, Norman being away in Capri for the winter, it could stay in the charge of Norman's housekeeper until May at least. Before May, however, they had found the shop in Ebury Street, fallen in love with it on sight and taken it recklessly on a twelve-year lease. Aubrey sighed. There had been anxious hours during those first few months. Then had come the sale of the Queen Anne set, broken chair and all, and then, almost as though Tate had suddenly determined to bewilder them with success, the bread trough and the Dutch candelabra were bought on the same day. You could never forget moments like that. The evening of celebration they'd had! Dinner at the Berkeley Grill and front-row stalls for the ballet.

After that the business had climbed steadily. They had always thought it would once they had a good start, and it did. During the ensuing years dinners at the Berkeley and stalls for the ballet became almost commonplace. But alas, even for amiable harmless lives like those of Aubrey and Maurice the laws of change are inexorable. In the year nineteen thirty-six the blow fell or, to be more accurate, a series of blows, beginning with Lady Brophy opening an elaborate interior decorating establishment five doors away from them. Lady Brophy was idle and rich, and with the heedless extravagance of the amateur, altered her window display completely every few weeks. She seldom arrived at her shop before noon, and then in a Rolls Royce, when Aubrey and Maurice had been at their post since nine o'clock as usual. Lady Brophy was undoubtedly the first blow. The drop in business within a few weeks of her arrival was only too apparent. The second blow was Maurice getting flu and then pneumonia and being sent to Sainte Maxime to convalesce where he first met Ivan. The third blow was a small but effective fire in the basement of the shop which demolished a Sheraton chair, two gate-legged tables, one good, the other so-so, a Jacobean corner cupboard, a set of Victorian engravings, two painted ostrich eggs circa 1850 and a really precious Spanish four-poster bed that Maurice had bought at an auction in Sevenoaks. The final and ultimately most decisive blow was Maurice's return to London with Ivan.

Ivan was more thoroughly Russian than any Russian Aubrey had ever seen. He was tall, melancholy, intellectual, given to spectacular outbursts of temperament and connected with the film business. Not, of course, in an active commercial way but on the experimental side. He was ardently at work upon a color film of shapes and sounds only, for which, he asserted positively, one of the principal companies in Hollywood was eagerly waiting. Aubrey often reproached himself for having been so nice to Ivan, if only he had known then what he knew later he would probably have been able to have nipped the whole thing in the bud, but then of course he could never have believed, unless it had been hammered into his brain by brutal reality, that Maurice could be so silly and, above all, so deceitful—but still there it was. Maurice suddenly announced that he wanted to give up the shop and lead a different sort of life entirely. You could have knocked Aubrey down with a feather. Maurice began the scene just as they were dressing to go to a first night at the Old Vic. Of course they hadn't gone. Even now Aubrey could hardly think of that awful evening without trembling. They had stayed in the flat, half dressed, just as they were and had the whole thing out. It had finally transpired that the root of the whole trouble was that Maurice was dissatisfied with himself. That, of course, was typical of Maurice—suddenly to be dissatisfied with himself when there was so much extra work to be done on account of the fire and a lot of new stuff to be bought. In vain Aubrey had remonstrated with him. In vain he had reiterated that what you are you are, and all the wishing in the world won't make you any different. Maurice had argued back that deep in his subconscious mind he had always had a conviction that what he was he wasn't really, that is to say at least not nearly so much as Aubrey was and that Ivan with his brilliant mind and wonderful view of life was the only person in the world who could really understand and help him; also, he added, he was an expert horseman. A few hours later they had gone out and had a chicken sandwich upstairs at the Café de Paris, both of them quite calm, purged of all emotion, but miserably aware that whatever the future might have in store for them, something very precious and important had been lost irretrievably.

That had all happened two and a half years ago. They had sold the shop jointly. Stock, lease, goodwill and everything. Aubrey had felt himself unable, even in the face of Maurice's pleading, to carry it on by himself or even with Norman, who had been quite keen to come in. The whole thing was over and that was that. Much better make a clean cut and embark on something new.

Maurice had, in due course, departed for America with Ivan, but there had apparently been some sort of hitch over the color film, for Aubrey had received a brief postcard from him some months later saying that he had obtained a position as assistant in Gump's Oriental Store in San Francisco and was very happy.

To embark on something new proved to be difficult for Aubrey for the simple reason that he had not the remotest idea what to embark on. He had a small amount of money saved from his share of the shop, and in order to husband this as carefully as possible he rejoined his family and stayed with them unenthusiastically for several months. He might have been less apathetic and devitalized had he but known at the time that those months at home with his parents, two unmarried sisters, a young brother and an elder brother with a wife and child, were the turning point in his life. *Animal Grab*, the comedy that had so entranced London and brought him such staggering success, had actually been written at his sister-in-law's request, for the local Amateur Dramatic Society to perform at the Town Hall for Christmas. There it had been seen, quite by chance, by Thornton Heatherly, who happened to be staying in the neighborhood and was taken to it. Thornton Heatherly, an enterprising young man with a harelip, had been running a small repertory theater at Hounslow for nearly two years at a loss although with a certain amount of critical réclame and *Animal Grab* impressed him, not so much by its wit or craftsmanship or story, but by its unabashed family appeal. There was a persistent vogue of family plays of all sorts in London. *Animal Grab* was as authentic and definitely noisier than most, in addition to which it had two surefire characters in it. A vague, lovable mother who always forgot people's names and a comedy cook who repeatedly gave notice.

Thornton Heatherly drove over to see Aubrey the next day, bought a year's option on the play with a minimum advance on account of royalties, and exactly eight weeks later, after a triumphant fortnight at Hounslow, it became the smash hit of the London season.

Since then Aubrey had had a busy time adjusting himself to his new circumstances. First he took the upper part of a small house in South Eaton Place, which he furnished bit by bit with impeccable taste, until, finally, for sheer perfection of Victorian atmosphere, it rivaled even Norman's famous flat in Clebe Place. Then he gradually acquired, with expensive clothes to go with it, a manner of cynical detachment, which was most effective and came in handy as an opening gambit when meeting strangers. "How extraordinary," they would exclaim. "One would never imagine that the author of *Animal Grab* looked in the least like you," to which he would reply with a light sophisticated smile and a certain disarming honesty—"Actually the play is based on my own family which only goes to prove how wickedly deceptive appearances can be!" Everyone, in the face of such amused candor, found him charming and he was invited everywhere. It was, of course, inevitable that the more intellectual of his friends shouldn't much care for *Animal Grab*. While having to admit its authenticity they were scornful of its excessive naïveté. Vivian Melrose, who contributed abstract poems and, occasionally, even more abstract dramatic criticisms to *The Weekly Revue* and ran a leftist bookshop in Marylebone summed it up very pungently, "*Animal Grab*," he said, "makes Puberty seem like Senile Decay!" Aubrey was smart enough to quote this with a wry laugh on several occasions, but in his heart he felt that Vivian had really gone a little too far. However, fortified by his weekly royalty checks, the sale of the amateur rights, the sale of the film rights and serialization in the *Evening Standard*, he could afford to ignore such gibes to a certain extent, but nevertheless a slight sting remained. He had signed an optional contract with Thornton Heatherly for the next two plays he wrote but as yet he had been unable to put pen to paper. After endless conversations with his intimate friends, such as Norman, and Elvira James, who was a literary agent and knew a thing or two, he had decided that his next effort should not be a play at all. He would first of all write a book of short stories, some of which need not be more than light sketches, in order to form an easy flexible style and then try his hand at a novel. He felt a strong urge—as indeed who doesn't?—to write a really good modern novel. Elvira and he had discussed this project very thoroughly. "To begin with," she had said, "it must not be about a family, either your own or anybody else's. The vogue for family life, although running strong at the moment, will not last for ever and there will be a reaction, mark my words." Aubrey agreed with her wholeheartedly, for truth to tell, family feeling, although charmingly expressed in *Animal Grab*, was not, and never had been, his strong point. "Then," went on Elvira relentlessly, "there must be no character in your book who is absentminded, your heroine must never say 'Come on, old Weasel, let's have another set,' and no old gentleman, father, uncle, vicar or professor must be called 'Boffles'!" Aubrey, recognizing the innate wisdom of this, promised. "Away with you," said Elvira, "go away and take notes, watch people, travel, look at Somerset Maugham!" This conversation had taken place a week ago and here he was alone in Switzerland having looked at Somerset Maugham steadfastly since leaving Victoria.

It must not be imagined that Aubrey intended to imitate anybody's particular style, he was far too intelligent for that, but he realized that a careful study of expert methods must in the long run be of some use to a beginner, and Aubrey had no illusions whatever as to his status as a writer. He only knew now, after the violent change that had occurred in his life during the last eighteen months, that he wanted, really wanted, to write. His notes, since leaving England, while not exactly copious, at least showed praiseworthy determination. "Old Lady on platform in wheelchair, probably French Duchess." "Man in dining car with elderly woman obviously German." He had had later to cross out German and put Scotch as he happened to hear them talking in the corridor. "The French countryside seen from a railway carriage looks strangely unfinished." That wasn't bad. "Indian Colonel and wife going to take cure in Wiesbaden suddenly have terrible row and he kills her in tunnel." This had been suggested by two disagreeable people at the next table to him at dinner in the Wagon restaurant.

Sitting outside this café in the afternoon sunshine his mind felt pleasantly alert. It had certainly been a good idea, this little continental jaunt; here he could sit, for hours if need be, just watching and listening and absorbing atmosphere. Later, of course, in the bar of the hotel or in the lounge after dinner, he would get into conversation with various people and draw them out subtly to talk about themselves, to tell him their stories. His knowledge of French being only adequate he hoped that should they wish to lay bare their lives in that language that they would not speak too rapidly. Of German he knew not a word, so whatever he gathered would have to be in English, slow French or by signs.

At this moment in his reflections his attention was caught by the seedy-looking man whom he had noticed before buying a ticket for the boat. Something in the way he was standing, or rather leaning against the railing, struck a familiar chord in his mind. He reminded him of somebody, that's what it was, but who? He scrutinized him carefully, the gray suit, the umbrella, the straggling moustache, the air of depressed resignation. Then he remembered—he was exactly like a commoner, foreign edition of Uncle Philip. Aubrey sighed with relief at having identified him; there is nothing so annoying as being tantalized by a resemblance. Uncle Philip! It might make quite an interesting little story if Uncle Philip, after all those years of marriage, suddenly left Aunt Freda and came here to live in some awful little pension with a French prostitute. Or perhaps not live with her, just meet her every afternoon here at the pier. His eyes would light up when she stepped off the boat (she worked in a café in a town on the other side of the lake and only had a few hours off), and they would walk away together under the chestnut trees, he timidly holding her arm. Then they would go to some sordid bedroom in the town somewhere and he, lying with her arms round him, would suddenly think of his life, those years at Exeter with Aunt Freda, and laugh madly. Aubrey looked at the Swiss Uncle Philip again; he was reading a newspaper now very intently. Perhaps, after all, he was a secret agent as he had at first thought and was waiting for the boat to take him down the lake to the town on the other side of the frontier, where he would sit in a bar with two men in bowler hats and talk very ostentatiously about his son who was ill in Zurich, which would give them to understand that Karl had received the papers satisfactorily in Amsterdam.

At this moment a bell rang loudly and a steamer sidled up to the pier. The man folded his paper, waved his hand and was immediately joined by a large woman in green and three children who had been sitting on a seat. They all went onto the boat together, the children making a good deal of noise. Aubrey sighed. Just another family.

While Aubrey was having his bath before dinner he visualized, on Somerset Maugham lines, the evening before him. A cocktail in the bar, then a table in the corner of the dining room commanding an excellent view of all the other tables. A distinguished-looking man, slightly gray at the temples eating alone at a table by the window, high cheekbones, skin yellowed by malaria and tropical suns.

Then later, in the lounge, "Perhaps you would do me the honor of taking a glass of brandy with me." Aubrey agreeing with an assured smile, noting the while those drawn lines of pain round the finely cut mouth, those hollow, rather haunted eyes. "One can at least say of this hotel that the brandy is of unparalleled excellence!" That slightly foreign accent, Russian perhaps or even Danish! Then the story—bit by bit, gradually unfolding—"I wonder if you ever knew the Baroness Fugier? A strange woman, dead now poor thing; I ran across her brother once in the Ukraine, that was just after the war, then later on, seven years to be exact, I ran across him again in Hankow; I happened to be there on business. He was probably the most brilliant scientist of his time. Has it ever occurred to you to reflect upon the strange passions that lie dormant in the minds of the most upright men?" The lounge emptying, still that level unemotional voice retailing the extraordinary, almost macabre, history of the Baroness Fugier's brother, the scandal in Hong Kong, the ruining of his career, his half-caste wife and finally the denouement.

Aubrey, at last rising. "Thank you so much—what a wonderful story. And what happened to the woman?" Then the sudden bitter chuckle, "The woman, my friend—happens to be my wife!"

2

Aubrey, immaculately dressed in a dinner jacket, descended to the bar, where he was discouraged to find no one whatever except the barman, who was totting up figures and absently eating potato salad. Aubrey suspected that there must be garlic in the potato salad as it smelt very strong. It was a rather dingy little bar, dimly lit, although modern in decoration to the extent that everything that looked as though it ought to be round was square or vice versa and there was a lot of red about. Aubrey hoisted himself on to a square stool and ordered a dry Martini and a packet of Player's. The barman, although quite willing to be pleasant, was not discoursive and turned on the radio. Aubrey sipped his Martini and listened, a trifle wistfully, to an Italian tenor singing "Santa Lucia," and when that was over "La Donna E Mobile." Presently several people came in together, they were elderly and without glamour, and they stood silently by the bar as though they were waiting for some catastrophe.

The barman glanced at the clock and then switched the radio to another station. A tremendous shriek ensued which he modulated until it became a German voice announcing the news. Aubrey could only pick out a word or two here and there such as "Einmal," "Americanische," "Freundschaft" and "Mussolini" so he ordered another dry Martini in a whisper. At the end of the news, which lasted half an hour, everybody bowed to the barman and filed out. Just as Aubrey was preparing to give up the whole thing and go and have dinner, a bald man of about fifty came in. He was obviously English and although not quite as sinister and distinguished as Aubrey would have wished, he was better than nobody. Aubrey noted the details of his appearance with swift professional accuracy. A long nose, eyes rather close together, a jutting underlip, slight jowl, as though at some time in his life someone had seized his face with both hands and pulled it downward. His clothes were quite good and his figure podgy without being exactly fat. He said "Good evening" in a voice that wasn't quite cockney but might have been a long while ago. Aubrey replied with alacrity and offered him a drink, whereupon the man said, "That's very nice of you, my name's Edmundson" as though the thought of accepting a drink from anyone who didn't know his name was Edmundson was not to be tolerated for a moment. Aubrey said that his name was Dakers and they shook hands cordially.

Mr. Edmundson was more than ready to talk, and before a quarter of an hour had passed Aubrey had docketed a number of facts. Mr. Edmundson was fifty-four and was in the silk business although he intended to retire shortly and let his son, who was married and had two children, a boy and a girl, take over for him. He also had two daughters both unmarried. One, however, was engaged to a nice young fellow in the Air Force, this was Sylvia the younger. The elder, Blanche, was having her voice trained with the object of becoming an opera singer. It was apparently a fine voice and very high indeed, and both Mr. and Mrs. Edmundson were at a loss to imagine where she had got it from as neither of them had any musical talent whatsoever. She was very good-looking too, although not so striking as Sylvia, who was the sort of girl people turn round to stare at in restaurants. Mr. Edmundson produced a snapshot from his note-case showing both girls with arms entwined against a sundial with somebody's foot and calf in the left-hand corner. "That's Mrs. Edmundson's foot," he said gaily, "she didn't get out of the way in time." Aubrey looked at the photograph with his head on one side and gave a little cluck of admiration. "They are nice-looking girls," he said as convincingly as he could. Thus encouraged, Mr. Edmundson went on about them a good deal more. Sylvia was the dashing one of the two and in many ways an absolute little minx; whatever she set her heart on she got, she was that sort of character; in fact, a few years ago when she was just beginning to be grown up, both he and Mrs. Edmundson had frequently been worried about her. Blanche, on the other hand, despite her musical gift, was more balanced and quiet, which was very odd really, because you would have thought it would have been just the other way round. Aubrey agreed that it certainly was most peculiar but there just wasn't any way of accounting for things like that. "This is my son Leonard," said Mr. Edmundson, producing another snapshot with the deftness of a card manipulator. "He's different again." Aubrey looked at it and admitted that he was. Leonard was short and sturdy with an under-slung jaw and eyebrows that went straight across his forehead in a black bar. On his lap he was holding, rather self-consciously, a mad baby. Mr. Edmundson discoursed for a long while upon Leonard's flair for engineering which apparently fell little short of genius. Ever since he was a tiny boy he had been unable to see a watch or a clockwork engine or a musical box without tearing it to pieces immediately, and when he was sixteen he had completely dismembered his new motorcycle on the front lawn within three hours of having received it.

During dinner, Mr. Edmundson having suggested that as they were both alone it would be pleasant to share a table, he explained that the reason he had come to Switzerland was to see a specialist on diseases of the bladder who had been recommended to him by a well-known doctor in Tonbridge. It appeared that for nearly a year past there had been a certain divergence of opinion as to whether he was forming a stone or not, and both he and his wife had decided, after mature consideration, that by far the wisest thing to do was to get an expert opinion once and for all. The Swiss specialist, who wasn't really Swiss but Austrian, had declared that as far as he could discover there were no indications of a stone having been formed or even beginning to form, but that in order to be on the safe side Mr. Edmundson must lead a perfectly normal life for ten days eating and drinking all that was habitual to him, which of course accounted for the three dry Martinis he had had in the bar, and then further tests would be made and we should see what we should see.

After dinner, in the lounge where they took their coffee, Mr. Edmundson reverted to his domestic affairs, discussing, at length, Blanche's prospects in Grand Opera; the problematical happiness of Sylvia when married to an aviator who might be killed at any minute; the advisability of forcing Leonard into the silk business where he would be certain of an assured income, or allowing him to continue with his experimental engineering; and last, but by no means least, whether Mrs. Edmundson's peculiar lassitude for the past few months was really caused by her teeth, which had been suggested, or whether it could be accounted for by those well-known biological changes that occur in all women of a certain age. He personally was in favor of the teeth theory and agreed with the doctor that she ought to have every man jack of them pulled out, and a nice set of artificial ones put in. The idea of this, however, somehow repelled Mrs. Edmundson, and so at the moment things were more or less at a deadlock.

Leaving them at a deadlock, Aubrey, increasingly aware that his head was splitting, almost abruptly said good night and departed, on leaden feet, to his room.

The next morning, round about half-past ten, Aubrey was sunning himself on his balcony, breathing in gratefully the fresh mountain air and enjoying the romantic tranquil beauty of the view. The lake was calm and blue and without a ripple except for the occasional passing of a steamer and a few little colored rowing boats sculling about close to the shore. Fleecy clouds lay around the peaks of the mountains and the morning was so still that the cow bells in the high pastures could be heard quite clearly. Presently Mr. Edmundson appeared on the next balcony about four feet away from him. "What a bit of luck," he said cheerfully. "I had no idea we were next-door neighbors." Conversation, or rather monologue, set in immediately. "I've had a postcard from Leonard's wife," he went on. "The younger child, the boy, woke up yesterday morning covered with spots and they're very worried, of course. I don't suppose it's anything serious, but you never know, do you? Anyhow, they sent for the doctor at once and kept the little girl away from school in case it might turn out to be something catching, and they're going to telegraph me during the day."

Aubrey endured this for a few minutes and then rose with a great air of decision. Mr. Edmundson, with the swiftness of a cat who perceives that the most enjoyable mouse it has met for weeks is about to vanish down a hole, pounced. "I thought we might take a little excursion on the lake; those skiffs are no trouble to handle."

Aubrey, shaken by the suggestion, replied that there would be nothing he would have liked better but that he was being called for by some friends who were driving him up to the mountains for lunch.

"Never mind," said Mr. Edmundson, "we're sure to meet later."

Aubrey lay on his bed for a while, shattered. He had been looking forward to a stroll through the town by himself and later a quiet lunch either on the hotel terrace or at a café down by the lake. Now, having committed himself to a drive in the mountains with his mythical friends, he was almost bound to be caught out. Why, oh why hadn't he been smart enough to think of a less concrete excuse? Suddenly he jumped up. The thing to do was to finish dressing and get out of the hotel immediately before Mr. Edmundson got downstairs. Once in the town he could keep a careful lookout and dart into a shop or something if he saw him coming. Fortunately, he had already bathed and shaved and in less than ten minutes he tiptoed out of his room. The coast was clear. He ran lightly down the stairs rather than use the lift which might take too long to come up. He was detained for a moment in the lounge by the hotel manager inquiring if he had slept well, but contrived to shake him off and sped through the palm garden on to the terrace. Mr. Edmundson rose from a chair at the top of the steps. 'No sign of your friend's car yet," he said. "Why not sit down and have a Tom Collins?"

"I'm afraid I can't," said Aubrey hurriedly. "I promised to meet them in the town and I'm late as it is."

"I'll come with you." Mr. Edmundson squared his shoulders. "I feel like a brisk walk."

Halfway to the town Aubrey gave an elaborate glance at his wristwatch. "I'm afraid I shall have to run," he said. "I promised to meet them at 11:15 and it's now twenty to twelve."

"Do us both good," said Mr. Edmundson and broke into a trot.

In the main square, which Aubrey had chosen at random as being the place where his friends were meeting him, there was, not unnaturally, no sign of them. Mr. Edmundson suggested sitting down outside a café and waiting. "They've probably been held up on the road," he said.

"I'm afraid," murmured Aubrey weakly, "that they're much more likely to have thought I wasn't coming and gone off without me."

"In that case," said Mr. Edmundson with a comforting smile, "we can take a little drive on our own and have lunch in the country somewhere."

During lunch, in a chalet restaurant high up on the side of a mountain, Mr. Edmundson spoke frankly of his early life. He had not, he said, always known the security, independence and comparative luxury that he enjoyed now, far from it. His childhood, most of which had been spent in a small house just off the Kennington Road, had been poverty-stricken in the extreme. Many a time he remembered having to climb a lamp-post in order to get a brief glimpse of a cricket match at the Oval, and many a time also he had been chased by the police for this and like misdemeanors; indeed on one occasion—

Aubrey listened and went on listening in a sort of desperate apathy. There was nothing else to do, no escape whatever. Incidents of Mr. Edmundson's life washed over him in a never-ending stream; his experiences in the war during which he hadn't got so much as a flesh wound in three years; his apprenticeship to the silk trade as a minor office clerk in Birmingham; his steady climb for several years until he arrived at being first a traveler and then manager of a department in a big shop in South London; his first meeting with the now Mrs. Edmundson at a dance in Maida Vale; his marriage; his honeymoon at Torquay; the birth of Blanche. By the time the doctor had arrived to deliver Mrs. Edmundson of Sylvia it had become quite chilly in the chalet restaurant and the shadows of the mountains were beginning to draw out over the lake. In the taxi driving back to the town Sylvia was safely delivered and Leonard well on the way.

Finally, having reached his room and shut and locked the door Aubrey flung himself down on the bed in a state of collapse. His whole body felt saturated with boredom and his limbs ached as though he had been running. Through the awful deadness of his despair he heard Mr. Edmundson in the next room humming a tune. Aubrey buried his head in the pillow and groaned.

3

Aubrey came down into the bar before dinner resolute and calm. He had had a hot bath, two aspirin, thought things out very carefully and made his decision. Consequently he was able to meet Mr. Edmundson's jocular salutation with equanimity. "I am leaving tomorrow evening," he said, graciously accepting a dry Martini. "For Venice."

Mr. Edmundson looked suitably disappointed. "What a shame," he said. "I thought you were staying for a week at least; in fact I was looking forward to being able to travel as far as Paris with you if my test turns out to be all right on Tuesday. You did say you were going to Paris from here, you know," he said reproachfully.

"I've changed my mind," said Aubrey. "I'm sick of Switzerland and I've always wanted to see Venice."

"Nice time of year for it anyhow," said Mr. Edmundson raising his glass. "Here goes."

The one thing that Aubrey had realized in the two hours' respite before dinner was that no compromise was possible. He couldn't very well stay on in the same hotel as Mr. Edmundson and refuse to eat with him or speak to him. That would be unkind and discourteous and hurt his feelings mortally. Aubrey shrank from rudeness and there was a confiding quality about Mr. Edmundson, a trusting belief that he was being good company which it would be dreadfully cruel to shatter. It was all Aubrey's own fault anyhow for having encouraged him in the first place. The only thing was to put up with things as they were for this evening and, he supposed, most of the next day and leave thankfully on the Rapide the next night. He had already arranged about his ticket and sleeper with the porter.

Mr. Edmundson banished melancholy by shrugging his shoulders, shooting his cuffs and giving a jolly laugh. "Anyway," he said, "it's all right about the baby's spots! I had a telegram this evening. The doctor said it was nothing but a rash, which only goes to show that there's no sense in being fussy until you know you've got something to be really fussy about. But that's typical of Nora, that's Leonard's wife, she's like that over everything, fuss, fuss, fuss. Sometimes I don't know how Len stands it and that's a fact; fortunately his head's screwed on the right way; it takes more than a few spots on baby's bottom to upset *his* apple-cart!"

Mr. Edmundson continued to be gay through dinner. He ordered a bottle of Swiss wine just to celebrate, "Hail and Farewell you know!" After dinner they went to the Kursaal and sat through an old and rather dull German movie. Mr. Edmundson seemed to enjoy it enormously and actually laughed once or twice, which irritated Aubrey, as he knew Mr. Edmundson understood German as little as he did. In the foyer on the way out a man in a bowler hat with a very foreign accent asked Mr. Edmundson for a light. "Right you are, me old cock robin," said Mr. Edmundson, and slapped him on the back. Aubrey hung his head in shame.

The next morning Aubrey woke with a great sense of relief, only one more day, one more lunch, one more dinner and then escape. He was careful, while dressing, not to venture out on to the balcony and, with amazing luck, managed to get out of the hotel and into town without seeing Mr. Edmundson at all. He chose a table, partially screened by a flowering shrub, outside the "Bienvenue," where he had sat the first afternoon of his arrival. It seemed incredible that it was only the day before yesterday—he felt as though he'd been living with Mr. Edmundson for weeks. The scene before him was as light and varied as ever, but he found after a while that he was looking at it with different eyes. A lot of the charm, the glitter of potential adventure had faded. He felt like some passionate virgin who had just had her first love affair and discovered it to have been both uncomfortable and dull. Rather pleased with this simile he jotted it down on the back of an envelope that he happened to have in his pocket. For instance, now, with this new, cynical disillusionment, he was certain that the man walking by with the pretty girl in a yellow beret was *not* her lover and had *not* just broken his leave in order to fly from Brussels to see her. Nor was the heavily made-up woman encased in black satin and wearing high-heeled white shoes the depraved Madame of a Brothel who had amassed a fortune out of the White Slave Traffic. Nor even was the ferrety-looking man in the gray raincoat carrying a violin case a secret agent. He was just a family man with five children. The made-up woman was probably the mother of six and the man and the girl were brother and sister and bored to tears with each other.

Elvira was wrong and so, damn it, was Somerset Maugham. The prospect of going through life alone in hotels and running the risk of meeting a series of Mr. Edmundsons was too awful to be contemplated. If that was the only way to gain material and inspiration he'd rather go back to antiques or write another play about his own family.

It depressed him to think that a man could live for fifty-four years like Mr. Edmundson and have nothing of the faintest interest happen to him at all beyond a problematical stone in the bladder. Of course he fully realized that a great writer with technique, humanity, warmth and vivid insight, such as Arnold Bennett, could make Mr. Edmundson an appealing hero for several hundred pages, but he himself felt that even though, in the far future, he should become a successful author, that sort of thing would, most emphatically, not be his line. He sipped a cup of delicious chocolate, with a large blob of cream on the top and anticipated the pleasures of Venice. He would sit on the terrace of a hotel on the Grand Canal and watch the sun setting over the lagoon, if it did, and the gondolas drifting by, and he wouldn't speak a word to anyone at all in any circumstances whatever unless they looked so madly attractive that he couldn't restrain himself.

He finished his chocolate, paid for it, scanned the horizon carefully and got up. There was an antique shop in a side street that he had noticed on his way to the café with some rather nice things in the window, and he thought he might go in and poke about a bit. He gave a little sigh. If only Maurice hadn't been so tiresome and were here with him, what fun it would be. But still, if Maurice hadn't been tiresome he would never have written *Animal Grab* and wouldn't be here at all, so there was no sense in being wistful about that. He turned up the little side street and shot back into an archway while Mr. Edmundson, fortunately looking the other way, passed within a few inches of him. Aubrey giggled with relief at his escape and fairly scampered off to the antique shop. The man in the shop greeted him politely. His English was very bad and Aubrey was certain he had heard his voice and seen his face before. He routed about for nearly an hour, not finding anything of interest apart from a very lovely Italian mirror that would have made Maurice's mouth water and some bits of rather fakey-looking cinque-cento jewelry. He bought a pair of malachite earrings for sixteen francs for Elvira, and was on his way out when his eye was caught by a small wooden Madonna. It was probably not older than eighteenth century or the beginning of the nineteenth and had once been painted in bright colors, but most of the paint had either faded or been rubbed off, giving the figure a pale almost ethereal quality. It was obviously of no particular value but certainly quite charming and might make a nice present for someone. He asked the man the price and was astonished to hear that it was two hundred francs. The man went off into a long rigmarole about it being very old and having belonged to the famous Marchesa something or other, but Aubrey, who wouldn't have paid more than ten shillings for it at most, cut him short with a polite bow and went out. On his way back to the hotel he suddenly remembered where he had seen the man before and gave a little gasp of remembered embarrassment. It was the man who had asked for a light in the foyer of the cinema last night, and to whom Mr. Edmundson with agonizing heartiness had said, "Right you are, me old cock robin!"

As he was walking through the lounge the underwaiter who generally served their coffee after dinner stopped him with information that his uncle was waiting for him in the bar. Aubrey laughed, repressing a shudder at the thought. "That's not my uncle," he said, "that's Mr. Edmundson." The waiter bowed politely and Aubrey went up to his room to wash.

At lunch Mr. Edmundson seemed a little less animated than usual. Aubrey, feeling that he could afford to be magnanimous as there were only a few hours to go, explained that the reason he hadn't seen him during the morning was that he had to get up early to go to Cook's about his passport and do a little shopping in town. He told him about the antique shop and also, with a little edge of malice, about recognizing the man. "You remember," he said, "the one you nearly knocked down in the Kursaal last night." Mr. Edmundson had the grace to look rather startled for a moment and then gave a shamefaced laugh. "I think I was a bit over the odds last night," he said. "That Swiss wine and the brandy after dinner." Then he changed the subject.

4

Mr. Edmundson insisted on coming with Aubrey to the station, merrily waving aside all protests. In the hotel bus his conversation was more domestic than ever. Apparently an aunt of Mrs. Edmundson's, hitherto concealed from Aubrey, had been living with them for nearly two years and was nothing more nor less than a damned nuisance. One of those whining women, always on the grumble and always causing trouble with the servants. They'd had altogether five parlormaids since she'd been in the house and now the present one was leaving, having told Mrs. Edmundson candidly that she just couldn't stand it and that was a fact. When the bus reached the station Mr. Edmundson was seriously considering whether or not it wouldn't be better and cheaper in the long run to set up the aunt on her own in a little flat in some seaside resort such as Herne Bay or Broadstairs. "After all," he said, "it isn't as if she's all that old, seventy-three's getting on I grant you, but she's in full possession of all her faculties, a bloody sight too full if you ask me, and she could live her own life and do what she pleased and grumble to her heart's content."

When Aubrey had got himself and his bags into his sleeper there were still a few minutes to spare before the train went, which Mr. Edmundson utilized by sitting on the bed and reverting briefly to the subject of Mrs. Edmundson's teeth. At last a whistle blew and he jumped up. "Well, bye-bye, old man," he said. "It's been jolly nice to have known you." Then, to Aubrey's embarrassment, he plunged his hand into the pocket of his coat and produced a small brown paper package. "I've bought you this this afternoon in the town just as a little souvenir. I know you like that sort of thing. No—" he held up his hand—"don't start thanking me, it isn't anything at all, just look at it every now and then and think of me and be good." The train started to move, and he dashed down the corridor and out on to the platform. Aubrey, feeling guilty and ashamed, opened the package and was appalled to discover that it was the little wooden Madonna he had seen in the antique shop that morning. He turned it over in his hands; the head had been broken off at some time or other and been stuck on again. Two hundred Swiss francs! That was about ten pounds! He closed his eyes and felt himself blushing with mortification at the cruel thoughts he had harbored against Mr. Edmundson. Poor Mr. Edmundson. Pathetic Mr. Edmundson. That was the worst of bores, they always turned out to have hearts of gold; it was awful. He undressed pensively and went to bed. In the night he was half wakened by the figure of a man stretching across to his luggage on the rack. Drowsily he realized that the train must be at the Italian Frontier.

"Nothing to declare," he muttered.

The man went away and he went to sleep again.

The next day, about a half an hour before the train was due to arrive in Venice, he unwrapped the Madonna again, which had been lying on the rack, and was in the act of putting it into his suitcase among his dirty washing when the head fell off and rolled under the seat. This tickled him enormously; he sat down and laughed until he cried. It really was too sad—poor Mr. Edmundson. He retrieved the head and tried to fix it on again, but it wouldn't stick without glue. The body was hollow and he shook it upside down just to see whether or not any priceless jewels might have been concealed inside, but it was quite empty. People like Mr. Edmundson, he reflected, are born unlucky, they can't even give a present without it being a failure.

Mr. Edmundson, on leaving the station, walked briskly down to the lake side and turned into the Bienvenue Café. It wasn't very crowded, but the air was smoky and thick and the radio was turned on full. He sat down and ordered a beer and an evening paper. Two men in bowler hats were seated at a table opposite to him playing dominoes, one of them was the proprietor of the antique shop. After a little while he looked across at Mr. Edmundson and raised his eyebrows inquiringly. Mr. Edmundson looked casually round the room, nodded briefly and went on reading his paper.

THE SHOW

Richmal Crompton

Richmal Crompton (1890–1969) was born in Lancashire but moved to London to train as a school mistress. Her first story about William Brown appeared in *Home* magazine in 1919, and the first collection was published three years later. In all, thirty-eight 'Just William' books were published, with the *Sunday Times* describing them as 'probably the funniest, toughest children's books ever written.'

T he Outlaws sat around the old barn, plunged in deep thought. Henry, the oldest member (aged 12¼), had said in a moment of inspiration:

'Let's think of – sumthin' else to do – sumthin' quite fresh from what we've ever done before.'

And the Outlaws were thinking.

They had engaged in mortal combat with one another, they had cooked strange ingredients over a smoking and reluctant flame with a fine disregard of culinary conventions, they had tracked each other over the countryside with gait and complexions intended to represent those of the aborigines of South America, they had even turned their attention to kidnapping (without any striking success), and these occupations had palled.

In all its activities the Society of Outlaws (comprising four members) aimed at a simple, unostentatious mode of procedure. In their shrinking from the glare of publicity they showed an example of unaffected modesty that many other public societies might profitably emulate. The parents of the members were unaware of the very existence of the society. The ill-timed and tactless interference of parents had nipped in the bud many a cherished plan, and by bitter experience the Outlaws had learnt that secrecy was their only protection. Owing to the rules and restrictions of an unsympathetic world that orders school hours from nine to four their meetings were confined to half-holidays and occasionally Sunday afternoons.

William, the ever ingenious, made the first suggestion.

'Let's shoot things with bows an' arrows same as real outlaws used to,' he said.

'What things?' and,

'What bows an' arrows?' said Henry and Ginger simultaneously.

'Oh, anything – birds an' cats an' hens an' things – an' buy bows an' arrows. You can buy them in shops.'

'We can make them,' said Douglas hopefully.

'Not like you can get them in shops. They'd shoot crooked or sumthin' if we made them. They've got to be jus' so to shoot straight. I saw some in Brook's window, too, jus' right – jus' same as real outlaws had.'

'How much?' said the Outlaws breathlessly.

'Five shillings – targets for learnin' on before we begin shootin' real things an' all.'

'Five shillings!' breathed Douglas. He might as well have said five pounds. 'We've not got five shillings. Henry's not having any money since he broke their drawing-room window an' Ginger only has a 3d a week an' has to give collection an' we've not paid for the guinea pig yet, the one that got into Ginger's sister's hat an' she was so mad at, an'—'

'Oh, never mind all that,' said William scornfully. 'We'll jus' get five shillings.'

'How?'

'Well,' uncertainly, 'grown-ups can always get money when they want it.'

'How?' again.

William disliked being tied down to details.

'Oh – bazaars an' things,' he said impatiently.

'Bazaars!' exploded Henry. 'Who'd come to a bazaar if we had one? Who would? Jus' tell me that if you're so clever! Who'd come to it? Besides, you've got to sell things at a bazaar, haven't you? What'd we sell? We've got nothin' to sell, have we? What's the good of havin' a bazaar with nothin' to sell and no one to buy it? Jus' tell me that!'

Henry always enjoyed scoring off William.

'Well – shows an' things,' said William desperately.

There was a moment's silence, then Ginger repeated thoughtfully, 'Shows!' and Douglas, whose eldest brother was home from college for his vacation, murmured self-consciously, 'By Jove!'

'We *could* do a show,' said Ginger. 'Get animals an' things an' charge money for lookin' at them.'

'Who'd pay it?' said Henry, the doubter.

'Anyone would. You'd pay to see animals, wouldn't you? Real animals. People do at the zoo, don't they? Well, we'll get some animals. That's easy enough, isn't it?'

A neighbouring church clock struck four and the meeting was adjourned.

'Well, we'll have a show an' get money and buy bows an' arrows an' shoot things,' summed up William, 'an we'll arrange the show next week.'

William returned home slowly and thoughtfully. He sat on his bed, his hands in his pockets, his brow drawn into a frown, his thoughts wandering in a dreamland of wonderful 'shows' and rare exotic beasts.

Suddenly from the next room came a thin sound that gathered volume till it seemed to fill the house like the roaring of a lion, then died gradually away and was followed by silence. But only for a second. It began again – a small whisper that grew louder and louder, became a raucous bellow, then faded slowly away to rise again after a moment's silence. In the next room William's mother's Aunt Emily was taking her afternoon nap. Aunt Emily had come down a month ago for a week's visit and had not yet referred to the date of her departure. William's father was growing anxious. She was a stout, healthy lady, who spent all her time recovering from a slight illness she had had two years ago.

Her life held two occupations, and only two. These were eating and sleeping. For William she possessed a subtle but irresistible fascination. Her stature, her appetite, her gloom, added to the fact that she utterly ignored him, attracted him strongly.

The tea-bell rang and the sound of the snoring ceased abruptly. This entertainment over, William descended to the dining-room, where his father was addressing his mother with some heat.

'Is she going to stay here for ever, or only for a few years? I'd like to know, because—'

Perceiving William, he stopped abruptly, and William's mother murmured:

'It's so nice to have her, dear.'

Then Aunt Emily entered.

'Have you slept well, Aunt?'

'Slept!' repeated Aunt Emily majestically. 'I hardly expect to sleep in my state of health. A little rest is all I can expect.'

'Sorry you're no better,' said William's father sardonically.

'*Better*?' she repeated again indignantly. 'It will be a long time before I'm better.'

She lowered her large, healthy frame into a chair, carefully selected a substantial piece of bread and butter and attacked it with vigour.

'I'm going to the post after tea,' said William's mother. 'Would you care to come with me?'

Aunt Emily took a large helping of jam.

'You hardly expect me to go out in the evening in my state of health, surely? It's years since I went out after tea. And I was at the post office this morning. There were a lot of people there, but they served me first. I suppose they saw I looked ill.'

William's father choked suddenly and apologised, but not humbly.

'Though I must say,' went on Aunt Emily, 'this place does suit me. I think after a few months here I should be a little stronger. Pass the jam, William.'

The glance that William's father fixed upon her would have made a stronger woman quail, but Aunt Emily was scraping out the last remnants of jam and did not notice.

'I'm a bit overtired today, I think,' she went on. 'I'm so apt to forget how weak I am and then I overdo it. I'm ready for the cake, William. I just sat out in the sun yesterday afternoon and sat a bit too long and overtired myself. I ought to write letters after tea, but I don't think I have the strength. Another piece of cake, William. I'll go upstairs to rest instead, I think. I hope you'll keep the house quiet. It's so rarely that I can get a bit of sleep.'

William's father left the room abruptly. William sat on and watched, with fascinated eyes, the cake disappear, and finally followed the large, portly figure upstairs and sat down in his room to plan the 'show' and incidentally listen, with a certain thrilled awe, for the sounds from next door.

The place and time of the 'show' presented no little difficulty. To hold it in the old barn would give away to the world the cherished secret of their meeting place. It was William who suggested his bedroom, to be entered, not by way of the front door and staircase, but by the less public way of the garden wall and scullery roof. Ever an optimist, he affirmed that no one would see or hear. The choice of a time was limited to Wednesday afternoon, Saturday afternoon, and Sunday. Sunday at first was ruled out as impossible. But there were difficulties about Wednesday afternoon and Saturday afternoon. On Wednesday afternoon Ginger and Douglas were unwilling and ungraceful pupils at a dancing class. On Saturday afternoon William's father gardened and would command a view of the garden wall and scullery roof. On these afternoons also Cook and Emma, both of a suspicious turn of mind, would be at large. On Sunday Cook and Emma went out, William's mother paid a regular weekly visit to an old friend and William's father spent the afternoon on the sofa, dead to the world.

Moreover, as he pointed out to the Outlaws, the members of the Sunday School could be waylaid and induced to attend the show and they would probably be provided with money for collection. The more

William thought over it, the more attractive became the idea of a Sunday afternoon in spite of superficial difficulties; therefore Sunday afternoon was finally chosen.

The day was fortunately a fine one, and William and the other Outlaws were at work early. William had asked his mother, with an expression of meekness and virtue that ought to have warned her of danger, if he might have 'jus' a few friends' in his room for the afternoon. His mother, glad that her husband should be spared his son's restless company, gave willing permission.

By half past two the exhibits were ready. In a cage by the window sat a white rat painted in faint alternate stripes of blue and pink. This was Douglas's contribution, handpainted by himself in watercolours. It wore a bewildered expression and occasionally licked its stripes and then obviously wished it hadn't. Its cage bore a notice printed on card-board:

> RAT FROM CHINA
> RATS ARE ALL
> LIKE THIS IN CHINA

Next came a cat belonging to William's sister, Smuts by name, now imprisoned beneath a basket chair. At the best of times Smuts was short-tempered, and all its life had cherished a bitter hatred of William. Now, enclosed by its enemy in a prison two feet square, its fury knew no bounds. It tore at the basketwork, it flew wildly round and round, scratching, spitting, swearing. Its chair bore the simple and appropriate notice:

> WILD CAT

William watched it with honest pride and prayed fervently that its indignation would not abate during the afternoon.

Next came a giant composed of Douglas upon Ginger's back, draped in two sheets tied tightly round Douglas's neck. This was labelled:

GENWIN GIANT

Ginger was already growing restive. His muffled voice was heard from the folds of the sheets informing the other Outlaws that it was a bit thick and he hadn't known it would be like this or he wouldn't have done it, and anyway he was going to change with Douglas half time or he'd chuck up the whole thing.

The next exhibit was a black fox fur of William's mother's, to which was fortunately attached a head and several feet, and which he had surreptitiously removed from her wardrobe. This had been tied up, stuffed with waste paper and wired by William till it was, in his eyes, remarkably lifelike. As the legs, even with the assistance of wire, refused to support the body and the head would only droop sadly to the ground, it was perforce exhibited in a recumbent attitude. It bore marks of sticky fingers, and of several side slips of the scissors when William was cutting the wire, but on the whole he was justly proud of it. It bore the striking but untruthful legend:

BEAR SHOT
BY OUTLAWS
IN RUSHER

Next came:

BLUE DOG

This was Henry's fox terrier, generally known as Chips. For Chips the world was very black. Henry's master mind had scorned his paintbox and his watercolours. Henry had 'borrowed' a blue bag and dabbed it liberally over Chips. Chips had, after the first wild frenzied struggle, offered no resistance. He now sat, a picture of black despair, turning every now and then a melancholy eye upon the still enraged Smuts. But for him cats and joy and life and fighting were no more. He was abject, shamed – a blue dog.

William himself, as showman, was an imposing figure. He was robed in a red dressing gown of his father's that trailed on the ground behind him and over whose cords in front he stumbled ungracefully as he walked. He had cut a few strands from the fringe of a rug and glued them to his lips to represent moustaches. They fell in two straight lines over his mouth. On his head was a tinsel crown, once worn by his sister as Fairy Queen.

The show had been widely advertised and all the neighbouring children had been individually canvassed, but under strict orders of secrecy. The threats of what the Outlaws would do if their secret were disclosed had kept many a child awake at night.

William surveyed the room proudly.

'Not a bad show for a penny, I *should* say. I guess there aren't many like it, anyway. Do shut up talkin', Ginger. It'll spoil it all, if folks hear the giant talking out of his stomach. It's Douglas that's got to do the giant's *talking*. Anyone could see that. I say, they're comin'! Look! They're comin'! Along the wall!'

There was a thin line of children climbing along the wall in single file on all fours. They ascended the scullery roof and approached the window. These were the first arrivals who had called on their way to Sunday School.

Henry took their pennies and William cleared his throat and began:

'White rat from China, ladies an' gentlemen, pink an' blue striped. All rats is pink an' blue striped in China. This is the only genwin China rat in England – brought over from China special las' week jus' for the show. It lives on China bread an' butter brought over special, too.'

'Wash it!' jeered an unbeliever. 'Jus' wash it an' let's see it then.'

'Wash it?' repeated the showman indignantly. 'It's gotter be washed. It's washed every morning an' night same as you or me. China rats have gotter be washed or they'd die right off. Washin' 'em don't make no difference to their stripes. Anyone knows that that knows anything about China rats, I guess.'

He laughed scornfully and turned to Smuts. Smuts had grown used to the basket chair and was settling down for a nap. William crouched down on all fours, ran his fingers along the basketwork, and, putting his face close to it, gave vent to a malicious howl. Smuts sprang at him, scratching and spitting.

'Wild cat,' said William triumphantly. 'Look at it! Kill anyone if it got out! Spring at their throats, it would, an' scratch their eyes out with its paws an' bite their necks till its teeth met. If I jus' moved away that chair it would spring out at you.' They moved hastily away from the chair. 'And I bet some of you would be dead pretty quick. It could have anyone's head right off with bitin' and scratchin'. Right off – separate from their bodies!'

There was an awestricken silence.

Then:

'Garn! It's Smuts. It's your sister's cat!'

William laughed as though vastly amused by this idea.

'Smuts!' he said, giving a surreptitious kick to the chair that infuriated its occupant still more. 'I guess there wouldn't be many of us left in this house if Smuts was like this.'

They passed on to the giant.

'A giant,' said William, rearranging the tinsel crown, which was slightly too big for him. 'Real giant. Look at it. As big as two of you put together. How d'you think he gets in at doors and things? Has to have everything made special. Look at him walk. Walk, Ginger.'

Ginger took two steps forward. Douglas clutched his shoulders and murmured anxiously, 'By Jove!'

'Go on,' urged William scornfully, 'that's not walkin'.'

The goaded Ginger's voice came from the giant's middle regions.

'If you go on talkin' at me, I'll drop him. I'm just about sick of it.'

'All right,' said William hastily.

'Anyway it's a giant,' he went on to his audience. 'A jolly fine giant.'

'It's got Douglas's face,' said one of his audience.

William was for a moment at a loss.

'Well,' he said at last, 'giant's got to have some sort of a face, hasn't it? Can't not have a face, can it?'

The Russian Bear, which had often been seen adorning the shoulders of William's mother and was promptly recognised, was greeted with ribald jeers, but there was no doubt as to the success of the Blue Dog. Chips advanced deprecatingly, blue head drooping, and blue tail between blue legs, making abject apologies for his horrible condition. But Henry had done his work well. They stood around in rapt admiration.

'Blue dog,' said the showman, walking forward proudly and stumbling violently over the cords of the dressing gown. 'Blue dog,' he repeated, recovering his balance and removing the tinsel crown from his nose to his brow. 'You never saw a blue dog before, did you? No, and you aren't likely to see one again, neither. It was made blue special for this show. It's the only blue dog in the world. Folks'll be comin' from all over the world to see this blue dog – an' thrown in in a penny show! If it was in the zoo you'd have to pay a shilling to see it, I bet. It's – it's jus' luck for you it's here. I guess the folks at the zoo wish they'd got it. Tain't many shows have blue dogs. Brown an' black an' white – but not blue. Why, folks pay money jus' to see shows of ornery dogs – so you're jus' lucky to see a blue dog *an'* a dead bear from Russia *an'* a giant, *an'* a wild cat, *an'* a China rat for jus' one penny.'

After each speech William had to remove from his mouth the rug fringe which persisted in obeying the force of gravity rather than William's idea of what a moustache should be.

'It's jus' paint. Henry's gate's being painted blue,' said one critic feebly, but on the whole the Outlaws had scored a distinct success in the blue dog.

Then, while they stood in silent admiration round the unhappy animal, came a sound from the next door, a gentle sound like the sighing of the wind through the trees. It rose and fell. It rose again and fell again. It increased in volume with each repetition, till at its height it sounded like a wild animal in pain.

'What's that?' asked the audience breathlessly.

William was slightly uneasy. He was not sure whether this fresh development would add lustre or dishonour to his show.

'Yes,' he said darkly to gain time, 'what is it? I guess you'd like to know what it is!'

'Garn! It's jus' snorin'.'

'Snorin'!' repeated William. 'It's not ornery snorin', that isn't. Jus' listen, that's all! You couldn't snore like that, I bet. Huh!'

They listened spellbound to the gentle sound, growing louder and louder till at its loudest it brought rapt smiles to their faces, then ceasing abruptly, then silence. Then again the gentle sound that grew and grew.

William asked Henry in a stage whisper if they oughtn't to charge extra for listening to it. The audience hastily explained that they weren't listening, they 'jus' couldn't help hearin'.'

A second batch of sightseers had arrived and were paying their entrance pennies, but the first batch refused to move. William, emboldened by success, opened the door and they crept out to the landing and listened with ears pressed to the magic door.

Henry now did the honours of showman. William stood, majestic in his glorious apparel, deep in thought. Then to his face came the faint smile that inspiration brings to her votaries. He ordered the audience back into the showroom and shut the door. Then he took off his shoes and softly and with bated breath opened Aunt Emily's door and peeped within. It was rather a close afternoon, and she lay on her bed on the top of her eiderdown. She had slipped off her dress skirt so as not to crush it, and she lay in her immense stature in a blouse and striped petticoat, while from her open mouth issued the fascinating sounds. In sleep Aunt Emily was not beautiful.

William thoughtfully propped up a cushion in the doorway and stood considering the situation.

In a few minutes the showroom was filled with a silent, expectant crowd. In a corner near the door was a new notice:

PLACE FOR TAKING
OFF SHOES AND TAKING
OTH OF SILENCE

William, after administering the oath of silence to a select party in his most impressive manner, led them shoeless and on tiptoe to the next room.

From Aunt Emily's bed hung another notice:

FAT WILD WOMAN
TORKIN NATIF
LANGWIDGE

They stood in a hushed, delighted group around her bed. The sounds never ceased, never abated. William only allowed them two minutes in the room. They came out reluctantly, paid more money, joined the end of the queue and re-entered. More and more children came to see the show, but the show now consisted solely in Aunt Emily.

The China rat had licked off all its stripes; Smuts was fast asleep; Ginger was sitting down on the seat of a chair and Douglas was on the back of it, and Ginger had insisted at last on air and sight and had put his head out where the two sheets joined; the Russian Bear had fallen on to the floor and no one had picked it up; Chips lay in a disconsolate heap, a victim of acute melancholia – and no one cared for any of these things. Newcomers passed by them hurriedly and stood shoeless in the queue outside Aunt Emily's room eagerly awaiting their turn. Those who came out simply went to the end again to wait another turn. Many returned home for more money, for Aunt Emily was 1d extra and each visit after the first, ½d. The Sunday School bell pealed forth its summons, but no one left the show. The vicar was depressed that evening. The attendance at Sunday School had been the worst on record. And still Aunt Emily slept and snored with a rapt, silent crowd around her. But William could never rest content. He possessed ambition that would have put many of his elders to shame. He cleared the room and reopened it after a few minutes, during which his clients waited in breathless suspense.

When they re-entered there was a fresh exhibit. William's keen eye had been searching out each detail of the room. On the table by her bed now stood a glass containing teeth, that William had discovered on the washstand, and a switch of hair and a toothless comb, that William had discovered on the dressing-table. These all bore notices:

FAT WILD WOMAN'S TEETH	FAT WILD WOMAN'S HARE	FAT WILD WOMAN'S KOME

Were it not that the slightest noise meant instant expulsion from the show (some of their number had already suffered that bitter fate) there would have been no restraining the audience. As it was, they crept in, silent, expectant, thrilled to watch and listen for the blissful two minutes. And Aunt Emily never failed them. Still she slept and snored. They borrowed money recklessly from each other. The poor sold their dearest treasures to the rich, and still they came again and again. And still Aunt Emily slept and snored. It would be interesting to know how long this would have gone on, had she not, on the top note of a peal that was a pure delight to her audience, awakened with a start and glanced around her. At first she thought that the cluster of small boys around her was a dream, especially as they turned and fled precipitately at once. Then she sat up and her eyes fell upon the table by her bed, the notices, and finally upon the petrified horror-stricken showman. She sprang up and, seizing him by the shoulders, shook him till his teeth chattered, the tinsel crown fell down, encircling ears and nose, and one of his moustaches fell limply at his feet.

'You wicked boy!' she said as she shook him. 'You *wicked, wicked, wicked* boy!'

He escaped from her grasp and fled to the showroom, where, in sheer self-defence, he moved a table and three chairs across the door. The room was empty except for Henry, the blue dog, and the still sleeping Smuts. All that was left of the giant was the crumpled sheets. Douglas had, with an awestricken 'By Jove!' snatched up his rat as he fled. The last of their clients was seen scrambling along the top of the garden wall on all fours with all possible speed.

Mechanically William straightened his crown.

'She's woke,' he said. 'She's mad wild.'

He listened apprehensively for angry footsteps descending the stairs and his father's dread summons, but none came. Aunt Emily could be heard moving about in her room, but that was all. A wild hope came to him that, given a little time, she might forget the incident.

'Let's count the money—' said Henry at last.

They counted.

'Four an' six!' screamed William. 'Four an' six! Jolly good, I *should* say! An' it would only have been about two shillings without Aunt Emily, an' I thought of her, didn't I? I guess you can all be jolly grateful to me.'

'All right,' said Henry unkindly. 'I'm not envying you, am I? You're welcome to it when she tells your father.'

And William's proud spirits dropped.

Then came the opening of the fateful door and heavy steps descending the stairs.

William's mother had returned from her weekly visit to her friend. She was placing her umbrella in the stand as Aunt Emily, hatted and coated and carrying a bag, descended. William's father had just awakened from his peaceful Sunday afternoon slumber, and, hearing his wife, had come into the hall.

Aunt Emily fixed her eye upon him.

'Will you be good enough to procure a conveyance?' she said. 'After the indignities to which I have been subjected in this house I refuse to remain in it a moment longer.'

Quivering with indignation she gave details of the indignities to which she had been subjected. William's mother pleaded, apologised, coaxed. William's father went quietly out to procure a conveyance. When he returned she was still talking in the hall.

'A crowd of vulgar little boys,' she was saying, 'and horrible indecent placards all over the room.'

He carried her bag down to the cab.

'And me in my state of health,' she said as she followed him. From the cab she gave her parting shot.

'And if this horrible thing hadn't happened, I might have stayed with you all the winter and perhaps part of the spring.'

William's father wiped his brow with his handkerchief as the cab drove off.

'How dreadful!' said his wife, but she avoided meeting his eye. 'It's – it's *disgraceful* of William,' she went on with sudden spirit. 'You must speak to him.'

'I will,' said his father determinedly. 'William!' he shouted sternly from the hall.

William's heart sank.

'She's told,' he murmured, his last hope gone.

'You'd better go and get it over,' advised Henry.

'William!' repeated the voice still more fiercely.

Henry moved nearer the window, prepared for instant flight if the voice's owner should follow it up the stairs.

'Go on,' he urged. 'He'll only come up for you.'

William slowly removed the barricade and descended the stairs. He had remembered to take off the crown and dressing gown, but his one-sided moustache still hung limply over his mouth.

His father was standing in the hall.

'What's that horrible thing on your face?' he began.

'Whiskers,' answered William laconically.

His father accepted the explanation.

'Is it true,' he went on, 'that you actually took your friends into your aunt's room without permission and hung vulgar placards around it?'

William glanced up into his father's face and suddenly took hope. Mr Brown was no actor.

'Yes,' he admitted.

'It's disgraceful,' said Mr Brown, '*disgraceful*! That's all.'

But it was not quite all. Something hard and round slipped into William's hand. He ran lightly upstairs.

'Hello!' said Henry, surprised. 'That's not taken long. What—'

William opened his hand and showed something that shone upon his extended palm.

'Look!' he said. 'Crumbs! Look!' It was a bright half-crown.

THE LORD OF THE FLIES

Marco Denevi

Marco Denevi (1922–1998) was an Argentine author, lawyer and journalist. His work is characterized by its criticism of human incompetence. His first novel, *Rosaura a las diez* (*Rosa at Ten O'Clock*), was a bestseller and his short story, 'Secret Ceremony', was made into a film starring Elizabeth Taylor.

The flies imagined their god. It was also a fly. The lord of the flies was a fly, now green, now black and gold, now pink, now white, now purple, an inconceivable fly, a beautiful fly, a monstrous fly, a terrible fly, a benevolent fly, a vengeful fly, a just fly, a youthful fly, but always a fly. Some embellished his size so that he was compared to an ox, others imagined him to be so small that you couldn't see him. In some religions, he was missing wings ("He flies," they argued, "but he doesn't need wings"), while in others he had infinite wings. Here it was said he had antennae like horns, and there that he had eyes that surrounded his entire head. For some he buzzed constantly, and for others he was mute, but he could communicate just the same. And for everyone, when flies died, he took them up to paradise. Paradise was a hunk of rotten meat, stinking and putrid, that souls of the dead flies could gnaw on for an eternity without devouring it; yes, this heavenly scrap of refuse would be constantly reborn and regenerated under the swarm of flies. For the good flies. Because there were also bad flies, and for them there was a hell. The hell for condemned flies was a place without excrement, without waste, trash, stink, without anything of anything; a place sparkling with cleanliness and illuminated by a bright white light; in other words, an ungodly place.

Translated by José Chaves

THE GIRL WHO FIXED THE UMLAUT

Nora Ephron

Nora Ephron (1941–2012) was an Academy Award-winning screen-writer and director and a *New York Times*-bestselling essayist, known for her biting wit and strong female characters. Starting out as a reporter for the *New York Post*, Ephron wrote humorous essays, which eventually led her to branch out into script writing. Her films, which include *When Harry Met Sally*, *Sleepless in Seattle* and *You've Got Mail*, essays, and autobiographical novel *Heartburn* have often drawn comparisons to Dorothy Parker. Ephron herself said, 'All I wanted in this world was to come to New York and be Dorothy Parker. The funny lady. The only lady at the table. The woman who made her living by her wit.'

There was a tap at the door at five in the morning. She woke up. *Shit. Now what?* She'd fallen asleep with her Palm Tungsten T3 in her hand. It would take only a moment to smash it against the wall and shove the battery up the nose of whoever was out there annoying her. She went to the door.

"I know you're home," he said.

Kalle fucking Blomkvist.

She tried to remember whether she was speaking to him or not. Probably not. She tried to remember why. No one knew why. It was undoubtedly because she'd been in a bad mood at some point. Lisbeth Salander was entitled to her bad moods on account of her miserable childhood and her tiny breasts, but it was starting to become confusing just how much irritability could be blamed on your slight figure and an abusive father you had once deliberately set on fire and then years later split open the head of with an axe.

Salander opened the door a crack and spent several paragraphs trying to decide whether to let Blomkvist in. Many italic thoughts flew through her mind. *Go away. Perhaps. So what.* Etc.

"Please," he said. "I must see you. The umlaut on my computer isn't working."

He was cradling an iBook in his arms. She looked at him. He looked at her. She looked at him. He looked at her. And then she did what she usually did when she had run out of italic thoughts: she shook her head.

"I can't really go on without an umlaut," he said. "We're in Sweden."

But where in Sweden were they? There was no way to know, especially if you'd never been to Sweden. A few chapters ago, for example, an unscrupulous agent from Swedish Intelligence had tailed Blomkvist by taking Stora Essingen and Gröndal into Södermalm, and then driving down Hornsgatan and across Bellmansgatan via Brännkyrkagatan, with a final left onto Tavastgatan. Who cared, but there it was, in black-and-white, taking up space. And now Blomkvist was standing in her doorway. Someone might still be following him—but who? There was no real way to be sure even when you found out, because people's names were so confusingly similar— Gullberg, Sandberg, and Holmberg; Nieminen and Niedermann; and, worst of all, Jonasson, Mårtensson, Torkelsson, Fredriksson, Svensson, Johansson, Svantesson, Fransson, and Paulsson.

"I need my umlaut," Blomkvist said. "What if I want to go to Svavelsjö? Or Strängnäs? Or Södertälje? What if I want to write to Wadensjö? Or Ekström or Nyström?"

It was a compelling argument.

She opened the door.

He handed her the computer and went to make coffee on her Jura Impressa X7.

She tried to get the umlaut to work. No luck. She pinged Plague and explained the problem. Plague was fat, but he would know what to do, and he would tell her, in Courier typeface.

<Where are you?> Plague wrote.

<Stockholm.>

<There's an Apple Store at the intersection of Kungsgatan and Sveavägen. Or you could try a Q-tip.>

She went to the bathroom and got a Q-tip and gently cleaned the area around the Alt key. It popped into place. Then she pressed "U." An umlaut danced before her eyes.

Finally, she spoke.

"It's fixed," she said.

"Thanks," he said.

She thought about smiling, but she'd smiled three hundred pages earlier, and once was enough.

THE LOCKED ROOM MYSTERY MYSTERY

Jasper Fforde

Jasper Fforde (1961–) spent his early career in the film industry before debuting on the *New York Times* bestseller list with *The Eyre Affair* in 2001. He is the author of several novels, which cross over genres, mixing elements of fantasy, crime thriller, satire and humour. They are noted for their literary allusions, wordplay and tight plots.

"So who's the victim?" asked Detective Inspector Jack Spratt, shaking his overcoat of the cold winter rain as he entered Usher Towers. "It's Locked Room Mystery," explained his amiable sidekick, Detective Sergeant Mary Mary. "He was found dead at 7.30pm. But get this: the library had been locked… *from the inside.*"

"Locked Room killed inside a locked room, eh?" murmured Spratt. "What was that tired old plot device doing out here anyway? I thought he was at the At the End of The Day retirement home for washed-up old cliches."

"It was the Mystery Contrivances Club annual dinner," explained Mary. "Locked Room was going to be given a long-service award – you know how they like to stick a gong on ideas before they die out completely. Last year it was the Identical Twins plot device."

"I always hated that one," said Jack.

They stepped into the spacious marble-lined entrance vestibule and a worried-looking individual ran up to them, wringing his hands in a desperate manner.

"Inspector Spratt!" he wailed. "This is a terrible business. You must help!"

"Jack," said Mary, "meet Red Herring, president of the club and owner of Usher Towers."

"Perhaps you'd better show me the body," said Jack quietly, "and tell me what happened."

"Of course, of course," replied Red Herring, leading them across the vestibule to a large oak-panelled door. "We were about to present Locked Room with his award but he'd gone missing. We eventually found his body in the library. I swear, the room was locked, the windows barred, and there is no other entrance."

"Hmm," replied Spratt thoughtfully. "You knew him well?"

"Locked Room and I have been friends for a long time," replied Red Herring, "despite the fact that he had an affair with my wife, fleeced me on a property deal in the 60s and has been secretly blackmailing me over my indiscretion with a Brazilian call girl named Conchita."

"Conchita, eh?"

"Damn," said Herring. "You know about her?"

"It's my business to know things," replied Spratt coolly. "I also know, for instance, that this mystery conforms to the Knox Convention."

"You mean—?"

"Right," said Jack. "There's no chance of someone we've not mentioned turning out to have done it."

"That also rules us out as the detectives," added Mary, "and there must be clues."

"And in a story this short," continued Jack, "some of them might be in italics – so keep a sharp eye out."

Jack turned back to Red Herring. "Who else was in the house at the time?"

Herring thought for a moment and counted the guests off on his fingers: "There was myself, Unshakeable Alibi, Cryptic Final Message, Least Likely Suspect, Overlooked Clue, and the butler, Flashback."

Spratt thought for a moment. "Tell everyone to wait in the drawing room and we'll speak to them one by one without a lawyer present and in clear contravention of any accepted police procedures."

Red Herring departed, and Jack and Mary ducked under the "Police line – do not cross" tape into the library. They cautiously approached the desk *where lay the corpse of the old lady, with her throat so entirely cut that, upon an attempt to raise her, the head fell off.*

"This MO seems somehow familiar," mused Spratt, looking around for a sharp object and finding nothing.

"Definitely locked from the inside," added Mary, having made an impossibly rapid examination of the room. Luckily for them both, the dark-humoured pathologist stereotype was the guest of honour at the Mystery Contrivances Club dinner, and was able to give an improbably precise time of death.

"About 7.02, give or take nine seconds," he said, munching on a sandwich.

The first suspect they spoke to was Unshakeable Alibi, who presented them with a photograph of herself taken earlier that evening – with a clock prominent in the background that read precisely 7.02.

"You knew Locked Room well?" asked Spratt.

"We were both there right at the beginning with Poe's Dupin mysteries," she mused. "Strange as it may seem now, Inspector, Locked Room was once the brightest star of the genre. He said he was going to make a comeback, but it never happened – it was all a bit sad, to be honest."

"And you are?" asked Jack as the next suspect walked in.

"Cryptic Final Message," replied the man, raising his hat. "Locked Room scribbled this note earlier today – I found it in the waste-paper basket."

Jack took the message and handed it to Mary.

"Okay, intimate nectar," she read. "Could be an anagram."

"Impossible," replied Spratt. "The Guild of Detectives have banned all anagram-related clues since 1998 – the same time we finally got rid of the ludicrous notion that albinos must always be homicidal lunatics."

"Well," purred Overlooked Clue, as she entered the room in a silk kimono. "Inspector Spratt – dahling – we meet again."

"Indeed," replied Jack. "You knew Locked Room?"

"Of course," she replied, draping herself with a fashionably decadent air upon the chaise longue. "We were close, but not intimate. He taught me all I know about misdirection. I always keep his first story close to my heart. Dearly missed, Inspector, dearly missed."

She sobbed and clasped a small volume of Poe short stories to her breast.

The next interviewee was Least Likely Suspect, a sweet old lady with white hair and clear blue eyes who spent her time gossiping and handing round photographs of her grandchildren. She asked Jack to hold a skein of wool so that she could wind some into a ball.

"I'm so sorry about Locked Room," she said sadly. "The finish of the Golden Age hit him badly. He always claimed he would make a dramatic comeback in the Christmas supplement of a leading daily newspaper, but I suppose it's too late for that now."

"Perhaps not," murmured Jack, leaning gently against the fourth wall. "I take it that you are still gainfully employed in the mystery thriller industry?"

"Me?" giggled the old lady. "What possible harm could a little old—"

She had stopped talking because a pearl-handled revolver had slipped from her purse and fallen to the floor with a clatter.

"I have a licence for that," she said quickly.

The next to be interviewed was Flashback the butler, who after taking them on an interesting but irrelevant excursion around a trivial incident in his childhood, gave no new information – except to say that Locked Room entered the library alone, and he heard the key being turned behind him.

"Tell me," said Jack slowly. "Was he carrying a small volume of short stories with him?"

"Why yes!" replied Flashback, "it's… it's all coming back to me now."

"I was initially baffled by the lack of a murder weapon within the locked room," intoned Spratt when all the suspects were conveniently arranged in the drawing room a few minutes later, "but after due consideration, it makes sense. All of you had reason to kill him. Red Herring was blackmailing him, Unshakeable Alibi was nervous that she might be eclipsed by his planned comeback, Overlooked Clue was still in love with him and Least Likely Suspect wanted to stay employed for ever."

They all looked nervously at one another as a log settled in the grate and sent a shower of sparks up the chimney.

"That's right," said Jack, "the killer was..."

Answer: It had to be a suicide. Locked Room, unable to come to terms with the loss of his literary stardom, wanted to re-establish the tired contrivance to full prominence in a final, totally unsolvable locked room mystery that would be discussed on a million bulletin boards for all eternity. Sadly, unable to come up with a decent description of his own mutilated body, he borrowed it word for word from Poe's "The Murders in the Rue Morgue", his first and keynote appearance.

Keen-eyed as usual, Jack noticed that in his haste, Locked Room had forgotten to change genders on the description and had inadvertently left the quote italicised. It was the book that Flashback saw him with, and also the same one later retrieved by Overlooked Clue as a keepsake. The anagram on the suicide note handed to Last Cryptic Message read: "I can't take it any more." Red Herring was indeed a red herring, and Flashback's attendance was entirely irrelevant – I just liked the joke.

From HANCOCK IN THE POLICE

Ray Galton and Alan Simpson

Ray Galton (1930–2018) and **Alan Simpson** (1929–2017) were an English comedy script-writing partnership. They met in 1948 whilst recuperating from tuberculosis at a sanatorium in Surrey. They are best known for their work with comedian Tony Hancock on radio and television, and for their long-running sitcom *Steptoe and Son*. The piece below is an extract from an episode of *Hancock's Half Hour* in which Hancock (played by Tony Hancock) and Bill (played by Bill Kerr) decide to become policemen. Their Bond Street beat is plagued by a thief, and so Superintendent Farmsworth (played by Kenneth Williams) hatches a plan to catch the devil red-handed.

SUPERINTENDENT FARMSWORTH. … Now, every Friday a young lady cashier leaves this shop with the week's takings and goes to the bank. My plan is this: we will employ a decoy. Another young lady will leave the shop at the correct time with an empty bag. We'll be lying in wait, and when the thieves strike, we will jump out and overpower them!

HANCOCK. Hooray!!

SUPERINTENDENT FARMSWORTH. The question is, who shall we use as a decoy?

HANCOCK. I know the very woman, my secretary. Just the girl. It'd take a gang of ten to knock her down.

[*Music*]

GRISELDA. No. I'm not risking my life to get you out of trouble.

HANCOCK. There's no risk, there'll be half the force ready to pounce on them the minute anybody tries anything.

GRISELDA. Honestly! The first time in my life anybody's likely to try anything, half the police force jump out and stop him.

HANCOCK. He's not going to try that sort of thing.

GRISELDA. After all these years, any sort of thing would be welcome.

HANCOCK. But Griselda! I've promised the Superintendent that you'll do it!

GRISELDA. Well, I'm not, so go away. I've got to finish sewing 'see you later alligator' on my sweater before the concert tonight. You'll just have to find someone else.

[*Music*]

HANCOCK. How do I look, Bill?

BILL. Sensational. The skirt's a little too baggy, and you haven't got the colouring for a blonde wig, but otherwise perfect.

HANCOCK. I'll be glad when I get out of these high heels; they're screwing up my bunions something horrible.

BILL. It won't be long, it's time to go down to the bank with the bag.

SUPERINTENDENT FARMSWORTH. Are you ready Hancock?

HANCOCK. I'm ready Super. I still think we ought to have found somebody else. It's not right you know: me, a policeman, dressed as a woman. It's overstepping the bounds of duty.

SUPERINTENDENT FARMSWORTH. Silence! Go out now, it's one o'clock, get down to the street. We'll be watching your every move. Good luck.

HANCOCK. Are my seams straight?

[*Door bangs*]

SUPERINTENDENT FARMSWORTH. Nothing suspicious so far. No one's taking any notice of him. Perhaps they're not going to try anything today.

BILL. Hey, wait a minute, look! There's a man following him. Look! The fellow in the trilby. He's crossing the road after him.

SUPERINTENDENT FARMSWORTH. Mm, I think we may be onto something here. Look! Hancock's stopped.

BILL. Yes, that was the fella. Oh gee, Tub looks worried.

SUPERINTENDENT FARMSWORTH. Get ready Kerr, I think this may be it.

BILL. No, wait until he actually snatches the bag. Yes, look! The fella's going up to Tub, he's tapping him on the shoulder, he's, he's saying something to him.

[*Footsteps*]

MAN. Good morning cheeky. Want to come to the pictures with me?

HANCOCK. Hop it, hop it! Go on, get out of it! Go on, go on. Go on home. Go home!

MAN. Don't be like that. I saw you wink at me.

HANCOCK. I didn't wink at you. Me false eyelash flopped down. Look, buzz off. Go on, hop it!

MAN. I think you're smashing.

HANCOCK. I'll smash you in a minute.

MAN. Ooooh, there see, I like girls with a bit of spirit. (A bit of fire. I bet you're Mexican or something aint you?

HANCOCK. I am not Mexican. I come from Cheam if it's any interest. Now clear off mate. There's a good boy. You might get hurt.

MAN. No, right little spitfire aren't you? You fascinating minx you.)* Come here…

* Text in brackets not included in original rehearsal script but appeared into the final radio recording of 'Hancock's Half Hour'.

HANCOCK. Do you mind! Let me go! How dare you! Unhand me!

MAN. Stop struggling! You girls are all the same. Tantalise a man until you drive him to distraction. Here, what about coming to the pictures?

HANCOCK. You're making a big mistake. Things aren't what they seem. Go and find somebody else!

MAN. No, I want you. I like them with a bit of meat on them.

HANCOCK. What do you mean a bit of meat? I'll fix you such a slosh across the face with my handbag in a minute.

MAN. Oh no. Stop messing about. What's your name, deary?

HANCOCK. Mind your own business!

MAN. I see you as a Laura.

HANCOCK. Do you? Well, I see you as a Charlie. Now, look! Let me give you a word of warning. There are a hundred policemen hiding in the shop doorways along here waiting to spring out on any man that talks to me.

MAN. Ooooh. You must be important. All those bodyguards, you must be an eastern princess or something.

HANCOCK. Do I look like an eastern princess?

MAN. A beauty like yours would fit in anywhere, my little goose. Come to the pictures with me.

HANCOCK. I'm not com— What's on? No, no, I can't go, I've got a job to do. Now go on, hop it, please.

MAN. Let me carry your bag then.

HANCOCK. No!

MAN. Oh give us it—

HANCOCK. No!

MAN. Oh go on.

HANCOCK. You'll be sorry! Give us it back!

MAN. No, no, the least a gentleman can do is carry a lady's handbag.

[*Whistles blowing*]

BILL. Alright, you're under arrest!

MAN. Me? What for?

BILL. We've been waiting for you to try and snatch that bag and now we've caught you in the act. Now come quietly.

MAN. But I haven't done anything. I'm just a young lad, trying to find himself a bit of fun.

BILL. You're wanted on a charge of robbing forty-nine shops, three factories, a warehouse and a bank. What have you got to say?

MAN. What are the girls like in prison?

SID'S MYSTERY TOURS

Ray Galton and Alan Simpson

Ray Galton (1930–2018) and **Alan Simpson** (1929–2017) were an English comedy script-writing partnership. They met in 1948 whilst recuperating from tuberculosis at a sanatorium in Surrey. They are best known for their work with comedian Tony Hancock on radio and television, and for their long-running sitcom *Steptoe and Son*.

CAST
Tony Hancock
Sidney James
Bill Kerr
Warren Mitchell
Errol Mckinnon
Mavis Villers

Grams. Signature tune... down for:

ANNOUNCER. We present Tony Hancock, Sidney James, and Bill Kerr in...

Grams. Sig. tune up and down for:

TONY. [*Breath*] "Hancock's Half Hour"

Grams. Sig tune up and out.

BILL. More tea, Tub?

TONY. Thank you, William, yes. Use the strainer this time. I do hate tea leaves floating about. It doesn't matter which way you turn the cup, they follow you round.

BILL. O.K. Do you want any more omelette Yugoslavian?

TONY. No thanks, I'll make do with the Cornflakes. Mediterranean.

BILL. What's that?

TONY. That's with milk on them.

BILL. Oh. What cornflakes do you want? The already sugared ones, or the ones you put the sugar on yourself?

TONY. The already sugared ones please. I don't like putting the sugar on myself. It goes right through and collects at the bottom of the plate. Those last two spoonfuls are like dredging the mouth of the Humber.

BILL. I'll have to open a fresh packet.

TONY. Bags me the little Tony Tiger badge. Oh god, he's riding a bike, I haven't got that one. Put it in the lapel of my clerical grey.

BILL. You can't do that.

TONY. I'm entitled to. I'm a club member. What? I've been whoofing cornflakes since before they started making a noise.

BILL. They've always made a noise.

TONY. Anything makes a noise when you eat it. Now keep quiet, I want to read the newspaper…

Effects: Newspaper.

TONY. Oh dear, oh dear, oh dear. Well I never. Doesn't it make you sick. Who do they think they are. Four times married, this time for keeps, ex-husband best man, and three of his ex-wives as bridesmaids. What a way to carry on. I don't know what the world's coming to. It's like a square dance. Once round the room and all change partners. I don't know why I buy this paper, I don't really, there's never any news in it. Hallo, I thought so, the dustmen have come out on strike in the Isle of Man. I knew that would happen, I could see it coming. You can't expect them to empty dustbins with motor bikes whipping by every five minutes. How would you like to keep crossing the road during the Junior T. T. If one of them was to be hit by Surtees on his Works Motorguzzi, he's had it. They haven't got much protection... a couple of dustbin lids, that's no good. Hallo, I see those two have got engaged. Dear oh dear... look at them, what a couple of charmers. What can he see in her. Look at her, what does she look like, beauty queen? Her. They don't say when, do they. Oh no. About 1932, I reckon. Look at it... all teeth and beauty spots.

BILL. Who?

TONY. I thought I told you to keep quiet.

BILL. Well, I only...

TONY. Do you want to go and stand outside?

BILL. No.

TONY. Well, be quiet then.

BILL. I thought we were going out today.

TONY. We are, there's plenty of time. I haven't read the gardening strip yet. There he is, old Harold the Gardener. Standing in the vegetable patch with bubbles coming out of his head. What's he saying. [*Dialect*] When you're planting your potatoes, make sure there aren't no wire worms about. He's right, he's dead right. Very nasty that is, wire worms in your spuds. Do you remember our spuds last year. We dug them out of the ground looking like bits of Henry Moore's statues. Disgusting it was. Thirty nine pounds of potatoes. We got five chips out of them.

BILL. Where are we going?

TONY. I haven't made up my mind yet. Hallo, that's a clever way of tying up your peas. Bits of string. Make a note of that. What's he doing in the last picture? Oh yes, how to get apples down from the top of the tree... Of course, garden shears on the end of big poles. I wish I'd known about that. I've been chopping ours down every year.

BILL. The time's getting on. It won't be worth going out in a minute.

TONY. Yes it will. You are a worryguts, aren't you?

BILL. Well, it's the first weekend we've had free for weeks. I want to go to the seaside.

TONY. Well, we're not going to the seaside. I don't like the seaside any more. You can't get near the sea for feet. Great bare plates pounding up and down the beach. You try and have a nice doze and wake up with your earholes full of sand… that's not my idea of enjoying ones self. No, if we go out, we'll have a nice quiet day in the country. We'll have a go at one of those excursions.

BILL. They'll be in the paper, in the small ads.

TONY. Yes, that'll be next to the horoscopes. Here we are. Page nine. Holidays and tours. Coach tour of the South Downs, thirty-two and six. De Luxe Coaches Ltd. Tour of the Western Highlands, twelve and six. That's very good. Oh… you've got to find your own way up to Aberdeen. Hallo, what's this? Free, Free, Free. Absolutely genuine offer, no obligations, guaranteed bona fide. Well, this sounds like a catch, doesn't it? Tour of the local district leaving Cheam High Street at two thirty.

BILL. Who's running it?

TONY. Er… Oh, I thought so.

BILL. What?

TONY. Sid James Mystery Tours. Isn't it marvellous. Every year it's the same. The minute the sun comes out he's got a racket going. You've got to hand it to him. He's got a fiddle worked out for every season of the year. Each Christmas we have the Old Mother James's Genuine Christmas puddings. Thirty bob each, made by him and Edwardian Fred in the bicycle shed, supply your own currants. Then at Easter we are confronted with the Great Easter Egg Take On. One cardboard egg painted brown with two bits of yellow cotton wool stuck on it which we are informed, are baby chickens. And inside crammed full of delicious sweets. Two peppermints with holes in and a liquorice shoelace… Thirty-five bob that lot. Then at Whitsun he's riding up and down the road selling set teas to motorists in traffic jams. Which wouldn't exist if it wasn't for the fake diversion signs that he sits up half the night painting. And now we have the Sid James Mystery Tours. The only mystery I can see is how the police haven't caught on to him yet.

BILL. Well, are we going to patronise him?

TONY. Certainly not. We'll go along and see what he's up to, but I'm not buying any tickets off him. I've been stung too many times. Hallo.

BILL. What?

TONY. My horoscope. Saggiteryus, Beware ugly looking man with frizzy hair. Money will undoubtedly change hands.

BILL. Show me mine. Leo the Lion. [*Reads*] That goes for you too.

TONY. Oh don't take any notice of him, he doesn't know what he's talking about. Herbert the Gipsy, I've never reckoned him. He's had my mother frightened to go out of the house six times since last march. Come on then, lay out my holiday outfit. Straw sandals, argyle socks plus fours, silk shirt and the blazer with the R.A.F. badge on it. Or shall I wear the blazer with the Royal Artillery badge?

BILL. I think you look best in the Oxford University blazer.

TONY. Yes, I think you're right. Although the Cambridge blazer looks rather chic when it's been cleaned up. Yes, I think the Cambridge University with the Old Etonian Tie... and my plastic mac.

Grams. Music link.

Grams. Street noises... and rain effect.

TONY. Now... Sid James Mystery Tours, 22a High Street East Cheam. Well, that's twenty, twenty-two... where's twenty-two A then?

BILL. It's not there.

TONY. I can see it's not there. That's why I said where is it? Why don't you listen? And get your feet off my plastic mac.

BILL. You shouldn't have it so long.

TONY. I like it long, do you mind. What's the point in having a plastic mac if your turn ups get wet. If you're going to have a mac, have a big 'un. Now get your feet off. You'll have the welded seams coming apart. Now... twenty-two A. Go and ask someone.

BILL. It's raining.

TONY. What difference does that make? They're not going to not know just because it's raining.

BILL. Wait a minute, would that be it?

TONY. Would what be it?

BILL. Over there. In between twenty-two and twenty-four, there's a gap.

TONY. That's right, that's the bomb site.

BILL. Well, there's a shed on it.

TONY. He's right, there is a shed on it. Well done, have a wine gum. There's no sign of life over there. Wait a minute, there's a flap coming down. Oh yes, there he is behind the counter, look at him, he looks like a dirty great spider in the middle of his web. Come on my old fly, let's go and see what it's all about.

BILL. I see he's got some customers already. We'll have to get on the queue...

[Fade]

SIDNEY. ... there you are sir, two tickets for the Grand Mystery Tour leaving here in ten minutes.

OLD MAN. Where are we going?

SIDNEY. Oh, I can't tell you that. It wouldn't be a mystery tour then would it? You have to chance your luck. That'll be thirty-five and six each please.

OLD MAN. That's a lot of money. It says seventeen and six on your board.

SIDNEY. You want to come back, don't you? Now go and stand

over there and wait for the others. We leave as soon as we've sold all the tickets. And the next gent please.

TONY. So you're at it again, eh?

SIDNEY. Oh, hallo Hancock. I haven't seen you for days. How's the tortoise I sold you?

TONY. It hasn't moved since I put it in the garden.

SIDNEY. Hasn't moved?

TONY. Not a step. I haven't even seen it yet. I haven't seen its head or its legs. I picked it up and shook it this morning, there's nothing in there.

SIDNEY. Of course there's something in there.

TONY. I don't care about something in there, is there a tortoise in there?

SIDNEY. Well, there should be.

TONY. Well, I don't think there is. I looked in through the front and I could see right out through his leg holes.

SIDNEY. Well, perhaps he was curled up.

TONY. They don't curl up.

SIDNEY. Well, give him a chance, he's only a baby, he's still growing, he hasn't filled the shell up yet.

TONY. The shell grows with them. There's nothing in there. I've been poking sticks in through every hole and there's nothing in there.

SIDNEY. Oh well, if you've been doing that, that explains it. He must have got a bit niggly. He probably lifted his shell up and ran for it.

TONY. Well, I'm not satisfied, I want my money back.

SIDNEY. No, I'm sorry. I never return money, you ought to know that.

TONY. Well, give me another one then. And no cheating. I want one with a head and four legs poking out.

SIDNEY. You're too late, mate, I'm not in the tortoise trade any more. They live too long. There's no replacement trade worth talking about.

BILL. Why don't you sell old ones?

TONY. Why don't you sell old ones? What a poltroon this man is. How can you tell how old a tortoise is?

BILL. You count the rings on its back.

TONY. That's a tree.

BILL. Oh. You count its teeth?

TONY. That's horses.

BILL. Well, you can't be right all the time.

TONY. No, no you're quite right, William. I wish I hadn't taken him in. Look, I wish to speak to Sidney you amuse yourself. Stand there and count the nails up the side of the shed.

BILL. One, two, three, four…

TONY. No, no, to yourself, eh? Quietly. That's a good lad. Well now, Sidney…

SIDNEY. Yeah, hurry up and get it over, I've got a business to run. Now, what can I do for you?

TONY. These tours of yours, what's the fiddle?

SIDNEY. There's no fiddle. Genuine legitimate business. I run mystery tours, that's all there is to it. How many tickets do you want?

TONY. Wait a minute… let's cut aside some of the mystery first. How does it work?

SIDNEY. Well, I've got all prices of tours, ranging from five bob right up to thirty-five and a tanner. You pay me the money and I give you the tour.

TONY. That sounds alright. I'll have two five-shilling ones.

SIDNEY. A very wise choice. A delightful tour you've chosen there. Not so long as a thirty-five and six one of course, but nonetheless interesting.

TONY. Good. When do we start?

SIDNEY. As soon as you like.

TONY. Alright then, I'll go now.

SIDNEY. Alright then, cheerio.

TONY. Cheeri... What do you mean, cheerio?

SIDNEY. You said you were off.

TONY. But where's the guide?

SIDNEY. I'm the guide.

TONY. Well, aren't you coming with us?

SIDNEY. No, I can't leave the office.

TONY. Well, how can you guide us then?

SIDNEY. Easy. You turn left at the traffic lights, up the High Street, first left, second right, first left round the gasworks, over the railway bridge, past the reservoir, round the back of the Town Hall, up an alleyway and back here.

TONY. That's not much of a tour, is it?

SIDNEY. What do you expect for five bob?

TONY. No, I suppose so. Alright then, where's the coach?

SIDNEY. What coach?

TONY. The coach we tour in.

SIDNEY. I didn't say anything about a coach. You have to walk.

TONY. I could do that for nothing. I don't have to pay you five bob to walk up the High Street.

SIDNEY. Ah yeah, if you want to wander aimlessly, but you're paying for the organisation. I've taken great care in drawing up a carefully detailed itinery.

TONY. Oh, there's an itinery.

SIDNEY. Certainly. All good tours have an itinery.

BILL. Hundred and ninety-eight.

TONY. Pardon?

BILL. There's a hundred and ninety-eight nails on this side.

TONY. Right, well count the nails on the other side, then you can start on the knotholes.

BILL. Right.

TONY. Now, where's this itinery?

SIDNEY. Here we are, Tour number Five, East Cheam High Street and the shops. Leave here at one o'clock. One 0 two, stop at the shoe shop and watch the blokes mending shoes in the windows, thirteen 0 three, all back in line to start off again.

TONY. Hang on, I want more than a minute to watch the shoe menders. They wouldn't have more than a quarter tip on in that time.

SIDNEY. I'm sorry, this is a strict timetable, you can't hold up the tour for individual members, you'll have to catch the others up outside the chemists shop.

TONY. What, and miss the greengrocers?

SIDNEY. That's the way it goes. Now then, thirteen 0 four, stop at the butchers shop and watch the sausages coming out of the machine.

TONY. Oh, that'll be an attraction.

SIDNEY. I've laid it on with Harry the Butcher. He makes a special batch of sausages for the benefit of my clients. We allow two minutes for that, then thirteen 0 six back in line for refreshments

TONY. Oh, we get refreshments?

SIDNEY. Yeah, all fixed up. I've arranged with the caterers for special parties of up to thirty.

TONY. What do we get?

SIDNEY. A glass of cherryade each at the sweetshop. Two minutes to get that down you, then a quick tour of the shop windows in King Street, walk past the gas works, round the resevoir, and round the back of the Town Hall. By this time we might be a bit tight on the schedule so you'll probably have to run the last half mile to be back here by thirteen 0 ten.

TONY. And that's it is it? That's the five-shilling mystery tour.

SIDNEY. Yeah, roughly. I mean, naturally I haven't put all the attractions down. You've got to create some of your own enjoyment, we like to leave our clients some freedom of choice. I mean, we don't tell you where you have to look, we've only made suggestions where to look. You can look where you like, you don't have to look in the shop windows if you don't want to.

TONY. As long as we keep in line.

SIDNEY. Exactly, and don't hold it up at all, keep it moving. There's a lot more in it than there is down there.

TONY. That's true, I mean, I could take my camera along, couldn't I?

SIDNEY. Certainly you could.

TONY. Make a pictorial record of the tour so to speak.

SIDNEY. That's it, a lot of people do just that.

TONY. You could take photos of the lamp posts, and the traffic lights, and the cars parked along the street.

SIDNEY. Then you can buy a projector, and entertain your friends, get a few drinks in, have a marvellous evening. I reckon it's fantastic value for five bob.

TONY. You do.

SIDNEY. Certainly. I realise it's not as comprehensive as some of the more expensive ones, but it's not bad for the money. It fulfills a certain demand in the popular price range.

TONY. You may be right. But personally… I mean this is only my opinion you realise…

SIDNEY. Quite.

TONY. Personally speaking, I would say at first sight… without going into it of course…! would say this is without a doubt the biggest take on I have ever come across.

SIDNEY. Well, everybody's entitled to their own opinion. Now are you going on the tour or not, 'cos you'd better get on the queue forming over there by the sandbin –they'll be off in five minutes, as soon as we've got a full load.

TONY. I'm not tramping round East Cheam looking in shop windows. What other tours have you got?

SIDNEY. There's our seven and six Class A tour.

TONY. What's that?

SIDNEY. That's the same as the other one only you walk slower. The ten bob de luxe tour, the windows you look in are a much better class of shop. Then there's the…

TONY. Don't go on. Am I to take it you're running about twelve Mystery Tours with not one single coach.

SIDNEY. I can't afford any, the season's only just started.

TONY. Well, I want my money back. I am a dissatisfied customer.

SIDNEY. How can you be dissatisfied, you haven't been on the tour yet.

TONY. I've been up and down this town thousands of times, and I know it's as miserable experience as one could wish to find. Give me my money back or I shall cause trouble.

SIDNEY. I'll tell you what I'll do. The estimated turnover of this company is fifty thousand nicker a year, but as I know you, I'll sell you a half share for ten bob.

TONY. Ten bob? Ten bob?

SIDNEY. Alright, seven and six. I'm not going any lower. Here, you sign here.

TONY. Wait a minute, there's something fishy here. Why should you have a contract already drawn up. Look at it, twenty-seven pages of illuminated parchment, this must have cost you more than seven and six... What's the catch?

SIDNEY. No catch. You're quite right, I can't give all my time to this little number, I've got so many other interests... I need somebody like you to take it over from me... It'll have to go, I'd sooner you, a friend of the family, than a stranger. Here you are... I'll give you fifty-one percent of the company... controlling interest... I keep forty-nine per cent. It's yours, then I can't do anything you don't agree with.

TONY. That's true. Fifty-one beats forty-nine. Has this company got all the trimmings. Office and all that?

SIDNEY. Certainly.

TONY. Has it got a long table with a big hammer at the end?

SIDNEY. Yeah. You'll be sitting at the end in your black coat and striped trousers on... Managing Director, intercom... send in Miss Krint, it's all there.

TONY. For seven and six.

SIDNEY. Yeah.

TONY. It's a deal. I've always fancied the big hammer. T. H., there's S. J. and B. K. to see you. Marvellous, a big row of note pads and three secretaries with funny glasses on… that's me, mate. Where do I sign?

SIDNEY. Just here, there and there. And a witness.

TONY. BILL. Where's he gone? I bet he's gone off picking up bus tickets again. Where is he?

BILL. Ninety-eight nails, and thirty-three knotholes. Shall I count the nails on the roof now?

TONY. In a minute. Sign this.

BILL. What is it?

TONY. Mind your own business… Sign it.

BILL. Oh, alright.

TONY. Come on now, no printing, real writing.

BILL. What, you mean joining all the letters together?

TONY. Yes.

BILL. Alright then. William Kerr. There.

TONY. Nothing like it. Could be anything. Looks like a line on a temperature chart.

BILL. That's good enough for me. Well, there it is, you now own a controlling interest in Sid James Mystery Tours Ltd.

TONY. Thank you very much. What do we do first then?

SIDNEY. Get a good lawyer.

BILL. What for?

SIDNEY. The police are after this firm.

TONY. The police?

SIDNEY. Certainly, what do you expect? Running a Mystery Tour Firm without any coaches. That's fraud. You ought to be ashamed of yourself.

TONY. But it's not my fault.

SIDNEY. Of course it is. You're the boss.

TONY. You didn't tell me anything about the police.

SIDNEY. It's in the minutes. You ought to read the minutes when you're Managing Director of a firm.

TONY. Well, where are they?

SIDNEY. They're in the files. You've got access to them.

TONY. I've only just taken the firm over.

SIDNEY. I don't think they'll take that as an excuse. I think you're in dead trouble, son.

TONY. What can I do about it?

SIDNEY. You'll have to buy a coach.

TONY. That'll cost over five thousand pounds.

SIDNEY. It's nothing to do with me, you're the boss. I just collect forty-nine per cent of the profits.

TONY. Oh I see, that's it, is it? I supply the coach which you couldn't afford, and you collect forty-nine per cent of it.

SIDNEY. I'm entitled to it. I built the firm up.

TONY. What do you mean, built it up. All you've got is one shed with two hundred and ninety-eight nails, thirty-three knot-holes, and a box of chalks for writing the tours out with.

SIDNEY. Well, it's up to you, if you want to go to prison, that's your look out.

TONY. I can't find five thousand pounds for a coach.

SIDNEY. How much can you find?

TONY. If I sold everything about a thousand pounds.

SIDNEY. Well, I don't know why I should help you, a frauder like you, but as you're a friend of the family… I might be able to get hold of one.

TONY. Where from?

SIDNEY. Sid James Scottish Tours Ltd. They've got a second-hand one going for a thousand nicker. I might be able to persuade the Board of Directors to let you have it.

TONY. I see. Sid James Scottish Tours have got a coach.

SIDNEY. Oh yes.

TONY. They probably bought it for … what? Two hundred?

SIDNEY. Somewhere round that. Of course it's an old one.

TONY. Oh, naturally. An open one, I expect, with solid tyres,

SIDNEY. Yeah, that's right.

TONY. Vintage, what?… 1926?

SIDNEY. 1917.

TONY. Seventeen. Oh, a very good year for motor coaches that was. Shall I tell you something, I'm not as dim as I look, I am not buying it… I am going to liquidate this firm as from now.

SIDNEY. You can't

TONY. I can, I own fifty-one per cent of the shares.

SIDNEY. Ah yes, that's A shares, not the B shares.

TONY. Oh cor… alright, come on, how does that work?

SIDNEY. Well, you only own Investing shares, that entitles you to put money into the firm… I own all the voting shares. You can't liquidate without the permission of the voting shareholders, and I withhold it.

TONY. That means the police are after you as well.

SIDNEY. No. I'm in the clear. I've got it in the minutes. Here it is, Saturday morning extraordinary General Meeting held outside the shed. The chief voting shareholder called upon the chief investing shareholder to invest in a coach and he refused. That'd clear me in any court of law that will.

TONY. I see. So what it amounts to is this… I've either got to buy from you for a thousand pounds a coach that's only worth two hundred or I go to prison, and if I buy the coach you take forty-nine per cent of the profits. And I paid you seven and six to put myself in this powerful position.

SIDNEY. That's about the size of it.

TONY. Hmmm. Bill, how would you like to buy a company for five shillings?

BILL. No thanks.

TONY. Two and six.

BILL. No, I don't want to go to prison.

TONY. How did you know? I thought you were counting the nails on the roof.

BILL. I was listening.

TONY. Why don't you mind your own business.

SIDNEY. Well, what about it then?

TONY. I don't appear to have any choice do I?

SIDNEY. No, not really.

TONY. Very well, I shall buy the coach. Here's your cheque.

SIDNEY. Thank you.

TONY. I shall build this company up and recoup my losses by honest means. I'll build it into one of the biggest coach tour companies in the country by sheer hard work and perseverance. Then, at the end of five years you'll want to buy it back off me.

SIDNEY. No I won't.

TONY. Why not?

SIDNEY. Our licence is up in a week.

BILL. I told you you shouldn't sign anything without reading it.

TONY. Oh shut up, it's all your fault, counting knotholes instead of advising me. We've got a week now to try and get our money back, go get out of it you ratbag, go on, go and get that coach, you're driving it. We'll get some Americans off the boat train.

Grams. Music link.

Grams. Old coach ticking over… Traffic noises.

TONY. Good afternoon, ladies and gentlemen visiting our shores from the far off Americas, and welcome to East Cheam, Surrey, England, Europe. My name is Anthony and I will be your guide for this tour of East Cheam and the surrounding districts, and I'm sure all you American ladies and gentlemen will find much of interest to you in this historic and beautiful slice of ye olde Merrie Englande.

HOVIS. [*An American*] Hey, these seats are hard, mac.

TONY. Exactly why I thought they may appeal to you, sir. You see this coach is the original coach that Dick Turpin held up on his ride to Grimsby to welcome home the herring fleets.

Omnes. Muttering of interest.

HOVIS. Aw gee, did you hear that, Hortense?

HORTENSE. I certainly did, Hovis honey, isn't that the cutest thing.

TONY. Well now, if you'll have your cameras at the ready we'll have a hundredweight of used film piled up at the back there before we get to the end of the High Street. Right you are, Sir William, off we go.

Effects. Old car starting and continues:

BILL. [*English*] Right you are, old bean, roger and all that, what?

HOVIS. Hey, is he a real lord?

TONY. What him. Lord Kerr. Oh my goodness me yes. He's the seventeenth Earl of West Chiswick. Very old family, he's on his hols from Eton you know… I suggest big tips for him at the end, he's got a castle to keep up you know.

HOVIS. Oh yeah, sure, sure. Hear that, Hortense, a real lord driving the coach for us.

HORTENSE. Oh gee, Hovis, just wait till the Women's Guild hear about this back in Grand Rapids, G. A.

TONY. As we pass along this historic High Street, mentioned in the Domesday Book, compiled by Alfred the Great, the well known king, in 793 at the request of the barons at Runnymede near Ascot Race Track…

HOVIS. I thought that was King William the Conqueror.

TONY. Ah yes, well it was in his name but he was away at the time, he couldn't attend, he was on a Crusade against the Vikings just outside Clacton. There's a good shot over there look…

Effects. Creak of car springs:

TONY. … don't all crowd on one side of the bus, you'll have the springs off. Notice the colourful local costumes of the native women as they go about their shopping. The rundown plat-form shoes, the quaint fag hanging from the corner of the mouth, serving as a constant reminder of that great explorer Sir Walter Drake who discovered a tobacco plant in Virginia the well-known part of America. And the colourful headscarf covering the traditional metal curlers in the hair. Note the headscarf is shaped in the form of a turban, as a tribute to our long-standing ties with India and the British Commonwealth, Turn left here, Sir William.

BILL. Right yob are, old bean, shall be done.

Effects. Screech of brakes.

TONY. I would like you to note the local tradesmen in their quaint shops as they carry on their ancient traditional crafts. Notice the centuries of skill that have gone into the way the old clock-maker levers open another crate of watches from Switzerland. Note the loving care devoted by the local butcher on the many sides of roast beef of Old England specially frozen for us in the Argentine. The natives love of their traditional dishes and local foods is evident in the grocers shop piled high with processed cheese, tinned fruit and frozen vegetables... Over the bridge across the picturesque polluted river down which floats impressive mountains of detergent foam... we can see the local house-wives attending to their weekly wash. Note the weary slump of their shoulders as they lean forward and peer through the little glass portholes to see if their sheets are done yet. Over there on the right we are passing one of our largest public buildings. A typical example of the more obsolete and generally accepted ugly periods of Victorian architecture... built in 1957. That tree you see over there with the railings round it is the Green Belt area of this district. Thanks to the great public spiritedness of the council and local businessmen, no one is allowed to build on it, and it will be preserved for the benefit and enjoyment of the public for all time. That concludes the first half of the tour, we will now stop at this picturesque, leaded-light, low-roofed, brass-filled horror known as Nan's Pantry for a farmhouse tea.

HORTENSE. Gee, Hovis, just think we're going to have a real English tea.

HOVIS. Oh gee, Hortense, and I hear they make it in a strange way over here. All loose and slopping about instead of in bags.

HORTENSE. Oh, what a shame, perhaps they can't afford the tea bags.

HOVIS. Yeah, I guess that's it.

HORTENSE. [*Whispers*] Hovis, now's your chance, ask the gentleman.

HOVIS. Oh yeah, sure. Er... excuse me – er, Anthony? I wonder if I could get a shot of my wife standing next to the English Me Lord.

TONY. Why certainly, by all means, [*calls*] Er – Sir William. [*To Hovis*] It'll cost you half a dollar.

HOVIS. Half a dollar, that's fifty cents.

TONY. Fifty cents, seven and twopence a dollar, that's three and seven... Yes, that's right, half a dollar, an Oxford scholar.

BILL. [*Terribly-terribly*] How would you like me to pose, old American bean?

HOVIS. Hey, what's this, ain't you got a monocle?

TONY. Oh, they don't all wear monocles, you know, oh dear me no, only the ones with duff eyes.

HOVIS. Oh well, I guess that'll be alright. Well, hold it your Lordship... That's fine, thank you very much.

BILL. Don't menchers, old sport. A pleasures, yes indeeders.

TONY. [*Calls*] In you go everybody for the farmhouse tea...

Effects. Small crowd.

TONY. ... everybody back on the coach in fifteen minutes. Well, how do you think it's going?

BILL. They seem to be enjoying it.

TONY. I can't think why. The load of old rubbish we've shown them. It's a bit of a liberty, you know, three pounds ten each.

BILL. We've got to get our money back somehow.

TONY. That's true. Needs must I suppose. Come on, let's nip in the Hand and Racquet. I can't stand that horrible tea she serves up.

MAN. Excuse me.

TONY. Oh, in Nan's Pantry with the rest, if you hurry you'll just be in time for a cup of varnish and a jam lardy.

MAN. I'm not on the tour, I'm from the London Transport Executive.

TONY. Oh I see, the rival mob, eh?

MAN. Is this your coach?

TONY. That is so, I'm the owner.

MAN. That's all we wanted to know. Constable, arrest these two men.

TONY. I beg your pardon, on what charge?

MAN. On a charge of stealing this vehicle from the London Transport Permanent Museum. We've been looking for this one for weeks.

TONY. This can be explained, I assure you.

MAN. I sincerely hope for your sake that it can. Take them away, Constable.

TONY. I protest... You see, when I say I'm the owner of the coach, that's not exactly true, it's owned by a company you see and...

BILL. Yeah, but you're the Managing Director of the company, aren't you?

TONY. Why don't you shut up?

MAN. I think that settles it, come along now, sir...

TONY. Oh, what can you do?

Grams. Music link.

SIDNEY. ... and over on the left you'll be interested to see the oldest municipal jail in these parts. Working in the fields you can see the first offenders, not dangerous, but nevertheless put out of the reach of the temptations of crime, and doing a service towards the economy of their country by heaving spuds.

HOVIS. Hey, Hortense, that fellow with the shovel, isn't he the guide from that last tour we made?

HORTENSE. Yeah, and that's the English Me Lord next to him. Take a shot of them, Hovis.

TONY. [*Off mike – calls*] Do you mind. Get your telephone lens off my person. Uncouth heathens. Go on, mind your own business. Go on home before I throw a spud at you. And as for you James, you wait till I get out. You'd better take the longest tour you've got, I'll have you, you wait. Bill, throw a cauliflower at him.

HORTENSE. Oh gee, what a nasty man.

SIDNEY. Yeah, well you get criminals in all countries, don't you. Continuing the eight pounds twelve and sixpenny tour, we see on the right the outskirts of Sherwood Forest where Robin Hood did sport with Maid Marian in days of yore... and on the left is the very spot where Abraham Lincoln's grandfather was born, over here we have the...

Grams. Closing sig starts on the word "Grandfather." Down for:

ANNOUNCER. That was "Hancock's Half Hour" starring Tony Hancock, with Sidney James, Bill Kerr, Warren Mitchell, Mavis Villers and Errol McKinnon. Theme and incidental music composed and conducted by Wally Stott. Alan Simpson and Ray Galton wrote the script and the programme, which was recorded, was produced by Tom Ronald.

Grams. Up and out... playout.

STORY TIME

Joyce Grenfell

Joyce Grenfell (1910–1979) was the daughter of the youngest of the Langhorne sisters, of whom the most celebrated was Nancy, Lady Astor. She spent her girlhood on the fringes of the famous Cliveden set, which included George Bernard Shaw and Noël Coward, but it wasn't until a dinner party in 1938 that her genius for dramatic monologue was discovered when she gave an impromptu imitation of a Women's Institute speaker. She was an accomplished actress and starred in many films, including the *St Trinian's* series. She was also a regular on television, radio and the stage, and entertained the troops during the war with her usual wit, charm and humour.

Children... pay attention, please. Free time is over, so put away your things and we are going to tell our nice story, so come over here and make a circle on the floor all around me, and we'll tell the story together. We've got a visitor today, so we can tell our story to her.

Will you be all right there, Mrs Binton? I think you'll get a good view of the proceedings.

Hurry up everybody. Don't push – there's lots of room for us all.

This group story-telling is quite a feature of our work here in the Nursery School, Mrs Binton. We like to feel that each little individual has a contribution to make to the world of make-believe, and of course many valuable lessons can be learned from team work. We're a happy band of brothers here!

Edgar, let go of Timmy's ear and settle down.

Come along, everybody.

Sidney, come out from under the table and join in the fun.

No, you're not in a space rocket.

You can't wait for the count-down, you come out now.

Don't you want to help us tell our nice story, Sidney?

Then say, 'No, thank you.' And stop machine-gunning everybody, please.

And Neville, stop being a train and sit down.

All right then, get into the station and then sit down.

George…

No…

Let's have some nice straight backs, shall we? What shall we tell our story about today?

Rachel, take your shoe off your head and put it on your foot.

Shall we tell it about a little mouse?

Or a big red bus?

About a dear little bunny rabbit! All right, Peggy, we'll tell it about a dear little bunny rabbit.

No, Sidney, he wasn't a cowboy bunny rabbit, and he didn't have a gun.

Why don't you come out from under the table and help us tell our nice story?

All right, stay where you are, but you must stop machine-gunning everybody. I don't want to have to tell you again.

One of our individualists! He does have little personality problems, of aggression, but we feel that when his energies are canalised in the right direction he is going to be a quite worthwhile person. That's what we hope…

Where did our bunny rabbit live?

No, he didn't live in a TV set.

No, not in a tree.

No, not in a flat.

Think please.

He lived in a HOLE.

Yes, Hazel, of course he did.

Only some of us call it a burrow, don't we?

He lived in a burrow with – who? His mummy bunny rabbit... and his?... Daddy bunny rabbit... and all his?... dear little sister and brother bunny rabbits. Wasn't that nice.

Yes, it was, Sidney.

No, Sidney, he wasn't a burglar bunny rabbit. Nor was his daddy. He was just an ordinary businessman bunny rabbit.

David, don't wander away like that.

Yes, I know the window is over there, but you don't want to look out of it now. Our story is getting much too exciting. Come and sit down by Neville.

Neville, don't pull your jersey down over your knees like that; you'll get it all out of shape.

Geoffrey, Lavinia, don't copy him. I don't want everybody pulling their sweaters down over their knees.

Now then, Peggy, you tell us, what was our bunny rabbit's name?

Yes, I know his name was bunny rabbit, but what did his mummy call him, I wonder?

Well, Piggy bunny isn't a very good name for a bunny rabbit. You see a piggy is a piggy and a bunny is a bunny, so we can't have a piggy bunny, can we?

Nor a pussy bunny.

Nor a doggie bunny.

Nor an elephant bunny.

Let's be sensible, please.

No, Sidney, Silly Old Fat Man isn't a good name for a bunny rabbit.

Nor is Wizzle Wuzzle.

No, it's not as funny as all that. There's no need to roll about on the floor.

Timmy, what have you got in your hand?

But we haven't had toast and marmalade for two days. Where did you find it?

In your pocket. No you can't eat it – it's all fuzzy. Now don't touch anything. Go and put it in the waste-paper basket and then wash your hands.

Peggy open the door for him. *Don't touch anything* and hurry back, please; we need you.

Now then, Hazel, what would you like our bunny rabbit to be called?

Yes, I think Princess Anne is a very pretty name, but I don't think it's a very good name for a boy bunny rabbit. We'll call him Billy Bunny Rabbit...

Because that's his name...

Well, because I happen to know. We're not going to discuss it any more.

Sue don't kiss Neville like that.

Because he doesn't like it.

Yes, I know you like it, but he doesn't.

I don't know why he doesn't like it, but he doesn't.

No, and you can't go under the table and kiss Sidney, because he doesn't like it either.

Well, you didn't like it yesterday, Sidney. You must learn to make up your mind, mustn't you?

George...

Lavinia, you tell us what our bunny rabbit was doing all day.

He was riding a horse, was he? That is unusual for a rabbit, isn't it? I expect he went gallopy-gallopy, don't you.

Oh good, Sidney, you are coming out to help us tell... no, Sidney, you cannot go gallopy-gallopy...

Neville, Susan, Peggy... everybody... come back here at once. You cannot go gallopy...

Sidney, come back here.

You know, sometimes I don't think love is enough with children.

COMMITTEE

Joyce Grenfell

Joyce Grenfell (1910–1979) was the daughter of the youngest of the Langhorne sisters, of whom the most celebrated was Nancy, Lady Astor. She spent her girlhood on the fringes of the famous Cliveden set, which included George Bernard Shaw and Noël Coward, but it wasn't until a dinner party in 1938 that her genius for dramatic monologue was discovered when she gave an impromptu imitation of a Women's Institute speaker. She was an accomplished actress and starred in many films, including the *St Trinian's* series. She was also a regular on television, radio and the stage, and entertained the troops during the war with her usual wit, charm and humour.

The ladies are assembled in Mrs Hailestones front room somewhere north of Birmingham. The telly is full on. It is time to start the meeting.

Well, let's get down to business, shall we?

Would you be so good as to turn off your telly, please, Mrs Hailestone? Thank you. That's better. It's very good of you to let us use your front room. I think we're all assembled. Mrs Brill, Miss Culch, Mrs Pell, Mrs Hailestone, May and me. All right then. May, let's have the minutes of the last meeting.

Oh, May. You're supposed to have them in that little book I gave you. I told you last time. You're supposed to write down everything we do and say and then read it out at the next meeting, and I sign it.

I know we all know what we said and did, dear, but you have to write it down. That's what minutes are for.

Don't cry, May, dear. Let's get on with the next item on the agenda. Apologies for Absence. You read out the excuses. Oh, May. Well, you must try and remember to bring your glasses next time. All right, I'll read them. Give them here. Cheer up.

Mrs Slope is very sorry she's caught up. Can't come.

Miss Heddle's got her mother again. Can't come.

Lady Widmore sent a telegram 'ALAS CANNOT BE WITH YOU DEVASTATED'. Can't come.

Well then. As you all know, this is *another* special meeting of the Ladies' Choral to talk about the forthcoming Festival and County Choral Competition. We know the date and we know the set song. Yes we do, May. It's in two parts for ladies' voices in E flat, 'My Bosom is a Nest'.

But of course what we are really here for tonight is this very important question of voices in the choir. Now, we don't want any unpleasantness. Friendly is what we are, and friendly is how we are going to go on. But it's no good beating about the bush, we all know there is *one* voice among the altos that did not ought to be there. And I think we all know to what I am referring.

Now, don't think that I don't like Mrs Codlin, because I do. Yes, she *is* a very nice woman. Look at how nice she is with her little car – giving us all lifts here and there. And she's a lovely lender – lends you her books, and her knitting patterns, recipes, anything. Lovely. Yes, she is a regular churchgoer *and* a most generous donator to the fund. But she just has this one fault: she does not blend.

May, dear, would you be so kind as to slip out and see if I left the lamp turned off on my bike? I don't want to waste the battery, and I can't remember if I did it. Thank you, May.

Ladies, I didn't like to say anything in front of May, but I must remind you that Mrs Codlin's voice is worse than what ever May's was; and you know what happened the last time we let May sing in the competition. We were disqualified. So you see it is very important and very serious.

Oh thank you, May, dear. Had I? I am a big silly, aren't I?

You see, it isn't as if Mrs Codlin had a voice you could ignore. I mean you can't drown her out. They can hear her all down the road, over the sopranos; yes, over your piano, Mrs Pell, over everything. You know, I was stood next to her at practice last week when we did 'The Wild Brown Bee is my Lover'. When we'd finished I said to her very tactfully, thinking she might like to take the hint, I said: 'I wonder who it is stands out so among the altos?' and she said she hadn't noticed. Hadn't noticed! Mrs Brill was on her other side and she said to me afterwards, didn't you, Mrs Brill? she said the vibrations were so considerable they made her chest hum.

No, I know she doesn't do it on purpose, May.

No, of course she didn't ought to have been let in in the first place. It's ridiculous. It makes a nonsense of music. But the thing is, it was her idea, wasn't it? She founded the choir.

Do you think if anyone was to ask her very nicely not to sing it might stop her? I mean we could let her come and just stand there. Yes, Mrs Hailestone, she does *look* like a singer, I'll give her that. That's the annoying part.

Would anybody like to ask her? Well, has anybody got any suggestions?

No, May, not anonymous letters. They aren't very nice.

May...?

I wonder... May, one of your jobs as secretary is watching the handbags and the coats at competitions, isn't it? I mean you have to stay in the cloakroom all during the competitions, don't you? I thought so. Look, May; now don't think we don't appreciate you as secretary – we do, dear, don't we ladies? – But would you like to resign? Just say yes now, and I'll explain it all later. Lovely.

Well, we accept your resignation, and I would like to propose that we appoint Mrs Codlin secretary and handbag-watcher for the next competition. Anybody second that? Thank you, Mrs Hailestone. Any against? Then that's passed unanimously. Lovely. Oh, I know it's not in order, Mrs Pell, but we haven't any minutes to prove it. May didn't have a pencil, did you, May?

Well, I think it's a very happy solution. We get rid of her and keep her at one and the same time.

What did you say, May? Can *you* sing if Mrs Codlin doesn't?

Oh, May, you've put us right back to square one.

THOUGHT FOR TODAY

Joyce Grenfell

Joyce Grenfell (1910–1979) was the daughter of the youngest of the Langhorne sisters, of whom the most celebrated was Nancy, Lady Astor. She spent her girlhood on the fringes of the famous Cliveden set, which included George Bernard Shaw and Noël Coward, but it wasn't until a dinner party in 1938 that her genius for dramatic monologue was discovered when she gave an impromptu imitation of a Women's Institute speaker. She was an accomplished actress and starred in many films, including the *St Trinian's* series. She was also a regular on television, radio and the stage, and entertained the troops during the war with her usual wit, charm and humour.

For the original, English version of this sketch, written in 1950 for 'Fenny Plain', the speaker used the same bright South-of-England suburban voice as the W.I. lecturer in 'Useful and Acceptable Gifts'. When I went to Broadway for the first time in 1954 I re-wrote the monologue and changed the background and income group of the enthusiastic speaker. This American woman has houses on Long Island and in Maine, a farm in Virginia and an apartment (or maybe a duplex?) in Manhattan, the scene of the sketch. She frequently crosses the Atlantic. The long drawling vowel sounds I used for this woman once indicated immense wealth. The same vowel sounds are heard in her fluent French.

Lily, darling... How divine to see you. Come right on in.
    Dimitri, voulez-vous apporter les drinks ici au librairie, toute suite. Oui, toutes les bouteilles. Isn't he divine, Lily? He's the

only white Russian butler left in the whole of New York. I found him in Paris and he's so typical. Moody and depressing. Just the way the Russians used to be. So much more fun. But Lily, come and sit down. I can't wait to tell you what's happened to me.

My dear, I am entirely different... Well, I am inside.

Lily, have you ever heard of Dr Pelting? My dear, you're going to. He is the most marvellous man in the whole world, and he knows the answer to everything.

Lily, you know how I worried? O, I mean I worried so I fell asleep all the time doing it... just talking to people or playing bridge... and I worried whether to go to California or get my hair cut. And I worried whether it was wrong to be so rich. But Dr Pelting says it isn't in the least wrong. He says it's fine to be rich.

You see he's made this marvellous discovery.

Lily, Dr Pelting's message to you, to me, to the whole world... is simply this:

Don't think.

Isn't it *exciting*? O, I know what you're going to say. What will happen if I don't think? And the marvellous answer is... Nothing! Because Earth Ray Thought Forces are going to think for you. It seems the earth is full of wonderful forces, but how to make contact?

Lily, where do we touch the earth most closely? Exactly... our feet. And what we get through our feet are Earth Ray Thought Forces.

I met him at Emily's. I'd had my face done, so I thought I might as well use it, and I put on a new little black dress I got at Balmain and some divine perfume called *Fiasco,* and honestly I didn't feel too unattractive. But this man came over to me, and he said 'You need help', and I said 'How do you *know*?' and he told me he had been guided to me by Earth Ray Thought Forces. And he told me that these forces enter the body through the soles of the feet, and that's the way they influence the mind. And he said anybody can renew supplies if they will only stand in earth night and morning, if possible facing north.

I said to him, 'Look, sweetie, I can do that out in the country down at the farm in Virginia, but I cannot do it here in New York, on the eighteenth floor. And anyway I don't know which way north is.'

But he said, 'Look, all you have to do is get yourself a little tray, fill it with earth and stand in that.' And, he said, any passing Girl Scout will tell you which way north is.

He is a man of such vision.

Well, we went to the country that weekend, and I stood in earth every day, night and morning, even when it rained. I did it in a flower-bed, and it certainly felt as if I was facing north.

Well, when I'd gotten over a silly little chest cold I came back to New York, and I got myself a little tray, and I use it all the time. Walthrop says he doesn't know me any more. I tried to make him do it too, but you know he is so blind to his basic needs, and he says he gets all he wants in life from Benzedrine.

But I couldn't do without E.R.T.F. – Earth Ray Thought Force; and Eddie – Dr Pelting – comes in here on his way home sometimes, and we do it together on my little tray. Well, because two people make twice as much force.

No, he's not good-looking. He's... he's just very vital.

Lily, you must try it. You'll love it. Let's go find my little tray right now.

O merci, Dimitri... mettez les drinks ici, là, sur le piano. O bon. Little cheesy things. *Merci. Non, c'est tout. Merci.*

You know, Lily, he's not as gloomy as he used to be. I wonder if he's been using my little tray...?

From THE DIARY OF A NOBODY

George and Weedon Grossmith

George (1847–1912) and **Weedon** (1854–1919) **Grossmith** were brothers, writers and actors. Both made names for themselves on the stage for their comic roles – in particular George, who worked frequently with Gilbert and Sullivan. The brothers collaborated on a column for *Punch* between 1888–9, which was published as *The Diary of a Nobody* in 1892. Cataloguing the quotidian events of lower-middle-class life towards the end of the Victorian period, this light-hearted yet acutely detailed account of Charsle Pooter's day-to-day life with his wife Caroline (Carrie) has never been out of print – and continues to attract new audiences.

A conversation with Mr. Merton on Society. Mr. and Mrs. James, of Sutton, come up. A miserable evening at the Tank Theatre. Experiments with enamel paint. I make another good joke; but Gowing and Cummings are unnecessarily offended. I paint the bath red, with unexpected result.

April 19.—Cummings called, bringing with him his friend Merton, who is in the wine trade. Gowing also called. Mr. Merton made himself at home at once, and Carrie and I were both struck with him immediately, and thoroughly approved of his sentiments.

He leaned back in his chair and said: "You must take me as I am;" and I replied: "Yes—and you must take us as we are. We're homely people, we are not swells."

He answered: "No, I can see that," and Gowing roared with laughter;

but Merton in a most gentlemanly manner said to Gowing: "I don't think you quite understand me. I intended to convey that our charming host and hostess were superior to the follies of fashion, and preferred leading a simple and wholesome life to gadding about to twopenny-halfpenny tea-drinking afternoons, and living above their incomes."

I was immensely pleased with these sensible remarks of Merton's, and concluded that subject by saying: "No, candidly, Mr. Merton, we don't go into Society, because we do not care for it; and what with the expense of cabs here and cabs there, and white gloves and white ties, etc., it doesn't seem worth the money."

Merton said in reference to *friends*: "My motto is 'Few and True;' and, by the way, I also apply that to wine, 'Little and Good.'" Gowing said: "Yes, and sometimes 'cheap and tasty,' eh, old man?" Merton, still continuing, said he should treat me as a friend, and put me down for a dozen of his "Lockanbar" whisky, and as I was an old friend of Gowing, I should have it for 36s., which was considerably under what he paid for it.

He booked his own order, and further said that at any time I wanted any passes for the theatre I was to let him know, as his name stood good for any theatre in London.

April 20.—Carrie reminded me that as her old school friend, Annie Fullers (now Mrs. James), and her husband had come up from Sutton for a few days, it would look kind to take them to the theatre, and would I drop a line to Mr. Merton asking him for passes for four, either for the Italian Opera, Haymarket, Savoy, or Lyceum. I wrote Merton to that effect.

April 21.—Got a reply from Merton, saying he was very busy, and just at present couldn't manage passes for the Italian Opera, Haymarket, Savoy, or Lyceum, but the best thing going on in London was the *Brown Bushes*, at the Tank Theatre, Islington, and enclosed seats for four; also bill for whisky.

April 23.—Mr. and Mrs. James (Miss Fullers that was) came to meat tea, and we left directly after for the Tank Theatre. We got a 'bus that took us to King's Cross, and then changed into one that took us to the "Angel." Mr. James each time insisted on paying for all, saying that I had paid for the tickets and that was quite enough.

We arrived at theatre, where, curiously enough, all our 'bus-load except an old woman with a basket seemed to be going in. I walked ahead and presented the tickets. The man looked at them, and called out: "Mr. Willowly! do you know anything about these?" holding up my tickets. The gentleman called to, came up and examined my tickets, and said: "Who gave you these?" I said, rather indignantly: "Mr. Merton, of course." He said: "Merton? Who's he?" I answered, rather sharply: "You ought to know, his name's good at any theatre in London." He replied: "Oh! is it? Well, it ain't no good here. These tickets, which are not dated, were issued under Mr. Swinstead's management, which has since changed hands." While I was having some very unpleasant words with the man, James, who had gone upstairs with the ladies, called out: "Come on!" I went up after them, and a very civil attendant said: "This way, please, box H." I said to James: "Why, how on earth did you manage it?" and to my horror he replied: "Why, paid for it of course."

This was humiliating enough, and I could scarcely follow the play, but I was doomed to still further humiliation. I was leaning out of the box, when my tie—a little black bow which fastened on to the stud by means of a new patent—fell into the pit below. A clumsy man not noticing it, had his foot on it for ever so long before he discovered it. He then picked it up and eventually flung it under the next seat in disgust. What with the box incident and the tie, I felt quite miserable. Mr. James, of Sutton, was very good. He said: "Don't worry—no one will notice it with your beard. That is the only advantage of growing one that I can see." There was no occasion for that remark, for Carrie is very proud of my beard.

To hide the absence of the tie I had to keep my chin down the rest of the evening, which caused a pain at the back of my neck.

April 24.—Could scarcely sleep a wink through thinking of having brought up Mr. and Mrs. James from the country to go to the theatre last night, and his having paid for a private box because our order was not honoured, and such a poor play too. I wrote a very satirical letter to Merton, the wine merchant, who gave us the pass, and said, "Considering we had to pay for our seats, we did our best to appreciate the performance." I thought this line rather cutting, and I asked Carrie how many p's there were in appreciate, and she said, "One." After I sent off the letter I looked at the dictionary and found there were two. Awfully vexed at this.

Decided not to worry myself any more about the James's; for, as Carrie wisely said, "We'll make it all right with them by asking them up from Sutton one evening next week to play at Bézique."

April 25.—In consequence of Brickwell telling me his wife was working wonders with the new Pinkford's enamel paint, I determined to try it. I bought two tins of red on my way home. I hastened through tea, went into the garden and painted some flower-pots. I called out Carrie, who said: "You've always got some new-fangled craze;" but she was obliged to admit that the flower-pots looked remarkably well. Went upstairs into the servant's bedroom and painted her washstand, towel-horse, and chest of drawers. To my mind it was an extraordinary improvement, but as an example of the ignorance of the lower classes in the matter of taste, our servant, Sarah, on seeing them, evinced no sign of pleasure, but merely said "she thought they looked very well as they was before."

April 26.—Got some more red enamel paint (red, to my mind, being the best colour), and painted the coal-scuttle, and the backs of our *Shakspeare*, the binding of which had almost worn out.

April 27.—Painted the bath red, and was delighted with the result. Sorry to say Carrie was not, in fact we had a few words about it. She said I ought to have consulted her, and she had never heard of such a thing as a bath being painted red. I replied: "It's merely a matter of taste."

Fortunately, further argument on the subject was stopped by a voice saying, "May I come in?" It was only Cummings, who said, "Your maid opened the door, and asked me to excuse her showing me in, as she was wringing out some socks." I was delighted to see him, and suggested we should have a game of whist with a dummy, and by way of merriment said: "You can be the dummy." Cummings (I thought rather ill-naturedly) replied: "Funny as usual." He said he couldn't stop, he only called to leave me the *Bicycle News*, as he had done with it.

Another ring at the bell; it was Gowing, who said he "must apologise for coming so often, and that one of these days we must come round to *him*." I said: "A very extraordinary thing has struck me." "Something funny, as usual," said Cummings. "Yes," I replied; "I think even you will say so this time. It's concerning you both; for doesn't it seem odd that Gowing's always coming and Cummings' always going?" Carrie, who had evidently quite forgotten about the bath, went into fits of laughter, and as for myself, I fairly doubled up in my chair, till it cracked beneath me. I think this was one of the best jokes I have ever made.

Then imagine my astonishment on perceiving both Cummings and Gowing perfectly silent, and without a smile on their faces. After rather an unpleasant pause, Cummings, who had opened a cigar-case, closed it up again and said: "Yes—I think, after that, I *shall* be going, and I am sorry I fail to see the fun of your jokes." Gowing said he didn't mind a joke when it wasn't rude, but a pun on a name, to his thinking, was certainly a little wanting in good taste. Cummings followed it up by saying, if it had been said by anyone else but myself, he shouldn't have entered the house again. This rather unpleasantly terminated what might have been a cheerful evening. However, it was as well they went, for the charwoman had finished up the remains of the cold pork.

April 28.—At the office, the new and very young clerk Pitt, who was very impudent to me a week or so ago, was late again. I told him it would be my duty to inform Mr. Perkupp, the principal. To my surprise, Pitt apologised most humbly and in a most gentlemanly fashion. I was unfeignedly pleased to notice this improvement in his manner towards me, and told him I would look over his unpunctuality. Passing down the room an hour later. I received a smart smack in the face from a rolled-up ball of hard foolscap. I turned round sharply, but all the clerks were apparently riveted to their work. I am not a rich man, but I would give half-a-sovereign to know whether that was thrown by accident or design. Went home early and bought some more enamel paint—black this time—and spent the evening touching up the fender, picture-frames, and an old pair of boots, making them look as good as new. Also painted Gowing's walking-stick, which he left behind, and made it look like ebony.

April 29, Sunday.—Woke up with a fearful headache and strong symptoms of a cold. Carrie, with a perversity which is just like her, said it was "painter's colic," and was the result of my having spent the last few days with my nose over a paint-pot. I told her firmly that I knew a great deal better what was the matter with me than she did. I had got a chill, and decided to have a bath as hot as I could bear it. Bath ready—could scarcely bear it so hot. I persevered, and got in; very hot, but very acceptable. I lay still for some time.

On moving my hand above the surface of the water, I experienced the greatest fright I ever received in the whole course of my life; for imagine my horror on discovering my hand, as I thought, full of blood. My first thought was that I had ruptured an artery, and was bleeding to death, and should be discovered, later on, looking like a second Marat, as I remember seeing him in Madame Tussaud's. My second thought was to ring the bell, but remembered there was no bell to ring. My third was, that there was nothing but the enamel paint, which had dissolved with boiling water. I stepped out of the bath, perfectly red all over, resembling the Red Indians I have seen depicted at an East-End theatre. I determined not to say a word to Carrie, but to tell Farmerson to come on Monday and paint the bath white.

A SIN CONFESSED

Giovanni Guareschi

Giovanni Guareschi (1908–1968) was an Italian journalist, cartoonist and humourist whose most famous creation is the priest Don Camillo. Guareschi trained as a lawyer but found his vocation when he sent some cartoons to the satirical magazine *Bartoldo*. Later, he founded his own magazine, *Candido*, and wrote 347 stories set in the "small world" of rural Italy after the war, featuring Don Camillo – a stalwart Italian priest – and his nemesis Peppone – the hot-headed communist mayor.

Don Camillo was one of those straight-talkers who are incapable of knowing when to hold back. On one occasion during Mass, after some unseemly goings-on in the village involving young girls and landowners far too old for them, he threw caution to the wind. Having started an agreeable homily on matters in general, he happened to catch sight of one of the guilty parties sitting right there in the front row. Breaking off from what he'd been saying, he draped a cloth over the Crucifix above the high altar, and planting his fists on his hips he finished his sermon in his own unique style. So blunt was the language of this great brute of a man and so thunderous the delivery that the very roof of the little church had appeared to shake.

Naturally, at election time, Don Camillo expressed his opinions about leftwing activists in a similarly explicit manner, with the consequence that, just about sunset, as he was coming back to the presbytery, a great hulk of a man wrapped in a cloak darted out from a hedge behind him and, making use of the fact that the priest was encumbered by his bicycle and a bundle of seventy' eggs hanging from the handlebars, gave him a whack with a stick before vanishing as if the earth had swallowed him up.

Don Camillo said nothing about this to anyone, but once he was back in the presbytery and the eggs were in a safe place, he went into the church to ask Jesus for advice, as he always did in moments of doubt.

'What should I do?' asked Don Camillo.

'Rub a bit of oil and water on your back and say nothing,' answered Jesus from above the altar. 'You must forgive those who offend you. That is the rule.'

'Yes, but in this case we're talking about beatings, not offences,' objected Don Camillo.

'And what does that mean?' whispered Jesus. 'That offences to the body are more painful than those done to the spirit?'

'All right, Signore. But you should bear in mind that by beating me, your minister, they have committed an offence against you... I'm more concerned for you than for me.'

'And am I not even more God's minister than you are? And did I not forgive those who nailed me to the cross?'

'It's pointless arguing with you, you're always right. Thy will be done. We'll forgive. But remember, if my silence makes that lot think they can get away with anything, and then they smash my head in, it'll be your responsibility. I could quote you passages from the Old Testament...'

'Don Camillo, you come here telling *me* about the Old Testament! I take full responsibility for whatever happens. But, just between ourselves, it serves you right. That little misfortune will teach you to play politics in my house.'

So Don Camillo forgave. But one thing stuck in his craw like a fishbone: the burning desire to know who had given him that tap on the back.

Time passed, and late one evening, while he was in the confessional, Don Camillo saw on the other side of the grille, the face of Peppone, the local boss of the far left.

Peppone coming to confession! – a jaw-dropping event. Don Camillo was delighted.

'God be with you, brother: with you who, more than any other, have need of His sacred blessing. Is it a long time since you have made a confession?'

'Not since 1918,' replied Peppone.

'Just imagine the sins you've committed in those twenty-eight years, with all those ideas filling your head.'

'Yes, well, quite a few,' sighed Peppone.

'For example?'

'For example, two months ago I hit you with a stick.'

'That is serious,' replied Don Camillo. 'By offending a minister of God you have offended God.'

'I regretted it afterwards,' Peppone exclaimed. 'I didn't beat you as a minister of God though, but as a political opponent. It was a moment of weakness.'

'Apart from this – and belonging to that diabolical Party of yours – do you have other serious sins to confess?'

Peppone spilled the beans.

All told, it wasn't much, and Don Camillo absolved him with ten Our Fathers and ten Hail Marys. Then while Peppone was kneeling at the altar rail to say his penance, Don Camillo went to kneel beneath the Crucifix.

'Jesus,' he said, 'forgive me, but I am going to beat him to a pulp.'

'Do not even dream of it,' answered Jesus. 'I have forgiven him, and so must you. Deep down he is a good man.'

'Don't trust the Reds, Jesus. They lure you in just so they can take advantage of you. Take a good look at him. Can't you see what a villainous mug he's got?'

'It is a face like any other. Don Camillo, you have let your heart be poisoned.'

'Jesus, if I have ever served you, grant me one thing: let me at least break that big candle over his back. Dear Jesus, what is one candle?'

'No,' replied Jesus. 'Your hands are made to bless, not to strike.'

Don Camillo sighed. He bowed and went through the little gate, turned towards the altar to make the sign of the cross again, and so found himself right behind Peppone who was kneeling there, deep in his prayers.

'Perfect,' groaned Don Camillo putting his hands together and looking at Jesus. 'My hands are made for blessing, but my feet aren't!'

'That is also true,' said Jesus from the high altar. 'But I am warning you, Don Camillo, just one!'

The kick flew like lightning and Peppone took it without batting an eye.

Then he stood up and sighed with relief: 'I've been waiting ten minutes for that,' he said. 'I feel better now.'

'Me too,' exclaimed Don Camillo, whose heart felt light and pure as the clear blue sky.

Jesus said nothing, but you could tell he was happy too.

THE BAPTISM

Giovanni Guareschi

Giovanni Guareschi (1908–1968) was an Italian journalist, cartoonist and humourist whose most famous creation is the priest Don Camillo. Guareschi trained as a lawyer but found his vocation when he sent some cartoons to the satirical magazine *Bartoldo*. Later, he founded his own magazine, *Candido*, and wrote 347 stories set in the "small world" of rural Italy after the war, featuring Don Camillo – a stalwart Italian priest – and his nemesis Peppone – the hot-headed communist mayor.

Out of the blue one day a man and two women came into the church. One of the women was the wife of Peppone, leader of the Reds.

Don Camillo, who was up a ladder polishing St Joseph's halo with Brasso, looked down and asked them what they wanted.

'This here needs baptising,' replied the man. And one of the women showed him a bundle with a baby inside.

'Whose is it?' asked Don Camillo, coming down.

'Mine,' said Peppone's wife.

'With your husband?' enquired Don Camillo.

'I should think so!' retorted Peppone's wife angrily. 'Who else would I have it with?'

'There's no need to get angry,' observed Don Camillo as he headed for the sacristy. 'I know a thing or two, and they say free love's all the rage in your Party.'

Passing the altar, Don Camillo bowed and winked at the crucified Christ.

'Did you hear that?' he chuckled. 'I slipped one to the Party of the Godless!'

'That is rubbish, Don Camillo,' replied Jesus in annoyance. 'If they were godless, they would not come here to have their children baptised. If Peppone's wife had slapped your face it would have been no more than you deserved.'

'If Peppone's wife had hit me I'd have grabbed all three of them by the neck and...'

'And?' asked Jesus sternly.

'Nothing, just a figure of speech,' said Don Camillo hurriedly as he stood up.

'Take care, Don Camillo,' Jesus warned.

Don Camillo put on his vestments and went up to the font.

'What do you want to call him?' asked Don Camillo.

'Lenin Libero Antonio,' replied Peppone's wife.

'Then go and have him baptised in Russia,' said Don Camillo, calmly replacing the cover on the font.

Don Camillo had hands as big as shovels, and the man and the two women left without a word. The priest then tried to sneak off to the sacristy, but a voice stopped him short.

'Don Camillo, you have done a terrible thing! Go and call those people back and baptise the child!'

'Jesus,' replied Don Camillo, 'baptism is no laughing matter. It is a sacrament. Baptism...'

'Don Camillo!' Jesus interrupted him. 'Are you seriously trying to teach me about baptism? I am the one who invented it! Now listen. You are behaving like an arrogant bully. Just suppose that baby were to die this moment, you'd be to blame if it was denied admission to Paradise!'

'Let's not over-dramatise the situation,' retorted Don Camillo. 'Why should the baby die? He's got ruddy cheeks like roses!'

'That has nothing to do with it,' Jesus countered. 'A roof tile could fall on his head; he could have an apoplectic fit. You *must* baptise him.'

Don Camillo flung wide his arms.

'Dear Lord, think about it for a moment. None of this would matter if we knew the child was definitely destined for Hell. But even though his parents are a bad lot, he could, if baptised, end up in Heaven. Now tell me this: how can I allow people called Lenin to join you in Heaven? I'm doing this for the good name of Heaven.'

'Leave the good name of Heaven to me,' cried Jesus in irritation. 'All I care about is that the child becomes an honest man. It does not matter to me if he is called Lenin or Coco the Clown. All you are entitled to do is point out to the parents that giving eccentric names to children can often cause them trouble, sometimes big trouble.'

'All right,' replied Don Camillo. 'It's always me who is wrong. We'll try and sort it out.'

Just then someone was heard entering the church. It was Peppone, alone but for the baby in his arms. He bolted the door behind him.

'I'm not leaving here,' he said, 'until my son is baptised with the name I want.'

'Well?' whispered Don Camillo to Jesus with a smile. 'You see now what these people are like? One can have nothing but the loftiest intentions, and look how they react.'

'Put yourself in his shoes,' replied Jesus. 'Peppone's way of life is not something for you to approve or disapprove, but to understand.'

Don Camillo shook his head.

'I said I'm not leaving until you baptise my son the way I want,' repeated Peppone, putting the bundle with the baby onto a pew. Then he took off his jacket, rolled up his sleeves, and came menacingly towards Don Camillo.

'Jesus,' implored Don Camillo, 'I appeal to you. If you think it right that one of your priests should assent to the threats of private individuals, then I will defer. But in that case, don't complain when they came back tomorrow with a calf they want baptised. You know as well as I do, precedents are dangerous...'

'Well,' said Jesus, 'in this case you must try to make him understand...'

'And if he attacks me?'

'Accept it, Don Camillo. Bear it. Suffer as I did.'

So Don Camillo turned around. 'All right, Peppone,' he said. 'The baby will leave here baptised, but not with that damnable name.'

'Don Camillo,' muttered Peppone, 'remember I've got a delicate stomach ever since I took that bullet in the mountains. No low blows, or I'll give you a good going over with a pew.'

'Don't worry, Peppone, I'll address myself only to your upper storey,' replied Don Camillo, landing a punch by Peppone's ear.

They were a pair of bruisers with arms of iron and their blows whistled through the air. After twenty minutes of furious, silent combat, Don Camillo heard a voice at his shoulder: 'Now, Don Camillo! Get him on the jaw!'

It came from above the altar. Don Camillo aimed a blow at the jaw, and Peppone fell to the ground.

He stayed sprawled out there for ten minutes, then he got up, massaged his chin, dusted himself off, put his jacket back on, retied his red kerchief, and picked up the baby.

Don Camillo, by then in his vestments, was waiting for him, solid as granite, beside the font.

'What shall we call him?' asked Don Camillo.

'Camillo Libero Antonio,' muttered Peppone.

Don Camillo shook his head.

'No, let's call him Libero Camillo Lenin,' he said. 'Yes, Lenin too. His sort cannot get up to mischief when he's got a Camillo as his neighbour.'

'Amen,' muttered Peppone, feeling his jaw.

When it was all done and Don Camillo was passing the altar, Jesus said smiling, 'Don Camillo, I have to admit it, you're better at politics than I am.'

'And at trading punches too,' answered Don Camillo loftily, putting a nonchalant finger to a big lump on his forehead.

THE PROCLAMATION

Giovanni Guareschi

Giovanni Guareschi (1908–1968) was an Italian journalist, cartoonist and humourist whose most famous creation is the priest Don Camillo. Guareschi trained as a lawyer but found his vocation when he sent some cartoons to the satirical magazine *Bartoldo*. Later, he founded his own magazine, *Candido*, and wrote 347 stories set in the "small world" of rural Italy after the war, featuring Don Camillo – a stalwart Italian priest – and his nemesis Peppone – the hot-headed communist mayor.

Late one evening, old Barchini turned up at the presbytery. He was the village stationer, but being also the proud owner of two cases of type and a foot-operated press from 1870, he had added the word 'Printer' above his shop. There must have been something big to report because he stayed in Don Camillo's study for quite a while.

When Barchini had gone, Don Camillo ran to share the information with Jesus above the altar.

'Important news!' he exclaimed. 'The enemy is going to publish an announcement tomorrow. Barchini's printing it and he's brought me a proof copy.'

Don Camillo pulled a freshly printed sheet of paper from his pocket and read it aloud:

FIRST AND LAST WARNING

Again yesterday evening a cowardly anonimus hand wrote an ofensive insult on our news buletin bord. That hand had better keep a lookout,

because if the good for nothing it belongs to, who takes advantage of
the shadows to preform acts of provocation, doesn't stop he will regret
it when its too late to make amends.

All patients has it's limits.

Branch Secretary
Giuseppe Bottazzi

Don Camillo gave a mocking laugh.

'What do you think of this? Quite a work of art isn't it? Just imagine the fun people will have tomorrow when these manifestoes go up. What's Peppone playing at, making such proclamations? It's enough to make you crack a rib laughing!'

Jesus made no reply, and Don Camillo stared in astonishment.

'Didn't you catch the style? Do you want me to read it again?'

'I heard you the first time,' said Jesus. 'People express themselves as best they can. It is hardly fair to expect someone who left school at the age of nine to cope with the subtleties of style.'

'Lord!' exclaimed Don Camillo, with his arms outspread. 'How can you speak of subtlety in the same breath as this verbal hotchpotch!'

'Don Camillo, the lowest tactic you can employ in a debate is to latch onto your opponent's spelling mistakes and bad grammar. What counts in a debate is the argument. You would do better to question his threatening tone.'

Don Camillo put the sheet of paper back into his pocket.

'Of course,' he mumbled. 'The really reprehensible thing is the threatening tone of the statement. But what can you expect from people like that? Violence is all they understand.'

'And yet,' observed Jesus, 'for all his exuberance, Peppone doesn't have the air of someone who is just a troublemaker.'

Don Camillo shrugged. 'It's like pouring good wine into a rotten barrel. When somebody gets himself into a certain kind of company and adopts the sacrilegious thinking of the rabble, he ends up fit for nothing.'

But Jesus did not seem convinced.

'I would say that in Peppone's case, you should look beyond appearances if you want to find out where the truth really lies. Is Peppone being mischievous or has he been provoked into this? Which do you think it is?'

Once again Don Camillo spread his arms. Who could possibly tell?

'All we need to know is what caused the offence,' insisted Jesus. 'He talks about an insult that someone wrote on his news bulletin yesterday evening. So, yesterday evening, when you went to the tobacconist, you didn't by any chance go past the notice board? Try and remember.'

'Well, yes I did go past it,' Don Camillo freely admitted.

'Good. And did you happen to stop for just a moment to read the bulletins?'

'Not to read them, definitely not: more a quick squint. Was that wrong?'

'Not in the least, Don Camillo. You need to keep in touch with what your flock is saying and writing and, if possible, thinking. I was only trying to find out if you noticed anything strange written on the board while you were there.'

Don Camillo shook his head.

'I can assure you that when I stopped there, I didn't see anything strange written on the notice board.'

Jesus thought for a while.

'And when you *left*, Don Camillo, did you see anything out of the ordinary written there?'

Don Camillo concentrated.

'Ah, yes,' he said at last. 'Thinking back, I have a feeling that as I left I did see something scribbled in red crayon on one of the bulletins. Oh! Please excuse me, I think I hear somebody in the presbytery.'

Don Camillo bowed hastily and made to slip away, but the voice from above the altar stopped him.

'Don Camillo!'

Don Camillo came slowly back and stopped sulkily in front of the altar.

'Well?' asked Jesus sternly.

'Well, yes,' mumbled Don Camillo. 'It may be that... I did happen to write "Peppone is an ass"... But if you'd read that bulletin, I'm sure you'd have...'

'Don Camillo, you seem to know nothing about your own actions, and yet you claim to know what the *Son of God* would do?'

'Forgive me. I've been foolish, I realise that. But now Peppone's being foolish too, sending out posters with threats, and so we're quits.'

'You are nothing of the kind!' exclaimed Jesus. 'You called Peppone an ass yesterday evening, and tomorrow the whole village will be doing the same. Just think of the people who will pour in from all directions to laugh at the howlers committed by local boss Peppone, of whom everyone is scared to death! And it is all your fault. Does that look good to you?'

Don Camillo plucked up the courage to say, 'You're right, but from the wider political point of view...'

Jesus cut him off. 'I care not at all about the wider political point of view! From the point of view of Christian charity, giving people an excuse to laugh at a man for no better reason than that he left school at the age of nine is a complete disgrace. And you, Don Camillo, are the cause of it!'

'Tell me, Lord,' sighed Don Camillo. 'What can I do?'

'Well it was not I who wrote "Peppone's an ass"! It is the sinner who must do the penance. See to it, Don Camillo!'

Don Camillo retreated to his study and started to walk up and down the room, imagining that he could hear people stopping in front of Peppone's proclamation to laugh. 'Idiots!' he exclaimed in fury.

He turned to the small statue of the Virgin Mary.

'Mother of God,' he prayed, 'help me.'

'This is strictly my Son's concern,' whispered the little Madonna. 'I cannot become involved.'

'Put in a good word for me.'

'I will try.'

And all of a sudden, in came Peppone.

'Listen,' he said. 'This has got nothing to do with politics. This is about a Christian who finds himself in trouble and comes to ask a priest for his advice. I'm sure...'

'I know my duty. Who have you killed?'

'I don't kill people, Don Camillo,' replied Peppone. 'But if someone treads on my corns, my fists are bound to blaze into action.'

'And how is little Libero Camillo Lenin?' inquired Don Camillo slyly. And Peppone, remembering the pounding he'd been given on the day of the baptism, shrugged his shoulders.

'You know how it is,' he grumbled. 'Fist fights go both ways. You win some, you lose some. But never mind that, this is a different matter. In short, the fact is that in the village there's a good-for-nothing lowdown coward, a Judas with poison fangs who, every time we pin up a bulletin on our board with my signature as Secretary, thinks it's amusing to write "Peppone's an ass" on it!'

'Is that all?' exclaimed Don Camillo. 'Not exactly a tragedy.'

'I'd like to know what *you'd* say if for twelve days on the trot you found someone writing "Don Camillo's an ass" on the order of service.'

Don Camillo said the comparison didn't stand up at all. A Church notice board was one thing, the news bulletin board of a political party quite another. It is one thing to call God's priest an ass, quite another so to discredit the leader of a bunch of rampaging lunatics.

Finally, he asked, 'Don't you have any idea who it might be?'

'It is better that I don't,' replied Peppone with some force. 'If I did, that Barabbas would be going around with both his eyes as black as his miserable soul. That vandal has been having his fun with me for twelve days – I'm certain it's always the same one – and now I'm warning him, it's gone far enough. He'd better watch out, because if I get hold of him it'll be the Messina earthquake all over again. And now I'm going to print some notices and put them up on every street corner, so he and his gang can't miss them.'

Don Camillo shrugged.

'I'm not a printer,' he said. 'What's it got to do with me? Go and find someone with a printing press.'

'I've already done that,' replied Peppone darkly. 'But since I don't like making an ass of myself, you'd better have a look at the draft of the announcement before Barchini prints it.'

'But Barchini's no fool. If there was something wrong with it, he'd have told you.'

'You think so?' Peppone gave a bitter laugh. 'He's the next worst thing to a priest... I mean, he's just as reactionary, black as his miserable soul. Even if he saw that I'd written "heart" with two aitches, he wouldn't think twice about making me look small.'

'But you've got your men,' returned Don Camillo.

'Do you really think I'm going to stoop so low as to let my inferiors correct me? Besides, it would be a joke. They don't have half the alphabet between them.'

'Let's see it then,' said Don Camillo. And Peppone gave him the proof sheet.

'Well, blunders aside, the tone does seem a bit strong.'

'Too strong?' cried Peppone. 'He's a damn lowlife, he's a hooligan, he's such a scoundrel of an *agent provocateur* that if I was to write it the way he deserves I'd need two dictionaries!'

Don Camillo picked up his pencil and carefully corrected the draft.

'Now go over the corrections in pen,' he said when he'd finished.

Peppone looked sadly at the paper covered with squiggles and crossings out.

'To think that wretch Barchini told me it was all fine... How much do I owe you?'

'Nothing. I'd rather you kept the whole thing under your hat. I don't like the idea of anyone knowing I do work for the Department of Propaganda.'

'I'll send you some eggs.'

Peppone left, and Don Camillo went to put his conscience to rest before the altar, before going to bed himself.

'Thank you for giving him the idea of coming to see me.'

'It's the least I could do,' replied Jesus, smiling. 'How did it go?'

'A bit tricky, but fine. He doesn't have the slightest idea that it was me yesterday evening.'

'Oh yes he does,' retorted Jesus. 'He knows perfectly well it was you. All twelve times. He even saw you on a couple of evenings. Stay alert, Don Camillo: think seven times before writing "Peppone's an ass"!'

'When I go out I'll leave my pencil behind,' promised Don Camillo solemnly.

'Amen,' concluded Jesus, smiling.

DO I UNDERSTAND THAT YOU ARE A HOMOSEXUAL, SIR?

Saleem Haddad

Saleem Haddad (1983–) was born in Kuwait City to an Iraqi-German mother and a Palestinian-Lebanese father. He has worked with Médecins Sans Frontières and other international organizations in Yemen, Syria, Iraq, Libya, Lebanon and Egypt. His debut novel, *Guapa*, received critical acclaim from the *New Yorker*, the *Guardian* and others. Haddad was selected as one of the top 100 Global Thinkers of 2016 by *Foreign Policy* magazine. He currently divides his time between London and the Middle East.

Y*ou might want to wear a floral sweatshirt. It will make you appear more optimistic. The one you have on from H&M is certainly a statement piece. Nothing says 'FUN' like a beige sweatshirt with enormous lavender and pink flower prints. You might be thinking that such high street attire might appear basic, perhaps a bit 'terrorist-y' even. But don't pontificate about fashion choices. It's too late for that now. You think a floral sweatshirt is going to change the fact that your middle name is Muhammad? We're too far gone for that. No, the sweatshirt is intended to make you seem easy, breezy, cover girl, and that's the vibe you need to project right now.*

If you want to get on this flight you'll have to follow my instructions carefully. First, stand up when they announce that they've begun to

*board passengers. Be cool. Maybe smooth out that sweatshirt. Pick up
your bag. Glance at the ticket. But only a casual glance. The gate is
there... and do you see him? That man in the suit, clean-shaven, buzzed
haircut. Yes, the one with his hands in his pockets, standing just behind
the stewardess who is checking boarding passes with an ennui so devastating it's poetic. That's him.*

Don't make eye contact.

Approach the stewardess. Act natural. Smile... wait, not that widely.

*You're showing too much teeth, you look like a lunatic. There you
go. Now hand the woman your boarding pass. She will scan your ticket
with her machine. The machine will beep. That's it. It beeped. Stay calm.
She's going to check your seat number against the list on her notepad,
and any minute now...*

'Sir, I'm going to have to ask you to step aside and speak to this
gentleman behind me.'

*What, did you think you were getting upgraded'? Oh habibi, please.
Now smile and say...*

'That's absolutely fine.'

*There you go. And there he is. The man. Standing between you and
the air bridge leading to the plane.*

'Good evening, sir. I work for the US Department of Homeland
Security. If you don't mind, I'd like to ask you a few questions before you
board the flight.'

*If you took my advice you should be about two Valiums deep right
about now. Don't act overly friendly, but don't be too standoffish either.
That's what the Valium is for.*

'Of course.'

'Have we stopped you before?'

*Of course they've stopped you. Every time you fly to the US they've
stopped you. But don't get smart...*

'Sometimes...'

'We do random checks.'

Yes, I realise this is patronising...

'I understand. You guys are mostly nice.'

'We try to be, sir. What is the purpose of your trip to the US?'

Don't overthink this. Just say something like…

'Vacation.'

Flawless.

'What do you intend to do while you're in the country?'

Your itinerary reveals everything about your character, so think this through carefully. Disneyland is good, but also difficult to pull off unless you've got kids. Americans always appreciate shopping, especially if you can name a few stores. Museums are also good. Everyone knows that terrorists don't like culture. Less appreciated are any references to build-ings or landmarks: the Statue of Liberty, the Empire State Building, the Golden Gate Bridge. These kinds of places scream terrorist.

'I'll be in New York for the week. I'm probably going to do some shopping… maybe see a show. Then I'll spend about a day or so in my Airbnb doing some productive crying. I also want to check out this ramen place in Brooklyn I saw on Instagram.'

Nice touch with the ramen.

'Do you know anyone in New York?'

Look, I don't want no 'Ahmad' or 'Ali' or 'Zubaida'. Give me a Mary! Give me a Jonathan! Give me an Angela! Give me an Andrew! Give me blonde hair, blue eyes, vanilla skin! Give me someone who knows how to ski! Give me—

'No. I'll be alone.'

Well that explains the crying.

'And when were you last in the United States?'

'About a year ago.'

'Can you tell me which countries you've visited in the last twelve months?'

Here we go. Now start with the good countries…

'I travel a lot for work.'

'Try and remember what you can, sir.'

I think Switzerland is a good one to start with. But wait isn't Europe overrun with Muslims? Okay, somewhere else. How about Malaysia? No, that's an Islamic country. Taiwan? Yes, Taiwan. No Muslims there. Go with Taiwan!

'Lebanon…'

'Lebanon?'

Really? Lebanon. That's the country you chose to start with?

'Yes. Lebanon.'

'What was the purpose of your travel to Lebanon?'

'Seeing friends.'

'And, sir, while you were in Lebanon, did you travel to any Hezbollah strongholds?'

Well you did sleep with that guy from Dahiyeh that you found on Grindr. He wasn't a Hezbollah supporter but he certainly had quite a 'strong hold' on you, pardon the pun. The first question he asked was which sect you were from and the second was whether you were a top or a bottom… Got to love the Lebanese.

'No.'

'Where else have you travelled?'

Give yourself a break, hayati…

'Paris. Milan. Ibiza. Dubai…'

Good boy.

'Hong Kong…'

'Is that it?'

'Ummm…'

Now it just looks like you're hiding something…

'Jordan, Turkey, Egypt…'

There you go. Just let it all out.

'Libya.'

'Libya?'

LIBYA?!

'Yes. Libya.'

'And what was the purpose of your trip to Libya?'

Make something up. Anything.

'I work between Libya and London...'

'Why is that?'

No, please... Don't say it.

'I work for my father's company. My father is Libyan.'

Oh honey. Tell him you've always wanted to go into fashion. Show him your Internet history. Do something, anything, to wash the Libya off you.

'Sir, do you have any other passports other than your British passport?'

Zip it.

'Not on me.'

'But do you have any?'

Not a word. Nothing.

'I have a Libyan passport.'

'May I see it?'

Please tell me you didn't bring it with you. Have I taught you nothing?

'I didn't bring it with me.'

Allahu Akbar, you're finally listening to me!

'Do you know, or have met with, any Islamist individuals or groups in your line of work in Libya?'

No. Nothing. Nada.

'No.'

'And personal life?'

Quick and easy...

'None.'

'Are you sure?'

'What do you mean exactly by "know"?'

You're thinking of that guy you had under the bridge, aren't you? The Misratan militia dude. Well, that's what you assumed he was, with his gun and his beard and his swagger. Kind of 'Islamic-y', I suppose, even if he did let you run your fingers through his beard.

'What do you mean by "what do you mean"?'

Wait, what are you doing? You didn't even have sex with him! That doesn't count as 'know'. In gay terms that barely counts as 'met'!

'I met some guy who was part of a Misratan militia. I guess it was an Islamic militia but I don't know the name of it.'

I give up.

'Just met, sir?'

You nearly had him, too. But then he asked if anyone had penetrated you before. You told the truth and he left, saying he only sleeps with virgins. Learned your lesson, didn't you? There are about fifty men walking around Libya right now thinking they've taken your virginity…

'Well… a bit more I suppose.'

… You're such a good actor. Trying to act all in pain. They hold you tenderly and say 'It's okay habibi, just relax and push, like you're making kaka…'

'What do you mean by "a bit more"?'

Don't say it.

'I gave him a blowjob.'

Well, there we go. It's all out now, isn't it?

'Excuse me?'

'I performed oral sex on him.'

He treated you with a roughness that was at moments tender, with a touch of pity that you had failed to reach his levels of manliness… Not so much like a man treats a woman, rather like a father would treat his stunted child…

'Do I understand that you are a homosexual, sir?'

Someone give this genius a Nobel Prize.

'Yes, I am.'

'And can someone be both a Libyan and a homosexual?'

'I think so, yes.'

'Sir, as you know with the new regulations, I have to ask you this…'

Here's your chance. Flap your wrists and tell him you've been exiled. Regale him with tales of 'suffering'. Don't you want to try that ramen place?

'… do you feel yourself to be more Libyan, or more homosexual?'

Okay, let's think about this carefully. I suppose your penis feels more homosexual. Doesn't your penis have a Cindy Crawford mole? That's such a homosexual thing for a penis to have… but then do you remember when you picked up that twink in that club in Soho, and you didn't know he was Israeli until you were both naked and staring at each other's circumcised penises, and then you finally noticed the Star of David tattoo on his wrist?

'Umm, do you want me to give percentages?'

'Well, I suppose that would help, sir.'

… Sure, that night you were both drunk enough and laughed it off. His lips were gorgeous and you spent the night making out. But, the next morning before you left, you wrote your name down so he could add you on Facebook. When he did, you went through his photos and there was a photo album dedicated to his military service, and you secretly wished you had fucked him so that perhaps you could have done your bit to liberate Palestine (is this your internalised misogyny talking?). Your penis felt very Libyan then, didn't it?

'I'll say 90 per cent homosexual and 10 per cent Libyan.'

'And, sir, like, in your heart… does the 10 per cent that is Libyan have positive feelings towards America?'

The flight is closing. Tell him about your Cindy Crawford mole!

'To be honest, America makes me feel anxious.'

What is it with you Arabs always making life difficult for yourselves?

'Anxiety over what? Like because of our freedoms?'

'No, because of your freeways. They are enormous and never-ending.'

'They are indeed, sir. Much like our freedoms. Anyway, thank you for your cooperation. Enjoy your trip.'

'Thank you.'

'Say… it must be tough to be a homosexual over there, no? So much hate and fear…'

I told you the floral sweatshirt would work.

ISLAM IS NOT SPIRITUAL, BUT IT IS A USEFUL IDENTITY

Omar Hamdi

Omar Hamdi (1990–) is a Welsh-Egyptian TV presenter, comedian and writer. He grew up in Cardiff before moving to London to perform stand-up full-time. He has completed a national UK tour, as well as performing at various festivals and clubs around the world. He has been recommended by the National Union of Journalists as 'a talented comic commentator on topical events,' and by the *Telegraph* for his 'shrewd insights into multiculturalism.'

Researchers at SSIC (School for the Study of Inferior Cultures) at London University have concluded, after an extensive one-week study, that Islam is 'just a useful identity' and 'not a spiritual tradition'.

Mariam Amélie, who led the study, said, 'There are some people out there who think Islam is a spiritual tradition, concerned with matters such as combating the ego, selflessness and purification of the heart. They're wrong. The results from our study undisputedly show that Islam is in actual fact, technically, an identity – like being black, or a goth (they're black too, but the first time I was talking about skin, not clothes).'

Ms Amélie's findings were welcomed by Dr Tariq Shaban of the campaign group Muslims with Attitude (MWA): 'It's very seventh century to think of Islam as a spiritual tradition – that's the kind of stuff Prophet Muhammad actually taught. I actually prefer to think of Islam as an identity. I'm a proud British Muslim – as of last week (the British bit, I mean). There's nowhere else in the world where I would be able to get so many angry brown people together to attend demonstrations on such a regular basis as in Britain. Most of those attending our demonstrations don't actually pray. The most important command in Islam is to be angry. And it is such a universal way of life – you can be angry about anything you like – Israel, Syria, silly cartoons... This is what makes it superior to western culture, where people are only allowed to be angry about unimportant things, like Oscar winners or dead gorillas.'

The long-awaited findings have been welcomed by politicians from across the political spectrum. Lianne Abbott MP, head of the All Party Parliamentary Group on Box-Ticking, said, 'I have a lot of Muslim constituents, so the more we can make them into a homogenous group without any individual opinions, the easier it is for me to stay in my seat in parliament – and I'm not planning on getting up any time soon. I welcome Ms Amélie's findings. She might even be made a Baroness on account of her labours (although she categorically hasn't been promised anything by our party leader).'

On the other side of the political divide, Lord Crinklebottom, founder of the BEAS (British Empire Appreciation Society), said, 'It makes much more sense to me that those bloody brown people have an identity – like a tribe – rather than a religion with actual spirituality, literature and music. Otherwise, they'd be just like Christians, and we all know that's simply not true is it?'

Ms Amélie has been forced to defend claims that her research lacks rigour. 'People think I don't know anything about Islam because I'm not a Muslim. But that's a spurious allegation because my ex is half Moroccan, and I love shisha, so I feel very close to the community. Plus, my father owns a house in Spain and that was ruled by the Moorish caliphate until 1492, so I understand ISIS better than anyone. Better than they understand themselves, in fact.

'I just want people to realise how great Islam is – as an identity of course, not as an actual spiritual tradition. Last year I told people I actually was Muslim, and it was amazing for my career. I was on TV, like, every Sunday morning, and all I had to do was put one of mum's Gucci pashminas on my head, and act angry. I've heard that if I go 'full-time Muslim' I could get tenure at Cambridge. It worked for Dr Shaban – he's got his own section at Waterstones shops up and down the country. Right now, I'm working on a hijabi dating show for a well-known youth channel – it's so important to raise awareness that girls in headscarves can be quite shaggable, especially considering the toxic rhetoric around Brexit. I would hope that one day members of the UK Separation Party will swipe right on a hijabi – far right. We're talking to Nike about a sponsorship deal.'

THE PLAN

Jack Handey

Jack Handey (1949–) is an American humourist, best-known for his *Deep Thoughts* – a large body of surreal one-liner jokes that first appeared on *Saturday Night Live*. Starting as a journalist, his first comic writing was with the comedian Steve Martin, who introduced him to SNL's creator. Handey's *Deep Thoughts* first appeared in a small comedy magazine, *Army Man*, and continued in *National Lampoon*, though they gained widespread popularity when they began to be featured on SNL in 1991.

The plan isn't foolproof. For it to work, certain things must happen:

—The door to the vault must have accidentally been left open by the cleaning woman.

—The guard must bend over to tie his shoes and somehow he gets all the shoelaces tied together. He can't get them apart, so he takes out his gun and shoots all his bullets at the knot. But he misses. Then he just lies down on the floor and goes to sleep.

—Most of the customers in the bank must happen to be wearing Nixon masks, so when we come in wearing our Nixon masks it doesn't alarm anyone.

—There must be an empty parking space right out in front. If it has a meter, there must be time left on it, because our outfits don't have pockets for change.

—The monkeys must grab the bags of money and not just shriek and go running all over the place, like they did in the practice run.

—The security cameras must be the early, old-timey kind that don't actually take pictures.

—When the big clock in the lobby strikes two, everyone must stop and stare at it for at least ten minutes.

—The bank alarm must have mistakenly been set to "Quiet." Or "Ebb tide."

—The gold bars must be made out of a lighter kind of gold that's just as valuable but easier to carry.

—If somebody runs out of the bank and yells, "Help! The bank is being robbed!," he must be a neighborhood crazy person who people just laugh at.

—If the police come, they don't notice that the historical mural on the wall is actually us, holding still.

—The bank's lost-and-found department must have a gun that fires a suction cup with a wire attached to it. Also a chainsaw and a hang glider.

—When we spray the lobby with knockout gas, for some reason the gas doesn't work on us.

—After the suction cup is stuck to the ceiling, it must hold long enough for Leon to pull himself up the wire while carrying the bags of money, the gold bars, and the hang glider. When he reaches the ceiling, he must be able to cut through it with the chainsaw and climb out.

—Any fingerprints we leave must be erased by the monkeys.

—Once on the roof, Leon must be able to hold on to the hang glider with one hand and the money and the gold bars with the other and launch himself off the roof. Then glide the twenty miles to the rendez-vous point.

—When we exit the bank, there must be a parade going by, so our get-away car, which is decorated to look like a float, can blend right in.

—During the parade, our car must not win a prize for best float, because then we'll have to have our picture taken with the award.

—At the rendezvous point, there must be an empty parking space with a meter that takes hundred-dollar bills.

—The robbery is blamed on the monkeys.

MY FIRST DAY IN HELL

Jack Handey

Jack Handey (1949–) is an American humourist, best-known for his *Deep Thoughts* – a large body of surreal one-liner jokes that first appeared on *Saturday Night Live*. Starting as a journalist, his first comic writing was with the comedian Steve Martin, who introduced him to SNL's creator. Handey's *Deep Thoughts* first appeared in a small comedy magazine, *Army Man*, and continued in *National Lampoon*, though they gained widespread popularity when they began to be featured on SNL in 1991.

My first day in Hell is drawing to a close. They don't really have a sunset here, but the fires seem to dim a bit, and the screaming gets more subdued. Most of the demons are asleep now, their pointy tails curled up around them. They look so innocent, it's hard to believe that just a few hours ago they were raping and torturing us.

The day started off at a party at the Chelsea Hotel, where some friends were daring me to do something. The next thing I knew, I was in Hell. At first, it seemed like a dream, but then I remembered that five-Martini dreams are usually a lot worse.

There's a kind of customs station when you arrive here, where a skeleton in a black robe checks a big book to make sure your name's there. And as he slowly scans the pages with his bony finger you can't help thinking, Why does a skeleton need a robe? Especially since it's so hot. That's the first thing you notice about Hell, how hot it is. I know it's a cliché, but it's true. Fortunately, it's a steamy, sulfury kind of hot. Like a spa or something.

You might think that people in Hell are all nude. But that's a myth. You wear what you were last wearing on earth. For instance, I am dressed like the German U-boat captain in the movie "Das Boot," because that's what I wore to the party. It's an easy costume, because all you really need is the hat. The bad part is, people are always asking you who you are, even in Hell. Come on! "Das Boot"!

The food here turns out to be surprisingly good. The trouble is, just about all of it is poisoned. So a few minutes after you finish eating you're doubled over in agony. The weird thing is, as soon as you recover you're ready to dig in all over again.

Despite the tasty food and warm weather, there's a dark side to Hell. For one thing, it's totally disorganized. That anything gets done down here is a miracle. You'll be herded along in one big line, then it'll separate into three lines, then the lines will all come back together again! For no apparent reason! It's crazy. You try to ask a demon a question, but he just looks at you. I don't mean to sound prejudiced, but you wonder if they even speak English.

To relieve the boredom, you can throw rocks at other people in line. They just think it was a demon. But I discovered the hard way that the demons don't like it when they're beating someone and you join in.

It's odd, but Hell can be a lonely place, even with so many people around. They all seem caught up in their own little worlds, running to and fro, wailing and tearing at their hair. You try to make conversation, but you can tell they're not listening.

A malaise set in within a couple hours of my arriving. I thought getting a job might help. It turns out I have a lot of relatives in Hell, and, using connections, I became the assistant to a demon who pulls people's teeth out. It wasn't actually a job, more of an internship. But I was eager. And at first it was kind of interesting. After a while, though, you start asking yourself: Is this what I came to Hell for, to hand different kinds of pliers to a demon? I started wondering if I should even have come to Hell at all. Maybe I should have lived my life differently and gone to Heaven instead.

I decided I had to get away—the endless lines, the senseless whipping, the forced sing-alongs. You get tired of trying to explain that you've already been branded, or that something that big won't fit in your ear, even with a hammer. I wandered off. I needed some *me* time. I came to a cave and went inside. Maybe I would find a place to meditate, or some gold nuggets.

That's when it happened, one of those moments which could only happen in Hell. I saw Satan. Some people have been in Hell for hundreds of years and have never seen Satan, but there he was: he was shorter than I thought he'd be, but he looked pretty good. He was standing on a big rock with his reading glasses on. I think he was practicing a speech. "Hey, Satan," I yelled out, "how's it going?" I was immediately set upon by demons. I can't begin to describe the tortures they inflicted on me, because apparently they are trade secrets. Suffice it to say that, even as you endure all the pain, you find yourself thinking, Wow, how did they think of *that*?

My stitches are a little itchy, but at least the demons sewed most of my parts back on. More important, my faith in Hell as an exciting place where anything can happen has been restored.

I had better get some rest. They say the bees will be out soon and that it's hard to sleep with the constant stinging. I lost my internship, but I was told I can reapply in a hundred years. Meanwhile, I've been assigned to a construction crew. Tomorrow we're supposed to build a huge monolith, then take picks and shovels and tear it down, then beat each other to death. It sounds pointless to me, but what do I know. I'm new here.

THE USES OF ENGLISH

Akinwumi Isola

> **Akinwumi Isola** (1939–2018) was a Nigerian playwright, novelist, actor, dramatist and scholar. He wrote almost exclusively in Yoruba, and translated many works by fellow Nigerian Wole Soyinka into the language. He was a fellow of the Nigerian Academy of Letters and received the Nigerian National Order of Merit.

It was a small village of about twenty-five houses with thatched roofs. Only the mission house, the school, and the church had corrugated iron roofs. It was a peaceful location in the middle of the agricultural belt that surrounded what was called Ibadanland.

There was a young man called Depo who had a wife called Asunle. No day passed without a noisy quarrel in their household. It was always more or less a shouting match because Depo always threatened his wife ferociously but he never really beat her. Asunle would maintain a safe distance and shout alarmingly, as if her life were in danger. Depo always looked annoyed and embarrassed. He seemed to be crying for help and salvation. His wife apparently enjoyed every bit of it; she would shout and curse to attract attention. Their neighbors would cry almost in unison: "There they go again!"

Asunle accused Depo of being obstinate and inconsiderate. Depo would insist on eating particular types of food at odd hours and always drank too much palm wine afterward. These habits were becoming intolerable to his wife, Some people thought that it was Asunle who was too defiant. She was always ready to pick a quarrel. She could, at will, turn the smallest domestic encounter into an irritating exchange.

She would struggle like a wild cat as she was being restrained, and hurl invectives at her husband in an endless exasperating stream that would make the peacemakers shout, "But that is enough!"

Elders in the village started looking for a solution. They spent long hours debating all relevant points, but no one suggested a divorce. Elders never did. At last Depo's close friends suggested what they thought was a foolproof plan: he should marry a second wife! With a co-wife in the household, they thought, Asunle would be forced to become more sensible. So, Depo and his friends began the anxious search; Asunle never seemed to worry. At last Atoke, the would-be second wife, was identified in a big village several kilometers away. Elders promptly proposed and received a favorable reply, including the consent of the girl herself. The ceremonies were performed, and even Asunle played her part as senior wife to her credit. The village heaved a sigh of relief, hoping for peace at last in Mr. Depo's household. But if the villagers were right in expecting peace after the marriage, they were naïve in thinking that other problems would not arise. It turned out that the battle lines only shifted from between husband and wife to between wife and co-wife. In their positive estimation of the new wife's character, villagers were grossly misled by her good looks. She was young, tall, and shapely, with a rich crop of hair, which she used to plait in beautiful, elaborate styles. There was a moderate gap between her upper front teeth and she smiled a lot. But beneath that alluring visage lay a sarcastic turbulence, amply fueled by a sharp tongue and an artful, dramatic disposition. In spite of Asunle's notorious, wily truculence, she could not duplicate half the repertoire of Atoke's creative acerbity. No one could tell whether Depo's choice of Atoke as second wife was by cruel accident or a calculated search for someone who would be more than a match for Asunle.

Trouble started when Atoke refused to duly acknowledge Asunle's superior position in the household. By tradition, it was Atoke's duty to cook for the whole household and it was Asunle's right to tell her what to cook, when to cook it, and how much. But Atoke refused to be ordered about by anyone. She would only cook for herself and her husband. Asunle was therefore forced to continue cooking for herself and her two children, Olu, a little boy in his third year of school, and Lara, a mere toddler. Before Asunle had realized it, Atoke's monopoly of their joint husband was complete. Atoke cooked the tastiest of foods, which endeared her all the more to Depo, who had by now learned to tap palm wine, most of which he consumed himself. The after-supper scenes between Depo and Atoke were enviable pictures of marital happiness. But Asunle was being excluded from it all!

The children adjusted quickly to the new domestic situation. Lara, the little girl, took to Atoke instantly, like a fish to water. She would follow Atoke everywhere in spite of her mother's attempts to restrain her. It was to Atoke's credit that she too liked Lara. She would carry her on her back; she would play little games with her. Lara preferred to join her father, Depo, and the new wife at mealtimes. She would sit in her father's lap and be indulged. Olu the schoolboy stuck by his mother, Asunle.

Soon Asunle could no longer endure this marginalization. She accused Depo of encouraging defiance on the part of Atoke, who was openly trampling tradition. But the gauntlet was taken up not by Depo, who was by then almost permanently inebriated, but by Atoke, who was not prepared to lose her favorable position. Rowdy quarrels quickly re-erupted in Depo's household and eventually regained their original position as the village's primary source of entertainment to the chagrin of elders and the delight of young ones.

Villagers were expecting Asunle to re-enact her past performances and promptly put the new wife in her place, but the very first public encounter left no doubt that Asunle was in trouble. Actually it was Asunle who fired the first salvos: three or four missiles of invective. Her style was to quickly boil over and assail her adversary with verbal abuse, gesticulating wildly. She would then refuse to go off the boil for a long time. She would make unpleasant remarks about her enemy's looks and behavior. When the opponent was her husband, she shone like a lone star.

When Asunle started this first fight, Atoke remained very calm. She came out of the house and stood outside. Asunle followed her. A small crowd was already gathering, attracted by Asunle's usual noise. Then Atoke asked Asunle to stop bleating like a sheep and wait for some response. At first she calmly agreed with Asunle on all the unpleasant remarks she had made about her bodily features and behavior. But she proceeded to demonstrate how all her own shortcomings would pale in comparison with the degree of ugliness of Asunle's features and the awkwardness of her behavior. She even gave a few examples.

Atoke was more sophisticated than Asunle. To Atoke, lips were not just thin, they had to be compared with a common phenomenon that would sharply paint the picture of incongruity. For example, Asunle's lips were as thin as a palm wine seller's drinking calabash! Her eyes were as sunken as a brook almost obscured under an evergreen bush. In other words, whereas Asunle would stop at just ridiculing an ugly part of the body, Atoke would go further and liken the part to some funny phenomenon. In addition, while Asunle's performances were angry and trumpet-tongued, Atoke's were calculated, spiteful, and expressed with great fluency. The truth soon became too apparent to be ignored. Asunle was no match for the great Atoke. Overnight, a new champion had wiped out all the records of a long reigning heroine. It was too bitter a pill for Asunle to swallow. Part of Atoke's advantage was that she came from a very big village where she had been exposed to greater variety in the art of vituperation than Asunle who had lived all her life in small villages. As the new wife's reputation spread, gossip was making the old wife's life unbearable. For the first time Asunle was not too keen to pick a quarrel. But these were trying times for the household as quarrels increased. One morning, Asunle discovered that there was no water in the family water pot. Normally she would have called on Atoke to go to the river and fetch some water, but she wanted to avoid any confrontation so early in the morning. So she picked a pot and ran to the river. When she returned, she did not pour the water into the big family water pot. She gave some to Olu to wash himself and get ready for school; she was also going to give Lara her morning bath and use the remaining to prepare breakfast for herself and the children. But while she was busy washing Lara in the backyard, Atoke took the remaining water, poured it into a cooking pot, and placed it on the fire to cook her own breakfast. When Asunle came back and discovered what had happened, she was furious. She wanted to know what gave Atoke the idea that she, Asunle, the senior wife, had become her errand girl to fetch water for her to cook food. Atoke just smiled, stoked the fire, and sat calmly without making any comment. The situation boiled over! Asunle picked up a small pestle and pushed the clay pot over. It overturned and broke, emptying its contents into the fire in a whirl of smoke and ashes. Atoke shot up and grabbed Asunle's clothes. They started a noisy struggle. Little Lara started to cry. Depo ran in from the backyard where he had gone to wash his face. He struggled to separate the fighters. Asunle pushed him off energetically and he fell. But he struggled up instantly. He forced himself between them. Atoke went out of the house followed by Asunle, and a grand performance of verbal abuse started in front of the house. The usual crowd gathered and seemed to be saying this time, "Not again!"

Both wives were equally angry and worked up. They reeled off abuse in a frenzied battle of wit and hate. Atoke had better control of her performance. Asunle was too angry to be effective. Atoke's performance was therefore entertaining. Atoke looked at Asunle, shook her head, and said, "Do you ever observe how you carry your body when you move about? You push that heavy mouth of yours forward like a timid stray dog venturing onto a dance floor." The audience would have applauded, but the elders suppressed all response, except a few muffled chuckles. Asunle had virtually lost her voice. She was going to cry! The villagers' sympathies instantly returned to her. An elderly lady came forward and shouted angrily at the two women. "What on earth do you think you are doing? Can't you see? People are laughing at you! Is this the kind of report you want sent back to your parents? Shut your mouths and go inside, now!"

The two ladies stopped shouting and went into their house. But the damage had been done to Asunle's reputation. She had been humiliated.

She went into her bedroom and cried. Depo had to take Olu to school to explain why he was coming so late that morning.

Asunle knew she had to do something to redeem herself. After some hard thinking, she smiled and carried on with the day's chores. Depo took his machete and went to the farm. The two ladies were not speaking to each other. That morning little Lara stayed with her mother.

It was two o'clock when Olu came home from school. Asunle had prepared a good lunch for him. He was eating hungrily because he hadn't had breakfast. Asunle sat watching him dotingly. Then a conversation began:

"Olu, my dear son."

"Yes, mother."

"How was school today?"

"We learned Bible stories and did arithmetic."

"Have you been learning any English?"

"Oh yes! We have learned a lot of English! Let me show you my book."

"No no! Don't worry. But you'll do something for me."

"An errand? You want to write a letter? Let me wash my hands."

"No, it's not a letter, but go and wash your hands."

Olu washed his hands and sat beside his mother.

"Now mother, what do you want me to do for you?"

"You said you have been learning some English?"

"Yes, we have learned a lot of English. Look at this book. Everything inside it is English!"

"Really!"

"Oh yes!"

"But can you insult someone in English?"

Olu hesitated a bit and said, "Well, yes! Oh yes! It is possible. There is so much English in my head!"

"Well then, you remember how that stupid Atoke abused me in the morning? Now, I want to show her that I tower above her in social standing. I have a son who can insult her in English! So, I want you to go to her now and insult her roundly in English."

Olu stood up calmly, tucked in his shirt, and adjusted his belt. He dashed to his bag and quickly checked something in his book. He nodded satisfactorily and marched smartly to face Atoke who was just entering the house. Olu stood right in Atoke's way, and Atoke was forced to stop and wonder.

Then Olu simply asked, "Why were you abusing my mother in the morning?"

The confrontation was unexpected, and it momentarily disorientated Atoke. But she quickly regained her balance. She shouted at him. "Shut your dirty mouth! Has your mother run out of ideas?"

Olu then moved a few steps back and with arms akimbo he started to speak English knowing full well that Atoke would not understand.

He said, "*What is this?*"

Atoke was taken aback. "What is he talking?"

Olu responded, "*It is a basket.*"

Atoke concluded that Olu must be insulting her in English. She warned mother and child: "If you want to abuse me in English, you'll get into trouble. And I hope you are listening, careless mother?"

Olu moved farther back before throwing another English missile: "*What are you doing?*"

Atoke was annoyed now. "I am warning you, little rat."

Olu just fired on: "*I am going to the door.*"

Atoke said, "This is a good-for-nothing boy!"

Olu continued. "*Sit on the chair. What are you doing? I am sitting on the chair.*"

Atoke said, with a lot of hatred in her voice, "That stupid English you are speaking will be the death of you."

Olu would not be deterred: "*Where is your book? It is on the desk.*"

Atoke then said, "I know that my God will surely throw back all those curses on your ill-fated head!"

At that point Asunle felt the need to protect her son. She had been sitting down, enjoying her son's special performance with tremendous pride. She now stood up to defend Olu: "Don't curse my son, shameless woman. His intelligence is a gift from God. I know you can't understand."

"There is nothing to understand," Atoke retorted. "You think he can succeed where you have failed? Where a calabash fails to bail out enough water, there is no job for the basket. It is one more step down the road to perdition for mother and child."

A big noisy quarrel ensued between the two wives, and a crowd quickly gathered. Now Olu had absolutely gone wild with English! He was reeling off original verbal insults in special English:

"Go to the door. What are you doing? I am going to the door! Put the basket on the table. Where is the basket? It is on the table."

The crowd grew bigger. Olu walked up and down the crowd, the left hand in his pocket, and the right held aloft as he nodded his head to emphasize the importance of each verbal missile in English!

Villagers tried to settle the quarrel. Atoke complained that Asunle had started asking her son to insult her in English! An elderly man wondered whether little Olu had acquired enough English to insult anyone. Before the man finished talking, Olu started rolling out his English again.

"What is this? It is a window."

When Atoke heard the word *window* she flew into a rage. Unfortunate coincidence! Yoruba had borrowed the word *window* from English and its meaning had been extended to describe gaps in teeth. Atoke shouted, "Did you all hear that? Is it right for this luckless little rat to ridicule the gap in my teeth?"

After more bitter exchanges villagers succeeded in pacifying the fighters. An old man shouted at Olu to quiet down, and he shut his frivolous mouth.

The oldest woman in the crowd wanted to know how Atoke, who never went to school, knew what Olu was saying in English. Atoke narrated how the fight started and reminded them that they were all witnesses to Olu's ridicule of the "window" in her teeth.

All this noise had attracted the attention of a teacher from the mission house. As the teacher approached, Olu cleverly went into hiding. Villagers sought the teacher's opinion on Olu's knowledge of English.

When another pupil in a higher class who witnessed part of Olu's performance explained what Olu had been saying to the teacher, they both burst into laughter. When the teacher explained it all to the villagers, everyone laughed.

The old man sighed and remarked: "This lack of English is a big embarrassment."

The teacher wanted to see Olu, but the little scholar had disappeared.

Noticing the improved atmosphere, little Lara quietly walked to Atoke and held on to her shawl. Atoke looked at her, smiled, and picked her up. The little girl smiled too. There was a gap in her tiny set of teeth.

Atoke laughed and said, "Well, look what we have here! I am not the only one with a window!"

Translated from the Yoruba by the author

MY FINANCIAL CAREER

Stephen Leacock

Stephen Leacock (1869–1944) was a Canadian teacher, political scientist and writer. Though not as well known now, during the early 1900s Leacock was the most famous humourist writing in the English language. At one point, it was claimed that more people had heard of Stephen Leacock than Canada.

When I go into a bank I get nervous. The clerks make me nervous; the little windows at the counters make me nervous; the sight of the money makes me nervous; everything makes me nervous.

The moment I go through the door of a bank and attempt to do business there, I become an irresponsible fool. I knew this before I went in, but my salary had been raised to fifty six dollars a month and I felt that the bank was the only place for it.

So I walked in with dragging feet and looked shyly round at the clerks. I had an idea that a person about to open an account was obliged to consult the manager.

I went up to a counter marked 'Accountant'. The Accountant was a tall, cool fellow. The very sight of him made me nervous. My voice was deep and hollow.

'Can I see the manager?' I said, and added solemnly, 'alone.' I don't know why I said 'alone.'

'Certainly,' said the accountant, and fetched him.

The manager was a grave, calm man. I held my fifty-six dollars clutched in a screwed-up ball in my pocket.

'Are you the manager?' I said. God knows I didn't doubt it.

'Yes,' he said.

'Can I see you,' I asked, 'alone?' I didn't want to say 'alone' again, but without it the thing seemed obvious.

The manager looked at me in some alarm. He felt that I had a terrible secret to reveal.

'Come in here,' he said, and led the way to a private room He turned the key in the lock.

'We are safe from interruption here,' he said: 'sit down.'

We both sat down and looked at each other. I found no voice to speak.

'You are one of Pinkerton's men, I suppose,' he said.

He had gathered from my mysterious manner that I was a detective. I knew what he was thinking, and it made me worse.

'No, not from Pinkerton's,' I said, seeming to suggest that I came from a rival agency.

'To tell the truth,' I went on, as if I had been tempted to lie about it, 'I am not a detective at all. I have come to open an account. I intend to keep all my money in this bank.'

The manager looked relieved but still serious; he concluded now that I was a son of Baron Rothschild or a young Gould.

'A large account, I suppose,' he said.

'Fairly large,' I whispered. 'I propose to deposit fifty-six dollars now and fifty dollars a month regularly.

The manager got up and opened the door. He called to the accountant.

'Mr. Montgomery,' he said unkindly loud, 'this gentleman is opening an account. He will deposit fifty-six dollars. Good morning.'

I rose.

A big iron door stood open at the side of the room.

'Good morning,' I said, and stepped into the safe.

'Come out,' said the manager coldly, and showed me the other way.

I went up to the accountant's counter and pushed the ball of money at him with a sudden, quick movement as if I were doing a conjuring trick.

My face was pale as death.

'Here,' I said, 'deposit it.' The tone of the words seemed to mean, 'Let us do this painful thing while we are in mood for it.'

He took the money and gave it to another clerk.

He made me write the sum on a piece of paper and sign my name in a book. I no longer knew what I was doing. The bank was going round and round before my eyes.

'Is it deposited?' I asked in a hollow, vibrating voice.

'It is,' said the accountant.

'Then I want to draw a cheque.'

My idea was to draw out six dollars of it for present use. Someone gave me a cheque-book through a little window and someone else began telling me how to write it out. The people in the bank had the impression that I was a millionaire who had something wrong with him. I wrote something on the cheque and thrust it in at the clerk. He looked at it.

'What! are you drawing it all out again?' he asked in surprise. Then I realized that I had written fifty six instead of six. I was too far gone to reason now. I had a feeling that it was impossible to explain the thing. All the clerks had stopped writing to look at me.

Reckless with misery, I made up my mind.

'Yes the whole thing.'

'You withdraw your money from the bank?'

'Every cent of it.'

'Are you not going to deposit any more?' said the clerk, astonished.

'Never.'

A foolish hope struck me that they might think something had insulted me while I was writing the cheque and that I had changed my mind. I made a wretched attempt to look like a man with a fearfully quick temper.

The clerk prepared to pay the money.

'How will you have it?' he said.

'What?'

'How will you have it?

'Oh' – I caught his meaning and answered without even trying to think – 'in fifties.'

He gave me a fifty-dollar bill.

'And the six?' he asked dryly.

'In sixes,' I said.

He gave it to me and I rushed out.

As the big door swung behind me I caught the echo of a roar of laughter that went up to the ceiling of the bank. Since then I bank no more. I keep my money in cash in my trousers pocket and my savings in silver dollars in a sock.

CONSUMING THE VIEW

Luigi Malerba

Luigi Malerba (1927–2008) wrote short stories, historical novels and screenplays and was a leader of Italy's Neoavanguardia literary movement. An original, linguistically inventive writer with a taste for satire, Umberto Eco called him 'maliciously ironic, unpredictable and ambiguous.'

The sky was clear and the air clean, yet from the telescopes on the Gianicolo hill the Roman panorama appeared hazy and out of focus. The first protests came from a group of Swiss tourists complaining that they had wasted their hundred lire on malfunctioning devices. The city sent out an expert technician, who had the lenses replaced. Nonetheless, protests kept coming, in writing and by phone. City Hall sent out another expert to test the telescopes again. A peculiar new element emerged: the panorama from the Gianicolo appeared blurry not only through the lenses of the telescopes but also to the naked eye. The city claimed the problem was no longer its responsibility, yet the tourists kept complaining, in writing and by phone. After gazing for a while at the expanse of rooftops, with the domes of Roman churches surfacing here and there and the white monument of the Piazza Venezia, many went to have their eyes checked. Some even started wearing glasses.

A professor of panoramology was called in, from the University of Minnesota at Minneapolis. She leaned over the Gianicolo wall at varying hours: dawn, daybreak, noon, sunset, even at night. Finally she wrote a lengthy report on the distribution of hydrogen in the photosphere, on phenomena of refraction, on carbon dioxide polluting the atmosphere, and even on the fragrance given off by exotic plants in the Botanical Garden below—without recommending any remedy.

A doorman at City Hall, who lived near the Gianicolo and who had learned of the problem, wrote a letter to the mayor explaining a theory of his. According to the doorman, the Roman panorama was being slowly worn away by the continuous gaze of tourists, and if no action were taken it would soon be entirely used up. In a footnote at the end of his letter, the doorman added that the same thing was happening to Leonardo da Vinci's *Last Supper* and other famous paintings. In a second footnote he emphasized, as proof of his thesis, how the view visibly worsened in the spring and summer, coinciding with the great crowds of tourists, while in the winter, when tourists were scant, one noticed no change for the worse; on the contrary, it seemed the panorama slowly regained its traditional limpidity.

Other expert panoramologists took photographs from the Gianicolo week after week, and these seemed to confirm the doorman's theory. The truth, however strange, now seemed crystal clear: the constant gaze of tourists was consuming the Roman panorama; a subtle leprosy was slowly corroding the image of the so-called Eternal City.

The City Hall public relations office launched a campaign, which, in order to discourage tourists, tried to ridicule the panorama in general, the very concept of a view. Their press releases had titles like "Stay Clear of the Panorama" and "The Banality of a View." Others, more aggressive, were entitled "Spitting on the Panorama," "Enough of This Panorama," "One Cannot Live on Views Alone." A famous semiologist wrote a long essay entitled "Panorama, Catastrophe of a Message." Some journalists abandoned themselves to malicious and gratuitous speculation on the greater corrosive power of Japanese or American or German tourists, according to their own whims or the antipathies of the newspapers in which the articles were published. Fierce discussions were unleashed, which, though noisy, achieved the opposite of the desired effect: all the publicity, though negative, ended up increasing the number of tourists crowding the Gianicolo hill.

Eventually, the Roman city government, following the advice of an expert brought in from China, resorted to the stealthy planting of a row of young cypresses under the Gianicolo wall, so that, within a few years, the famous panorama would be completely hidden behind a thick, ever-green barrier.

Translated by Lesley Riva

THE DAUGHTERS OF THE LATE COLONEL

Katherine Mansfield

Katherine Mansfield (1888–1923) was born in New Zealand and settled in London in 1908. A recognised master of the short story, her prose style was celebrated for being innovative, accessible and psychologically acute. She died at thirty-four of tuberculosis. On her death, Virginia Woolf – her close friend and rival – wrote 'I was jealous of her writing – the only writing I have ever been jealous of.'

I

The week after was one of the busiest weeks of their lives. Even when they went to bed it was only their bodies that lay down and rested; their minds went on, thinking things out, talking things over, wondering, deciding, trying to remember where…

Constantia lay like a statue, her hands by her sides, her feet just overlapping each other, the sheet up to her chin. She stared at the ceiling.

"Do you think father would mind if we gave his top-hat to the porter?"

"The porter?" snapped Josephine. "Why ever the porter? What a very extraordinary idea!"

"Because," said Constantia slowly, "he must often have to go to funerals. And I noticed at—at the cemetery that he only had a bowler." She paused. "I thought then how very much he'd appreciate a top-hat. We ought to give him a present, too. He was always very nice to father."

"But," cried Josephine, flouncing on her pillow and staring across the dark at Constantia, "father's head!" And suddenly, for one awful moment, she nearly giggled. Not, of course, that she felt in the least like giggling. It must have been habit. Years ago, when they had stayed awake at night talking, their beds had simply heaved. And now the porter's head, disappearing, popped out, like a candle, under father's hat... The giggle mounted, mounted; she clenched her hands; she fought it down; she frowned fiercely at the dark and said "Remember" terribly sternly.

"We can decide tomorrow," she said.

Constantia had noticed nothing; she sighed.

"Do you think we ought to have our dressing-gowns dyed as well?"

"Black?" almost shrieked Josephine.

"Well, what else?" said Constantia. "I was thinking—it doesn't seem quite sincere, in a way, to wear black out of doors and when we're fully dressed, and then when we're at home—"

"But nobody sees us," said Josephine. She gave the bedclothes such a twitch that both her feet became uncovered and she had to creep up the pillows to get them well under again.

"Kate does," said Constantia. "And the postman very well might."

Josephine though of her dark-red slippers, which matched her dressing-gown, and of Constantia's favourite indefinite green ones which went with hers. Black! Two black dressing-gowns and two pairs of black woolly slippers, creeping off to the bathroom like black cats.

"I don't think it's absolutely necessary," said she.

Silence. Then Constantia said, "We shall have to post the papers with the notice in them tomorrow to catch the Ceylon mail... How many letters have we had up till now?"

"Twenty-three."

Josephine had replied to them all, and twenty-three times when she came to "We miss our dear father so much" she had broken down and had to use her handkerchief, and on some of them even to soak up a very light-blue tear with an edge of blotting-paper. Strange! She couldn't have put it on—but twenty-three times. Even now, though, when she said over to herself sadly "We miss our dear father so much," she could have cried if she'd wanted to.

"Have you got enough stamps?" came from Constantia.

"Oh, how can I tell?" said Josephine crossly. "What's the good of asking me that now?"

"I was just wondering," said Constantia mildly.

Silence again. There came a little rustle, a scurry, a hop.

"A mouse," said Constantia.

"It can't be a mouse because there aren't any crumbs," said Josephine.

"But it doesn't know there aren't," said Constantia.

A spasm of pity squeezed her heart. Poor little thing! She wished she'd left a tiny piece of biscuit on the dressing-table. It was awful to think of it not finding anything. What would it do?

"I can't think how they manage to live at all," she said slowly.

"Who?" demanded Josephine.

And Constantia said more loudly than she meant to, "Mice."

Josephine was furious. "Oh, what nonsense, Con!" she said. "What have mice got to do with it? You're asleep."

"I don't think I am," said Constantia. She shut her eyes to make sure. She was.

Josephine arched her spine, pulled up her knees, folded her arms so that her fists came under her ears, and pressed her cheek hard against the pillow.

II

Another thing which complicated matters was they had Nurse Andrews staying on with them that week. It was their own fault; they had asked her. It was Josephine's idea. On the morning—well, on the last morning, when the doctor had gone, Josephine had said to Constantia, "Don't you think it would be rather nice if we asked Nurse Andrews to stay on for a week as our guest?"

"Very nice," said Constantia.

"I thought," went on Josephine quickly, "I should just say this after-noon, after I've paid her, 'My sister and I would be very pleased, after all you've done for us, Nurse Andrews, if you would stay on for a week as our guest.' I'd have to put that in about being our guest in case—"

"Oh, but she could hardly expect to be paid!" cried Constantia.

"One never knows," said Josephine sagely.

Nurse Andrews had, of course, jumped at the idea. But it was a bother. It meant they had to have regular sit-down meals at the proper times, whereas if they'd been alone they could just have asked Kate if she wouldn't have minded bringing them a tray wherever they were. And meal-times now that the strain was over were rather a trial.

Nurse Andrews was simply fearful about butter. Really they couldn't help feeling that about butter, at least, she took advantage of their kindness. And she had that maddening habit of asking for just an inch more of bread to finish what she had on her plate, and then, at the last mouthful, absent-mindedly—of course it wasn't absent-mindedly—taking another helping. Josephine got very red when this happened, and she fastened her small, bead-like eyes on the table cloth as if she saw a minute strange insect creeping through the web of it. But Constantia's long, pale face lengthened and set, and she gazed away—away—far over the desert, to where that line of camels unwound like a thread of wool…

"When I was with Lady Tukes," said Nurse Andrews, "she had such a dainty little contrayvance for the buttah. It was a silvah Cupid balanced on the—on the bordah of a glass dish, holding a tayny fork. And when you wanted some buttah you simply pressed his foot and he bent down and speared you a piece. It was quite a gayme."

Josephine could hardly bear that. But "I think those things are very extravagant" was all she said.

"But whey?" asked Nurse Andrews, beaming through her eyeglasses. "No one, surely, would take more buttah than one wanted—would one?"

"Ring, Con," cried Josephine. She couldn't trust herself to reply.

And proud young Kate, the enchanted princess, came in to see what the old tabbies wanted now. She snatched away their plates of mock something or other and slapped down a white, terrified blancmange.

"Jam, please, Kate," said Josephine kindly.

Kate knelt and burst open the sideboard, lifted the lid of the jam-pot, saw it was empty, put it on the table, and stalked off.

"I'm afraid," said Nurse Andrews a moment later, "there isn't any."

"Oh, what a bother!" said Josephine. She bit her lip. "What had we better do?"

Constantia looked dubious. "We can't disturb Kate again," she said softly.

Nurse Andrews waited, smiling at them both. Her eyes wandered, spying at everything behind her eyeglasses. Constantia in despair went back to her camels. Josephine frowned heavily—concentrated. If it hadn't been for this idiotic woman she and Con would, of course, have eaten their blancamange without. Suddenly the idea came.

"I know," she said. "Marmalade. There's some marmalade in the sideboard. Get it, Con."

"I hope," laughed Nurse Andrews—and her laugh was like a spoon tinkling against a medicine-glass—"I hope it's not very bittah marma-layde."

III

But, after all, it was not long now, and then she'd be gone for good. And there was no getting over the fact that she had been very kind to father. She had nursed him day and night at the end. Indeed, both Constantia and Josephine felt privately she had rather overdone the not leaving him at the very last. For when they had gone in to say good-bye Nurse Andrews had sat beside his bed the whole time, holding his wrist and pretending to look at her watch. It couldn't have been necessary. It was so tactless, too. Supposing father had wanted to say something—something private to them. Not that he had. Oh, far from it! He lay there, purple, a dark, angry purple in the face, and never even looked at them when they came in. Then, as they were standing there, wondering what to do, he had suddenly opened one eye. Oh, what a difference it would have made, what a difference to their memory of him, how much easier to tell people about it, if he had only opened both! But no—one eye only. It glared at them a moment and then… went out.

IV

It had made it very awkward for them when Mr. Farolles, of St. John's, called the same afternoon.

"The end was quite peaceful, I trust?" were the first words he said as he glided towards them through the dark drawing-room.

"Quite," said Josephine faintly. They both hung their heads. Both of them felt certain that eye wasn't at all a peaceful eye.

"Won't you sit down?" said Josephine.

"Thank you, Miss Pinner," said Mr. Farolles gratefully. He folded his coat-tails and began to lower himself into Father's arm-chair, but just as he touched it he almost sprang up and slid into the next chair instead.

He coughed. Josephine clasped her hands; Constantia looked vague.

"I want you to feel, Miss Pinner," said Mr. Farolles, "and you, Miss Constantia, that I'm trying to be helpful. I want to be helpful to you both, if you will let me. These are the times," said Mr Farolles, very simply and earnestly, "when God means us to be helpful to one another."

"Thank you very much, Mr. Farolles," said Josephine and Constantia.

"Not at all," said Mr. Farolles gently. He drew his kid gloves through his fingers and leaned forward. "And if either of you would like a little Communion, either or both of you, here and now, you have only to tell me. A little Communion is often very help—a great comfort," he added tenderly.

But the idea of a little Communion terrified them. What! In the drawing-room by themselves—with no—no altar or anything! The piano would be much too high, thought Constantia, and Mr. Farolles could not possibly lean over it with the chalice. And Kate would be sure to come bursting in and interrupt them, thought Josephine. And supposing the bell rang in the middle? It might be somebody important—about their mourning. Would they get up reverently and go out, or would they have to wait... in torture?

"Perhaps you will send round a note by your good Kate if you would care for it later," said Mr. Farolles.

"Oh yes, thank you very much!" they both said.

Mr. Farolles got up and took his black straw hat from the round table.

"And about the funeral," he said softly. "I may arrange that—as your dear father's old friend and yours, Miss Pinner—and Miss Constantia?"

Josephine and Constantia got up too.

"I should like it to be quite simple," said Josephine firmly, "and not too expensive. At the same time, I should like—"

"A good one that will last," thought dreamy Constantia, as if Josephine were buying a nightgown. But, of course, Josephine didn't say that. "One suitable to our father's position." She was very nervous.

"I'll run round to our good friend Mr. Knight," said Mr. Farolles soothingly. "I will ask him to come and see you. I am sure you will find him very helpful indeed."

V

Well, at any rate, all that part of it was over, though neither of them could possibly believe that father was never coming back. Josephine had had a moment of absolute terror at the cemetery, while the coffin was lowered, to think that she and Constantia had done this thing without asking his permission. What would father say when he found out? For he was bound to find out sooner or later. He always did. "Buried. You two girls had me buried! "She heard his stick thumping. Oh, what would they say? What possible excuse could they make? It sounded such an appallingly heartless thing to do. Such a wicked advantage to take of a person because he happened to be helpless at the moment. The other people seemed to treat it all as a matter of course. They were strangers; they couldn't be expected to understand that father was the very last person for such a thing to happen to. No, the entire blame for it all would fall on her and Constantia. And the expense, she thought, stepping into the tight-buttoned cab. When she had to show him the bills. What would he say then?

She heard him absolutely roaring. "And do you expect me to pay for this gimcrack excursion of yours?"

"Oh," groaned poor Josephine aloud, "we shouldn't have done it, Con!"

And Constantia, pale as a lemon in all that blackness, said in a frightened whisper, "Done what, Jug?"

"Let them bu-bury father like that," said Josephine, breaking down and crying into her new, queer-smelling mourning handkerchief.

"But what else could we have done?" asked Constantia wonderingly. "We couldn't have kept him unburied. At any rate, not in a flat that size."

Josephine blew her nose; the cab was dreadfully stuffy.

"I don't know," she said forlornly. "It is all so dreadful. I feel we ought to have tried to, just for a time at least. To make perfectly sure. One thing's certain"—and her tears sprang out again—"father will never forgive us for this—never!"

VI

Father would never forgive them. That was what they felt more than ever when, two mornings later, they went into his room to go through his things. They had discussed it quite calmly. It was even down on Josephine's list of things to be done. Go through father's things and settle about them. But that was a very different matter from saying after breakfast:

"Well, are you ready, Con?"

"Yes, Jug—when you are."

"Then I think we'd better get it over."

It was dark in the hall. It had been a rule for years never to disturb father in the morning, whatever happened. And now they were going to open the door without knocking even... Constantia's eyes were enormous at the idea; Josephine felt weak in the knees.

"You—you go first," she gasped, pushing Constantia.

But Constantia said, as she always had said on those occasions, "No, Jug, that's not fair. You're the eldest."

Josephine was just going to say—what at other times she wouldn't have owned to for the world—what she kept for her very last weapon, "But you're the tallest," when they noticed that the kitchen door was open, and there stood Kate...

"Very stiff," said Josephine, grasping the door-handle and doing her best to turn it. As if anything ever deceived Kate!

It couldn't be helped. That girl was... Then the door was shut behind them, but—but they weren't in father's room at all. They might have suddenly walked through the wall by mistake into a different flat altogether. Was the door just behind them? They were too frightened to look. Josephine knew that if it was it was holding itself tight shut; Constantia felt that, like the doors in dreams, it hadn't any handle at all. It was the coldness which made it so awful. Or the whiteness—which? Everything was covered. The blinds were down, a cloth hung over the mirror, a sheet hid the bed; a huge fan of white paper filled the fireplace. Constantia timidly put out her hand; she almost expected a snowflake to fall. Josephine felt a queer tingling in her nose, as if her nose was freezing. Then a cab klop-klopped over the cobbles below, and the quiet seemed to shake into little pieces.

"I had better pull up a blind," said Josephine bravely.

"Yes, it might be a good idea," whispered Constantia.

They only gave the blind a touch, but it flew up and the cord flew after, rolling round the blind-stick, and the little tassel tapped as if trying to get free. That was too much for Constantia.

"Don't you think—don't you think we might put it off for another day?" she whispered.

"Why?" snapped Josephine, feeling, as usual, much better now that she knew for certain that Constantia was terrified. "It's got to be done. But I do wish you wouldn't whisper, Con."

"I didn't know I was whispering," whispered Constantia.

"And why do you keep staring at the bed?" said Josephine, raising her voice almost defiantly. "There's nothing on the bed."

"Oh, Jug, don't say so!" said poor Connie. "At any rate, not so loudly."

Josephine felt herself that she had gone too far. She took a wide swerve over to the chest of drawers, put out her hand, but quickly drew it back again.

"Connie!" she gasped, and she wheeled round and leaned with her back against the chest of drawers.

"Oh, Jug—what?"

Josephine could only glare. She had the most extraordinary feeling that she had just escaped something simply awful. But how could she explain to Constantia that father was in the chest of drawers? He was in the top drawer with his handkerchiefs and neckties, or in the next with his shirts and pyjamas, or in the lowest of them all with his suits. He was watching there, hidden away—just behind the door-handle— ready to spring.

She pulled a funny old-fashioned face at Constantia, just as she used to in the old days when she was going to cry.

"I can't open," she nearly wailed.

"No, don't, Jug," whispered Constantia earnestly. "It's much better not to. Don't let's open anything. At any rate, not for a long time."

"But—but it seems so weak," said Josephine, breaking down.

"But why not be weak for once, Jug?" argued Constantia, whispering quite fiercely. "If it is weak." And her pale stare flew from the locked writing-table—so safe—to the huge glittering wardrobe, and she began to breathe in a queer, panting away. "Why shouldn't we be weak for once in our lives, Jug? It's quite excusable. Let's be weak—be weak, Jug. It's much nicer to be weak than to be strong."

And then she did one of those amazingly bold things that she'd done about twice before in their lives: she marched over to the wardrobe, turned the key, and took it out of the lock. Took it out of the lock and held it up to Josephine, showing Josephine by her extraordinary smile that she knew what she'd done—she'd risked deliberately father being in there among his overcoats.

If the huge wardrobe had lurched forward, had crashed down on Constantia, Josephine wouldn't have been surprised. On the contrary, she would have thought it the only suitable thing to happen. But nothing happened. Only the room seemed quieter than ever, and the bigger flakes of cold air fell on Josephine's shoulders and knees. She began to shiver.

"Come, Jug," said Constantia, still with that awful callous smile; and Josephine followed just as she had that last time, when Constantia had pushed Benny into the round pond.

VII

But the strain told on them when they were back in the dining-room. They sat down, very shaky, and looked at each other.

"I don't feel I can settle to anything," said Josephine, "until I've had something. Do you think we could ask Kate for two cups of hot water?"

"I really don't see why we shouldn't," said Constantia carefully. She was quite normal again. "I won't ring. I'll go to the kitchen door and ask her."

"Yes, do," said Josephine, sinking down into a chair. "Tell her, just two cups, Con, nothing else—on a tray."

"She needn't even put the jug on, need she?" said Constantia, as though Kate might very well complain if the jug had been there.

"Oh no, certainly not! The jug's not at all necessary. She can pour it direct out of the kettle," cried Josephine, feeling that would be a labour-saving indeed.

Their cold lips quivered at the greenish brims. Josephine curved her small red hands round the cup; Constantia sat up and blew on the wavy steam, making it flutter from one side to the other.

"Speaking of Benny," said Josephine.

And though Benny hadn't been mentioned Constantia immediately looked as though he had.

"He'll expect us to send him something of Father's, of course. But it's so difficult to know what to send to Ceylon."

"You mean things get unstuck so on the voyage," murmured Constantia.

"No, lost," said Josephine sharply. "You know there's no post. Only runners."

Both paused to watch a black man in white linen drawers running through the pale fields for dear life, with a large brown-paper parcel in his hands. Josephine's black man was tiny; he scurried along glistening like an ant. But there was something blind and tireless about Constantia's tall, thin fellow, which made him, she decided, a very unpleasant person indeed... On the veranda, dressed all in white and wearing a cork helmet, stood Benny. His right hand shook up and down, as Father's did when he was impatient. And behind him, not in the least interested, sat Hilda, the unknown sister-in-law. She swung in a cane rocker and flicked over the leaves of the *Tatler*.

"I think his watch would be the most suitable present," said Josephine.

Constantia looked up; she seemed surprised.

"Oh, would you trust a gold watch to a native?"

"But of course, I'd disguise it," said Josephine. "No one would know it was a watch." She liked the idea of having to make a parcel such a curious shape that no one could possibly guess what it was. She even thought for a moment of hiding the watch in a narrow cardboard corset-box that she'd kept by her for a long time, waiting for it to come in for something. It was such beautiful, firm cardboard. But, no, it wouldn't be appropriate for this occasion. It had lettering on it: *Medium Women's 28. Extra Firm Busks.* It would be almost too much of a surprise for Benny to open that and find father's watch inside.

"And, of course, it isn't as though it would be going—ticking, I mean," said Constantia, who was still thinking of the native love of jewellery. "At least," she added, "it would be very strange if after all that time it was."

VIII

Josephine made no reply. She had flown off on one of her tangents. She had suddenly thought of Cyril. Wasn't it more usual for the only grandson to have the watch? And then dear Cyril was so appreciative and a gold watch meant so much to a young man. Benny, in all probability, had quite got out of the habit of watches; men so seldom wore waistcoats in those hot climates. Whereas Cyril in London wore them from year's end to year's end. And it would be so nice for her and Constantia, when he came to tea, to know it was there. "I see you've got on Grandfather's watch, Cyril." It would be somehow so satisfactory.

Dear boy! What a blow his sweet, sympathetic little note had been! Of course they quite understood; but it was most unfortunate.

"It would have been such a point, having him," said Josephine. "And he would have enjoyed it so," said Constantia, not thinking what she was saying.

However, as soon as he got back he was coming to tea with his aunties. Cyril to tea was one of their rare treats.

"Now, Cyril, you mustn't be frightened of our cakes. Your Auntie Con and I bought them at Buszard's this morning. We know what a man's appetite is. So don't be ashamed of making a good tea."

Josephine cut recklessly into the rich dark cake that stood for her winter gloves or the soling and heeling of Constantia's only respectable shoes. But Cyril was most unmanlike in appetite.

"I say, Aunt Josephine, I simply can't. I've only just had lunch, you know."

"Oh, Cyril, that can't be true! It's after four," cried Josephine. Constantia sat with her knife poised over the chocolate-roll.

"It is, all the same," said Cyril. "I had to meet a man at Victoria, and he kept me hanging about till... there was only time to get lunch and to come on here. And he gave me—phew"—Cyril put his hand to his forehead—"a terrific blow-out," he said.

It was disappointing—today of all days. But still he couldn't be expected to know.

"But you'll have a meringue, won't you, Cyril?" said Aunt Josephine. "These meringues were bought specially for you. Your dear father was so fond of them. We were sure you are, too."

"I *am*, Aunt Josephine," cried Cyril ardently. "Do you mind if I take half to begin with?"

"Not at all, dear boy; but we mustn't let you off with that."

"Is your dear father still so fond of meringues?" asked Auntie Con gently. She winced faintly as she broke through the shell of hers.

"Well, I don't quite know, Auntie Con," said Cyril breezily.

At that they both looked up.

"Don't know?" almost snapped Josephine. "Don't know a thing like that about your own father, Cyril?"

"Surely," said Auntie Con softly.

Cyril tried to laugh it off. "Oh, well," he said, "it's such a long time since—" He faltered. He stopped. Their faces were too much for him.

"Even *so*," said Josephine.

And Auntie Con looked.

Cyril put down his teacup. "Wait a bit," he cried. "Wait a bit, Aunt Josephine. What am I thinking of?"

He looked up. They were beginning to brighten. Cyril slapped his knee.

"Of course," he said, "it was meringues. How could I have forgotten?

Yes, Aunt Josephine, you're perfectly right. Father's most frightfully keen on meringues."

They didn't only beam. Aunt Josephine went scarlet with pleasure; Auntie Con gave a deep, deep sigh.

"And now, Cyril, you must come and see father," said Josephine. "He knows you were coming today."

"Right," said Cyril, very firmly and heartily. He got up from his chair; suddenly he glanced at the clock.

"I say, Auntie Con, isn't your clock a bit slow? I've got to meet a man at—at Paddington just after five. I'm afraid I shan't be able to stay very long with grandfather."

"Oh, he won't expect you to stay *very* long!" said Aunt Josephine.

Constantia was still gazing at the clock. She couldn't make up her mind if it was fast or slow. It was one or the other, she felt almost certain of that. At any rate, it had been.

Cyril still lingered. "Aren't you coming along, Auntie Con?"

"Of course," said Josephine, "we shall all go. Come on, Con."

IX

They knocked at the door, and Cyril followed his aunts into grandfather's hot, sweetish room.

"Come on," said Grandfather Pinner. "Don't hang about. What is it? What've you been up to?"

He was sitting in front of a roaring fire, clasping his stick. He had a thick rug over his knees. On his lap there lay a beautiful pale yellow silk handkerchief.

"It's Cyril, father," said Josephine shyly. And she took Cyril's hand and led him forward.

"Good afternoon, Grandfather," said Cyril, trying to take his hand out of Aunt Josephine's. Grandfather Pinner shot his eyes at Cyril in the way he was famous for. Where was Auntie Con? She stood on the other side of Aunt Josephine; her long arms hung down in front of her; her hands were clasped. She never took her eyes off grandfather.

"Well," said Grandfather Pinner, beginning to thump, "what have you got to tell me?"

What had he, what had he got to tell him? Cyril felt himself smiling like a perfect imbecile. The room was stifling, too.

But Aunt Josephine came to his rescue. She cried brightly, "Cyril says his father is still very fond of meringues, Father dear."

"Eh?" said Grandfather Pinner, curving his hand like a purple meringue-shell over one ear.

Josephine repeated, "Cyril says his father is still very fond of meringues."

"Can't hear," said old Colonel Pinner. And he waved Josephine away with his stick, then pointed with his stick to Cyril. "Tell me what she's trying to say," he said.

(My God!) "Must I?" said Cyril, blushing and staring at Aunt Josephine.

"Do, dear," she smiled. "It will please him so much."

"Come on, out with it!" cried Colonel Pinner testily, beginning to thump again.

And Cyril leaned forward and yelled, "Father's still very fond of meringues."

At that Grandfather Pinner jumped as though he had been shot.

"Don't shout!" he cried. "What's the matter with the boy? *Meringues*! What about 'em?"

"Oh, Aunt Josephine, must we go on?" groaned Cyril desperately.

"It's quite all right, dear boy," said Aunt Josephine, as though he and she were at the dentist's together. "He'll understand in a minute." And she whispered to Cyril, "He's getting a bit deaf, you know." Then she leaned forward and really bawled at Grandfather Pinner, "Cyril only wanted to tell you, Father dear, that his father is still very fond of meringues."

Colonel Pinner heard that time, heard and brooded, looking Cyril up and down.

"What an esstrordinary thing!" said old Grandfather Pinner. "What an esstrordinary thing to come all this way here to tell me!"

And Cyril felt it *was*.

"Yes, I shall send Cyril the watch," said Josephine.

"That would be very nice," said Constantia. "I seem to remember last time he came there was some little trouble about the time."

X

They were interrupted by Kate bursting through the door in her usual fashion, as though she had discovered some secret panel in the wall.

"Fried or boiled?" asked the bold voice.

Fried or boiled? Josephine and Constantia were quite bewildered for the moment. They could hardly take it in.

"Fried or boiled what, Kate?" asked Josephine, trying to begin to concentrate.

Kate gave a loud sniff. "Fish."

"Well, why didn't you say so immediately?" Josephine reproached her gently. "How could you expect us to understand, Kate? There are a great many things in this world, you know, which are fried or boiled." And after such a display of courage she said quite brightly to Constantia, "Which do you prefer, Con?"

"I think it might be nice to have it fried," said Constantia. "On the other hand, of course, boiled fish is very nice. I think I prefer both equally well... Unless you... In that case—"

"I shall fry it," said Kate, and she bounced back, leaving their door open and slamming the door of her kitchen.

Josephine gazed at Constantia; she raised her pale eyebrows until they rippled away into her pale hair. She got up. She said in a very lofty, imposing way, "Do you mind following me into the drawing-room, Constantia? I've got something of great importance to discuss with you."

For it was always to the drawing-room they retired when they wanted to talk over Kate.

Josephine closed the door meaningly. "Sit down, Constantia," she said, still very grand. She might have been receiving Constantia for the first time. And Con looked round vaguely for a chair, as though she felt indeed quite a stranger.

"Now the question is," said Josephine, bending forward, "whether we shall keep her or not."

"That is the question," agreed Constantia.

"And this time," said Josephine firmly, "we must come to a definite decision."

Constantia looked for a moment as though she might begin going over all the other times, but she pulled herself together and said, "Yes, Jug."

"You see, Con," explained Josephine, "everything is so changed now." Constantia looked up quickly. "I mean," went on Josephine, "we're not dependent on Kate as we were." And she blushed faintly. "There's not father to cook for."

"That is perfectly true," agreed Constantia. "Father certainly doesn't want any cooking now whatever else—"

Josephine broke in sharply, "You're not sleepy, are you, Con?"

"Sleepy, Jug?" Constantia was wide-eyed.

"Well, concentrate more," said Josephine sharply, and she returned to the subject. "What it comes to is, if we did"—and this she barely breathed, glancing at the door—"give Kate notice"—she raised her voice again—"we could manage our own food."

"Why not?" cried Constantia. She couldn't help smiling. The idea was so exciting. She clasped her hands. "What should we live on, Jug?"

"Oh, eggs in various forms!" said Jug, lofty again. "And, besides, there are all the cooked foods."

"But I've always heard," said Constantia, "they are considered so very expensive."

"Not if one buys them in moderation," said Josephine. But she tore herself away from this fascinating bypath and dragged Constantia after her.

"What we've got to decide now, however, is whether we really do trust Kate or not."

Constantia leaned back. Her flat little laugh flew from her lips.

"Isn't it curious, Jug," said she, "that just on this one subject I've never been able to quite make up my mind?"

XI

She never had. The whole difficulty was to prove anything. How did one prove things, how could one? Suppose Kate had stood in front of her and deliberately made a face. Mightn't she very well have been in pain? Wasn't it impossible, at any rate, to ask Kate if she was making a face at her? If Kate answered "No"—and, of course, she would say "No"— what a position! How undignified! Then, again, Constantia suspected, she was almost certain that Kate went to her chest of drawers when she and Josephine were out, not to take things but to spy. Many times she had come back to find her amethyst cross in the most unlikely places, under her lace ties or on top of her evening Bertha. More than once she had laid a trap for Kate. She had arranged things in a special order and then called Josephine to witness.

"You see, Jug?"

"Quite, Con."

"Now we shall be able to tell."

But, oh dear, when she did go to look, she was as far off from a proof as ever! If anything was displaced, it might so very well have happened as she closed the drawer; a jolt might have done it so easily.

"You come, Jug, and decide. I really can't. It's too difficult."

But after a pause and a long glare Josephine would sigh, "Now you've put the doubt into my mind, Con, I'm sure I can't tell myself."

"Well, we can't postpone it again," said Josephine. "If we postpone it this time—"

XII

But at that moment in the street below a barrel-organ struck up. Josephine and Constantia sprang to their feet together.

"Run, Con," said Josephine. "Run quickly. There's sixpence on the—"

Then they remembered. It didn't matter. They would never have to stop the organ-grinder again. Never again would she and Constantia be told to make that monkey take his noise somewhere else. Never would sound that loud, strange bellow when father thought they were not hurrying enough. The organ-grinder might play there all day and the stick would not thump.

It never will thump again,

It never will thump again,

played the barrel-organ.

What was Constantia thinking? She had such a strange smile; she looked different. She couldn't be going to cry.

"Jug, Jug," said Constantia softly, pressing her hands together. "Do you know what day it is? It's Saturday. It's a week today, a whole week."

A week since father died,

A week since father died,

cried the barrel-organ. And Josephine, too, forgot to be practical and sensible; she smiled faintly, strangely. On the Indian carpet there fell a square of sunlight, pale red; it came and went and came—and stayed, deepened—until it shone almost golden.

"The sun's out," said Josephine, as though it really mattered.

A perfect fountain of bubbling notes shook from the barrel-organ, round, bright notes, carelessly scattered. Constantia lifted her big, cold hands as if to catch them, and then her hands fell again. She walked over to the mantelpiece to her favourite Buddha. And the stone and gilt image, whose smile always gave her such a queer feeling, almost a pain and yet a pleasant pain, seemed today to be more than smiling. He knew something; he had a secret. "I know something that you don't know," said her Buddha. Oh, what was it, what could it be? And yet she had always felt there was… something.

The sunlight pressed through the windows, thieved its way in, flashed its light over the furniture and the photographs. Josephine watched it. When it came to mother's photograph, the enlargement over the piano, it lingered as though puzzled to find so little remained of mother, except the ear-rings shaped like tiny pagodas and a black feather boa. Why did the photographs of dead people always fade so? wondered Josephine. As soon as a person was dead their photograph died too. But, of course, this one of mother was very old. It was thirty-five years old. Josephine remembered standing on a chair and pointing out that feather boa to Constantia and telling her that it was a snake that had killed their mother in Ceylon... Would everything have been different if mother hadn't died? She didn't see why. Aunt Florence had lived with them until they had left school, and they had moved three times and had their yearly holiday and... and there'd been changes of servants, of course.

Some little sparrows, young sparrows they sounded, chirped on the window-ledge. *Yeep–eyeep–yeep.* But Josephine felt they were not sparrows, not on the window-ledge. It was inside her, that queer little crying noise. *Yeep–eyeep–yeep.* Ah, what was it crying, so weak and forlorn?

If mother had lived, might they have married? But there had been nobody for them to marry. There had been father's Anglo-Indian friends before he quarrelled with them. But after that she and Constantia never met a single man except clergymen. How did one meet men? Or even if they'd met them, how could they have got to know men well enough to be more than strangers? One read of people having adventures, being followed, and so on. But nobody had ever followed Constantia and her. Oh yes, there had been one year at Eastbourne a mysterious man at their boarding-house who had put a note on the jug of hot water outside their bedroom door! But by the time Connie had found it the steam had made the writing too faint to read; they couldn't even make out to which of them it was addressed. And he had left next day. And that was all. The rest had been looking after father and at the same time keeping out of father's way. But now? But now? The thieving sun touched Josephine gently. She lifted her face. She was drawn over to the window by gentle beams.

Until the barrel-organ stopped playing Constantia stayed before the Buddha, wondering, but not as usual, not vaguely. This time her wonder was like longing. She remembered the times she had come in here, crept out of bed in her nightgown when the moon was full, and lain on the floor with her arms outstretched, as though she was crucified. Why? The big, pale moon had made her do it. The horrible dancing figures on the carved screen had leered at her and she hadn't minded. She remembered too how, whenever they were at the seaside, she had gone off by herself and got as close to the sea as she could, and sung something, something she had made up, while she gazed all over that restless water. There had been this other life, running out, bringing things home in bags, getting things on approval, discussing them with Jug, and taking them back to get more things on approval, and arranging father's trays and trying not to annoy father. But it all seemed to have happened in a kind of tunnel. It wasn't real. It was only when she came out of the tunnel into the moonlight or by the sea or into a thunderstorm that she really felt herself. What did it mean? What was it she was always wanting? What did it all lead to? Now? Now?

She turned away from the Buddha with one of her vague gestures. She went over to where Josephine was standing. She wanted to say something to Josephine, something frightfully important, about—about the future and what…

"Don't you think perhaps—" she began.

But Josephine interrupted her. "I was wondering if now—" she murmured. They stopped; they waited for each other.

"Go on, Con," said Josephine.

"No, no, Jug; after you," said Constantia.

"No, say what you were going to say. You began," said Josephine.

"I… I'd rather hear what you were going to say first," said Constantia.

"Don't be absurd, Con."

"Really, Jug."

"Connie!"

"Oh, *Jug!*"

A pause. Then Constantia said faintly, "I can't say what I was going to say, Jug, because I've forgotten what it was... that I was going to say."

Josephine was silent for a moment. She stared at a big cloud where the sun had been. Then she replied shortly, "I've forgotten too."

THE 40-LITRE MONKEY

Adam Marek

Adam Marek (1974–) is an award-winning British short story writer. He won the 2011 Arts Foundation Short Story Fellowship, and was shortlisted for the inaugural *Sunday Times* EFG Short Story Award and the Edge Hill Short Story Prize. His stories have appeared on BBC Radio 4, and in many magazines and anthologies, including *Prospect* and *The Sunday Times Magazine*, and *The Penguin Book of the British Short Story*. His short story collections *The Stone Thrower* and *Instruction Manual for Swallowing* are published by Comma Press.

I once met a man with a forty-litre monkey. He measured all his animals by volume. His Dalmatian was small, only eighteen litres, but his cat, a Prussian Blue, was huge — five litres, when most cats are three. He owned a pet shop just off Portobello Road. I needed a new pet for my girlfriend because our last two had just killed each other.

'The ideal pet,' the owner told me, 'is twelve litres. That makes them easy enough to pick up, but substantial enough for romping without risk of injury. What did you have?'

'A gecko,' I replied. 'I guess he was about half a pint.'

'You use imperial?' The man smirked and gestured towards a large vivarium in the corner. 'Iguana,' he said. 'Six litres, and still growing.'

'Oh right,' I said. 'I also had a cat. She must have been four litres, maybe more.'

'Are you sure?' he asked. 'Was she a longhair, because they look big, but when you dunk them they're small, like skinny rats.'

'She was a short hair,' I said.

'How old?'

'Four.'

'That volume would have dropped anyway, unless you mixed tripe with her food. Did you do that?'

'No,' I said. 'She ate tuna fish.'

'No pet ever got voluminous eating tuna,' he smiled, almost sympathetic.

'What's the biggest thing you've got?' I asked.

'That would have to be my forty-litre monkey,' he smiled.

'May I see it?'

'You doubt my veracity?'

'Not at all. Is it a secret monkey?'

'No, he's not a secret monkey. I've shown him in South America, Russia, and most of Western Europe.'

'What sort of monkey is it?'

'He is a baboon,' he said, raising his eyebrows.

'A baboon? What do they usually scale in at?'

'Twenty-three litres.'

'How did yours get so big?'

'I won't tell you. Have you any idea how many thirty-litre monkeys I got through before I hit on the right combination?'

I shrugged my shoulders. The man rubbed his brow between his thumb and forefinger, as if wondering why he was even talking to me, the owner of a dead half-pint gecko. I was getting claustrophobic and started to leave, when he grabbed my arm and said, 'Would you like to see my monkey?'

I nodded that I would. He locked the front door and led me up a narrow staircase. Names were written on every step, and alongside, a volume: Edgar 29 litres; Wallace 32 litres; Merian 34 litres. Also on every step were paper bags of feed, books and files, stacked up against the wall, so that I had to put each foot directly in front of the other to walk up, and I kept catching my ankle with the edge of my heel.

'So how did your pets die, anyway?' the man asked.

'The cat managed to slide the door of the gecko's tank open. She tried to eat him whole, and he stuck in her throat.'

'Hmph,' the man laughed.

The man took me to a door, which was covered in stickers of various animal organisations I'd never heard of: Big Possums of Australasia, American Tiny Titans. The door had a keypad, which he shielded with one hand as he punched the code with the other. A pungent stench of meat and straw and bleach poured out of the room, and I heard a soft sucking noise, like air drawn into a broken vacuum, but I may have imagined this.

Being in the room felt like being suffocated in an armpit. Something was shuffling about in a cage in the corner, grunting softly. The perimeter of the room was like the staircase, with books, files and bags of dried food-stuffs piled up the walls. The floor was covered in black linoleum, and the section in front of the door was rough with thousands of scratches. Opposite the door was an archway, which led into a bright bathroom. He had a huge glass tank in there with units of measurement running up the sides and extra marks and comments written in marker pen.

'He's over there,' the man said. 'Stay here, and I'll let him out.'

'Does he bite?' I asked.

'Not any more.'

The man took a key from his back pocket, which was attached to a chain and belt loop. The lock undid with a satisfying click. He opened the cage door a little and crouched in front. He whispered something to the baboon, but I couldn't hear what he said. He nodded his head, as if receiving a response from the monkey, then moved back, staying in his crouched position.

The bad air in the room was making me feel sick.

'Why is it so dark in here?' I asked.

'Light makes him too active. He burns off all that volume when the light's on,' he replied.

The man stayed crouched down, and began to bob his backside up and down, as if he were rubbing an itch up against a tree. He patted the floor with his hands, staring all the while into the cage.

A shape shuffled out. I'd never seen a regular-size baboon, so had no point of reference for his size, but he was big, big and greasy.

'Why is his fur all slicked down like that?' I asked. 'Vaseline,' the man replied. 'Baboon hair is slightly absorbent. If he soaks up water that makes less volume.'

'So you grease him up to make him waterproof?'

'Yes.'

'Is that legal?'

The man looked at me like I was an idiot.

The baboon came further out of the cage. The man put something in his own mouth. The baboon shifted back nervously at first, but then skipped in and took the food from his lips. He looked at me while he ate. His face seemed to be saying, 'I know I look ridiculous, but if you say anything, I'll pull your arm off.'

'What's his name?' I asked.

'Don't speak so loudly,' he whisper-spat. 'He's called Cooper.'

'So what's next,' I asked. 'A fifty-litre monkey?'

'You can't get a baboon that size. Not without steroids.'

'Do they make monkey steroids?'

'Are you mocking me?' The man stood up. The baboon raised his arms and hooted. The man squatted down again and bowed his head, looking back at me and suggesting I do the same.

I squatted down. The smell became worse. It hung near the floor like a fog.

'Do many people do this, grow big monkeys, I mean?'

'Not many. In this country anyway.'

'How many would you say there are around the world?'

'It's hard to say,' the man said. 'Not everyone competes, but there are about sixty regulars I guess.'

'And is this a record monkey?'

'By half a litre.'

'So have you got like an arch rival? An enemy monkey grower?' I couldn't help smiling when I said this. The man seemed to be having a crisis. He didn't know whether to be angry, or to be excited. I think this must have been the first time anyone had wanted to see his monkey.

'There's a guy from Thailand. He claimed he had a forty-three-litre monkey, but he'd put putty in its armpits and stuffed golfballs up its bum.'

'You're kidding.'

'It's quite common. They're a lot stricter about it now though.'

The baboon settled close to the man and allowed him to stroke its greasy head.

'Who's they?' I asked. 'Is there some kind of governing body?'

'Yes, the BMG.'

'What's that stand for, the Big Monkey Group?' I laughed.

'Yes. They're a part of the Big Animal Group. People compete with almost every animal you could think of. I specialise in baboons, but I dabble in cats and guinea pigs too. They're cheaper to transport long distance, and they take less time to grow.'

I was glad that it was dark because my eyes were watering.

'Do you want me to measure him?' the man asked.

'What, now? In the tank?'

The man nodded.

'No, don't worry. You're okay. I wouldn't want to get Cooper all wet for nothing.'

'It's no trouble.'

'No really. It's fine,' I said.

'But how do you know I'm not lying to you?'

'I trust you.'

'Would you know a forty-litre monkey when you saw one?'

'No, but at a guess, I'm sure that he's about…'

'Not about. Exactly. He's exactly forty litres. I'll show you.'

The man scooped Cooper up in his arms. The baboon wrapped his long arms around the man's neck. His blue shirt became smeared with Vaseline.

'It's really okay. I believe you,' I said.

The man ignored me and went into the bathroom. He pointed to the water level, which was exactly on the zero position, and then lowered the monkey in. I expected him to freak out, but instead, he went limp, as if dead.

'How come he's like that?' I asked.

'If he moved around, he might splash water out of the tank. Instant disqualification. Getting them to be still can be even harder than getting them large,' he said.

Cooper grasped the man's index fingers and remained still as the water covered his throat, his mouth, and then his whole head. When the water level cut a line across the baboon's forearms, the man let him go. Cooper pulled his arms down below the surface. The water made a soft plopping sound. The man ducked down to look at the monkey through the tank. He clapped his hands twice, and Cooper stuck his arms out to either side, pressing against the glass and holding himself below the water.

His hair stayed flat against his body. Air bubbles clung to the corners of his eyes and to his nostrils. His black-ringed eyes darted around while his head stayed still, as if the monkey was just a suit, and there was something alive inside it, something that didn't like water.

'There, you see?' the man said.

I looked at the water level. 'It says thirty-nine,' I said.

'Don't be stupid,' he snapped, but then he looked at the meniscus and gasped. It was a sound of pain, of betrayal. His intake of breath and the way he stared at the baboon were loaded with hurt.

The baboon stayed beneath the surface of the water. The man looked him up and down and around the tank, looking for a reason for the reading. He walked around the tank, looking for spilt water.

'Is he waiting for some kind of signal to come up?' I asked. Cooper's eyes were frantic.

The man ignored me, still trying to see a reason why the reading would be low. He scrambled around the tank, his hands wrestling each other.

'Should I clap or something?' I asked.

The man looked at me, and then at the monkey, and clapped twice. The baboon let go of the sides of the tank and rose up. His head broke the surface and he wheezed for breath, panic over his face, as if he knew he was guilty of something awful.

The man grabbed his wrists and dragged him out. He was being much less delicate with Cooper than before he went in the tank.

'What did you do?' he snapped. 'What did you do?' The baboon shook some of the water off of his oiled skin. 'Did you make yourself sick?'

'Bastard monkey,' he spat.

'Surely it's not his fault,' I said.

'Oh, you think?' The man smiled, and then turned nasty. 'What the hell do you know about monkeys, huh?'

I shrugged my shoulders, and the man turned his attention back to the monkey. He dropped Cooper to the ground, and the baboon bounded across the room. The man muttered to himself as he grabbed a paper sack from the floor. He poured something that looked like muesli into a bowl, and then squeezed a bright yellow liquid over it. He dumped the bowl on the floor while he used both hands to unscrew a large tub, out of which he scooped two spoonfuls of a gelatinous substance. He mixed this into the bowl, all the while muttering to himself. He took the bowl to a cabinet, which was full of droppers and bottles like a medicine cabinet. He put drops of this in and a sprinkling of that, and popped a capsule of something else in, then stirred it all up and slid it across the floor to the baboon.

The baboon looked at the bowl, and then at the man. He turned away and slunk into the cage.

'Oh, you're not hungry,' he said. 'Maybe you're happy being a thirty-nine litre monkey? Is that what you're telling me? Why are you doing this?'

The man looked like he was caught between crying and bleeding from his ears.

'I should probably go,' I said. 'Thanks for showing me your monkey.'

'Is that some kind of joke?' The man turned to me. 'Thanks for showing me your thirty-nine-litre monkey? Is that what you're trying to say?' His fists were bunched.

'I'm not trying to say anything. I think you've got a lovely monkey, whatever volume he is.'

I don't know what I'd said to him, but he went crazy. His face flushed bright red and the tendons in his neck went taut. He actually reached his arms out towards me and stretched his fingers, as if he were going to strangle me. I backed away towards the door, preparing myself to sprint.

But then a cloud seemed to pass behind his eyes. He began tapping the side of his left palm and whispering to himself. And this had an immediate calming effect. He took a deep breath.

'I apologise for displaying inappropriate emotion,' he said.

'That's… okay,' I said.

The man locked up Cooper's cage, shoulders hunched, and his posture repentant. He spoke to Cooper in a soft voice. I could not hear the words, or see the baboon's face, but the shuffling sounds in the cage calmed, giving me the impression that they were making their peace. 'Let us sort out a new pet for your girlfriend,' the man said as he stood up and ushered me to the door, huffing air through his nose.

The air in the shop, which had been thick when I first entered, was fresh compared to the poisonous fug of Cooper's room. 'Look around,' he said. 'I'll give you a very good deal.'

I paced around the shop, sidestepping to get through the tight spaces between display shelves, and looked at the eyes of cockatoos and kittens and rabbits and snakes. Nothing made an impression on me. My mind was blank. I couldn't shake the image from my head of Cooper beneath the water, his hands pressed against the glass sides of the tank.

'I don't know,' I said. 'You're the expert. What do you think my girl-friend would like?'

At this, the muscular plates of his face slid around an expression of pure delight. 'Yes. Yes!' He said, jabbing a triumphant finger into the air. 'I have it.' And he went through a beaded curtain into a back room, coming back moments later with a small cage covered in a thick, dark cloth.

The man lifted up the corner of the cloth and urged me to peer inside. I could see nothing in there at first, but as I pressed my nose against the metal bars, my eyes adjusted and I could see, sat on a smooth branch, a small possum-like creature. Its long tail was wrapped around the branch, and as I inhaled, it turned its enormous eyes to me.

'Wow,' I said. 'What is it?'

'She is a Madagascan nightingale lemur. Very rare. At dusk, she sings a song that would send lions to sleep.'

'That's perfect,' I said. 'Thank you.'

We were discussing the price, when the man put one palm up in the air, and the index finger of his other hand to his lips. 'Wait,' he said. 'Do you hear that? She is about to start singing.'

LA BAMBA HOT LINE

Bobbie Ann Mason

Bobbie Ann Mason (1940–) is an American novelist and short story writer. Her first short stories were published in *The New Yorker* in the 1980s and she has published two novels, *In Country* and *The Girl in the Blue Beret*. Her memoir, *Clear Springs*, about an American farm family throughout the twentieth century, was a finalist for the Pulitzer prize.

"Hello. La Bamba Hot Line."

"Is it true that 'La Bamba' is derived from the Icelandic Younger Edda, set to music by Spanish sailors and transported via the Caribbean to America in 1665?"

"No, not even close. La Bamba Hot Line. Go ahead, please."

"When is the next Louie Louie Parade scheduled?"

"You want the Louie Louie Hot Line. This is the La Bamba Hot Line."

"Oh."

"La Bamba Hot Line."

"This is Senator Sethspeaks in Washington, on the Committee for the Investigation of Obscene Rock Lyrics."

"State your business, please."

"Uh—I was wondering, just what are the words to 'La Bamba'?"

"Do you have the record?"

"Yes, I do."

"Well, listen to it."

"But I can't tell if the words are obscene or not."

"That's your problem. La Bamba Hot Line."

"My teen-age daughter has been acting funny lately. She refuses to eat, and she has frown lines on her face. She's become aggressive with her parrot and when you talk to her she just says everything is geeky. The doctor can't find anything wrong with her. What should I do?"

"I'm glad you asked. The La Bamba Hot Line has a special pamphlet dealing with problems of teen-agers. Just send a self-addressed stamped envelope to La Bamba Hot Line, P.O. Box 4700. But first, I'd have a heart-to-heart with that parrot."

"Much obliged."

"Likewise, I'm sure. La Bamba Hot Line."

"This is Phil Donahue. Is it true that the La Bamba Hot Line is having a lip-sync contest?"

"Absolutely. October the ninth."

"What do I have to do to win?"

"What do you think? Perform 'La Bamba' till your eyes bug out, do it like a rockin' fool, blow the house down."

"Do you think I've got a chance?"

"Everybody has a chance in life, Mr. Donahue."

You wouldn't believe the stuff I get on the La Bamba Hot Line. I work twelve to four. It's an intensive job and can burn you out quick. Two short breaks, while all the calls stack up. They get a message, "All the La Bamba Hot Lines are temporarily busy. Please try again." It's unfair that people have to keep calling and calling, dialling till their nails split in order to get the La Bamba Hot Line. We need help! We need somebody to handle the genuine emergencies, weed out the crazies. The things people want to know; they want to know are they going to get cancer, will the plane they have a ticket on for tomorrow crash, which stores are giving double coupons this week? We try to answer what we can, but I mean we're not God. I tell them play "La Bamba" thirty-two times in a dark room, then improvise thirty-two versions, then listen to it standing on their head. I tell them to walk down the street muttering

"*Yo no soy marinero/Soy capitán.*" Count the number of people who recognize the lines and multiply by four, and whatever number that is, that's Ollie North's secret Swiss bank account. I mean, some things are so simple you wonder why anybody would bother calling up. We deal with a lot of that. Little kids call just to be funny, try to catch us off guard. Is your refrigerator running, that kind of thing. I'm on to them. I start screaming a wild, cacophonous sort of schizo "La Bamba." Blows them right out of the water.

But mostly it's scholars. Academic stuff. People wanting to know about roots, symbolism, the double-entendre of the *marinero/capitán* lines, etc. Idea stuff. I spend my mornings at the library just to stay even with these people. Man, they're sharp. One guy had a beaut—a positive beaut. The way he traced the Paul-is-dead hoax back to the lost Shakespearean sonnets, twisting it around and back through "Poor Ritchie's Almanac" straight up to the chord progressions of "La Bamba"—it was breathtaking. The switchboard was lit up like the stars in the open desert sky on a clear night while I listened and kept all those calls on hold. I was humbled right to my knees. Unfortunately, his spiel didn't get recorded and I didn't get the guy's name. But he'll call again. I'm sure he will.

Some of the ideas that come in are just junk, of course. Did Idi Amin record "La Bamba"? Of course not. But former President Jimmy Carter did. Some stuff you hear is so unbelievable. No, the Voyager is not carrying "La Bamba" out to the end of the universe. Don't I wish. That's sort of my job really, to carry "La Bamba" to the end of the universe.

My boyfriend is giving me a hard time. He says I take my work too seriously. We'll be watching "Washington Week in Review" and I'll say, "Look at those guys. Talk about serious. Don't they ever get down?" He says, "All day it's your La Bamba duties, your La Bamba research, your La Bamba outfits. You go off in the morning with your La Bamba briefcase. When are we ever going to talk about us?"

He says, "This La Bamba thing is going to blow over any minute. It may be blown over by Friday. Things are that fast these days."

"Don't say that!" I cry. "Buddy Holly. 'American Pie.' The Big Bopper. Elvis. Things last longer than you think."

We're going through crisis time, I guess. But we'll work it out. I have faith in that. Right now, my work is at a critical juncture. I'm talking demographics. Market potentializing. La Bamba aerobics, theme weddings, instructional software. We were represented at the harmonic convergence. We met on the boardwalk at Atlantic City, an overflow crowd of La Bamba regulars. We played the song over and over and concentrated on fibre optics, sending our vibes out all over the universe.

The special thing is, my boyfriend can sing "La Bamba." He's not allowed to enter the lip-sync contest because it would be sort of a conflict of interest. He doesn't just lip-sync. He sings it a cappella. He sounds so sincere when he sings it. He makes up the words—he's not a purist—but they sound right; he has the right tune. That is the secret of "La Bamba," inventing it as you go along. That is the true soul of La Bamba. La Bamba lives.

THE VERGER

W. Somerset Maugham

William Somerset Maugham (1874–1965) trained and qualified as a physician but, following the success of his first novel in 1897, he gave up medicine to write full time. One of the most successful writers of the twentieth century, his novels include *Of Human Bondage*, *The Moon and Sixpence* and *The Painted Veil*, and he also wrote a number of short story collections and plays. In 1947 he founded a prize in his name awarded to the best British writer under thirty-five.

There had been a christening that afternoon at St Peter's, Neville Square, and Albert Edward Foreman still wore his verger's gown. He kept his new one, its folds as full and stiff as though it were made not of alpaca but of perennial bronze, for funerals and weddings (St Peter's, Neville Square, was a church much favoured by the fashionable for these ceremonies) and now he wore only his second-best. He wore it with complacence, for it was the dignified symbol of his office, and without it (when he took it off to go home) he had the disconcerting sensation of being somewhat insufficiently clad. He took pains with it; he pressed it and ironed it himself. During the sixteen years he had been verger of this church he had had a succession of such gowns, but he had never been able to throw them away when they were worn out and the complete series, neatly wrapped up in brown paper, lay in the bottom drawers of the wardrobe in his bedroom.

The verger busied himself quietly, replacing the painted wooden cover on the marble font, taking away a chair that had been brought for an infirm old lady, and waited for the vicar to have finished in the vestry so that he could tidy up in there and go home. Presently he saw him walk across the chancel, genuflect in front of the high altar, and come down the aisle; but he still wore his cassock.

'What's he 'anging about for?' the verger said to himself. 'Don't'e know I want my tea?'

The vicar had been but recently appointed, a red-faced energetic man in the early forties, and Albert Edward still regretted his predecessor, a clergyman of the old school who preached leisurely sermons in a silvery voice and dined out a great deal with his more aristocratic parishioners. He liked things in church to be just so, but he never fussed; he was not like this new man who wanted to have his finger in every pie. But Albert Edward was tolerant. St Peter's was in a very good neighbourhood and the parishioners were a very nice class of people. The new vicar had come from the East End and he couldn't be expected to fall in all at once with the discreet ways of his fashionable congregation.

'All this 'ustle.' said Albert Edward. 'But give 'im time, he'll learn.'

When the vicar had walked down the aisle so far that he could address the verger without raising his voice more than was becoming in a place of worship he stopped.

'Foreman, will you come into the vestry for a minute. I have something to say to you.'

'Very good, sir.'

The vicar waited for him to come up and they walked up the church together.

'A very nice christening, I thought, sir. Funny 'ow the baby stopped cryin' the moment you took him.'

'I've noticed they very often do,' said the vicar, with a little smile. 'After all I've had a good deal of practice with them.'

It was a source of subdued pride to him that he could nearly always quiet a whimpering infant by the manner in which he held it and he was not unconscious of the amused admiration with which mothers and nurses watched him settle the baby in the crook of his surpliced arm. The verger knew that it pleased him to be complimented on his talent.

The vicar preceded Albert Edward into the vestry. Albert Edward was a trifle surprised to find the two churchwardens there. He had not seen them come in. They gave him pleasant nods.

'Good afternoon, my lord. Good afternoon, sir,' he said to one after the other.

They were elderly men, both of them, and they had been church-wardens almost as long as Albert Edward had been verger. They were sitting now at a handsome refectory table that the old vicar had brought many years before from Italy and the vicar sat down in the vacant chair between them. Albert Edward faced them, the table between him and them, and wondered with slight uneasiness what was the matter. He remembered still the occasion on which the organist had got into trouble and the bother they had all had to hush things up. In a church like St Peter's, Neville Square, they couldn't afford a scandal. On the vicar's red face was a look of resolute benignity, but the others bore an expression that was slightly troubled.

'He's been naggin' them, he 'as,' said the verger to himself. 'He's jock-eyed them into doin' something, but they don't 'alf like it. That's what it is, you mark my words.'

But his thoughts did not appear on Albert Edward's clean-cut and distinguished features. He stood in a respectful but not obsequious attitude. He had been in service before he was appointed to his ecclesi-astical office, but only in very good houses, and his deportment was irreproachable. Starting as a page-boy in the household of a merchant prince, he had risen by due degrees from the position of fourth to first footman, for a year he had been single-handed butler to a widowed peeress, and, till the vacancy occurred at St Peter's, butler with two men under him in the house of a retired ambassador. He was tall, spare, grave, and dignified. He looked, if not like a duke, at least like an actor of the old school who specialized in dukes' parts. He had tact, firmness, and self-assurance. His character was unimpeachable.

The vicar began briskly.

'Foreman, we've got something rather unpleasant to say to you.

You've been here a great many years and I think his lordship and the general agree with me that you've fulfilled the duties of your office to the satisfaction of everybody concerned.'

The two churchwardens nodded.

'But a most extraordinary circumstance came to my knowledge the other day and I felt it my duty to impart it to the churchwardens. I discovered to my astonishment that you could neither read nor write.'

The verger's face betrayed no sign of embarrassment.

'The last vicar knew that, sir,' he replied. 'He said it didn't make no difference. He always said there was a great deal too much education in the world for 'is taste.'

'It's the most amazing thing I ever heard,' cried the general. 'Do you mean to say that you've been verger of this church for sixteen years and never learned to read or write.'

'I went into service when I was twelve, sir. The cook in the first place tried to teach me once, but I didn't seem to 'ave the knack for it, and then what with one thing and another I never seemed to 'ave the time. I've never really found the want of it. I think a lot of these young fellows waste a rare lot of time readin' when they might be doin' something useful.'

'But don't you want to know the news? said the other churchwarden. 'Don't you ever want to write a letter?'

'No, me lord, I seem to manage very well without. And of late years now they've all these pictures in the papers I get to know what's goin' on pretty well. Me wife's quite a scholar and if I want to write a letter she writes it for me. It's not as if I was a bettin' man.' The two churchwardens gave the vicar a troubled glance and then looked down at the table.

'Well, Foreman, I've talked the matter over with these gentlemen and they quite agree with me that the situation is impossible. At a church like St Peter's, Neville Square, we cannot have a verger who can neither read nor write.'

Albert Edward's thin, sallow face reddened and he moved uneasily on his feet, but he made no reply.

'Understand me, Foreman, I have no complaint to make against you.

You do your work quite satisfactorily; I have the highest opinion both of your character and of your capacity; but we haven't the right to take the risk of some accident that might happen owing to your lamentable ignorance. It's a matter of prudence as well as of principle.'

'But couldn't you learn, Foreman? asked the general.

'No, sir, I'm afraid I couldn't, not now. You see, I'm not as young as I was and if I couldn't seem able to get the letters in me 'ead when I was a nipper I don't think there's much chance of it now.'

'We don't want to be harsh with you, Foreman,' said the vicar. 'But the churchwardens and I have quite made up our minds. We'll give you three months and if at the end of that time you cannot read and write I'm afraid you'll have to go.'

Albert Edward had never liked the new vicar. He'd said from the beginning that they'd made a mistake when they gave him St Peter's. He wasn't the type of man they wanted with a classy congregation like that. And now he straightened himself a little. He knew his value and he wasn't going to allow himself to be put upon. 'I'm very sorry, sir. I'm afraid it's no good. I'm too old a dog to learn new tricks. I've lived a good many years without knowin' 'ow to read and write, and without wishin' to praise myself, self praise is no recommendation, I don't mind sayin' I've done my duty in that state of life in which it 'as pleased a merciful providence to place me, and if I could learn now I don't know as I'd want to.'

'In that case. Foreman, I'm afraid you must go.'

'Yes, sir, I quite understand. I shall be 'appy to 'and in my resignation as soon as you've found somebody to take my place.'

But when Albert Edward with his usual politeness had closed the church door behind the vicar and the two churchwardens he could not sustain the air of unruffled dignity with which he had borne the blow inflicted upon him and his lips quivered. He walked slowly back to the vestry and hung up on its proper peg his verger's gown. He sighed as he thought of all the grand funerals and smart weddings it had seen. He tidied everything up, put on his coat, and hat in hand walked down the aisle. He locked the church door behind him. He strolled across the square, but deep in his sad thoughts he did not take the street that led him home, where a nice strong cup of tea awaited him; he took the wrong turning. He walked slowly along. His heart was heavy. He did not know what he should do with himself. He did not fancy the notion of going back to domestic service; after being his own master for so many years, for the vicar and churchwardens could say what they liked, it was he that had run St Peter's, Neville Square, he could scarcely demean himself by accepting a situation. He had saved a tidy sum, but not enough to live on without doing something, and life seemed to cost more every year. He had never thought to be troubled with such questions. The vergers of St Peter's, like the popes of Rome, were there for life. He had often thought of the pleasant reference the vicar would make in his sermon at even-song the first Sunday after his death to the long and faithful service, and the exemplary character of their late verger, Albert Edward Foreman. He sighed deeply. Albert Edward was a non-smoker and a total abstainer, but with a certain latitude; that is to say he liked a glass of beer with his dinner and when he was tired he enjoyed a cigarette. It occurred to him now that one would comfort him and since he did not carry them he looked about him for a shop where he could buy a packet of Gold Flake. He did not at once see one and walked on a little. It was a long street, with all sorts of shops in it, but there was not a single one where you could buy cigarettes.

'That's strange,' said Albert Edward.

To make sure he walked right up the street again. No, there was no doubt about it.

He stopped and looked reflectively up and down.

'I can't be the only man as walks along this street and wants a fag,' he said. 'I shouldn't wonder but what a fellow might do very well with a little shop here. Tobacco and sweets, you know.'

He gave a sudden start.

'That's an idea,' he said. 'Strange 'ow things come to you when you least expect it.'

'You're very silent this afternoon, Albert,' his wife remarked.

'I'm thinkin',' he said.

He considered the matter from every point of view and next day he went along the street and by good luck found a little shop to let that looked as though it would exactly suit him. Twenty-four hours later he had taken it, and when a month after that he left St Peter's, Neville Square, for ever, Albert Edward Foreman set up in business as a tobacconist and newsagent. His wife said it was a dreadful come-down after being verger of St Peter's, but he answered that you had to move with the times, the church wasn't what it was, and 'enceforward he was going to render unto Caesar what was Caesar's. Albert Edward did very well. He did so well that in a year or so it struck him that he might take a second shop and put a manager in. He looked for another long street that hadn't got a tobacconist in it and when he found it, and a shop to let, took it and stocked it. This was a success too. Then it occurred to him that if he could run two he could run half a dozen, so he began walking about London, and whenever he found a long street that had no tobacconist and a shop to let he took it. In the course of ten years he had acquired no less than ten shops and he was making money hand over fist. He went round to all of them himself every Monday, collected the week's takings, and took them to the bank.

One morning when he was there paying in a bundle of notes and a heavy bag of silver the cashier told him that the manager would like to see him. He was shown into an office and the manager shook hands with him.

'Mr Foreman, I wanted to have a talk to you about the money you've got on deposit with us. D'you know exactly how much it is?'

'Not within a pound or two, sir; but I've got a pretty rough idea.'

'Apart from what you paid in this morning it's a little over thirty thousand pounds. That's a very large sum to have on deposit and I should have thought you'd do better to invest it.'

'I wouldn't want to take no risk, sir. I know it's safe in the bank.'

'You needn't have the least anxiety. We'll make you out a list of absolutely gilt-edged securities. They'll bring you in a better rate of interest than we can possibly afford to give you.'

A troubled look settled on Mr Foreman's distinguished face. 'I've never 'ad anything to do with stocks and shares and I'd 'ave to leave it all in your 'ands,' he said.

The manager smiled. 'We'll do everything. All you'll have to do next time you come in is just to sign the transfers.'

'I could do that all right,' said Albert uncertainly. 'But 'ow should I know what I was signin'?'

'I suppose you can read,' said the manager a trifle sharply.

Mr Foreman gave him a disarming smile.

'Well, sir, that's just it. I can't. I know it sounds funny-like, but there it is, I can't read or write, only me name, an' I only learnt to do that when I went into business.'

The manager was so surprised that he jumped up from his chair.

'That's the most extraordinary thing I ever heard.'

'You see, it's like this, sir, I never 'ad the opportunity until it was too late and then some'ow I wouldn't. I got obstinate-like.'

The manager stared at him as though he were a prehistoric monster.

'And do you mean to say that you've built up this important business and amassed a fortune of thirty thousand pounds without being able to read or write? Good God, man, what would you be now if you had been able to?'

'I can tell you that, sir,' said Mr Foreman, a little smile on his still aristocratic features. 'I'd be verger of St Peter's, Neville Square.'

HITLER'S SECRET DAIRY

Bruce McCall

Bruce McCall (1935–) is a Canadian expatriate who began his career in a commercial art studio, switched to journalism and then advertising, and began writing and painting humorous subjects in the seventies, first with *National Lampoon* and ultimately for *The New Yorker*. He lives in New York.

JUNE 25, 1933

Telepathic vibrations have relayed the electrokinetic force of my will into the minds of others! Today, E. led me out into the dooryard and presented me with a cow! Female, classically Rubenesque, black-and-white camouflage! Tomorrow, like a cowboy, I will pat her head!

JUNE 27, 1933

E. says a Brown Swiss would match my shirt, but I remind her that the Holstein is the more German animal. Only the left-handed and others in the grip of the world riboflavin trust, which I will smash, would dare argue to the contrary!

AUGUST 16, 1933

I will not refuse Destiny's mandate! The cow has had a cub today, the two-hundredth anniversary of Frederick the Great's marriage to Elizabeth of Brunswick-Bevern! Führer, architect, artist, dairyman!

NOVEMBER 12, 1934

I confer with my milking instructor, who insists that I must have been a milkman in my previous incarnation, so quickly have I mastered the tricky Friesian Squeeze! No sign of Himmler (22:30 hrs.)! He should have finished cleaning the stalls by now.

April 17, 1935
Göring *again* lets his straw make disgusting noises as he finishes up his milkshake. I am forced to decree that hereafter only E. and I are to be served milkshakes. E. begs me to hear her ukulele recital of highlights from "Die Walküre," but I am in no mood for culture festivals!

August 2, 1937
Bormann brings me a Belted Galloway heifer to inspect. It steps on von Rundstedt's nice shiny boots! Ha ha!

February 6, 1938
That Goebbels is a didactic little pettifogger and an advertising man! He wastes an hour of my time tonight attempting to convince me that cowboys should correctly be called horseboys. But he has his uses. Tonight he showed me a film. The Adolf Hitler Bovine Battalion has trained its entire crack herd to wag their tails in unison forty-eight times on command, in honor of my age! I insisted that Goebbels run this stirring tribute several times, once backward. E. claims that my eyes were brimming. This I will not deny!

September 1, 1939
Busy day. Nevertheless showed Speer my sketches of an underground dairy, which future difficulties may make advisable. He must design the largest and grandest dairy in the entire history of the human and bovine races, not omitting a Rotunda of the Germanic Bovines, large enough that the Great Pyramid of Cheops could easily fit beneath its ceiling! I shall call it "Lactia." It will last a thousand years. Who can tell? With good management, perhaps even longer!

OCTOBER 23, 1939

My first public milking attempt is sabotaged by Ribbentrop's coughing fit, which startles the cow, Irmtraud, who is high-strung. Hess tries making a joke of this, knowing well how I despise jokes—and jokesters who make jokes! He should clip his eyebrows. Ribbentrop is a dandified weasel who incessantly puffs on English cigarettes, and never gives me the little cards inside with pictures of ocean liners and aircraft and trains. Hess leaps to light Ribbentrop's infernal smokes. So! The two *are* in cahoots after all!

OCTOBER 24, 1939

Such incidents as yesterday's would be grist for the mills of that hack Sunday painter Churchill and other smart-aleck cads. I have ordered that my dairy interests and activities must henceforth be an official secret of the Reich. E. must tell the locals that she is Frau Schicklgruber, a lost aviatrix.

MARCH 4, 1940

The chubby hat collector Göring swears never to use a straw if he is again permitted to drink milkshakes. E. says his hands feel like blancmange and that he would make a poor dairyman. She says I have fine hands for milking, as the perspiration makes an ideal lubricant. I believe she is correct in this!

JUNE 30, 1940

Hess bursts in with a look of pure triumph, swiftly erased. When I demanded the Jerseys and Guernseys, I meant the *animals!*

AUGUST 21, 1940

Old Pétain, along with Laval, visits. The French know nothing of cows or milking. I explained to Schacht afterward that great dairy undertakings have been historically alien in all cultures with vowel-dominant languages. He was fascinated.

MARCH 12, 1941

The fatheaded scientific masterminds plead that my design for a rocket-powered milking machine is "impractical." That is what they think, is it? Is that what they think? I think "Ha ha."

MAY 15, 1941

Is the Aberdeen a beef cow or a milk cow? Tonight at supper (cheese, buttermilk, yogurt), Rosenberg and Funk answered yes. Bormann asked which I wanted it to be. Only Hess offered to find out. Perhaps I have misjudged him; a chowderhead, but a chowder-head with initiative!

MAY 16, 1941

The chowderhead went to Scotland!

JANUARY 21, 1942

A pair of silk milking gloves from Mussolini. Wrong size! How I wish to cuff that popinjay fibber-deluxe of a Duce with them!

SEPTEMBER 16, 1943

Doenitz claimed today that cottage cheese is not made from dairy products. Raeder disagreed violently. I let them argue it out.

NOVEMBER 8, 1944

E. insists the cows are saying "moo," not "boo." I have ordered recordings to be made and analyzed. It is just like those dumb walking milk-bags to turn on one the moment adversity strikes! They bear watching!!

JANUARY 11, 1945

Treacheries afoot! I caught the entire herd red-handed today, all facing in the same direction, toward the west and the advancing Allied forces! Bormann failed to prove to my satisfaction that they were *not* British cattle parachuted in. I left him with orders to monitor the movements of Irmtraud, the walleyed Holstein—*or her double!*

FEBRUARY 2, 1945

I have today ordered Lactia to be converted immediately into a practice rink for the new roller-skating regiments that will soon reverse events—*if* Speer can get enough ball bearings!!!

MARCH 12, 1945

Up all night designing a new kind of cow. Upon it depends the future!

APRIL 27, 1945

Midget cows on rocket-powered roller skates! Firing concentrated lactic acids! Penetrating tank armor from a range of ten thousand metres!

HOW TO TAKE YOUR PLEASURE SADLY

George Mikes

George Mikes (1912–1987) was born in Siklós, Hungary. He studied law at Budapest University, then became a journalist and was sent to London as a correspondent to cover the Munich crisis. He came for a fortnight but stayed on and made England his home. During the Second World War, he broadcast for the BBC Hungarian Service where he remained until 1951. In 1946 he published *How to be an Alien*, which identified him as a humourist, though he hadn't intended the book to be funny. It sold more than 450,000 copies and led to three more books – *How to be Inimitable*, *How to be Decadent* and *How to be a Brit*.

I do not know how the silly phrase 'the English take their pleasures sadly' originated. Slavs take their pleasures sadly. A Russian cannot really enjoy himself without sobbing for an hour or two on another Slavonic bosom. But Englishmen? They, in their moments of pleasure, may be unemotional, shy, phlegmatic – but sad? Oh no, not sad.

The English, instead of taking their pleasures sadly, endure them bravely, in a spirit worthy of their Puritan ancestors. I often imagine a modern Grand Inquisitor summoning an Englishman and sending him on a normal summer holiday. He pronounces sentence:

'One: tomorrow morning you will get into your car and take twelve and a half hours to cover a four-hour journey. The journey back will take you fifteen hours and the fumes will nearly choke you.

'Two: when you reach your destination, you will queue up twelve times a day: three times for ice-cream, twice for deck-chairs, three times for beer, once for tea, twice for swings for the children and once just for the hell of it.

'Three: whenever you feel unbearably hot, I order you to accept the additional torture of drinking hot tea.

'Four: when it gets still hotter, you will drive down to the seaside and sit in the oven of your car, for two hours and a half.

'Five: wherever you go, there will never be less than two thousand people around you. They will shout and shriek into your ear and trample on your feet and your only consolation will be that you, too, trample on *their* feet. There is no escape from them. You may try the country-side but the countryside, too, will be transformed into an ever-lasting Bank Holiday fairground, strewn with paper bags and empty tins and bottles. Furthermore, to add to your sufferings, I order you to take a portable radio everywhere with you and listen to "Housewives' Choice" and "Mrs Dale's Diary" incessantly!'

If all this were meted out as dire punishment, proud, free Englishmen everywhere would rise against it as they have always risen against foul oppression. But as, on top of it all, they have to spend a whole year's savings on these pleasures, they are delighted if they can join the devotees anywhere.

Britain has been the marvel-country of the world for a long time. Many people used to regard her as decadent, decaying and exhausted until they learned better. How has Britain come out of her many trials, not only victorious but rejuvenated? The secret of the British is very simple: if they can endure their summer holidays, they can endure anything.

HOW TO DIE

George Mikes

George Mikes (1912–1987) was born in Siklós, Hungary. He studied law at Budapest University, then became a journalist and was sent to London as a correspondent to cover the Munich crisis. He came for a fortnight but stayed on and made England his home. During the Second World War, he broadcast for the BBC Hungarian Service where he remained until 1951. In 1946 he published *How to be an Alien*, which identified him as a humourist, though he hadn't intended the book to be funny. It sold more than 450,000 copies and led to three more books – *How to be Inimitable*, *How to be Decadent* and *How to be a Brit*.

The English are the only race in the world who enjoy dying. Most other peoples contemplate death with abject and rather contemptible fear; the English look forward to it with gusto.

They speak of death as if it were something natural. It is, of course, more natural than birth. Hundreds of millions of people are not born; but all who are born, die. During the bombing raids of the last war people on the Continent prayed: 'God, even if I have to be hit and maimed, please spare my life.' The English said: 'If I have to die, well, I couldn't care less. But I don't want to be made an invalid and I don't want to suffer.' Foreign insurance agents speak of 'certain possibilities' and the 'eventuality' that 'something might happen to you'; the English make careful calculations and the thought that the insurance company will have to pay up always sweetens their last hours. Nowhere in the world do people make so many cruel jokes about the aged and the weak as here. In continental families you simply do not refer to the fact that a parent or a grandparent is not immortal. But not long ago my two children burst into my room and asked me:

'Daddy, which of us will get your camera when you die?'

'I'll let you know,' I replied. 'By the way, I am sorry to be still alive. It's not my fault. I can't help it.'

They were a little hurt.

'Don't be silly. We don't really mind at all. We only wanted to know who'll get the camera.'

And when the moment comes, the English make no fuss. Dead or alive, they hate being conspicuous or saying anything unconventional. They are not a great people for famous last words.

I shall never forget the poor gentleman who once travelled with me on the Channel boat. Only the two of us were on deck as a violent storm was raging. A tremendous gale was lashing mountainous seas. We huddled there for a while, without saying anything. Suddenly a fearful gust blew him overboard. His head emerged just once from the water below me. He looked at me calmly and remarked somewhat casually:

'Rather windy, isn't it?'

FOILED BY PRESIDENT FRED

Spike Milligan

Terence Alan 'Spike' Milligan (1918–2002) was born in India, where his father was a soldier, and came to England in 1934. Early jobs ranged from factory hand to scrubber in a laundry; he was also a trumpet player in a band for a while, then a trumpet player not in a band. He met Harry Secombe in the army, teamed up for concerts, began to write, met Peter Sellers – and so began *The Goon Show* from which the text below is taken. He appeared in many films and West End plays. His other writings include the novel *Puckoon*, various books of children's and comic verse, and the bestselling *Adolf Hitler – My Part in His Downfall*.

BILL. This is the BBC Home Service. And candidly, I'm fed up with it.

HARRY. Have a care there, Wallace, otherwise I'll be forced to speak to John Snagge.

BILL. My dear fellow, everybody has to be forced to speak to John Snagge.

HARRY. Come, curb those biting cynicisms and permit me to present the highly esteemed Goon Show.

Grams. Aeolian clarinet (or old dance music record).

SPIKE. Stop that sinful music! Secombe? Take off those carbon-paper plus fours and listen to the story entitled—'In Honour Bound'.

Orchestra. Traditional English hero theme.

SEAGOON. My name is Neddie Seagoon. I was a gas meter inspector. It all began the day of the annual general board meeting of the South Balham Gas Board.

Effects. Murmurs – gavel.

CRUN. Gentlemen—I have here the books for the—mnk—financial year—mnk—just ended—mnk—mnk—and by the look of them gas is here to stay. I am glad to say that the South Balham Gas Colossus has made a gross profit of no less than three pounds twelve shillings and nine.

Grams. Clapping.

CRUN. It proves that hard work pays. Now, I'll read the vital balance sheet. Credits—sales of gas, eighteen pounds. Expenses—one bag of coke, eight and sixpence; electric fire for office heating, two pounds, eleven and fourpence; replacing light bulbs in Gas Board's premises, thirteen shillings and tenpence; saxophone lessons for Chairman's wife, three pounds, eight shillings and ninepence...

MINNIE. [*Off*] Do we have to pay for saxophone lessons, buddy?

CRUN. Ah—yes—you never know when it comes in useful—mnk—mnk—next we have the—oh!—ah!—oh! I overlooked an entry here—an outstanding debt of four pounds, nineteen shillings and sixpence!

GRAMS. Sensation.

CRUN. Don't worry! I shall set this right at once. [*Calls*] Ned Seagoon?

Effects. Door opens.

SEAGOON. Gas meter inspector Seagoon reporting for duty, sir.

CRUN. Seagoon, go to this address and—mnk—serve them a seven-day final notice.

SEAGOON. Yes sir. What's this? President Fred, Casa Rosa, Avenida Varest, Buenos Aires, Argentina? Argentina? That's South America.

CRUN. Ohhoho—is it? Then you'd better borrow the Gas Board's bicycle.

SEAGOON. But sir, it's overseas.

CRUN. [*Angry*] What's our bicycle doing overseas?

SEAGOON. No, no. I mean *Argentina* is overseas. How can I get there on a bicycle?

CRUN. Well, you must have it waterproofed.

SEAGOON. Oh, thank you, sir. I hadn't thought of that. Goodbye, sir.

OMNES. Goodbye—Ta ta.

BILL. Dear listeners, you doubtless are wondering how it is that the South Balham Gas Board supplies gas to Argentina. It was thanks to the enterprise of a British Major who, in 1939, shipped a cylinder of gas there.

SEAGOON. Yes, on arrival in Argentina it was this man I contacted.

Orchestra. Bloodnok theme.

Grams. Record of Flamenco guitar.

BLOODNOK. Ah! Oh! The heat! Gladys?

RAY. Si, señor?

BLOODNOK. Turn off one of those women and put some more ice on the fire—ah!

Effects. Knock on door.

BLOODNOK. [*Suspicious*] Who's there?

SEAGOON. [*Off*] Ned Seagoon, South Balham Gas Board.

BLOODNOK. Quick! Burn the books. Tear up those revolting postcards. Chase those women out of my room. Take all those 'For Sale' signs off the furniture and help me get the floor back under this carpet. [*Makes huge effort*] Come in!

Effects. Door opens.

SEAGOON. Good morning.

BLOODNOK. I'm sorry your journey's all been wasted. I posted the account books back to Balham this morning. Goodbye.

Effects. Door slams. Loud knocking.

BLOODNOK. You can't come in. I'm in the bath.

SEAGOON. [*Off*] What are you doing in the bath?

BLOODNOK. I'm—I'm watching television.

SEAGOON. [*Off*] What's showing?

BLOODNOK. My dear fellow—nothing. I've got a towel round me.

Effects. Door opens.

SEAGOON. Look here. Major, enough of this tomfoolery.

BLOODNOK. Do you play the saxophone?

SEAGOON. No. I'm here to deliver a final demand notice to a President Fred—how do I contact him?

BLOODNOK. Come to the window, lad...

Effects. Window raised. Distant shots and sounds of warfare.

BLOODNOK. That white house in the square is President Fred's headquarters.

SEAGOON. But how can I get through that hail of bullets?

BLOODNOK. Be outside the back door at midnight. I shall send a man to guide you.

SEAGOON. Very well. But remember—if I'm not back within seven days, don't hesitate to cut off their gas supply. Farewell!

Effects. Door slams. Phone up.

BLOODNOK. Hello, Moriarty?

MORIARTY. Yes.

BLOODNOK. Listen, there's a Charlie from Balham coming over to collect a gas bill from President Fred. It's only three pounds, twelve shillings and ninepence.

MORIARTY. Bloodnok, that money was paid to *you* last month.

BLOODNOK. I know, but I don't want any trouble with the South Balham Gas fellows. Be a good feller and settle it up.

MORIARTY. Sapristi galamnackos! How *can* we pay him? President Fred has vanished with all the money. I think you'd better come over here at once.

BLOODNOK. Very well. I'll pause only for Max Geldray.

Max & Orchestra. 'Have You Ever Been Lonely'.

[*Applause*]

SEAGOON. That night at midnight I waited in a specially darkened doorway for the coming of the stranger who was to guide me on my perilous mission. I was so heavily disguised that not even my own mother would have recognised me.

MOTHER. Good evening, Neddie.

SEAGOON. Good evening, Mum. [*Embarrassed cough*] But wait! Who is this approaching, wearing an anthracite tie, lead waistcoat, with an electric guitar plugged into the tram lines?

ECCLES. Ahem—psst!

SEAGOON. Are you pssting at me?

ECCLES. Yeah. You Neddie Seagoon?

SEAGOON. I am.

ECCLES. Been waiting long?

SEAGOON. Yes.

ECCLES. Who for?

SEAGOON. You, you idiot. Now, how do I get through the firing line to President Fred's headquarters?

ECCLES. Go straight up that road there.

SEAGOON. But they're shooting down it.

ECCLES. Oh. Don't go that way. Take this road here. They're not shooting down that.

SEAGOON. That road doesn't lead to it.

ECCLES. No, don't take that one.

[*Pause*]

SEAGOON. Any other ideas?

ECCLES. Do you play the saxophone?

SEAGOON. No.

ECCLES. Well—I'd better be getting along now.

SEAGOON. Don't go. The sewers! That's how we'll get there. Quick. Down this manhole.

Effects. Manhole cover. Two splashes. Wading [*continues*].

SEAGOON. [*Proud*] Now—I'm going to roll up my trousers.

ECCLES. Why?

SEAGOON. I've got nice legs. Wait! What's that ahead?

ECCLES. It's a head.

SEAGOON. Yes, but whose it is?

BLUEBOTTLE. It is mine, my capting.

SEAGOON. Who are you, little cardboard-clad frogman?

BLUEBOTTLE. I will give you a musical clue. Close your eyes. Moves right, picks up flannel zither. [*Sings*] Plunka-plunka-plunka-plunk ... etc. ['*Harry Lime*']

ECCLES. I know. The Man from Laramie.

BLUEBOTTLE. [*Heartbroken*] You rotten swine, you. I'm not the Laramie man. I'm the Harry Lime-type man. Goes into second chorus. [*Sing as before*]

SEAGOON. Save that lovely voice, little widget. Tonight is not the Harry Lime game Tonight is the South American President Fred game.

BLUEBOTTLE. Oh! Do not go. Wait for me. Quickly throws away silly zither, makes brown paper lariat, reverses Mum's old bloomers to make cowboy trousers and picks up hair and fibre banjo. Olé! Am ready for new game. Ride, vaquero, ride!

SEAGOON. Well done, little thrice-adolescent hybrid. Lead me to President Fred's headquarters and this quarter of liquorice all-sorts is yours.

BLUEBOTTLE. Oooh! Licorish! Thinks. I must be careful how many of these I eat. Right, Captain, quick—jump into this cardboard bootbox. Hurriedly wraps up captain in brown paper parcel labelled "Explosives" and stuffs him through headquarters letter box. Jumps on to passing dustcart and exits left to buy bowler before price goes up. Thinks—that wasn't a very big part for Bluebottle.

BILL. By the magic of inconsequence the scene now changes to the Suspicious Parcels Testing Chamber in President Fred's head-quarters.

MORIARTY. Grytpype, this mysterious parcel has just arrived by mysterious parcel post—mysteriously.

GRYTPYPE-THYNNE. Right, Moriarty. Steam the stamp off and cash it.

MORIARTY. Sapristi Muchos! I don't like the expression on this parcel's label. I wonder what's in it.

Effects. Phone rings. Receiver up.

GRYTPYPE-THYNNE. Hello?

SEAGOON. [*Distort*] I'll tell you what's in the parcel. It's me, gas meter Inspector Neddie Seagoon, South Balham Gas Board. You have seven days to pay a gas bill of three pounds, twelve and nine.

GRYTPYPE-THYNNE. Um! Do you play the saxophone?

SEAGOON. [*Distort*] No. Now listen, you have seven days to pay. You can post your cheque to me care of this parcel.

Effects. Phone down.

GRYTPYPE-THYNNE. Mmm! Moriarty, hand me that forty-ton steam hammer.

Effects. Psst! Thud! Phone rings and receiver up.

SEAGOON. [*Distort*] Ow!

Effects. Receiver down.

GRYTPYPE-THYNNE. Yes—Moriarty, make a hole in the parcel, insert the nozzle of this hose and turn it on—so!

Effects. Running water. Phone rings and receiver up.

GRYTPYPE-THYNNE. Hello?

SEAGOON. [*Through water*] Bobbleobbleobbleobble—plumber!

Effects. Phone down.

GRYTPYPE-THYNNE. That'll do, Moriarty. I think he's had enough. Open it.

Effects. Paper torn.

SEAGOON. Thank heaven you've arrived. The roof was leaking. Now then—what about this gas bill? President Fred owes the South Balham Gas Board three pounds, twelve shillings and ninepence.

GRYTPYPE-THYNNE. Oh—I tell you what. Go down to the basement and read the meter and make sure.

SEAGOON. Right. Come, Eccles—

Effects. Door shuts.

GRYTPYPE-THYNNE. Good. That gives us a breathing space. I say, how empty the room is without him.

Effects. Background shooting.

MORIARTY. Sapristi—the counter-revolutionaries with tanks are attacking.

GRYTPYPE-THYNNE. We've got to evacuate.

MORIARTY. Why?

GRYTPYPE-THYNNE. The rent's too high here. Pack the floor. We're leaving.

Effects. Door shuts. Door broken down. Shots.

OMNES. [*Shouts*]

GENERAL ASTON VILLA. Well, the cowardly swines have run away. They are frightened of Il Heneral Aston Villa. Run up my personal flag. Ssh! Someone's coming upstairs.

Effects. Door opens.

SEAGOON. Right, gentlemen, I've checked the meter, and the bill is exactly four pounds.

GENERAL ASTON VILLA. What are you talking about, you miserable English creep?

SEAGOON. Come, come, Mr. Grytpype, you can't fool the South Balham Gas Board with those childish disguises and silly changes of voice. Four pounds, please.

GENERAL ASTON VILLA. There is some mistake, señor. We have just taken possession here this very minute. We only just lit the gas.

SEAGOON. Good heavens, I'm dreadfully sorry. In that case you couldn't have used more than a therm or two. I'll go down and read the meter again. Excuse me...

Effects. Door closes.

GENERAL ASTON VILLA. Now—when he comes up—pay the bill—then keel heem.

Effects. Burst of firing.

OBREGON. Queeck! The President Fredists are attacking.

GENERAL ASTON VILLA. Everybody retreat.

Effects. General stampede out and door closes.

[*Pause*]

Effects. Door opens.

GRYTPYPE-THYNNE. Well done, Moriarty. What a beautiful counter-attack. We couldn't have continued to hold *their* headquarters anyway. Three pounds, ten shillings a week? Impossible!

Effects. Door opens.

SEAGOON. Well, gentlemen, I've read the meter. And you were quite right. You'd only put on one more therm—one and six please.

GRYTPYPE-THYNNE. Right. Here's a photograph of two shillings.

SEAGOON. Thank you. And here's a photograph of sixpence—change.

GRYTPYPE-THYNNE. Can't you do it in coppers?

SEAGOON. By all means—here's a photograph of sixpence in coppers.

GRYTPYPE-THYNNE. Thank you.

SEAGOON. No—wait! It's you back again! You've cheated me. You're the people who owe the three pounds, twelve shillings and ninepence.

GRYTPYPE-THYNNE. That's President Fred's responsibility. Go and see him. Room 509.

SEAGOON. I will. But wait! Who is this approaching, riding a kilted monkey and carrying a mackintosh sackbut? It's Ray Ellington!

Quartet. 'Birth of The Blues'.

[*Applause*]

BILL. Here for idiots is a resumé. The revolution so far.

Effects. Shooting.

BILL. Thank you. Chapter Two.

Effects. Knocking on the door.

BLOODNOK. Heavens-o! El knocko on the door-o. Come in-o.

Effects. Door opens.

SEAGOON. Good morning, President Fred Peron. I've come to collect—wait a minute. You don't look like President Fred Peron.

BLOODNOK. What a coincidence! Neither do you!

SEAGOON. But I'm not supposed to be him.

BLOODNOK. Oh! So that's your excuse, is it? By the way, do you play the saxophone?

SEAGOON. No.

BLOODNOK. I'll give you a lesson.

Saxophone. Solo—'Valse Vanité'.

SEAGOON. Stop that! I'm convinced you're not President Fred. You're Major Bloodnok.

BLOODNOK. Nonsense. And you can soon find out. Phone him on the telefonico at this number-o: three-o nine-o.

SEAGOON. By gad, I will...

Effects. Receiver up. Dialling.

SEAGOON. [*Over*] I'll soon call this cunning bluff.

Effects. Phone rings.

SEAGOON. Excuse me a moment.

Effects. Phone up.

BLOODNOK. Hello. Three-o nine-o here.

SEAGOON. Who's that speaking?

BLOODNOK. Major Denis Bloodnok.

SEAGOON. Oh! I'm sorry. There's a man here whom I've accused of being you.

BLOODNOK. Why?

SEAGOON. He's your living image. He even sounds like you.

BLOODNOK. Nonsense—goodbye—

Effects. Phone down.

BLOODNOK. [*To Seagoon*] Well, you doubter? You see?

SEAGOON. I'm sorry. But if you're President Fred, there's a gas bill here which now stands at four pounds.

BLOODNOK. Oh! Right, I'll pay you. Here's a photograph of a four pound note.

SEAGOON. Thank you. Now I can report back to Major Bloodnok, 'Mission completed. Gas bill paid in full'.

Effects. Door slams.

BLOODNOK. Good, he's gone.

[*Pause*]

Effects. Door opens.

MORIARTY. Ah! Bloodnok! You got rid of him, then. Splendid. And we for our part we've got rid of President Fred Peron.

BLOODNOK. You mean…?

MORIARTY. Yes. He gave us all his money to smuggle him out of the country.

BLOODNOK. Well done. Now to divide his fifty million.

MORIARTY. Yes. I have it here in this red sack.

BLOODNOK. Good. We'll split evenly. I'll take the money and you take the sack.

MORIARTY. No. Why should I get the lion's share? You have the sack and I'll take the money.

BLOODNOK. Listen, Moriarty. Let us settle this thing amicably.

Effects. Shot.

MORIARTY. Oh, Sapristi Nuckos! Dead!

Effects. Thud.

BLOODNOK. Good heavens! That pistol was loaded. Poor Moriarty. I wonder if he played the saxophone. Taxi!

Effects. Taxi drives off.

[*Pause*]

Effects. Door opens.

GRYTPYPE-THYNNE. Has he gone?

MORIARTY. Yes. He swallowed the bait, hook, line and sinker. I gave him a pistol with a blank cartridge and he took the red sack full of the forged banknotes.

GRYTPYPE-THYNNE. Splendid. I've got the genuine money here in this blue sack. Now, you go to the airport, Moriarty, and buy two air tickets.

MORIARTY. Right.

Effects. Whoosh. Door shuts.

GRYTPYPE-THYNNE. Fifty million, eh? [*Sings softly*] Christmas in Capri, millions of moulah…

Effects. Door opens.

ECCLES. Hello, Mr. Grytpype. I see you got that old red sack full of those forged notes ready to fool old Bloodnok, then. That was a good idea of yours having me pack those two sacks. Where's the *blue* sack with the *real* stuff.

GRYTPYPE-THYNNE. This *is* the blue one.

ECCLES. Oh! That man was right then.

GRYTPYPE-THYNNE. What man?

ECCLES. That oculist fellow who said I was colour-blind.

GRYTPYPE-THYNNE. You mean Bloodnok has the *real* money?

ECCLES. Yeah.

GRYTPYPE-THYNNE. Moriarty! Quick!

Effects. Whoosh! Whoosh!

ECCLES. [*Sings*] I talk to der trees—dat's why… [*etc.*]

Effects. Door opens.

BLUEBOTTLE. Has Mr. Grytpype gone, Eccles?

ECCLES. Yup. Yup. [*Sings*]

BLUEBOTTLE. And left us the blue sack with all the real money?

ECCLES. Yup. [*Sings*]

ECCLES & BLUEBOTTLE. Ha. Ha. Ha.

BLUEBOTTLE. Oh, I like this game, don't you, Eccles?

ECCLES. Yup, it's fine—fine.

BOTH. [*Sing*] Christmas in Capri, plenty of money…

[*Fade*]

Effects. Door opens.

BLOODNOK. [*Breathlessly*] Juan! Pack everything. I've millions of moulah. I must leave before Neddie gets back…

RAY. You'd better take that President Fred Peron make up off.

BLOODNOK. Yes, there!

Effects. Door bursts open.

SEAGOON. Major Bloodnok! My mission's completed. Here's a photo of a four pound note.

BLOODNOK. Wait! This note in the photograph—it's a forgery!

SEAGOON. Gad, I've been tricked! Bloodnok, I'll go right back!

Effects. Door slams.

BLOODNOK. [*Hums*] Christmas in Capri—let's count the moolah.

Effects. Door opens.

MORIARTY. Hands up!

BLOODNOK. Ah! Great thundering widgets of Kludge! Put down that double-action hydraulic-recoil eighteen-inch Howitzer.

MORIARTY. No. It belonged to my mother.

BLOODNOK. What do you want?

MORIARTY. Give me that sack of money.

BLOODNOK. Come, come, Moriarty. Old friends mustn't fall out.

MORIARTY. Very well, we'll settle this amicably.

BLOODNOK. How?

MORIARTY. Like this.

Effects. Shot.

BLOODNOK. Ah! Shot through me gaiters!

MORIARTY. Got him.

Effects. Door opens.

GRYTPYPE-THYNNE. Is he dead?

MORIARTY. Yes.

Effects. Shot.

MORIARTY. Ooooh! Shot in the kringe!

Effects. Thud.

GRYTPYPE-THYNNE. Got him!

Effects. Door opens.

SEAGOON. Grytpype!

GRYTPYPE-THYNNE. Hello, Neddie.

SEAGOON. What are these men lying on the floor for?

GRYTPYPE-THYNNE. We haven't got any carpets.

SEAGOON. Eccles told me that Bloodnok ran off with a red sack full of banknotes, believing them to be real.

GRYTPYPE-THYNNE. And—weren't they?

SEAGOON. No. The real ones are with Eccles.

Effects. Whoosh. Door shuts. [Pause] Door opens.

ECCLES. Hullo. Has he gone?

SEAGOON. Yes.

ECCLES. Fine, fine, fine. You know, I'm not really colour-blind at all. I only said that to fool Bluebottle. That blue sack you're holding is full of the real stuff.

SEAGOON. Blue? This is a red sack.

ECCLES. Ooooh! Then you got the wrong stuff. Bluebottle's got the real stuff.

SEAGOON. Then I must find him and collect the Gas Board's four pounds from President Fred's treasure. Farewell.

Effects. Door shuts. [Pause]

Effects. Door opens.

BLUEBOTTLE. Has he gone, Eccles?

ECCLES. Yup, yup.

BLUEBOTTLE. And now we have both sacks—the red one and the blue one. Heehee! This is a good game. Eccles, which sack has the real money?

ECCLES. The blue one.

BLUEBOTTLE. Then we will split it fifty-fifty. You take the red one and I'll take the blue one.

ECCLES. Fine, fine.

BLUEBOTTLE. And you're sure you're not colour-blind?

ECCLES. No, no.

BLUEBOTTLE. Well, goodbye Eccles.

Effects. Door shuts.

ECCLES. Goodbye, Redbottle.

BILL. Three weeks later, at the head office of the South Balham Gas Board.

Effects. Knock on door.

MANAGER. Come in.

Effects. Door opens.

Violin. 'Hearts and Flowers'.

MANAGER. Seagoon, put that blasted violin down and get up off your knees. Here—I'll hold that celluloid baby.

Music out.

SEAGOON. Please sir, I know I failed to collect that bill, but— couldn't I have my old job back?

MANAGER. I'm sorry, it's gone. Allow me to introduce our new gas meter inspector, Balham area—President Fred.

BLOODNOK. Ah! Pleased to meet you.

SEAGOON. Oh no!

Orchestra. Link.

BILL. Meantime, on the Isle of Capri...

Music accompaniment.

ECCLES. [*Hums*] "O Sole Mio" etc... [*Calls*] Hey, Manager! My bill!

GRYTPYPE-THYNNE. Yes, sir. Let me see now, sir. Egg on toast and small pot of tea—that makes just fifty million pesos.

ECCLES. Oh, that's okay. I've got it all here in this blue sack.

GRYTPYPE-THYNNE. But that's a red sack.

ECCLES. Oooh!

Orchestra. Signature tune: up and down for:—

BILL. Stop! Stop, please!

Music out.

BILL. If the cast will just gather round, the BBC cashier will pay them for the last overseas repeat in pesos from this blue sack.

HARRY. But that's a red sack.

PETER. Blue.

SPIKE. It's green.

Orchestra. Signature tune: up and down for:—

BILL. That was The Goon Show—a BBC recorded programme featuring Peter Sellers, Harry Secombe and Spike Milligan with the Ray Ellington Quartet and Max Geldray. The orchestra was conducted by Wally Stott. Script by Spike Milligan. Announcer Wallace Greenslade. The programme was produced by Peter Eton.

Orchestra. Signature tune up to end.

[*Applause*]

Max & Orchestra. 'Crazy Rhythm' playout.

THE ELEPHANT

Sławomir Mrożek

Sławomir Mrożek (1930–2013) was a Polish playwright and author
noted for his subtle parody and stylized language. Working first as a
journalist and cartoonist, writing short humorous articles full of word
play, his celebrated short story collection, *Elephant*, was first published in 1957. Having condemned Poland's role in the 1968 invasion
of Czechoslovakia, his work was banned there and he left the country,
living first in France and then in Mexico.

The director of the Zoological Gardens has shown himself to be
an upstart. He regarded his animals simply as stepping stones on
the road of his own career. He was indifferent to the educational
importance of his establishment. In his Zoo the giraffe had a short neck,
the badger had no burrow and the whistlers, having lost all interest,
whistled rarely and with some reluctance. These shortcomings should
not have been allowed, especially as the Zoo was often visited by parties
of schoolchildren.

The Zoo was in a provincial town, and it was short of some of
the most important animals, among them the elephant. Three thousand rabbits were a poor substitute for the noble giant. However, as
our country developed, the gaps were being filled in a well-planned
manner. On the occasion of the anniversary of the liberation, on 22nd
July, the Zoo was notified that it had at long last been allocated an
elephant. All the staff, who were devoted to their work, rejoiced at
this news. All the greater was their surprise when they learnt that the
director had sent a letter to Warsaw, renouncing the allocation and

putting forward a plan for obtaining an elephant by more economic means.

"I, and all the staff," he had written, "are fully aware how heavy a burden falls upon the shoulders of Polish miners and foundry men because of the elephant. Desirous of reducing our costs, I suggest that the elephant mentioned in your communication should be replaced by one of our own procurement. We can make an elephant out of rubber, of the correct size, fill it with air and place it behind railings. It will be carefully painted the correct colour and even on close inspection will be indistinguishable from the real animal. It is well known that the elephant is a sluggish animal and it does not run and jump about. In the notice on the railings we can state that this particular elephant is exceptionally sluggish. The money saved in this way can be turned to the purchase of a jet plane or the conservation of some church monument.

"Kindly note that both the idea and its execution are my modest contribution to the common task and struggle.

"I am, etc."

This communication must have reached a soulless official, who regarded his duties in a purely bureaucratic manner and did not examine the heart of the matter but, following only the directive about reduction of expenditure, accepted the director's plan. On hearing the Ministry's approval, the director issued instructions for the making of the rubber elephant.

The carcase was to have been filled with air by two keepers blowing into it from opposite ends. To keep the operation secret the work was to be completed during the night because the people of the town, having heard that an elephant was joining the Zoo, were anxious to see it. The director insisted on haste also because he expected a bonus, should his idea turn out to be a success.

The two keepers locked themselves in a shed normally housing a workshop, and began to blow. After two hours of hard blowing they discovered that the rubber skin had risen only a few inches above the floor and its bulge in no way resembled an elephant. The night progressed.

Outside, human voices were stilled and only the cry of the jackass interrupted the silence. Exhausted, the keepers stopped blowing and made sure that the air already inside the elephant should not escape. They were not young and were unaccustomed to this kind of work.

"If we go on at this rate," said one of them, "we shan't finish before the morning. And what am I to tell my Missus? She'll never believe me if I say that I spent the night blowing up an elephant."

"Quite right," agreed the second keeper. "Blowing up an elephant is not an everyday job. And it's all because our director is a leftist."

They resumed their blowing, but after another half-an- hour they felt too tired to continue. The bulge on the floor was larger but still nothing like the shape of an elephant.

"It's getting harder all the time," said the first keeper.

"It's an uphill job, all right," agreed the second. "Let's have a little rest."

While they were resting, one of them noticed a gas pipe ending in a valve. Could they not fill the elephant with gas? He suggested it to his mate.

They decided to try. They connected the elephant to the gas pipe, turned the valve, and to their joy in a few minutes there was a full-sized beast standing in the shed. It looked real: the enormous body, legs like columns, huge ears and the inevitable trunk. Driven by ambition the director had made sure of having in his Zoo a very large elephant indeed.

"First class," declared the keeper who had the idea of using gas. "Now we can go home."

In the morning the elephant was moved to a special run in a central position, next to the monkey cage. Placed in front of a large real rock it looked fierce and magnificent. A big notice proclaimed: "Particularly sluggish. Hardly moves."

Among the first visitors that morning was a party of children from the local school. The teacher in charge of them was planning to give them an object-lesson about the elephant. He halted the group in front of the animal and began:

"The elephant is a herbivorous mammal. By means of its trunk it pulls out young trees and eats their leaves."

The children were looking at the elephant with enraptured admiration. They were waiting for it to pull out a young tree, but the beast stood still behind its railings.

"... The elephant is a direct descendant of the now extinct mammoth. It's not surprising, therefore, that it's the largest living land animal."

The more conscientious pupils were making notes.

"... Only the whale is heavier than the elephant, but then the whale lives in the sea. We can safely say that on land the elephant reigns supreme."

A slight breeze moved the branches of the trees in the Zoo. "... The weight of a fully grown elephant is between nine and thirteen thousand pounds."

At that moment the elephant shuddered and rose in the air. For a few seconds it swayed just above the ground but a gust of wind blew it upwards until its mighty silhouette was against the sky. For a short while people on the ground could still see the four circles of its feet, its bulging belly and the trunk, but soon, propelled by the wind, the elephant sailed above the fence and disappeared above the tree-tops. Astonished monkeys in the cage continued staring into the sky.

They found the elephant in the neighbouring botanical gardens. It had landed on a cactus and punctured its rubber hide.

The schoolchildren who had witnessed the scene in the Zoo soon started neglecting their studies and turned into hooligans. It is reported that they drink liquor and break windows. And they no longer believe in elephants.

THE MAN WHO INVENTED THE CALENDAR

B.J. Novak

B.J. Novak (1979–) is an American writer and actor best known for his work on the Emmy Award-winning comedy series *The Office* as an actor, writer, director and executive producer. He is also known for his stand-up comedy performances. His first book of stories, *One More Thing*, from which this one is taken, was a *New York Times* bestseller.

January 1st—Ha, that feels fun to write! I'm excited. I've been thinking about doing this for so long, too—I went through all my old diaries, and it turns out I came up with this idea all the way back on Day After Day After Very Cloudy Day.

January 2nd—I'm still so excited about this calendar thing. It just makes so much sense! One thousand days a year, divided into 25 months, 40 days a month. Why didn't anyone think of this before?

January 3rd—Getting so many compliments on the calendar. One guy came up to me today and said he's going to organize his whole life around it—literally, someone said that!

January 4th—Best day ever (or at least so far in recorded history)! I was talking to Alice at the bonfire for such a long time— yes, *that* Alice. It seemed like she was into me, but I didn't want to be presumptuous. Finally I asked if she wanted to come back to my place and hang out more. She winked at me and said, "I don't know… I guess I'll have to check my *calendar*" (!!!!!!!!!!!!!!)

January 30th—People really hate January and want it to be over right away. I tried to explain that it's just the way we choose to label things and that it wouldn't make any difference, but no one got it. Finally, I just told everyone that this would be the last day of January, and months would be just 30 days instead of 40. But there wasn't enough time to get the word out. So to be safe, we have to make this month 31 days, and then we'll make the rest 30. Not a big deal. Everyone is excited to see Febuary—including me!

February 1st—Another small fuck-up: I put an extra *r* in all the copies I handed out of the calendar, so it said "FebRuary," even though I already told everyone the next month coming was called "FebUary." I felt so stupid—but Alice came up with the best solution! She said: "Just tell everyone it's spelled *February* but pronounced 'Feb-u-ary.' That way, *they'll* feel stupid!" Alice is the best.

February 14th—Alice stuff weird. Tonight we were having a nice dinner at the same place we always go, but she was being unusually quiet. Finally I asked if anything was wrong, and she said, "Do you know what day today is?" I said, "Yes, of course I do, I invented the calendar. It's February 14th. Why?" She smiled a really tense smile, said, "Yes. Yes, it is"—and then just walked away right in the middle of dinner! What's that about?

February 15th—So cold.

February 28th—I hate this month. I just can't take one more day of it. This month will just have to be shorter than the rest, and if people don't like it, they can go fuck themselves.

March 1st—Feeling much better! I don't know if it's just symbolic, but I'm glad February is over. I have a really good feeling about March.

March 9th—There's this new type of berry that looks soooo good, but somebody told me it's poison. Oh well.

April 1st—A lot of shenanigans today, like pranks (which are lies-for-no-reason). People say it has something to do with the calendar, which I wasn't crazy about hearing, because to be honest I think the whole thing is kind of lame. It's just not my style. But I guess that's good, when your invention takes on a life you never expected. That's what the inventor of the scarf told me—it was originally supposed to be a weapon.

April 12th—Someone should invent a new type of clock. Really simple. No cuckoo, no sun business, just numbers.

April 30th—I think 31 days was a mistake. You can't divide anything into 31, so you can't make anything half a month or half a week or anything (because 7 is the same way). There should be a word for numbers like that. So: 30 days it is. Glad to be done with this decision.

May 2nd—Ahhh, now maybe I want months to be 31 days. (Why am I so obsessed with this?)

May 20th—Ran into Alice again, and I played it so cool! She congratulated me on the calendar stuff and asked if I ever thought of putting pictures on it—she could maybe pose for it or something. I said that I'd think about it but that it sounded kind of cheesy. She asked when I could hang out more and catch up, and I told her I was busy, but I'd let her know in August. "What's August?" she said. "Oh, it's a month I've been kicking around—you're going to love it," I said. I could not have played it better!

June 29th—Met this really cool girl Jane at a stoning. Will write more later!

October 9th—Can't believe I haven't written in so long! Summer was amazing. Harvest amazing! People keep asking if I can make the days longer during the harvest season, just by an hour or two. I told them that they should just wake up earlier if it was so important to them, but everyone was too drunk to understand, so eventually I just said, "Sure, maybe one hour, maybe someday," and everyone cheered. "More sleep!" Huh? None of it made any sense.

October 21st—Things are still going strong with Jane. This year has been so amazing, and it's only October! So much has already happened, and there's still November, December, Latrember, Faunus, Rogibus, Neptember, Stonk...

October 26th—Got all excited about the clock thing last night and built an early prototype! I did it in a hurry, though, and I wrote too big and ran out of space for numbers halfway through. Jane tried to be supportive. "Maybe you can just have every number count twice," she said. Then how will they know which "six o'clock" it is, for instance? I asked. "They… they'd just have to know, I guess. From context?" she suggested. I really liked how supportive she was trying to be, but I knew this was too lazy to be a real solution. Alice would have known what to say.

November 5th—Stuff with Jane getting a little tense. She keeps wanting to push the relationship forward. She says that we've been together "forever." I said that maybe it feels that way, but that I kept track of it on the calendar and it's actually been less than five months. She just stared at me. Then to change the subject I told her this new idea I was excited about: we'd choose a date in the future to make things official, and then every year after that, that day on the calendar would be like our own personal holiday—for just the two of us. Good idea, right? "You'd never remember it," she said.

November 6th—Things with Jane getting better. I think we're going to work this out. I love Jane. That's all that matters.

November 11th—They sacrificed Jane today. Really happy for the Sun God.

November 12th—Cold.

November 13th—Dark.

November 18th—Turns out those berries aren't poison. So, now I'm the guy who discovered that.

November 23rd—Alice came by and said she felt bad about the Jane stuff, and that I should hang out with her and her friends. Then it turned out her friends included this new guy she's seeing who—get this—invented the diary. Anyway, to be the mature one, I said, "Oh, that's great, I use that almost every day." Guess what he says: "Oh, really? I invented that for girls." *What a dick.* Then he said, "So, what else have you done?" and I said I have been totally distraught about Jane being sacrificed (I kind of exaggerated, but whatever) but that I plan on pulling it together soon and working on something new, maybe something with clocks. He said: "Well, you know what tomorrow is?" I said, yes, November 24th. He said, "No, tomorrow is the first day of the rest of your life." And everyone said, "Awwww" and I was like *Are you kidding me?! Do you know how long it took me to get people to stop talking like that?*

December 1st—I think the key to feeling better is to really just focus on work. Starting tomorrow, I am going to choose a new project to work on every day. It doesn't have to be clocks; it just has to be something. Let's go!!!!

December 23rd—It seems like Alice and Diary Guy are really close this week. Really happy for them. Hard to see other people so happy this week for some reason. Ahhhh. Going to focus on work.

December 25th—Why do I feel so lonely today?

December 26th—Why am I so fat?

December 30th—I told everyone I'm ending the year early. I know it was impulsive, but I just had to do it. I was ready for everyone to make fun of me, but it turned out people were way cooler about it than I thought they would be. "That's great," "About time," "Just what I need." It was actually the most praise I got since I invented the calendar in the first place.

This year just got away from me somehow. Looking back, I realize how much I got sidetracked and how many months slipped by that I can't even remember. The one nice thing is seeing how I used to be so worked up about Alice, and now I realize I really don't care at all anymore. We're going to be friends in the New Year, and I'm really looking forward to that. And the Jane thing ended the right way, I think—better than some long, drawn-out breakup.

So this year wasn't everything I hoped it would be, and I didn't get all the months in that I wanted, but I know next year is going to be totally different. When the New Year starts, I'm going to wake up at dawn every day and get to work—see, I'd love to put a number on "dawn," that's why I think this new clock thing could be really big. I have so many ideas for it. For example: I either want seconds to be timed to a blink of an eye so people don't have to say "in the blink of an eye"—they can just say "one second"—or I want to double the length of a second so people don't always say, "Can you give me two seconds?!" They can just say "one second." I have a lot of ideas like that.

December 31st—So many parties going on tonight. On a Tuesday?! Not complaining, just saying.

January 1st—Woke up at sun-past-mountain with a headache. So much for the "dawn" thing. But I still feel good.

TWO IN ONE

Flann O'Brien

Flann O'Brien (1911–1966), whose real name was Brian O'Nolan, and who wrote under multiple pen names, was an Irish novelist, playwright and satirist. He wrote satirical columns for the *Irish Times* as well as novels, the most famous of which are *At Swim-Two-Birds* and *The Third Policeman*. O'Brien's bizarre humour and modernist metafiction has attracted a wide following. Though he was influenced by James Joyce he was, nonetheless, sceptical of the cult surrounding him, saying 'I declare to God if I hear that name Joyce one more time I will surely froth at the gob.' This story was originally credited to his pseudonym Myles na Gopaleen.

The story I have to tell is a strange one, perhaps unbelievable. I will try to set it down as simply as I can. I do not expect to be disturbed in my literary labours, for I am writing this in the condemned cell.

Let us say my name is Murphy. The unusual occurrence which led me here concerns my relations with another man whom we shall call Kelly. Both of us were taxidermists.

I will not attempt a treatise on what a taxidermist is. The word is ugly and inadequate. Certainly it does not convey to the layman that such an operator must combine the qualities of zoologist, naturalist, chemist, sculptor, artist, and carpenter. Who would blame such a person for showing some temperament now and again, as I did?

It is necessary, however, to say a brief word about this science. First, there is no such thing in modern practice as "stuffing" an animal. There is a record of stuffed gorillas having been in Carthage in the 5th century, and it is a fact that an Austrian prince, Siegmund Herberstein, had stuffed bison in the great hall of his castle in the 16th century—it was then the practice to draw the entrails of animals and to substitute spices and various preservative substances. There is a variety of methods in use today but, except in particular cases—snakes, for example, where preserving the translucency of the skin is a problem calling for special measures—the basis of all modern methods is simply this: you skin the animal very carefully according to a certain pattern, and you encase the skinless body in plaster of Paris. You bisect the plaster when cast providing yourself with two complementary moulds from which you can make a casting of the animal's body—there are several substances, all very light, from which such castings can be made. The next step, calling for infinite skill and patience, is to mount the skin on the casting of the body. That is all I need explain here, I think.

Kelly carried on a taxidermy business and I was his assistant. He was the boss—a swinish, overbearing mean boss, a bully, a sadist. He hated me, but enjoyed his hatred too much to sack me. He knew I had a real interest in the work, and a desire to broaden my experience. For that reason, he threw me all the common-place jobs that came in. If some old lady sent her favourite terrier to be done, that was me; foxes and cats and Shetland ponies and white rabbits—they were all strictly *my* department. I could do a perfect job on such animals in my sleep, and got to hate them. But if a crocodile came in, or a Great Borneo spider, or (as once happened) a giraffe—Kelly kept them all for himself. In the meantime he would treat my own painstaking work with sourness and sneers and complaints.

One day the atmosphere in the workshop had been even fouler than usual, with Kelly in a filthier temper than usual. I had spent the fore-noon finishing a cat, and at about lunch-time put it on the shelf where he left completed orders.

I could nearly *hear* him glaring at it. Where was the tail? I told him there was no tail, that it was a Manx cat. How did I know it was a

Manx cat, how did I know it was not an ordinary cat which had lost its tail in a motor accident or something? I got so mad that I permitted myself a disquisition on cats in general, mentioning the distinctions as between *Felis manul*, *Felis silvestris*, and *Felis lybica*, and on the unique structure of the Manx cat. His reply to that? He called me a slob. That was the sort of life *I* was having.

On this occasion something within me snapped. I was sure I could hear the snap. I had moved up to where he was to answer his last insult. The loathsome creature had his back to me, bending down to put on his bicycle clips. Just to my hand on the bench was one of the long, flat, steel instruments we use for certain operations with plaster. I picked it up and hit him a blow with it on the back of the head. He gave a cry and slumped forward. I hit him again. I rained blow after blow on him. Then I threw the tool away. I was upset. I went out into the yard and looked around. I remembered he had a weak heart. Was he dead? I remember adjusting the position of a barrel we had in the yard to catch rainwater, the only sort of water suitable for some of the mixtures we used. I found I was in a cold sweat but strangely calm. I went back into the workshop.

Kelly was just as I had left him. I could find no pulse. I rolled him over on his back and examined his eyes, for I have seen more lifeless eyes in my day than most people. Yes, there was no doubt: Kelly was dead. I had killed him. I was a murderer. I put on my coat and hat and left the place. I walked the streets for a while, trying to avoid panic, trying to think rationally. Inevitably, I was soon in a public house. I drank a lot of whiskey and finally went home to my digs. The next morning I was very sick indeed from this terrible mixture of drink and worry. Was the Kelly affair merely a fancy, a drunken fancy? No, there was no consolation in that sort of hope. He was dead all right.

It was as I lay in bed there, shaking, thinking, and smoking, that the mad idea came into my head. No doubt this sounds incredible, grotesque, even disgusting, but I decided I would treat Kelly the same as any other dead creature that found its way to the workshop.

Once one enters a climate of horror, distinction of degree as between one infamy and another seems slight, sometimes undetectable. That evening I went to the workshop and made my preparations. I worked steadily all next day. I will not appall the reader with gruesome detail. I need only say that I applied the general technique and flaying pattern appropriate to apes. The job took me four days at the end of which I had a perfect skin, face and all. I made the usual castings before committing the remains of, so to speak, the remains, to the furnace. My plan was to have Kelly on view asleep on a chair, for the benefit of anybody who might call. Reflection convinced me that this would be far too dangerous. I had to think again.

A further idea began to form. It was so macabre that it shocked even myself. For days I had been treating the inside of the skin with the usual preservatives—cellulose acetate and the like—thinking all the time. The new illumination came upon me like a thunderbolt. *I would don his skin and, when the need arose, BECOME Kelly!* His clothes fitted me. So would his skin. Why not?

Another day's agonised work went on various alterations and adjustments but that night I was able to look into a glass and see Kelly looking back at me, perfect in every detail except for the teeth and eyes, which had to be my own but which I knew other people would never notice.

Naturally I wore Kelly's clothes, and had no trouble in imitating his unpleasant voice and mannerisms. On the second day, having "dressed," so to speak, I went for a walk, receiving salutes from newsboys and other people who had known Kelly. And on the day after, I was foolhardy enough to visit Kelly's lodgings. Where on earth had I been, his landlady wanted to know. (She had noticed nothing.) What, I asked— had that fool Murphy not told her that I had to go to the country for a few days? No? I had told the good-for-nothing to convey the message.

I slept that night in Kelly's bed. I was a little worried about what the other landlady would think of my own absence. I decided not to remove Kelly's skin the first night I spent in his bed but to try to get the rest of my plan of campaign perfected and into sharper focus. I eventually decided that Kelly should announce to various people that he was going to a very good job in Canada, and that he had sold his business to his assistant Murphy. I would then burn the skin, I would own a business and—what is more stupid than vanity!—I could secretly flatter myself that I had committed the perfect crime.

Need I say that I had overlooked something?

The mummifying preparation with which I had dressed the inside of the skin was, of course, quite stable for the ordinary purposes of taxidermy. It had not occurred to me that a night in a warm bed would make it behave differently. The horrible truth dawned on me the next day when I reached the workshop and tried to take the skin off. *It wouldn't come off!* It had literally fused with my own! And in the days that followed, this process kept rapidly advancing. Kelly's skin got to live again, to breathe, to perspire.

Then followed more days of terrible tension. My own landlady called one day, inquiring about me of "Kelly." I told her I had been on the point of calling on *her* to find out where I was. She was disturbed about my disappearance—it was so unlike me—and said she thought she should inform the police. I thought it wise not to try to dissuade her. My disappearance would eventually come to be accepted, I thought. My Kelliness, so to speak, was permanent. It was horrible, but it was a choice of that or the scaffold.

I kept drinking a lot. One night, after many drinks, I went to the club for a game of snooker. This club was in fact one of the causes of Kelly's bitterness towards me. I had joined it without having been aware that Kelly was a member. His resentment was boundless. He thought I was watching him, and taking note of the attentions he paid the lady members.

On this occasion I nearly made a catastrophic mistake. It is a simple fact that I am a very good snooker player, easily the best in that club. As I was standing watching another game in progress awaiting my turn for the table, *I suddenly realised that Kelly did not play snooker at all!* For some moments, a cold sweat stood out on Kelly's brow at the narrowness of this escape. I went to the bar. There, a garrulous lady (who thinks her unsolicited conversation is a fair exchange for a drink) began talking to me. She remarked the long absence of my nice Mr. Murphy. She said he was missed a lot in the snooker room. I was hot and embarrassed and soon went home. To Kelly's place, of course.

Not embarrassment, but a real sense of danger, was to be my next portion in this adventure. One afternoon, two very casual strangers strolled into the workshop, saying they would like a little chat with me. Cigarettes were produced. Yes indeed, they were plain-clothes-men making a few routine inquiries. This man Murphy had been reported missing by several people. Any idea where he was? None at all. When had I last seen him? Did he seem upset or disturbed? No, but he was an impetuous type. I had recently reprimanded him for bad work. On similar other occasions he had threatened to leave and seek work in England. Had I been away for a few days myself? Yes, down in Cork for a few days. On business. Yes… yes… some people thinking of starting a natural museum down there, technical school people—that sort of thing.

The casual manner of these men worried me, but I was sure they did not suspect the truth and that they were genuinely interested in tracing Murphy. Still, I knew I was in danger, without knowing the exact nature of the threat I had to counter. Whiskey cheered me somewhat.

Then it happened. The two detectives came back accompanied by two other men in uniform. They showed me a search warrant. It was purely a formality; it had to be done in the case of all missing persons. They had already searched Murphy's digs and had found nothing of interest. They were very sorry for upsetting the place during my working hours.

A few days later the casual gentlemen called and put me under arrest for the wilful murder of Murphy, of myself. They proved the charge in due course with all sorts of painfully amassed evidence, including the remains of human bones in the furnace. I was sentenced to be hanged. Even if I could now prove that Murphy still lived by shedding the accursed skin, what help would that be? Where, they would ask, is Kelly?

This is my strange and tragic story. And I end it with the thought that if Kelly and I must each be either murderer or murdered, it is perhaps better to accept my present fate as philosophically as I can and be cherished in the public mind as the victim of this murderous monster, Kelly. He *was* a murderer, anyway.

SCENES IN A NOVEL

Flann O'Brien

Flann O'Brien (1911–1966), whose real name was Brian O'Nolan, and who wrote under multiple pen names, was an Irish novelist, playwright and satirist. He wrote satirical columns for the *Irish Times* as well as novels, the most famous of which are *At Swim-Two-Birds* and *The Third Policeman*. O'Brien's bizarre humour and modernist metafiction has attracted a wide following. Though he was influenced by James Joyce he was, nonetheless, sceptical of the cult surrounding him, saying 'I declare to God if I hear that name Joyce one more time I will surely froth at the gob.' This story was originally credited to his pseudonym Brother Barnabas.

I am penning these lines, dear reader, under conditions of great emotional stress, being engaged, as I am, in the composition of a posthumous article. The great blots of sweat which gather on my brow are instantly decanted into a big red handkerchief, though I know the practice is ruinous to the complexion, having regard to the open pores and the poisonous vegetable dyes that are used nowadays in the Japanese sweat-shops. By the time these lines are in neat rows of print, with no damn over-lapping at the edges, the writer will be in Kingdom Come.*

---

* "Truagh sin, a leabhair bhig bháin
Tiocfaidh lá, is ba fíor,
Déarfaidh neach os cionn do chláir
Ní mhaireann an lámh do scríobh."

["It is a pity, beloved little book
A day will come, to be sure,
Someone will inscribe over your contents
'The hand that wrote this lives not.'" (Trans. Jack Fennell)]

I have rented Trotsky's villa in Paris, though there are four defects in the lease (three reckoning by British law) and the drains are—what shall I say?—just a *leetle* bit Gallic. Last week, I set about the melancholy task of selling up my little home. Auction followed auction. Priceless books went for a mere song, and invaluable songs, many of them of my own composition, were ruthlessly exchanged for loads of books. Stomach-pumps and stallions went for next to nothing, whilst my ingenious home-made typewriter, in perfect order except for two faulty characters, was knocked down for four and tuppence. I was finally stripped of all my possessions, except for a few old articles of clothing upon which I had waggishly placed an enormous reserve price. I was in some doubt about a dappled dressing-gown of red fustian, bordered with a pleasing grey piping. I finally decided to present it to the Nation. The Nation, however, acting through one of its accredited Sanitary Inspectors, declined the gift—rather churlishly I thought—and pleading certain statutory prerogatives, caused the thing to be burnt in a yard off Chatham Street within a stone's throw of the house where the Brothers Sheares played their last game of *taiplis* [draughts]. Think of that! When such things come to pass, as Walt Whitman says, you re-examine philosophies and religions. Suggestions as to compensation were pooh-poohed and sallies were made touching on the compulsory acquisition of slum property. You see? If a great mind is to be rotted and deranged, no meanness or no outrage is too despicable, no maggot of officialdom is too contemptible to perpetrate it... the ash of my dressing-gown, a sickly wheaten colour, and indeed, the whole incident reminded me forcibly of Carruthers McDaid* Carruthers McDaid is a man I created one night when I had swallowed nine stouts and felt vaguely blasphemous. I gave him a good but worn-out mother and an industrious father, and coolly negativing fifty years of eugenics, made him a worthless scoundrel, a betrayer of women and a secret drinker. He had a sickly wheaten head, the watery blue eyes of the weakling. For if the truth must be told I had

* Who is Carruthers McDaid, you ask?

started to compose a novel and McDaid was the kernel or the fulcrum of it. Some writers have started with a good and noble hero and traced his weakening, his degradation and his eventual downfall; others have introduced a degenerate villain to be ennobled and uplifted to the tune of twenty-two chapters, usually at the hands of a woman—"She was not beautiful, but a shortened nose, a slightly crooked mouth and eyes that seemed brimful of a simple complexity seemed to spell a curious attraction, an inexplicable charm." In my own case, McDaid, starting off as a rank waster and a rotter, was meant to sink slowly to absolutely the last extremities of human degradation. Nothing, absolutely nothing, was to be too low for him, the wheaten-headed hound…

I shall never forget the Thursday when the thing happened. I retired to my room at about six o'clock, fortified with a pony of porter and two threepenny cigars, and manfully addressed myself to the achievement of Chapter Five. McDaid, who for a whole week had been living precariously by selling kittens to foolish old ladies and who could be said to be existing on the immoral earnings of his cat, was required to rob a poor-box in a church. But no! Plot or no plot, it was not to be.

"Sorry, old chap," he said, "but I absolutely can't do it."

"What's this, Mac," said I, "getting squeamish in your old age?"

"Not squeamish exactly," he replied, "but I bar poor-boxes. Dammit, you can't call me squeamish. Think of that bedroom business in Chapter Two, you old dog."

"Not another word," said I sternly, "you remember that new shaving brush you bought?"

"Yes."

"Very well, you burst the poor-box or it's anthrax in two days."

"But, I say, old chap, that's a bit thick."

"You think so? Well, I'm old-fashioned enough to believe that your opinions don't matter."

We left it at that. Each of us firm, outwardly polite, perhaps, but determined to yield not one tittle of our inalienable rights. It was only afterwards that the whole thing came out. Knowing that he was a dyed-in-the-wool atheist, I had sent him to a revivalist prayer-meeting, purely for the purpose of scoffing and showing the reader the blackness of his soul. It appears that he remained to pray. Two days afterwards I caught him sneaking out to Gardiner Street at seven in the morning. Furthermore, a contribution to the funds of a well-known charity, a matter of four-and-sixpence in the name of Miles Caritatis was not, I understand, unconnected with our proselyte. A character ratting on his creator and exchanging the pre-destined hangman's rope for a halo is something new. It is, however, only one factor in my impending dissolution. Shaun Svoolish, my hero, the composition of whose heroics have cost me many a sleepless day, has formed an alliance with a slavey in Griffith Avenue; and Shiela, his "steady," an exquisite creature I produced for the sole purpose of loving him and becoming his wife, is apparently to be given the air. You see? My carefully thought-out plot is turned inside out and goodness knows where this individualist flummery is going to end. Imagine sitting down to finish a chapter and running bang into an unexplained slavey at the turn of a page! I reproached Shaun, of course.

"Frankly, Shaun," I said, "I don't like it."

"I'm sorry," he said. "My brains, my brawn, my hands, my body are willing to work for you, but the heart! Who shall say yea or nay to the timeless passions of a man's heart? Have you ever been in love? Have you ever—?"

"What about Shiela, you shameless rotter? I gave her dimples, blue eyes, blonde hair and a beautiful soul. The last time she met you, I rigged her out in a blue swagger outfit, brand new. You now throw the whole lot back in my face… Call it cricket if you like, Shaun, but don't expect me to agree."

"I may be a prig," he replied, "but I know what I like. Why can't I marry Bridie and have a shot at the Civil Service?"

"Railway accidents are fortunately rare," I said finally, "but when they happen they are horrible. Think it over."

"You wouldn't dare!"

"O, wouldn't I? Maybe you'd like a new shaving brush as well."

And that was that.

Treason is equally widespread among the minor characters. I have been confronted with a Burmese shanachy, two corner-boys, a barmaid, and five bus-drivers, none of whom could give a satisfactory explanation of their existence or a plausible account of their movements. They are evidently "friends" of my characters. The only character to yield me undivided and steadfast allegiance is a drunken hedonist who is destined to be killed with kindness in Chapter Twelve. *And he knows it!* Not that he is any way lacking in cheek, of course. He started nagging me one evening.

"I say, about the dust-jacket—"

"Yes?"

"No damn vulgarity, mind. Something subtle, refined. If the thing was garish or cheap, I'd die of shame."

"Felix," I snapped, "mind your own business."

Just one long round of annoyance and petty persecution. What is troubling me just at the moment, however, is a paper-knife. I introduced it in an early scene to give Father Hennessy something to fiddle with on a parochial call. It is now in the hands of McDaid. It has a dull steel blade, and there is evidently something going on. The book is seething with conspiracy and there have been at least two whispered consultations between all the characters, including two who have not yet been officially created. Posterity taking a hand in the destiny of its ancestors, if you know what I mean. It is too bad. The only objector, I understand, has been Captain Fowler, the drunken hedonist, who insists that there shall be no foul play until Chapter Twelve has been completed; and he has been over-ruled.

Candidly, reader, I fear my number's up.

I sit at my window thinking, remembering, dreaming. Soon I go to my room to write. A cool breeze has sprung up from the west, a clean wind that plays on men at work, on boys at play and on women who seek to police the corridors, live in Stephen's Green and feel the heat of buck-shee turf…

It is a strange world, but beautiful. How hard it is, the hour of parting. I cannot call in the Guards, for we authors have our foolish pride. The destiny of Brother Barnabas is sealed, sealed for aye.

I must write!

These, dear reader, are my last words. Keep them and cherish them. Never again can you read my deathless prose, for my day that has been a good day is past.

Remember me and pray for me.

Adieu!

WELCOME TO FRIENDLY SKIES!

Joyce Carol Oates

Joyce Carol Oates (1938–) is an American novelist, short story writer and essayist noted for her vast literary output in a variety of styles and genres. She has won a host of prizes, including the National Book Award, two O. Henry Awards, the National Humanities Medal and the Jerusalem Prize. Oates has taught at Princeton University since 1978.

Ladies and gentlemen WELCOME to our friendly skies! WELCOME aboard our North American Airways Boeing 878 Classic Aircraft! This is North American Airways Flight 443 to Amchitka, Alaska—Birdwatchers and Environmental Activists Special!

Our 182-passenger Boeing Classic this morning is under the able command of Captain Hiram Slatt, discharged from service in the United States Air Force mission in Afghanistan after six heroic deployments and now returned, following a restorative sabbatical at the VA Neuropsychiatric Hospital in Wheeling, West Virginia to his "first love"—civilian piloting for North American Airways.

Captain Slatt has informed us that, once we are cleared for *takeoff*, our flying time will be between approximately seventeen and twenty-two hours depending upon ever-shifting Pacific Ocean air currents and the ability of our seasoned Classic 878 to withstand gale-force winds of 90 knots roaring "like a vast army of demons" (in Captain Slatt's colorful terminology) over the Arctic Circle.

As you have perhaps noticed Flight 443 is a full—i.e., "overbooked"—flight. Actually most North American Airways flights *are* overbooked—it is Airways protocol to persist in assuming that a certain percentage of passengers will simply fail to show up at the gate having somehow expired, or disappeared, en route. For those of you who boarded with tickets for seats already taken—North American Airways apologizes for this unforeseeable development. We have dealt with the emergency situation by assigning seats in four lavatories as well as in the hold and in designated areas of the overhead bin.

Therefore our request to passengers in Economy Plus, Economy, and Economy Minus is that you force your carry-ons beneath the seat in front of you; and what cannot be crammed into that space, or in the overhead bin, if no one is occupying the overhead bin, you must grip securely on your lap for the duration of the flight.

Passengers in First Class may give their drink orders now.

SECURITY:

Our Classic 878 aircraft is fully "secured": that is, we have on board several (unidentified, incognito) Federal Marshals for the protection of our passengers. Under Federal Aviation Regulations, no Federal Marshal, pilot or co-pilot, or crewmember is allowed a firearm on board any aircraft, for obvious reasons. However, under extenuating circumstances, in the event of the aircraft being forced to land unlawfully, a pilot of the rank of captain or above is allowed one "concealed weapon" (in Captain Slatt's case, a .45-caliber handgun worn on his person); with the captain's permission, his co-pilot is similarly allowed a concealed weapon. (In this case, copilot Lieutenant M. Crisco, much-decorated ex-Navy pilot, is also armed with a .45-caliber handgun.) Federal Marshals are armed with tasers of the highest voltage, virtually as lethal as more conventional weapons, which, as they say, they "will not hesitate to use if provoked."

As passenger security comes first with us, all passengers are fore-warned that it is not in their best interests to behave in any way that might be construed as "aggressive"—"threatening"—"subversive"—"suspicious" by security officers. All passengers are urged to report to the nearest flight attendant any suspicious behavior, verbal expressions, facial tics and mannerisms exhibited by fellow passengers; this includes the perusal of suspicious and "subversive" reading material. As Home-land Security advises us: "If you see something, say something."

To which Captain Slatt has amended grimly: "See it, slay it."

Note also: Federal Aviation Regulations require passengers to comply with the lighted information signs and crewmember instructions. Please observe the NO SMOKING sign which will remain illuminated through the duration of the flight; smoking is prohibited throughout the cabin and in the lavatories though allowed, under special circumstances, in the cockpit. All lavatories are equipped with smoke detection systems and Federal Law prohibits tampering with, disabling, or destroying these systems; accordingly, Federal Marshals are deputized to punish violators of this regulation at once, and harshly.

We will quote Captain Slatt in a more waggish mood: "If you smoke, you croak."

We crewmembers of North American Airways are here to ensure that you have a comfortable trip but we are primarily concerned about your SAFETY. With that in mind we ask that you take the North American Airways Safety Information Card out of the seat pocket in front of you and follow along as we perform our SAFETY demonstration.

SEAT BELT:

Our first and most important safety feature is the SEAT BELT.

Now that you are all comfortably seated please follow instructions: to fasten your seat belt, insert the metal fitting into the buckle until you hear a sharp *click!* If some of you are (as we noticed with derisive little chuckles as you'd shuffled on board) "plus-size" you may have some difficulty fitting your belt across your paunch; simply ring your overhead service bell and an airflight attendant, or two, or three as the case may be, will force the belt in place. The ensuing *click!* means that the belt is *securely locked in place.* Next, adjust your SEAT BELT to fit snugly with the loose end of the strap. Your SEAT BELT should be worn low and tight across your lap like a leather belt that has, for some obscure reason, slipped from your waist to bind you tightly across the thighs like a vise that will prevent your pants from "falling down" as well as pulling them taut to assure a proper crease even in the event of aircraft catastrophe.

Yes, your SEAT BELT *is* locked in place. (Didn't I just tell you this? Why are some of you struggling to *unlock your locked* seat belts, if you have been listening?) Flight 443 to Amchitka, Alaska is a very special flight. Article 19 of Homeland Security Provisions allows for specially regulated flights over "nondomestic" (i.e., foreign) territories to suspend "buckle release" privileges for such duration of time as the captain of the aircraft deems necessary for purposes of safety and passenger control.

Use of lavatories on this flight has been suspended, for reasons explained. So you can see there is no practical purpose in your seat belts not being *locked.*

In any case you have all signed waivers (perhaps under the impression that you were signing up for Frequent Flyer credits) that grant to the flight captain a wide range of discriminatory powers for security purposes. (Such waivers are fully legal documents under Federal Statute 9384, Homeland Security.)

EMERGENCY EXITS:

Those passengers who unwittingly find themselves in "emergency exit rows" are expected to assist our (badly understaffed) flight attendant team in the (unlikely) event of an emergency. Namely, you will be expected to *struggle to open the very heavy exit door* which might be warped, stuck, or in some other way unopenable, even as terrified fellow passengers are pushing against you and trampling you amid the chaos of a crash or forced landing.

Passengers who believe that they are not capable of such courageous and selfless altruism in a time of emergency should raise their hands at once to have their seats reassigned.

("Reassigned" where?—that, you will discover.)

EMERGENCY MEASURES:

In the (unlikely) event of an EMERGENCY your seat belts are guaranteed to 'pop open" to free you. And in the (unlikely) event that your seat belt is malfunctioning and remains in *lock* mode, a flight attendant will help you extricate yourself, if there are any flight attendants still remaining in the cabin after the emergency announcement.

As you are on a Boeing 878 Classic aircraft you will find that there are ten emergency exits of which the majority are in the First Class and Economy Plus compartments. A map of the aircraft will indicate five doors on the left and five doors on the right, each clearly marked with a red EXIT sign overhead.

All doors (except the overwing doors at 3 left and 3 right) are equipped with slide/ rafts (except in those instances in which the overwing doors are at 5 left and 7 right). These rafts are intended to be detached in the event of a WATER EVACUATION. The overwing doors are equipped with a ramp and an off-wing slide. (A thirty-foot 'slide" into icy waters is an astonishing visceral experience, survivors have claimed. Some have confirmed that the slide was a "life-altering" experience not unlike the euphoria induced by an epileptic attack or a "near-death" experience and that they "believe they are more spiritual persons for having lived through it").

Life rafts are located in "pull-down" ceiling compartments at the overwing doors. For our passengers in First Class, your escape routes near the front of the aircraft are clearly marked: FIRST CLASS EXIT. Passengers in Economy Plus, Economy, Economy Minus, Overhead Bin, and Hold are advised to locate the two exits nearest you, if you can find them; two exits is preferable to one, or none, in case one exit is blocked by crammed and crushed bodies or by flaming debris. Detailed instructions regarding slides and rafts are available in cartoon illustrations in the safety information card for slower-witted passengers or for passengers in states of extreme apprehension.

Though the odds of survival in the freezing waters of the Pacific Ocean even amid flaming wreckage are not high you will find in our air flight magazine *Friendly Skies Forever!* a monthly feature of interviews with passengers who somehow managed just this miraculous feat, in such hostile yet scenic environments as the Cape of Good Horn, the northern seacoast of Antarctica, the Bering Strait, and our destination today, the murky turbulent shark-infested icy waters of the Aleutian Islands strangely beloved by birdwatchers and environmentalists.

FLOOR-PATH LIGHTING:

This state-of-the-art aircraft is equipped with aisle-path lighting, which is located on the floor in the left and right aisles. In the event that "cabin visibility" is impaired—that is, in the event of a "black-out"—the exit path should be illuminated by these lights, except in those instances in which the "black-out" is total.

"White lights lead to red lights"—keep this favorite Zen koan of Captain Slatt in mind as the red light will indicate that you have reached or are near an emergency exit. If, that is, the red light is *on*.

*

OXYGEN:

Cabin pressure is controlled for your comfort. However, it may not be to everyone's comfort. North American Airways is mandated to maintain an air supply containing at least 18% oxygen (which may present difficulties for passengers with weak respiratory systems, asthma, extreme anxiety, or expectations of air with a minimum of 21% oxygen which is the "civilian norm"). Should the air pressure change radically in flight, which will happen at times, unpredictably, though at other times predictably, compartments are designed to automatically open in the panel above your head. In the event of this emergency simply reach up—calmly!—and pull the mask to your face. Do not snatch at the mask desperately for masks made of flimsy materials have been known to "shred" in such situations.

Once the mask is on your face, oxygen should begin to flow.

In the event that oxygen does not "flow" you may simply be, as Captain Slatt says, "out of luck"; or, if so minded, you may try to inveigle your seat mate into surrendering his or her mask, quickly before oxygen deprivation sets in and you begin to hallucinate.

Or, to raise the probability of your oxygen flowing unimpeded, you may purchase our OxFloLifeSave feature for just $400. (Airflight staff will move among you to take orders now. Please raise your hands if you are interested in signing up for OxFloLifeSave rather than take your chances with "economy oxygen.")

Once you have firmly seized your mask place it carefully over your mouth and nose and secure with the elastic band as your flight attendant is demonstrating. Next, tighten by pulling on both ends of the elastic bands—not too hard, and not too hesitantly. In situations of chaos and terror "he who hesitates is lost"—but also, paradoxically, as Captain Slatt cautions, "he who acts impulsively is lost as well." Even though oxygen is flowing, at least in theory, the plastic bag may not inflate. This is estimated to occur in approximately 27% of aircraft emergency situations and it is just unfortunate! If you are traveling with children, or are seated next to someone who needs assistance, this is bad luck for them since you're obviously having enough trouble trying to secure your mask to your own face, and to breathe without hyperventilating; you certainly have no time for anyone else.

Warning: pure oxygen can be deleterious to the human brain, causing hallucinations, convulsions, black-outs, or stroke. Thus, while you should breathe deeply through your oxygen mask, *you should not breathe too deeply.*

Continue breathing through the mask until advised by a uniformed crewmember to remove it. Do not—repeat: *do not*— surrender your oxygen mask to any individual who requests it if he or she is not in easily recognizable *North American Airways uniform.*

LIFE VEST:

Your life vest is located in a pouch beneath your seat. You may locate it now, to give yourself a "sense of security."

Should life vest use become necessary, remove your vest from the plastic packet as efficiently as possible, using both fingernails and incisors as required, but do not— repeat: *do not*—paw desperately at the packet which has been made toughly "childproof" for the protection of our youngest passengers.

Once you have succeeded in tearing open the packet remove the life vest by using both hands, with a firm tug; slip the vest over your (lowered) head and pull smartly downward on the front panel with both hands exerting equal pressure. (Do not favor your strong hand over your weak hand as this may interfere with the operation of the life vest.) Next, bring the strap around your waist and insert it into the buckle on the front. (If there is no buckle on the front, you will have to fashion a "buckle" with the fingers and thumb of one hand—use your imagination!) Next, pull on the loose strap until the vest fits snugly—as I am now demonstrating. If you are a "plus-size"—and your life vest does not fit—this is an unfortunate development you should have considered before you purchased your ticket to Amchitka, Alaska!

If you are a "minus-size" and it looks as if you are "drowning" in the life vest— this is very witty of you! You may well be quoted in *Friendly Skies Forever!* With your oxygen mask and your life vest you are now prepared to attempt to exit the aircraft amid a Dante-esque chaos of flames, boiling black smoke, dangling live electric wires, the screams and pleadings of your fellow passengers—or to, as Captain Slatt says, "walk the walk of Hell."

As you make your way out of the aircraft, by whatever desperate and improvised means, assuming you have located an exit that is unblocked, do not forget to INFLATE the vest by pulling down firmly on the red tabs. It is very important that you remember to INFLATE the life vest as an uninflated life vest is of no more worth in the choppy seas that await you than a soggy copy of *The New York Times* would be.

(In some rare cases, if the vest fails to INFLATE by way of the red tabs, it may be orally inflated by a strenuous, superhuman blowing into the inflation tubes at shoulder level, roughly equivalent, it has been esti- mated, to the effort required to blow up three hundred average-sized party balloons within a few minutes. Good luck with this!) For First Class passengers each vest is equipped with a "rescue light" on the shoulder for night use, which is water-activated by removing the Pull to Light tab located on the battery. In this way your life vest will provide for you a tiny, near-invisible "rescue light" in the choppy shark-infested waters of the nighttime Pacific Ocean.

(It *is* complicated, isn't it! Each time we give our life vest demonstra- tion something goes wrong, but it is never the same "something" from one time to another and so we have not the privilege of "learning from our mistakes"!)

*

"RETURN":

No Frequent Flyer mileage is available for the "Return Flight 443"—
there is no scheduled "Return Flight 443."

This "No Return" from Amchitka, Alaska is stipulated in the waiver
you cheerfully signed before boarding our aircraft without (it seems)
having read, or perhaps even seen, the fine print.

APPLICATION:

Some of you are looking alarmed at the possibility of "No Return"—
for reasons having to do with the Defense Department s Amchitka Bio-
Labs Research Project which covers six hundred acres on the island
though not marked on any (nonclassified) map, and which is your destination upon arrival at Amchitka.

Yes, this is a "surprise." Yes, it is too late to "exit."

Please note, however: less than 83% of passengers will be taken into
custody as *subjects* in the bio-lab experiments; the remainder of you
will be drafted as lab assistants and security staff, for there is considerable employee turnover at Amchitka. Applications for these coveted
positions should be filled out as soon as possible, as hiring decisions
will be made before our arrival at Amchitka.

Please don't hesitate to raise your hand if you would like an application.

Note that the application requires a complete resume of education,
background, employment, and financial assets. Now is not the time for
"false modesty"!

PREPARATION FOR TAKEOFF:

Captain Slatt reports from the cockpit that the "mysterious" technical
difficulties the aircraft has been exhibiting since your boarding ninety

minutes ago have been deemed solved (at least by Homeland Security) and the aircraft is now ready for *takeoff*.

Accordingly, all doors have been locked; all SEAT BELTS are in *lock mode*; attendants, please be seated.

As some of you have discovered it is too late to change your mind about your exotic "birdwatching" expedition to the North Polar region. It was too late, in fact, as soon as you boarded the plane and took your seats. Therefore, please ensure that your seat backs and tray tables are in their full upright and stowed positions and all your carry-on items in secure places where they will not fly up suddenly and injure you or your hapless neighbors.

Ladies and gentlemen, we are now prepared to take off. We thank you for choosing North American Airways. Settle back in your seats, take a deep breath, and enjoy our friendly skies!

JUST A LITTLE ONE

Dorothy Parker

Dorothy Parker (1893–1967) was a New Yorker famous for her hard drinking, stinging repartee and endlessly quotable one-liners. In 1915 one of her poems was purchased by *Vanity Fair*, and she then went on to work for *Vogue* and *Vanity Fair*. In 1925, she began writing for the brand new magazine *The New Yorker*, establishing a connection that would last for over thirty years. She and her second husband, the actor Alan Campbell, were Oscar-nominated for their screenplay of the movie *A Star is Born*. Trying to define what humour means to her, Parker wrote, 'There must be a magnificent disregard of your reader, for if he cannot follow you, there is nothing you can do about it.'

I like this place, Fred. This is a nice place. How did you ever find it? I think you're perfectly marvelous, discovering a speakeasy in the year 1928. And they let you right in, without asking you a single question. I bet you could get into the subway without using anybody's name. Couldn't you, Fred?

Oh, I like this place better and better, now that my eyes are getting accustomed to it. You mustn't let them tell you this lighting system is original with them, Fred; they got the idea from the Mammoth Cave. This is you sitting next to me, isn't it? Oh, you can't fool me. I'd know that knee anywhere.

You know what I like about this place? It's got atmosphere. That's what it's got. If you would ask the waiter to bring a fairly sharp knife, I could cut off a nice little block of the atmosphere, to take home with me. It would be interesting to have for my memory book. I'm going to start keeping a memory book tomorrow. Don't let me forget.

Why, I don't know, Fred—what are you going to have? Then I guess I'll have a highball, too; please, just a little one. Is it really real Scotch? Well, that will be a new experience for me. You ought to see the Scotch I've got home in my cupboard; at least it was in the cupboard this morning—it's probably eaten its way out by now. I got it for my birthday. Well, it was something. The birthday before, all I got was a year older.

This is a nice highball, isn't it? Well, well, well, to think of me having real Scotch; I'm out of the bush leagues at last. Are you going to have another one? Well, I shouldn't like to see you drinking all by yourself, Fred. Solitary drinking is what causes half the crime in the country. That's what's responsible for the failure of prohibition. But please, Fred, tell him to make mine just a little one. Make it awfully weak; just cambric Scotch.

It will be nice to see the effect of veritable whisky upon one who has been accustomed only to the simpler forms of entertainment. You'll like that, Fred. You'll stay by me if anything happens, won't you? I don't think there will be anything spectacular, but I want to ask you one thing, just in case. Don't let me take any horses home with me. It doesn't matter so much about stray dogs and kittens, but elevator boys get awfully stuffy when you try to bring in a horse. You might just as well know that about me now, Fred. You can always tell that the crash is coming when I start getting tender about Our Dumb Friends. Three highballs, and I think I'm St. Francis of Assisi.

But I don't believe anything is going to happen to me on these. That's because they're made of real stuff. That's what the difference is. This just makes you feel fine. Oh, I feel swell, Fred. You do too, don't you? I knew you did, because you look better. I love that tie you have on. Oh, did Edith give it to you? Ah, wasn't that nice of her? You know, Fred, most people are really awfully nice. There are dam few that aren't pretty fine at heart. You've got a beautiful heart, Fred. You'd be the first person I'd go to if I were in trouble. I guess you are just about the best friend I've got in the world. But I worry about you, Fred. I do so, too. I don't think you take enough care of yourself. You ought to take care of yourself for your friends' sake. You oughtn't to drink all this terrible stuff that's around; you owe it to your friends to be careful. You don't mind my talking to you like this, do you? You see, dear, it's because I'm your friend that I hate to see you not taking care of yourself. It hurts me to see you batting around the way you've been doing. You ought to stick to this place, where they have real Scotch that can't do you any harm. Oh, darling, do you really think I ought to? Well, you tell him just a little bit of a one. Tell him, sweet.

Do you come here often, Fred? I shouldn't worry about you so much if I knew you were in a safe place like this. Oh, is this where you were Thursday night? I see. Why, no, it didn't make a bit of difference, only you told me to call you up, and like a fool I broke a date I had, just because I thought I was going to see you. I just sort of naturally thought so, when you said to call you up. Oh, good Lord, don't make all that fuss about it. It really didn't make the slightest difference. It just didn't seem a very friendly way to behave, that's all. I don't know—I'd been believing we were such good friends. I'm an awful idiot about people, Fred. There aren't many who are really your friend at heart. Practically anybody would play you dirt for a nickel. Oh, yes, they would.

Was Edith here with you, Thursday night? This place must be very becoming to her. Next to being in a coal mine, I can't think of anywhere she could go that the light would be more flattering to that pan of hers. Do you really know a lot of people that say she's good-looking? You must have a wide acquaintance among the astigmatic, haven't you, Freddie, dear? Why, I'm not being any way at all—it's simply one of those things, either you can see it or you can't. Now to me, Edith looks like something that would eat her young. Dresses well? *Edith* dresses well? Are you trying to kid me, Fred, at my age? You mean you mean it? Oh, my God. You mean those clothes of hers are *intentional*? My heavens, I always thought she was on her way out of a burning building.

Well, we live and learn. Edith dresses well! Edith's got good taste!

Yes, she's got sweet taste in neckties. I don't suppose I ought to say it about such a dear friend of yours, Fred, but she is the lousiest necktie-picker-out I ever saw. I never saw anything could touch that thing you have around your neck. All right, suppose I did say I liked it. I just said that because I felt sorry for you. I'd feel sorry for anybody with a thing like that on. I just wanted to try to make you feel good, because I thought you were my friend. My friend! I haven't got a friend in the world. Do you know that, Fred? Not one single friend in this world.

All right, what do you care if I'm crying? I can cry if I want to, can't I? I guess you'd cry, too, if you didn't have a friend in the world. Is my face very bad? I suppose that damned mascara has run all over it. I've got to give up using mascara, Fred; life's too sad. Isn't life terrible? Oh, my God, isn't life awful? Ah, don't cry, Fred. Please don't. Don't you care, baby. Life's terrible, but don't you care. You've got friends. I'm the one that hasn't got any friends. I am so. No, it's me. I'm the one.

I don't think another drink would make me feel any better. I don't know whether I want to feel any better. What's the sense of feeling good, when life's so terrible? Oh, all right, then. But please tell him just a little one, if it isn't too much trouble. I don't want to stay here much longer. I don't like this place. It's all dark and stuffy. It's the kind of place Edith would be crazy about—that's all I can say about this place. I know I oughtn't to talk about your best friend, Fred, but that's a terrible woman. That woman is the louse of this world. It makes me feel just awful that you trust that woman, Fred. I hate to see anybody play you dirt I'd hate to see you get hurt. That's what makes me feel so terrible. That's why I'm getting mascara all over my face. No, please don't, Fred. You mustn't hold my hand. It wouldn't be fair to Edith. We've got to play fair with the big louse. After all, she's your best friend, isn't she?

Honestly? Do you honestly mean it, Fred? Yes, but how could I help thinking so, when you're with her all the time—when you bring her here every night in the week? Really, only Thursday? Oh, I know— I know how those things are. You simply can't help it, when you get stuck with a person that way. Lord, I'm glad you realize what an awful thing that woman is. I was worried about it, Fred. It's because I'm your friend. Why, of course I am, darling. You know I am. Oh, that's just silly, Freddie. You've got heaps of friends. Only you'll never find a better friend than I am. No, I know that I know I'll never find a better friend than you are to me. Just give me back my hand a second, till I get this damned mascara out of my eye.

Yes, I think we ought to, honey. I think we ought to have a little drink, on account of our being friends. Just a little one, because it's real Scotch, and we're real friends. After all, friends are the greatest things in the world, aren't they, Fred? Gee, it makes you feel good to know you have a friend. I feel great, don't you, dear? And you look great, too. I'm proud to have you for a friend. Do you realize, Fred, what a rare thing a friend is, when you think of all the terrible people there are in this world? Animals are much better than people. God, I love animals. That's what I like about you, Fred. You're so fond of animals.

Look, I'll tell you what let's do, after we've had just a little highball. Let's go out and pick up a lot of stray dogs. I never had enough dogs in my life, did you? We ought to have more dogs. And maybe there'd be some cats around, if we looked. And a horse, I've never had one single horse, Fred. Isn't that rotten? Not one single horse. Ah, I'd like a nice old cab-horse, Fred. Wouldn't you? I'd like to take care of it and comb its hair and everything. Ah, don't be stuffy about it, Fred, please don't. I need a horse, honestly I do. Wouldn't you like one? It would be so sweet and kind. Let's have a drink and then let's you and I go out and get a horsie, Freddie—just a little one, darling, just a little one.

YOU WERE PERFECTLY FINE

Dorothy Parker

Dorothy Parker (1893–1967) was a New Yorker famous for her hard drinking, stinging repartee and endlessly quotable one-liners. In 1915 one of her poems was purchased by *Vanity Fair*, and she then went on to work for *Vogue* and *Vanity Fair*. In 1925, she began writing for the brand new magazine *The New Yorker*, establishing a connection that would last for over thirty years. She and her second husband, the actor Alan Campbell, were Oscar-nominated for their screenplay of the movie *A Star is Born*. Trying to define what humour means to her, Parker wrote, 'There must be a magnificent disregard of your reader, for if he cannot follow you, there is nothing you can do about it.'

The pale young man eased himself carefully into the low chair, and rolled his head to the side, so that the cool chintz comforted his cheek and temple.

"Oh, dear," he said. "Oh, dear, oh, dear, oh, dear. Oh."

The clear-eyed girl, sitting light and erect on the couch, smiled brightly at him.

"Not feeling so well to-day?" she said.

"Oh, I'm great," he said. "Corking, I am. Know' what time I got up? Four o'clock this afternoon, sharp. I kept trying to make it, and every time I took my head off the pillow, it would roll under the bed. This isn't my head I've got on now. I think this is something that used to belong to Walt Whitman. Oh, dear, oh, dear, oh, dear."

"Do you think maybe a drink would make you feel better?" she said.

"The hair of the mastiff that bit me?" he said. "Oh, no, thank you. Please never speak of anything like that again. I'm through. I'm all, all through. Look at that hand; steady as a humming-bird. Tell me, was I very terrible last night?"

"Oh, goodness," she said, "everybody was feeling pretty high. You were all right."

"Yeah," he said. "I must have been dandy. Is everybody sore at me?"

"Good heavens, no," she said. "Everyone thought you were terribly funny. Of course, Jim Pierson got a little stuffy, there for a minute at dinner. But people sort of held him back in his chair, and got him calmed down. I don't think anybody at the other tables noticed it at all. Hardly anybody."

"He was going to sock me?" he said. "Oh, Lord. What did I do to him?"

"Why, you didn't do a thing," she said. "You were perfectly fine. But you know how silly Jim gets, when he thinks anybody is making too much fuss over Elinor."

"Was I making a pass at Elinor?" he said. "Did I do that?"

"Of course you didn't," she said. "You were only fooling, that's all. She thought you were awfully amusing. She was having a marvelous time. She only got a little tiny bit annoyed just once, when you poured the clam-juice down her back."

"My God," he said. "Clam-juice down that back. And every vertebra a little Cabot. Dear God. What'll I ever do?"

"Oh, she'll be all right," she said. "Just send her some flowers, or something. Don't worry about it. It isn't anything."

"No, I won't worry," he said. "I haven't got a care in the world. I'm sitting pretty. Oh, dear, oh, dear. Did I do any other amusing tricks at dinner?"

"You were fine," she said. "Don't be so foolish about it. Everybody was crazy about you. The maître d'hôtel was a little worried because you wouldn't stop singing, but he really didn't mind. All he said was, he was afraid they'd close the place again, if there was so much noise. But he didn't care a bit, himself. I think he loved seeing you have such a good time. Oh, you were just singing away, there, for about an hour. It wasn't so terribly loud, at all."

"So I sang," he said. "That must have been a treat. I sang."

"Don't you remember?" she said. "You just sang one song after another. Everybody in the place was listening. They loved it. Only you kept insisting that you wanted to sing some song about some kind of fusiliers or other, and everybody kept shushing you, and you'd keep trying to start it again. You were wonderful. We were all trying to make you stop singing for a minute, and eat something, but you wouldn't hear of it. My, you were funny."

"Didn't I eat any dinner?" he said.

"Oh, not a thing," she said. "Every time the waiter would offer you something, you'd give it right back to him, because you said that he was your long-lost brother, changed in the cradle by a gypsy band, and that anything you had was his. You had him simply roaring at you."

"I bet I did,"' he said. "I bet I was comical. Society's Pet, I must have been. And what happened then, after my overwhelming success with the waiter?"

"Why, nothing much," she said. "You took a sort of dislike to some old man with white hair, sitting across the room, because you didn't like his necktie and you wanted to tell him about it. But we got you out, before he got really mad."

"Oh, we got out," he said. "Did I walk?"

"Walk! Of course you did," she said. "You were absolutely all right. There was that nasty stretch of ice on the sidewalk, and you did sit down awfully hard, you poor dear. But good heavens, that might have happened to anybody."

"Oh surely," he said. "Mrs. Coolidge or anybody. So I fell down on the sidewalk. That would explain what's the matter with my—Yes. I see. And then what, if you don't mind?"

"Ah, now, Peter!" she said. "You can't sit there and say you don't remember what happened after that! I did think that maybe you were just a little tight at dinner—oh, you were perfectly all right, and all that, but I did know you were feeling pretty gay. But you were so serious, from the time you fell down—I never knew you to be that way. Don't you know, how you told me I had never seen your real self before? Oh, Peter, I just couldn't bear it, if you didn't remember that lovely long ride we took together in the taxi! Please, you do remember that, don't you? I think it would simply kill me, if you didn't."

"Oh, yes," he said. "Riding in the taxi. Oh, yes, sure. Pretty long ride, hmm?"

"Round and round and round the Park," she said. "Oh, and the trees were shining so in the moonlight. And you said you never knew before that you really had a soul."

"Yes," he said. "I said that. That was me."

"You said such lovely, lovely things," she said. "And I'd never known, all this time, how you had been feeling about me, and I'd never dared to let you see how I felt about you. And then last night—oh, Peter dear, I think that taxi ride was the most important thing that ever happened to us in our lives."

"Yes," he said. "I guess it must have been."

"And we're going to be so happy," she said. "Oh, I just want to tell everybody! But I don't know—I think maybe it would be sweeter to keep it all to ourselves."

"I think it would be," he said.

"Isn't it lovely?" she said.

"Yes," he said. "Swell."

"Lovely!" she said.

"Look here," he said, "do you mind if I have a drink? I mean, just medicinally, you know. I'm off the stuff for life, so help me. But I think I feel a collapse coming on."

"Oh, I think it would do you good," she said. "You poor boy, it's a shame you feel so awful. I'll go make you a highball."

"Honestly," he said, "I don't see how you could ever want to speak to me again, after I made such a fool of myself, last night. I think I'd better go join a monastery in Thibet."

"You crazy idiot! " she said. "As if I could ever let you go away now! Stop talking like that. You were perfectly fine."

She jumped up from the couch, kissed him quickly on the forehead, and ran out of the room.

The pale young man looked after her, and shook his head long and slowly, then dropped it in his damp and trembling hands.

"Oh, dear," he said. "Oh, dear, oh, dear, oh, dear."

SWINDLE SHEET WITH BLUEBLOOD ENGRAILED, ARRANT FIBS RAMPANT

S.J. Perelman

Sidney Joseph Perelman (1904–1979) was born into a Russian Jewish immigrant family in Brooklyn. He attended Brown University in 1922 where he became the cartoonist of the college magazine and finally its editor. After publishing his first two books he was invited to Hollywood by Groucho Marx to script two films: *Monkey Business* and *Horse Feathers*. A contributor to *The New Yorker* from 1935, he soon became the magazine's most successful humourist.

I promise you I hadn't a clue, when I unfolded my *Times* one recent morning at the bootblack's, that it would contain the most electrifying news to come out of England in a generation—the biggest, indeed, since the relief of Lucknow. As invariably happens after one passes forty, the paper sagged open to the obituary page; I skimmed it quickly to make sure I wasn't listed, and then, having winnowed the theatrical, movie, and book gossip, began reading the paper as every enlightened coward does nowadays, back to front. There, prominently boxed in the second section, was the particular dispatch—terse and devoid of bravura, yet charged with a kind of ragged dignity. "BRITAIN'S INDIGENT LORDS ASK EXPENSE ACCOUNTS," it announced over a London dateline, and went on, "Some peers are too impoverished in the highly taxed present-day welfare state to travel to London and do their duty without pay, the

House of Lords was told today. The Upper House, shorn by the last Labor Government of much of its power, was debating its own possible reform. One of its proposals was for giving expense money to those members who do trouble to come to Westminster. At present the Lords get no salaries and nothing but bare traveling expenses. On an average day no more than one peer in ten is present."

"Well, well!" I exclaimed involuntarily. "It's high time, if you ask me."

"What'd you say?" inquired the bootblack with a start, almost spilling the jonquil-colored dye with which he was defacing my shoes.

"This story about the British peers," I replied. "Poor chaps are practically on the dole—beggars-on-horseback sort of thing. Pretty ironical situation, what?"

He threw me a sidelong glance, plainly uncertain whether it was safe to commit himself. "You a peer?" he asked cautiously.

"No," I said, "but I do think England's in a hell of a state when your Gloucesters and your Somersets have to get down on their knees and scrounge expense money."

"Yeah, the whole world's falling apart," he said, scratching his ear reflectively with his dauber. "A couple of shmos like you and me, we can't even get up our rent, whereas them dukes and earls and all those other highbinders over there are rolling in dough."

"But they're not," I objected. "Judging from this, they've hardly enough carfare to get from their ancestral seats to London."

"That's what I said—it's all topsy-turvy," he returned. His inflection made it abundantly clear that he was humoring an imbecile. "Look, should I put some new laces in here? These are full of knots."

"I prefer them that way," I said icily, and retired behind the paper. The snub, though momentarily soothing to my ego, cost me dear; in retaliation, he gave me such a flamboyant shine that an old gorgon on the sidewalk mistook me for a minstrel and demanded to know where I was hiding my tambourine.

Fletcherizing the news item subsequently in a more tranquil setting, it occurred to me that while the projected expense accounts might seem a godsend at first glance, they could also be a potential source of embarrassment to the noble lords. No matter how august their lineage, they will eventually have to undergo the scrutiny of, and explain every last deduction to, a corps of income-tax ferrets rated among the keenest in the world. I have been speculating about just how, in these circumstances, one applies the thumbscrews to a man whose title dates back four or five centuries—how, in other words, the British tax inquisitor manages to grovel and browbeat at the same time. Obviously, the best way to find out is to secrete ourselves behind the arras at such an examination. Softly, then, and remember, everything you see or hear henceforth is in strictest confidence.

SCENE: The office of Simon Auger, an inspector in the review division of the Board of Inland Revenue. A small, cheerless room equipped with the standard instruments of torture—a desk, two chairs, a filing cabinet. As a decorative touch rather than for its psychological effect, someone has hung on the wall a kiboko, or rhinoceros-hide whip. When the curtain rises, Auger, a dyspeptic of forty-odd, is finishing a frugal lunch of Holland Rusk, wheat germ, and parsnips, a copy of Burke's Peerage *propped up before him. For the most part, his face is expressionless, but occasionally it betrays a wintry smile of the kind observable in barracudas. At length, he sighs deeply, stashes the book in the desk, and, withdrawing a bottle of Lucknow's Instant Relief, downs a spoonful. The phone rings.*

AUGER: Auger here... Who?... Ah, yes. Please ask His Lordship to come in, won't you? [*The door opens to admit Llewellyn Fitzpoultice, ninth Viscount Zeugma. He is in his mid-sixties, ramrod-straight, affects a white cavalry mustache and a buttonhole, and is well dressed to the point of dandyism. Having fortified himself with four brandy-and-sodas at lunch, his complexion—already bronzed by twenty-five years on the Northwest Frontier—glows like an old mahogany sideboard.*]

ZEUGMA [*Jauntily*]. Afternoon. Hope I'm not terribly late.

AUGER: Not at all. No more than three-quarters of an hour or so.

ZEUGMA: Frightfully sorry. This filthy traffic, you know. I defy anyone to find a cab in Greek Street.

AUGER: Your Lordship was lunching in Soho?

ZEUGMA: Yes, I found a rather decent little place there—Stiletto's. They do you quite well for five guineas—*coquilles St. Jacques*, snails, a tart, and a passable *rosé*. You must try it sometime.

AUGER: I could hardly afford to, at my salary.

ZEUGMA: Between ourselves, I can't either, but the Crown pays for it—ha ha ha. [*Blandly*] Necessary business expense in connection with my duties in the Upper House.

AUGER: Indeed. [*He jots down a note.*] By the way, I believe I had the pleasure of meeting a relative of yours about a fortnight ago—the Right Honourable Anthony de Profundis.

ZEUGMA. Wild young cub—Tony. What's the boy been up to?

AUGER. Little matter of evasion and fraud. He was sly, but we specialize in those sly ones—ha ha ha. [*Opening a dossier*] Well, let's get on with it, shall we? Your address remains the same, I take it—The Grange, Regurgingham-supra-Mare, Dotards, Broome Abbas, Warwickshire.

ZEUGMA. That's right. But why do you ask?

AUGER. Because your nephew changed his unexpectedly last week, if you follow me.

ZEUGMA. I—I say, it seems dreadfully warm in here. Could we open a window?

AUGER. I'm afraid not. Whoever designed this stage set forgot to include one. However, to resume. According to your return, you made thirty-one trips here from Warwickshire during the last Parliamentary session.

ZEUGMA [*Muffled*]. Whole avalanche of measures directly affecting my constituency. Crucial decisions. No time for shillyshallying.

AUGER. I have no doubt. Still, in glancing over the minutes of the Upper House I notice Your Lordship didn't speak once in all that period.

ZEUGMA. Blasted committees chained me down. Paperwork from dawn to dark. Closeted with Winnie weeks on end. Barely able to snatch a sandwich.

AUGER. Yes, few of us realize how unselfishly England's public men give of their energy. Notwithstanding, you did find time to squeeze in sixty-three meals, excluding breakfasts, for a total of four hundred fifty-seven pounds thirteen shillings. These were all concerned with legislative matters?

ZEUGMA. Every blessed one. [*Spluttering*] Confound it, are you questioning my word?

AUGER. I wouldn't dream of it. I was merely giving you what we call a surface probe—to make certain there was no aura of peculation, as it were. Now suppose we cast an eye at your hotel appropriation. These five-room suites you habitually took at the Dorchester—weren't they a bit grandiose for an overnight stay?

ZEUGMA. By Gad, sir, if you expect me to crawl into some greasy boarding house in Kensington and fry my own kippers—

AUGER. Certainly not, certainly not. One can't conceivably imagine Lady Zeugma in such an atmosphere.

ZEUGMA [*Unwarily*]. She wasn't with me—er, that is, I was batching it most of the term—

AUGER [*Smoothly*]. I see. And the rest of the time you shared the accommodations with another legislator?

ZEUGMA. Well—uh—in a way. My staff secretary— or, rather, my secretarial adviser. Mrs. Thistle Fotheringay, of Stoke Poges.

AUGER. Ah, that explains these miscellaneous charges—one hundred eighteen quid for champagne, forty-two pounds ten for caviar, and so on. Naturally, neither you nor Mrs. Fotheringay ever partook of these delicacies paid for by the state?

ZEUGMA [*Struggling to dislodge an emery board from his trachea*]. N-no, of course not. I just kept 'em on hand for colleagues— for other viscounts, you understand. Haven't touched a drop of bubbly in years. It's death to my liver.

AUGER. Really. Then perhaps you'd care to examine this cutting from a recent issue of the *Tatler*. It shows you and your-ahem-secretarial adviser with upraised champagne glasses, dining at the Bagatelle.

ZEUGMA. Demnition... I say, old man, mind if I pass it along to Mrs. Fotheringay? Women like to preserve sentimental slop like this.

AUGER. I know. That's why I thought of sending it to Lady Zeugma.

ZEUGMA [*Agitatedly*]. Wait a bit, let's not—We mustn't go off half—By Jove, I've just had an absolutely wizard idea!

AUGER. Amazing how they pop out of nowhere, isn't it?

ZEUGMA. You revenue blokes have some kind of fraternal organization, don't you? I mean where you take the missus to Blackpool, toffee for the kiddies, all that drill?

AUGER. Quite. And if I may anticipate Your Lordship, you'd like to make a small donation to our outing fund.

ZEUGMA. Why, how did you guess?

AUGER. One becomes surprisingly clairvoyant in this line of work.

ZEUGMA. Fancy that. Well, suppose you put me down for about five hundred pounds. Needn't use my name, necessarily. Call it "Compliments of a Friend."

AUGER. Very magnanimous of you, I'm sure.

ZEUGMA. Nonsense—live and let live's my motto. Let sleeping dogs lie, I always say.

AUGER. Yes, and whilst you're raking up proverbs, don't forget there's no fool like an old fool. [*He replaces the dossier in the desk, extends a packaged handkerchief to his illustrious caller.*] Would you care for one of these? Your own seems to be wringing wet.

ZEUGMA [*Undone*]. Ah, yes, many tax—that is, you're most welcome. Pip-pip. Cheerio. [*He exits, tripping over his stick and ricocheting off the filing cabinet. Auger's eyes crinkle up at the corners and he hums two or three bars of a tuneless little melody. Then, reopening* Burke's Peerage, *he begins nibbling a carrot reflectively as the curtain falls.*]

WHY BOYS LEAVE HOME

S.J. Perelman

Sidney Joseph Perelman (1904–1979) was born into a Russian Jewish immigrant family in Brooklyn. He attended Brown University in 1922 where he became the cartoonist of the college magazine and finally its editor. After publishing his first two books he was invited to Hollywood by Groucho Marx to script two films: *Monkey Business* and *Horse Feathers*. A contributor to *The New Yorker* from 1935, he soon became the magazine's most successful humourist.

Every woman worth her salt, and even the few unsalted ones I have known, cherishes somewhere in her heart midway between the auricle and the ventricle a lovely, pastel-tinted dream. Maid or matron, she longs to dress up her man in a velvet smoking jacket and red morocco slippers, plant him in his favourite easy chair with a pipe and a rattling good detective story, and then, the moment his eyes freeze over, launch into a catalogue of bargains available at the stores. My own chocolate drop is no exception. One evening a while ago, I tottered in from a gruelling afternoon at the bookmaker's and collapsed heavily in my Morris chair. I barely had time to sluice my larynx with a healing emollient of honey, orange bitters and a drop of cognac to allay the insupportable sweetness before the nightly overture struck up.

"Well, I vum," began my helpmate, unfolding her newspaper. "Do you remember those cunning little doilies Sandra Vermifuge bought two years ago at Neimann & Marcus, in Dallas? She paid a dollar forty-nine for them, and here they are at McCreery's for only a dollar forty-three. I can't wait to see her face!"

"Neither can I," I giggled. "Let's call her up and tease her! Where does she live now?"

"In Spokane, I think," said my wife doubtfully. "But you don't really intend—"

"Why not?" I urged. "Oh, come on, it's only a twenty-three-dollar toll call!" My proposal was received with an icy silence that melted forty-five seconds later, just as I had relaxed my neck muscles and begun a realistic imitation of a transcontinental truck puffing up a grade.

"Macy's is holding its annual clearance of barbecue aprons," the Voice resumed. "We've got four, but I don't think you can have too many barbecue aprons, do you?... And look at this: there's a sacrifice of poplin-covered steamer chairs at Altman's, eighty-nine dollars and ninety-eight cents, only twenty-two to a customer... Genuine quilted-rayon cheese strainers, marked down to four fifty-four... Now here's something we really need!... Are you awake?"

"Urg," I replied, to indicate I was drinking in every word.

"GIMBEL'S JACKS UP YOUR CAR!" she read breathlessly. "GIMBEL'S COVERS UP YOUR CAR. If you're going into the service or to Florida, leave your car protected, so it will stay spick-and-span until you return. Jack it up on our plywood jacks—they'll hold an eight-ton truck for the duration. Then cover it from stem to stern with our paper coverall to keep out dust, soot, grit and grime; it's sturdy kraft paper—"

"Listen!" I roared. "I like the car the way it is! I like it down there in the country with mushrooms in the clutch and chickens roosting in the glove compartment! And if you think I'm going to travel sixty-four miles in the dead of winter to dress up a '37 Plymouth in a paper tent, you can jolly well—"

"Of course not, gingerbread boy," agreed Circe soothingly, "but it can't hurt if I stop in tomorrow and look at it, can it?"

Which may explain how I came to reel into the railroad station at Frogtown, New Jersey, yesterday morning in a sub-arctic dawn, my spectacles opaque with steam and my pigmy frame bent double under a massive carton. The freight agent squirted tobacco juice over my shoes in welcome.

"Back for the summer, eh?" he inquired. "Say, you certainly look awful. What are those big circles under your eyes?"

"Glasses," I said evenly. "What the hell do you think they are?"

"You never got 'em drinkin' milk," he guffawed, slapping his thigh. "Say, what's in that there box?"

"A body," I snapped. "The body of a freight agent with a long nose that he kept sticking into other people's business." There was a short, pregnant silence during which our eyes stood toe-to-toe and slugged it out. Then, humming a nonchalant air, I sauntered into a snowdrift outside and dawdled a scant hour and a half wondering how to cover the seven miles to my duchy without a car. At last a friendly chicken farmer drew up, attracted by my humorous carrot nose, stovepipe hat and lumps of coal simulating buttons.

"Ain't no room up front here," he said hospitably, leaning out of the warm, cosy cab of his truck, "but you can ride back there with them pullets."

For the first couple of miles, it was a novel experience to travel with a boutonnière of Rhode Island Reds pecking at my cravat, but eventually their silly feminine chatter bored me, and averting my face, I drank in great healing lungfuls of the exhaust. With the perfect sense of timing that characterises everything I do, I arranged matters so that my chariot was exactly abreast of the post office as a group of neighbourhood louts emerged.

"Pretty good-sized capon you raised there, Zeb," they complimented my ferryman. "Figger on butcherin' him now or feedin' him through the winter?"

Their good-natured derision was infectious, and averting my face, I drank in great healing lungfuls of the pullets. Soon, however, the spires of my château came into sight and I vaulted nimbly into a puddle, slashing a jagged rent in my overcoat, and trudged up the glare ice to Lacklustre Farm. Time had wrought few changes in the old place; one or two chimneys had fallen down and passing sportsmen had blown out every pane of glass in the windows, but there was nothing amiss that fifty thousand dollars would not cure.

Divesting myself of my coat to insure a spanking case of pneumonia, I gamely caught up the carton and staggered to the barn where the car was housed. Fortunately, there was no need to waste time opening doors, as the wind had obligingly torn them from their tracks. The trip along the dark threshing floor was uneventful, except that I adroitly involved myself in a rope hanging from the beams and conceived the ridiculous notion that someone was trying to garrote me. I emitted a few piercing cries, however, and it shook itself loose. The car itself seemed more streamlined than I remembered it, until I realised that parties unknown had removed the tyres, along with the wheels. I rarely give way to my feelings, but in the irritation of the moment, I gave those axles a kick they will remember for many a day to come. As soon as my foot stopped throbbing, I routed out an old broom and transferred the dust and wheat chaff which had settled down over the body to my own. Then, arms akimbo, I shrewdly laid out my plan of campaign.

The first thing to do, I said to myself, was to get the car up on the wooden jacks. To accomplish this, I would need a stout tyre jack, which must be in the luggage compartment. The key to the luggage compartment, though, was on my bureau sixty-four miles away, where I had prudently left it. Ergo, I must force the lock— child's play to one whose knowledge of mechanics was a household word for ten feet around. I procured a pinch bar from the toolroom, inserted it under the door of the luggage compartment, and heaved my weight downward as outlined in first-year physics.

After picking myself up from the floor, I twisted my handkerchief into a makeshift tourniquet and decided that the wooden jacks would be superfluous anyhow, as the car already stood staunchly on its transmission. The next step hence was to envelop it in the paper coverall. I clawed up the carton and eventually succeeded in setting up the coverall, though several times the wind sweeping through the barn bore me off into the fields like a box kite.

"Now, easy does it," I said cunningly—I had reached the stage where I was addressing myself aloud—and holding the coverall above my head like Paul and Virginia fleeing before the storm, I crept up over the top of the car and dropped it neatly into place. Unluckily, this left me pinned on my stomach in the dark, slowly throttling under sturdy kraft paper; and acting on a sudden obscure impulse, I decided not to linger. I went through the side of the coverall biting, gouging and scratching, and when I hit the lane, I kept on going. The natives are still talking about the meteor covered with chicken feathers that flashed across the Delaware River yesterday afternoon. And the minute he gets his breath back, the meteor's going to do a little talking himself— to Mrs. Meteor.

From far away, I could hear my wife's voice bravely trying to control her anxiety.

"What if he becomes restless, Doctor?"

"Get him a detective story," returned the leech. "Or better still, a nice, soothing picture puzzle—something he can do with his hands."

WHOSE LADY NICOTINE?

S.J. Perelman

Sidney Joseph Perelman (1904–1979) was born into a Russian Jewish immigrant family in Brooklyn. He attended Brown University in 1922 where he became the cartoonist of the college magazine and finally its editor. After publishing his first two books he was invited to Hollywood by Groucho Marx to script two films: *Monkey Business* and *Horse Feathers*. A contributor to *The New Yorker* from 1935, he soon became the magazine's most successful humourist.

At approximately four o'clock yesterday afternoon, the present troubadour, a one-story taxpayer in a wrinkled alpaca jacket and a repossessed Panama, was gaping into the window of Alfred Buntwell Inc., the celebrated tobacconist in Radio City. Above his balding, gargoyle head floated a feathery cloud containing a Mazda bulb labelled "Idea!" Buntwell is a name revered by pipe smokers everywhere; his briars have probably penetrated farther into the earth's far places than the Union Jack. From the steaming jungles of the Gran Chaco to the snows of Kanchanjanga, from the Hook of Holland to the Great Barrier Reef, the white dot on the Buntwell pipe stem is the sign of the sahib. Deep in equatorial Africa, surrounded by head-hunters, Mungo Park clenched a Buntwell pipe between his teeth to maintain his fortitude; it was a battered Buntwell mouthpiece that yielded up the fate of the Franklin polar expedition.

Peering into the shop, jostled by crisp, well-fed executives hurrying toward million-dollar deals, it suddenly struck me that a Buntwell pipe was the key to my future. Here at last was a magic talisman that would transform me from a wormy, chopfallen cipher into a forceful, grim-lipped tycoon. A wave of exultation swept over me; I saw myself in the club car of the Twentieth Century Limited puffing a silver-mounted Buntwell and merging directorates with a careless nod. I too could become one of those enviable types who lounged against knotty-pine interiors in four-colour advertisements, smoking their Buntwells and fiercely demanding Old Peg-leg Whisky. "Give me Old Peg-leg's satin smoothness every time," I would growl. "I like a *blended* rye."

I squared my tiny shoulders and, baring my teeth in the half-snarl befitting a major industrialist, entered the shrine. To my chagrin, no obsequious lackey sprang forward to measure my features for the correct model. A cathedral hush enveloped the shop, which had the restrained elegance of a Park Avenue jeweller's. At a chaste showcase displaying a box of panatelas marked down to a thousand dollars, a glacial salesman was attending a fierce old party with white cavalry mustaches redolent of Napoleon brandy. In the background, another was languidly demonstrating a cigarette lighter to a dowager weighed down under several pounds of diamonds. I coughed apologetically and gave the salesman a winning smile to indicate that I knew my place. The old grenadier scowled at me from under beetling brows. "Confound it, sir," he roared, "you're not at a cock fight! Blasted place is gettin' noisier than the durbar!" I cleared my throat, in which a fish bone had mysteriously lodged, and made myself as inconspicuous as possible. The salesman hastily explained that the war had brought an influx of foreigners, but his client refused to be mollified.

"Should have caned the bounder," he sputtered. "Country's goin' to the demnition bow-wows, dash it all! Now then, Harkrider, what's this infernal nonsense about my Burma cheroots?" He waved aside the salesman's excuse that a convoy had been sunk, commanded that Buntwell himself be summoned.

"But Mr. Buntwell's been dead sixty years, major," Harkrider protested.

"None of your poppycock!" barked the major. "You tell Buntwell to bring 'em around personally by noon tomorrow or I close my account!"

He stamped out, his wattles crimson with rage, and I sidled forward timidly. In a few badly chosen words, I indicated that I required a pipe.

"H'm-m-m-," murmured Harkrider grudgingly, surveying my clothes. "Just a moment." He disappeared through a curtain and engaged in a whispered consultation with the manager. I dimly overheard a phrase that sounded like "butter-snipe"; the two were obviously discussing their lunch. At length the salesman re-entered and conducted me sullenly to a showcase. After some deliberation, he extracted what appeared to be an old sycamore root fitted with a steel flange that covered the bowl.

"Know anything about pipes?" he inquired patronisingly.

"Well, not exactly," I hesitated. "I had a corncob when I was a little boy—"

"I'm not interested in reminiscences of your youth," he snapped. "Hold still." With a quick gesture, he jammed the root into my mouth and backed off, studying my face critically.

"Wh-what is it for?" I stammered.

"Big-game hunting," he returned loftily. I was screwing up my courage to inquire out of which end the bullet came when he suddenly plucked it from my teeth. "No, I don't care for you in that. Let's see now—what's your club?"

"Why—er—uh—the Williams After-Shave Club," I replied politely. "You know, for men whose skins welcome that zestful, bracing tang—

"No, no," he broke in irritably. "Where do you keep your yacht?" His face darkened and he took a threatening step forward. "You have a yacht, haven't you?" "Oh-why—er—bub—certainly," I lied skilfully. "He's—I mean, she's laid up right now, the man's scraping her chimney. It got full of seaweeds."

Harkrider glared at me suspiciously, clearly unconvinced.

"Yo heave ho, blow the man down," I hummed nonchalantly, executing a few steps of the sailor's hornpipe. "Thar she blows and sparm at that! A double ration of plum duff for all hands, matey!" The stratagem was successful; with a baffled grunt, Harkrider produced a green velvet jewel case and exhibited a small, charred stub encrusted with salt.

"That's been used before, hasn't it?" I faltered.

"Of course it's been used," he grated. "You don't think you're going to get a new pipe for sixty-seven dollars, do you?"

"Oh, no, naturally," I agreed. "Tell you the truth, I had in mind something a bit smaller."

"Smaller?" snorted Harkrider. "You ought to have a calabash to go with that jaw of yours!"

"That's what I was telling the wife only this morning," I chuckled. "Gee, did you ever see anything like it? It's worse than an English bull-dog's."

"Well, do you want a calabash or not?" he interrupted. "They're twenty dollars—though I guess you don't see that much money in a year, do you?" Blushing like a lovely long-stemmed American Beauty rose, I explained that I merely wanted something to knock around in, a homely old jimmy pipe I could suck on while dispensing salty aphorisms like Velvet Joe. After a heartrending plea, he finally consented to part with a factory second for thirteen dollars, equipped with an ingenious aluminum coil which conveyed the nicotine juice directly into the throat before it lost its potency. To prove my gratitude, I immediately bought a tobacco jar in the shape of a human skull, two pounds of Buntwell's Special Blend of chopped amethysts and attar of roses, and a cunning all-purpose reamer equally useful for removing carbon from a pipe or barnacles from a boat. Peeling eighty-three rugs from my skinny little roll, I caught up my purchases and coursed homeward whistling gems from The Bartered Bride. Right after dinner, I disposed myself in my favourite easy chair, lit a cheery blaze in the pipe and picked up the evening paper.

When I regained consciousness, there was a smell in the apartment like a Hindu suttee, and an angel in starched denim was taking my pulse and what remained of my roll. If I go on improving at this rate, she's promised I can get up tomorrow. That means I can go out Wednesday and go to jail on Thursday, because in the meantime I've got a date to heave a brick through a plate-glass window in Radio City. See you in Alcatraz, bud.

YOU'RE LAUGHING

Luigi Pirandello

Luigi Pirandello (1867–1936) was an Italian dramatist, novelist, poet and short story writer, who was awarded the 1934 Nobel Prize in Literature. Pirandello broke decisively with the conventions of realist theatre with his two major plays, *Six Characters in Search of an Author* (1921) and *Henry IV* (1922). His relationship with Mussolini has been the subject of much debate, and his last play, *The Mountain Goats*, reflects his growing anxiety about artistic integrity under a fascist regime.

Shaken by his wife with an angry tug on the arm, jolted out of his sleep again that night, was poor Mister Anselmo.

"You're laughing!"

Dazed, and with his nose still stuffy from sleep, and wheezing a bit from the sudden alarm, he swallowed; he scratched his hairy chest; then said irked:

"And... my God... again tonight?"

"Every night! Every night!" his wife shouted, livid with annoyance.

Mister Anselmo raised himself on an elbow, and continuing with the other hand to scratch his chest, asked with exasperation:

"But are you really sure about it? I might make some sound with my lips, because of my stomach rumbling; and it seems to you that I'm laughing."

"No, you're laughing, laughing, laughing," she reaffirmed those three times. "Want to hear how? Like this..."

And she mimicked the deep bubbling laughter which her husband made in his sleep every night.

Stunned, embarrassed and almost incredulous, Mister Anselmo turned to ask:

"Like that?"

"Like that! Like that!"

And his wife, after the effort of that laugh, exhausted, let her head fall back onto the pillows and her arms over the covers, moaning:

"Oh God, my head…"

In the bedroom, sputtering, and about to go out was a votive candle before of an image of the Madonna of Loreto, on the chest of drawers. At every sputter of light, it seemed as though all the furniture jumped.

Irritation and humiliation, anger and worry leapt up in the same way in the overburdened soul of Mister Anselmo, for those incredible laughs of his every night, in his sleep, which made his wife suspect that he, sleeping, wallowed in who knows what delights, while she, lying there beside him, was sleepless, and angry from the perpetual headache and neurotic asthma, heart palpitations, and in short, all the disorders possible and imaginable in an emotional woman nearing her fifties.

"Do you want me to light the candle?"

"Light it, yes, light it! And give me the drops right away: twenty, in an inch of water."

Mister Anselmo lit the candle and got out of bed as quick as he could. So in his nightgown and barefoot, passing in front of the wardrobe to get from the dresser the little bottle of anti-hysteric liquid and the dropper, he saw himself in the mirror, and instinctively raised his hand to tidy up on his head the long lock of hair, with which he deluded himself in some way hid his baldness.

From the bed his wife noticed it.

"He's fixing his hair!" she sneered. "He has the nerve to fix his hair, even in the dead of night, in his nightgown, while I'm here dying!"

Mister Anselmo turned around, as if a snake had bit him in betrayal; he pointed the index finger of one hand towards his wife and shouted at her:

"You're dying?"

"I wish," she lamented then, "that the Lord would make you feel, I don't say much, a little of what I'm suffering at this moment!"

"Eh, my dear, no," grumbled Mister Anselmo. "If you really felt ill, you wouldn't pay attention to scold me for an involuntary gesture. I only lifted my hand, I lifted... Dang it! How many of them did I let fall in?"

And he threw to the floor in an impulse of anger the water of the glass, into which, instead of twenty, who knows how many drops of that anti-hysteric mixture had fallen. And he had to go into the kitchen, like that, barefoot and in his nightgown, to get more water.

"I laugh...! Ladies and gentlemen, I laugh...," he said to himself passing through, on tiptoe, with the candle in hand, the long corridor.

A small voice from the shadows came out from an opening onto the hallway.

"Grandpa..."

It was the voice of one of the five granddaughters, the voice of Susanna, the oldest, and the dearest to Mister Anselmo, whom he called Susì.

He had taken into his home for two years those five granddaughters, together with the daughter-in-law, upon death of his only son. The daughter-in-law, a sad disagreeable woman, who at eighteen had snared him, that poor son of his, by luck had escaped from the house for some months with a certain gentleman, an intimate friend of the deceased husband; and so the five little orphan girls (of which the oldest, Susì, was only eight years old) were left in the arms of Mister Anselmo, really in his own arms, because in those of the grandmother, afflicted with so many maladies, it is clear that they couldn't rest.

The grandmother didn't even have strength to mind herself.

But mind, yes, if Mister Anselmo unconsciously lifted a hand to readjust on his pate the twenty-five hairs that had left. Because, over-coming all those illnesses, she had the audacity, the grandmother, to still be ferociously jealous of him, as if at the tender age of fifty-six, with his white beard, and bald head, in the midst of all the delights that lady destiny had lavished on him; and those five granddaughters in his arms, for whom, with his meager salary he didn't know how to provide, with a heart that was still bleeding over the death of his disgraced son, he could in fact attend to making love to pretty women!

Wasn't he laughing perhaps for this? But yes! But yes! Who knows how many women canoodled with him in dreams, every night!

The fury which with his wife shook him, the vehement rage with which she shouted, "You're laughing!"

Which… nothing, away with it!… what was it? a trifle… a ridiculous little sliver of brimstone, bestowed by that lady-luck friend of his through the hand of his wife, because she enjoyed salting his wounds, all those wounds, the existence of which he had wished to neatly whisk away.

Mister Anselmo put the candle on the floor near the door, so as not to wake the other grandchildren with the light, and went into the little bedroom, at Susì's call.

With the greatest empathy of her grandfather, who loved her so much, Susì grew awkwardly; one shoulder taller than the other and crooked, and day by day her neck became ever more like a stem too slender to support her head, [which was] just too big. Ah, that head of Susì's…

Mister Anselmo bent over the bed, to allow the thin arm of his granddaughter to encircle his neck; he told her:

"Do you know what, Susì? I laughed!"

Susì looked into his face with pained surprise.

"Again tonight?"

"Yes, again tonight. A big belly la-ha-ha-augh… Enough, let me go, dear, to get water for grandma… Sleep, sleep, and try to laugh too, you know? Good night."

He kissed his granddaughter on the hair, tucked her snugly inside the covers, and went in the kitchen to get the water.

Helped along so much by his devoted fate, Mister Anselmo had succeeded (always for his greater consolation) to raise his spirits by philosophical considerations, which, in fact without at all harming the faith in honest feelings rooted deeply in his heart, nevertheless had taken away from him the comfort of trusting in that God, who awards and rewards from above. And not trusting in God, he couldn't either consequently believe anymore, as he would have liked, in some evil demonic prankster who lurked inside his body and would amuse himself every night by laughing, to arouse the saddest suspicions in the mind of his jealous wife.

He was certain, very certain, Mister Anselmo not to have ever had any dream, that could cause those laughs. He didn't dream at all! He never dreamed! He fell every evening, at the usual time, in a black, leaden sleep, hard and very deep, from which it cost him so much effort and so much pain to rouse himself! His eyelids weighed on his eyes like two tombstones.

And therefore, excluding the devil, excluding the dreams, there remained no other explanation for those laughs but some illness of a new kind; maybe an abdominal spasm, that was manifesting itself in that sonorous eruption of laughter.

The following day, he wanted to consult the young physician, specialist of nervous diseases, who every other day came to visit his wife.

Besides the expertise that they paid for, this young specialist doctor's clients got his blond hair which because of too much studying had been falling out prematurely, and his vision which, for the same reason, had already been prematurely weakened.

And he had, other than his specialized knowledge of nervous ailments, another specialty, which he offered free to his clients: his eyes, behind the glasses, of different colors: one yellow and one green.

He closed his yellow one, blinked with the green, and explained everything. Ah, he explained everything, with a marvelous clarity, to give to his genteel clients, even in the case that they should have to die, complete satisfaction.

"Tell me, doctor, can it happen that someone laughs in his sleep, without dreaming? Loud, you know?"

Those deep loud la-ha-ha-aughs....

The young doctor began to explain to Mister Anselmo the most recent and reasoned theories on sleep and on dreams; for about half an hour he spoke, inserting into his discourse all that Greek terminology that makes the profession of the physician so respectable, and at the end concluded that – no – it could not be.

Without dreaming, someone could not laugh that way in their sleep.

"But I swear to you, doctor, that I really do not dream, do not dream, haven't ever dreamed!" exclaimed Mister Anselmo testily, noticing the sardonic laugh with which his wife had welcomed the conclusion of the young doctor.

"Eh no, you believe! So it seems to you," added the doctor, going back to closing his yellow eye and blinking with the green. "So it seems to you... but you dream. It's positive. Only, the memory of the dreams doesn't remain, because you're deeply asleep. Normally, as I explained it to you, we don't remember the dreams that we have, when the veils, so to speak, of sleep are somewhat dispersed."

"So I laugh at the dreams I have?"

"Without a doubt. You dream happy things and laugh."

"What nonsense!" Mister Anselmo let slip out then. "I mean to be happy, at least in dreams, doctor, and not to be able to know it! Because I swear to you that I don't know a thing. My wife shakes me, yells at me 'You're laughing', and I'm left stunned looking at her in the face, because I really don't know that I laughed, nor what I laughed about."

But look, there, there it was at the end. Yes, yes. It had to be like that. Providentially, nature, secretly, aided you in your sleep. As soon as you closed your eyes on the spectacle of your miseries, nature, you see, undressed your soul of all its sorrowful crepe, and led it away, very gently, like a feather, towards the fresh valleys of happier dreams. Denied to you, it is true, cruelly, is the memory of who knows what exhilarating delights; but surely, in every way, it compensated you, restored your mind without your knowing it, so that the following day you would be able to bear the worries and the adversities of fate.

And now, returned from his office, Mister Anselmo took Susì on his knees, who knew how to imitate so well the bellowing laugh that he made every night, because she'd heard it repeated so many times by her grandmother; he kissed the mature little face and asked her:

"Susì, how do I laugh? Come on, dear, let me hear it, my nice laugh."

And Susì, throwing back her head and exposing her slender rachitic neck, burst out in the joyous laughter, deep, full, and warm-hearted.

Mister Anselmo, blissful, listened to it, savored it, even with tears about to fall because of the sight of that little girl's misshapen neck; and shaking his head and looking out the window, sighed:

"Who knows how happy I am, Susì! Who knows how happy I am, dreaming, when I laugh like that."

Unfortunately, though, Mister Anselmo had to lose even this illusion.

It happened to him once, coincidentally, to remember one of his dreams, that made him laugh so much every night.

Here: He saw a wide staircase, up which was climbing with much difficulty, leaning on a cane, a certain Torella, his old companion from the office, with crooked legs. Behind Torella, was, climbing quickly, his boss, cavalier Ridotti, who was amusing himself by cruelly hitting with his cane Torella's cane that, because of those crooked legs of his, he needed, climbing, to support himself upon steadily. In the end, that poor man Torella, unable to do anything else, bent forward, with both hands grabbed onto a step of the stairway and began to kick backwards, like a mule, towards cavalier Ridotti. Ridotti laughed scornfully and, ably dodging those kicks, tried to stick the tip of his cruel cane into the exposed rear end of poor Torella, there, right in the middle, and finally he succeeded.

To such a vision, Mister Anselmo, waking himself, with the laugh on his lips suddenly cut off, heard the breath and joy fall away from him. Oh God, was it because of this he was laughing, for such absurdities?

He constricted his mouth into a smirk of deep disgust, and remained gazing ahead of himself.

For this he was laughing! This was all the happiness, that he had believed he was enjoying in dreams!

Oh God... Oh God...

If not that, the philosophical spirit, which already for many years had begun speaking inside of him, this time again, came to his aid, and showed him that, of course, it was certainly natural that he would laugh at stupid things.

What did he want to laugh about? In his condition, he needed to become stupid, too, in order to laugh.

How would he have been able to laugh otherwise?

Translated by John Galletta

THE ANGEL OF THE ODD – AN EXTRAVAGANZA

Edgar Allan Poe

Edgar Allan Poe (1809–1849) wrote poetry, novels and criticism, and is seen as one of the earliest practitioners of the short story, working in all genres, including mystery and science fiction. He was the first well-known American writer to earn a living through writing alone, resulting in a financially difficult life and career.

It was a chilly November afternoon. I had just consummated an unusually hearty dinner, of which the dyspeptic truffe formed not the least important item, and was sitting alone in the dining-room, with my feet upon the fender, and at my elbow a small table which I had rolled up to the fire, and upon which were some apologies for dessert, with some miscellaneous bottles of wine, spirit, and liqueur. In the morning I had been reading Glover's "Leonidas," Wilkies "Epigoniad," Lamartine's "Pilgrimage," Barlow's "Columbiad," Tuckermann's "Sicily," and Griswold's "Curiosities"; I am willing to confess, therefore, that I now felt a little stupid. I made effort to arouse myself by aid of frequent Lafitte, and, all failing, I betook myself to a stray newspaper in despair. Having carefully perused the column of "houses to let," and the column of "dogs lost," and then the two columns of "wives and apprentices runaway," I attacked with great resolution the editorial matter, and, reading it from beginning to end without understanding a syllable, conceived the possibility of its being Chinese, and so re-read it from the end to the beginning, but with no more satisfactory result. I was about to throw away, in disgust,

This folio of four pages, happy work
Which not even poets criticise,

When I felt my attention somewhat aroused by the paragraph which follows:

"The avenues to death are numerous and strange. A London paper mentions the decease of a person from a singular cause. He was playing at 'puff the dart,' which is played with a long needle inserted in some worsted, and blown at a target through a tin tube. He placed the needle at the wrong end of the tube, and drawing his breath strongly to puff the dart forward with force, drew the needle into his throat. It entered the lungs, and in a few days killed him."

Upon seeing this I fell into a great rage, without exactly knowing why. "This thing," I exclaimed, "is a contemptible falsehood – a poor hoax – the lees of the invention of some pitiable penny-a-liner of some wretched concoctor of accidents in Cocaigne. These fellows, knowing the extravagant gullibility of the age, set their wits to work in the imagination of improbable possibilities – of odd accidents, as they term them; but to a reflecting intellect (like mine," I added, in parenthesis, putting my forefinger unconsciously to the side of my nose), "to a contemplative understanding such as I myself possess, it seems evident at once that the marvellous increase of late in these 'odd accidents' is by far the oddest accident of all. For my own part, I intend to believe nothing henceforward that has anything of the 'singular' about it.

"Mein Gott, den, vat a vool you bees for dat!" replied one of the most remarkable voices I ever heard. At first I took it for a rumbling in my ears – such as man sometimes experiences when getting very drunk – but, upon second thought, I considered the sound as more nearly resembling that which proceeds from an empty barrel beaten with a big stick; and, in fact, this I should have concluded it to be, but for the articulation of the syllables and words. I am by no means naturally nervous, and the very few glasses of Lafitte which I had sipped served to embolden me a little, so that I felt nothing of trepidation, but merely uplifted my eyes with a leisurely movement, and looked carefully around the room for the intruder. I could not, however, perceive any one at all.

"Humph!" resumed the voice, as I continued my survey, "you mus pe so dronk as de pig, den, for not zee me as I zit here at your zide."

Hereupon I bethought me of looking immediately before my nose, and there, sure enough, confronting me at the table sat a personage non-descript, although not altogether indescribable. His body was a wine-pipe, or a rum-puncheon, or something of that character, and had a truly Falstaffian air. In its nether extremity were inserted two kegs, which seemed to answer all the purposes of legs. For arms there dangled from the upper portion of the carcass two tolerably long bottles, with the necks outward for hands. All the head that I saw the monster possessed of was one of those Hessian canteens which resemble a large snuff-box with a hole in the middle of the lid. This canteen (with a funnel on its top, like a cavalier cap slouched over the eyes) was set on edge upon the puncheon, with the hole toward myself; and through this hole, which seemed puckered up like the mouth of a very precise old maid, the creature was emitting certain rumbling and grumbling noises which he evidently intended for intelligible talk.

"I zay," said he, "you mos pe dronk as de pig, vor zit dare and not zee me zit ere; and I zay, doo, you most pe pigger vool as de goose, vor to dispelief vat iz print in de print. 'Tiz de troof – dat it iz – eberry vord ob it."

"Who are you, pray?" said I, with much dignity, although somewhat puzzled; "how did you get here? And what is it you are talking about?"

"Az vor ow I com'd ere," replied the figure, "dat iz none of your pizz-ness; and as vor vat I be talking apout, I be talk apout vot I tink proper; and as vor who I be, vy dat is de very ting I com'd here for to let you zee for yourzelf."

"You are a drunken vagabond," said I, "and I shall ring the bell and order my footman to kick you into the street."

"He! he! he!" said the fellow, "Hu! Hu! Hu! Dat you can't do."

"Can't do!" said I, "What do you mean? Can't do what?"

"Ring de pell," he replied, attempting a grin with his little villainous mouth.

Upon this I made an effort to get up, in order to put my threat into execution; but the ruffian just reached across the table very deliberately, and hitting me a tap on the forehead with the neck of one of the long bottles, knocked me back into the arm-chair from which I had half arisen. I was utterly astounded; and, for a moment, was quite at a loss what to do. In the meantime, he continued his talk.

"You zee," said he, "It iz te bess vor zit still; and now you shall know who I pe. Look at me! Zee! I am te Angel ov te Odd!"

"And odd enough, too," I ventured to reply; "but I was always under the impression that an angel had wings."

"Te wing!" he cried, highly incensed, "vat I pe do mit te wing? Mein Gott! Do you take me vor a shicken?"

"No – oh, no!" I replied, much alarmed, "you are no chicken – certainly not."

"Well, den, zit still and pehabe yourself, or I'll rap you again mid me vist. It iz te shicken ab te wing, und te owl ab te wing, und te imp ab te wing, und te headteuffel ab te wing. Te angel ab not te wing, and I am te Angel ov te Odd."

"And your business with me at present is… is—"

"My pizzness!" ejaculated the thing, "vy vot a low bred puppy you mos pe vor to ask a gentleman und an angel apout his pizzness!"

This language was rather more than I could bear, even from an angel; so, plucking up courage, I seized a salt-cellar which lay within reach, and hurled it at the head of the intruder. Either he dodged, however, or my aim was inaccurate; for all I accomplished was the demolition of the crystal which protected the dial of the clock upon the mantelpiece. As for the Angel, he evinced his sense of my assault by giving me two or three hard consecutive raps upon the forehead as before. These reduced me at once to submission, and I am almost ashamed to confess that, either through pain or vexation, there came a few tears into my eyes.

"Mein Gott!" said the Angel of the Odd, apparently much softened at my distress; "mein Gott, te man is eder ferry dronck or ferry sorry. You mos not trink it so strong – you mos put de water in te wine. Here, trink dis, like a goot veller, und don't gry now – don't!"

Hereupon the Angel of the Odd replenished my goblet (which was about a third full of Port) with a colorless fluid that he poured from one of his hand bottles. I observed that these bottles had labels about their necks, and that these labels were inscribed "Kirschenwasser."

The considerate kindness of the Angel mollified me in no little measure; and, aided by the water with which he diluted my Port more than once, I at length regained sufficient temper to listen to his very extraordinary discourse. I cannot pretend to recount all that he told me, but I gleaned from what he said that he was the genius who presided over the contre temps of mankind, and whose business it was to bring about the odd accidents which are continually astonishing the skeptic. Once or twice, upon my venturing to express my total incredulity in respect to his pretensions, he grew very angry indeed, so that at length I considered it the wiser policy to say nothing at all, and let him have his own way. He talked on, therefore, at great length, while I merely leaned back in my chair with my eyes shut, and amused myself with munching raisins and flipping the stems about the room. But, by and by, the Angel suddenly construed this behavior of mine into contempt. He arose in a terrible passion, slouched his funnel down over his eyes, swore a vast oath, uttered a threat of some character which I did not precisely comprehend, and finally made me a low bow and departed, wishing me, in the language of the archbishop in Gil-Blas, "beaucoup de bonheur et un peu plus de bon sens."

His departure afforded me relief. The very few glasses of Lafitte that I had sipped had the effect of rendering me drowsy, and I felt inclined to take a nap of some fifteen or twenty minutes, as is my custom after dinner. At six I had an appointment of consequence, which it was quite indispensable that I should keep. The policy of insurance for my dwelling house had expired the day before; and, some dispute having arisen, it was agreed that, at six, I should meet the board of directors of the company and settle the terms of a renewal. Glancing upward at the clock on the mantel-piece (for I felt too drowsy to take out my watch), I had the pleasure to find that I had still twenty-five minutes to spare. It was half past five; I could easily walk to the insurance office in five minutes; and my usual post prandian siestas had never been known to exceed five and twenty. I felt sufficiently safe, therefore, and composed myself to my slumbers forthwith.

Having completed them to my satisfaction, I again looked toward the time-piece, and was half inclined to believe in the possibility of odd accidents when I found that, instead of my ordinary fifteen or twenty minutes, I had been dozing only three; for it still wanted seven and twenty of the appointed hour. I betook myself again to my nap, and at length a second time awoke, when, to my utter amazement, it still wanted twenty-seven minutes of six. I jumped up to examine the clock, and found that it had ceased running. My watch informed me that it was half past seven; and, of course, having slept two hours, I was too late for my appointment "It will make no difference," I said; "I can call at the office in the morning and apologize; in the meantime what can be the matter with the clock?" Upon examining it I discovered that one of the raisin-stems which I had been flipping about the room during the discourse of the Angel of the Odd had flown through the fractured crystal, and lodging, singularly enough, in the key-hole, with an end projecting outward, had thus arrested the revolution of the minute-hand.

"Ah!" said I; "I see how it is. This thing speaks for itself. A natural accident, such as will happen now and then!"

I gave the matter no further consideration, and at my usual hour retired to bed. Here, having placed a candle upon a reading-stand at the bed-head, and having made an attempt to peruse some pages of the "Omnipresence of the Deity," I unfortunately fell asleep in less than twenty seconds, leaving the light burning as it was.

My dreams were terrifically disturbed by visions of the Angel of the Odd. Methought he stood at the foot of the couch, drew aside the curtains, and, in the hollow, detestable tones of a rum-puncheon, menaced me with the bitterest vengeance for the contempt with which I had treated him. He concluded a long harrangue by taking off his funnelcap, inserting the tube into my gullet, and thus deluging me with an ocean of Kirschenwasser, which he poured, in a continuous flood, from one of the long-necked bottles that stood him instead of an arm. My agony was at length insufferable, and I awoke just in time to perceive that a rat had ran off with the lighted candle from the stand, but not in season to prevent his making his escape with it through the hole. Very soon, a strong suffocating odor assailed my nostrils; the house, I clearly perceived, was on fire. In a few minutes the blaze broke forth with violence, and in an incredibly brief period the entire building was wrapped in flames. All egress from my chamber, except through a window, was cut off. The crowd, however, quickly procured and raised a long ladder. By means of this I was descending rapidly, and in apparent safety, when a huge hog, about whose rotund stomach, and indeed about whose whole air and physiognomy, there was something which reminded me of the Angel of the Odd, when this hog, I say, which hitherto had been quietly slumbering in the mud, took it suddenly into his head that his left shoulder needed scratching, and could find no more convenient rubbing post than that afforded by the foot of the ladder. In an instant I was precipitated, and had the misfortune to fracture my arm.

This accident, with the loss of my insurance, and with the more serious loss of my hair, the whole of which had been singed off by the fire, predisposed me to serious impressions, so that, finally, I made up my mind to take a wife. There was a rich widow disconsolate for the loss of her seventh husband, and to her wounded spirit I offered the balm of my vows. She yielded a reluctant consent to my prayers. I knelt at her feet in gratitude and adoration. She blushed, and bowed her luxuriant tresse into close contact with those supplied me, temporarily, by Grandjean. I know not how the entanglement took place, but so it was. I arose with a shining pate, wigless, she in disdain and wrath, half buried in alien hair. Thus ended my hopes of the widow by an accident which could not have been anticipated, to be sure, but which the natural sequence of events had brought about.

Without despairing, however, I undertook the siege of a less implacable heart. The fates were again propitious for a brief period; but again a trivial incident interfered. Meeting my betrothed in an avenue thronged with the elite of the city, I was hastening to greet her with one of my best considered bows, when a small particle of some foreign matter lodging in the corner of my eye, rendered me, for the moment, completely blind. Before I could recover my sight, the lady of my love had disappeared – irreparably affronted at what she chose to consider my premeditated rudeness in passing her by ungreeted. While I stood bewildered at the suddenness of this accident (which might have happened, nevertheless, to any one under the sun), and while I still continued incapable of sight, I was accosted by the Angel of the Odd, who proffered me his aid with a civility which I had no reason to expect. He examined my disordered eye with much gentleness and skill, informed me that I had a drop in it, and (whatever a "drop" was) took it out, and afforded me relief.

I now considered it time to die, (since fortune had so determined to persecute me,) and accordingly made my way to the nearest river. Here, divesting myself of my clothes, (for there is no reason why we cannot die as we were born,) I threw myself headlong into the current; the sole witness of my fate being a solitary crow that had been seduced into the eating of brandy-saturated corn, and so had staggered away from his fellows. No sooner had I entered the water than this bird took it into its head to fly away with the most indispensable portion of my apparel. Postponing, therefore, for the present, my suicidal design, I just slipped my nether extremities into the sleeves of my coat, and betook myself to a pursuit of the felon with all the nimbleness which the case required and its circumstances would admit. But my evil destiny attended me still. As I ran at full speed, with my nose up in the atmosphere, and intent only upon the purloiner of my property, I suddenly perceived that my feet rested no longer upon terre firma; the fact is, I had thrown myself over a precipice, and should inevitably have been dashed to pieces, but for my good fortune in grasping the end of a long guide-rope, which descended from a passing balloon.

As soon as I sufficiently recovered my senses to comprehend the terrific predicament in which I stood or rather hung, I exerted all the power of my lungs to make that predicament known to the aeronaut overhead. But for a long time I exerted myself in vain. Either the fool could not, or the villain would not perceive me. Meantime the machine rapidly soared, while my strength even more rapidly failed. I was soon upon the point of resigning myself to my fate, and dropping quietly into the sea, when my spirits were suddenly revived by hearing a hollow voice from above, which seemed to be lazily humming an opera air. Looking up, I perceived the Angel of the Odd. He was leaning with his arms folded, over the rim of the car, and with a pipe in his mouth, at which he puffed leisurely, seemed to be upon excellent terms with himself and the universe. I was too much exhausted to speak, so I merely regarded him with an imploring air. For several minutes, although he looked me full in the face, he said nothing. At length removing carefully his meerschaum from the right to the left corner of his mouth, he condescended to speak.

"Who pe you?" he asked, "und what der teuffel you pe do dare?"

To this piece of impudence, cruelty, and affectation, I could reply only by ejaculating the monosyllable "Help!"

"Elp!" echoed the ruffian – "not I. Dare iz te pottle – elp yourself, und pe tam'd!"

With these words he let fall a heavy bottle of Kirschenwasser which, dropping precisely upon the crown of my head, caused me to imagine that my brains were entirely knocked out. Impressed with this idea, I was about to relinquish my hold and give up the ghost with a good grace, when I was arrested by the cry of the Angel, who bade me hold on.

"Old on!" he said; "don't pe in te urry – don't. Will you pe take de odder pottle, or ave you pe got zober yet and come to your zenzes?"

I made haste, hereupon, to nod my head twice – once in the negative, meaning thereby that I would prefer not taking the other bottle at present – and once in the affirmative, intending thus to imply that I was sober and had positively come to my senses. By these means I somewhat softened the Angel.

"Und you pelief, ten," he inquired, "at te last? You pelief, ten, in te possibilty of te odd?"

I again nodded my head in assent.

"Und you ave pelief in me, te Angel of te Odd?"

I nodded again.

"Und you acknowledge tat you pe te blind dronk and te vool?"

I nodded once more.

"Put your right hand into your left hand preeches pocket, ten, in token oy your vull zubmission unto te Angel ov te Odd."

This thing, for very obvious reasons, I found it quite impossible to do. In the first place, my left arm had been broken in my fall from the ladder, and, therefore, had I let go my hold with the right hand, I must have let go altogether. In the second place, I could have no breeches until I came across the crow. I was therefore obliged, much to my regret, to shake my head in the negative – intending thus to give the Angel to understand that I found it inconvenient, just at that moment, to comply with his very reasonable demand! No sooner, however, had I ceased shaking my head than—

"Go to der teuffel ten!" roared the Angel of the Odd.

In pronouncing these words, he drew a sharp knife across the guide rope by which I was suspended, and as we then happened to be precisely over my own house, (which, during my peregrinations, had been hand-somely rebuilt,) it so occurred that I tumbled headlong down the ample chimney and alit upon the dining-room hearth. Upon coming to my senses, (for the fall had very thoroughly stunned me,) I found it about four o'clock in the morning. I lay outstretched where I had fallen from the balloon. My head grovelled in the ashes of an extinguished fire, while my feet reposed upon the wreck of a small table, overthrown, and amid the fragments of a miscellaneous dessert, intermingled with a news-paper, some broken glass and shattered bottles, and an empty jug of the Schiedam Kirschenwasser. Thus revenged himself the Angel of the Odd.

THE TWO COMEDIANS

Satyajit Ray

Satyajit Ray (1921–1992) was born in Calcutta. Widely regarded as one of the greatest filmmakers of the twentieth century, he established the Calcutta Film Society in 1947, and, during a trip to Europe in 1950 he managed to see ninety-nine films in only four and a half months. He completed his first film, *Pather Panchali*, in 1955, which established Ray as a director of international stature. In 1987 he made the documentary *Sukumar Ray* to commemorate his father, Bengal's most famous writer of nonsense verse and children's books, and in 1992 he was awarded the Oscar for Lifetime Achievement. As well as his film work, Ray was a respected author, writing numerous poems, stories and essays published in both Bengali and English.

'Today, I'm going to talk about a film star,' said Uncle Tarini, sipping his tea.

'Which film star? What's his name?' we cried in unison.

'You wouldn't have heard of him,' he replied. 'You were probably born only after he retired.'

'Even so, do tell us his name,' Napla insisted, reluctant to give up easily. 'We often see old films on TV, and know the names of many old stars.'

'All right, his name was Ratanlal Raxit.'

'Yes, I know who you mean,' Napla nodded sagely. 'I saw a film called *Joy Porajoy* (Victory and Defeat) on TV about three months ago. Ratan Raxit played the hero's father.'

'Well then, if you have seen him in a film, you'll be able to enjoy the story all the more.'

'Is it a ghost story?'

'No, but it is about something dead and gone. In that sense, I suppose you could call it a ghost story. It concerns the past; events from days gone by.'

'Very well. Please begin.'

Uncle Tarini pulled a bolster closer to lean against, and began his story:

'Ratanlal Raxit retired in 1970, at the age of seventy. His health was not very good, so his doctor prescribed complete rest. He had worked in films for forty-five years, right from the era of silent films. He had made a great deal of money, and knew how to put it to good use. He had three houses in Calcutta and lived in the one in Amherst Street. The others he let out on rent.

'One day, after his retirement, Ratanlal put an advertisement in the papers for a secretary. I was in Calcutta then, and was almost fifty years old at that time. Having spent all my life travelling and trying my hand at a variety of jobs, I was wondering whether it was time to settle down once and for all in my own homeland, when I spotted that ad. So I applied. The name of Ratanlal Raxit was well known to me. I had seen many of his films and, besides, you know I have a special interest in films.

'I received a reply within a week. I was to appear for an interview.

'I went to Mr Raxit's house. I knew he was unwell, but there was no sign of illness in his appearance. His skin was smooth, and his teeth appeared to be his own. The first thing he asked me was whether I had seen any of his films. I told him that I had, not just his later films, but also some of the earliest ones, made in the silent era, when Mr Raxit used to act in comedies.

'My answer seemed to please him. He said, "I have managed to collect, over the last few years, copies of most of my silent films. A room in this house now acts as a mini-cinema. I've got a projector in that room, and appointed someone to run it. It is very difficult to get hold of silent films. Perhaps you know about the fire in the main warehouse that destroyed copies of most silent films in Bengal? It happened not once, but twice.

As a result, it is almost impossible to find prints of those films. But I refused to give up without trying. I advertised in the papers, and came to know eventually that many of my films were kept safe in the warehouse of one of my producers called Mirchandani. The reason for this was simply that Mirchandani was not just the producer, but also a fan of mine. He died four years ago. I spoke to his son, and bought from him what films he had. Then I advertised again, and over a period of time, collected the rest. My failing health has forced me to retire, but I cannot possibly stay away from films. So I watch my own films, and pass a pleasant evening every day. Your job will be to look after my film library, make a catalogue of all my films, and find out which ones are missing from my present collection. Can you do it?"

'I said I would certainly do my best. It would not be too difficult to make a catalogue of the films he already had. Looking for the ones he didn't would naturally be a bigger challenge. "I am not talking only of my silent films," Mr Raxit added. "Some of the early talkies are missing as well. But I think if you went to the offices of a few producers and distributors in the Dharamtola area, you'd definitely be able to get copies of what you need. I want my collection to be complete, with not a single film missing. In my old age, I wish to entertain myself only by watching my own films."

'I got the job. Mr Raxit was an unusual man. His wife had died fifteen years ago. He had two sons, both of whom lived in south Calcutta. His only daughter was in Allahabad. Her husband was a doctor there. Occasionally, his grandchildren came to visit him. So did his sons, at times, but Mr Raxit was not really in close contact with his family. He lived with two servants, a cook, and a special personal bearer called Lakshmikant. Lakshmikant was in his sixties, and totally devoted to his master. Mr Raxit was lucky to have someone like him.

'I began my work, and with Lakshmikant's help, managed to produce a catalogue of all the films in the collection within ten days. Then I made a round of the film distributors' offices in Dharamtola and located many of the early talkies Mr Raxit had featured in. He bought a print of each.

'I worked from ten in the morning to five in the evening. But sometimes, I spent the evening with Mr Raxit, instead of going home at five. He usually started seeing his films at half past six, and finished at eight-thirty. The projectionist was called Ashu Babu, a cheerful man. The audience comprised only three people—Mr Raxit, Lakshmikant and myself. The bearer had to be present, for Mr Raxit liked smoking a hookah. Lakshmikant was required to take it away from time to time to refill it. Although it was always dark in the room, I could tell by glancing at Lakshmikant's face that he enjoyed watching the films very much.

'The silent films were the best of all. I've told you already that Mr Raxit had acted in comedies in the silent era. Many of these were short films. There were only two reels, which ran for twenty minutes. They showed the escapades of a duo called Bishu and Shibu, a bit like Laurel and Hardy. Mr Raxit played Bishu, and Shibu was played by an actor called Sharat Kundu. Twenty minutes simply flew when we began watching the antics of these two. In some films they appeared as businessmen, or gamblers. In others, they were clowns in a circus, or a zamindar and his hanger-on. I knew how popular they Were in their time. These short films were often shown before a longer feature film.

'What I enjoyed watching more than these films, however, was Mr Raxit's response to his own acting. He would roll around laughing every time he saw himself clowning on the screen. Sometimes, I found it hard to believe that a comedian could laugh so much at his own acting. Naturally, I had to laugh with him. He said to me at times, "You know, Tarini, when I acted in these films, I did not find them funny at all. In fact, they struck me often as slapstick, and the humour seemed forced. It used to annoy me. But now, I can see that these films contain a lot of pure, innocent fun which is far better than what you get to see in modern comedies."

'One day, I asked him something that had been bothering me for some time. "I am very curious about one thing, sir," I said. "You played Bishu. But what about Sharat Kundu, who played Shibu? What happened to him? Aren't you in touch?"

'Mr Raxit shook his head. "As far as I know, Sharat Kundu stopped acting in films when the talkies started. We were quite close when we worked together. We used to rack our brains and plan our acts ourselves. There was a director, but only in name. We did everything, including providing the props and costumes. Then, one day, we read in a press report that films in Hollywood were being made with sound; so when the characters spoke, the audience could now hear their voices. That was in either 1928 or 1929. Three or four years later, the same thing happened in Indian films. It created a major stir. The entire process of film-making changed, as did the style of acting. Personally, I did not find that a problem. I had a good voice, so the talkies could do me no harm. I was then in my early thirties. The film industry in Bengal needed a hero with a good voice, and I had no difficulty in meeting that demand. That put an end to clowning around for twenty minutes. I became a hero. But, for some reason, Sharat Kundu disappeared. I asked a few people about him, but no one could tell me where he was. God knows if he died young."

'If that was the case, naturally, there would be no point in looking for him. But something told me I should make a few enquiries about Sharat Kundu. Judging by those twenty-minute films, he was no less gifted an actor than Ratanlal Raxit.

'I went to Tollygunge and asked a few people I knew. I learnt that a journalist called Naresh Sanyal was doing research on the very early films made in Bengal, with a view to writing a definitive book on them and their makers.

I managed to get his address, and turned up at his house one Sunday morning. Mr Sanyal admitted to knowing a few things about Sharat Kundu. Apparently, about five years ago, he had obtained Sharat Kundu's address, after considerable difficulty, and visited him to conduct an interview. "Where did you find him?" I asked.

'"In a slum in Goabagan," Mr Sanyal told me. "He was almost a pauper at the time."

'"Are you interviewing all the actors who had appeared in silent films?" I wanted to know.

'"As many as I can. Very few are still alive," Mr Sanyal replied.

'I told him about Ratanlal Raxit, adding that I could arrange an interview with him. Mr Sanyal greeted this news with great enthusiasm.

'Now I asked him what I really wanted to know: "Did Sharat Kundu stop acting once the talkies started?"

"'Yes. He was rejected after a voice test. He did not tell me how he survived after that, possibly because he did not want to talk about a bitter struggle. But I learnt a lot of facts about the silent era from him."

'After that, I went back to Tollygunge and spoke to some other people. It turned out that Sharat Kundu had continued to visit the studios for quite a while, even after it became clear that there was no future for him in the talkies. His financial situation had become grave. The manager of the Mayapuri Studio in Tollygunge told me that, just occasionally, Sharat Kundu was given a role as an extra, which brought him an income of just a few rupees. An extra is usually required to stand in the background in a crowd. He does not have to speak.

'It was in the same Mayapuri Studio that I learnt something else from an old production manager called Dwarik Chakravarty. "Go to Nataraj Cabin in Bentinck Street," he said. "I saw Sharat Kundu there, just a few years ago."

'By this time I was determined to drag Sharat Kundu out of oblivion. So I went to Nataraj Cabin. Before doing so—I forgot to mention this—I had been to Goabagan and learnt that he no longer lived there. Needless to say, in my efforts at rediscovering Sharat Kundu, I had the full support of Ratanlal Raxit. He was as enthusiastic as me, and seemed to have caught my obsession for Sharat Kundu, as if it was some sort of a contagious disease. He began telling me about their close friendship, and how popular their short films had been. When people went to the cinema, they were more interested in watching Bishu and Shibu than the main feature film. They had been an enormously popular duo, but now only one of them was around. This was not fair. The other had to be found.

'Pulin Datta, the manager of Nataraj Cabin, said to me, "Three years ago, Sharat-da was a regular visitor here. But I haven't seen him since."

"'Did he have a job?"

'"I don't know. I tried asking him, but never got a straight answer. All he ever said was, 'There's nothing that I haven't done, just to keep myself from starving.' But he stopped working in films, or even watching films, for that matter. Perhaps he could never forget that the arrival of talkies destroyed his career."

'A month passed after my meeting with Pulin Datta. I made some more enquiries, but drew a blank everywhere. Sharat Kundu seemed to have vanished into thin air. Mr Raxit was genuinely disappointed to hear that I had failed to find him. "He was such a talented actor!" he lamented. "Finished by the talkies, and now totally forgotten. Who would recognize his name today? Isn't it as bad as being dead?"

'I decided to drop the subject of Sharat Kundu since there was nothing more that I could do. I broached a different matter. "Would you mind giving an interview?" I asked.

'"An interview? Who wants it?"

'I told him about Naresh Sanyal. Mr Sanyal had called me that morning saying he wanted to come the next day.

'"All right, tell him to come at ten. But I cannot spend a long time talking to him, tell him that." I rang Naresh Sanyal, and passed on the message.

'That evening, I remained in the projection room to watch the antics of Bishu and Shibu. There were forty-two films in all. Thirty-seven of them were already in Mr Raxit's collection when I started my job. I had managed to get the remaining five. That day, watching some of these films, I was struck again by Sharat Kundu's acting prowess. He was truly a gifted comedian. I heard Mr Raxit click his tongue in regret at the disappearance of his partner.

'The following morning, Mr Sanyal turned up within ten minutes of my own arrival. Mr Raxit was ready to receive his visitor. "Let's have some tea before our interview," said Mr Raxit. Mr Sanyal raised no objection.

'It was our daily practice to have a cup of tea at ten o'clock. Usually, this was the time when Mr Raxit and I discussed what needed to be done. Then I started on my job, and he went back to his room to rest.

I had finished making the catalogue. Now I was making a synopsis of each of the films featuring Bishu and Shibu, and a list of other actors, the director, the cameraman and other crew. Such a list is known as filmography.

'Anyway, today a plate of hot kachauris arrived with the tea, in honour of our visitor. Mr Sanyal was speaking when the tea was brought. He broke off abruptly the instant the tray was placed on the table. I saw him staring at the bearer who had brought it in. It was Mr Raxit's personal attendant, Lakshmikant.

'I, too, found myself looking closely at him; and so did Mr Raxit. Lakshmikant's nose, his chin, his broad forehead, and that sharp look in his eyes… where had I seen those before? Why, I had never looked properly at him in all these months! There was no reason to. When do we ever look closely at a servant, unless there is a specific reason to do so?

'The same name escaped from our lips, almost in unison: "Sharat Kundu!"

'No, there could possibly be no doubt about it. Sharat Kundu, once his partner, was now Mr Raxit's personal attendant.

'"What is this, Sharat?" Mr Raxit shouted. "Is it really you? All this time… in my house…?"

'Sharat Kundu took some time to find his tongue. "What could I do?" he said finally, wiping his perspiring forehead. "How was I to know this gentleman would recognize me? If he didn't, you certainly wouldn't have. You didn't realize who I was, did you? How could you, it's been forty years since you last saw me. What happened was simply that I went to Mirchandani's office one day to look for a job. There I heard that you had bought copies of all our old films. So I thought I might get the chance to watch my own films again, if I could work for you in your house. I didn't even know those films were still available. So I came here and asked if you needed a bearer. Luckily for me, you did. So I got the job, although you did not recognize me. I did not mind at all. I have worked as a coolie in the past. The job of a bearer is sheer heaven after that, I can tell you. Besides, I really enjoyed being here. All those films that we made before the talkies started… they weren't bad, were they? But now, I guess I won't get to see them any more."

"'Why? Why shouldn't you?" Mr Raxit jumped to his feet. "From now on, you are going to be my manager. You will sit in the same room as Tarini, and you'll live here with me in my house. We'll watch our films together every evening. A stroke of misfortune may have broken the famous duo, but that breakage has now been put to right. What do you say, Tarini?"'

'I looked at Naresh Sanyal. I had never seen anyone look so totally dumbstruck. But what could be a better scoop, from a journalist's point of view?'

Translated by Gopa Majumdar

IS IT JUST ME?

Simon Rich

Simon Rich (1984–) is an American humourist, novelist and screen-writer. He has published two novels and three collections of stories, several of which appeared in *The New Yorker*. Rich was one of the youngest writers ever hired on *Saturday Night Live*, and has written for Pixar and *The Simpsons*.

When I found out my ex-girlfriend was dating Adolf Hitler, I couldn't believe it. I always knew on some level that she'd find another boyfriend. She's smart, cool, incredibly attractive—a girl like that doesn't stay single forever. Still, I have to admit, the news really took me by surprise.

I first found out about them from my friend Paul. We were at Murphy's Pub, watching the World Cup. Argentina was playing, and when they showed a close-up of the crowd, he chuckled.

"I wonder if we'll see Anna and Adolf!"

I could tell by how casually the names rolled off his tongue that they'd been a couple for a while. Everyone, apparently, had been keeping the news from me. I took a sip of bourbon and forced a smile.

"Yeah," I said. "I wonder if we'll see them."

Paul's eyes widened.

"You knew they were dating, right?"

"Of course!" I lied. "I mean, everyone knows *that*."

*

That night, with some help from Facebook, I pieced it all together. Anna met Hitler a few months after dumping me while vacationing in Buenos Aires. He'd been in hiding there ever since the war, earning money as a German-language tutor. She saw him at a café, recognized his moustache, and struck up a conversation. They hit it off almost immediately.

The relationship progressed quickly, and within a few months, he'd agreed to move into her place in Prospect Heights. It made me nauseous to think about them sharing that apartment. I could still picture it vividly—the clanging of her radiator, the smell of her toothpaste, the softness of her sheets. He'd taken all of it away from me. I knew it was irrational, but I couldn't help hating the guy.

A few weeks later, I was at a friend's party when Anna strolled in with the fuehrer. I bolted for the kitchen and closed the door behind me. I hadn't seen Anna since we broke up. What was I going to say to her? And what was I going to say to Hitler?

"You've got to at least say hi to them," Paul begged me. "If you don't, things will get weird."

"Things are already weird," I said. "She's dating Adolf Hitler!"

Paul stared at me blankly.

"So?"

I closed my eyes and massaged my temples.

"Well, for starters, he's a hundred and twenty-four. That makes him old enough to be her great-great-grandfather."

Paul shrugged.

"Other than the wheelchair, he seems pretty youthful."

I craned my head out the door just in time to hear Hitler quote a line from *Parks and Recreation*. His accent was pretty thick, but Anna burst into laughter anyway. The sound of it made my stomach hurt. We'd dated for almost two years and I couldn't remember ever making her laugh like that.

"I just don't like that guy," I whispered. "I mean, he murdered millions of people."

Paul laughed.

"You don't like him because he's dating Anna."

I sighed.

"Maybe," I admitted. "But don't you think it's weird she's dating him, of all people? I mean, I'm Jewish—he hates Jews."

"Don't make this about you," Paul said. "Come on, you need to be adult about this."

He grabbed my shoulder and shoved me into the living room. As soon as Anna saw me, she sprinted over and hooked her skinny arms around my torso.

"How are you!" she cooed.

"Great!" I answered, my body tensing. "Really great!"

Hitler wheeled over and stretched out his palm.

"Nice to meet you," he said. "Adolf Hitler."

"Hi," I said, shaking his hand. "Seth Greenberg."

Hitler's pale lips curled into a grin.

"Greenberg?" he said. "Uh-oh!"

Everyone laughed, and I had no choice but to join in. I looked down at my cup; somehow, I was already out of bourbon.

"Seth's an artist," Anna told Hitler. "You should buy some of his paintings."

I started to protest but she ignored me.

"Adolf's got a great collection, but I keep telling him, he needs to get some postwar pieces."

I watched as she ran her fingers across his scalp, delicately massaging his spotted, wrinkled head.

"I used to paint when I was your age," Hitler told me, clearly trying to be polite. "Do you have a website?"

"Come on," Anna urged me. "Tell him."

"It's sethgreenbergpaints.com," I mumbled.

Hitler neatly copied it down in his address book. Then he wheeled to the bar, grabbed a nearly empty bottle of Jim Beam, and poured the last of it into his red plastic cup.

Anna had cut her hair short, but otherwise she looked better than ever. Her skin was tan from her trips to Argentina, and her smile was wide and bright.

"I miss you," I said, in spite of myself.

She chuckled.

"Seth, you're drunk! Let's get you a glass of water."

She started to walk to the kitchen—and I grabbed her elbow.

"Why are you with this guy? Is it just to hurt me?"

She shook me off.

"My relationship with Adolf has nothing to do with you. Okay? We're just two people who fell in love."

"Why can't you give me another shot?"

I could tell my voice was slurred, but I couldn't stop myself from talking.

"I won't spend as much time at the studio," I rambled. "I'll be better with your friends. I'm a different person now—I'm more relaxed, more fun—I'm better than this Hitler guy!"

"Seth—"

"I mean, seriously, he's the worst! Why can't everyone see that? How is it just me?"

"Seth!" she hissed. "You're embarrassing yourself."

I looked around. Half the people at the party were staring at me.

"I'm sorry," I murmured.

Anna's fists were clenched; I could tell she was furious at me.

"Please," I begged. "I said I was sorry."

She rolled her eyes.

"Okay," she said, finally. "I forgive you."

TOBERMORY

Saki

Saki (1870–1916), or Hector Hugh Munro, was a British writer whose witty, mischievous and sometimes macabre stories satirised Edwardian society and culture. Though born in Burma, he was brought up mainly in England by his grandmother and aunts in a strict puritanical household. When the war broke out, Munro refused a commission and joined the army as a regular trooper. He was killed in action by a German sniper. His last words were, reportedly, 'Put that bloody cigarette out!' A master of the short form, he was influenced by Oscar Wilde, Lewis Carroll and Rudyard Kipling, and he himself influenced A.A. Milne, Noël Coward and P.G. Wodehouse.

It was a chill, rain-washed afternoon of a late August day, that indefinite season when partridges are still in security or cold storage, and there is nothing to hunt—unless one is bounded on the north by the Bristol Channel, in which case one may lawfully gallop after fat red stags. Lady Blemley's house-party was not bounded on the north by the Bristol Channel, hence there was a full gathering of her guests round the tea-table on this particular afternoon. And, in spite of the blankness of the season and the triteness of the occasion, there was no trace in the company of that fatigued restlessness which means a dread of the pianola and a subdued hankering for auction bridge. The undisguised open-mouthed attention of the entire party was fixed on the homely negative personality of Mr. Cornelius Appin. Of all her guests, he was the one who had come to Lady Blemley with the vaguest reputation. Some one had said he was "clever," and he had got his invitation in the moderate expectation, on the part of his hostess, that some portion at least of his cleverness would be contributed to the general entertainment. Until tea-time that day she had been unable to discover in what direction, if any, his cleverness lay. He was neither a wit nor a croquet champion, a hypnotic force nor a begetter of amateur theatricals. Neither did his exterior suggest the sort of man in whom women are willing to pardon a generous measure of mental deficiency. He had subsided into mere Mr. Appin, and the Cornelius seemed a piece of transparent baptismal bluff. And now he was claiming to have launched on the world a discovery beside which the invention of gunpowder, of the printing-press, and of steam locomotion were inconsiderable trifles. Science had made bewildering strides in many directions during recent decades, but this thing seemed to belong to the domain of miracle rather than to scientific achievement.

"And do you really ask us to believe," Sir Wilfrid was saying, "that you have discovered a means for instructing animals in the art of human speech, and that dear old Tobermory has proved your first successful pupil?"

"It is a problem at which I have worked for the last seventeen years," said Mr. Appin, "but only during the last eight or nine months have I been rewarded with glimmerings of success. Of course I have experimented with thousands of animals, but latterly only with cats, those wonderful creatures which have assimilated themselves so marvelously with our civilization while retaining all their highly developed feral instincts. Here and there among cats one comes across an outstanding superior intellect, just as one does among the ruck of human beings, and when I made the acquaintance of Tobermory a week ago I saw at once that I was in contact with a "Beyond-cat" of extraordinary intelligence. I had gone far along the road to success in recent experiments; with Tobermory, as you call him, I have reached the goal."

Mr. Appin concluded his remarkable statement in a voice which he strove to divest of a triumphant inflection. No one said "Rats," though Clovis's lips moved in a monosyllabic contortion, which probably invoked those rodents of disbelief.

"And do you mean to say," asked Miss Resker, after a slight pause, "that you have taught Tobermory to say and understand easy sentences of one syllable?"

"My dear Miss Resker," said the wonder-worker patiently, "one teaches little children and savages and backward adults in that piecemeal fashion; when one has once solved the problem of making a beginning with an animal of highly developed intelligence one has no need for those halting methods. Tobermory can speak our language with perfect correctness."

This time Clovis very distinctly said, "Beyond-rats!" Sir Wilfred was more polite but equally sceptical.

"Hadn't we better have the cat in and judge for ourselves?" suggested Lady Blemley.

Sir Wilfred went in search of the animal, and the company settled themselves down to the languid expectation of witnessing some more or less adroit drawing-room ventriloquism.

In a minute Sir Wilfred was back in the room, his face white beneath its tan and his eyes dilated with excitement.

"By Gad, it's true!"

His agitation was unmistakably genuine, and his hearers started forward in a thrill of wakened interest.

Collapsing into an armchair he continued breathlessly:

"I found him dozing in the smoking-room, and called out to him to come for his tea. He blinked at me in his usual way, and I said, 'Come on, Toby; don't keep us waiting' and, by Gad! he drawled out in a most horribly natural voice that he'd come when he dashed well pleased! I nearly jumped out of my skin!"

Appin had preached to absolutely incredulous hearers; Sir Wilfred's statement carried instant conviction. A Babel-like chorus of startled exclamation arose, amid which the scientist sat mutely enjoying the first fruit of his stupendous discovery.

In the midst of the clamour Tobermory entered the room and made his way with velvet tread and studied unconcern across the group seated round the tea-table.

A sudden hush of awkwardness and constraint fell on the company. Somehow there seemed an element of embarrassment in addressing on equal terms a domestic cat of acknowledged dental ability.

"Will you have some milk, Tobermory?" asked Lady Blemley in a rather strained voice.

"I don't mind if I do," was the response, couched in a tone of even indifference. A shiver of suppressed excitement went through the listeners, and Lady Blemley might be excused for pouring out the saucerful of milk rather unsteadily.

"I'm afraid I've spilt a good deal of it," she said apologetically.

"After all, it's not my Axminster," was Tobermory's rejoinder.

Another silence fell on the group, and then Miss Resker, in her best district-visitor manner, asked if the human language had been difficult to learn. Tobermory looked squarely at her for a moment and then fixed his gaze serenely on the middle distance. It was obvious that boring questions lay outside his scheme of life.

"What do you think of human intelligence?" asked Mavis Pellington lamely.

"Of whose intelligence in particular?" asked Tobermory coldly.

"Oh, well, mine for instance," said Mavis with a feeble laugh.

"You put me in an embarrassing position," said Tobermory, whose tone and attitude certainly did not suggest a shred of embarrassment. "When your inclusion in this house-party was suggested Sir Wilfrid protested that you were the most brainless woman of his acquaintance, and that there was a wide distinction between hospitality and the care of the feeble-minded. Lady Blemley replied that your lack of brain-power was the precise quality which had earned you your invitation, as you were the only person she could think of who might be idiotic enough to buy their old car. You know, the one they call 'The Envy of Sisyphus,' because it goes quite nicely up-hill if you push it."

Lady Blemley's protestations would have had greater effect if she had not casually suggested to Mavis only that morning that the car in question would be just the thing for her down at her Devonshire home.

Major Barfield plunged in heavily to effect a diversion.

"How about your carryings-on with the tortoise-shell puss up at the stables, eh?"

The moment he had said it every one realized the blunder.

"One does not usually discuss these matters in public," said Tobermory frigidly. "From a slight observation of your ways since you've been in this house I should imagine you'd find it inconvenient if I were to shift the conversation to your own little affairs."

The panic which ensued was not confined to the Major.

"Would you like to go and see if cook has got your dinner ready?" suggested Lady Blemley hurriedly, affecting to ignore the fact that it wanted at least two hours to Tobermory's dinner-time.

"Thanks," said Tobermory, "not quite so soon after my tea. I don't want to die of indigestion."

"Cats have nine lives, you know," said Sir Wilfred heartily.

"Possibly," answered Tobermory; "but only one liver."

"Adelaide!" said Mrs. Cornett, "do you mean to encourage that cat to go out and gossip about us in the servants' hall?"

The panic had indeed become general. A narrow ornamental balustrade ran in front of most of the bedroom windows at the Towers, and it was recalled with dismay that this had formed a favourite promenade for Tobermory at all hours, whence he could watch the pigeons—and heaven knew what else besides. If he intended to become reminiscent in his present outspoken strain the effect would be something more than disconcerting. Mrs. Cornett, who spent much time at her toilet table, and whose complexion was reputed to be of a nomadic though punctual disposition, looked as ill at ease as the Major. Miss Scrawen, who wrote fiercely sensuous poetry and led a blameless life, merely displayed irritation; if you are methodical and virtuous in private you don't necessarily want everyone to know it. Bertie van Tahn, who was so depraved at 17 that he had long ago given up trying to be any worse, turned a dull shade of gardenia white, but he did not commit the error of dashing out of the room like Odo Finsberry, a young gentleman who was understood to be reading for the Church and who was possibly disturbed at the thought of scandals he might hear concerning other people. Clovis had the presence of mind to maintain a composed exterior; privately he was calculating how long it would take to procure a box of fancy mice through the agency of the Exchange and Mart as a species of hush-money.

Even in a delicate situation like the present, Agnes Resker could not endure to remain long in the background.

"Why did I ever come down here?" she asked dramatically.

Tobermory immediately accepted the opening.

"Judging by what you said to Mrs. Cornett on the croquet-lawn yesterday, you were out of food. You described the Blemleys as the dullest people to stay with that you knew, but said they were clever enough to employ a first-rate cook; otherwise they'd find it difficult to get any one to come down a second time."

"There's not a word of truth in it! I appeal to Mrs. Cornett—" exclaimed the discomfited Agnes.

"Mrs. Cornett repeated your remark afterwards to Bertie van Tahn," continued Tobermory, "and said, 'That woman is a regular Hunger Marcher; she'd go anywhere for four square meals a day,' and Bertie van Tahn said—"

At this point the chronicle mercifully ceased. Tobermory had caught a glimpse of the big yellow tom from the Rectory working his way through the shrubbery towards the stable wing. In a flash he had vanished through the open French window.

With the disappearance of his too brilliant pupil Cornelius Appin found himself beset by a hurricane of bitter upbraiding, anxious inquiry, and frightened entreaty. The responsibility for the situation lay with him, and he must prevent matters from becoming worse. Could Tobermory impart his dangerous gift to other cats? was the first question he had to answer. It was possible, he replied, that he might have initiated his intimate friend the stable puss into his new accomplishment, but it was unlikely that his teaching could have taken a wider range as yet.

"Then," said Mrs. Cornett, "Tobermory may be a valuable cat and a great pet; but I'm sure you'll agree, Adelaide, that both he and the stable cat must be done away with without delay."

"You don't suppose I've enjoyed the last quarter of an hour, do you?" said Lady Blemley bitterly. "My husband and I are very fond of Tobermory—at least, we were before this horrible accomplishment was infused into him; but now, of course, the only thing is to have him destroyed as soon as possible."

"We can put some strychnine in the scraps he always gets at dinner-time," said Sir Wilfred, "and I will go and drown the stable cat myself. The coachman will be very sore at losing his pet, but I'll say a very catching form of mange has broken out in both cats and we're afraid of it spreading to the kennels."

"But my great discovery!" expostulated Mr. Appin; "after all my years of research and experiment—"

"You can go and experiment on the short-horns at the farm, who are under proper control," said Mrs. Cornett, "or the elephants at the Zoological Gardens. They're said to be highly intelligent, and they have this recommendation, that they don't come creeping about our bedrooms and under chairs, and so forth."

An archangel ecstatically proclaiming the Millennium, and then finding that it clashed unpardonably with Henley and would have to be indefinitely postponed, could hardly have felt more crestfallen than Cornelius Appin at the reception of his wonderful achievement. Public opinion, however, was against him—in fact, had the general voice been consulted on the subject it is probable that a strong minority vote would have been in favour of including him in the strychnine diet.

Defective train arrangements and a nervous desire to see matters brought to a finish prevented an immediate dispersal of the party, but dinner that evening was not a social success. Sir Wilfred had had rather a trying time with the stable cat and subsequently with the coachman. Agnes Resker ostentatiously limited her repast to a morsel of dry toast, which she bit as though it were a personal enemy; while Mavis Pellington maintained a vindictive silence throughout the meal. Lady

Blemley kept up a flow of what she hoped was conversation, but her attention was fixed on the doorway. A plateful of carefully dosed fish scraps was in readiness on the sideboard, but the sweets and savoury and dessert went their way, and no Tobermory appeared in the dining-room or kitchen.

The sepulchral dinner was cheerful compared with the subsequent vigil in the smoking-room. Eating and drinking had at least supplied a distraction and cloak to the prevailing embarrassment. Bridge was out of the question in the general tension of nerves and tempers, and after Odo Finsberry had given a lugubrious rendering of 'Melisande in the Wood' to a frigid audience, music was tacitly avoided. At eleven the servants went to bed, announcing that the small window in the pantry had been left open as usual for Tobermory's private use. The guests read steadily through the current batch of magazines, and fell back gradu-ally on the "Badminton Library" and bound volumes of Punch. Lady Blemley made periodic visits to the pantry, returning each time with an expression of listless depression which forestalled questioning.

At two o'clock Clovis broke the dominating silence.

"He won't turn up tonight. He's probably in the local newspaper office at the present moment, dictating the first installment of his reminiscences. Lady What's-her-name's book won't be in it. It will be the event of the day."

Having made this contribution to the general cheerfulness, Clovis went to bed. At long intervals the various members of the house-party followed his example.

The servants taking round the early tea made a uniform announce-ment in reply to a uniform question. Tobermory had not returned.

Breakfast was, if anything, a more unpleasant function than dinner had been, but before its conclusion the situation was relieved. Tobermory's corpse was brought in from the shrubbery, where a gardener had just discovered it. From the bites on his throat and the yellow fur which coated his claws it was evident that he had fallen in unequal combat with the big Tom from the Rectory.

By midday most of the guests had quitted the Towers, and after lunch

Lady Blemley had sufficiently recovered her spirits to write an extremely nasty letter to the Rectory about the loss of her valuable pet.

Tobermory had been Appin's one successful pupil, and he was destined to have no successor. A few weeks later an elephant in the Dresden Zoological Garden, which had shown no previous signs of irritability, broke loose and killed an Englishman who had apparently been teasing it. The victim's name was variously reported in the papers as Oppin and Eppelin, but his front name was faithfully rendered Cornelius.

"If he was trying German irregular verbs on the poor beast," said Clovis, "he deserved all he got."

FILBOID STUDGE, THE STORY OF A MOUSE THAT HELPED

Saki

Saki (1870–1916), or Hector Hugh Munro, was a British writer whose witty, mischievous and sometimes macabre stories satirised Edwardian society and culture. Though born in Burma, he was brought up mainly in England by his grandmother and aunts in a strict puritanical household. When the war broke out, Munro refused a commission and joined the army as a regular trooper. He was killed in action by a German sniper. His last words were, reportedly, 'Put that bloody cigarette out!' A master of the short form, he was influenced by Oscar Wilde, Lewis Carroll and Rudyard Kipling, and he himself influenced A.A. Milne, Noël Coward and P.G. Wodehouse.

'I want to marry your daughter,' said Mark Spayley with faltering eagerness. 'I am only an artist with an income of two hundred a year, and she is the daughter of an enormously wealthy man, so I suppose you will think my offer a piece of presumption.'

Duncan Dullamy, the great company inflator, showed no outward sign of displeasure. As a matter of fact, he was secretly relieved at the prospect of finding even a two-hundred-a-year husband for his daughter, Leonore. A crisis was rapidly rushing upon him, from which he knew he would emerge with neither money nor credit; all his recent ventures had fallen flat, and flattest of all had gone the wonderful new breakfast food, Pipenta, on the advertisement of which he had sunk such huge sums. It could scarcely be called a drug in the market; people bought drugs, but no one bought Pipenta.

'Would you marry Leonore if she were a poor man's daughter?' asked the man of phantom wealth.

'Yes,' said Mark, wisely avoiding the error of over-protestation. And to his astonishment Leonore's father not only gave his consent, but suggested a fairly early date for the wedding. 'I wish I could show my gratitude in some way,' said Mark with genuine emotion. 'I'm afraid it's rather like the mouse proposing to help the lion.'

'Get people to buy that beastly muck,' said Dullamy, nodding savagely at a poster of the despised Pipenta, 'and you'll have done more than any of my agents have been able to accomplish.'

'It wants a better name,' said Mark reflectively, 'and something distinctive in the poster line. Anyway, I'll have a shot at it.'

Three weeks later the world was advised of the coming of a new breakfast food, heralded under the resounding name of 'Filboid Studge'. Spayley put forth no pictures of massive babies springing up with fungus-like rapidity under its forcing influence, or of representatives of the leading nations of the world scrambling with fatuous eagerness for its possession. One huge sombre poster depicted the Damned in Hell suffering a new torment from their inability to get at the Filboid Studge which elegant young fiends held in transparent bowls just beyond their reach. The scene was rendered even more gruesome by a subtle suggestion of the features of leading men and women of the day in the portrayal of the Lost Souls; prominent individuals of both political parties, Society hostesses, well-known dramatic authors and novelists, and distinguished aeroplanists were dimly recognizable in that doomed throng; noted lights of the musical-comedy stage flickered wanly in the shades of the Inferno, smiling still from force of habit, but with the fearsome smiling rage of baffled effort. The poster bore no fulsome allusions to the merits of the new breakfast food, but a single grim statement ran in bold letters along its base: 'They cannot buy it now'.

Spayley had grasped the fact that people will do things from a sense of duty which they would never attempt as a pleasure. There are thousands of respectable middle-class men who, if you found them unexpectedly in a Turkish bath, would explain in all sincerity that a doctor had ordered them to take Turkish baths; if you told them in return that you went there because you liked it, they would stare in pained wonder at the frivolity of your motive. In the same way, whenever a massacre of Armenians is reported from Asia Minor, everyone assumes that it has been carried out 'under orders' from somewhere or another; no one seems to think that there are people who might like to kill their neighbours now and then.

And so it was with the new breakfast food. No one would have eaten Filboid Studge as a pleasure, but the grim austerity of its advertisement drove housewives in shoals to the grocers' shops to clamour for an immediate supply. In small kitchens solemn pig-tailed daughters helped depressed mothers to perform the primitive ritual of its preparation. On the breakfast-tables of cheerless parlours it was partaken of in silence. Once the womenfolk discovered that it was thoroughly unpalatable, their zeal in forcing it on their households knew no bounds. 'You haven't eaten your Filboid Studge!' would be screamed at the appetiteless clerk as he hurried wearily from the breakfast-table, and his evening meal would be prefaced by a warmed-up mess which would be explained as 'your Filboid Studge that you didn't eat this morning.' Those strange fanatics who ostentatiously mortify themselves, inwardly and outwardly, with health biscuits and health garments, battened aggressively on the new food. Earnest spectacled young men devoured it on the steps of the National Liberal Club. A bishop who did not believe in a future state preached against the poster, and a peer's daughter died from eating too much of the compound. A further advertisement was obtained when an infantry regiment mutinied and shot its officers rather than eat the nauseous mess; fortunately, Lord Birrell of Blatherstone, who was War Minister at the moment, saved the situation by his happy epigram, that 'Discipline to be effective must be optional.'

Filboid Studge had become a household word, but Dullamy wisely realized that it was not necessarily the last word in breakfast dietary; its supremacy would be challenged as soon as some yet more unpalatable food should be put on the market. There might even be a reaction in favour of something tasty and appetizing, and the Puritan austerity of the moment might be banished from domestic cookery. At an opportune moment, therefore, he sold out his interests in the article which had brought him in colossal wealth at a critical juncture, and placed his financial reputation beyond the reach of cavil. As for Leonore, who was now an heiress on a far greater scale than ever before, he naturally found her something a vast deal higher in the husband market than a two-hundred-a-year poster designer. Mark Spayley, the brainmouse who had helped the financial lion with such untoward effect, was left to curse the day he produced the wonder-working poster.

'After all,' said Clovis, meeting him shortly afterwards at his club, 'you have this doubtful consolation, that 'tis not in mortals to countermand success.'

THE TOYS OF PEACE

Saki

Saki (1870–1916), or Hector Hugh Munro, was a British writer whose witty, mischievous and sometimes macabre stories satirised Edwardian society and culture. Though born in Burma, he was brought up mainly in England by his grandmother and aunts in a strict puritanical household. When the war broke out, Munro refused a commission and joined the army as a regular trooper. He was killed in action by a German sniper. His last words were, reportedly, 'Put that bloody cigarette out!' A master of the short form, he was influenced by Oscar Wilde, Lewis Carroll and Rudyard Kipling, and he himself influenced A.A. Milne, Noël Coward and P.G. Wodehouse.

'Harvey,' said Eleanor Bope, handing her brother a cutting from a London morning paper of the 19th of March, 'just read this about children's toys, please; it exactly carries out some of our ideas about influence and upbringing.'

'In the view of the National Peace Council,' ran the extract, 'there are grave objections to presenting our boys with regiments of fighting men, batteries of guns, and squadrons of "Dreadnoughts." Boys, the Council admits, naturally love fighting and all the panoply of war... but that is no reason for encouraging, and perhaps giving permanent form to, their primitive instincts. At the Children's Welfare Exhibition, which opens at Olympia in three weeks' time, the Peace Council will make an alternative suggestion to parents in the shape of an exhibition of "peace toys." In front of a specially-painted representation of the Peace Palace at The Hague will be grouped, not miniature soldiers but miniature civilians, not guns but ploughs and the tools of industry... It is hoped that manufacturers may take a hint from the exhibit, which will bear fruit in the toy shops.'

'The idea is certainly an interesting and very well-meaning one,' said Harvey; 'whether it would succeed well in practice—'

'We must try,' interrupted his sister; 'you are coming down to us at Easter, and you always bring the boys some toys, so that will be an excellent opportunity for you to inaugurate the new experiment. Go about in the shops and buy any little toys and models that have special bearing on civilian life in its more peaceful aspects. Of course you must explain the toys to the children and interest them in the new idea. I regret to say that the "Siege of Adrianople" toy, that their Aunt Susan sent them, didn't need any explanation; they knew all the uniforms and flags, and even the names of the respective commanders, and when I heard them one day using what seemed to be the most objectionable language they said it was Bulgarian words of command; of course it *may* have been, but at any rate I took the toy away from them. Now I shall expect your Easter gifts to give quite a new impulse and direction to the children's minds; Eric is not eleven yet, and Bertie is only nine-and-a-half, so they are really at a most impressionable age.'

'There is primitive instinct to be taken into consideration, you know,' said Henry doubtfully, 'and hereditary tendencies as well. One of their great-uncles fought in the most intolerant fashion at Inkerman – he was specially mentioned in dispatches, I believe – and their great-grandfather smashed all his Whig neighbours' hot houses when the great Reform Bill was passed. Still, as you say, they are at an impressionable age. I will do my best.'

On Easter Saturday Harvey Bope unpacked a large, promising-looking red cardboard box under the expectant eyes of his nephews. 'Your uncle has brought you the newest thing in toys,' Eleanor had said impressively, and youthful anticipation had been anxiously divided between Albanian soldiery and a Somali camel-corps. Eric was hotly in favour of the latter contingency. 'There would be Arabs on horseback,' he whispered; 'the

Albanians have got jolly uniforms, and they fight all day long, and all night, too, when there's a moon, but the country's rocky, so they've got no cavalry.'

A quantity of crinkly paper shavings was the first thing that met the view when the lid was removed; the most exiting toys always began like that. Harvey pushed back the top layer and drew forth a square, rather featureless building.

'It's a fort!' exclaimed Bertie.

'It isn't, it's the palace of the Mpret of Albania,' said Eric, immensely proud of his knowledge of the exotic title; 'it's got no windows, you see, so that passers-by can't fire in at the Royal Family.'

'It's a municipal dust-bin,' said Harvey hurriedly; 'you see all the refuse and litter of a town is collected there, instead of lying about and injuring the health of the citizens.'

In an awful silence he disinterred a little lead figure of a man in black clothes.

'That,' he said, 'is a distinguished civilian, John Stuart Mill. He was an authority on political economy.'

'Why?' asked Bertie.

'Well, he wanted to be; he thought it was a useful thing to be.'

Bertie gave an expressive grunt, which conveyed his opinion that there was no accounting for tastes.

Another square building came out, this time with windows and chimneys.

'A model of the Manchester branch of the Young Women's Christian Association,' said Harvey.

'Are there any lions?' asked Eric hopefully. He had been reading Roman history and thought that where you found Christians you might reasonably expect to find a few lions.

'There are no lions,' said Harvey. 'Here is another civilian, Robert Raikes, the founder of Sunday schools, and here is a model of a municipal wash-house. These little round things are loaves backed in a sanitary bakehouse. That lead figure is a sanitary inspector, this one is a district councillor, and this one is an official of the Local Government Board.'

'What does he do?' asked Eric wearily.

'He sees to things connected with his Department,' said Harvey. 'This box with a slit in it is a ballot-box. Votes are put into it at election times.'

'What is put into it at other times?' asked Bertie.

'Nothing. And here are some tools of industry, a wheelbarrow and a hoe, and I think these are meant for hop-poles. This is a model beehive, and that is a ventilator, for ventilating sewers. This seems to be another municipal dust-bin – no, it is a model of a school of art and public library. This little lead figure is Mrs. Hemans, a poetess, and this is Rowland Hill, who introduced the system of penny postage. This is Sir John Herschel, the eminent astrologer.'

'Are we to play with these civilian figures?' asked Eric.

'Of course,' said Harvey, 'these are toys; they are meant to be played with.'

'But how?'

It was rather a poser. 'You might make two of them contest a seat in Parliament,' said Harvey, 'and have an election—'

'With rotten eggs, and free fights, and ever so many broken heads!' exclaimed Eric.

'And noses all bleeding and everybody drunk as can be,' echoed Bertie, who had carefully studied one of Hogarth's pictures.

'Nothing of the kind,' said Harvey, 'nothing in the least like that. Votes will be put in the ballot-box, and the Mayor will count them – and he will say which has received the most votes, and then the two candidates will thank him for presiding, and each will say that the contest has been conducted throughout in the pleasantest and most straightforward fashion, and they part with expressions of mutual esteem. There's a jolly game for you boys to play. I never had such toys when I was young.'

'I don't think we'll play with them just now,' said Eric, with an entire absence of the enthusiasm that his uncle had shown; 'I think perhaps we ought to do a little of our holiday task. It's history this time; we've got to learn up something about the Bourbon period in France.'

'The Bourbon period,' said Harvey, with some disapproval in his voice.

'We've got to know something about Louis the Fourteenth,' continued Eric; 'I've learnt the names of all the principal battles already.'

This would never do. 'There were, of course, some battles fought during his reign,' said Harvey, 'but I fancy the accounts of them were much exaggerated; news was very unreliable in those days, and there were practically no war correspondents, so generals and commanders could magnify every little skirmish they engaged in till they reached the proportions of decisive battles. Louis was really famous, now, as a landscape gardener; the way he laid out Versailles was so much admired that it was copied all over Europe.'

'Do you know anything about Madame Du Barry?' asked Eric; 'didn't she have her head chopped off?'

'She was another great lover of gardening,' said Harvey, evasively; 'in fact, I believe the well known rose Du Barry was named after her, and now I think you had better play for a little and leave your lessons till later.'

Harvey retreated to the library and spent some thirty or forty minutes in wondering whether it would be possible to compile a history, for use in elementary schools, in which there should be no prominent mention of battles, massacres, murderous intrigues, and violent deaths. The York and Lancaster period and the Napoleonic era would, he admitted to himself, present considerable difficulties, and the Thirty Years' War would entail something of a gap if you left it out altogether. Still, it would be something gained if, at a highly impressionable age, children could be got to fix their attention on the invention of calico printing instead of the Spanish Armada or the Battle of Waterloo.

It was time, he thought, to go back to the boys' room, and see how they were getting on with their peace toys. As he stood outside the door he could hear Eric's voice raised in command; Bertie chimed in now and again with a helpful suggestion.

'That is Louis the Fourteenth,' Eric was saying, 'that one in knee-breeches, that Uncle said invented Sunday schools. It isn't a bit like him, but it'll have to do.'

'We'll give him a purple coat from my paintbox by and by,' said Bertie.

'Yes, an' red heels. That is Madame de Maintenon, that one he called Mrs. Hemans. She begs Louis not to go on this expedition, but he turns a deaf ear. He takes Marshal Saxe with him, and we must pretend that they have thousands of men with them. The watchword is Qui vive? and the answer is L'etat c'est moi – that was one of his favourite remarks, you know. They land at Manchester in the dead of the night, and a Jacobite conspirator gives them the keys of the fortress.'

Peeping in through the doorway Harvey observed that the municipal dustbin had been pierced with holes to accommodate the muzzles of imaginary cannon, and now represented the principal fortified position in Manchester; John Stuart Mill had been dipped in red ink, and apparently stood for Marshal Saxe.

'Louis orders his troops to surround the Young Women's Christian Association and seize the lot of them. "Once back at the Louvre and the girls are mine," he exclaims. We must use Mrs. Hemans again for one of the girls; she says "Never," and stabs Marshal Saxe to the heart.'

'He bleeds dreadfully,' exclaimed Bertie, splashing red ink liberally over the facade of the Association building.

'The soldiers rush in and avenge his death with the utmost savagery. A hundred girls are killed' – here Bertie emptied the remainder of the red ink over the devoted building – 'and the surviving five hundred are dragged off to the French ships. "I have lost a Marshal," says Louis, "but I do not go back empty-handed."'

Harvey stole away from the room, and sought out his sister.

'Eleanor,' he said, 'the experiment—'

'Yes?'

'Has failed. We have begun too late.'

THE INSTITUTE FOR FACIAL REFORM (A FANTASTICAL STORY)

Getsl Selikovich

Getsl (George) Selikovich (1855–1926) was a writer, scholar and Egyptologist born in Rietavas (Riteve) in what is now Lithuania. In 1885, he served as an Arabic interpreter for the British military in Egypt, but he left the expedition early after he was accused of sympathising with the Egyptians. He moved to the United States to take up the position of professor of Egyptology at the University of Pennsylvania, but he was forced to leave on account of 'intrigues'. He then began a long career as a Yiddish and Hebrew journalist, during which he published erudite articles as well as a number of humoresques.

"Faces twisted, noses extended
Foreheads short, Lips distended
Go one and all to Dr. Skinner DeLintz,
He'll make you handsome as a prince."

This poetic phrase written in large letters alongside a nice picture hung in front of the door to the office of Dr. Skinner DeLintz, the director of "The Institute for Facial Reform," as he titled himself and his medical institution.

Instead of just describing the outside of this medical institute, let's take a look inside.

Dr. Skinner DeLintz sat with a cigar in his mouth and explained in a serious tone to his assistant that his Institute for Facial Reform had already achieved the highest artistry in changing any face, just like a good tailor can transform any item of clothing into whatever he likes. Now it was time for them to come up with a brand-new sensation in their profession. It was time to make a lot more money.

"I'll tell you, Dr. Skinner," Dr. Skimmer began, "as soon as you compared us to tailors, this question came to me: Who are the best tailors in the world? Certainly not those who make clothing according to what's in fashion. Instead, it's those who themselves come up with a new fashion whenever they want, and convince the public to go after whatever fashion they release. Now I ask you, Skinner my friend, why should we not do what the great tailors do? Why should we not be bothered when a client comes to us and says that his nose is too short or too long, or his chin too pointy, and we should fix it the way he likes? No, Doctor, we ourselves should decide between us that one season it should be the fashion to wear long noses, and another season we'll come out with short noses, and yet another season pug noses, and so forth, like the tailors do. And this way we'll be showered with millions. Right?"

"This is really a terrific plan!" cried out Dr. Skinner DeLintz. "But we must first create a mold for a face that will please everyone, and we will copyright this handsome face in Washington, D.C. First let's search for a model of a manly face. When we have succeeded, we will start with the women, because we have to be more careful with women. So, first a handsome model of a face for men."

Dr. Skimmer went out and walked along Broadway, down Forty-Second Street, and on Fifth Avenue. He went to every neighborhood in order to find an inspiration, a model for a perfectly handsome face that would please everyone, and that could serve as a prototype for the Institute for Facial Reform. After Dr. Skimmer strolled around for several hours he noticed in a photography gallery a picture with a remarkably attractive man's face: a face that was not only handsome, but also noble, pleasant, friendly, and attractive. Dr. Skimmer did not have to take much time to consider before he bought the picture in order to bring it to a good sculptor. He was sure that with only a few improvements by the sculptor the head in plaster would be the beautiful model that would please everyone! Several days later, when the sculptor finished the stunning head, both doctors were highly pleased with their model, and they began enthusiastically to announce their new plan in all of the newspapers. The advertisement, which was in rhyme, was phrased eloquently:

"Do you want a face as fresh as spring
And to be as handsome as a king?
Do you want to be solemn as an academician,
Dreamy as a poet or a musician?
Do you want to look like an aristocrat,
A wise man, a wealthy man, or a diplomat,
A trust-fund magnate or a prince?
Then go to Dr. Skinner DeLintz."

To the side of this "poetry" was the picture of the handsome, noble face, and under it was the address of the Institute for Facial Reform on Broadway. They waited for the result. The very next day, several people showed up who wanted their faces to be "reformed" according to the face that they saw on the advertisement. The first patient that the doctor took into the operating room had a terrible face. He looked like some kind of bandit. "He must be a thief from the forest," the doctor thought. When the patient told to him that he was a financier who lent money and earned interest, the doctor said to himself with a smile that he had guessed perfectly. The lender explained that he had a bank counter and did good business. But he would do ten times better business without his hideous face that drove people away.

The two doctors did most of the work in less than an hour, while the lender was unconscious. They poured potent wax onto the skin of his forehead so that it should be smooth and without bumps, like on the noble face from their advertisement. With other means they took care of the lender's nose, chin, and lips, until his whole face was entirely changed into a very sympathetic countenance. When the patient came to and they gave him a mirror, he was beside himself with joy and paid the $50 fee with pleasure.

The next patient was a bartender, also with a grotesque appearance. He said that he wanted to marry a girl whom he loved with his whole heart, but she was not attracted to his strange and wild appearance. This bartender also wanted to have a handsome face like the one in the doctor's advertisement. They put him to sleep and performed the same operation as they had done with the lender. The patient left the doctor's institute with a face like an ideal philanthropist. The third patient was a politician, who was a candidate to become a judge and was almost sure that he could win, if only his face did not stand in his way.

Already on the first day there were twelve people walking around New York with faces identical to the doctor's model, and that's without counting the thirteenth man, on whom the model was based! Dr. Skinner and Dr. Skimmer were busy day and night, and by the end of the week there were 116 people walking around New York whose faces looked exactly the same!

But the next Sunday something happened in New York that shook up the whole city. When the famous Reverend Doctor Flim Flam finished preaching in his Temple, two secret policemen came up to him and arrested him as the man who gave a false check to a farmer. Dr. Flim Flam looked at them as though he didn't know what to say, but his arguments were of no avail: the policemen had a detailed description of the culprit's face, according to the farmer's description, a face that matched Doctor Flim Flam's down to the last hair. So, did they need any better evidence?

On Broadway, at the exact time of Dr. Flim Flam's arrest, it happened that two other policemen arrested a famous tenor from the Metropolitan Opera House for the same crime of the false check, written to the same farmer. And there was a rumor that a millionaire on Wall Street was also arrested for the same false check to the same farmer.

But the great sensation came the next day, Monday morning, when dozens of detectives brought into court together with Dr. Flim Flam no fewer than sixty suspects, all sixty with the same face, and each one of them accused of the same crime of the false check! The laughter in court was indescribable. They say that the policemen and the detectives rolled with laughter. What kind of a trick was this? Was it a dream? But how could a hundred people in court have the same dream? The judge barely had the strength to say "dismissed" before he quickly fainted.

When Dr. Skinner DeLintz read in the paper the next day about this comedy in court, he wrote a letter of apology to Dr. Flim Flam. He decided then and there with his friend Skimmer to quickly abandon, at least for a while, the plan that "all faces should look like one race."

Translated by Jessica Kirzane

DEAR MOUNTAIN ROOM PARENTS

Maria Semple

Maria Semple (1964–) is the internationally bestselling author of *This One is Mine*, *Where'd You Go, Bernadette* and *Today Will Be Different*. Before writing fiction, she wrote for TV shows including *90210*, *Mad About You* and *Arrested Development*.

Hi, everyone!

The Mountain Room is gearing up for its Day of the Dead celebration on Friday. Please send in photos of loved ones for our altar. All parents are welcome to come by on Wednesday afternoon to help us make candles and decorate skulls.

Thanks!

Emily

Hi again.

Because I've gotten some questions about my last e-mail, there is nothing "wrong" with Halloween. The Day of the Dead is the Mexican version, a time of remembrance. Many of you chose Little Learners because of our emphasis on global awareness. Our celebration on Friday is an example of that. The skulls we're decorating are sugar skulls. I should have made that more clear.

Emily

Parents:

Some of you have expressed concern about your children celebrating a holiday with the word "dead" in it. I asked Eleanor's mom, who's a pediatrician, and here's what she said: "Preschoolers tend to see death as temporary and reversible. Therefore, I see nothing traumatic about the Day of the Dead." I hope this helps.

Emily

Dear Parents:

In response to the e-mail we all received from Maddie's parents, in which they shared their decision to raise their daughter dogma-free, yes, there will be an altar, but please be assured that the Day of the Dead is a pagan celebration of life and has nothing to do with God. Keep those photos coming!

Emily

Hello.

Perhaps "pagan" was a poor word choice. I feel like we're veering a bit off track, so here's what I'll do. I'll start setting up our altar now, so that today at pickup you can see for yourselves how colorful and harmless the Day of the Dead truly is.

Emily

Parents:

The photos should be of loved ones who have passed. Max's grandma was understandably shaken when she came in and saw a photo of herself on our altar.

But the candles and skulls were cute, right?

Emily

Mountain Room Parents:

It's late and I can't possibly respond to each and every e-mail. (Not that it comes up a lot in conversation, but I have children, too.) As the skulls have clearly become a distraction, I decided to throw them away. They're in the compost. I'm looking at them now. You can, too, tomorrow at drop-off. I just placed a "no basura" card on the bin to make sure it doesn't get emptied. Finally, to those parents who are offended by our Day of the Dead celebration, I'd like to point out that there are parents who are offended that you are offended.

Emily

Dear Parents:

Thanks to their group e-mail, we now know that the families of Millie and Jaden M. recognize Jesus Christ as their Saviour. There still seems to be some confusion about why, if we want to celebrate life, we're actually celebrating death. To better explain this "bewildering detour," I've asked Adela, who works in the office and makes waffles for us on Wednesdays, and who was born in Mexico, to write you directly.

Emily

Hola a los Padres:

El Día de los Muertos begins with a parade through the zócalo, where we toss oranges into decorated coffins. The skeletons drive us in the bus to the cemetery and we molest the spirits from under the ground with candy and traditional Mexican music. We write poems called calaveras, which laugh at the living. In Mexico, it is a rejoicing time of ofrendas, picnics, and dancing on graves.

Adela

Parents:

I sincerely apologize for Adela's e-mail. I would have looked it over, but I was at my daughter's piano recital. (Three kids, in case you're wondering, one who's allergic to everything, even wind.) For now, let's agree that e-mail has reached its limits. How about we process our feelings face to face? 9 A.M. tomorrow?

Emily

Dear Parents:

Some of you chose to engage in our dialogue. Some chose to form a human chain. Others had jobs (!) to go to. So we're all up to speed, let me recap this morning's discussion:

—Satan isn't driving our bus. Little Learners does not have a bus. If we did, I wouldn't still need parent drivers for the field trip to the cider mill. Anyone? I didn't think so.

—Ofrenda means "offering." It's just a thing we put on the altar. Any random thing. A bottle of Fanta. Unopened, not poisoned. Just a bottle of Fanta.

—We're moving past the word "altar" and calling it what it really is: a Seahawks blanket draped over some cinder blocks.

—Adela will not be preparing food anymore and Waffle Wednesdays will be suspended. (That didn't make us any new friends in the Rainbow and Sunshine Rooms!)

—On Friday morning, I will divide the Mountain Room into three groups: those who wish to celebrate the Day of the Dead; those who wish to celebrate Halloween; and Maddie, who will make nondenominational potato prints in the corner.

Dear Mountain Room Parents:

Today I learned not to have open flames in the same room as a costume parade. I learned that a five-dollar belly-dancer outfit purchased at a pop-up costume store can easily catch fire, but, really, I knew that just by looking at it. I learned that Fanta is effective in putting out fires. I learned that a child's emerging completely unscathed from a burning costume isn't a good enough outcome for some parents. I learned that I will be unemployed on Monday. For me, the Day of the Dead will always be a time of remembrance.

Happy Halloween!

Emily

TALKING CHIMP GIVES HIS FIRST PRESS CONFERENCE

Paul Simms

Paul Simms (1966–) is an American television writer and producer. He began his career writing for *Late Night with David Letterman* and later wrote for *The Larry Sanders Show*. More recently, he has directed and produced *Flight of the Conchords* and *Atlanta*. His short stories have appeared in *The New Yorker*.

Hello? Can everyone hear me? Anyone?

Check, check. Check, one two.

Is this thing on?

Not the microphone—I mean my Electronic Larynx Implant device. Is it working? Hit the "Reboot" button, and see if that ook ook-ook ook.

Ook? Ook? Ook-ook.

Ook!

Ook-ook-oo—why does it seem like it always takes an eternity for the ELI to reboot? I mean, isn't this something we should have ironed out a long time ago?

Oh. O.K. We're back online now? Good. You can all hear me out there? Great.

I'd like to apologize for the technical difficulties up here. One would think that the most important part of setting up the world's first talking chimp demonstration is making sure that the P.A. is working, but... O.K. I guess.

Can I get a bowl of water, please? Thank you. Is the sound guy here? The sound guy. The P.A. technician. Is he here? He's in the back? Just as well. It's just that… you know how sometimes you get the feeling that you'd like to bite bite bite bite bite someone? Anyone? Nothing? Whatever. It'll pass.

Well, anyway: Hello, male humans and female humans! I am indeed what you call a chimpanzee. I do have a human-given proper name— something that sounds like Timmy or Jimmy or Bimmy or Immy—but, for some reason, recognizing and pronouncing human-given proper names is virtually impossible for me. So, yeah, all you skeptics can go ahead and make hay with that one, but I'm doing my best up here.

I guess I should start by acknowledging Dr. Female-Human-Lemon-Colored-Hair and her partner Dr. Male-Human-Persistent-Territory-Threatener for all the great work they've done with me—or, rather, *on* me—in the past few years.

The development of the ELI was a long and arduous process, and there were more than a few times—usually after being shot with a tranquillizer dart and then waking up hours later with excruciatingly painful bleeding stitch holes in my neck and chest regions—when I wasn't sure if it was worth it. But I guess it was, because here we are today, in this beautiful conference room at the Sheraton.

In fact, there were some days when I felt nothing but the desire to bite bite bite bite bite everyone involved, including, if you can believe it, Mr. Male-Human-Black-Skin-Food-Bringer. Who, for my money, is the true unsung hero of this interminable experiment. This guy is the male human who not only brings me my kibble every morning but also delivers to my cage a metal bucket full of orange wedges every afternoon.

So give him a round of applause, if you would. Stand up, Mr. Male-Human-Black-Skin-Food-Bringer! Don't be shy!

He's not here? O.K., then. I'm not sure why he wasn't invited to share in the limelight today, but I guess we all have our different ways of doing things. Or something. Let's just move right along.

I had planned today to speak mainly about the similarities between humans and chimpanzees. How we're all members of the same family, and so on and so forth.

I feel like I have to take a dump right now.

But instead of speaking about the similarities between humans and—

Ahh. That's better. Dump taken. Where was I?

Similarities. Right. But instead of speaking about similarities I'd like to take this time to—

I'm sorry, you people in the first few rows. Apparently, my dump somehow offends you? Perhaps if I gather it up and fling it at you, you'll think twice next time before you wrinkle your dinky noses at my healthy and natural exudate. Is that what I should do? Because it's very easy. All I have to do is scoop it up like this and—

Ow!

Take it easy with the leash, Mr. Male-Human-Leash-Puller-If-He-Ever-Turns-His-Back-Bite-Bite-Bite! I wasn't actually going to do it! Sheesh. Why this guy is here but my kibble-and-orange-wedge-bringing buddy isn't, I have no idea.

Where was I?

Could I get another bowl of water, please? Thank you. Give me a moment here.

Ah… that's the stuff. The elixir of life, which soothes all but the most surgery-ravaged monkey throat.

Anyway, let's just go to your questions and get this over with, because I'm pretty eager to get back to my cage at this point.

Yes, right here in the front—Mr. Male-Human-Small-Torso-No-Threat?

Right. As I said, I am eager to get back to my cage. That surprises you somehow? Let me explain. I like my cage. My cage is small and manageable. Unlike your cage here, which makes me uneasy. Who needs a cage this large? I mean, come on! How can you be comfortable in a cage so large that the entrance and egress points are so far away that sometimes I think they might not even exist? With a cage this large, any random taker-of-food or biter-of-chimpanzees could enter at any time and take your kibble—or, even worse, your orange wedges—and/or bite bite bite you.

I mean, I know: your human needs are more complex than mine, because you're all fancy and shit. But as for me and my kind? Give me a full kibble trough every morning and regular delivery of orange wedges every afternoon, and I'm good. Maybe an empty beer keg to push from one side of my cage to the other and back again. And of course the presence of (or at least the promise of) a potential female copulation partner within the immediate smellable vicinity.

Now, if you'll excuse me for a moment, I am experiencing a feeling that virtually compels me to try to eat this microphone.

Ow! There's really no reason to go nuts with the leash like that, Mr. Bite-Bite-Bite-Bite-Bite-As-Soon-As-Possible! No one told me the microphone was a "Bad-Boy-Don't-Eat" item. So work with me a little—O.K., Mr. Gouge-Eyes-Eat-Fingers?

Wow, folks. I guess it takes all kinds, huh? Give me a minute while I simultaneously finish off this bowl of water and take another dump.

Ahh.

And ahh again.

Another question?

Yes—you, Ms. Female-Human-Copulation-Candidate, right here on the left. Your question?

Mm-hmm? That's an excellent question. But, before I answer, may I ask you something? When was the last time you copulated?

I can tell by the way you cover your bared teeth with your hand while your cheeks fill with color that my question intrigues you. I like that. Your copulation partner must be gigantic and have a virtually bottomless supply of orange wedges to have snared a mate like you. But I tell you this: one hour with me and my long stick, and you'd be—

Ow! Again with the leash! Always with the leash, Mr. Male-Human-Mount-And-Copulate-With-To-Humiliate-Before-Killing!

You know what? Go ahead with the leash. Seriously, keep it up. Go down in history as the male human who strangled the world's first talking chimpanzee. What do I care?

I happened to be referring to my termite stick, for your kind information. It's a sophisticated food-gathering tool? Maybe you've heard of it? No?

Figures.

All right, I'm done with this now. Take me back to my cage, please. ASAP. Yes, I know that many of you have more questions, but I'm afraid I'm experiencing a strong, unsettling feeling that the empty beer keg back in my cage is currently on exactly the wrong side and needs to be pushed back to the other side as soon as possible. So let me get back to my job, and maybe we can talk again another time.

THE CHILD

Ali Smith

Ali Smith (1962–) was born in Inverness. She is the author of numerous novels and short story collections, including most recently *Autumn*, *Winter* and *Spring* in the 'Seasonal' quartet. Her 2014 novel *How to Be Both* won the Baileys Women's Prize for Fiction, the Goldsmiths Prize and the Costa Novel of the Year Award. She has been shortlisted once for the Orwell Prize, twice for the Orange Prize and four times for the Man Booker Prize.

I went to Waitrose as usual in my lunchbreak to get the weekly stuff. I left my trolley by the vegetables and went to find bouquet garni for the soup. But when I came back to the vegetables again I couldn't find my trolley. It seemed to have been moved. In its place was someone else's shopping trolley, with a child sitting in the little child seat, its fat little legs through the leg-places.

Then I glanced into the trolley in which the child was sitting and saw in there the few things I'd already picked up: the three bags of oranges, the apricots, the organic apples, the folded copy of the Guardian and the tub of Kalamata olives. They were definitely my things. It was definitely my trolley.

The child in it was blond and curly-haired, very fair-skinned and flushed, big-cheeked like a cupid or a chub-fingered angel on a Christmas card or a child out of an old-fashioned English children's book, the kind of book where they wear sunhats to stop themselves getting sunstroke all the postwar summer. This child was wearing a little blue tracksuit with a hood and blue shoes and was quite clean, though a little crusty round the nose. Its lips were very pink and perfectly bow-shaped; its eyes were blue and clear and blank. It was an almost embarrassingly beautiful child.

Hello, I said. Where's your mother?

The child looked at me blankly.

I stood next to the potatoes and waited for a while. There were people shopping all round. One of them had clearly placed this child in my trolley and when he or she came to push the trolley away I could explain these were my things and we could swap trolleys or whatever and laugh about it and I could get on with my shopping as usual.

I stood for five minutes or so. After five minutes I wheeled the child in the trolley to the Customer Services desk.

I think someone somewhere may be looking for this, I said to the woman behind the desk, who was busy on a computer.

Looking for what, Madam? she said.

I presume you've had someone losing their mind over losing him, I said. I think it's a him. Blue for a boy, etc.

The Customer Services woman was called Marilyn Monroe. It said so on her name-badge.

Quite a name, I said pointing to the badge.

I'm sorry? she said.

Your name, I said. You know. Monroe, Marilyn.

Yes, she said. That's my name.

She looked at me like I was saying something dangerously foreign-sounding to her.

How exactly can I help you? she said in a singsong voice.

Well, as I say, this child, I said.

What a lovely boy! she said. He's very like his mum.

Well, I wouldn't know, I said. He's not mine.

Oh, she said. She looked offended. But he's so like you. Aren't you? Aren't you, darling? Aren't you, sweetheart?

She waved the curly red wire attached to her keyring at the child, who watched it swing inches away from its face, nonplussed. I couldn't imagine what she meant. The child looked nothing like me at all.

No, I said. I went round the corner to get something and when I got back to my trolley he was there, in it.

Oh, she said. She looked very surprised. We've had no reports of a missing child, she said.

She pressed some buttons on an intercom thing.

Hello? she said. It's Marilyn on Customers. Good, thanks, how are you? Anything up there on a missing child? No? Nothing on a child? Missing, or lost? Lady here claims she found one.

She put the intercom down. No, Madam, I'm afraid nobody's reported any child that's lost or missing, she said.

A small crowd had gathered behind us. He's adorable, one woman said. Is he your first?

He's not mine, I said.

How old is he? another said.

I don't know, I said.

You don't? she said. She looked shocked.

Aw, he's lovely, an old man, who seemed rather too poor a person to be shopping in Waitrose, said. He got a fifty-pence piece out of his pocket, held it up to me and said: Here you are. A piece of silver for good luck.

He tucked it into the child's shoe.

I wouldn't do that, Marilyn Monroe said. He'll get it out of there and swallow it and choke on it.

He'll never get it out of there, the old man said. Will you? You're a lovely boy. He's a lovely boy, he is. What's your name? What's his name? I bet you're like your dad. Is he like his dad, is he?

I've no idea, I said.

No idea! the old man said. Such a lovely boy! What a thing for his mum to say!

No, I said. Really. He's nothing to do with me, he's not mine. I just found him in my trolley when I came back with the—

At this point the child sitting in the trolley looked at me, raised its little fat arms in the air and said, straight at me: Mammuttm.

Everybody round me in the little circle of baby admirers looked at me. Some of them looked knowing and sly. One or two nodded at each other.

The child did it again. It reached its arms up, almost as if to pull itself up out of the trolley seat and lunge straight at me through the air.

Mummaam, it said.

The woman called Marilyn Monroe picked up her intercom again and spoke into it. Meanwhile the child had started to cry. It screamed and bawled. It shouted its word for mother at me over and over again and shook the trolley with its shouting.

Give him your car keys, a lady said. They love to play with car keys.

Bewildered, I gave the child my keys. It threw them to the ground and screamed all the more.

Lift him out, a woman in a Chanel suit said. He just wants a little cuddle.

It's not my child, I explained again. I've never seen it before in my life.

Here, she said.

She pulled the child out of the wire basket of the trolley seat, holding it at arm's length so her little suit wouldn't get smeared. It screamed even more as its legs came out of the wire seat; its face got redder and redder and the whole shop resounded with the screaming. (I was embarrassed. I felt peculiarly responsible. I'm so sorry, I said to the people round me.) The Chanel woman shoved the child hard into my arms. Immediately it put its arms around me and quietened to fretful cooing.

Jesus Christ, I said because I had never felt so powerful in all my life.

The crowd round us made knowing noises. See? a woman said. I nodded. There, the old man said. That'll always do it. You don't need to be scared, love. Such a pretty child, a passing woman said. The first three years are a nightmare, another said, wheeling her trolley past me towards the fine wines. Yes, Marilyn Monroe was saying into the intercom. Claiming it wasn't hers. But I think it's all right now. Isn't it, Madam? All right now? Madam?

Yes, I said through a mouthful of the child's blond hair.

Go on home, love, the old man said. Give him his supper and he'll be right as rain.

Teething, a woman ten years younger than me said. She shook her head; she was a veteran. It can drive you crazy, she said, but it's not forever. Don't worry. Go home now and have a nice cup of herb tea and it'll all settle down, he'll be asleep as soon as you know it.

Yes, I said. Thanks very much. What a day.

A couple of women gave me encouraging smiles; one patted me on the arm. The old man patted me on the back, squeezed the child's foot inside its shoe. Fifty pence, he said. That used to be ten shillings. Long before your time, little soldier. Used to buy a week's worth of food, ten shillings did. In the old days, eh? Ah well, some things change and some others never do. Eh? Eh, Mum?

Yes. Ha ha. Don't I know it, I said shaking my head.

I carried the child out into the car park. It weighed a ton.

I thought about leaving it right there in the car park behind the recycling bins, where it couldn't do too much damage to itself and someone would easily find it before it starved or anything. But I knew that if I did this the people in the store would remember me and track me down after all the fuss we'd just had. So I laid it on the back seat of the car, buckled it in with one of the seatbelts and the blanket off the back window, and got in the front. I started the engine.

I would drive it out of town to one of the villages, I decided, and leave it there, on a doorstep or outside a shop or something, when no one was looking, where someone else would report it found and its real parents or whoever had lost it would be able to claim it back. I would have to leave it somewhere without being seen, though, so no one would think I was abandoning it.

Or I could simply take it straight to the police. But then I would be further implicated. Maybe the police would think I had stolen the child, especially now that I had left the supermarket openly carrying it as if it were mine after all.

I looked at my watch. I was already late for work.

I cruised out past the garden centre and towards the motorway and decided I'd turn left at the first signpost and deposit it in the first quiet, safe, vaguely peopled place I found then race back into town. I stayed in the inside lane and watched for village signs.

You're a really rubbish driver, a voice said from the back of the car. I could do better than that, and I can't even drive. Are you for instance representative of all women drivers or is it just you among all women who's so rubbish at driving?

It was the child speaking. But it spoke with so surprisingly charming a little voice that it made me want to laugh, a voice as young and clear as a series of ringing bells arranged into a pretty melody. It said the complicated words, representative and for instance, with an innocence that sounded-ancient, centuries old, and at the same time as if it had only just discovered their meaning and was trying out their usage and I was privileged to be present when it did.

I slewed the car over to the side of the motorway, switched the engine off and leaned over the front seat into the back. The child still lay there helpless, rolled up in the tartan blanket, held in place by the seatbelt. It didn't look old enough to be able to speak. It looked barely a year old.

It's terrible. Asylum-seekers and foreigners come here and take all our jobs and all our benefits, it said preternaturally, sweetly. They should all be sent back to where they come from.

There was a slight endearing lisp on the s sounds in the words asylum and seekers and foreigners and jobs and benefits and sent.

What? I said.

Can't you hear? Cloth in your ears? it said. The real terrorists are people who aren't properly English. They will sneak into football stadiums and blow up innocent Christian people supporting innocent English teams.

The little words slipped out of its ruby-red mouth. I could just see the glint of its little coming teeth.

It said: The pound is our rightful heritage. We deserve our heritage. Women shouldn't work if they're going to have babies. Women shouldn't work at all. It's not the natural order of things. And as for gay weddings. Don't make me laugh.

Then it laughed, blondly, beautifully, as if only for me. Its big blue eyes were open and looking straight up at me as if I were the most delightful thing it had ever seen.

I was enchanted. I laughed back.

From nowhere a black cloud crossed the sun over its face, it screwed up its eyes and kicked its legs, waved its one free arm around outside the blanket, its hand clenched in a tiny fist, and began to bawl and wail.

It's hungry, I thought and my hand went down to my shirt and before I knew what I was doing I was unbuttoning it, getting myself out, and planning how to ensure the child's later enrolment in one of the area's better secondary schools.

I turned the car around and headed for home. I had decided to keep the beautiful child. I would feed it. I would love it. The neighbours would be amazed that I had hidden a pregnancy from them so well, and everyone would agree that the child was the most beautiful child ever to grace our street. My father would dandle the child on his knee. About time too, he'd say. I thought you were never going to make me a grandfather. Now I can die happy.

The beautiful child's melodious voice, in its pure RP pronunciation, the pronunciation of a child who's already been to an excellent public school and learned how exactly to speak, broke in on my dream.

Why do women wear white on their wedding day? it asked from the back of the car.

What do you mean? I said.

Why do women wear white on their wedding day? it said again.

Because white signifies purity, I said. Because it signifies—

To match the stove and the fridge when they get home, the child interrupted. An Englishman, an Irishman, a Chineseman and a Jew are all in an aeroplane flying over the Atlantic.

What? I said.

What's the difference between a pussy and a cunt? the child said in its innocent pealing voice.

Language! please! I said.

I bought my mother-in-law a chair, but she refused to plug it in, the child said. I wouldn't say my mother-in-law is fat, but we had to stop buying her Malcolm X t-shirts because helicopters kept trying to land on her.

I hadn't heard a fat mother-in-law joke for more than twenty years. I laughed. I couldn't not.

Why did they send premenstrual women into the desert to fight the Iraqis? Because they can retain water for four days. What do you call an Iraqi with a paper bag over his head?

Right, I said. That's it. That's as far as I go.

I braked the car and stopped dead on the inside lane. Cars squealed and roared past us with their drivers leaning on their horns. I switched on the hazard lights. The child sighed.

You're so politically correct, it said behind me charmingly. And you're a terrible driver. How do you make a woman blind? Put a windscreen in front of her.

Ha ha, I said. That's an old one.

I took the B roads and drove to the middle of a dense wood. I opened the back door of the car and bundled the beautiful blond child out. I locked the car. I carried the child for half a mile or so until I found a sheltered spot, where I left it in the tartan blanket under the trees.

I've been here before, you know, the child told me. S'not my first time.

Goodbye, I said. I hope wild animals find you and raise you well.

I drove home.

But all that night I couldn't stop thinking about the helpless child in the woods, in the cold, with nothing to eat and nobody knowing it was there. I got up at four a.m. and wandered round in my bedroom. Sick with worry, I drove back out to the wood road, stopped the car in exactly the same place and walked the half-mile back into the trees.

There was the child, still there, still wrapped in the tartan travel rug.

You took your time, it said. I'm fine, thanks for asking. I knew you'd be back. You can't resist me.

I put it in the back seat of the car again.

Here we go again. Where to now? the child said.

Guess, I said.

Can we go somewhere with broadband or wifi so I can look at some porn? the beautiful child said beautifully.

I drove to the next city and pulled into the first supermarket car park I passed. It was 6.45 a.m. and it was open.

Ooh, the child said. My first 24-hour Tesco's. I've had an Asda and a Sainsbury's and a Waitrose but I've not been to a Tesco's before.

I pulled the brim of my hat down over my eyes to evade being identifiable on the CCTV and carried the tartan bundle in through the out doors when two other people were leaving. The supermarket was very quiet but there was a reasonable number of people shopping. I found a trolley, half-full of good things, French butter, Italian olive oil, a folded new copy of the Guardian, left standing in the biscuits aisle, and emptied the child into it out of the blanket, slipped its pretty little legs in through the gaps in the child-seat.

There you go, I said. Good luck. All the best. I hope you get what you need.

I know what you need all right, the child whispered after me, but quietly, in case anybody should hear. Psst, it hissed. What do you call a woman with two brain cells? Pregnant! Why were shopping trolleys invented? To teach women to walk on their hind legs!

Then it laughed its charming peal of a pure childish laugh and I slipped away out of the aisle and out of the doors past the shopgirls cutting open the plastic binding on the morning's new tabloids and arranging them on the newspaper shelves, and out of the supermarket, back to my car, and out of the car park, while all over England the bells rang out in the morning churches and the British birdsong welcomed the new day, God in his heaven, and all being right with the world.

THE EXECUTOR

Muriel Spark

Muriel Spark (1918–2006) was a Scottish writer known for the satire and wit with which the serious themes of her novels are presented. She worked as a teacher, and then in the Foreign Office during the war, before becoming the editor of *Poetry Review* and turning to writing in earnest. Initially writing only poetry, she published her first novel, *The Comforters*, in 1957. She went on to write many acclaimed novels, the most famous of which, *The Prime of Miss Jean Brodie*, was made into a film starring Maggie Smith.

When my uncle died all the literary manuscripts went to a university foundation, except one. The correspondence went too, and the whole of his library. They came (a white-haired man and a young girl) and surveyed his study. Everything, they said, would be desirable and it would make a good price if I let the whole room go – his chair, his desk, the carpet, even his ashtrays. I agreed to this. I left everything in the drawers of the desk just as it was when my uncle died, including the bottle of Librium and a rusty razor blade.

My uncle died this way: he was sitting on the bank of the river, playing a fish. As the afternoon faded a man passed by, and then a young couple who made pottery passed him. As they said later, he was sitting peacefully awaiting the catch and of course they didn't disturb him. As night fell the colonel and his wife passed by; they were on their way home from their daily walk. They knew it was too late for my uncle to be simply sitting there, so they went to look. He had been dead, the doctor pronounced, from two to two and a half hours. The fish was still struggling with the bait. It was a mild heart attack. Everything my uncle did was mild, so different from everything he wrote. Yet perhaps not so different. He was supposed to be "far out", so one didn't know what went on out there. Besides, he had not long returned from a trip to London. They say, still waters run deep.

But far out was how he saw himself. He once said that if you could imagine modern literature as a painting, perhaps by Brueghel the Elder, the people and the action were in the foreground, full of colour, eating, stealing, copulating, laughing, courting each other, excreting, and stabbing each other, selling things, climbing trees. Then in the distance, at the far end of a vast plain, there he would be, a speck on the horizon, always receding and always there, and always a necessary and mysterious component of the picture; always there and never to be taken away, essential to the picture... a speck in the distance, which if you were to blow up the detail would simply be a vague figure, plodding on the other way.

I am no fool, and he knew it. He didn't know it at first, but he had seven months in which to learn that fact. I gave up my job in Edinburgh in the government office, a job with a pension, to come here to the lonely house among the Pentland Hills to live with him and take care of things. I think he imagined I was going to be another Elaine when he suggested the arrangement. He had no idea how much better I was for him than Elaine. Elaine was his mistress, that is the stark truth. "My commonlaw wife," he called her, explaining that in Scotland, by tradition, the woman you are living with is your wife. As if I didn't know all that nineteenth-century folklore; and it's long died out. Nowadays you have to do more than say "I marry you, I marry you, I marry you," to make a woman your wife. Of course, my uncle was a genius and a character. I allowed for that. Anyway, Elaine died and I came here a month later. Within a month I had cleared up the best part of the disorder. He called me a Scottish puritan girl, and at forty-one it was nice to be a girl and I wasn't against the Scottish puritanical attribution either since I am proud to be a Scot; I feel nationalistic about it. He always had that smile of his when he said it, so I don't know how he meant it. They say he had that smile of his when he was found dead, fishing.

"I appoint my niece Susan Kyle to be my sole literary executor." I don't wonder he decided on this course after I had been with him for three months. Probably for the first time in his life all his papers were in order. I went into Edinburgh and bought box-files and cover-files and I filed away all that mountain of papers, each under its separate heading. And I knew what was what. You didn't catch me filing away a letter from Angus Wilson or Saul Bellow in the same place as an ordinary "W" or "B", a Miss Mary Whitelaw or a Mrs Jonathan Brown. I knew the value of these letters, they went into a famous-persons file, bulging and of value. So that in a short time my uncle said, "There's little for me to do now, Susan, but die." Which I thought was melodramatic, and said so. But I could see he was forced to admire my good sense. He said, "You remind me of my mother, who prepared her shroud all ready for her funeral." His mother was my grandmother Janet Kyle. Why shouldn't she have sat and sewn her shroud? People in those days had very little to do, and here I was running the house and looking after my uncle's papers with only the help of Mrs Donaldson three mornings a week, where my grandmother had four pairs of hands for indoor help and three out. The rest of the family never went near the house after my grandmother died, for Elaine was always there with my uncle.

The property was distributed among the family, but I was the sole literary executor. And it was up to me to do what I liked with his literary remains. It was a good thing I had everything inventoried and filed, ready for sale. They came and took the total archive as they called it away, all the correspondence and manuscripts except one. That one I kept for myself. It was the novel he was writing when he died, an unfinished manuscript. I thought, Why not? Maybe I will finish it myself and publish it. I am no fool, and my uncle must have known how the book was going to end. I never read any of his correspondence, mind you; I was too busy those months filing it all in order. I did think, however, that I would read this manuscript and perhaps put an ending to it. There were already ten chapters. My uncle had told me there was only another chapter to go. So I said nothing to the Foundation about that one unfinished manuscript; I was only too glad when they had come and gone, and the papers were out of the house. I got the painters in to clean the study. Mrs Donaldson said she had never seen the house looking so like a house should be.

Under my uncle's will I inherited the house, and I planned eventually to rent rooms to tourists in the summer, bed and breakfast. In the meantime I set about reading the unfinished manuscript, for it was only April, and I'm not a one to let the grass grow under my feet. I had learnt to decipher that old-fashioned handwriting of his which looked good on the page but was not too clear. My uncle had a treasure in me those last months of his life, although he said I was like a book without an index – all information, and no way of getting at it. I asked him to tell me what information he ever got out of Elaine, who never passed an exam in her life.

This last work of my uncle's was an unusual story for him, set in the seventeenth century here among the Pentland Hills. He had told me only that he was writing something strong and cruel, and that this was easier to accomplish in a historical novel. It was about the slow identification and final trapping of a witch, and I could see as I read it that he hadn't been joking when he said it was strong and cruel; he had often said things to frighten and alarm me, I don't know why. By chapter ten the trial of the witch in Edinburgh was only halfway through. Her fate depended entirely on chapter eleven, and on the negotiations that were being conducted behind the scenes by the opposing factions of intrigue. My uncle had left a pile of notes he had accumulated towards this novel, and I retained these along with the manuscript. But there was no sign in the notes as to how my uncle had decided to resolve the fate of the witch – whose name was Edith but that is by the way. I put the notebooks and papers away, for there were many other things to be done following the death of my famous uncle. The novel itself was written by hand in twelve notebooks. In the twelfth only the first two pages had been filled, the rest of the pages were blank; I am sure of this. The two filled pages came to the end of chapter ten. At the top of the next page was written "Chapter Eleven". I looked through the rest of the notebook to make sure my uncle had not made some note there on how he intended to continue; all blank, I am sure of it. I put the twelve notebooks, together with the sheaf of loose notes, in a drawer of the solid-mahogany dining-room sideboard.

A few weeks later I brought the notebooks out again, intending to consider how I might proceed with the completion of the book and so enhance its value. I read again through chapter ten; then, when I turned to the page where "Chapter Eleven" was written, there in my uncle's handwriting was the following:

Well, Susan, how do you feel about finishing my novel? Aren't you a greedy little snoot, holding back my unfinished work, when you know the Foundation paid for the lot? What about your puritanical principles? Elaine and I are waiting to see how you manage to write Chapter Eleven. Elaine asks me to add it's lovely to see you scouring and cleaning those neglected corners of the house. But don't you know, Jaimie is having you on. Where does he go after lunch? Your affec Uncle.

I could hardly believe my eyes. The first shock I got was the bit about Jaimie, and then came the second shock, that the words were there at all. It was twelve-thirty at night and Jaimie had gone home. Jaimie Donaldson is the son of Mrs Donaldson, and it isn't his fault he's out of work. We have had experiences together, but nobody is to know that, least of all Mrs Donaldson who introduced him into the household merely to clean the windows and stoke the boiler. But the words? Where did they come from?

It is a lonely house, here in a fold of the Pentlands, surrounded by woods, five miles to the nearest cottage, six to Mrs Donaldson's, and the buses stop at ten p.m. I felt a great fear there in the dining-room, with the twelve notebooks on the table, and the pile of papers, a great cold, and a panic. I ran to the hall and lifted the telephone but didn't know how to explain myself or whom to phone. My story would sound like that of a woman gone crazy. Mrs Donaldson? The police? I couldn't think what to say to them at that hour of night. "I have found some words that weren't there before in my uncle's manuscript, and in his own hand." It was unthinkable. Then I thought perhaps someone had played me a trick. Oh no, I knew that this couldn't be. Only Mrs Donaldson had been in the dining-room, and only to dust, with me to help her. Jaimie had no chance to go there, not at all. I never used the dining-room now and had meals in the kitchen. But in fact I knew it wasn't them, it was Uncle. I wished with all my heart that I was a strong woman, as I had always felt I was, strong and sensible. I stood in the hall by the telephone, shaking. "O God, everlasting and almighty," I prayed, "make me strong, and guide and lead me as to how Mrs Thatcher would conduct herself in circumstances of this nature."

I didn't sleep all night. I sat in the big kitchen stoking up the fire. Only once I moved, to go back into the dining-room and make sure that those words were there. Beyond a doubt they were, and in my uncle's handwriting – that handwriting it would take an expert forger to copy. I put the manuscript back in the drawer; I locked the dining-room door and took the key. My uncle's study, now absolutely empty, was above the kitchen. If he was haunting the house, I heard no sound from there or from anywhere else. It was a fearful night, waiting there by the fire.

Mrs Donaldson arrived in the morning, complaining that Jaimie was getting lazy; he wouldn't rise. Too many late nights.

"Where does he go after lunch?" I said.

"Oh, he goes for a round of golf after his dinner," she said. "He's always ready for a round of golf no matter what else there is to do. Golf is the curse of Scotland."

I had a good idea who Jaimie was meeting on the golf course, and I could almost have been grateful to Uncle for pointing out to me in that sly way of his that Jaimie wandered in the hours after the midday meal which we called lunch and they called their dinner. By five o'clock in the afternoon Jaimie would come here to the house to fetch up the coal, bank the fire, and so forth. But all afternoon he would be on the links with that girl who works at the manse, Greta, younger sister of Elaine, the one who moved in here openly, ruining my uncle's morals, leaving the house to rot. I always suspected that family. After Elaine died it came out he had even introduced her to all his friends; I could tell from the letters of condolence, how they said things like "He never got over the loss of Elaine" and "He couldn't live without her". And sometimes he called me Elaine by mistake. I was furious. Once, for example, I said, "Uncle, stop pacing about down here. Go up to your study and do your scribbling; I'll bring you a cup of cocoa." He said, with that glaze-eyed look he always had when he was interrupted in his thoughts, "What's come over you, Elaine?" I said, "I'm not Elaine, thank you very much." "Oh, of course," he said, "you are not Elaine, you are most certainly not her." If the public that read his books by the tens of thousands could have seen behind the scenes, I often wondered what they would have thought. I told him so many a time, but he smiled in that sly way, that smile he still had on his face when they found him fishing and stone dead.

After Mrs Donaldson left the house, at noon, I went up to my bedroom, half dropping from lack of sleep. Mrs Donaldson hadn't noticed anything; you could be falling down dead – they never look at you. I slept till four. It was still light. I got up and locked the doors, front and back. I pulled the curtains shut, and when Jaimie rang the bell at five o'clock I didn't open, I just let him ring. Eventually he went away. I expect he had plenty to wonder about. But I wasn't going to make him welcome before the fire and get him his supper, and take off my clothes there in the back room on the divan with him, in front of the television, while Uncle and Elaine were looking on, even though it is only Nature. No, I turned on the television for myself. You would never believe, it was a programme on the Scottish BBC about Uncle. I switched to TV One, and got a quiz show. And I felt hungry, for I'd eaten nothing since the night before.

But I couldn't face any supper until I had assured myself about that manuscript. I was fairly certain by now that it was a dream. "Maybe I've been overworking," I thought to myself. I had the key of the dining-room in my pocket and I took it and opened the door; I closed the curtains, and I went to the drawer and took out the notebook.

Not only were the words that I had read last night there, new words were added, a whole paragraph:

Look up the Acts of the Apostles, Chapter 5, verses 1 to 10. See what happened to Ananias and Sapphira his wife. You're not getting on very fast with your scribbling, are you, Susan? Elaine and I were under the impression you were going to write Chapter Eleven. Why don't you take a cup of cocoa and get on with it? First read Acts, V, 1.10. Your affec Uncle.

Well, I shoved the book in the drawer and looked round the dining-room. I looked under the table and behind the curtains. It didn't look as if anything had been touched. I got out of the room and locked the door, I don't know how. I went to fetch my Bible, praying, "O God omnipotent and allseeing, direct and instruct me as to the way out of this situation, astonishing as it must appear to Thee." I looked up the passage:

But a certain man named Ananias, with Sapphira his wife, sold a possession. And kept back part of the price, his wife also being privy to it, and brought a certain part and laid it at the apostles' feet. But Peter said, Ananias, why hath Satan filled thine heart to lie to the Holy Ghost, and to keep back part of the land?

I didn't read any more because I knew how it went on. Ananias and Sapphira, his wife, were both struck dead for holding back the portion of the sale for themselves. This was Uncle getting at me for holding back his manuscript from the Foundation. That's an impudence, I thought, to make such a comparison from the Bible, when he was an open and avowed sinner himself.

I thought it all over for a while. Then I went into the dining-room and got out that last notebook. Something else had been written since I had put it away, not half an hour before:

Why don't you get on with Chapter Eleven? We're waiting for it.

I tore out the page, put the book away and locked the door. I took the page to the fire and put it on to burn. Then I went to bed.

This went on for a month. My uncle always started the page afresh with "Chapter Eleven", followed by a new message. He even went so far as to put in that I had kept back bits of the housekeeping money, although, he wrote, I was well paid enough. That's a matter of opinion, and who did the economising, anyway? Always, after reading Uncle's disrespectful comments, I burned the page, and we were getting near the end of the notebook. He would say things to show he followed me round the house, and even knew my dreams. When I went into Edinburgh for some shopping he knew exactly where I had been and what I'd bought. He and Elaine listened in to my conversations on the telephone if I rang up an old friend. I didn't let anyone in the house except Mrs Donaldson. No more Jaimie. He even knew if I took a dose of salts and how long I had sat in the bathroom, the awful old man.

Mrs Donaldson one morning said she was leaving. She said to me, "Why don't you see a doctor?" I said, "Why?" But she wouldn't speak.

One day soon afterwards a man rang me up from the Foundation. They didn't want to bother me, they said, but they were rather puzzled. They had found in Uncle's letters many references to a novel, The Witch of the Pentlands, which he had been writing just before his death; and they had found among the papers a final chapter to this novel, which he had evidently written on loose pages on a train, for a letter of his, kindly provided by one of his many correspondents, proved this. Only they had no idea where the rest of the manuscript could be. In the end the witch Edith is condemned to be burned, but dies of her own will power before the execution, he said, but there must be ten more chapters leading up to it. This was Uncle's most metaphysical work, and based on a true history, the man said, and he must stress that it was very important.

I said that I would have a look. I rang back that afternoon and said I had found the whole book in a drawer in the dining-room.

So the man came to get it. On the phone he sounded very suspicious, in case there were more manuscripts. "Are you sure that's everything? You know, the Foundation's price included the whole archive. No, don't trust it to the mail, I'll be there tomorrow at two."

Just before he arrived I took a good drink, whisky and soda, as, indeed, I had been taking from sheer need all the past month. I had brought out the notebooks. On the blank page was written:

Good-bye, Susan. It's lovely being a speck in the distance.
Your affec Uncle.

FIRST IMPRESSIONS

Ricardo Sumalavia

Ricardo Sumalavia (1968–), born in Lima, is a professor at the Catholic
University of Peru and coordinator of its Centre for Oriental Studies.
He is the author of three short story collections and a novel – *Que la
tierra te sea leve* ('may the earth lie lightly upon you'). He teaches at
the Université Michel de Montaigne in Bordeaux.

In the months before the end of my last year of high school, I began
working in the afternoons at a small printing press. My mother was
not opposed. I was friendly with the owner as well as his wife, an
enormous and attractive woman who visited my house now and then so
my mother could cut her hair or dye it in whatever color current style
demanded. I learned the publishing trade with the enthusiasm of one who
hoped to see his own poems in print one day. For the time being, I was
only in charge of placing letters of lead type, and I was always careful not
to get them out of order, so that I wouldn't have to place them all again,
line by line, as tended to happen whenever Señora Leonor, the owner's
wife, came by the print shop. Her presence was always a bit unsettling
to me, and she was well aware of this. I suspect she had always known
it, even before I did, ever since I was a child, when I didn't understand
the transitory pleasure that came from brushing against her legs or her
hips on the pretext of playing with my little cars, before I was sent out
to the patio, leaving Señora Leonor and that smile that would electrify
me years later in her husband's print shop. If her visits were sporadic, it
only made the effect more disconcerting: an unease that I tried to pour
into my adolescent poems, to be transferred later onto an old plank of

wood in the composition box that I kept hidden beneath the other work of the day—that is, if my shame didn't force me to undo it all.

In this way the months passed, and, with the end of the year, my schooling, too, came to a close. It was natural, then, that the print shop should become my full-time job, at a higher salary and with all the respect accorded an adult employee—or so the owner informed me in early January. His wife, with short, red hair and a miniskirt of the kind worn at the end of the sixties—justified by the intense heat of that summer— came to visit more and more often. I should confess that the color of her hair, contrasted with her pale skin, inspired what I considered to be my best poem. And the longest. The only one I was, without misgivings, able to set in type, and the only one I was prepared to show to its muse. Of course, I imagined a thousand ways of offering her the poem, certain that her only response would be to keep me in suspense with a kiss on the cheek perhaps, or with the touch of her fingernail along my chin.

Until the appropriate afternoon came. It was a Thursday, the day of her usual visits, and her husband had gone out to pick up a few rolls of paper. I had used the opportunity to typeset and ink my poem when Señora Leonor appeared, red-haired and wearing a miniskirt, intensely pale in spite of the summer sun. I don't recall exactly what she said, I only know that she ordered me to close the door of the shop, and then called me to the back. She stood before me, contemplating me for a moment, with a hint of that smile I knew so well, and then she kissed me. She used her hands to guide mine, so that I might caress her body, lift her miniskirt easily, and drop her underwear, which may or not have been fashionable in those days but which shook me the very moment I saw it. In this state of intoxication I pushed her to the worktable, where I leaned her back and climbed on top of her, on top of the impressive Señora Leonor, who received me with moans and tremors of excitement.

We stayed that way for a long while, until satisfaction and good sense separated us. It was when she got up from the table that I discovered, perplexed, the fate of my poem. It was printed on the woman's back. In truth, the opening, which was on her lumbar region, could be read very clearly, while the final verses, which spread to her expansive ass, were blurry, nothing more than senseless marks of ink. Though I've tried to explain it to myself, I still can't quite understand my silence. I let her get dressed, let her bid me farewell with an affectionate kiss. It was the only time I managed to reshuffle the lead type on the plank that had held my poem. I could reshuffle others, I told myself, in the free moments of some future employment.

Translated by Daniel Alarcón

THE SECRET LIFE OF WALTER MITTY

James Thurber

James Thurber (1894–1961) was an American writer, cartoonist, playwright and wit. He published many stories in *The New Yorker* and was one of the most popular humourists of his time, celebrating the comic frustrations and eccentricities of ordinary people. He wrote the Broadway comedy *The Male Animal* in collaboration with Elliott Nugent, which was later adapted into a film starring Henry Fonda and Olivia de Havilland, and his short story 'The Secret Life of Walter Mitty' has been adapted for film twice.

"We're going through!" The Commander's voice was like thin ice breaking. He wore his full-dress uniform, with the heavily braided white cap pulled down rakishly over one cold gray eye. "We can't make it, sir. It's spoiling for a hurricane, if you ask me." "I'm not asking you, Lieutenant Berg," said the Commander. "Throw on the power lights! Rev her up to 8,500! We're going through!" The pounding of the cylinders increased: ta-pocketa-pocketa-pocketa-*pocketa-pocketa*. The Commander stared at the ice forming on the pilot window. He walked over and twisted a row of complicated dials. "Switch on No. 8 auxiliary!" he shouted. "Switch on No. 8 auxiliary!" repeated Lieutenant Berg. "Full strength in No. 3 turret!" shouted the Commander. "Full strength in No. 3 turret!" The crew, bending to their various tasks in the huge, hurtling eight-engined Navy hydroplane, looked at each other and grinned. "The Old Man'll get us through," they said to one another. "The Old Man ain't afraid of Hell!"...

"Not so fast! You're driving too fast!" said Mrs. Mitty. "What are you driving so fast for?"

"Hmm?" said Walter Mitty. He looked at his wife, in the seat beside him, with shocked astonishment. She seemed grossly unfamiliar, like a strange woman who had yelled at him in a crowd. "You were up to fifty-five," she said. "You know I don't like to go more than forty. You were up to fifty-five." Walter Mitty drove on toward Waterbury in silence, the roaring of the SN202 through the worst storm in twenty years of Navy flying fading in the remote, intimate airways of his mind. "You're tensed up again," said Mrs. Mitty. "It's one of your days. I wish you'd let Dr. Renshaw look you over."

Walter Mitty stopped the car in front of the building where his wife went to have her hair done. "Remember to get those overshoes while I'm having my hair done," she said. "I don't need overshoes," said Mitty. She put her mirror back into her bag. "We've been all through that," she said, getting out of the car. "You're not a young man any longer." He raced the engine a little. "Why don't you wear your gloves? Have you lost your gloves?" Walter Mitty reached in a pocket and brought out the gloves. He put them on, but after she had turned and gone into the building and he had driven on to a red light, he took them off again. "Pick it up, brother!" snapped a cop as the light changed, and Mitty hastily pulled on his gloves and lurched ahead. He drove around the streets aimlessly for a time, and then he drove past the hospital on his way to the parking lot.

... "It's the millionaire banker, Wellington McMillan," said the pretty nurse. "Yes?" said Walter Mitty, removing his gloves slowly. "Who has the case?" "Dr. Renshaw and Dr. Benbow, but there are two specialists here, Dr. Remington from New York and Dr. Pritchard-Mitford from London. He flew over." A door opened down a long, cool corridor and Dr. Renshaw came out. He looked distraught and haggard. "Hello, Mitty," he said. "We're having the devil's own time with McMillan, the millionaire banker and close personal friend of Roosevelt. Obstreosis of the ductal tract. Tertiary. Wish you'd take a look at him." "Glad to," said Mitty.

In the operating room there were whispered introductions: "Dr. Remington, Dr. Mitty. Dr. Pritchard-Mitford, Dr. Mitty." "I've read your book on streptothricosis," said Pritchard-Mitford, shaking hands. "A brilliant performance, sir." "Thank you," said Walter Mitty. "Didn't know you were in the States, Mitty," grumbled Remington. "Coals to Newcastle, bringing Mitford and me up here for a tertiary." "You are very kind," said Mitty. A huge, complicated machine, connected to the operating table, with many tubes and wires, began at this moment to go pocketa-pocketa-pocketa. "The new anaesthetizer is giving way!" shouted an intern. "There is no one in the East who knows how to fix it!" "Quiet, man!" said Mitty, in a low, cool voice. He sprang to the machine, which was now going pocketa-pocketa-queep-pocketa-queep. He began fingering delicately a row of glistening dials. "Give me a fountain pen!" he snapped. Someone handed him a fountain pen. He pulled a faulty piston out of the machine and inserted the pen in its place. "That will hold for ten minutes," he said. "Get on with the operation." A nurse hurried over and whispered to Renshaw, and Mitty saw the man turn pale. "Coreopsis has set in," said Renshaw nervously. "If you would take over, Mitty?" Mitty looked at him and at the craven figure of Benbow, who drank, and at the grave, uncertain faces of the two great specialists. "If you wish," he said. They slipped a white gown on him; he adjusted a mask and drew on thin gloves; nurses handed him shining…

"Back it up, Mac! Look out for that Buick!" Walter Mitty jammed on the brakes. "Wrong lane, Mac," said the parking-lot attendant, looking at Mitty closely. "Gee. Yeh," muttered Mitty. He began cautiously to back out of the lane marked "Exit Only." "Leave her sit there," said the attendant. "I'll put her away." Mitty got out of the car. "Hey, better leave the key." "Oh," said Mitty, handing the man the ignition key. The attendant vaulted into the car, backed it up with insolent skill, and put it where it belonged.

They're so damn cocky, thought Walter Mitty, walking along Main

Street; they think they know everything. Once he had tried to take his chains off, outside New Milford, and he had got them wound around the axles. A man had had to come out in a wrecking car and unwind them, a young, grinning garageman. Since then Mrs. Mitty always made him drive to a garage to have the chains taken off. The next time, he thought, I'll wear my right arm in a sling; they won't grin at me then. I'll have my right arm in a sling and they'll see I couldn't possibly take the chains off myself. He kicked at the slush on the sidewalk. "Overshoes," he said to himself, and he began looking for a shoe store.

When he came out into the street again, with the overshoes in a box under his arm, Walter Mitty began to wonder what the other thing was his wife had told him to get. She had told him, twice, before they set out from their house for Waterbury. In a way he hated these weekly trips to town—he was always getting something wrong. Kleenex, he thought, Squibb's, razor blades? No. Toothpaste, toothbrush, bicarbonate, carborundum, initiative and referendum? He gave it up. But she would remember it. "Where's the what's-its-name?" she would ask. "Don't tell me you forgot the what's-its-name." A newsboy went by shouting something about the Waterbury trial.

… "Perhaps this will refresh your memory." The District Attorney suddenly thrust a heavy automatic at the quiet figure on the witness stand. "Have you ever seen this before?" Walter Mitty took the gun and examined it expertly. "This is my Webley-Vickers 50.80," he said calmly. An excited buzz ran around the courtroom. The Judge rapped for order. "You are a crack shot with any sort of firearms, I believe?" said the District Attorney, insinuatingly. "Objection!" shouted Mitty's attorney. "We have shown that the defendant could not have fired the shot. We have shown that he wore his right arm in a sling on the night of the fourteenth of July." Walter Mitty raised his hand briefly and the bickering attorneys were stilled. "With any known make of gun," he said evenly, "I could have killed Gregory Fitzhurst at three hundred feet *with my left hand*." Pandemonium broke loose in the courtroom. A woman's scream rose above the bedlam and suddenly a lovely, dark-haired girl was in Walter Mitty's arms. The District Attorney struck at her savagely. Without rising from his chair, Mitty let the man have it on the point of the chin. "You miserable cur!"...

"Puppy biscuit," said Walter Mitty. He stopped walking and the buildings of Waterbury rose up out of the misty courtroom and surrounded him again. A woman who was passing laughed. "He said 'Puppy biscuit,'" she said to her companion. "That man said 'Puppy biscuit' to himself." Walter Mitty hurried on. He went into an A. & P., not the first one he came to but a smaller one farther up the street. "I want some biscuit for small, young dogs," he said to the clerk. "Any special brand, sir?" The greatest pistol shot in the world thought a moment. "It says 'Puppies Bark for It' on the box," said Walter Mitty.

His wife would be through at the hairdresser's in fifteen minutes, Mitty saw in looking at his watch, unless they had trouble drying it; sometimes they had trouble drying it. She didn't like to get to the hotel first; she would want him to be there waiting for her as usual. He found a big leather chair in the lobby, facing a window, and he put the overshoes and the puppy biscuit on the floor beside it. He picked up an old copy of *Liberty* and sank down into the chair. "Can Germany Conquer the World Through the Air?" Walter Mitty looked at the pictures of bombing planes and of ruined streets.

... "The cannonading has got the wind up in young Raleigh, sir," said the sergeant. Captain Mitty looked up at him through touselled hair. "Get him to bed," he said wearily. "With the others. I'll fly alone." "But you can't, sir," said the sergeant anxiously. "It takes two men to handle that bomber and the Archies are pounding hell out of the air. Von Richtman's circus is between here and Saulier." "Somebody's got to get that ammunition dump," said Mitty. "I'm going over. Spot of brandy?" He poured a drink for the sergeant and one for himself. War thundered and whined around the dugout and battered at the door. There was a rending of wood and splinters flew through the room. "A bit of a near thing," said Captain Mitty carelessly. "The box barrage is closing in," said the sergeant. "We only live once, Sergeant," said Mitty, with his faint, fleeting smile. "Or do we?" He poured another brandy and tossed it off. "I never see a man could hold his brandy like you, sir," said the sergeant. "Begging your pardon, sir." Captain Mitty stood up and strapped on his huge Webley-Vickers automatic. "It's forty kilometres through hell, sir," said the sergeant. Mitty finished one last brandy. "After all," he said softly, "what isn't?" The pounding of the cannon increased; there was the rat-tat-tatting of machine guns, and from somewhere came the menacing pocketa-pocketa-pocketa of the new flame-throwers. Walter Mitty walked to the door of the dugout humming "Auprès de Ma Blonde." He turned and waved to the sergeant. "Cheerio!" he said…

Something struck his shoulder. "I've been looking all over this hotel for you," said Mrs. Mitty. "Why do you have to hide in this old chair? How did you expect me to find you?" "Things close in," said Walter Mitty vaguely. "What?" Mrs. Mitty said. "Did you get the what's-its-name? The puppy biscuit? What's in that box?" "Overshoes," said Mitty. "Couldn't you have put them on in the store?" "I was thinking," said Walter Mitty. "Does it ever occur to you that I am sometimes thinking?" She looked at him. "I'm going to take your temperature when I get you home," she said.

They went out through the revolving doors that made a faintly derisive whistling sound when you pushed them. It was two blocks to the parking lot. At the drugstore on the corner she said, "Wait here for me. I forgot something. I won't be a minute." She was more than a minute. Walter Mitty lighted a cigarette. It began to rain, rain with sleet in it. He stood up against the wall of the drugstore, smoking… He put his shoulders back and his heels together. "To hell with the handkerchief," said Walter Mitty scornfully. He took one last drag on his cigarette and snapped it away. Then, with that faint, fleeting smile playing about his lips, he faced the firing squad; erect and motionless, proud and disdainful, Walter Mitty the Undefeated, inscrutable to the last.

From THE SECRET DIARY OF ADRIAN MOLE, AGED 13¾

Sue Townsend

Sue Townsend (1946–2014) was an English writer and humourist, best known for creating the character Adrian Mole. Born in Leicester, she left school at fifteen and worked in a variety of jobs including factory worker and shop assistant, joining a writers' group at the Phoenix Theatre in her thirties. She won the Thames Television Playwright Award for her play *Womberang*, which kick-started her writing career. *The Secret Diary of Adrian Mole aged 13¾* was published in 1982 and was followed by *The Growing Pains of Adrian Mole* in 1984. These two books made her the bestselling novelist of the 1980s.

Thursday   January 1st
BANK HOLIDAY IN ENGLAND,
IRELAND, SCOTLAND AND WALES

These are my New Year's resolutions:
1. I will help the blind across the road.
2. I will hang my trousers up.
3. I will put the sleeves back on my records.
4. I will not start smoking.
5. I will stop squeezing my spots.
6. I will be kind to the dog.
7. I will help the poor and ignorant.
8. After hearing the disgusting noises from downstairs last night, I have also vowed never to drink alcohol.

My father got the dog drunk on cherry brandy at the party last night. If the RSPCA hear about it he could get done. Eight days have gone by since Christmas Day but my mother still hasn't worn the green lurex apron I bought her for Christmas! She will get bathcubes next year.

Just my luck, I've got a spot on my chin for the first day of the New Year!

Friday   January 2nd

BANK HOLIDAY IN SCOTLAND. FULL MOON

I felt rotten today. It's my mother's fault for singing 'My Way' at two o'clock in the morning at the top of the stairs. Just my luck to have a mother like her. There is a chance my parents could be alcoholics. Next year I could be in a children's home.

The dog got its own back on my father. It jumped up and knocked down his model ship, then ran into the garden with the rigging tangled in its feet. My father kept saying, 'Three months' work down the drain', over and over again.

The spot on my chin is getting bigger. It's my mother's fault for not knowing about vitamins.

Saturday   January 3rd

I shall go mad through lack of sleep! My father has banned the dog from the house so it barked outside my window all night. Just my luck! My father shouted a swear-word at it. If he's not careful he will get done by the police for obscene language.

I think the spot is a boil. Just my luck to have it where everybody can see it. I pointed out to my mother that I hadn't had any vitamin C today. She said, 'Go and buy an orange, then'. This is typical.

She still hasn't worn the lurex apron.

I will be glad to get back to school.

Sunday   January 4th

SECOND AFTER CHRISTMAS

My father has got the flu. I'm not surprised with the diet we get. My mother went out in the rain to get him a vitamin C drink, but as I told her, 'It's too late now'. It's a miracle we don't get scurvy. My mother says she can't see anything on my chin, but this is guilt because of the diet.

The dog has run off because my mother didn't close the gate. I have broken the arm on the stereo. Nobody knows yet, and with a bit of luck my father will be ill for a long time. He is the only one who uses it apart from me. No sign of the apron.

Monday   January 5th

The dog hasn't come back yet. It is peaceful without it. My mother rang the police and gave a description of the dog. She made it sound worse than it actually is: straggly hair over its eyes and all that. I really think the police have got better things to do than look for dogs, such as catching murderers. I told my mother this but she still rang them. Serve her right if she was murdered because of the dog.

My father is still lazing about in bed. He is supposed to be ill, but I noticed he is still smoking!

Nigel came round today. He has got a tan from his Christmas holiday. I think Nigel will be ill soon from the shock of the cold in England. I think Nigel's parents were wrong to take him abroad.

He hasn't got a single spot yet.

Tuesday   January 6th

EPIPHANY. NEW MOON

The dog is in trouble!

It knocked a meter-reader off his bike and messed all the cards up. So now we will all end up in court I expect. A policeman said we must keep the dog under control and asked how long it had been lame. My mother said it wasn't lame, and examined it. There was a tiny model pirate trapped in its left front paw.

The dog was pleased when my mother took the pirate out and it jumped up the policeman's tunic with its muddy paws. My mother fetched a cloth from the kitchen but it had strawberry jam on it where I had wiped the knife, so the tunic was worse than ever. The policeman went then. I'm sure he swore. I could report him for that.

I will look up 'Epiphany' in my new dictionary.

Wednesday   January 7th

Nigel came round on his new bike this morning. It has got a water bottle, a milometer, a speedometer, a yellow saddle, and very thin racing wheels. It's wasted on Nigel. He only goes to the shops and back on it. If I had it, I would go all over the country and have an experience.

My spot or boil has reached its peak. Surely it can't get any bigger!

I found a word in my dictionary that describes my father. It is *malingerer*. He is still in bed guzzling vitamin C.

The dog is locked in the coal shed.

Epiphany is something to do with the three wise men. Big deal!

Thursday   January 8th

Now my mother has got the flu. This means that I have to look after them both. Just my luck!

I have been up and down the stairs all day. I cooked a big dinner for them tonight: two poached eggs with beans, and tinned semolina pudding. (It's a good job I wore the green lurex apron because the poached eggs escaped out of the pan and got all over me.) I nearly said something when I saw they hadn't eaten *any* of it. They can't be that ill. I gave it to the dog in the coal shed. My grandmother is coming tomorrow morning, so I had to clean the burnt saucepans, then take the dog for a walk. It was half-past eleven before I got to bed. No wonder I am short for my age.

I have decided against medicine for a career.

Friday   January 9th

It was cough, cough, cough last night. If it wasn't one it was the other. You'd think they'd show some consideration after the hard day I'd had.

My grandma came and was disgusted with the state of the house. I showed her my room which is always neat and tidy and she gave me fifty pence. I showed her all the empty drink bottles in the dustbin and she was disgusted.

My grandma let the dog out of the coal shed. She said my mother was cruel to lock it up. The dog was sick on the kitchen floor. My grandma locked it up again.

She squeezed the spot on my chin. It has made it worse. I told grandma about the green apron and grandma said that she bought my mother a one hundred per cent acrylic cardigan every Christmas and my mother had *never ever* worn one of them!

Saturday   January 10th

a.m. Now the dog is ill! It keeps being sick so the vet has got to come. My father told me not to tell the vet that the dog had been locked in the coal shed for two days.

I have put a plaster over the spot to stop germs getting in it from the dog.

The vet has taken the dog away. He says he thinks it has got an obstruction and will need an emergency operation.

My grandma has had a row with my mother and gone home. My grandma found the Christmas cardigans all cut up in the duster bag. It is disgusting when people are starving.

Mr Lucas from next door has been in to see my mother and father who are still in bed. He brought a 'get well' card and some flowers for my mother. My mother sat up in bed in a nightie that showed a lot of her chest. She talked to Mr Lucas in a yukky voice. My father pretended to be asleep.

Nigel brought his records round. He is into punk, but I don't see the point if you can't hear the words. Anyway I think I'm turning into an intellectual. It must be all the worry.

p.m. I went to see how the dog is. It has had its operation. The vet showed me a plastic bag with lots of yukky things in it. There was a lump of coal, the fir tree from the Christmas cake, and the model pirates from my father's ship. One of the pirates was waving a cutlass which must have been very painful for the dog. The dog looks a lot better. It can come home in two days, worse luck.

My father was having a row with my grandma on the phone about the empty bottles in the dustbin when I got home.

Mr Lucas was upstairs talking to my mother. When Mr Lucas went, my father went upstairs and had an argument with my mother and made her cry. My father is in a bad mood. This means he is feeling better. I made my mother a cup of tea without her asking. This made her cry as well. You can't please some people!

The spot is still there.

Sunday   January 11th

FIRST AFTER EPIPHANY

Now I *know* I am an intellectual. I saw Malcolm Muggeridge on the television last night, and I understood nearly every word. It all adds up. A bad home, poor diet, not liking punk. I think I will join the library and see what happens.

It is a pity there aren't any more intellectuals living round here. Mr Lucas wears corduroy trousers, but he's an insurance man. Just my luck.

The first what after Epiphany?

Monday   January 12th

The dog is back. It keeps licking its stitches, so when I am eating I sit with my back to it.

My mother got up this morning to make the dog a bed to sleep in until it's better. It is made out of a cardboard box that used to contain packets of soap powder. My father said this would make the dog sneeze and burst its stitches, and the vet would charge even more to stitch it back up again. They had a row about the box, then my father went on about Mr Lucas. Though what Mr Lucas has to do with the dog's bed is a mystery to me.

Tuesday   January 13th

My father has gone back to work. Thank God! I don't know how my mother sticks him.

Mr Lucas came in this morning to see if my mother needed any help in the house. He is very kind. Mrs Lucas was next door cleaning the outside windows. The ladder didn't look very safe. I have written to Malcolm Muggeridge, c/o the BBC, asking him what to do about being an intellectual. I hope he writes back soon because I'm getting fed up being one on my own. I have written a poem, and it only took me two minutes. Even the famous poets take longer than that. It is called 'The Tap', but it isn't really about a tap, it's very deep, and about life and stuff like that.

The Tap, by Adrian Mole
The tap drips and keeps me awake,
In the morning there will be a lake.
For the want of a washer the carpet will spoil,
Then for another my father will toil.
My father could snuff it while he is at work.
Dad, fit a washer don't be a burk!

I showed it to my mother, but she laughed. She isn't very bright. She still hasn't washed my PE shorts, and it is school tomorrow. She is not like the mothers on television.

Wednesday   January 14th

Joined the library. Got *Care of the Skin*, *Origin of Species*, and a book by a woman my mother is always going on about. It is called *Pride and Prejudice*, by a woman called Jane Austen. I could tell the librarian was impressed. Perhaps she is an intellectual like me. She didn't look at my spot, so perhaps it is getting smaller. About time!

Mr Lucas was in the kitchen drinking coffee with my mother. The room was full of smoke. They were laughing, but when I went in, they stopped.

Mrs Lucas was next door cleaning the drains. She looked as if she was in a bad mood. I think Mr and Mrs Lucas have got an unhappy marriage. Poor Mr Lucas!

None of the teachers at school have noticed that I am an intellectual. They will be sorry when I am famous. There is a new girl in our class. She sits next to me in Geography. She is all right. Her name is Pandora, but she likes being called 'Box'. Don't ask me why. I might fall in love with her. It's time I fell in love, after all I am 13¾ years old.

Thursday   January 15th

Pandora has got hair the colour of treacle, and it's long like girls' hair should be. She has quite a good figure. I saw her playing netball and her chest was wobbling. I felt a bit funny.

I think this is it!

The dog has had its stitches out. It bit the vet, but I expect he's used to it. (The vet I mean; I know the dog is.)

My father found out about the arm on the stereo. I told a lie. I said the dog jumped up and broke it. My father said he will wait until the dog is completely cured of its operation then kick it. I hope this is a joke.

Mr Lucas was in the kitchen again when I got home from school. My mother is better now, so why he keeps coming round is a mystery to me. Mrs Lucas was planting trees in the dark. I read a bit of *Pride and Prejudice*, but it was very old-fashioned. I think Jane Austen should write something a bit more modern.

The dog has got the same colour eyes as Pandora. I only noticed because my mother cut the dog's hair. It looks worse than ever. Mr Lucas and my mother were laughing at the dog's new haircut which is not very nice, because dogs can't answer back, just like the Royal Family.

I am going to bed early to think about Pandora and do my back-stretching exercises. I haven't grown for two weeks. If this carries on I will be a midget.

I will go to the doctor's on Saturday if the spot is still there. I can't live like this with everybody staring.

Friday   January 16th

Mr Lucas came round and offered to take my mother shopping in the car. They dropped me off at school. I was glad to get out of the car what with all the laughing and cigarette smoke. We saw Mrs Lucas on the way. She was carrying big bags of shopping. My mother waved, but Mrs Lucas couldn't wave back.

It was Geography today so I sat next to Pandora for a whole hour. She looks better every day. I told her about her eyes being the same as the dog's. She asked what kind of dog it was. I told her it was a mongrel.

I lent Pandora my blue felt-tip pen to colour round the British Isles.

I think she appreciates these small attentions.

I started *Origin of Species* today, but it's not as good as the television series. *Care of the Skin* is dead good. I have left it open on the pages about vitamins. I hope my mother takes the hint. I have left it on the kitchen table near the ashtray, so she is bound to see it.

I have made an appointment about the spot. It has turned purple.

Saturday   January 17th

I was woken up early this morning. Mrs Lucas is concreting the front of their house and the concrete lorry had to keep its engine running while she shovelled the concrete round before it set. Mr Lucas made her a cup of tea. He really is kind.

Nigel came round to see if I wanted to go to the pictures but I told him I couldn't, because I was going to the doctor's about the spot. He said he couldn't see a spot, but he was just being polite because the spot is massive today.

Dr Taylor must be one of those overworked GPs you are always reading about. He didn't examine the spot, he just said I mustn't worry and was everything all right at home. I told him about my bad home life and my poor diet, but he said I was well nourished and to go home and count my blessings. So much for the National Health Service.

I will get a paper-round and go private.

AURELIA'S UNFORTUNATE YOUNG MAN

Mark Twain

Mark Twain (1835–1910), born Samuel Langhorne Clemens, is one of America's most beloved writers, famous for his novels, *The Adventures of Tom Sawyer* and *The Adventures of Huckleberry Finn*. An adventurer himself, Twain left school at twelve, travelled through North and South America, became a steamboat captain on the Mississippi, served in the Confederate army, and became a successful journalist. His two novels made him wildly rich and famous, but he then lost his fortune on a typesetting machine he invented. Undeterred, he made another fortune, and lost it again. Lauded as 'the father of American Literature', he was witty, entertaining, irascible and superstitious. Born shortly after an appearance of Halley's Comet, he predicted he would go out with it as well. He died a day after the comet returned.

The facts in the following case come to me by letter from a young lady who lives in the beautiful city of San Jose; she is perfectly unknown to me, and simply signs herself "Aurelia Maria," which may possibly be a fictitious name. But no matter, the poor girl is almost heart-broken by the misfortunes she has undergone, and so confused by the conflicting counsels of misguided friends and insidious enemies, that she does not know what course to pursue in order to extricate herself from the web of difficulties in which she seems almost hopelessly involved. In this dilemma she turns to me for help, and supplicates for my guidance and instruction with a moving eloquence that would touch the heart of a statue. Hear her sad story:

She says that when she was sixteen years old she met and loved, with all the devotion of a passionate nature, a young man from New-Jersey, named Williamson Breckinridge Caruthers, who was some six years her senior. They were engaged, with the free consent of their friends and relatives, and for a time it seemed as if their career was destined to be characterized by an immunity from sorrow beyond the usual lot of humanity. But at last the tide of fortune turned; young Caruthers became infected with small-pox of the most virulent type, and when he recovered from his illness, his face was pitted like a waffle-mould and his comeliness gone forever. Aurelia thought to break off the engagement at first, but pity for her unfortunate lover caused her to postpone the marriage-day for a season, and give him another trial.

The very day before the wedding was to have taken place, Breckinridge, while absorbed in watching the flight of a balloon, walked into a well and fractured one of his legs, and it had to be taken off above the knee. Again Aurelia was moved to break the engagement, but again love triumphed, and she set the day forward and gave him another chance to reform.

And again misfortune overtook the unhappy youth. He lost one arm by the premature discharge charge of a Fourth-of-July cannon, and within three months he got the other pulled out by a carding-machine. Aurelia's heart was almost crushed by these latter calamities. She could not but be deeply grieved to see her lover passing from her by piecemeal, feeling, as she did, that he could not last forever under this disastrous process of reduction, yet knowing of no way to stop its dreadful career, and in her tearful despair she almost regretted, like brokers who hold on and lose, that she had not taken him at first, before he had suffered such an alarming depreciation. Still, her brave soul bore her up, and she resolved to bear with her friend's unnatural disposition yet a little longer.

Again the wedding-day approached, and again disappointment over-shadowed it: Caruthers fell ill with the erysipelas, and lost the use of one of his eyes entirely. The friends and relatives of the bride, consid-ering that she had already put up with more than could reasonably be expected of her, now came forward and insisted that the match should be broken off; but after wavering awhile, Aurelia, with a generous spirit which did her credit, said she had reflected calmly upon the matter, and could not discover that Breckinridge was to blame.

So she extended the time once more, and he broke his other leg.

It was a sad day for the poor girl when she saw the surgeons reverently bearing away the sack whose uses she had learned by previous experience, and her heart told her the bitter truth that some more of her lover was gone. She felt that the field of her affections was growing more and more circumscribed every day, but once more she frowned down her relatives and renewed her betrothal.

Shortly before the time set for the nuptials another disaster occurred. There was but one man scalped by the Owens River Indians last year. That man was Williamson Breckinridge Caruthers, of New-Jersey. He was hurrying home with happiness in his heart, when he lost his hair forever, and in that hour of bitterness he almost cursed the mistaken mercy that had spared his head.

At last Aurelia is in serious perplexity as to what she ought to do. She still loves her Breckinridge, she writes, with true womanly feeling—she still loves what is left of him—-but her parents are bitterly opposed to the match, because he has no property and is disabled from working, and she has not sufficient means to support both comfortably. "Now, what should she do?" she asks with painful and anxious solicitude.

It is a delicate question; it is one which involves the lifelong happiness of a woman, and that of nearly two thirds of a man, and I feel that it would be assuming too great a responsibility to do more than make a mere suggestion in the case. How would it do to build to him? If Aurelia can afford the expense, let her furnish her mutilated lover with wooden arms and wooden legs, and a glass eye and a wig, and give him another show; give him ninety days, without grace, and if he does not break his neck in the mean time, marry him and take the chances. It does not seem to me that there is much risk, any way, Aurelia, because if he sticks to his infernal propensity for damaging himself every time he sees a good opportunity, his next experiment is bound to finish him, and then you are all right, you know, married or single. If married, the wooden legs and such other valuables as he may possess, revert to the widow, and you see you sustain no actual loss save the cherished fragment of a noble but most unfortunate husband, who honestly strove to do right, but whose extraordinary instincts were against him. Try it, Maria! I have thought the matter over carefully and well, and it is the only chance I see for you. It would have been a happy conceit on the part of Caruthers if he had started with his neck and broken that first; but since he has seen fit to choose a different policy and string himself out as long as possible, I do not think we ought to upbraid him for it if he has enjoyed it. We must do the best we can under the circumstances, and try not to feel exasperated at him.

TOM EDISON'S SHAGGY DOG

Kurt Vonnegut

Kurt Vonnegut (1922–2007) was an American writer, known for his black humour and satirical voice. Enlisting in the air force in 1943, Vonnegut survived the bombing of Dresden, an experience he captured in his most famous novel, *The Slaughterhouse Five*. First published in 1950, he went on to write fourteen novels, four plays and three short story collections in addition to countless works of non-fiction.

Two old men sat on a park bench one morning in the sunshine of Tampa, Florida—one trying doggedly to read a book he was plainly enjoying while the other, Harold K. Bullard, told him the story of his life in the full, round, head tones of a public address system. At their feet lay Bullard's Labrador retriever, who further tormented the aged listener by probing his ankles with a large, wet nose.

Bullard, who had been, before he retired, successful in many fields, enjoyed reviewing his important past. But he faced the problem that complicates the lives of cannibals—namely: that a single victim cannot be used over and over. Anyone who had passed the time of day with him and his dog refused to share a bench with them again.

So Bullard and his dog set out through the park each day in quest of new faces. They had had good luck this morning, for they had found this stranger right away, clearly a new arrival in Florida, still buttoned up tight in heavy serge, stiff collar and necktie, and with nothing better to do than read.

"Yes," said Bullard, rounding out the first hour of his lecture, "made and lost five fortunes in my time."

"So you said," said the stranger, whose name Bullard had neglected to ask. "Easy, boy. No, no, no, boy," he said to the dog, who was growing more aggressive toward his ankles.

"Oh? Already told you that, did I?" said Bullard.

"Twice."

"Two in real estate, one in scrap iron, and one in oil and one in trucking."

"So you said."

"I did? Yes, guess I did. Two in real estate, one in scrap iron, one in oil, and one in trucking. Wouldn't take back a day of it."

"No, I suppose not," said the stranger. "Pardon me, but do you suppose you could move your dog somewhere else? He keeps—"

"Him?" said Bullard, heartily. "Friendliest dog in the world. Don't need to be afraid of him."

"I'm not afraid of him. It's just that he drives me crazy, sniffing at my ankles."

"Plastic," said Bullard, chuckling.

"What?"

"Plastic. Must be something plastic on your garters. By golly. I'll bet it's those little buttons. Sure as we're sitting here, those buttons must be plastic. That dog is nuts about plastic. Don't know why that is, but he'll sniff it out and find it if there's a speck around. Must be a deficiency in his diet, though, by gosh, he eats better than I do. Once he chewed up a whole plastic humidor. Can you beat it? *That's* the business I'd go into now, by glory, if the pill rollers hadn't told me to let up, to give the old ticker a rest."

"You could tie the dog to that tree over there," said the stranger.

"I get so darn' sore at all the youngsters these days!" said Bullard. "All of 'em mooning around about no frontiers any more. There never have been so many frontiers as there are today. You know what Horace Greeley would say today?"

"His nose is wet," said the stranger, and he pulled his ankles away, but the dog humped forward in patient pursuit. "Stop it, boy!"

"His wet nose shows he's healthy," said Bullard. "'Go plastic, young man!' That's what Greeley'd say. 'Go atom, young man!'"

The dog had definitely located the plastic buttons on the stranger's garters and was cocking his head one way and another, thinking out ways of bringing his teeth to bear on those delicacies.

"Scat!" said the stranger.

"'Go electronic, young man!'" said Bullard. "Don't talk to me about no opportunity any more. Opportunity's knocking down every door in the country, trying to get in. When I was young, a man had to go out and find opportunity and drag it home by the ears. Nowadays—"

"Sorry," said the stranger, evenly. He slammed his book shut, stood and jerked his ankle away from the dog. "I've got to be on my way. So good day, sir."

He stalked across the park, found another bench, sat down with a sigh and began to read. His respiration had just returned to normal, when he felt the wet sponge of the dog's nose on his ankles again.

"Oh—it's you!" said Bullard, sitting down beside him. "He was tracking you. He was on the scent of something, and I just let him have his head. What'd I tell you about plastic?" He looked about contentedly. "Don't blame you for moving on. It was stuffy back there. No shade to speak of and not a sign of a breeze."

"Would the dog go away if I bought him a humidor?" said the stranger.

"Pretty good joke, pretty good joke," said Bullard, amiably. Suddenly he clapped the stranger on his knee. "Sa-ay, you aren't in plastics, are you? Here I've been blowing off about plastics, and for all I know that's your line."

"My line?" said the stranger crisply, laying down his book. "Sorry—I've never had a line. I've been a drifter since the age of nine, since Edison set up his laboratory next to my home, and showed me the intelligence analyzer."

"Edison?" said Bullard. "Thomas Edison, the inventor?"

"If you want to call him that, go ahead," said the stranger.

"If I *want* to call him that?"—Bullard guffawed—"I guess I just will! Father of the light bulb and I don't know what all."

"If you want to think he invented the light bulb, go ahead. No harm in it." The stranger resumed his reading.

"Say, what is this?" said Bullard, suspiciously. "You pulling my leg? What's this about an intelligence analyzer? I never heard of that."

"Of course you haven't," said the stranger. "Mr. Edison and I promised to keep it a secret. I've never told anyone. Mr. Edison broke his promise and told Henry Ford, but Ford made him promise not to tell anybody else—for the good of humanity."

Bullard was entranced. "Uh, this intelligence analyzer," he said, "it analyzed intelligence, did it?"

"It was an electric butter churn," said the stranger.

"Seriously now," Bullard coaxed.

"Maybe it *would* be better to talk it over with someone," said the stranger. "It's a terrible thing to keep bottled up inside me, year in and year out. But how can I be sure that it won't go any further?"

"My word as a gentleman," Bullard assured him.

"I don't suppose I could find a stronger guarantee than that, could I?" said the stranger, judiciously.

"There is no stronger guarantee," said Bullard, proudly. "Cross my heart and hope to die!"

"Very well." The stranger leaned back and closed his eyes, seeming to travel backward through time. He was silent for a full minute, during which Bullard watched with respect.

"It was back in the fall of eighteen seventy-nine," said the stranger at last, softly. "Back in the village of Menlo Park, New Jersey. I was a boy of nine. A young man we all thought was a wizard had set up a laboratory next door to my home, and there were flashes and crashes inside, and all sorts of scary goings on. The neighborhood children were warned to keep away, not to make any noise that would bother the wizard."

"I didn't get to know Edison right off, but his dog Sparky and I got to be steady pals. A dog a whole lot like yours, Sparky was, and we used to wrestle all over the neighborhood. Yes, sir, your dog is the image of Sparky."

"Is that so?" said Bullard, flattered.

"Gospel," replied the stranger. "Well, one day Sparky and I were wrestling around, and we wrestled right up to the door of Edison's laboratory. The next thing I knew, Sparky had pushed me in through the door, and bam! I was sitting on the laboratory floor, looking up at Mr. Edison himself."

"Bet he was sore," said Bullard, delighted.

"You can bet I was scared," said the stranger. "I thought I was face to face with Satan himself. Edison had wires hooked to his ears and running down to a little black box in his lap! I started to scoot, but he caught me by my collar and made me sit down.

"'Boy,' said Edison, 'it's always darkest before the dawn. I want you to remember that.'

"'Yes, sir,' I said.

"'For over a year, my boy,' Edison said to me, 'I've been trying to find a filament that will last in an incandescent lamp. Hair, string, splinters—nothing works. So while I was trying to think of something else to try, I started tinkering with another idea of mine, just letting off steam. I put this together,' he said, showing me the little black box. 'I thought maybe intelligence was just a certain kind of electricity, so I made this intelligence analyzer here. It works! You're the first one to know about it, my boy. But I don't know why you shouldn't be. It will be your generation that will grow up in the glorious new era when people will be as easily graded as oranges.'"

"I don't believe it!" said Bullard.

"May I be struck by lightning this very instant!" said the stranger. "And it did work, too. Edison had tried out the analyzer on the men in his shop, without telling them what he was up to. The smarter a man was, by gosh, the farther the needle on the indicator in the little black box swung to the right. I let him try it on me, and the needle just lay where it was and trembled. But dumb as I was, then is when I made my one and only contribution to the world. As I say, I haven't lifted a finger since."

"Whadja do?" said Bullard, eagerly.

"I said, 'Mr. Edison, sir, let's try it on the dog.' And I wish you could have seen the show that dog put on when I said it! Old Sparky barked and howled and scratched to get out. When he saw we meant business, that he wasn't going to get out, he made a beeline right for the intelligence analyzer and knocked it out of Edison's hands. But we cornered him, and Edison held him down while I touched the wires to his ears. And would you believe it, that needle sailed clear across the dial, way past a little red pencil mark on the dial face!"

"The dog busted it," said Bullard.

"'Mr. Edison, sir,' I said, 'what's that red mark mean?'

"'My boy,' said Edison, 'it means that the instrument is broken, because that red mark is me.'"

"I'll say it was broken," said Bullard.

The stranger said gravely, "But it wasn't broken. No, sir. Edison checked the whole thing, and it was in apple-pie order. When Edison told me that, it was then that Sparky, crazy to get out, gave himself away."

"How?" said Bullard, suspiciously.

"We really had him locked in, see? There were three locks on the door—a hook and eye, a bolt, and a regular knob and latch. That dog stood up, unhooked the hook, pushed the bolt back and had the knob in his teeth when Edison stopped him."

"No!" said Bullard.

"Yes!" said the stranger, his eyes shining. "And then is when Edison showed me what a great scientist he was. He was willing to face the truth, no matter how unpleasant it might be.

"'So!' said Edison to Sparky. 'Man's best friend, huh? Dumb animal, huh?'

"That Sparky was a caution. He pretended not to hear. He scratched himself and bit fleas and went around growling at ratholes—anything to get out of looking Edison in the eye.

"'Pretty soft, isn't it, Sparky?' said Edison. 'Let somebody else worry about getting food, building shelters and keeping warm, while you sleep in front of a fire or go chasing after the girls or raise hell with the boys. No mortgages, no politics, no war, no work, no worry. Just wag the old tail or lick a hand, and you're all taken care of.'

"'Mr. Edison,' I said, 'do you mean to tell me that dogs are smarter than people?'

"'Smarter?' said Edison. 'I'll tell the world! And what have I been doing for the past year? Slaving to work out a light bulb so dogs can play at night!'

"'Look, Mr. Edison,' said Sparky, 'why not—'"

"Hold on!" roared Bullard.

"Silence!" shouted the stranger, triumphantly. "'Look, Mr. Edison,' said Sparky, 'why not keep quiet about this? It's been working out to everybody's satisfaction for hundreds of thousands of years; Let sleeping dogs lie. You forget all about it, destroy the intelligence analyzer, and I'll tell you what to use for a lamp filament.'"

"Hogwash!" said Bullard, his face purple.

The stranger stood. "You have my solemn word as a gentleman. That dog rewarded *me* for my silence with a stock-market tip that made me independently wealthy for the rest of my days. And the last words that Sparky ever spoke were to Thomas Edison. 'Try a piece of carbonized cotton thread,' he said. Later, he was torn to bits by a pack of dogs that had gathered outside the door, listening."

The stranger removed his garters and handed them to Bullard's dog. "A small token of esteem, sir, for an ancestor of yours who talked himself to death. Good day." He tucked his book under his arm and walked away.

THE MAN WHO COULD WORK MIRACLES

H.G. Wells

Herbert George Wells (1866–1946) was a prolific English writer, producing dozens of novels, short stories, essays, satire, biography and autobiography. He is best remembered for his science fiction novels and is often called the father of the genre. A forward-looking social critic and utopian, he foresaw the advent of aircraft, tanks, space travel, nuclear weapons, satellite television and something resembling the internet. His most notable books include *The Time Machine*, *The Invisible Man* and *The War of the Worlds*. He was nominated for the Nobel Prize in Literature four times.

It is doubtful whether the gift was innate. For my own part, I think it came to him suddenly. Indeed, until he was thirty he was a sceptic, and did not believe in miraculous powers. And here, since it is the most convenient place, I must mention that he was a little man, and had eyes of a hot brown, very erect red hair, a moustache with ends that he twisted up, and freckles. His name was George McWhirter Fotheringay—not the sort of name by any means to lead to any expectation of miracles—and he was clerk at Gomshott's. He was greatly addicted to assertive argument. It was while he was asserting the impossibility of miracles that he had his first intimation of his extraordinary powers. This particular argument was being held in the bar of the Long Dragon, and Toddy Beamish was conducting the opposition by a monotonous but effective "So you say," that drove Mr. Fotheringay to the very limit of his patience.

There were present, besides these two, a very dusty cyclist, landlord

Cox, and Miss Maybridge, the perfectly respectable and rather portly barmaid of the Dragon. Miss Maybridge was standing with her back to Mr. Fotheringay, washing glasses; the others were watching him, more or less amused by the present ineffectiveness of the assertive method. Goaded by the Torres Vedras tactics of Mr. Beamish, Mr. Fotheringay determined to make an unusual rhetorical effort. "Looky here, Mr. Beamish," said Mr. Fotheringay. "Let us clearly understand what a miracle is. It's something contrariwise to the course of nature done by power of Will, something what couldn't happen without being specially willed."

"So you say," said Mr. Beamish, repulsing him.

Mr. Fotheringay appealed to the cyclist, who had hitherto been a silent auditor, and received his assent—given with a hesitating cough and a glance at Mr. Beamish. The landlord would express no opinion, and Mr. Fotheringay, returning to Mr. Beamish, received the unexpected concession of a qualified assent to his definition of a miracle.

"For instance," said Mr. Fotheringay, greatly encouraged. "Here would be a miracle. That lamp, in the natural course of nature, couldn't burn like that upsy-down, could it, Beamish?"

"You say it couldn't," said Beamish.

"And you?" said Fotheringay. "You don't mean to say—eh?"

"No," said Beamish reluctantly. "No, it couldn't."

"Very well," said Mr. Fotheringay. "Then here comes someone, as it might be me, along here, and stands as it might be here, and says to that lamp, as I might do, collecting all my will—Turn upsy-down without breaking, and go on burning steady, and—Hullo!"

It was enough to make anyone say "Hullo!" The impossible, the incredible, was visible to them all. The lamp hung inverted in the air, burning quietly with its flame pointing down. It was as solid, as indisputable as ever a lamp was, the prosaic common lamp of the Long Dragon bar.

Mr. Fotheringay stood with an extended forefinger and the knitted brows of one anticipating a catastrophic smash. The cyclist, who was sitting next the lamp, ducked and jumped across the bar. Everybody jumped, more or less. Miss Maybridge turned and screamed. For nearly three seconds the lamp remained still. A faint cry of mental distress came from Mr. Fotheringay. "I can't keep it up," he said, "any longer." He staggered back, and the inverted lamp suddenly flared, fell against the corner of the bar, bounced aside, smashed upon the floor, and went out.

It was lucky it had a metal receiver, or the whole place would have been in a blaze. Mr. Cox was the first to speak, and his remark, shorn of needless excrescences, was to the effect that Fotheringay was a fool. Fotheringay was beyond disputing even so fundamental a proposition as that! He was astonished beyond measure at the thing that had occurred. The subsequent conversation threw absolutely no light on the matter so far as Fotheringay was concerned; the general opinion not only followed Mr. Cox very closely but very vehemently. Everyone accused Fotheringay of a silly trick, and presented him to himself as a foolish destroyer of comfort and security. His mind was in a tornado of perplexity, he was himself inclined to agree with them, and he made a remarkably ineffectual opposition to the proposal of his departure.

He went home flushed and heated, coat-collar crumpled, eyes smarting and ears red. He watched each of the ten street lamps nervously as he passed it. It was only when he found himself alone in his little bed-room in Church Row that he was able to grapple seriously with his memories of the occurrence, and ask, "What on earth happened?"

He had removed his coat and boots, and was sitting on the bed with his hands in his pockets repeating the text of his defence for the seventeenth time, "I didn't want the confounded thing to upset," when it occurred to him that at the precise moment he had said the commanding words he had inadvertently willed the thing he said, and that when he had seen the lamp in the air he had felt it depended on him to maintain it there without being clear how this was to be done. He had not a particularly complex mind, or he might have stuck for a time at that "inadvertently willed," embracing, as it does, the abstrusest problems of voluntary action; but as it was, the idea came to him with a quite acceptable haziness. And from that, following, as I must admit, no clear logical path, he came to the test of experiment.

He pointed resolutely to his candle and collected his mind, though he felt he did a foolish thing. "Be raised up," he said. But in a second that feeling vanished. The candle was raised, hung in the air one giddy moment, and as Mr. Fotheringay gasped, fell with a smash on his toilet-table, leaving him in darkness save for the expiring glow of its wick.

For a time Mr. Fotheringay sat in the darkness, perfectly still. "It did happen, after all," he said. "And 'ow I'm to explain it I don't know." He sighed heavily, and began feeling in his pockets for a match. He could find none, and he rose and groped about the toilet-table. "I wish I had a match," he said. He resorted to his coat, and there was none there, and then it dawned upon him that miracles were possible even with matches. He extended a hand and scowled at it in the dark. "Let there be a match in that hand," he said. He felt some light object fall across his palm, and his fingers closed upon a match.

After several ineffectual attempts to light this, he discovered it was a safety-match. He threw it down, and then it occurred to him that he might have willed it lit. He did, and perceived it burning in the midst of his toilet-table mat. He caught it up hastily, and it went out. His perception of possibilities enlarged, and he felt for and replaced the candle in its candlestick. "Here! you be lit," said Mr. Fotheringay, and forthwith the candle was flaring, and he saw a little black hole in the toilet-cover, with a wisp of smoke rising from it. For a time he stared from this to the little flame and back, and then looked up and met his own gaze in the looking glass. By this help he communed with himself in silence for a time.

"How about miracles now?" said Mr. Fotheringay at last, addressing his reflection.

The subsequent meditations of Mr. Fotheringay were of a severe but confused description. So far, he could see it was a case of pure willing with him. The nature of his experiences so far disinclined him for any further experiments, at least until he had reconsidered them. But he lifted a sheet of paper, and turned a glass of water pink and then green, and he created a snail, which he miraculously annihilated, and got himself a miraculous new tooth-brush. Somewhen in the small hours he had reached the fact that his will-power must be of a particularly rare and pungent quality, a fact of which he had certainly had inklings before, but no certain assurance. The scare and perplexity of his first discovery was now qualified by pride in this evidence of singularity and by vague intimations of advantage. He became aware that the church clock was striking one, and as it did not occur to him that his daily duties at Gomshott's might be miraculously dispensed with, he resumed undressing, in order to get to bed without further delay. As he struggled to get his shirt over his head, he was struck with a brilliant idea. "Let me be in bed," he said, and found himself so. "Undressed," he stipulated; and, finding the sheets cold, added hastily, "and in my nightshirt—no, in a nice soft woollen nightshirt. Ah!" he said with immense enjoyment. "And now let me be comfortably asleep…"

He awoke at his usual hour and was pensive all through breakfast-time, wondering whether his overnight experience might not be a particularly vivid dream. At length his mind turned again to cautious experiments. For instance, he had three eggs for breakfast; two his landlady had supplied, good, but shoppy, and one was a delicious fresh goose-egg, laid, cooked, and served by his extraordinary will. He hurried off to Gomshott's in a state of profound but carefully concealed excitement, and only remembered the shell of the third egg when his landlady spoke of it that night. All day he could do no work because of this astonishingly new self-knowledge, but this caused him no inconvenience, because he made up for it miraculously in his last ten minutes.

As the day wore on his state of mind passed from wonder to elation, albeit the circumstances of his dismissal from the Long Dragon were still disagreeable to recall, and a garbled account of the matter that had reached his colleagues led to some badinage. It was evident he must be careful how he lifted frangible articles, but in other ways his gift promised more and more as he turned it over in his mind.

He intended among other things to increase his personal property by unostentatious acts of creation. He called into existence a pair of very splendid diamond studs, and hastily annihilated them again as young

Gomshott came across the counting-house to his desk. He was afraid young Gomshott might wonder how he had come by them. He saw quite clearly the gift required caution and watchfulness in its exercise, but so far as he could judge the difficulties attending its mastery would be no greater than those he had already faced in the study of cycling. It was that analogy, perhaps, quite as much as the feeling that he would be unwelcome in the Long Dragon, that drove him out after supper into the lane beyond the gas-works, to rehearse a few miracles in private.

There was possibly a certain want of originality in his attempts, for apart from his will-power Mr. Fotheringay was not a very exceptional man. The miracle of Moses' rod came to his mind, but the night was dark and unfavourable to the proper control of large miraculous snakes. Then he recollected the story of "Tannhauser" that he had read on the back of the Philharmonic programme. That seemed to him singularly attractive and harmless. He stuck his walking-stick—a very nice Poona-Penang lawyer—into the turf that edged the footpath, and commanded the dry wood to blossom. The air was immediately full of the scent of roses, and by means of a match he saw for himself that this beautiful miracle was indeed accomplished. His satisfaction was ended by advancing footsteps. Afraid of a premature discovery of his powers, he addressed the blossoming stick hastily: "Go back." What he meant was "Change back;" but of course he was confused. The stick receded at a considerable velocity, and incontinently came a cry of anger and a bad word from the approaching person. "Who are you throwing brambles at, you fool?" cried a voice. "That got me on the shin."

"I'm sorry, old chap," said Mr. Fotheringay, and then realising the awkward nature of the explanation, caught nervously at his moustache. He saw Winch, one of the three Immering constables, advancing.

"What d'yer mean by it?" asked the constable. "Hullo! it's you, is it? The gent that broke the lamp at the Long Dragon!"

"I don't mean anything by it," said Mr. Fotheringay. "Nothing at all."

"What d'yer do it for then?"

"Oh, bother!" said Mr. Fotheringay.

"Bother indeed! D'yer know that stick hurt? What d'yer do it for, eh?"

For the moment Mr. Fotheringay could not think what he had done it for. His silence seemed to irritate Mr. Winch. "You've been assaulting the police, young man, this time. That's what you done."

"Look here, Mr. Winch," said Mr. Fotheringay, annoyed and confused, "I'm very sorry. The fact is—"

"Well?"

He could think of no way but the truth. "I was working a miracle." He tried to speak in an off-hand way, but try as he would he couldn't.

"Working a—! 'Ere, don't you talk rot. Working a miracle, indeed! Miracle! Well, that's downright funny! Why, you's the chap that don't believe in miracles... Fact is, this is another of your silly conjuring tricks—that's what this is. Now, I tell you—"

But Mr. Fotheringay never heard what Mr. Winch was going to tell him. He realised he had given himself away, flung his valuable secret to all the winds of heaven. A violent gust of irritation swept him to action. He turned on the constable swiftly and fiercely. "Here," he said, "I've had enough of this, I have! I'll show you a silly conjuring trick, I will! Go to Hades! Go, now!"

He was alone!

Mr. Fotheringay performed no more miracles that night nor did he trouble to see what had become of his flowering stick. He returned to the town, scared and very quiet, and went to his bed-room. "Lord!" he said, "it's a powerful gift—an extremely powerful gift. I didn't hardly mean as much as that. Not really... I wonder what Hades is like!"

He sat on the bed taking off his boots. Struck by a happy thought he transferred the constable to San Francisco, and without any more interference with normal causation went soberly to bed. In the night he dreamt of the anger of Winch.

The next day Mr. Fotheringay heard two interesting items of news. Someone had planted a most beautiful climbing rose against the elder Mr. Gomshott's private house in the Lullaborough Road, and the river as far as Rawling's Mill was to be dragged for Constable Winch.

Mr. Fotheringay was abstracted and thoughtful all that day, and performed no miracles except certain provisions for Winch, and the miracle of completing his day's work with punctual perfection in spite of all the bee-swarm of thoughts that hummed through his mind. And the extraordinary abstraction and meekness of his manner was remarked by several people, and made a matter for jesting. For the most part he was thinking of Winch.

On Sunday evening he went to chapel and oddly enough, Mr. Maydig, who took a certain interest in occult matters, preached about "things that are not lawful." Mr. Fotheringay was not a regular chapel goer, but the system of assertive scepticism, to which I have already alluded, was now very much shaken. The tenor of the sermon threw an entirely new light on these novel gifts, and he suddenly decided to consult Mr. Maydig immediately after the service. So soon as that was determined, he found himself wondering why he had not done so before.

Mr. Maydig, a lean, excitable man with quite remarkably long wrists and neck, was gratified at a request for a private conversation from a young man whose carelessness in religious matters was a subject for general remark in the town. After a few necessary delays, he conducted him to the study of the Manse, which was contiguous to the chapel, seated him comfortably, and, standing in front of a cheerful fire—his legs threw a Rhodian arch of shadow on the opposite wall—requested Mr. Fotheringay to state his business.

At first Mr. Fotheringay was a little abashed, and found some difficulty in opening the matter. "You will scarcely believe me, Mr. Maydig, I am afraid"—and so forth for some time. He tried a question at last, and asked Mr. Maydig his opinion of miracles.

Mr. Maydig was still saying "Well" in an extremely judicial tone, when Mr. Fotheringay interrupted again: "You don't believe, I suppose, that some common sort of person—like myself, for instance—as it might be sitting here now, might have some sort of twist inside him that made him able to do things by his will."

"It's possible," said Mr. Maydig. "Something of the sort, perhaps, is possible."

"If I might make free with something here, I think I might show you by a sort of experiment," said Mr. Fotheringay. "Now, take that tobacco-jar on the table, for instance. What I want to know is whether what I am going to do with it is a miracle or not. Just half a minute, Mr. Maydig, please."

He knitted his brows, pointed to the tobacco-jar and said: "Be a bowl of violets."

The tobacco-jar did as it was ordered.

Mr. Maydig started violently at the change, and stood looking from the thaumaturgist to the bowl of flowers. He said nothing. Presently he ventured to lean over the table and smell the violets; they were fresh-picked and very fine ones. Then he stared at Mr. Fotheringay again.

"How did you do that?" he asked.

Mr. Fotheringay pulled his moustache. "Just told it—and there you are. Is that a miracle, or is it black art, or what is it? And what do you think's the matter with me? That's what I want to ask."

"It's a most extraordinary occurrence."

"And this day last week I knew no more that I could do things like that than you did. It came quite sudden. It's something odd about my will, I suppose, and that's as far as I can see."

"Is that—the only thing? Could you do other things besides that?"

"Lord, yes! said Mr. Fotheringay. "Just anything." He thought, and suddenly recalled a conjuring entertainment he had seen. "Here!" He pointed. "Change into a bowl of fish—no, not that—change into a glass bowl full of water with goldfish swimming in it. That's better! You see that, Mr. Maydig?"

"It's astonishing. It's incredible. You are either a most extraordinary... But no—"

"I could change it into anything," said Mr. Fotheringay. "Just anything. Here! be a pigeon, will you?"

In another moment a blue pigeon was fluttering round the room and making Mr. Maydig duck every time it came near him. "Stop there, will you," said Mr. Fotheringay; and the pigeon hung motionless in the air. "I could change it back to a bowl of flowers," he said, and after replacing the pigeon on the table worked that miracle. "I expect you will want your pipe in a bit," he said, and restored the tobacco-jar.

Mr. Maydig had followed all these later changes in a sort of ejaculatory silence. He stared at Mr. Fotheringay and, in a very gingerly manner, picked up the tobacco-jar, examined it, replaced it on the table. "Well!" was the only expression of his feelings.

"Now, after that it's easier to explain what I came about," said Mr. Fotheringay; and proceeded to a lengthy and involved narrative of his strange experiences, beginning with the affair of the lamp in the Long Dragon and complicated by persistent allusions to Winch. As he went on, the transient pride Mr. Maydig's consternation had caused passed away; he became the very ordinary Mr. Fotheringay of everyday intercourse again. Mr. Maydig listened intently, the tobacco-jar in his hand, and his bearing changed also with the course of the narrative. Presently, while Mr. Fotheringay was dealing with the miracle of the third egg, the minister interrupted with a fluttering extended hand—

"It is possible," he said. "It is credible. It is amazing, of course, but it reconciles a number of amazing difficulties. The power to work miracles is a gift—a peculiar quality like genius or second sight—hitherto it has come very rarely and to exceptional people. But in this case... I have always wondered at the miracles of Mahomet, and at Yogi's miracles, and the miracles of Madame Blavatsky. But, of course! Yes, it is simply a gift! It carries out so beautifully the arguments of that great thinker"— Mr. Maydig's voice sank—"his Grace the Duke of Argyll. Here we plumb some profounder law—deeper than the ordinary laws of nature. Yes— yes. Go on. Go on!"

Mr. Fotheringay proceeded to tell of his misadventure with Winch, and Mr. Maydig, no longer overawed or scared, began to jerk his limbs about and interject astonishment. "It's this what troubled me most," proceeded Mr. Fotheringay; "it's this I'm most mijitly in want of advice for; of course he's at San Francisco—wherever San Francisco may be—but of course it's awkward for both of us, as you'll see, Mr. Maydig. I don't see how he can understand what has happened, and I daresay he's scared and exasperated something tremendous, and trying to get at me. I daresay he keeps on starting off to come here. I send him back, by a miracle, every few hours, when I think of it. And of course, that's a thing he won't be able to understand, and it's bound to annoy him; and, of course, if he takes a ticket every time it will cost him a lot of money. I done the best I could for him, but of course it's difficult for him to put himself in my place. I thought afterwards that his clothes might have got scorched, you know—if Hades is all it's supposed to be—before I shifted him. In that case I suppose they'd have locked him up in San Francisco. Of course I willed him a new suit of clothes on him directly I thought of it. But, you see, I'm already in a deuce of a tangle—"

Mr. Maydig looked serious. "I see you are in a tangle. Yes, it's a difficult position. How you are to end it…" He became diffuse and inconclusive.

"However, we'll leave Winch for a little and discuss the larger question. I don't think this is a case of the black art or anything of the sort. I don't think there is any taint of criminality about it at all, Mr. Fotheringay—none whatever, unless you are suppressing material facts. No, it's miracles—pure miracles—miracles, if I may say so, of the very highest class."

He began to pace the hearthrug and gesticulate, while Mr. Fotheringay sat with his arm on the table and his head on his arm, looking worried. "I don't see how I'm to manage about Winch," he said.

"A gift of working miracles—apparently a very powerful gift," said Mr. Maydig, "will find a way about Winch—never fear. My dear Sir, you are a most important man—a man of the most astonishing possibilities. As evidence, for example! And—in other ways, the things you may do…"

"Yes, I've thought of a thing or two," said Mr. Fotheringay. "But—some of the things came a bit twisty. You saw that fish at first? Wrong sort of bowl and wrong sort of fish. And I thought I'd ask someone."

"A proper course," said Mr. Maydig, "a very proper course—altogether the proper course." He stopped and looked at Mr. Fotheringay. "It's practically an unlimited gift. Let us test your powers, for instance. If they really are… If they really are all they seem to be."

And so, incredible as it may seem, in the study of the little house behind the Congregational Chapel, on the evening of Sunday, Nov. 10, 1896, Mr. Fotheringay, egged on and inspired by Mr. Maydig, began to work miracles. The reader's attention is specially and definitely called to the date. He will object, probably has already objected, that certain points in this story are improbable, that if any things of the sort already described had indeed occurred, they would have been in all the papers a year ago. The details immediately following he will find particularly hard to accept, because among other things they involve the conclusion that he or she, the reader in question, must have been killed in a violent and unprecedented manner more than a year ago. Now a miracle is nothing if not improbable, and as a matter of fact the reader was killed in a violent and unprecedented manner a year ago. In the subsequent course of this story that will become perfectly clear and credible, as every right-minded and reasonable reader will admit. But this is not the place for the end of the story, being but little beyond the hither side of the middle. And at first the miracles worked by Mr. Fotheringay were timid little miracles—little things with the cups and parlour fitments—as feeble as the miracles of Theosophists, and, feeble as they were, they were received with awe by his collaborator. He would have preferred to settle the Winch business out of hand, but Mr. Maydig would not let him. But after they had worked a dozen of these domestic trivialities, their sense of power grew, their imagination began to show signs of stimulation, and their ambition enlarged. Their first larger enterprise was due to hunger and the negligence of Mrs. Minchin, Mr. Maydig's housekeeper. The meal to which the minister conducted Mr. Fotheringay was certainly ill-laid and uninviting as refreshment for two industrious miracle-workers; but they were seated, and Mr. Maydig was descanting in sorrow rather than in anger upon his housekeeper's shortcomings, before it occurred to Mr. Fotheringay that an opportunity lay before him. "Don't you think, Mr. Maydig," he said; "if it isn't a liberty, I—"

"My dear Mr. Fotheringay! Of course! No—I didn't think."

Mr. Fotheringay waved his hand. "What shall we have?" he said, in a large, inclusive spirit, and, at Mr. Maydig's order, revised the supper very thoroughly. "As for me," he said, eyeing Mr. Maydig's selection, "I am always particularly fond of a tankard of stout and a nice Welsh rarebit, and I'll order that. I ain't much given to Burgundy," and forthwith stout and Welsh rarebit promptly appeared at his command. They sat long at their supper, talking like equals, as Mr. Fotheringay presently perceived, with a glow of surprise and gratification, of all the miracles they would presently do. "And, by the by, Mr. Maydig," said Mr. Fotheringay, "I might perhaps be able to help you—in a domestic way."

"Don't quite follow," said Mr. Maydig pouring out a glass of miraculous old Burgundy.

Mr. Fotheringay helped himself to a second Welsh rarebit out of vacancy, and took a mouthful. "I was thinking," he said, "I might be able (chum, chum) to work (chum, chum) a miracle with Mrs. Minchin (chum, chum)—make her a better woman."

Mr. Maydig put down the glass and looked doubtful. "She's—She strongly objects to interference, you know, Mr. Fotheringay. And—as a matter of fact—it's well past eleven and she's probably in bed and asleep. Do you think, on the whole—"

Mr. Fotheringay considered these objections. "I don't see that it shouldn't be done in her sleep."

For a time Mr. Maydig opposed the idea, and then he yielded. Mr. Fotheringay issued his orders, and a little less at their ease, perhaps, the two gentlemen proceeded with their repast. Mr. Maydig was enlarging on the changes he might expect in his housekeeper next day, with an optimism that seemed even to Mr. Fotheringay's supper senses a little forced and hectic, when a series of confused noises from upstairs began. Their eyes exchanged interrogations, and Mr. Maydig left the room hastily. Mr. Fotheringay heard him calling up to his housekeeper and then his footsteps going softly up to her.

In a minute or so the minister returned, his step light, his face radiant. "Wonderful!" he said, "and touching! Most touching!"

He began pacing the hearthrug. "A repentance—a most touching repentance—through the crack of the door. Poor woman! A most wonderful change! She had got up. She must have got up at once. She had got up out of her sleep to smash a private bottle of brandy in her box. And to confess it too!... But this gives us—it opens—a most amazing vista of possibilities. If we can work this miraculous change in her..."

"The thing's unlimited seemingly," said Mr. Fotheringay. "And about Mr. Winch—"

"Altogether unlimited." And from the hearthrug Mr. Maydig, waving the Winch difficulty aside, unfolded a series of wonderful proposals— proposals he invented as he went along.

Now what those proposals were does not concern the essentials of this story. Suffice it that they were designed in a spirit of infinite benevolence, the sort of benevolence that used to be called post-prandial. Suffice it, too, that the problem of Winch remained unsolved. Nor is it necessary to describe how far that series got to its fulfilment. There were astonishing changes. The small hours found Mr. Maydig and Mr. Fotheringay careering across the chilly market-square under the still moon, in a sort of ecstasy of thaumaturgy, Mr. Maydig all flap and gesture, Mr. Fotheringay short and bristling, and no longer abashed at his greatness. They had reformed every drunkard in the Parliamentary division, changed all the beer and alcohol to water (Mr. Maydig had overruled Mr. Fotheringay on this point); they had, further, greatly improved the railway communication of the place, drained Flinder's swamp, improved the soil of One Tree Hill, and cured the Vicar's wart. And they were going to see what could be done with the injured pier at South Bridge. "The place," gasped Mr. Maydig, "won't be the same place to-morrow. How surprised and thankful everyone will be!" And just at that moment the church clock struck three.

"I say," said Mr. Fotheringay, "that's three o'clock! I must be getting back. I've got to be at business by eight. And besides, Mrs. Wimms—"

"We're only beginning," said Mr. Maydig, full of the sweetness of unlimited power. "We're only beginning. Think of all the good we're doing. When people wake—"

"But—" said Mr. Fotheringay.

Mr. Maydig gripped his arm suddenly. His eyes were bright and wild. "My dear chap," he said, "there's no hurry. "Look"—he pointed to the moon at the zenith—"Joshua!"

"Joshua?" said Mr. Fotheringay.

"Joshua," said Mr. Maydig. "Why not? Stop it."

Mr. Fotheringay looked at the moon.

"That's a bit tall," he said after a pause.

"Why not?" said Mr. Maydig. "Of course it doesn't stop. You stop the rotation of the earth, you know. Time stops. It isn't as if we were doing harm."

"H'm!" said Mr. Fotheringay. "Well." He sighed. "I'll try. Here—"

He buttoned up his jacket and addressed himself to the habitable globe, with as good an assumption of confidence as lay in his power. "Jest stop rotating, will you," said Mr. Fotheringay.

Incontinently he was flying head over heels through the air at the rate of dozens of miles a minute. In spite of the innumerable circles he was describing per second, he thought; for thought is wonderful—sometimes as sluggish as flowing pitch, sometimes as instantaneous as light. He thought in a second, and willed. "Let me come down safe and sound. Whatever else happens, let me down safe and sound."

He willed it only just in time, for his clothes, heated by his rapid flight through the air, were already beginning to singe. He came down with a forcible, but by no means injurious bump in what appeared to be a mound of fresh-turned earth. A large mass of metal and masonry, extraordinarily like the clock-tower in the middle of the market-square, hit the earth near him, ricochetted over him, and flew into stonework, bricks, and masonry, like a bursting bomb. A hurtling cow hit one of the larger blocks and smashed like an egg. There was a crash that made all the most violent crashes of his past life seem like the sound of falling dust, and this was followed by a descending series of lesser crashes. A vast wind roared throughout earth and heaven so that he could scarcely lift his head to look. For a while he was too breathless and astonished even to see where he was or what had happened. And his first movement was to feel his head and reassure himself that his streaming hair was still his own.

"Lord!" gasped Mr. Fotheringay, scarce able to speak for the gale, "I've had a squeak! What's gone wrong? Storms and thunder. And only a minute ago a fine night. It's Maydig set me on to this sort of thing. What a wind! If I go on fooling in this way I'm bound to have a thundering accident!...

"Where's Maydig?

"What a confounded mess everything's in!"

He looked about him so far as his flapping jacket would permit. The appearance of things was really extremely strange. "The sky's all right anyhow," said Mr. Fotheringay. "And that's about all that is all right. And even there it looks like a terrific gale coming up. But there's the moon overhead, just as it was just now. Bright as midday. But as for the rest—Where's the village? Where's—where's anything? And what on earth set this wind a-blowing? I didn't order no wind."

Mr. Fotheringay struggled to get to his feet in vain, and after one failure, remained on all fours, holding on. He surveyed the moonlit world to leeward, with the tails of his jacket streaming over his head. "There's something seriously wrong," said Mr. Fotheringay. "And what it is—goodness knows."

Far and wide nothing was visible in the white glare through the haze of dust that drove before a screaming gale but tumbled masses of earth and heaps of inchoate ruins, no trees, no houses, no familiar shapes, only a wilderness of disorder vanishing at last into the darkness beneath the whirling columns and streamers, the lightnings and thunderings of a swiftly rising storm. Near him in the livid glare was something that might once have been an elm-tree, a smashed mass of splinters, shivered from boughs to base, and further a twisted mass of iron girders—only too evidently the viaduct—rose out of the piled confusion.

You see when Mr. Fotheringay had arrested the rotation of the solid globe, he had made no stipulation concerning the trifling movables upon its surface. And the earth spins so fast that the surface at its equator is travelling at rather more than a thousand miles an hour, and in these latitudes at more than half that pace. So that the village, and Mr. Maydig, and Mr. Fotheringay, and everybody and everything had been jerked violently forward at about nine miles per second—that is to say, much more violently than if they had been fired out of a cannon. And every human being, every living creature, every house, and every tree—all the world as we know it—had been so jerked and smashed and utterly destroyed. That was all.

These things Mr. Fotheringay did not, of course, fully appreciate. But he perceived that his miracle had miscarried, and with that a great disgust of miracles came upon him. He was in darkness now, for the clouds had swept together and blotted out his momentary glimpse of the moon, and the air was full of fitful struggling tortured wraiths of hail. A great roaring of wind and waters filled earth and sky, and, peering under his hand through the dust and sleet to windward, he saw by the play of the lightnings a vast wall of water pouring towards him.

"Maydig!" screamed Mr. Fotheringay's feeble voice amid the elemental uproar. "Here!—Maydig!"

"Stop!" cried Mr. Fotheringay to the advancing water. "Oh, for goodness' sake, stop!"

"Just a moment," said Mr. Fotheringay to the lightnings and thunder. "Stop jest a moment while I collect my thoughts… And now what shall I do?" he said. "What shall I do? Lord! I wish Maydig was about."

"I know," said Mr. Fotheringay. "And for goodness' sake let's have it right this time."

He remained on all fours, leaning against the wind, very intent to have everything right.

"Ah!" he said. "Let nothing what I'm going to order happen until I say 'Off!'… Lord! I wish I'd thought of that before!"

He lifted his little voice against the whirlwind, shouting louder and louder in the vain desire to hear himself speak. "Now then!—here goes! Mind about that what I said just now. In the first place, when all I've got to say is done, let me lose my miraculous power, let my will become just like anybody else's will, and all these dangerous miracles be stopped. I don't like them. I'd rather I didn't work 'em. Ever so much. That's the first thing. And the second is—let me be back just before the miracles begin; let everything be just as it was before that blessed lamp turned up. It's a big job, but it's the last. Have you got it? No more miracles, everything as it was—me back in the Long Dragon just before I drank my half-pint. That's it! Yes."

He dug his fingers into the mould, closed his eyes, and said "Off!"

Everything became perfectly still. He perceived that he was standing erect.

"So you say," said a voice.

He opened his eyes. He was in the bar of the Long Dragon, arguing about miracles with Toddy Beamish. He had a vague sense of some great thing forgotten that instantaneously passed. You see, except for the loss of his miraculous powers, everything was back as it had been; his mind and memory therefore were now just as they had been at the time when this story began. So that he knew absolutely nothing of all that is told here, knows nothing of all that is told here to this day. And among other things, of course, he still did not believe in miracles.

"I tell you that miracles, properly speaking, can't possibly happen," he said, "whatever you like to hold. And I'm prepared to prove it up to the hilt."

"That's what you think," said Toddy Beamish, and "Prove it if you can."

"Looky here, Mr. Beamish," said Mr. Fotheringay. "Let us clearly understand what a miracle is. It's something contrariwise to the course of nature done by power of Will…"

ARISTOTLE AT AFTERNOON TEA

Oscar Wilde

Oscar Wilde (1854–1900) was an Irish poet, playwright and celebrity, best remembered for his witty epigrams and plays, and for his novel *The Picture of Dorian Gray*. He was a spokesman for the late nineteenth-century Aesthetic movement in England, which advocated art for art's sake, and was known for his biting wit, flamboyant dress and glittering conversational skill. At the height of his fame and success, Wilde had the Marquess of Queensberry prosecuted for criminal libel, which unearthed evidence leading to his own arrest and trial for gross indecency with men. He was eventually convicted and sentenced to two years' hard labour. He died destitute in Paris at the age of forty-six.

In society, says Mr Mahaffy, every civilized man and woman ought to feel it their duty to say something, even when there is hardly anything to be said, and, in order to encourage this delightful art of brilliant chatter, he has published a social guide without which no *débutante* or dandy should ever dream of going out to dine. Not that Mr Mahaffy's book can be said to be, in any sense of the word, popular. In discussing this important subject of conversation, he has not merely followed the scientific method of Aristotle which is, perhaps, excusable, but he has adopted the literary style of Aristotle for which no excuse is possible. There is, also, hardly a single anecdote, hardly a single illustration, and the reader is left to put the Professor's abstract rules into practice, without either the examples or the warnings of history to encourage or to dissuade him in his reckless career. Still, the book can be warmly recommended to all who propose to substitute the vice of verbosity for the stupidity of silence. It fascinates in spite of its form and pleases in spite of its pedantry, and is the nearest approach, that we know of, in modern literature to meeting Aristotle at an afternoon tea.

As regards physical conditions, the only one that is considered by Mr Mahaffy as being absolutely essential to a good conversationalist, is the possession of a musical voice. Some learned writers have been of opinion that a slight stammer often gives peculiar zest to conversation, but Mr Mahaffy rejects this view and is extremely severe on every eccentricity from a native brogue to an artificial catchword. With his remarks on the latter point, the meaningless repetition of phrases, we entirely agree. Nothing can be more irritating than the scientific person who is always saying '*Exactly so,*' or the commonplace person who ends every sentence with '*I Don't you know?*' or the pseudo-artistic person who murmurs '*Charming, charming,*' on the smallest provocation. It is, however, with the mental and moral qualifications for conversation that Mr Mahaffy specially deals. Knowledge he, naturally, regards as an absolute essential, for, as he most justly observes, 'an ignorant man is seldom agreeable, except as a butt.' Upon the other hand, strict accuracy should be avoided. 'Even a consummate liar,' says Mr Mahaffy, is a better ingredient in a company than 'the scrupulously truthful man, who weighs every statement, questions every fact, and corrects every inaccuracy.' The liar at any rate recognizes that recreation, not instruction, is the aim of conversation, and is a far more civilized being than the blockhead who loudly expresses his disbelief in a story which is told simply for the amusement of the company. Mr Mahaffy, however, makes an exception in favour of the eminent specialist and tells us that intelligent questions addressed to an astronomer, or a pure mathematician, will elicit many curious facts which will pleasantly beguile the time. Here, in the interest of Society, we feel bound to enter a formal protest. Nobody, even in the provinces, should ever be allowed to ask an intelligent question about pure mathematics across a dinner table. A question of this kind is quite as bad as enquiring suddenly about the state of a man's soul, a sort of *coup* which, as Mr Mahaffy remarks elsewhere, 'many pious people have actually thought a decent introduction to a conversation'.

As for the moral qualifications of a good talker, Mr Mahaffy, following the example of his great master, warns us against any disproportionate excess of virtue. Modesty, for instance, may easily become a social vice, and to be continually apologizing for one's ignorance or stupidity is a grave injury to conversation, for, 'what we want to learn from each member is his free opinion on the subject in hand, not his own estimate of the value of that opinion.' Simplicity, too, is not without its dangers. The *enfant terrible*, with his shameless love of truth, the raw country-bred girl who always says what she means, and the plain, blunt man who makes a point of speaking his mind on every possible occasion, without ever considering whether he has a mind at all, are the fatal examples of what simplicity leads to. Shyness may be a form of vanity, and reserve a development of pride, and as for sympathy, what can be more detestable than the man, or woman, who insists on agreeing with everybody, and so makes 'a discussion, which implies differences in opinion', absolutely impossible? Even the unselfish listener is apt to become a bore. 'These silent people,' says Mr Mahaffy, 'not only take all they can get in Society for nothing, but they take it without the smallest gratitude, and have the audacity afterwards to censure those who have laboured for their amusement.' Tact, which is an exquisite sense of the symmetry of things, is, according to Mr Mahaffy, the highest and best of all the moral conditions for conversation. The man of tact, he most wisely remarks, 'will instinctively avoid jokes about Blue Beard' in the company of a woman who is a man's third wife; he will never be guilty of talking like a book, but will rather avoid too careful an attention to grammar and the rounding of periods; he will cultivate the art of graceful interruption, so as to prevent a subject being worn threadbare by the aged or the inexperienced; and should he be desirous of telling a story, he will look round and consider each member of the party, and if there be a single stranger present will forgo the pleasure of anecdotage rather than make the social mistake of hurting even one of the guests. As for prepared or premeditated art, Mr Mahaffy has a great contempt for it and tells us of a certain college don (let us hope not at Oxford or Cambridge) who always carried a jest-book in his pocket and had to refer to it when he wished to make a repartee. Great wits, too, are often very cruel, and great humorists often very vulgar, so it will be better to try and 'make good conversation without any large help from these brilliant but dangerous gifts.'

In a *tête-à-tête* one should talk about persons, and in general society about things. The state of the weather is always an excusable exordium, but it is convenient to have a paradox or heresy on the subject always ready so as to direct the conversation into other channels. Really domestic people are almost invariably bad talkers as their very virtues in home life have dulled their interest in outer things. The very best mothers will insist on chattering of their babies and prattling about infant education. In fact, most women do not take sufficient interest in politics, just as most men are deficient in general reading. Still, anybody can be made to talk, except the very obstinate, and even a commercial traveller may be drawn out and become quite interesting. As for Society small talk, it is impossible, Mr Mahaffy tells us, for any sound theory of conversation to depreciate gossip, 'which is perhaps the main factor in agreeable talk throughout Society.' The retailing of small personal points about great people always gives pleasure, and if one is not fortunate enough to be an Arctic traveller or an escaped Nihilist, the best thing one can do is to relate some anecdote of 'Prince Bismarck, or King Victor Emmanuel, or Mr Gladstone'. In the case of meeting a genius and a Duke at dinner, the good talker will try to raise himself to the level of the former and to bring the latter down to his own level. To succeed among one's social superiors one must have no hesitation in contradicting them. Indeed, one should make bold criticisms and introduce a bright and free tone into a Society whose grandeur and extreme respectability make it, Mr Mahaffy remarks, as pathetically as inaccurately, 'perhaps somewhat dull'. The best conversationalists are those whose ancestors have been bilingual, like the French and Irish, but the art of conversation is really within the reach of almost every one, except those who are morbidly truthful, or whose high moral worth requires to be sustained by a permanent gravity of demeanour and a general dulness of mind.

These are the broad principles contained in Mr Mahaffy's clever little book, and many of them will, no doubt, commend themselves to our readers. The maxim, 'If you find the company dull, blame yourself,' seems to us somewhat optimistic, and we have no sympathy at all with the professional storyteller who is really a great bore at a dinner table; but Mr Mahaffy is quite right in insisting that no bright social intercourse is possible without equality, and it is no objection to his book to say that it will not teach people how to talk cleverly. It is not logic that makes men reasonable, nor the science of ethics that makes men good, but it is always useful to analyse, to formularize and to investigate. The only thing to be regretted in the volume is the arid and jejune character of the style. If Mr Mahaffy would only write as he talks, his book would be much pleasanter reading.

The Principles of the Art of Conversation: A Social Essay.
By J. P. Mahaffy. (Macmillan and Co.)

LONDON MODELS

Oscar Wilde

Oscar Wilde (1854–1900) was an Irish poet, playwright and celebrity, best remembered for his witty epigrams and plays, and for his novel *The Picture of Dorian Gray*. He was a spokesman for the late nineteenth-century Aesthetic movement in England, which advocated art for art's sake, and was known for his biting wit, flamboyant dress and glittering conversational skill. At the height of his fame and success, Wilde had the Marquess of Queensberry prosecuted for criminal libel, which unearthed evidence leading to his own arrest and trial for gross indecency with men. He was eventually convicted and sentenced to two years' hard labour. He died destitute in Paris at the age of forty-six.

Professional models are a purely modern invention. To the Greeks, for instance, they were quite unknown. Mr Mahaffy, it is true, tells us that Pericles used to present peacocks to the great ladies of Athenian society in order to induce them to sit to his friend Phidias, and we know that Polygnotus introduced into his picture of the Trojan women the face of Elpinice, the celebrated sister of the great Conservative leader of the day, but these *grandes dames* clearly do not come under our category. As for the old masters, they undoubtedly made constant studies from their pupils and apprentices, and even their religious pictures are full of the portraits of their friends and relations, but they do not seem to have had the inestimable advantage of the existence of a class of people whose sole profession is to pose. In fact the model, in our sense of the word, is the direct creation of Academic Schools.

Every country now has its own models, except America. In New York, and even in Boston, a good model is so great a rarity that most of the artists are reduced to painting Niagara and millionaires. In Europe, however, it is different. Here we have plenty of models, and of every nationality. The Italian models are the best. The natural grace of their attitudes, as well as the wonderful picturesqueness of their colouring, makes them facile – often too facile – subjects for the painter's brush. The French models, though not so beautiful as the Italian, possess a quickness of intellectual sympathy, a capacity, in fact, of understanding the artist, which is quite remarkable. They have also a great command over the varieties of facial expression, are peculiarly dramatic, and can chatter the *argot* of the *atelier* as cleverly as the critic of the *Gil Blas*. The English models form a class entirely by themselves. They are not so picturesque as the Italian, nor so clever as the French, and they have absolutely no tradition, so to speak, of their order. Now and then some old veteran knocks at a studio door, and proposes to sit as Ajax defying the lightning, or as King Lear upon the blasted heath. One of them some time ago called on a popular painter who, happening at the moment to require his services, engaged him, and told him to begin by kneeling down in the attitude of prayer. 'Shall I be Biblical or Shakespearean, sir?' asked the veteran. 'Well – Shakespearean,' answered the artist, wondering by what subtle *nuance* of expression the model would convey the difference. 'All right, sir,' said the professor of posing, and he solemnly knelt down and began to wink with his left eye! This class, however, is dying out. As a rule the model, nowadays, is a pretty girl, from about twelve to twenty-five years of age, who knows nothing about art, cares less, and is merely anxious to earn seven or eight shillings a day without much trouble. English models rarely look at a picture, and never venture on any aesthetic theories. In fact, they realize very completely Mr Whistler's idea of the function of an art critic, for they pass no criticisms at all. They accept all schools of art with the grand catholicity of the auctioneer, and sit to a fantastic young impressionist as readily as to a learned and laborious academician. They are neither for the Whistlerites nor against them; the quarrel between the school of facts and the school of effects touches them not; idealistic and naturalistic are words that convey no meaning to their ears; they merely desire that the studio shall be warm, and the lunch hot, for all charming artists give their models lunch.

As to what they are asked to do they are equally indifferent. On Monday they will don the rags of a beggar-girl for Mr Pumper, whose pathetic pictures of modern life draw such tears from the public, and on Tuesday they will pose in a peplum for Mr Phoebus, who thinks that all really artistic subjects are necessarily BC. They career gaily through all centuries and through all costumes, and, like actors, are interesting only when they are not themselves. They are extremely good-natured, and very accommodating. 'What do you sit for?' said a young artist to a model who had sent him in her card (all models, by the way, have cards and a small black bag). 'Oh, for anything you like, sir,' said the girl, 'landscape if necessary!'

Intellectually, it must be acknowledged, they are Philistines, but physically they are perfect – at least some are. Though none of them can talk Greek, many can look Greek, which to a nineteenth-century painter is naturally of great importance. If they are allowed, they chatter a great deal, but they never say anything. Their observations are the only *banalités* heard in Bohemia. However, though they cannot appreciate the artist as artist, they are quite ready to appreciate the artist as a man. They are very sensitive to kindness, respect and generosity. A beautiful model who had sat for two years to one of our most distinguished English painters, got engaged to a street vendor of penny ices. On her marriage the painter sent her a pretty wedding present, and received in return a nice letter of thanks with the following remarkable postscript: 'Never eat the green ices!'

When they are tired a wise artist gives them a rest. Then they sit in a chair and read penny dreadfuls, till they are roused from the tragedy of literature to take their place again in the tragedy of art. A few of them smoke cigarettes. This, however, is regarded by the other models as showing a want of seriousness, and is not generally approved of. They are engaged by the day and by the half day. The tariff is a shilling an hour, to which great artists usually add an omnibus fare. The two best things about them are their extraordinary prettiness, and their extreme respectability. As a class they are very well behaved, particularly those who sit for the figure, a fact which is curious or natural according to the view one takes of human nature. They usually marry well, and sometimes they marry the artist. For an artist to marry his model is as fatal as for a *gourmet* to marry his cook: the one gets no sittings, and the other gets no dinners.

On the whole the English female models are very naïve, very natural and very good-humoured. The virtues which the artist values most in them are prettiness and punctuality. Every sensible model consequently keeps a diary of her engagements, and dresses neatly. The bad season is, of course, the summer, when the artists are out of town. However, of late years some artists have engaged their models to follow them, and the wife of one of our most charming painters has often had three or four models under her charge in the country, so that the work of her husband and his friends should not be interrupted. In France the models migrate *en masse* to the little seaport villages or forest hamlets where the painters congregate. The English models, however, wait patiently in London, as a rule, till the artists come back. Nearly all of them live with their parents, and help to support the house. They have every qualification for being immortalized in art except that of beautiful hands. The hands of the English model are nearly always coarse and red.

As for the male models, there is the veteran whom we have mentioned above. He has all the traditions of the grand style, and is rapidly disappearing with the school he represents. An old man who talks about Fuseli is, of course, unendurable, and, besides, patriarchs have ceased to be fashionable subjects. Then there is the true Academy model. He is usually a man of thirty, rarely good-looking, but a perfect miracle of muscles. In fact he is the apotheosis of anatomy, and is so conscious of his own splendour that he tells you of his tibia and his thorax, as if no one else had anything of the kind. Then come the Oriental models. The supply of these is limited, but there are always about a dozen in London. They are very much sought after as they can remain immobile for hours, and generally possess lovely costumes. However, they have a very poor opinion of English art, which they regard as something between a vulgar personality and a commonplace photograph. Next we have the Italian youth who has come over specially to be a model, or takes to it when his organ is out of repair. He is often quite charming with his large melancholy eyes, his crisp hair, and his slim brown figure. It is true he eats garlic, but then he can stand like a faun and couch like a leopard, so he is forgiven. He is always full of pretty compliments, and has been known to have kind words of encouragement for even our greatest artists. As for the English lad of the same age, he never sits at all. Apparently he does not regard the career of a model as a serious profession. In any case he is rarely, if ever, to be got hold of. English boys, too, are difficult to find. Sometimes an ex-model who has a son will curl his hair, and wash his face, and bring him the round of the studios, all soap and shininess. The young school don't like him, but the older school do, and when he appears on the walls of the Royal Academy he is called *The Infant Samuel*. Occasionally also an artist catches a couple of *gamins* in the gutter and asks them to come to his studio. The first time they always appear, but after that they don't keep their appointments. They dislike sitting still, and have a strong and perhaps natural objection to looking pathetic. Besides, they are always under the impression that the artist is laughing at them. It is a sad fact, but there is no doubt that the poor are completely unconscious of their own picturesqueness. Those of them who can be induced to sit do so with the idea that the artist is merely a benevolent philanthropist who has chosen an eccentric method of distributing alms to the undeserving. Perhaps the School Board will teach the London *gamin* his own artistic value, and then they will be better models than they are now. One remarkable privilege belongs to the Academy model, that of extorting a sovereign from any newly elected Associate or RA. They wait at Burlington House till the announcement is made, and then race to the hapless artist's house. The one who arrives first receives the money. They have of late been much troubled at the long distances they have had to run, and they look with disfavour on the election of artists who live at Hampstead or at Bedford Park, for it is considered a point of honour not to employ the underground railway, omnibuses, or any artificial means of locomotion. The race is to the swift.

Besides the professional posers of the studio there are posers of the Row, the posers at afternoon teas, the posers in politics and the circus posers. All four classes are delightful, but only the last class is ever really decorative. Acrobats and gymnasts can give the young painter infinite suggestions, for they bring into their art an element of swiftness of motion and of constant change that the studio model necessarily lacks. What is interesting in these 'slaves of the ring' is that with them Beauty is an unconscious result not a conscious aim, the result in fact of the mathematical calculation of curves and distances, of absolute precision of eye, of the scientific knowledge of the equilibrium of forces, and of perfect physical training. A good acrobat is always graceful, though grace is never his object; he is graceful because he does what he has to do in the best way in which it can be done – graceful because he is natural. If an ancient Greek were to come to life now, which considering the probable severity of his criticisms would be rather trying to our conceit, he would be found far oftener at the circus than at the theatre. A good circus is an oasis of Hellenism in a world that reads too much to be wise, and thinks too much to be beautiful. If it were not for the running-ground at Eton, the towing-path at Oxford, the Thames swimming-baths, and the yearly circuses, humanity would forget the plastic perfection of its own form, and degenerate into a race of short-sighted professors and spectacled *précieuses*. Not that the circus proprietors are, as a rule, conscious of their high mission. Do they not bore us with the *haute école*, and weary us with Shakespearean clowns? Still, at least, they give us acrobats, and the acrobat is an artist. The mere fact that he never speaks to the audience shows how well he appreciates the great truth that the aim of, art is not to reveal personality but to please. The clown may be blatant, but the acrobat is always beautiful. He is an interesting combination of the spirit of Greek sculpture with the spangles of the modern costumier. He has even had his niche in the novels of our age, and if *Manette Salomon* be the unmasking of the model, *Les Frères Zemganno* is the apotheosis of the acrobat.

As regards the influence of the ordinary model on our English school of painting, it cannot be said that it is altogether good. It is, of course, an advantage for the young artist sitting in his studio to be able to isolate 'a little corner of life', as the French say, from disturbing surroundings, and to study it under certain effects of light and shade. But this very isolation leads often to mere mannerism in the painter, and robs him of that broad acceptance of the general facts of life which is the very essence of art. Model-painting, in a word, while it may be the condition of art, is not by any means its aim. It is simply practice, not perfection. Its use trains the eye and the hand of the painter, its abuse produces in his work an effect of mere posing and prettiness. It is the secret of much of the artificiality of modern art, this constant posing of pretty people, and when art becomes artificial it becomes monotonous. Outside the little world of the studio, with its draperies and its *bric-à-brac,* lies the world of life with its infinite, its Shakespearean variety. We must, however, distinguish between the two kinds of models, those who sit for the figure and those who sit for the costume. The study of the first is always excellent, but the costume-model is becoming rather wearisome in modern pictures. It is really of very little use to dress up a London girl in Greek draperies and to paint her as a goddess. The robe may be the robe of Athens, but the face is usually the face of Brompton. Now and then, it is true, one comes across a model whose face is an exquisite anachronism, and who looks lovely and natural in the dress of any century but her own. This, however, is rather rare. As a rule models are absolutely *de notre siècle,* and should be painted as such. Unfortunately they are not, and, as a consequence, we are shown every year a series of scenes from fancy dress balls which are called historical pictures, but are little more than mediocre representations of modern people masquerading. In France they are wiser. The French painter uses the model simply for study; for the finished picture he goes direct to life.

However, we must not blame the sitters for the shortcomings of the artists. The English models are a well-behaved and hardworking class, and if they are more interested in artists than in art, a large section of the public is in the same condition, and most of our modern exhibitions seem to justify its choice.

THE CANTERVILLE GHOST

Oscar Wilde

Oscar Wilde (1854–1900) was an Irish poet, playwright and celebrity, best remembered for his witty epigrams and plays, and for his novel *The Picture of Dorian Gray*. He was a spokesman for the late nineteenth-century Aesthetic movement in England, which advocated art for art's sake, and was known for his biting wit, flamboyant dress and glittering conversational skill. At the height of his fame and success, Wilde had the Marquess of Queensberry prosecuted for criminal libel, which unearthed evidence leading to his own arrest and trial for gross indecency with men. He was eventually convicted and sentenced to two years' hard labour. He died destitute in Paris at the age of forty-six.

I

When Mr. Hiram B. Otis, the American Minister, bought Canterville Chase, every one told him he was doing a very foolish thing, as there was no doubt at all that the place was haunted. Indeed, Lord Canterville himself, who was a man of the most punctilious honour, had felt it his duty to mention the fact to Mr. Otis when they came to discuss terms.

"We have not cared to live in the place ourselves," said Lord Canterville, "since my grandaunt, the Dowager Duchess of Bolton, was frightened into a fit, from which she never really recovered, by two skeleton hands being placed on her shoulders as she was dressing for dinner, and I feel bound to tell you, Mr. Otis, that the ghost has been seen by several living members of my family, as well as by the rector of the parish, the Rev. Augustus Dampier, who is a Fellow of King's College, Cambridge. After the unfortunate accident to the Duchess, none of our younger servants would stay with us, and Lady Canterville often got very little sleep at night, in consequence of the mysterious noises that came from the corridor and the library."

"My Lord," answered the Minister, "I will take the furniture and the ghost at a valuation. I have come from a modern country, where we have everything that money can buy; and with all our spry young fellows painting the Old World red, and carrying off your best actors and prima-donnas, I reckon that if there were such a thing as a ghost in Europe, we'd have it at home in a very short time in one of our public museums, or on the road as a show."

"I fear that the ghost exists," said Lord Canterville, smiling, "though it may have resisted the overtures of your enterprising impresarios. It has been well known for three centuries, since 1584 in fact, and always makes its appearance before the death of any member of our family."

"Well, so does the family doctor for that matter, Lord Canterville. But there is no such thing, sir, as a ghost, and I guess the laws of Nature are not going to be suspended for the British aristocracy."

"You are certainly very natural in America," answered Lord Canterville, who did not quite understand Mr. Otis's last observation, "and if you don't mind a ghost in the house, it is all right. Only you must remember I warned you."

A few weeks after this, the purchase was concluded, and at the close of the season the Minister and his family went down to Canterville Chase. Mrs. Otis, who, as Miss Lucretia R. Tappan, of West 53d Street, had been a celebrated New York belle, was now a very handsome, middle-aged woman, with fine eyes, and a superb profile. Many American ladies on leaving their native land adopt an appearance of chronic ill-health, under the impression that it is a form of European refinement, but Mrs. Otis had never fallen into this error. She had a magnificent constitution, and a really wonderful amount of animal spirits. Indeed, in many respects, she was quite English, and was an excellent example of the fact that we have really everything in common with America nowadays, except, of course, language. Her eldest son, christened Washington by his parents in a moment of patriotism, which he never ceased to regret, was a fair-haired, rather good-looking young man, who had qualified himself for American diplomacy by leading the German at the Newport Casino for three successive seasons, and even in London was well known as an excellent dancer. Gardenias and the peerage were his only weaknesses. Otherwise he was extremely sensible. Miss Virginia E. Otis was a little girl of fifteen, lithe and lovely as a fawn, and with a fine freedom in her large blue eyes. She was a wonderful Amazon, and had once raced old Lord Bilton on her pony twice round the park, winning by a length and a half, just in front of the Achilles statue, to the huge delight of the young Duke of Cheshire, who proposed for her on the spot, and was sent back to Eton that very night by his guardians, in floods of tears. After Virginia came the twins, who were usually called "The Star and Stripes," as they were always getting swished. They were delightful boys, and, with the exception of the worthy Minister, the only true republicans of the family.

As Canterville Chase is seven miles from Ascot, the nearest railway station, Mr. Otis had telegraphed for a waggonette to meet them, and they started on their drive in high spirits. It was a lovely July evening, and the air was delicate with the scent of the pinewoods. Now and then they heard a wood-pigeon brooding over its own sweet voice, or saw, deep in the rustling fern, the burnished breast of the pheasant. Little squirrels peered at them from the beech-trees as they went by, and the rabbits scudded away through the brushwood and over the mossy knolls, with their white tails in the air. As they entered the avenue of Canterville Chase, however, the sky became suddenly overcast with clouds, a curious stillness seemed to hold the atmosphere, a great flight of rooks passed silently over their heads, and, before they reached the house, some big drops of rain had fallen.

Standing on the steps to receive them was an old woman, neatly dressed in black silk, with a white cap and apron. This was Mrs. Umney, the housekeeper, whom Mrs. Otis, at Lady Canterville's earnest request, had consented to keep in her former position. She made them each a low curtsey as they alighted, and said in a quaint, old-fashioned manner, "I bid you welcome to Canterville Chase." Following her, they passed through the fine Tudor hall into the library, a long, low room, panelled in black oak, at the end of which was a large stained glass window. Here they found tea laid out for them, and, after taking off their wraps, they sat down and began to look round, while Mrs. Umney waited on them.

Suddenly Mrs. Otis caught sight of a dull red stain on the floor just by the fireplace, and, quite unconscious of what it really signified, said to Mrs. Umney, "I am afraid something has been spilt there."

"Yes, madam," replied the old housekeeper in a low voice, "blood has been spilt on that spot."

"How horrid!" cried Mrs. Otis; "I don't at all care for blood-stains in a sitting-room. It must be removed at once."

The old woman smiled, and answered in the same low, mysterious voice, "It is the blood of Lady Eleanore de Canterville, who was murdered on that very spot by her own husband, Sir Simon de Canterville, in 1575. Sir Simon survived her nine years, and disappeared suddenly under very mysterious circumstances. His body has never been discovered, but his guilty spirit still haunts the Chase. The blood-stain has been much admired by tourists and others, and cannot be removed."

"That is all nonsense," cried Washington Otis; "Pinkerton's Champion Stain Remover and Paragon Detergent will clean it up in no time," and before the terrified housekeeper could interfere, he had fallen upon his knees, and was rapidly scouring the floor with a small stick of what looked like a black cosmetic. In a few moments no trace of the blood-stain could be seen.

"I knew Pinkerton would do it," he exclaimed, triumphantly, as he looked round at his admiring family; but no sooner had he said these words than a terrible flash of lightning lit up the sombre room, a fearful peal of thunder made them all start to their feet, and Mrs. Umney fainted.

"What a monstrous climate!" said the American Minister, calmly, as he lit a long cheroot. "I guess the old country is so overpopulated that they have not enough decent weather for everybody. I have always been of opinion that emigration is the only thing for England."

"My dear Hiram," cried Mrs. Otis, "what can we do with a woman who faints?"

"Charge it to her like breakages," answered the Minister; "she won't faint after that;" and in a few moments Mrs. Umney certainly came to. There was no doubt, however, that she was extremely upset, and she sternly warned Mr. Otis to beware of some trouble coming to the house.

"I have seen things with my own eyes, sir," she said, "that would make any Christian's hair stand on end, and many and many a night I have not closed my eyes in sleep for the awful things that are done here." Mr. Otis, however, and his wife warmly assured the honest soul that they were not afraid of ghosts, and, after invoking the blessings of Providence on her new master and mistress, and making arrangements for an increase of salary, the old housekeeper tottered off to her own room.

II

The storm raged fiercely all that night, but nothing of particular note occurred. The next morning, however, when they came down to breakfast, they found the terrible stain of blood once again on the floor. "I don't think it can be the fault of the Paragon Detergent," said Washington, "for I have tried it with everything. It must be the ghost." He accordingly rubbed out the stain a second time, but the second morning it appeared again. The third morning also it was there, though the library had been locked up at night by Mr. Otis himself, and the key carried up-stairs. The whole family were now quite interested; Mr. Otis began to suspect that he had been too dogmatic in his denial of the existence of ghosts, Mrs. Otis expressed her intention of joining the Psychical Society, and Washington prepared a long letter to Messrs. Myers and Podmore on the subject of the Permanence of Sanguineous Stains when connected with Crime. That night all doubts about the objective existence of phantasmata were removed for ever.

The day had been warm and sunny; and, in the cool of the evening, the whole family went out to drive. They did not return home till nine o'clock, when they had a light supper. The conversation in no way turned upon ghosts, so there were not even those primary conditions of receptive expectations which so often precede the presentation of psychical phenomena. The subjects discussed, as I have since learned from Mr. Otis, were merely such as form the ordinary conversation of cultured Americans of the better class, such as the immense superiority of Miss Fanny Devonport over Sarah Bernhardt as an actress; the difficulty of obtaining green corn, buckwheat cakes, and hominy, even in the best English houses; the importance of Boston in the development of the world-soul; the advantages of the baggage-check system in railway travelling; and the sweetness of the New York accent as compared to the London drawl. No mention at all was made of the supernatural, nor was Sir Simon de Canterville alluded to in any way. At eleven o'clock the family retired, and by half-past all the lights were out. Some time after, Mr. Otis was awakened by a curious noise in the corridor, outside his room. It sounded like the clank of metal, and seemed to be coming nearer every moment. He got up at once, struck a match, and looked at the time. It was exactly one o'clock. He was quite calm, and felt his pulse, which was not at all feverish. The strange noise still continued, and with it he heard distinctly the sound of footsteps. He put on his slippers, took a small oblong phial out of his dressing-case, and opened the door. Right in front of him he saw, in the wan moonlight, an old man of terrible aspect. His eyes were as red burning coals; long grey hair fell over his shoulders in matted coils; his garments, which were of antique cut, were soiled and ragged, and from his wrists and ankles hung heavy manacles and rusty gyves.

"My dear sir," said Mr. Otis, "I really must insist on your oiling those chains, and have brought you for that purpose a small bottle of the Tammany Rising Sun Lubricator. It is said to be completely efficacious upon one application, and there are several testimonials to that effect on the wrapper from some of our most eminent native divines. I shall leave it here for you by the bedroom candles, and will be happy to supply you with more, should you require it." With these words the United States Minister laid the bottle down on a marble table, and, closing his door, retired to rest.

For a moment the Canterville ghost stood quite motionless in natural indignation; then, dashing the bottle violently upon the polished floor, he fled down the corridor, uttering hollow groans, and emitting a ghastly green light. Just, however, as he reached the top of the great oak staircase, a door was flung open, two little white-robed figures appeared, and a large pillow whizzed past his head! There was evidently no time to be lost, so, hastily adopting the Fourth dimension of Space as a means of escape, he vanished through the wainscoting, and the house became quite quiet. On reaching a small secret chamber in the left wing, he leaned up against a moonbeam to recover his breath, and began to try and realize his position. Never, in a brilliant and uninterrupted career of three hundred years, had he been so grossly insulted. He thought of the Dowager Duchess, whom he had frightened into a fit as she stood before the glass in her lace and diamonds; of the four housemaids, who had gone into hysterics when he merely grinned at them through the curtains on one of the spare bedrooms; of the rector of the parish, whose candle he had blown out as he was coming late one night from the library, and who had been under the care of Sir William Gull ever since, a perfect martyr to nervous disorders; and of old Madame de Tremouillac, who, having wakened up one morning early and seen a skeleton seated in an armchair by the fire reading her diary, had been confined to her bed for six weeks with an attack of brain fever, and, on her recovery, had become reconciled to the Church, and broken off her connection with that notorious sceptic, Monsieur de Voltaire. He remembered the terrible night when the wicked Lord Canterville was found choking in his dressing-room, with the knave of diamonds half-way down his throat, and confessed, just before he died, that he had cheated Charles

James Fox out of £50,000 at Crockford's by means of that very card, and swore that the ghost had made him swallow it. All his great achievements came back to him again, from the butler who had shot himself in the pantry because he had seen a green hand tapping at the window-pane, to the beautiful Lady Stutfield, who was always obliged to wear a black velvet band round her throat to hide the mark of five fingers burnt upon her white skin, and who drowned herself at last in the carp-pond at the end of the King's Walk. With the enthusiastic egotism of the true artist, he went over his most celebrated performances, and smiled bitterly to himself as he recalled to mind his last appearance as "Red Reuben, or the Strangled Babe," his debut as "Guant Gibeon, the Blood-sucker of Bexley Moor," and the *furore* he had excited one lovely June evening by merely playing ninepins with his own bones upon the lawn-tennis ground. And after all this some wretched modern Americans were to come and offer him the Rising Sun Lubricator, and throw pillows at his head! It was quite unbearable. Besides, no ghost in history had ever been treated in this manner. Accordingly, he determined to have vengeance, and remained till daylight in an attitude of deep thought.

III

The next morning, when the Otis family met at breakfast, they discussed the ghost at some length. The United States Minister was naturally a little annoyed to find that his present had not been accepted. "I have no wish," he said, "to do the ghost any personal injury, and I must say that, considering the length of time he has been in the house, I don't think it is at all polite to throw pillows at him,"—a very just remark, at which, I am sorry to say, the twins burst into shouts of laughter. "Upon the other hand," he continued, "if he really declines to use the Rising Sun Lubricator, we shall have to take his chains from him. It would be quite impossible to sleep, with such a noise going on outside the bedrooms."

For the rest of the week, however, they were undisturbed, the only thing that excited any attention being the continual renewal of the blood-stain on the library floor. This certainly was very strange, as the door was always locked at night by Mr. Otis, and the windows kept closely barred. The chameleon-like colour, also, of the stain excited a good deal of comment. Some mornings it was a dull (almost Indian) red, then it would be vermilion, then a rich purple, and once when they came down for family prayers, according to the simple rites of the Free American Reformed Episcopalian Church, they found it a bright emerald-green. These kaleidoscopic changes naturally amused the party very much, and bets on the subject were freely made every evening. The only person who did not enter into the joke was little Virginia, who, for some unexplained reason, was always a good deal distressed at the sight of the blood-stain, and very nearly cried the morning it was emerald-green.

The second appearance of the ghost was on Sunday night. Shortly after they had gone to bed they were suddenly alarmed by a fearful crash in the hall. Rushing down-stairs, they found that a large suit of old armour had become detached from its stand, and had fallen on the stone floor, while seated in a high-backed chair was the Canterville ghost, rubbing his knees with an expression of acute agony on his face. The twins, having brought their pea-shooters with them, at once discharged two pellets on him, with that accuracy of aim which can only be attained by long and careful practice on a writing-master, while the United States Minister covered him with his revolver, and called upon him, in accordance with Californian etiquette, to hold up his hands! The ghost started up with a wild shriek of rage, and swept through them like a mist, extinguishing Washington Otis's candle as he passed, and so leaving them all in total darkness. On reaching the top of the staircase he recovered himself, and determined to give his celebrated peal of demoniac laughter. This he had on more than one occasion found extremely useful. It was said to have turned Lord Raker's wig grey in a single night, and had certainly made three of Lady Canterville's French governesses give warning before their month was up. He accordingly laughed his most horrible laugh, till the old vaulted roof rang and rang again, but hardly had the fearful echo died away when a door opened, and Mrs. Otis came out in a light blue dressing-gown. "I am afraid you are far from well," she said, "and have brought you a bottle of Doctor Dobell's tincture. If it is indigestion, you will find it a most excellent remedy." The ghost glared at her in fury, and began at once to make preparations for turning himself into a large black dog, an accomplishment for which he was justly renowned, and to which the family doctor always attributed the permanent idiocy of Lord Canterville's uncle, the Hon. Thomas Horton. The sound of approaching footsteps, however, made him hesitate in his fell purpose, so he contented himself with becoming faintly phosphorescent, and vanished with a deep churchyard groan, just as the twins had come up to him.

On reaching his room he entirely broke down, and became a prey to the most violent agitation. The vulgarity of the twins, and the gross materialism of Mrs. Otis, were naturally extremely annoying, but what really distressed him most was that he had been unable to wear the suit of mail. He had hoped that even modern Americans would be thrilled by the sight of a Spectre in armour, if for no more sensible reason, at least out of respect for their natural poet Longfellow, over whose graceful and attractive poetry he himself had whiled away many a weary hour when the Cantervilles were up in town. Besides it was his own suit. He had worn it with great success at the Kenilworth tournament, and had been highly complimented on it by no less a person than the Virgin Queen herself. Yet when he had put it on, he had been completely over-powered by the weight of the huge breastplate and steel casque, and had fallen heavily on the stone pavement, barking both his knees severely, and bruising the knuckles of his right hand.

For some days after this he was extremely ill, and hardly stirred out of his room at all, except to keep the blood-stain in proper repair. However, by taking great care of himself, he recovered, and resolved to make a third attempt to frighten the United States Minister and his family. He selected Friday, August 17th, for his appearance, and spent most of that day in looking over his wardrobe, ultimately deciding in favour of a large slouched hat with a red feather, a winding-sheet frilled at the wrists and neck, and a rusty dagger. Towards evening a violent storm of rain came on, and the wind was so high that all the windows and doors in the old house shook and rattled. In fact, it was just such weather as he loved. His plan of action was this. He was to make his way quietly to Washington Otis's room, gibber at him from the foot of the bed, and stab himself three times in the throat to the sound of low music. He bore Washington a special grudge, being quite aware that it was he who was in the habit of removing the famous Canterville blood-stain by means of Pinkerton's Paragon Detergent. Having reduced the reckless and foolhardy youth to a condition of abject terror, he was then to proceed to the room occupied by the United States Minister and his wife, and there to place a clammy hand on Mrs. Otis's forehead, while he hissed into her trembling husband's ear the awful secrets of the charnel-house. With regard to little Virginia, he had not quite made up his mind. She had never insulted him in any way, and was pretty and gentle. A few hollow groans from the wardrobe, he thought, would be more than sufficient, or, if that failed to wake her, he might grabble at the counterpane with palsy-twitching fingers. As for the twins, he was quite determined to teach them a lesson. The first thing to be done was, of course, to sit upon their chests, so as to produce the stifling sensation of nightmare. Then, as their beds were quite close to each other, to stand between them in the form of a green, icy-cold corpse, till they became paralyzed with fear, and finally, to throw off the winding-sheet, and crawl round the room, with white, bleached bones and one rolling eyeball, in the character of "Dumb Daniel, or the Suicide's Skeleton," a *rôle* in which he had on more than one occasion produced a great effect, and which he considered quite equal to his famous part of "Martin the Maniac, or the Masked Mystery."

At half-past ten he heard the family going to bed. For some time he was disturbed by wild shrieks of laughter from the twins, who, with the light-hearted gaiety of schoolboys, were evidently amusing themselves before they retired to rest, but at a quarter-past eleven all was still, and, as midnight sounded, he sallied forth. The owl beat against the window-panes, the raven croaked from the old yew-tree, and the wind wandered moaning round the house like a lost soul; but the Otis family slept unconscious of their doom, and high above the rain and storm he could hear the steady snoring of the Minister for the United States. He stepped stealthily out of the wainscoting, with an evil smile on his cruel, wrinkled mouth, and the moon hid her face in a cloud as he stole past the great oriel window, where his own arms and those of his murdered wife were blazoned in azure and gold. On and on he glided, like an evil shadow, the very darkness seeming to loathe him as he passed. Once he thought he heard something call, and stopped; but it was only the baying of a dog from the Red Farm, and he went on, muttering strange sixteenth-century curses, and ever and anon brandishing the rusty dagger in the midnight air. Finally he reached the corner of the passage that led to luckless Washington's room. For a moment he paused there, the wind blowing his long grey locks about his head, and twisting into grotesque and fantastic folds the nameless horror of the dead man's shroud. Then the clock struck the quarter, and he felt the time was come. He chuckled to himself, and turned the corner; but no sooner had he done so than, with a piteous wail of terror, he fell back, and hid his blanched face in his long, bony hands. Right in front of him was standing a horrible spectre, motionless as a carven image, and monstrous as a madman's dream! Its head was bald and burnished; its face round, and fat, and white; and hideous laughter seemed to have writhed its features into an eternal grin. From the eyes streamed rays of scarlet light, the mouth was a wide well of fire, and a hideous garment, like to his own, swathed with its silent snows the Titan form. On its breast was a placard with strange writing in antique characters, some scroll of shame it seemed, some record of wild sins, some awful calendar of crime, and, with its right hand, it bore aloft a falchion of gleaming steel.

Never having seen a ghost before, he naturally was terribly frightened, and, after a second hasty glance at the awful phantom, he fled back to his room, tripping up in his long winding-sheet as he sped down the corridor, and finally dropping the rusty dagger into the Minister's jack-boots, where it was found in the morning by the butler. Once in the privacy of his own apartment, he flung himself down on a small pallet-bed, and hid his face under the clothes. After a time, however, the brave old Canterville spirit asserted itself, and he determined to go and speak to the other ghost as soon as it was daylight. Accordingly, just as the dawn was touching the hills with silver, he returned towards the spot where he had first laid eyes on the grisly phantom, feeling that, after all, two ghosts were better than one, and that, by the aid of his new friend, he might safely grapple with the twins. On reaching the spot, however, a terrible sight met his gaze. Something had evidently happened to the spectre, for the light had entirely faded from its hollow eyes, the gleaming falchion had fallen from its hand, and it was leaning up against the wall in a strained and uncomfortable attitude. He rushed forward and seized it in his arms, when, to his horror, the head slipped off and rolled on the floor, the body assumed a recumbent posture, and he found himself clasping a white dimity bed-curtain, with a sweeping-brush, a kitchen cleaver, and a hollow turnip lying at his feet! Unable to understand this curious transformation, he clutched the placard with feverish haste, and there, in the grey morning light, he read these fearful words:—

YE OTIS GHOSTE
Ye Onlie True and Originale Spook,
Beware of Ye Imitationes.
All others are counterfeite.

The whole thing flashed across him. He had been tricked, foiled, and out-witted! The old Canterville look came into his eyes; he ground his toothless gums together; and, raising his withered hands high above his head, swore according to the picturesque phraseology of the antique school, that, when Chanticleer had sounded twice his merry horn, deeds of blood would be wrought, and murder walk abroad with silent feet.

Hardly had he finished this awful oath when, from the red-tiled roof of a distant homestead, a cock crew. He laughed a long, low, bitter laugh, and waited. Hour after hour he waited, but the cock, for some strange reason, did not crow again. Finally, at half-past seven, the arrival of the housemaids made him give up his fearful vigil, and he stalked back to his room, thinking of his vain oath and baffled purpose. There he consulted several books of ancient chivalry, of which he was exceedingly fond, and found that, on every occasion on which this oath had been used, Chanticleer had always crowed a second time. "Perdition seize the naughty fowl," he muttered, "I have seen the day when, with my stout spear, I would have run him through the gorge, and made him crow for me an 'twere in death!" He then retired to a comfortable lead coffin, and stayed there till evening.

IV

The next day the ghost was very weak and tired. The terrible excitement of the last four weeks was beginning to have its effect. His nerves were completely shattered, and he started at the slightest noise. For five days he kept his room, and at last made up his mind to give up the point of the bloodstain on the library floor. If the Otis family did not want it, they clearly did not deserve it. They were evidently people on a low, material plane of existence, and quite incapable of appreciating the symbolic value of sensuous phenomena. The question of phantasmic apparitions, and the development of astral bodies, was of course quite a different matter, and really not under his control. It was his solemn duty to appear in the corridor once a week, and to gibber from the large oriel window on the first and third Wednesdays in every month, and he did not see how he could honourably escape from his obligations. It is quite true that his life had been very evil, but, upon the other hand, he was most conscientious in all things connected with the supernatural. For the next three Saturdays, accordingly, he traversed the corridor as usual between midnight and three o'clock, taking every possible precaution against being either heard or seen. He removed his boots, trod as lightly as possible on the old worm-eaten boards, wore a large black velvet cloak, and was careful to use the Rising Sun Lubricator for oiling his chains. I am bound to acknowledge that it was with a good deal of difficulty that he brought himself to adopt this last mode of protection. However, one night, while the family were at dinner, he slipped into Mr. Otis's bedroom and carried off the bottle. He felt a little humiliated at first, but afterwards was sensible enough to see that there was a great deal to be said for the invention, and, to a certain degree, it served his purpose. Still in spite of everything he was not left unmolested. Strings were continually being stretched across the corridor, over which he tripped in the dark, and on one occasion, while dressed for the part of "Black Isaac, or the Huntsman of Hogley Woods," he met with a severe fall, through treading on a butter-slide, which the twins had constructed from the entrance of the Tapestry Chamber to the top of the oak stair-case. This last insult so enraged him, that he resolved to make one final effort to assert his dignity and social position, and determined to visit the insolent young Etonians the next night in his celebrated character of "Reckless Rupert, or the Headless Earl."

He had not appeared in this disguise for more than seventy years; in fact, not since he had so frightened pretty Lady Barbara Modish by means of it, that she suddenly broke off her engagement with the present Lord Canterville's grandfather, and ran away to Gretna Green with handsome Jack Castletown, declaring that nothing in the world would induce her to marry into a family that allowed such a horrible phantom to walk up and down the terrace at twilight. Poor Jack was afterwards shot in a duel by Lord Canterville on Wandsworth Common, and Lady Barbara died of a broken heart at Tunbridge Wells before the year was out, so, in every way, it had been a great success. It was, however an extremely difficult "make-up," if I may use such a theatrical expression in connection with one of the greatest mysteries of the supernatural, or, to employ a more scientific term, the higher-natural world, and it took him fully three hours to make his preparations. At last everything was ready, and he was very pleased with his appearance. The big leather riding-boots that went with the dress were just a little too large for him, and he could only find one of the two horse-pistols, but, on the whole, he was quite satisfied, and at a quarter-past one he glided out of the wainscoting and crept down the corridor. On reaching the room occupied by the twins, which I should mention was called the Blue Bed Chamber, on account of the colour of its hangings, he found the door just ajar. Wishing to make an effective entrance, he flung it wide open, when a heavy jug of water fell right down on him, wetting him to the skin, and just missing his left shoulder by a couple of inches. At the same moment he heard stifled shrieks of laughter proceeding from the four-post bed. The shock to his nervous system was so great that he fled back to his room as hard as he could go, and the next day he was laid up with a severe cold. The only thing that at all consoled him in the whole affair was the fact that he had not brought his head with him, for, had he done so, the consequences might have been very serious.

He now gave up all hope of ever frightening this rude American family, and contented himself, as a rule, with creeping about the passages in list slippers, with a thick red muffler round his throat for fear of draughts, and a small arquebuse, in case he should be attacked by the twins. The final blow he received occurred on the 19th of September. He had gone down-stairs to the great entrance-hall, feeling sure that there, at any rate, he would be quite unmolested, and was amusing himself by making satirical remarks on the large Saroni photographs of the United States Minister and his wife which had now taken the place of the Canterville family pictures. He was simply but neatly clad in a long shroud, spotted with churchyard mould, had tied up his jaw with a strip of yellow linen, and carried a small lantern and a sexton's spade. In fact, he was dressed for the character of "Jonas the Graveless, or the Corpse-Snatcher of Chertsey Barn," one of his most remarkable impersonations, and one which the Cantervilles had every reason to remember, as it was the real origin of their quarrel with their neighbour. Lord Rufford. It was about a quarter-past two o'clock in the morning, and, as far as he could ascertain, no one was stirring. As he was strolling towards the library, however, to see if there were any traces left of the blood-stain, suddenly there leaped out on him from a dark corner two figures, who waved their arms wildly above their heads, and shrieked out "BOO!" in his ear.

Seized with a panic, which, under the circumstances, was only natural, he rushed for the staircase, but found Washington Otis waiting for him there with the big garden-syringe, and being thus hemmed in by his enemies on every side, and driven almost to bay, he vanished into the great iron stove, which, fortunately for him, was not lit, and had to make his way home through the flues and chimneys, arriving at his own room in a terrible state of dirt, disorder, and despair.

After this he was not seen again on any nocturnal expedition. The twins lay in wait for him on several occasions, and strewed the passages with nutshells every night to the great annoyance of their parents and the servants, but it was of no avail. It was quite evident that his feelings were so wounded that he would not appear. Mr. Otis consequently resumed his great work on the history of the Democratic Party, on which he had been engaged for some years; Mrs. Otis organized a wonderful clam-bake, which amazed the whole county; the boys took to lacrosse euchre, poker, and other American national games, and Virginia rode about the lanes on her pony, accompanied by the young Duke of Cheshire, who had come to spend the last week of his holidays at Canterville Chase. It was generally assumed that the ghost had gone away, and, in fact, Mr. Otis wrote a letter to that effect to Lord Canterville, who, in reply, expressed his great pleasure at the news, and sent his best congratulations to the Minister's worthy wife.

The Otises, however, were deceived, for the ghost was still in the house, and though now almost an invalid, was by no means ready to let matters rest, particularly as he heard that among the guests was the young Duke of Cheshire, whose grand-uncle, Lord Francis Stilton, had once bet a hundred guineas with Colonel Carbury that he would play dice with the Canterville ghost, and was found the next morning lying on the floor of the card-room in such a helpless paralytic state that, though he lived on to a great age, he was never able to say anything again but "Double

Sixes." The story was well known at the time, though, of course, out of respect to the feelings of the two noble families, every attempt was made to hush it up, and a full account of all the circumstances connected with it will be found in the third volume of Lord Tattle's *Recollections of the Prince Regent and his Friends*. The ghost, then, was naturally very anxious to show that he had not lost his influence over the Stiltons, with whom, indeed, he was distantly connected, his own first cousin having been married *en secondes noces* to the Sieur de Bulkeley, from whom, as every one knows, the Dukes of Cheshire are lineally descended. Accordingly, he made arrangements for appearing to Virginia's little lover in his celebrated impersonation of "The Vampire Monk, or the Bloodless Benedictine," a performance so horrible that when old Lady Startup saw it, which she did on one fatal New Year's Eve, in the year 1764, she went off into the most piercing shrieks, which culminated in violent apoplexy, and died in three days, after disinheriting the Cantervilles, who were her nearest relations, and leaving all her money to her London apothecary. At the last moment, however, his terror of the twins prevented his leaving his room, and the little Duke slept in peace under the great feathered canopy in the Royal Bedchamber, and dreamed of Virginia.

V

A few days after this, Virginia and her curly-haired cavalier went out riding on Brockley meadows, where she tore her habit so badly in getting through a hedge that, on their return home, she made up her mind to go up by the back staircase so as not to be seen. As she was running past the Tapestry Chamber, the door of which happened to be open, she fancied she saw some one inside, and thinking it was her mother's maid, who sometimes used to bring her work there, looked in to ask her to mend her habit. To her immense surprise, however, it was the Canterville Ghost himself! He was sitting by the window, watching the ruined gold of the yellowing trees fly through the air, and the red leaves dancing madly down the long avenue. His head was leaning on his hand, and his whole attitude was one of extreme depression. Indeed, so forlorn, and so much out of repair did he look, that little Virginia, whose first idea had been to run away and lock herself in her room, was filled with pity, and determined to try and comfort him. So light was her footfall, and so deep his melancholy, that he was not aware of her presence till she spoke to him.

"I am so sorry for you," she said, "but my brothers are going back to Eton to-morrow, and then, if you behave yourself, no one will annoy you."

"It is absurd asking me to behave myself," he answered, looking round in astonishment at the pretty little girl who had ventured to address him, "quite absurd. I must rattle my chains, and groan through keyholes, and walk about at night, if that is what you mean. It is my only reason for existing."

"It is no reason at all for existing, and you know you have been very wicked. Mrs. Umney told us, the first day we arrived here, that you had killed your wife."

"Well, I quite admit it," said the Ghost, petulantly, "but it was a purely family matter, and concerned no one else."

"It is very wrong to kill any one," said Virginia, who at times had a sweet puritan gravity, caught from some old New England ancestor.

"Oh, I hate the cheap severity of abstract ethics! My wife was very plain, never had my ruffs properly starched, and knew nothing about cookery. Why, there was a buck I had shot in Hogley Woods, a magnificent pricket, and do you know how she had it sent to table? However, it is no matter now, for it is all over, and I don't think it was very nice of her brothers to starve me to death, though I did kill her."

"Starve you to death? Oh, Mr. Ghost—I mean Sir Simon, are you hungry? I have a sandwich in my case. Would you like it?"

"No, thank you, I never eat anything now; but it is very kind of you, all the same, and you are much nicer than the rest of your horrid, rude, vulgar, dishonest family."

"Stop!" cried Virginia, stamping her foot, "it is you who are rude, and horrid, and vulgar, and as for dishonesty, you know you stole the paints out of my box to try and furbish up that ridiculous bloodstain in the library. First you took all my reds, including the vermilion, and I couldn't do any more sunsets, then you took the emerald-green and the chrome-yellow, and finally I had nothing left but indigo and Chinese white, and could only do moonlight scenes, which are always depressing to look at, and not at all easy to paint. I never told on you, though I was very much annoyed, and it was most ridiculous, the whole thing; for who ever heard of emerald-green blood?"

"Well, really," said the Ghost, rather meekly, "what was I to do? It is a very difficult thing to get real blood nowadays, and, as your brother began it all with his Paragon Detergent, I certainly saw no reason why I should not have your paints. As for colour, that is always a matter of taste: the Cantervilles have blue blood, for instance, the very bluest in England; but I know you Americans don't care for things of this kind."

"You know nothing about it, and the best thing you can do is to emigrate and improve your mind. My father will be only too happy to give you a free passage, and though there is a heavy duty on spirits of every kind, there will be no difficulty about the Custom House, as the officers are all Democrats. Once in New York, you are sure to be a great success. I know lots of people there who would give a hundred thousand dollars to have a grandfather, and much more than that to have a family ghost."

"I don't think I should like America."

"I suppose because we have no ruins and no curiosities," said Virginia, satirically.

"No ruins! no curiosities!" answered the Ghost; "you have your navy and your manners."

"Good evening; I will go and ask papa to get the twins an extra week's holiday."

"Please don't go. Miss Virginia," he cried; "I am so lonely and so unhappy, and I really don't know what to do. I want to go to sleep and I cannot."

"That's quite absurd! You have merely to go to bed and blow out the candle. It is very difficult sometimes to keep awake, especially at church, but there is no difficulty at all about sleeping. Why, even babies know how to do that, and they are not very clever."

"I have not slept for three hundred years," he said sadly, and Virginia's beautiful blue eyes opened in wonder; "for three hundred years I have not slept, and I am so tired."

Virginia grew quite grave, and her little lips trembled like rose-leaves. She came towards him, and kneeling down at his side, looked up into his old withered face.

"Poor, poor Ghost," she murmured; "have you no place where you can sleep?"

"Far away beyond the pine-woods," he answered, in a low, dreamy voice, "there is a little garden. There the grass grows long and deep, there are the great white stars of the hemlock flower, there the nightingale sings all night long. All night long he sings, and the cold crystal moon looks down, and the yew-tree spreads out its giant arms over the sleepers."

Virginia's eyes grew dim with tears, and she hid her face in her hands.

"You mean the Garden of Death," she whispered.

"Yes, death. Death must be so beautiful. To lie in the soft brown earth, with the grasses waving above one's head, and listen to silence. To have no yesterday, and no to-morrow. To forget time, to forget life, to be at peace. You can help me. You can open for me the portals of death's house, for love is always with you, and love is stronger than death is."

Virginia trembled, a cold shudder ran through her, and for a few moments there was silence. She felt as if she was in a terrible dream.

Then the ghost spoke again, and his voice sounded like the sighing of the wind.

"Have you ever read the old prophecy on the library window?"

"Oh, often," cried the little girl, looking up; "I know it quite well. It is painted in curious black letters, and is difficult to read. There are only six lines:

"'When a golden girl can win
Prayer from out the lips of sin,
When the barren almond bears.
And a little child gives away its tears,
Then shall all the house be still
And peace come to Canterville.'

But I don't know what they mean."

"They mean," he said, sadly, "that you must weep with me for my sins, because I have no tears, and pray with me for my soul, because I have no faith, and then, if you have always been sweet, and good, and gentle, the angel of death will have mercy on me. You will see fearful shapes in darkness, and wicked voices will whisper in your ear, but they will not harm you, for against the purity of a little child the powers of Hell cannot prevail."

Virginia made no answer, and the ghost wrung his hands in wild despair as he looked down at her bowed golden head. Suddenly she stood up, very pale, and with a strange light in her eyes. "I am not afraid," she said firmly, "and I will ask the angel to have mercy on you."

He rose from his seat with a faint cry of joy, and taking her hand bent over it with old-fashioned grace and kissed it. His fingers were as cold as ice, and his lips burned like fire, but Virginia did not falter, as he led her across the dusky room. On the faded green tapestry were broidered little huntsmen. They blew their tasselled horns and with their tiny hands waved to her to go back. "Go back! little Virginia," they cried, "go back!" but the ghost clutched her hand more tightly, and she shut her eyes against them. Horrible animals with lizard tails and goggle eyes blinked at her from the carven chimneypiece, and murmured, "Beware! little Virginia, beware! we may never see you again," but the Ghost glided on more swiftly, and Virginia did not listen. When they reached the end of the room he stopped, and muttered some words she could not understand. She opened her eyes, and saw the wall slowly fading away like a mist, and a great black cavern in front of her. A bitter cold wind swept round them, and she felt something pulling at her dress. "Quick, quick," cried the Ghost, "or it will be too late," and in a moment the wainscoting had closed behind them, and the Tapestry Chamber was empty.

VI

About ten minutes later, the bell rang for tea, and, as Virginia did not come down, Mrs. Otis sent up one of the footmen to tell her. After a little time he returned and said that he could not find Miss Virginia anywhere. As she was in the habit of going out to the garden every evening to get flowers for the dinner-table, Mrs. Otis was not at all alarmed at first, but when six o'clock struck, and Virginia did not appear, she became really agitated, and sent the boys out to look for her, while she herself and Mr. Otis searched every room in the house. At half-past six the boys came back and said that they could find no trace of their sister anywhere. They were all now in the greatest state of excitement, and did not know what to do, when Mr. Otis suddenly remembered that, some few days before, he had given a band of gipsies permission to camp in the park. He accordingly at once set off for Blackfell Hollow, where he knew they were, accompanied by his eldest son and two of the farm-servants. The little Duke of Cheshire, who was perfectly frantic with anxiety, begged hard to be allowed to go too, but Mr. Otis would not allow him, as he was afraid there might be a scuffle. On arriving at the spot, however, he found that the gipsies had gone, and it was evident that their departure had been rather sudden, as the fire was still burning, and some plates were lying on the grass. Having sent off Washington and the two men to scour the district, he ran home, and despatched telegrams to all the police inspectors in the county, telling them to look out for a little girl who had been kidnapped by tramps or gipsies. He then ordered his horse to be brought round, and, after insisting on his wife and the three boys sitting down to dinner, rode off down the Ascot road with a groom. He had hardly, however, gone a couple of miles, when he heard somebody galloping after him, and, looking round, saw the little Duke coming up on his pony, with his face very flushed, and no hat. "I'm awfully sorry, Mr. Otis," gasped out the boy, "but I can't eat any dinner as long as Virginia is lost. Please don't be angry with me; if you had let us be engaged last year, there would never have been all this trouble. You won't send me back, will you? I can't go! I won't go!"

The Minister could not help smiling at the handsome young scapegrace, and was a good deal touched at his devotion to Virginia, so leaning down from his horse, he patted him kindly on the shoulders, and said, "Well, Cecil, if you won't go back, I suppose you must come with me, but I must get you a hat at Ascot."

"Oh, bother my hat! I want Virginia!" cried the little Duke, laughing, and they galloped on to the railway station. There Mr. Otis inquired of the station-master if any one answering to the description of Virginia had been seen on the platform, but could get no news of her. The station-master, however, wired up and down the line, and assured him that a strict watch would be kept for her, and, after having bought a hat for the little Duke from a linen-draper, who was just putting up his shutters, Mr. Otis rode off to Bexley, a village about four miles away, which he was told was a well-known haunt of the gipsies, as there was a large common next to it. Here they roused up the rural policeman, but could get no information from him, and, after riding all over the common, they turned their horses' heads homewards, and reached the Chase about eleven o'clock, dead-tired and almost heart-broken. They found Washington and the twins waiting for them at the gate-house with lanterns, as the avenue was very dark. Not the slightest trace of Virginia had been discovered. The gipsies had been caught on Brockley meadows, but she was not with them, and they had explained their sudden departure by saying that they had mistaken the date of Chorton Fair, and had gone off in a hurry for fear they should be late. Indeed, they had been quite distressed at hearing of Virginia's disappearance, as they were very grateful to Mr. Otis for having allowed them to camp in his park, and four of their number had stayed behind to help in the search. The carp-pond had been dragged, and the whole Chase thoroughly gone over, but without any result. It was evident that, for that night at any rate, Virginia was lost to them; and it was in a state of the deepest depression that Mr. Otis and the boys walked up to the house, the groom following behind with the two horses and the pony. In the hall they found a group of frightened servants, and lying on a sofa in the library was poor Mrs. Otis, almost out of her mind with terror and anxiety, and having her forehead bathed with eau de cologne by the old housekeeper. Mr. Otis at once insisted on her having something to eat, and ordered up supper for the whole party. It was a melancholy meal, as hardly any one spoke, and even the twins were awestruck and subdued, as they were very fond of their sister. When they had finished, Mr. Otis, in spite of the entreaties of the little Duke, ordered them all to bed, saying that nothing more could be done that night, and that he would telegraph in the morning to Scotland Yard for some detectives to be sent down immediately. Just as they were passing out of the dining-room, midnight began to boom from the clock tower, and when the last stroke sounded they heard a crash and a sudden shrill cry; a dreadful peal of thunder shook the house, a strain of unearthly music floated through the air, a panel at the top of the staircase flew back with a loud noise, and out on the landing, looking very pale and white, with a little casket in her hand, stepped Virginia. In a moment they had all rushed up to her. Mrs. Otis clasped her passion-ately in her arms, the Duke smothered her with violent kisses, and the twins executed a wild war-dance round the group.

"Good heavens! child, where have you been?" said Mr. Otis, rather angrily, thinking that she had been playing some foolish trick on them. "Cecil and I have been riding all over the country looking for you, and your mother has been frightened to death. You must never play these practical jokes any more."

"Except on the Ghost! except on the Ghost!" shrieked the twins, as they capered about.

"My own darling, thank God you are found; you must never leave my side again," murmured Mrs. Otis, as she kissed the trembling child, and smoothed the tangled gold of her hair.

"Papa," said Virginia, quietly, "I have been with the Ghost. He is dead, and you must come and see him. He had been very wicked, but he was really sorry for all that he had done, and he gave me this box of beautiful jewels before he died."

The whole family gazed at her in mute amazement, but she was quite grave and serious; and, turning round, she led them through the opening in the wainscoting down a narrow secret corridor, Washington following with a lighted candle, which he had caught up from the table. Finally, they came to a great oak door, studded with rusty nails. When Virginia touched it, it swung back on its heavy hinges, and they found themselves in a little low room, with a vaulted ceiling, and one tiny grated window. Imbedded in the wall was a huge iron ring, and chained to it was a gaunt skeleton, that was stretched out at full length on the stone floor, and seemed to be trying to grasp with its long fleshless fingers an old-fashioned trencher and ewer, that were placed just out of its reach. The jug had evidently been once filled with water, as it was covered inside with green mould. There was nothing on the trencher but a pile of dust. Virginia knelt down beside the skeleton, and, folding her little hands together, began to pray silently, while the rest of the party looked on in wonder at the terrible tragedy whose secret was now disclosed to them.

"Hallo!" suddenly exclaimed one of the twins, who had been looking out of the window to try and discover in what wing of the house the room was situated. "Hallo! the old withered almond-tree has blossomed. I can see the flowers quite plainly in the moonlight."

"God has forgiven him," said Virginia, gravely, as she rose to her feet, and a beautiful light seemed to illumine her face.

"What an angel you are!" cried the young Duke, and he put his arm round her neck, and kissed her.

*

VII

Four days after these curious incidents, a funeral started from Canterville Chase at about eleven o'clock at night. The hearse was drawn by eight black horses, each of which carried on its head a great tuft of nodding ostrich-plumes, and the leaden coffin was covered by a rich purple pall, on which was embroidered in gold the Canterville coat-of-arms. By the side of the hearse and the coaches walked the servants with lighted torches, and the whole procession was wonderfully impressive. Lord Canterville was the chief mourner, having come up specially from Wales to attend the funeral, and sat in the first carriage along with little Virginia. Then came the United States Minister and his wife, then Washington and the three boys, and in the last carriage was Mrs. Umney. It was generally felt that, as she had been frightened by the ghost for more than fifty years of her life, she had a right to see the last of him. A deep grave had been dug in the corner of the churchyard, just under the old yew-tree, and the service was read in the most impressive manner by the Rev. Augustus Dampier. When the ceremony was over, the servants, according to an old custom observed in the Canterville family, extinguished their torches, and, as the coffin was being lowered into the grave, Virginia stepped forward, and laid on it a large cross made of white and pink almond-blossoms. As she did so, the moon came out from behind a cloud, and flooded with its silent silver the little churchyard, and from a distant copse a nightingale began to sing. She thought of the ghost's description of the Garden of Death, her eyes became dim with tears, and she hardly spoke a word during the drive home.

The next morning, before Lord Canterville went up to town, Mr. Otis had an interview with him on the subject of the jewels the ghost had given to Virginia. They were perfectly magnificent, especially a certain ruby necklace with old Venetian setting, which was really a superb specimen of sixteenth-century work, and their value was so great that Mr. Otis felt considerable scruples about allowing his daughter to accept them.

"My lord," he said, "I know that in this country mortmain is held to apply to trinkets as well as to land, and it is quite clear to me that these jewels are, or should be, heirlooms in your family. I must beg you, accordingly, to take them to London with you, and to regard them simply as a portion of your property which has been restored to you under certain strange conditions. As for my daughter, she is merely a child, and has as yet, I am glad to say, but little interest in such appurtenances of idle luxury. I am also informed by Mrs. Otis, who, I may say, is no mean authority upon Art,—having had the privilege of spending several winters in Boston when she was a girl,—that these gems are of great monetary worth, and if offered for sale would fetch a tall price. Under these circumstances, Lord Canterville, I feel sure that you will recognize how impossible it would be for me to allow them to remain in the possession of any member of my family; and, indeed, all such vain gauds and toys, however suitable or necessary to the dignity of the British aristocracy, would be completely out of place among those who have been brought up on the severe, and I believe immortal, principles of Republican simplicity. Perhaps I should mention that Virginia is very anxious that you should allow her to retain the box, as a memento of your unfortunate but misguided ancestor. As it is extremely old, and consequently a good deal out of repair, you may perhaps think fit to comply with her request. For my own part, I confess I am a good deal surprised to find a child of mine expressing sympathy with mediaevalism in any form, and can only account for it by the fact that Virginia was born in one of your London suburbs shortly after Mrs. Otis had returned from a trip to Athens."

Lord Canterville listened very gravely to the worthy Minister's speech, pulling his grey moustache now and then to hide an involuntary smile, and when Mr. Otis had ended, he shook him cordially by the hand, and said: "My dear sir, your charming little daughter rendered my unlucky ancestor, Sir Simon, a very important service, and I and my family are much indebted to her for her marvellous courage and pluck. The jewels are clearly hers, and, egad, I believe that if I were heartless enough to take them from her, the wicked old fellow would be out of his grave in a fortnight, leading me the devil of a life. As for their being heirlooms, nothing is an heirloom that is not so mentioned in a will or legal document, and the existence of these jewels has been quite unknown. I assure you I have no more claim on them than your butler, and when Miss Virginia grows up, I dare say she will be pleased to have pretty things to wear. Besides, you forget, Mr. Otis, that you took the furniture and the ghost at a valuation, and anything that belonged to the ghost passed at once into your possession, as, whatever activity Sir Simon may have shown in the corridor at night, in point of law he was really dead, and you acquired his property by purchase."

Mr. Otis was a good deal distressed at Lord Canterville's refusal, and begged him to reconsider his decision, but the good-natured peer was quite firm, and finally induced the Minister to allow his daughter to retain the present the ghost had given her, and when, in the spring of 1890, the young Duchess of Cheshire was presented at the Queen's first drawing-room on the occasion of her marriage, her jewels were the universal theme of admiration. For Virginia received the coronet, which is the reward of all good little American girls, and was married to her boy-lover as soon as he came of age. They were both so charming, and they loved each other so much, that every one was delighted at the match, except the old Marchioness of Dumbleton, who had tried to catch the Duke for one of her seven unmarried daughters, and had given no less than three expensive dinner-parties for that purpose, and, strange to say, Mr. Otis himself. Mr. Otis was extremely fond of the young Duke personally, but, theoretically, he objected to titles, and, to use his own words, "was not without apprehension lest, amid the enervating influences of a pleasure-loving aristocracy, the true principles of Republican simplicity should be forgotten." His objections, however, were completely overruled, and I believe that when he walked up the aisle of St. George's, Hanover Square, with his daughter leaning on his arm, there was not a prouder man in the whole length and breadth of England.

The Duke and Duchess, after the honeymoon was over, went down to Canterville Chase, and on the day after their arrival they walked over in the afternoon to the lonely churchyard by the pine-woods. There had been a great deal of difficulty at first about the inscription on Sir Simon's tombstone, but finally it had been decided to engrave on it simply the initials of the old gentleman's name, and the verse from the library window. The Duchess had brought with her some lovely roses, which she strewed upon the grave, and after they had stood by it for some time they strolled into the ruined chancel of the old abbey. There the Duchess sat down on a fallen pillar, while her husband lay at her feet smoking a cigarette and looking up at her beautiful eyes. Suddenly he threw his cigarette away, took hold of her hand, and said to her, "Virginia, a wife should have no secrets from her husband."

"Dear Cecil! I have no secrets from you."

"Yes, you have," he answered, smiling, "you have never told me what happened to you when you were locked up with the ghost."

"I have never told any one, Cecil," said Virginia, gravely.

"I know that, but you might tell me."

"Please don't ask me, Cecil, I cannot tell you. Poor Sir Simon! I owe him a great deal. Yes, don't laugh, Cecil, I really do. He made me see what Life is, and what Death signifies, and why Love is stronger than both."

The Duke rose and kissed his wife lovingly.

You can have your secret as long as I have your heart," he murmured.

"You have always had that, Cecil."

"And you will tell our children some day, won't you?"

Virginia blushed.

THE BEST OF BETTY

Jincy Willett

Jincy Willett (1946–) is the author of *Jenny and the Jaws of Life*, winner of the National Book Award, and *The Writing Class*, both of which have been translated and sold internationally. Her stories have been published in *Cosmopolitan*, *McSweeney's Quarterly* and other magazines. She frequently reviews for *The New York Times Book Review*.

DEAR BETTY:

I'm only forty-two years old and already going through the Change. I tried for twenty years to get pregnant and now I never will. Also, I get horrible cluster migraines now. The worst ones feel like a huge tarantula is clamped to my head with his legs sticking into my eyes and ears, and I have to scream with the pain. Next Tuesday I'm going to have all my teeth pulled, because the hormones have rotted my gums. I'm forty-two years old and for the rest of my life I'm going to sleep with my teeth in a glass by the bed. I hate being a woman. I hate my life. I hate Iowa. If I didn't believe in hell I'd kill myself.

Hopeless in the Heartland

DEAR HOPELESS:

What's the question?

Sorry, Readers. It's broken record time again. (1) Seek the aid of a competent therapist or clergyman, (2) Keep busy, (3) Above all, don't think about yourself so much, because (4) WHINING DOESNT ADVANCE THE BALL

For starters, Hopeless, why don't you rewrite this letter, only instead of cataloguing your complaints, include everything you have to be grateful for. You'll be amazed at how well this works.

DEAR BETTY:

Calling all Tooth Fairies! Don't throw away your kids' teeth! Save them up until you have a good third cupful, then scatter them around your tulip beds come spring, and you won't lose one bulb to marauding squirrels. Scares the dickens out of them, I guess!

Petunia

DEAR PETUNIA:

I guess it would! Thanks for another of your timely and original gardening tips.

DEAR BETTY:

Lately, at parties, my husband has started calling me "Lard-bottom." I know he loves me, and he says he doesn't mean anything by it, but he hurts me terribly. Last night, at the bowling alley with some of his trucker buddies, he kept referring to me as "Wide Load." Betty, I cried all night.

We're both big fans of yours. Would you comment on his cruel behavior? He'd pay attention to you. Tell him that I may have put on weight, but I'm still a

Human Being

DEAR HUMAN:

Yes, a human being with an enormous behind. Sorry, Toots. If I read correctly between the lines, hubby's worried sick about your health. Try a little self-control. Quit stuffing your face.

DEAR BETTY:

Last winter my sister and I moved out here to Drygulch, Arizona, for her health. She's doing well, but I've developed tic douloureux, of all things, and the spasms are unpredictable and agonizing. Our nearest doctor is fifty miles away, as is, for that matter, our nearest neighbor. I can't help feeling I'd be better off in Tucson or Phoenix, near a large medical center, but my sister, who's quite reclusive, says that if we moved her emphysema would just kick up again. Should we split up? Do I have the right to leave her, on account of a disease which, though painful, is not life-threatening?

Dolorous in Drygulch

DEAR DOLOROUS:

Why not join a tic douloureux support group? If there isn't already one in the area, why not start one? (The company might bring Sis out of her shell!)

DEAR BETTY:

Isn't it about time for a rerun of "Betty Believes"? I'd love to get a new copy laminated for my niece.

Happiness Is

DEAR HAPPINESS:

Of course. Here goes:

BETTY BELIEVES

1. That everything has a funny side to it.
2. That whining doesn't advance the ball.
3. That there's always somebody worse off than you.
4. That there's such a thing as being too smart for your own good.

5. That there are worse things in the world than ignorance and mediocrity.
6. That it takes all kinds.
7. That nobody's opinion is worth more than anybody else's.
8. That the more things stay the same, the better.
9. That everything happens for a good reason.
10. That no one ever died from an insult to the intelligence.

DEAR BETTY:

My Grandma Claire used to read your column every morning with her first cup of coffee and cigarette of the day. She called "Ask Betty" the real news. She said that following the progress of your career over the years was her only truly wicked pleasure, and that it was like watching a massacre through a telescope. What did she mean by that? She got throat cancer and died, and the last thing she said to me was, "There are too atheists in foxholes." My mom says she was out of her mind. What do you think?

Fourteen and Wondering

DEAR WONDERING:

That your Grandma Claire will not have died in vain if you will heed the lesson of her life: *Don't smoke.*

CONFIDENTIAL to *First Person Singular.*

Is it worth it, kid? Is it really?

Sure, on the one side you have money—obscene amounts of money—not to mention job security, reputation, celebrity. But... what about the numbing boredom? What about self-respect? What about, you should pardon the expression, honor? Huh, Toots?

I mean, who's really contemptible here? Them, or you?

Hint: Who's got the ulcer?

Who's got the whim-whams?
Who's got the blues in the night?

DEAR BETTY:

This is going to sound ridiculous, but hear me out. My husband smacks his lips in his sleep and it's driving me batty. If he were only snoring or gnashing his teeth, but this is a licking sound, a lapping, sipping, slurping sound, like a huge baby gumming pureed peas in the dark, and it makes my flesh crawl. I've tried nudging him awake, but he just looks at me so pitifully, and then I feel guilty. Imagine how he'd feel if I told him what I really want, which is my own bed in my own separate bedroom! Help!

Nauseous in Nashville

DEAR NAUSEOUS:

Sounds like hubby has some deep dark cravings, or so my sleep disorder experts tell me. Why not fix him up a yummy bowl of butter-scotch pudding (from scratch) just before bedtime?

By the way… you mean "nauseated," dear.

DEAR BETTY:

You want to know what burns me up? Inconsiderate bozos who jam up the speedy checkout line with grocery carts loaded to the brim, and moronic bimbos who let their children rip open bags of candy and cereal boxes and knock over jelly jars, and don't even have the decency to tell the stockboy to clean up their disgusting mess. I just got back from two hours at the grocery store and my new pumps are covered with mince-meat. What do you think of these lunkheads?

Burned Up

DEAR BURNED:

These people are not bozos, bimbos, or lunkheads. They are trash.

DEAR BETTY:

I am 135 pounds of screaming muscle in crepe-soled shoes. I groan under enormous trays laden with exotic delicacies I shall never taste, as they are beyond my meager economic means. Having seen your face once I am able to connect it with the food and drink of your choice. I smile when you are rude to me and apologize when the fault lies in the kitchen. I walk the equivalent of five miles each night on throbbing feet to satisfy your every whim, and when you are stuffed and have no further need of me, I act grateful for a substandard tip, if at all. I am

Your Waitress

DEAR WAITRESS:

Thank you.
What's the question?

DEAR BETTY:

You hear from so many unfortunates with serious problems that I feel a bit ashamed to take up your time this way. I am an attractive woman of 59; my thighs are perfectly smooth, my waist unthickened, I still have both my breasts and all my teeth; in fact I am two dress sizes smaller than I was at eighteen. My three grown daughters are intelligent, healthy, and independent. My husband and I are as much in love as when we first were married, despite the depth of our familiarity, and the, by now, considerable conflation of our tastes, political beliefs, preferences in music and art, and, of course, memories. He still interests and pleasures me; miraculously our sexual life remains joyous, inventive, and mutually fulfilling. I continue to adore the challenge and variety of my career as an ethnic dance therapist. We have never had to worry about money. Our country home is lovely, and very old, and solidly set down in a place of incomparable, ever shifting beauty; our many friends, old and new, are delightful people, amusing and wise, and every one of them honorable and a source of strength to us.

And yet, with all of this, and more, I am frequently very sad, and cannot rid myself of a growing, formless, yet very real sense of devastating loss, no less hideous for its utter irrationality. Forgive me, but does this make any sense to you?

Niobe

DEAR NIOBE:

Certainly. You're lying about the sex.

DEAR BETTY:

Why not scissor the cups out of your old brassieres and set them out in your annual garden as little domes to protect fragile seedlings? It looks wacky but it sure does the trick!

Petunia

DEAR PETUNIA:

Why the heck not? And hey, don't throw away those brassiere *straps*! Kids love to carry their schoolbooks in them, especially once you've disguised their embarrassing identity with precision-cut strips of silver mylar cemented front and back with epoxy, then adorned with tiny hand-sewn appliques in animal or rock-star designs. Use your imagination!

CONFIDENTIAL to *Smarting and Smiling*:

What you describe is not a "richly deserved comeuppance" but a sexual perversion, which, aside from being your own business and none of mine, is harmless enough and, if I read accurately between the lines, apparently works well for both of you.

You might just try these thought experiments, though: Imagine the effect upon your sex life of: a business failure, the birth of a child; rheumatoid arthritis (his); a positive biopsy (yours); the death of a child; a sudden terrifying sense of vastation that comes to either of you at three in the morning; a Conelrad Alert. In what ways would it differ from the experience of a couple for whom the concepts of integrity, maturity, valor and dignity retained actual relevance and power?

DEAR BETTY:

You deserve a swift kick in the pants for your bum advice to *Fretting in Spokane*. Where do you get off telling that lady to iron her dustcloths? Dollars to doughnuts you've got a maid to keep *your* rags shipshape, but most of us aren't so lucky.

And another thing. These days there's getting to be a snotty, know-it-all, lah-dee-dah, cynical tone to your column. I can't put my finger on it, but I'm not the only one who thinks you're getting "too big for your britches." Don't kid yourself. You need us more than we need you. So bend over, Betty, if you know what's good for you, and get ready for a

Washington Wallop

DEAR WALLOP:

For what it's worth, I agree with you about the dustcloths. But I sincerely regret having ever unwittingly encouraged your brand of coarse familiarity. And may I suggest that you take yourself to the nearest dictionary—you can find one in any public library—and "put your finger" on the distinction between cynicism and irony. Think about it, Wallop. And tell me how it turns out.

Dear Betty:

Many years ago you ran a column that started off "The Other Woman is a sponging parasitic succubus…" I clipped it and kept it magnetized to my freezer, but it finally fell apart. Do you know the one I mean? Would you mind running it again?

Sister Sue

Dear Sis:

Not at all. Here goes:

"The Other Woman is a sponging parasitic succubus, a proper role model for young people, a vacuous nitwit, a manic-depressive, a Republican, a good mother, an international terrorist, or what-have-you, depending, of course, upon the facts of her particular character and life.

"Though this much should be obvious, there are those who believe that any woman sexually involved with a man she is not married to can be, for social and moral purposes, reduced to a cheap stereotype. *This is dangerous nonsense. This is a terrible habit of thought.* For who among us has fewer than three dimensions? In the history of the human race, has there ever existed a single person, besides Hitler, who could slip beneath closed doors, disappear when viewed from the side, and settle comfortably, with room to spare, between the pages of a bad novel?

"Therefore let us rejoice in our variety! Let every one of us celebrate the special homeliness of her own history! Let us wonder, and be surprised, and admit to possibilities, and get on with it, and *stop being so damn stupid!*"

Dear Betty:

Are you nuts? You can't get away with this. Even if you do, what's the point?

First Person Singular

DEAR F.P.S.:

The point is, watch my smoke.

DEAR BETTY:

I need you to settle an argument. My brother-in-law says you're not the original Betty and that you're not even a *person*. He says Betty died two years ago in a car wreck and they covered it up and this column is being carried on by a committee, hush-hush. I say he's all wet. (He's one of those conspiracy nuts.) Anyway, what's the poop? (Hint: There's a lobster dinner riding on this.)

No Skeptic

DEAR NO:

This is a stumper. I've been staring for so long at the wonderful phrase "original Betty" that the words have become nonsensical and even the letters look strange. Who, I wonder, is or was the "original Betty"? I'm not making fun of you, dear. I honestly don't know what to say. If it's any help to you, I do have the same fingerprints as the infant born prematurely to Mary Alice Feeney in 1927, and the vivacious coed who won first prize in the national "My Country Because" essay contest of 1946, and the woman who put this column into syndication in 1952. So I suppose you deserve the lobster; although how you're going to convince your brother-in-law is anybody's guess. I wonder what he'd take as proof. I've got to think about this.

DEAR BETTY:

It's *him* I can't stand. In *bed*! And he knows it, too. I just don't want him *touching* me, I can't bear it! And *I still love him*! But there's *nothing* left any more, and how the hell is homemade butterscotch pudding going to help that? My God! My God! And don't tell me it's just a phase, because I know better and so does he. God, I'm so unhappy.

Nauseated, All Right? in Nashville

DEAR N:

That's much better. Awful, isn't it? The death of desire? And you're probably right, there's no help for it. Though if you can stomach the notion that intimacy is nothing more than a perfectable technique, you might try what they call a "reputable sex therapist."

Of all the foolish, ignoble, even evil acts I have committed in my long life, including the "My Country Because" essay, the single event that most shames me, so that I flush from chest to scalp even as I write this, was when I sat, of my own free will, in the offices of one of these technicians, and in the presence of a pink, beaming, gleaming young man, a total stranger, took my husband's hands in mine, and stared into his face, his poor face, crimson like my own, transfixed with humiliation and disbelief, and said—oh, this is dreadful; my husband of twenty-three years!—and said, in public, "I love it when you lick my nipples."

My God! *My God!*

DEAR BETTY:

Our family recently spent a weekend in our nation's Capital. While there we visited the moving Vietnam Memorial. Upon our return home I penned the following lines, which I would like to share with you.

You Could Have Been a Son of Ours
You could have been a son of ours
    If we had ever had a son,
You could have been our pride and joy
    But someone shot you with a gun
        And now your work is done.

You perished in a jungle wild
  So that our freedoms might be insured.
You risked your life without complaint
  You laid it down without a word.

And now upon a long black stone
  Are chiseled words that give you fame,
You could have been a son of ours—
  Were proud to say, "We know your name."

Emily

READERS:

Policy change! Policy change! Pay attention, now, because I'm not kidding around. Hereafter this column will continue to run the usual advice letters, recipes, and household hints, but we will no longer publish original verse. There will be no exceptions. Don't even think about it.

DEAR BETTY:

I guess you think you're pretty funny. I guess you think we're all hicks and idiots out here.

Well, maybe you're right, but I'll tell you one thing. That old letter I asked for about "The Other Woman"? It's not the one you ran before, even though you said it was, or you changed it in some way. I may not be super intelligent but I've got a good memory, and what's more I know when I'm being made fun of.

You know what? You really hurt me. Congratulations.

Sister Sue

DEAR SIS:

I am ashamed.

I, too, have an excellent memory, and for this reason my recordkeeping has never been systematic. And very occasionally I confuse genuine mail with letters I have concocted for one reason or another. This is what happened in your case. I had you down as a fiction.

I can't apologize enough.

DEAR BETTY:

Aren't you taking a big chance, admitting that you make up some of this stuff? Also, you haven't dealt with Sister Sue's real complaint, which is that now, inexplicably, after spending three decades securing the trust and affection of middle American women, you expose yourself as a misanthrope, misogynist, intellectual snob, and cheat. What are you up to, anyway?

F.P.S.

DEAR F:

Look, nobody reads this but us gals, so I'm hardly "taking a big chance." And it should be obvious, especially to you, that I'm "up to" no good.

DEAR BETTY:

Do you believe in God? I don't. Also, do you ever sit in front of a mirror and stare at your face? My face is so blobby that I can't figure out how even my own parents can recognize me. Lastly, do you think we should be selling weapons to Jordan?

Fifteen and Wondering

DEAR WONDERING:

Take five years off after you graduate from high school. Move away from home, get a menial job, fall for as many unworthy young men as it takes to get all that nonsense out of your system. Don't even think about college until your mind is parched and you are frantic to learn. Don't marry in your twenties. Don't be kind to yourself. *Keep in touch.*

DEAR BETTY:

I was not "lying about the sex", nor do I for a minute imagine that you thought I was. You simply could not resist making a flip wisecrack at my expense.

I was lying about my friends, who have gradually lost their affection for me but continue to socialize with us because they value my husband's company. He is aging well. I am turning into a fool. I'm one of those handsome old beauties with a gravelly, post-menopausal voice and a terrible laugh. I never had much of a sense of humor, but once I had a smoky, provocative laugh, which has now somehow become the sort of theatrical bray that hushes crowds. Strangers, accosted by me at parties, attacked at lunch counters and in elevators, shift and squirm in alarm: even the most obtuse knows he's about to be mugged, that he will not be allowed to pass until I have exacted my tribute. I am all affectation, obvious need and naked ego: just that kind of horrible woman who imagines herself an unforgettable character. I tell off-color jokes and hold my breath after the punch line, threatening to asphyxiate if you fail to applaud my remarkably emancipated attitude. During the past forty years I have told countless people about the stillbirth of my son, to show that I Have Known Great Sorrow. I parade my political beliefs, all liberal and unexamined, as evidence of my wisdom. I am a deeply boring, fatuous woman, and strangers pity me, friends lose patience with me, and my family loves me because it never occurs to any of them that I know it. I am the emperor in his new clothes, who knew perfectly well he was naked, who just needed a little attention, that's all, merely the transfixed attention of the entire populace, not an unreasonable request, just unlimited lifetime use of the cosmic footlights.

Don't try to tell me I can change. Of course I can't. And don't for an instant presume that I'm not all that bad. I am. Believe it.

Niobe

DEAR NIOBE:

Yes, but on the other hand your astonishing self-awareness makes you a genuinely tragic figure. And, Honey, cling to this: you're not ordinary. Commonplace sufferers find themselves trapped in homely, deformed, or dying bodies; you're trapped in an inferior *soul*. You really *are* a remarkable woman. Bravo!

How about it, Ladies? Isn't she something?

DEAR BETTY:

Just who the hell do you think you are?

Washington Wallop

DEAR WALLOP:

I am 147 pounds of despair in a fifty-pound mail sack. Though over-paid I groan with ennui beneath the negligible weight of your all too modest expectations, and when I fail to counter one of your clichés with another twice as mindless I apologize, even though the fault, God knows, is yours. I am

Betty

DEAR BETTY:

Temper, temper.

F.P.S.

DEAR F:

I can't help it. That broad really frosts my butt.

DEAR BETTY:

Do I have an inner life? I think I read somewhere that women don't. Also, what does it mean? Do you think we're capable of original thought?

Fifteen and Still Wondering

DEAR WONDERING:

I love you, and wish you were my own daughter. I have in fact two daughters, but neither of them has an inner life. I am what they call nowadays a "controlling personality." (Believe me, dear, that's not what they used to call it.) I was one of those omniscient mothers—the ones who always claim to know what their children are thinking, what they've just done, what they are planning to do. Not for any sinister reasons, mind you, but I got so good at guessing and predicting that, without intending to, I actually convinced them both of their utter transparency. They are each adrift, goalless and pathetic. They are big soft women, big criers, especially when they spend much time with me. I think I should feel worse about this than I actually do. Do you think this is Darwinian of me? (Hint: Go to a good library, and take out some books on Darwin.)

DEAR BETTY:

It's me again! Do you have any suggestions as to what I can do with a ten-foot length of old garden hose?

Petunia

DEAR PETUNIA:

Do you ever just sit still? Do you ever just sit in front of a mirror, for instance, and stare at your face? It's none of my business, but—and I say this with no snide intent; I am trying to be good, so that my teeth are literally clenched as I write this—I seriously think you should calm down. Petunia, even the Athenians threw things away. Let the garden hose be what it is, a piece of garbage. Now sit very very very still and try to think of nothing but the weight of your eyelids. Come to rest. Let your muscles slip and slide. Easy does it, girl. Easy. *Sbhhhhhbhbbhh.*

DEAR BETTY:

Maybe you should stop "trying to be good" if that's the best you can do. If I were Petunia, I'd rather get a wisecrack than a lot of patronizing advice based upon a snap analysis of my character and the circumstances of my life. You're a fine one to exhort them to wonder, be surprised, and admit to possibilities. On the basis of little evidence you've turned the woman into a cartoon. You don't see her as a person at all, just a type Early thirties, right? Hyperthyroid, narrow-shouldered, big-bottomed, frantically cheery, classically obsessive-compulsive, a churchgoing, choir-singing, Brownie troop mothering Total Woman with a soft sweet high voice; darting panic behind her deep-set eyes, an awful cornball sense of humor, and an overbite like a prairie dog. Am I right? Boy, how trite can you get! And how presumptuous you've become! I've tried to see it your way, but it's no go. I say, bring back the Original Betty.

F.P.S.

DEAR F:

Look, we know for a fact she's a cornball. No one who asks what she should do with a ten-foot length of hose could possibly have a sense of humor. As for the rest, well, I stayed up half the night trying to imagine another psychological context for her question (which, I must object, is hardly "a little evidence"), so that if I have failed it isn't for lack of trying.

Oh, all right, I admit it. I did see her as a type. But it becomes so difficult to believe that Petunia, or any of them, has any kind of independent existence. Remember, these folks are just words on a page; of course they're full-fleshed and complex, but I have to take this on faith. Most of them probably think they're revealing their true selves, whereas really they tell me almost nothing, and with every letter I'm supposed to make up a whole person, out of *scraps*.

I don't like to complain, but this doesn't get any easier with practice, and I'm tiring now, and losing my nerve. I can live with not being nice— nobody nice would do what I do—but what if I'm not any *good*?

READERS:

Do you think that failure of the imagination can have moral significance? I mean, is it a character flaw or just an insufficiency of skill? Is triteness a *sin*? Or what?

DEAR BETTY:

Last night my husband woke me up at 2:00 A.M. with a strange request. Then after awhile this old song started going through my head that I hadn't thought about for thirty years. I must have gone through the darn thing ten thousand times. It got so I was following the words with a bouncing ball, so that even when I blocked out the sound that old ball was still bobbing away in my head and I never did get to sleep until sunrise. The question is, does anybody out there know the missing words?

 Herman the German and Frenchie the Swede
  Set out for the Alkali Flats—Oh!
 Herman did follow and Frenchie did lead
  And they carried something in, or on, their hats—Oh!

 Now Herman said, "Frenchie, let's rest for a while,
  "My pony has something the matter with it—Oh!"

Now Frenchie said, "Herman, we'll rest in a mile,
 "On the banks of the River Something—Oh!"*

*(*If I could get the name of the
river I'd be all set here)*

Now Hattie McGurk was a sorrowful gal,
 Something something something.
She had a dirt camp in the high chaparral
 And a something as wide as Nebraska.

There's more, but I never did know the other verses, so they don't matter so much.

Betty, we sure do love you out here in Elko.

Sleepytime Sal

DEAR BETTY:

One time I was at this Tupperware party at my girlfriend's. Actually, it was just like a Tupperware party, only it was marital underwear, but it was run the same way. Anyway, everybody was drinking beer and passing around the items, and cutting up, you know, laughing about the candy pants and whatnot, and having a real good time. Only all of a sudden this feeling came over me. I started feeling real sorry for everybody, even though they were screaming and acting silly I thought about how much work it was to have fun, and how brave we all were for going to the trouble, since the easiest thing would be to just moan and cry and bite the walls, because we're all going to die anyway, sooner or later. Isn't that sad? I saw how every human life is a story, and the story always ends badly. It came to me that there wasn't any God at all and that we've always known this, but most of us are too polite and kind to talk about it. Finally I got so blue that I had to go into the bathroom and bawl. Then I was all right.

Partly Sunny

DEAR BETTY:

When I was first married you ran a recipe in your column called "How to Preserve Your Mate." It had all kinds of stuff in it like "fold in a generous dollop of forgiveness" and "add plenty of spice." I thought it was so cute that I copied it out on a sampler. Time went by, and I got a divorce, and finished high school, and then I got a university scholarship, and eventually a masters degree in business administration. Now I'm married again, to a corporate tax lawyer, and we live in a charming old pre-Revolutionary farmhouse, and all our pillows are made of goose down, and our potholders and coffee mugs and the bedspreads and curtains in the children's rooms all have Marimekko prints, and every item of clothing I own is made of natural fiber. But I never threw that old sampler away, and every now and then, when I'm all alone, I take it out and look at it and laugh my head off about what an incredible middle-class jerk I used to be.

Save the Whales

DEAR BETTY:

This is the end of the line for you and the rest of your ilk. We shall no longer seek the counsel of false matriarchs, keepers of the Old Order, quislings whose sole power derives from the continuing bondage of their sisters. Like the dinosaurs, your bodies will fuel the new society, where each woman shall be sovereign, and acknowledge her rage, and validate her neighbor's rage, and rejoice in everybody's rage, and caper and dance widdershins beneath the gibbous moon.

Turning and Turning in the Widening Gyre

DEAR BETTY:

I did what you said and sat real quiet and let myself go. Then you know what happened? I got real nutty and started wondering if I was just an idea in the mind of God. Is this an original thought? 'Cause if it is, you can keep it.

Hey, are you all right?

Petunia

DEAR PETUNIA:

No, since you ask. My mother is dying. My husband's mistress has myesthenia gravis. My younger daughter just gave all of her trust money to the Church of the Famous Maker. And I, like Niobe, am not aging well. My ulcer is bleeding, I can't sleep, and I'm not so much depressed as humiliated, both by slapstick catastrophe and by the minute tragedy of my wasted talents. To tell you the truth, I feel like hell.

DEAR BETTY:

I can see you have problems, dear, but whining doesn't advance the ball. Why not make a list of all your blessings and tape it to your medicine chest? Or send an anonymous houseplant to your oldest enemy? Why not expose yourself to the clergyman of your choice? Or, you could surprise hubby with a yummy devil's food layer cake, made from scratch in the nude.

Or, if nothing seems to work, you can put your head down and suffer like any other dumb animal. This always does the trick for me.

Ha ha ha. How do you like it, Sister? Ha ha ha ha ha.

Bitterly Laughing in the Heartland

DEAR BETTY:

See? They're closing in. You had to try it, didn't you, you got them going, and now all hell's breaking loose. You took a sweet racket and ruined it, and for what? Honor? Integrity? *Aesthetic principle?* Well, go ahead and martyr yourself, but leave me out of it.

F.P.S.

READERS.

For what it's worth,

BETTY REALLY BELIEVES

1. That God is criminally irresponsible.
2. That nobility is possible.
3. That hope is necessary.
4. That courage is commonplace.
5. That sentimentality is wicked.
6. That cynicism is worse.
7. That most people are surprisingly good sports.
8. That some people are irredeemable idiots.
9. That everybody on the Board of Directors of CM, Ford, Chrysler, and U.S. Steel, and every third member of Congress and the Cabinet ought to be taken out, lined up against a wall and shot.
10. That whining, though ugly, sometimes advances the ball.

How about it, Readers? What do *you* believe?

DEAR BETTY:

Does anybody have the recipe for Kooky Cake?

Kooky in Dubuque

DEAR KOOKY:

Forget the cake. The cake is terrible. What we're trying for here is a community of souls, a free exchange of original thoughts, an unrehearsed, raucous, a cappella chorus of Middle American women.

A Symphony of Gals!

Kooky, for God's sake, tell me your fears, your dreams, your awfullest secrets, and I'll tell you mine. Tell me, for instance, why you use that degrading nickname. I'm sending you my private phone number. Use it. Call me, Kooky. Call me anytime. Call collect. *Call soon.*

That goes for everybody else. All my dear readers, the loyal and the hateful, the genuine and the fictional, the rich and the strange. Call me anytime. Or, I'll send you my home address. Drop in. I'm serious. Let's talk.

Serious? You're critical. These people are going to kill you.

These people are my dearest friends. I love them all.

You do not! You don't even know them!

What's the question?

But... sentimentality is wicked.

But cynicism is worse.

THE SPOT OF ART

P.G. Wodehouse

P.G. Wodehouse (1881–1975) was the author of almost a hundred
books and the creator of Jeeves, Blandings Castle, Psmith, Ukridge,
Uncle Fred and Mr Mulliner. Born in London, he spent two years in
banking before becoming a full-time writer, contributing to periodicals
including *Punch* and the *Globe*. As well as his novels and short stories,
he wrote lyrics for musical comedies with Guy Bolton and Jerome
Kern, and at one time had five musicals running simultaneously on
Broadway. His time in Hollywood also provided much source material
for fiction.

I was lunching at my Aunt Dahlia's, and despite the fact that Anatole,
her outstanding cook, had rather excelled himself in the matter of
the bill-of-fare, I'm bound to say the food was more or less turning
to ashes in my mouth. You see, I had some bad news to break to her—
always a prospect that takes the edge off the appetite. She wouldn't
be pleased, I knew, and when not pleased Aunt Dahlia, having spent
most of her youth in the hunting-field, has a crispish way of expressing
herself.

However, I supposed I had better have a dash at it and get it over.

'Aunt Dahlia,' I said, facing the issue squarely.

'Hullo?'

'You know that cruise of yours?'

'Yes.'

'That yachting-cruise you are planning?'

'Yes.'

'That jolly cruise in your yacht in the Mediterranean to which you so kindly invited me and to which I have been looking forward with such keen anticipation?'

'Get on, fathead, what about it?'

I swallowed a chunk of *côtelette-suprème-avec-choux-fleurs* and slipped her the distressing info'.

'I'm frightfully sorry, Aunt Dahlia,' I said, 'but I shan't be able to come.'

As I had foreseen, she goggled.

'What!'

'I'm afraid not.'

'You poor, miserable hell-hound, what do you mean, you won't be able to come?'

'Well, I won't.'

'Why not?'

'Matters of the most extreme urgency render my presence in the Metropolis imperative.'

She sniffed.

'I supposed what you really mean is that you're hanging round some unfortunate girl again?'

I didn't like the way she put it, but I admit I was stunned by her penetration, if that's the word I want. I mean the sort of thing detectives have.

Yes, Aunt Dahlia,' I said, 'you have guessed my secret. I do indeed love.'

'Who is she?'

'A Miss Pendlebury. Christian name, Gwladys. She spells it with a "*w*".

'With a "g", you mean.'

'With a "w" *and* a "g".'

'Not Gwladys?'

'That's it.'

The relative uttered a yowl.

'You sit there and tell me you haven't enough sense to steer clear of a girl who calls herself Gwladys? Listen, Bertie,' said Aunt Dahlia earnestly, 'I'm an older woman than you are—well, you know what I mean—and I can tell you a thing or two. And one of them is that no good can come of association with anything labelled Gwladys or Ysobel or Ethyl or Mabelle or Kathryn. But particularly Gwladys. What sort of girl is she?'

'Slightly divine.'

'She isn't that female I saw driving you at sixty miles p.h. in the Park the other day. In a red two-seater?'

'She did drive me in the Park the other day. I thought it rather a hopeful sign. And her Widgeon Seven is red.'

Aunt Dahlia looked relieved.

'Oh well, then, she'll probably break your silly fat neck before she can get you to the altar. That's some consolation. Where did you meet her?'

'At a party in Chelsea. She's an artist.'

'Ye gods!'

'And swings a jolly fine brush, let me tell you. She's painted a portrait of me. Jeeves and I hung it up in the flat this morning. I have an idea Jeeves doesn't like it.'

'Well, if it's anything like you I don't see why he should. An artist! Calls herself Gwladys! And drives a car in the sort of way Segrave would if he were pressed for time.' She brooded awhile. 'Well, it's all very sad, but I can't see why you won't come on the yacht.'

I explained.

'It would be madness to leave the metrop. at this juncture,' I said. 'You know what girls are. They forget the absent face. And I'm not at all easy in my mind about a certain cove of the name of Lucius Pim. Apart from the fact that he's an artist, too, which forms a bond, his hair waves. One must never discount wavy hair, Aunt Dahlia. Moreover, this bloke is one of those strong, masterful men. He treats Gwladys as if she were less than the dust beneath his taxi wheels. He criticizes her hats and says nasty things about her chiaroscuro. For some reason, I've often noticed, this always seems to fascinate girls, and it has sometimes occurred to me that, being myself more the parfait gentle knight, if you know what I mean, I am in grave danger of getting the short end. Taking all these things into consideration, then, I cannot breeze off to the Mediterranean, leaving this Pim a clear field. You must see that?'

Aunt Dahlia laughed. Rather a nasty laugh. Scorn in its *timbre*, or so it seemed to me.

'I shouldn't worry,' she said. You don't suppose for a moment that Jeeves will sanction the match?'

I was stung.

'Do you imply, Aunt Dahlia,' I said—and I can't remember if I rapped the table with the handle of my fork or not, but I rather think I did—'that I allow Jeeves to boss me to the extent of stopping me marrying somebody I want to marry?'

'Well, he stopped you wearing a moustache, didn't he? And purple socks. And soft-fronted shirts with dress-clothes.'

'That is a different matter altogether.'

'Well, I'm prepared to make a small bet with you, Bertie. Jeeves will stop this match.'

'What absolute rot!'

'And if he doesn't like that portrait, he will get rid of it.'

'I never heard such dashed nonsense in my life.'

'And, finally, you wretched, pie-faced wambler, he will present you on board my yacht at the appointed hour. I don't know how he will do it, but you will be there, all complete with yachting-cap and spare pair of socks.'

'Let us change the subject, Aunt Dahlia,' I said coldly.

Being a good deal stirred up by the attitude of the flesh-and-blood at the luncheon-table, I had to go for a bit of a walk in the Park after leaving, to soothe the nervous system. By about four-thirty the ganglions had ceased to vibrate, and I returned to the flat. Jeeves was in the sitting-room, looking at the portrait.

I felt a trifle embarrassed in the man's presence, because just before leaving I had informed him of my intention to scratch the yacht-trip, and he had taken it on the chin a bit. You see, he had been looking forward to it rather. From the moment I had accepted the invitation, there had been a sort of nautical glitter in his eye, and I'm not sure I hadn't heard him trolling Chanties in the kitchen. I think some ancestor of his must have been one of Nelson's tars or something, for he has always had the urge of the salt sea in his blood. I have noticed him on liners, when we were going to America, striding the deck with a sailorly roll and giving the distinct impression of being just about to heave the main-brace or splice the binnacle.

So, though I had explained my reasons, taking the man fully into my confidence and concealing nothing, I knew that he was distinctly peeved; and my first act, on entering, was to do the cheery a bit. I joined him in front of the portrait.

'Looks good, Jeeves, what?'

Yes, sir.'

'Nothing like a spot of art for brightening the home.'

'No, sir.'

'Seems to lend the room a certain—what shall I say—'

'Yes, sir.'

The responses were all right, but his manner was far from hearty, and I decided to tackle him squarely. I mean, dash it. I mean, I don't know if you have ever had your portrait painted, but if you have you will understand my feelings. The spectacle of one's portrait hanging on the wall creates in one a sort of paternal fondness for the thing: and what you demand from the outside public is approval and enthusiasm—not the curling lip, the twitching nostril, and the kind of supercilious look which you see in the eye of a dead mackerel. Especially is this so when the artist is a girl for whom you have conceived sentiments deeper and warmer than those of ordinary friendship.

'Jeeves,' I said, 'you don't like this spot of art.'

'Oh, yes, sir.'

'No. Subterfuge is useless. I can read you like a book. For some reason this spot of art fails to appeal to you. What do you object to about it?'

'Is not the colour-scheme a trifle bright, sir?'

'I had not observed it, Jeeves. Anything else?'

'Well, in my opinion, sir, Miss Pendlebury has given you a somewhat too hungry expression.'

'Hungry?'

'A little like that of a dog regarding a distant bone, sir.'

I checked the fellow.

'There is no resemblance whatever, Jeeves, to a dog regarding a distant bone. The look to which you allude is wistful and denotes Soul.'

'I see, sir.'

I proceeded to another subject.

'Miss Pendlebury said she might look in this afternoon to inspect the portrait. Did she turn up?'

'Yes, sir.'

'But has left?'

'Yes, sir.'

'You mean she's gone, what?'

'Precisely, sir.'

'She didn't say anything about coming back, I suppose?'

'No, sir. I received the impression that it was not Miss Pendlebury's intention to return. She was a little upset, sir, and expressed a desire to go to her studio and rest.'

'Upset? What was she upset about?'

'The accident, sir.'

I didn't actually clutch the brow, but I did a bit of mental brow-clutching, as it were.

'Don't tell me she had an accident!'

'Yes, sir.'

'What sort of accident?'

'Automobile, sir.'

'Was she hurt?'

'No, sir. Only the gentleman.'

'What gentleman?'

'Miss Pendlebury had the misfortune to run over a gentleman in her car almost immediately opposite this building. He sustained a slight fracture of the leg.'

'Too bad! But Miss Pendlebury is all right?'

'Physically, sir, her condition appeared to be satisfactory. She was suffering a certain distress of mind.'

'Of course, with her beautiful, sympathetic nature. Naturally. It's a hard world for a girl, Jeeves, with fellows flinging themselves under the wheels of her car in one long, unending stream. It must have been a great shock to her. What became of the chump?'

'The gentleman, sir?'

'Yes.'

'He is in your spare bedroom, sir.'

'What!'

"Yes, sir.'

'In my spare bedroom?'

'Yes, sir. It was Miss Pendlebury's desire that he should be taken there. She instructed me to telegraph to the gentleman's sister, sir, who is in Paris, advising her of the accident. I also summoned a medical man, who gave it as his opinion that the patient should remain for the time being *in statu quo*.'

'You mean, the corpse is on the premises for an indefinite visit?'

'Yes, sir.'

'Jeeves, this is a bit thick!'

'Yes, sir.'

And I meant it, dash it. I mean to say, a girl can be pretty heftily divine and ensnare the heart and what not, but she's no right to turn a fellow's flat into a morgue. I'm bound to say that for a moment passion ebbed a trifle.

'Well, I suppose I'd better go and introduce myself to the blighter. After all, I am his host. Has he a name?'

'Mr Pim, sir.'

'Pim!'

'Yes, sir. And the young lady addressed him as Lucius. It was owing to the fact that he was on his way here to examine the portrait which she had painted that Mr Pim happened to be in the roadway at the moment when Miss Pendlebury turned the corner.'

I headed for the spare bedroom. I was perturbed to a degree. I don't know if you have ever loved and been handicapped in your wooing by a wavy-haired rival, but one of the things you don't want in such circs is the rival parking himself on the premises with a broken leg. Apart from anything else, the advantage the position gives him is obviously terrific. There he is, sitting up and toying with a grape and looking pale and interesting, the object of the girl's pity and concern, and where do you get off, bounding about the place in morning costume and spats and with the rude flush of health on the cheek? It seemed to me that things were beginning to look pretty mouldy.

I found Lucius Pim lying in bed, draped in a suit of my pyjamas, smoking one of my cigarettes, and reading a detective story. He waved the cigarette at me in what I considered a dashed patronizing manner.

'Ah, Wooster!' he said.

'Not so much of the "Ah, Wooster!"' I replied brusquely. 'How soon can you be moved?'

'In a week or so, I fancy.'

'In a week!'

'Or so. For the moment, the doctor insists on perfect quiet and repose. So forgive me, old man, for asking you not to raise your voice. A hushed whisper is the stuff to give the troops. And now, Wooster, about this accident. We must come to an understanding.'

'Are you sure you can't be moved?'

'Quite. The doctor said so.'

'I think we ought to get a second opinion.'

'Useless, my dear fellow. He was most emphatic, and evidently a man who knew his job. Don't worry about my not being comfortable here. I shall be quite all right. I like this bed. And now, to return to the subject of this accident. My sister will be arriving to-morrow. She will be greatly upset. I am her favourite brother.'

'You are?'

'I am.'

'How many of you are there?'

'Six.'

'And you're her favourite?'

'I am.'

It seemed to me that the other five must be pretty fairly subhuman, but I didn't say so. We Woosters can curb the tongue.

'She married a bird named Slingsby. Slingsby's Superb Soups. He rolls in money. But do you think I can get him to lend a trifle from time to time to a needy brother-in-law?' said Lucius Pim bitterly. 'No, sir! However, that is neither here nor there. The point is that my sister loves me devotedly: and, this being the case, she might try to prosecute and persecute and generally bite pieces out of poor little Gwladys if she knew that it was she who was driving the car that laid me out. She must never know, Wooster. I appeal to you as a man of honour to keep your mouth shut.'

'Naturally.'

'I'm glad you grasp the point so readily, Wooster. You are not the fool people take you for.'

'Who takes me for a fool?'

The Pim raised his eyebrows slightly.

'Don't people?' he said. 'Well, well. Anyway, that's settled. Unless I can think of something better I shall tell my sister that I was knocked down by a car which drove on without stopping and I didn't get its number. And now perhaps you had better leave me. The doctor made a point of quiet and repose. Moreover, I want to go on with this story. The villain has just dropped a cobra down the heroine's chimney, and I must be at her side. It is impossible not to be thrilled by Edgar Wallace. I'll ring if I want anything.'

I headed for the sitting-room. I found Jeeves there, staring at the portrait in rather a marked manner, as if it hurt him.

'Jeeves,' I said, 'Mr Pim appears to be a fixture.'

'Yes, sir.'

'For the nonce, at any rate. And to-morrow we shall have his sister, Mrs Slingsby, of Slingsby's Superb Soups, in our midst.'

'Yes, sir. I telegraphed to Mrs Slingsby shortly before four. Assuming her to have been at her hotel in Paris at the moment of the telegram's delivery, she will no doubt take a boat early to-morrow afternoon, reaching Dover—or, should she prefer the alternative route, Folkestone— in time to begin the railway journey at an hour which will enable her to arrive in London at about seven. She will possibly proceed first to her London residence—'

'Yes, Jeeves,' I said, 'yes. A gripping story, full of action and human interest. You must have it set to music some time and sing it. Meanwhile, get this into your head. It is imperative that Mrs Slingsby does not learn that it was Miss Pendlebury who broke her brother in two places. I shall require you, therefore, to approach Mr Pim before she arrives, ascertain exactly what tale he intends to tell, and be prepared to back it up in every particular.'

'Very good, sir.'

'And now, Jeeves, what of Miss Pendlebury?'

'Sir?'

'She's sure to call to make inquiries.'

'Yes, sir.'

'Well, she mustn't find me here. You know all about women, Jeeves?'

'Yes, sir.'

'Then tell me this. Am I not right in supposing that if Miss Pendlebury is in a position to go into the sick-room, take a long look at the inter- esting invalid, and then pop out, with the memory of that look fresh in her mind, and get a square sight of me lounging about in sponge-bag trousers, she will draw damaging comparisons? You see what I mean? Look on this picture and on that—the one romantic, the other not… Eh?'

'Very true, sir. It is a point which I had intended to bring to your attention. An invalid undoubtedly exercises a powerful appeal to the motherliness which exists in every woman's heart, sir. Invalids seem to stir their deepest feelings. The poet Scott has put the matter neatly in the lines—"Oh, Woman in our hours of ease uncertain, coy, and hard to please… When pain and anguish rack the brow—"'

I held up a hand.

'At some other time, Jeeves,' I said, 'I shall be delighted to hear you say your piece, but just now I am not in the mood. The position being as I have outlined, I propose to clear out early to-morrow morning and not to reappear until nightfall. I shall take the car and dash down to Brighton for the day.'

'Very good, sir.'

'It is better so, is it not, Jeeves?'

'Indubitably, sir.'

'I think so, too. The sea breezes will tone up my system, which sadly needs a dollop of toning. I leave you in charge of the old home.'

'Very good, sir.'

'Convey my regrets and sympathy to Miss Pendlebury and tell her I have been called away on business.'

'Yes, sir.'

'Should the Slingsby require refreshment, feed her in moderation.'

'Very good, sir.'

'And, in poisoning Mr Pim's soup, don't use arsenic, which is readily detected. Go to a good chemist and get something that leaves no traces.'

I sighed, and cocked an eye at the portrait.

'All this is very wonky, Jeeves.'

'Yes, sir.'

'When that portrait was painted, I was a happy man.'

'Yes, sir.'

'Ah, well, Jeeves!'

'Very true, sir.'

And we left it at that.

It was lateish when I got back on the following evening. What with a bit of ozone-sniffing, a good dinner, and a nice run home in the moonlight with the old car going as sweet as a nut, I was feeling in pretty good shape once more. In fact, coming through Purley, I went so far as to sing a trifle. The spirit of the Woosters is a buoyant spirit, and optimism had begun to reign again in the W. bosom.

The way I looked at it was, I saw I had been mistaken in assuming that a girl must necessarily love a fellow just because he has broken a leg. At first, no doubt, Gwladys Pendlebury would feel strangely drawn to the Pim when she saw him lying there a more or less total loss. But it would not be long before other reflections crept in. She would ask herself if she were wise in trusting her life's happiness to a man who hadn't enough sense to leap out of the way when he saw a car coming. She would tell herself that, if this sort of thing had happened once, who knew that it might not go on happening again and again all down the long years. And she would recoil from a married life which consisted entirely of going to hospitals and taking her husband fruit. She would realize how much better off she would be, teamed up with a fellow like Bertram Wooster, who, whatever his faults, at least walked on the pavement and looked up and down a street before he crossed it.

It was in excellent spirits, accordingly, that I put the car in the garage, and it was with a merry Tra-la on my lips that I let myself into the flat as Big Ben began to strike eleven. I rang the bell and presently, as if he had divined my wishes, Jeeves came in with siphon and decanter.

'Home again, Jeeves,' I said, mixing a spot.

'Yes, sir.'

'What has been happening in my absence? Did Miss Pendlebury call?'

'Yes, sir. At about two o'clock.'

'And left?'

'At about six, sir.'

I didn't like this so much. A four-hour visit struck me as a bit sinister. However, there was nothing to be done about it.

'And Mrs Slingsby?'

'She arrived shortly after eight and left at ten, sir.'

'Ah? Agitated?'

'Yes, sir. Particularly when she left. She was very desirous of seeing you, sir.'

'Seeing me?'

'Yes, sir.'

'Wanted to thank me brokenly, I suppose, for so courteously allowing her favourite brother a place to have his game legs in. Eh?'

'Possibly, sir. On the other hand, she alluded to you in terms suggestive of disapprobation, sir.'

'She—what?'

'"Feckless idiot" was one of the expressions she employed, sir.'

'Feckless idiot?'

'Yes, sir.'

I couldn't make it out. I simply couldn't see what the woman had based her judgement on. My Aunt Agatha has frequently said that sort of thing about me, but she has known me from a boy.

'I must look into this, Jeeves. Is Mr Pim asleep?'

'No, sir. He rang the bell a moment ago to inquire if we had not a better brand of cigarette in the flat.'

'He did, did he?'

'Yes, sir.'

'The accident doesn't seem to have affected his nerve.'

'No, sir.'

I found Lucius Pim sitting propped up among the pillows, reading his detective story.

'Ah, Wooster,' he said. 'Welcome home. I say, in case you were worrying, it's all right about that cobra. The hero had got at it without the villain's knowledge and extracted its poison-fangs. With the result that when it fell down the chimney and started trying to bite the heroine its efforts were null and void. I doubt if a cobra has ever felt so silly.'

'Never mind about cobras.'

'It's no good saying "Never mind about cobras",' said Lucius Pim in a gentle, rebuking sort of voice. 'You've jolly well *got* to mind about cobras, if they haven't had their poison-fangs extracted. Ask anyone. By the way, my sister looked in. She wants to have a word with you.'

'And I want to have a word with her.'

'"Two minds with but a single thought". What she wants to talk to you about is this accident of mine. You remember that story I was to tell her? About the car driving on? Well the understanding was, if you recollect, that I was only to tell it if I couldn't think of something better. Fortunately, I thought of something much better. It came to me in a flash as I lay in bed looking at the ceiling. You see, that driving-on story was thin. People don't knock fellows down and break their legs and go driving on. The thing wouldn't have held water for a minute. So I told her you did it.'

'What!'

'I said it was you who did it in your car. Much more likely. Makes the whole thing neat and well-rounded. I knew you would approve. At all costs we have got to keep it from her that I was outed by Gwladys. I made it as easy for you as I could, saying that you were a bit pickled at the time and so not to be blamed for what you did. Some fellows wouldn't have thought of that. Still,' said Lucius Pim with a sigh, 'I'm afraid she's not any too pleased with you.'

'She isn't, isn't she?'

'No, she is not. And I strongly recommend you, if you want anything like a pleasant interview to-morrow, to sweeten her a bit overnight.'

'How do you mean, sweeten her?'

'I'd suggest you sent her some flowers. It would be a graceful gesture. Roses are her favourites. Shoot her in a few roses—Number Three, Hill Street is the address—and it may make all the difference. I think it my duty to inform you, old man, that my sister Beatrice is rather a tough egg, when roused. My brother-in-law is due back from New York at any moment, and the danger, as I see it, is that Beatrice, unless sweetened, will get at him and make him bring actions against you for torts and malfeasances and what not and get thumping damages. He isn't over-fond of me and, left to himself, would rather approve than otherwise of people who broke my legs: but he's crazy about Beatrice and will do anything she asks him to. So my advice is, Gather ye rose-buds, while ye may and bung them in to Number Three, Hill Street. Otherwise, the case of Slingsby *v.* Wooster will be on the calendar before you can say "What-ho".'

I gave the fellow a look. Lost on him, of course.

'It's a pity you didn't think of all that before,' I said. And it wasn't so much the actual words, if you know what I mean, as the way I said it.

'I thought of it all right,' said Lucius Pim. 'But, as we were both agreed that at all costs—'

'Oh, all right,' I said. 'All right, all right.'

'You aren't annoyed?' said Lucius Pim, looking at me with a touch of surprise.

'Oh, no!'

'Splendid,' said Lucius Pim, relieved. 'I knew you would feel that I had done the only possible thing. It would have been awful if Beatrice had found out about Gwladys. I daresay you have noticed, Wooster, that when women find themselves in a position to take a running kick at one of their own sex they are twice as rough on her as they would be on a man. Now, you, being of the male persuasion, will find everything made nice and smooth for you. A quart of assorted roses, a few smiles, a tactful word or two, and she'll have melted before you know where you are. Play your cards properly, and you and Beatrice will be laughing merrily and having a game of Round and Round the Mulberry Bush together in about five minutes. Better not let Slingsby's Soups catch you at it, however. He's very jealous where Beatrice is concerned. And now you'll forgive me, old chap, if I send you away. The doctor says I ought not to talk too much for a day or two. Besides, it's time for bye-bye.'

The more I thought it over, the better that idea of sending those roses looked. Lucius Pim was not a man I was fond of—in fact, if I had had to choose between him and a cockroach as a companion for a walking-tour, the cockroach would have had it by a short head—but there was no doubt that he had outlined the right policy. His advice was good, and I decided to follow it. Rising next morning at ten-fifteen, I swallowed a strengthening breakfast and legged it off to that flower-shop in Piccadilly. I couldn't leave the thing to Jeeves. It was essentially a mission that demanded the personal touch. I laid out a couple of quid on a sizeable bouquet, sent it with my card to Hill Street, and then looked in at the Drones for a brief refresher. It is a thing I don't often do in the morning, but this threatened to be rather a special morning.

It was about noon when I got back to the flat. I went into the sitting-room and tried to adjust the mind to the coming interview. It had to be faced, of course, but it wasn't any good my telling myself that it was going to be one of those jolly scenes the memory of which cheer you up as you sit toasting your toes at the fire in your old age. I stood or fell by the roses. If they sweetened the Slingsby, all would be well. If they failed to sweeten her, Bertram was undoubtedly for it.

The clock ticked on, but she did not come. A late riser, I took it, and was slightly encouraged by the reflection. My experience of women has been that the earlier they leave the hay the more vicious specimens they are apt to be. My Aunt Agatha, for instance, is always up with the lark, and look at her.

Still, you couldn't be sure that this rule always worked, and after a while the suspense began to get in amongst me a bit. To divert the mind, I fetched the old putter out of its bag and began to practice putts into a glass. After all, even if the Slingsby turned out to be all that I had pictured her in my gloomier moments, I should have improved my close-to-the-hole work on the green and be that much up, at any rate.

It was while I was shaping for a rather tricky shot that the front-door bell went.

I picked up the glass and shoved the putter behind the settee. It struck me that if the woman found me engaged on what you might call a frivolous pursuit she might take it to indicate lack of remorse and proper feeling. I straightened the collar, pulled down the waistcoat, and managed to fasten on the face a sort of sad half-smile which was welcoming without being actually jovial. It looked all right in the mirror, and I held it as the door opened.

'Mr Slingsby,' announced Jeeves.

And, having spoken these words, he closed the door and left us alone together.

For quite a time there wasn't anything in the way of chit-chat. The shock of expecting Mrs Slingsby and finding myself confronted by something entirely different—in fact, not the same thing at all—seemed to have affected the vocal cords. And the visitor didn't appear to be disposed to make light conversation himself. He stood there looking strong and silent. I suppose you have to be like that if you want to manufacture anything in the nature of a really convincing soup.

Slingsby's Superb Soups was a Roman Emperor-looking sort of bird, with keen, penetrating eyes and one of those jutting chins. The eyes seemed to be fixed on me in a dashed unpleasant stare and, unless I was mistaken, he was grinding his teeth a trifle. For some reason he appeared to have taken a strong dislike to me at sight, and I'm bound to say this rather puzzled me. I don't pretend to have one of those Fascinating Personalities which you get from studying the booklets advertised in the back pages of the magazines, but I couldn't recall another case in the whole of my career where a single glimpse of the old map had been enough to make anyone look as if he wanted to foam at the mouth. Usually, when people meet me for the first time, they don't seem to know I'm there.

However, I exerted myself to play the host.

'Mr Slingsby?'

'That is my name.'

'Just got back from America?'

'I landed this morning.'

'Sooner than you were expected, what?'

'So I imagine.'

'Very glad to see you.'

"You will not be long.'

I took time off to do a bit of gulping. I saw now what had happened. This bloke had been home, seen his wife, heard the story of the accident, and had hastened round to the flat to slip it across me. Evidently those roses had not sweetened the female of the species. The only thing to do now seemed to be to take a stab at sweetening the male.

'Have a drink?' I said.

'No!'

'A cigarette?'

'No!'

'A chair?'

'No!'

I went into the silence once more. These non-drinking, non-smoking non-sitters are hard birds to handle.

'Don't grin at me, sir!'

I shot a glance at myself in the mirror, and saw what he meant. The sad half-smile *had* slopped over a bit. I adjusted it, and there was another pause.

'Now, sir,' said the Superb Souper. 'To business. I think I need scarcely tell you why I am here.'

'No. Of course. Absolutely. It's about that little matter—'

He gave a snort which nearly upset a vase on the mantelpiece. 'Little matter? So you consider it a little matter, do you?'

'Well—'

'Let me tell you, sir, that when I find that during my absence from the country a man has been annoying my wife with his importunities I regard it as anything but a little matter. And I shall endeavour,' said the Souper, the eyes gleaming a trifle brighter as he rubbed his hands together in a hideous, menacing way, 'to make you see the thing in the same light.'

I couldn't make head or tail of this. I simply couldn't follow him. The lemon began to swim.

'Eh?' I said. 'Your wife?'

'You heard me.'

'There must be some mistake.'

'There is. You made it.'

'But I don't know your wife.'

'Ha!'

'I've never even met her.'

'Tchah!'

'Honestly, I haven't.'

'Bah!'

He drank me in for a moment.

'Do you deny you sent her flowers?'

I felt the heart turn a double somersault. I began to catch his drift.

'Flowers!' he proceeded. 'Roses, sir. Great, fat, beastly roses. Enough of them to sink a ship. Your card was attached to them by a small pin—'

His voice died away in a sort of gurgle, and I saw that he was staring at something behind me. I spun round, and there, in the doorway—I hadn't seen it open, because during the last spasm of dialogue I had been backing cautiously towards it—there in the doorway stood a female. One glance was enough to tell me who she was. No woman could look so like Lucius Pim who hadn't the misfortune to be related to him. It was Sister Beatrice, the tough egg. I saw all. She had left home before the flowers had arrived: she had sneaked, unsweetened, into the flat, while I was fortifying the system at the Drones: and here she was.

'Er—' I said.

'Alexander!' said the female.

'Goo!' said the Souper. Or it may have been 'Coo'.

Whatever it was, it was in the nature of a battle-cry or slogan of war. The Souper's worst suspicions had obviously been confirmed. His eyes shone with a strange light. His chin pushed itself out another couple of inches. He clenched and unclenched his fingers once or twice, as if to make sure that they were working properly and could be relied on to do a good, clean job of strangling. Then, once more observing 'Coo!' (or 'Goo!'), he sprang forward, trod on the golf-ball I had been practising putting with, and took one of the finest tosses I have ever witnessed. The purler of a lifetime. For a moment the air seemed to be full of arms and legs, and then, with a thud that nearly dislocated the flat, he made a forced landing against the wall.

And, feeling I had had about all I wanted, I oiled from the room and was in the act of grabbing my hat from the rack in the hall, when Jeeves appeared.

'I fancied I heard a noise, sir,' said Jeeves.

'Quite possibly,' I said. 'It was Mr Slingsby.'

'Sir?'

'Mr Slingsby practicing Russian dances,' I explained. 'I rather think he has fractured an assortment of limbs. Better go in and see.'

'Very good, sir.'

'If he is the wreck I imagine, put him in my room and send for the doctor. The flat is filling up nicely with the various units of the Pim family and its connections, eh, Jeeves?'

'Yes, sir.'

'I think the supply is about exhausted, but should any aunts or uncles by marriage come along and break their limbs, bed them out on the Chesterfield.'

'Very good, sir.'

'I, personally, Jeeves,' I said, opening the front door and pausing on the threshold, 'am off to Paris. I will wire you the address. Notify me in due course when the place is free from Pims and completely purged of Slingsbys, and I will return. Oh, and Jeeves.'

'Sir?'

'Spare no effort to mollify these birds. They think—at least, Slingsby (female) thinks, and what she thinks to-day he will think to-morrow— that it was I who ran over Mr Pim in my car. Endeavour during my absence to sweeten them.'

'Very good, sir.'

'And now perhaps you had better be going in and viewing the body I shall proceed to the Drones, where I shall lunch, subsequently catching the two o'clock train at Charing Cross. Meet me there with an assortment of luggage.'

It was a matter of three weeks or so before Jeeves sent me the 'All clear' signal. I spent the time pottering pretty perturbedly about Paris and environs. It is a city I am fairly fond of, but I was glad to be able to return to the old home. I hopped on to a passing aeroplane and a couple of hours later was bowling through Croydon on my way to the centre of things. It was somewhere down in the Sloane Square neighbourhood that I first caught sight of the posters.

A traffic block had occurred, and I was glancing idly this way and that, when suddenly my eye was caught by something that looked familiar. And then I saw what it was.

Pasted on a blank wall and measuring about a hundred feet each way was an enormous poster, mostly red and blue. At the top of it were the words:

SLINGSBY'S SUPERB SOUPS

and at the bottom:

SUCCULENT AND STRENGTHENING

And, in between, me. Yes, dash it, Bertram Wooster in person. A reproduction of the Pendlebury portrait, perfect in every detail.

It was the sort of thing to make a fellow's eyes flicker, and mine flickered. You might say a mist seemed to roll before them. Then it lifted, and I was able to get a good long look before the traffic moved on.

Of all the absolutely foul sights I have ever seen, this took the biscuit with ridiculous ease. The thing was a bally libel on the Wooster face, and yet it was as unmistakable as if it had had my name under it. I saw now what Jeeves had meant when he said that the portrait had given me a hungry look. In the poster this look had become one of bestial greed. There I sat absolutely slavering through a monocle about six inches in circumference at a plateful of soup, looking as if I hadn't had a meal for weeks. The whole thing seemed to take one straight away into a different and a dreadful world.

I woke from a species of trance or coma to find myself at the door of the block of flats. To buzz upstairs and charge into the home was with me the work of a moment.

Jeeves came shimmering down the hall, the respectful beam of welcome on his face.

'I am glad to see you back, sir.'

'Never mind about that,' I yipped. 'What about—?'

'The posters, sir? I was wondering if you might have observed them.'

'I observed them!'

'Striking, sir?'

'Very striking. Now, perhaps you'll kindly explain—'

'You instructed me, if you recollect, sir, to spare no effort to mollify Mr Slingsby.'

'Yes, but—'

'It proved a somewhat difficult task, sir. For some time Mr Slingsby, on the advice and owing to the persuasion of Mrs Slingsby, appeared to be resolved to institute an action in law against you—a procedure which I knew you would find most distasteful.'

'Yes, but—'

'And then, the first day he was able to leave his bed, he observed the portrait, and it seemed to me judicious to point out to him its possibilities as an advertising medium. He readily fell in with the suggestion and, on my assurance that, should he abandon the projected action in law, you would willingly permit the use of the portrait, he entered into negotiations with Miss Pendlebury for the purchase of the copyright.'

'Oh? Well, I hope she's got something out of it, at any rate?'

'Yes, sir. Mr Pim, acting as Miss Pendlebury's agent, drove, I under-stand, an extremely satisfactory bargain.'

'He acted as her agent, eh?'

'Yes, sir. In his capacity as fiancé to the young lady, sir.'

'Fiancé!'

'Yes, sir.'

It shows how the sight of that poster had got into my ribs when I state that, instead of being laid out cold by this announcement, I merely said 'Ha!' or 'Ho!' or it may have been 'H'm'. After the poster, nothing seemed to matter.

'After that poster, Jeeves,' I said, 'nothing seems to matter.'

'No, sir?'

'No, Jeeves. A woman has tossed my heart lightly away, but what of it?'

'Exactly, sir.'

'The voice of Love seemed to call to me, but it was a wrong number. Is that going to crush me?'

'No, sir.'

'No, Jeeves. It is not. But what does matter is this ghastly business of my face being spread from end to end of the Metropolis with the eyes fixed on a plate of Slingsby's Superb Soup. I must leave London. The lads at the Drones will kid me without ceasing.'

'Yes, sir. And Mrs Spenser Gregson—'

I paled visibly. I hadn't thought of Aunt Agatha and what she might have to say about letting down the family prestige.

'You don't mean to say she has been ringing up?'

'Several times daily, sir.'

'Jeeves, flight is the only resource.'

'Yes, sir.'

'Back to Paris, what?'

'I should not recommend the move, sir. The posters are, I understand, shortly to appear in that city also, advertising the *Bouillon Suprême*. Mr Slingsby's products command a large sale in France. The sight would be painful for you, sir.'

'Then where?'

'If I might make a suggestion, sir, why not adhere to your original intention of cruising in Mrs Travers' yacht in the Mediterranean? On the yacht you would be free from the annoyance of these advertising displays.'

The man seemed to me to be drivelling.

'But the yacht started weeks ago. It may be anywhere by now.'

'No, sir. The cruise was postponed for a month owing to the illness of Mr Travers' chef, Anatole, who contracted influenza. Mr Travers refused to sail without him.'

'You mean they haven't started?'

'Not yet, sir. The yacht sails from Southampton on Tuesday next.'

'Why, then, dash it, nothing could be sweeter.'

'No, sir.'

'Ring up Aunt Dahlia and tell her we'll be there.'

'I ventured to take the liberty of doing so a few moments before you arrived, sir.'

'You did?'

'Yes, sir. I thought it probable that the plan would meet with your approval.'

'It does! I've wished all along I was going on that cruise.'

'I, too, sir. It should be extremely pleasant.'

'The tang of the salt breezes, Jeeves!'

'Yes, sir.'

'The moonlight on the water!'

'Precisely, sir.'

'The gentle heaving of the waves!'

'Exactly, sir.'

I felt absolutely in the pink. Gwladys—pah! The posters—bah! That was the way I looked at it.

'Yo-ho-ho, Jeeves!' I said, giving the trousers a bit of a hitch.

'Yes, sir.'

'In fact, I will go further. Yo-ho-ho and a bottle of rum!'

'Very good, sir. I will bring it immediately.'

MULLINER'S BUCK-U-UPPO

P.G. Wodehouse

P.G. Wodehouse (1881–1975) was the author of almost a hundred books and the creator of Jeeves, Blandings Castle, Psmith, Ukridge, Uncle Fred and Mr Mulliner. Born in London, he spent two years in banking before becoming a full-time writer, contributing to periodicals including *Punch* and the *Globe*. As well as his novels and short stories, he wrote lyrics for musical comedies with Guy Bolton and Jerome Kern, and at one time had five musicals running simultaneously on Broadway. His time in Hollywood also provided much source material for fiction.

The village Choral Society had been giving a performance of Gilbert and Sullivan's *Sorcerer* in aid of the Church Organ Fund; and, as we sat in the window of the Anglers' Rest, smoking our pipes, the audience came streaming past us down the little street. Snatches of song floated to our ears, and Mr Mulliner began to croon in unison.

'"Ah me! I was a pa-ale you-oung curate then!",' chanted Mr Mulliner in the rather snuffling voice in which the amateur singer seems to find it necessary to render the old songs.

'Remarkable,' he said, resuming his natural tones, 'how fashions change, even in clergymen. There are very few pale young curates nowadays.'

'True,' I agreed. 'Most of them are beefy young fellows who rowed for their colleges. I don't believe I have ever seen a pale young curate.'

'You never met my nephew Augustine, I think?'

'Never.'

'The description in the song would have fitted him perfectly. You will want to hear all about my nephew Augustine.'

At the time of which I am speaking (said Mr Mulliner) my nephew Augustine was a curate, and very young and extremely pale. As a boy he had completely outgrown his strength, and I rather think at his Theological College some of the wilder spirits must have bullied him; for when he went to Lower Briskett-in-the-Midden to assist the vicar, the Rev. Stanley Brandon, in his cure of souls, he was as meek and mild a young man as you could meet in a day's journey. He had flaxen hair, weak blue eyes, and the general demeanour of a saintly but timid cod-fish. Precisely, in short, the sort of young curate who seems to have been so common in the Eighties, or whenever it was that Gilbert wrote *The Sorcerer*.

The personality of his immediate superior did little or nothing to help him to overcome his native diffidence. The Rev. Stanley Brandon was a huge and sinewy man of violent temper, whose red face and glittering eyes might well have intimidated the toughest curate. The Rev. Stanley had been a heavyweight boxer at Cambridge, and I gather from Augustine that he seemed to be always on the point of introducing into debates on parish matters the methods which had made him so successful in the roped ring. I remember Augustine telling me that once, on the occasion when he had ventured to oppose the other's views in the matter of decorating the church for the Harvest Festival, he thought for a moment that the vicar was going to drop him with a right hook to the chin. It was some quite trivial point that had come up – a question as to whether the pumpkin would look better in the apse or the clerestory, if I recollect rightly – but for several seconds it seemed as if blood was about to be shed.

Such was the Rev. Stanley Brandon. And yet it was to the daughter of this formidable man that Augustine Mulliner had permitted himself to lose his heart. Truly, Cupid makes heroes of us all.

Jane was a very nice girl, and just as fond of Augustine as he was of her. But, as each lacked the nerve to go to the girl's father and put him abreast of the position of affairs, they were forced to meet surreptitiously. This jarred upon Augustine who, like all the Mulliners, loved the truth and hated any form of deception. And one evening, as they paced beside the laurels at the bottom of the vicarage garden, he rebelled.

'My dearest,' said Augustine, 'I can no longer brook this secrecy. I shall go into the house immediately and ask your father for your hand.'

Jane paled and clung to his arm. She knew so well that it was not her hand but her father's foot which he would receive if he carried out this mad scheme.

'No, no, Augustine! You must not!'

'But, darling, it is the only straightforward course.'

'But not tonight. I beg of you, not tonight.'

'Why not?'

'Because father is in a very bad temper. He has just had a letter from the bishop, rebuking him for wearing too many orphreys on his chasuble, and it has upset him terribly. You see, he and the bishop were at school together, and father can never forget it. He said at dinner that if old Boko Bickerton thought he was going to order him about he would jolly well show him.'

'And the bishop comes here tomorrow for the Confirmation services!' gasped Augustine.

'Yes. And I'm so afraid they will quarrel. It's such a pity father hasn't some other bishop over him. He always remembers that he once hit this one in the eye for pouring ink on his collar, and this lowers his respect for his spiritual authority. So you won't go in and tell him tonight will you?'

'I will not,' Augustine assured her with a slight shiver.

'And you will be sure to put your feet in hot mustard and water when you get home? The dew has made the grass so wet.'

'I will indeed, dearest.'

'You are not strong, you know.'

'No, I am not strong.'

'You ought to take some really good tonic.'

'Perhaps I ought. Goodnight, Jane.'

'Goodnight, Augustine.'

The lovers parted. Jane slipped back into the vicarage, and Augustine made his way to his cosy rooms in the High Street. And the first thing he noticed on entering was a parcel on the table, and beside it a letter.

He opened it listlessly, his thoughts far away.

'*My dear Augustine.*'

He turned to the last page and glanced at the signature. The letter was from his Aunt Angela, the wife of my brother, Wilfred Mulliner. You may remember that I once told you the story of how these two came together. If so, you will recall that my brother Wilfred was the eminent chemical researcher who had invented, among other specifics, such world-famous preparations as Mulliner's Raven Gipsy Face Cream and the Mulliner Snow of the Mountains Lotion. He and Augustine had never been particularly intimate, but between Augustine and his aunt there had always existed a warm friendship.

My dear Augustine (wrote Angela Mulliner],

I have been thinking so much about you lately, and I cannot forget that, when I saw you last, you seemed very fragile and deficient in vitamins. I do hope you take care of yourself.

I have been feeling for some time that you ought to take a tonic, and by a lucky chance Wilfred has just invented one which he tells me is the finest thing he has ever done. It is called Buck-U-Uppo, and acts directly on the red corpuscles. It is not yet on the market, but I have managed to smuggle a sample bottle from Wilfred's laboratory, and I want you to try it at once. I am sure it is just what you need.

Your affectionate aunt,

Angela Mulliner.

P.S. – You take a tablespoonful before going to bed, and another just before breakfast.

Augustine was not an unduly superstitious young man, but the coincidence of this tonic arriving so soon after Jane had told him that a tonic was what he needed affected him deeply. It seemed to him that this thing must have been meant. He shook the bottle, uncorked it, and, pouring out a liberal tablespoonful, shut his eyes and swallowed it.

The medicine, he was glad to find, was not unpleasant to the taste. It had a slightly pungent flavour, rather like old boot-soles beaten up in sherry. Having taken the dose, he read for a while in a book of theological essays, and then went to bed.

And as his feet slipped between the sheets, he was annoyed to find that Mrs Wardle, his housekeeper, had once more forgotten his hot-water bottle.

'Oh, dash!' said Augustine.

He was thoroughly upset. He had told the woman over and over again that he suffered from cold feet and could not get to sleep unless the dogs were properly warmed up. He sprang out of bed and went to the head of the stairs.

'Mrs Wardle!' he cried.

There was no reply.

'Mrs Wardle!' bellowed Augustine in a voice that rattled the window panes like a strong nor'-easter. Until tonight he had always been very much afraid of his housekeeper and had both walked and talked softly in her presence. But now he was conscious of a strange new fortitude. His head was singing a little, and he felt equal to a dozen Mrs Wardles.

Shuffling footsteps made themselves heard.

'Well, what is it now?' asked a querulous voice.

Augustine snorted.

'I'll tell you what it is now,' he roared. 'How many times have I told you always to put a hot-water bottle in my bed? You've forgotten it again, you old cloth-head!'

Mrs Wardle peered up, astounded and militant.

'Mr Mulliner, I am not accustomed—'

'Shut up!' thundered Augustine. 'What I want from you is less backchat and more hot-water bottles. Bring it up at once, or I leave tomorrow. Let me endeavour to get it into your concrete skull that you aren't the only person letting rooms in this village. Any more lip and I walk straight round the corner, where I'll be appreciated. Hot-water bottle ho! And look slippy about it.'

'Yes, Mr Mulliner. Certainly, Mr Mulliner. In one moment, Mr Mulliner.'

'Action! Action!' boomed Augustine. 'Show some speed. Put a little snap into it.'

'Yes, yes, most decidedly, Mr Mulliner,' replied the chastened voice from below.

An hour later, as he was dropping off to sleep, a thought crept into Augustine's mind. Had he not been a little brusque with Mrs Wardle? Had there not been in his manner something a shade abrupt – almost rude? Yes, he decided regretfully, there had. He lit a candle and reached for the diary which lay on the table at his bedside.

He made an entry.

The meek shall inherit the earth. Am I sufficiently meek? I wonder. This evening, when reproaching Mrs Wardle, my worthy housekeeper, for omitting to place a hot-water bottle in my bed, I spoke quite crossly. The provocation was severe, but still I was surely to blame for allowing my passions to run riot. Mem: Must guard agst. this.

But when he woke next morning, different feelings prevailed. He took his ante-breakfast dose of Buck-U-Uppo: and looking at the entry in the diary, could scarcely believe that it was he who had written it. 'Quite cross'? Of course he had been quite cross. Wouldn't anybody be quite cross who was for ever being persecuted by beetle-wits who forgot hot-water bottles?

Erasing the words with one strong dash of a thick-leaded pencil, he scribbled in the margin a hasty 'Mashed potatoes! Served the old idiot right!' and went down to breakfast.

He felt amazingly fit. Undoubtedly, in asserting that this tonic of his acted forcefully upon the red corpuscles, his Uncle Wilfred had been right. Until that moment Augustine had never supposed that he had any red corpuscles; but now, as he sat waiting for Mrs Wardle to bring him his fried egg, he could feel them dancing about all over him. They seemed to be forming rowdy parties and sliding down his spine. His eyes sparkled, and from sheer joy of living he sang a few bars from the hymn for those of riper years at sea.

He was still singing when Mrs Wardle entered with a dish. 'What's this?' demanded Augustine, eyeing it dangerously.

'A nice fried egg, sir.'

'And what, pray, do you mean by nice? It may be an amiable egg. It may be a civil, well-meaning egg. But if you think it is fit for human consumption, adjust that impression. Go back to your kitchen, woman; select another; and remember this time that you are a cook, not an incinerating machine. Between an egg that is fried and an egg that is cremated there is a wide and substantial difference. This difference, if you wish to retain me as a lodger in these far too expensive rooms, you will endeavour to appreciate.'

The glowing sense of well-being with which Augustine had begun the day did not diminish with the passage of time. It seemed, indeed, to increase. So full of effervescing energy did the young man feel that, departing from his usual custom of spending the morning crouched over the fire, he picked up his hat, stuck it at a rakish angle on his head, and sallied out for a healthy tramp across the fields.

It was while he was returning, flushed and rosy, that he observed a sight which is rare in the country districts of England – the spectacle of a bishop running. It is not often in a place like Lower Briskett-in-the-Midden that you see a bishop at all; and when you do he is either riding in a stately car or pacing at a dignified walk. This one was sprinting like a Derby winner, and Augustine paused to drink in the sight.

The bishop was a large, burly bishop, built for endurance rather than speed; but he was making excellent going. He flashed past Augustine in a whirl of flying gaiters: and then, proving himself thereby no mere specialist but a versatile all-round athlete, suddenly dived for a tree and climbed rapidly into its branches. His motive, Augustine readily divined, was to elude a rough, hairy dog which was toiling in his wake. The dog reached the tree a moment after his quarry had climbed it, and stood there, barking.

Augustine strolled up.

'Having a little trouble with the dumb friend, bish?' he asked, genially.

The bishop peered down from his eyrie.

'Young man,' he said, 'save me!'

'Right most indubitably ho!' replied Augustine. 'Leave it to me.'

Until today he had always been terrified of dogs, but now he did not hesitate. Almost quicker than words can tell, he picked up a stone, discharged it at the animal, and whooped cheerily as it got home with a thud. The dog, knowing when he had had enough, removed himself at some forty-five mph; and the bishop, descending cautiously, clasped Augustine's hand in his.

'My preserver!' said the bishop.

'Don't give it another thought,' said Augustine, cheerily. 'Always glad to do a pal a good turn. We clergymen must stick together.'

'I thought he had me for a minute.'

'Quite a nasty customer. Full of rude energy.'

The bishop nodded.

'His eye was not dim, nor his natural force abated. Deuteronomy xxxiv. 7,' he agreed. 'I wonder if you can direct me to the vicarage? I fear I have come a little out of my way.'

'I'll take you there.'

'Thank you. Perhaps it would be as well if you did not come in. I have a serious matter to discuss with old Pieface – I mean, with the Rev. Stanley Brandon.'

'I have a serious matter to discuss with his daughter. I'll just hang about the garden.'

'You are a very excellent young man,' said the bishop, as they walked along. 'You are a curate, eh?'

'At present. But,' said Augustine, tapping his companion on the chest, 'just watch my smoke. That's all I ask you to do – just watch my smoke.'

'I will. You should rise to great heights – to the very top of the tree.'

'Like you did just now, eh? Ha, ha!'

'Ha, ha!' said the bishop. 'You young rogue!'

He poked Augustine in the ribs.

'Ha, ha, ha!' said Augustine.

He slapped the bishop on the back.

'But all joking aside,' said the bishop as they entered the vicarage grounds, 'I really shall keep my eye on you and see that you receive the swift preferment which your talents and character deserve. I say to you, my dear young friend, speaking seriously and weighing my words, that the way you picked that dog off with that stone was the smoothest thing I ever saw. And I am a man who always tells the strict truth.'

'Great is truth and mighty above all things. Esdras iv. 41,' said Augustine.

He turned away and strolled towards the laurel bushes, which were his customary meeting-place with Jane. The bishop went on to the front door and rang the bell.

Although they had made no definite appointment, Augustine was surprised when the minutes passed and no Jane appeared. He did not know that she had been told off by her father to entertain the bishop's wife that morning, and show her the sights of Lower Briskett-in-the-Midden. He waited some quarter of an hour with growing impatience, and was about to leave when suddenly from the house there came to his ears the sound of voices raised angrily.

He stopped. The voices appeared to proceed from a room on the ground floor facing the garden.

Running lightly over the turf, Augustine paused outside the window and listened. The window was open at the bottom, and he could hear quite distinctly.

The vicar was speaking in a voice that vibrated through the room.

'Is that so?' said the vicar.

'Yes, it is!' said the bishop.

'Ha, ha!'

'Ha, ha! to you, and see how you like it!' rejoined the bishop with spirit.

Augustine drew a step closer. It was plain that Jane's fears had been justified and that there was serious trouble afoot between these two old schoolfellows. He peeped in. The vicar, his hands behind his coat-tails, was striding up and down the carpet, while the bishop, his back to the fireplace, glared defiance at him from the hearthrug.

'Who ever told you you were an authority on chasubles?' demanded the vicar.

'That's all right who told me,' rejoined the bishop.

'I don't believe you know what a chasuble is.'

'Is that so?'

'Well, what is it, then?'

'It's a circular cloak hanging from the shoulders, elaborately embroidered with a pattern and with orphreys. And you can argue as much as you like, young Pieface, but you can't get away from the fact that there are too many orphreys on yours. And what I'm telling you is that you've jolly well got to switch off a few of these orphreys or you'll get it in the neck.'

The vicar's eyes glittered furiously.

'Is that so?' he said. 'Well, I just won't, so there! And it's like your cheek coming here and trying to high-hat me. You seem to have forgotten that I knew you when you were an inky-faced kid at school and that, if I liked, I could tell the world one or two things about you which would probably amuse it.'

'My past is an open book.'

'Is it?' The vicar laughed malevolently. 'Who put the white mouse in the French master's desk?'

The bishop started.

'Who put jam in the dormitory prefect's bed?' he retorted.

'Who couldn't keep his collar clean?'

'Who used to wear a dickey?' The bishop's wonderful organ-like voice, whose softest whisper could be heard throughout a vast cathedral, rang out in tones of thunder. 'Who was sick at the house supper?'

The vicar quivered from head to foot. His rubicund face turned a deeper crimson.

'You know jolly well,' he said, in shaking accents, 'that there was something wrong with the turkey. Might have upset anyone.'

'The only thing wrong with the turkey was that you ate too much of it. If you had paid as much attention to developing your soul as you did to developing your tummy, you might by now,' said the bishop, 'have risen to my own eminence.'

'Oh, might I?'

'No, perhaps I am wrong. You never had the brain.'

The vicar uttered another discordant laugh.

'Brain is good! We know all about your eminence, as you call it, and how you rose to that eminence.'

'What do you mean?'

'You are a bishop. How you became one we will not inquire.'

'What do you mean?'

'What I say. We will not inquire.'

'Why don't you inquire?'

'Because,' said the vicar, 'it is better not!'

The bishop's self-control left him. His face contorted with fury, he took a step forward. And simultaneously Augustine sprang lightly into the room.

'Now, now, now!' said Augustine. 'Now, now, now, now, now!'

The two men stood transfixed. They stared at the intruder dumbly.

'Come, come!' said Augustine.

The vicar was the first to recover. He glowered at Augustine.

'What do you mean by jumping through my window?' he thundered. 'Are you a curate or a harlequin?'

Augustine met his gaze with an unfaltering eye.

I am a curate,' he replied, with a dignity that well became him. 'And, as a curate, I cannot stand by and see two superiors of the cloth, who are moreover old schoolfellows, forgetting themselves. It isn't right. Absolutely not right, my old superiors of the cloth.'

The vicar bit his lip. The bishop bowed his head.

'Listen,' proceeded Augustine, placing a hand on the shoulder of each. 'I hate to see you two dear good chaps quarrelling like this.'

'He started it,' said the vicar, sullenly.

'Never mind who started it.' Augustine silenced the bishop with a curt gesture as he made to speak. 'Be sensible, my dear fellows. Respect the decencies of debate. Exercise a little good-humoured give-and-take. You say,' he went on, turning to the bishop, 'that our good friend here has too many orphreys on his chasuble?'

'I do. And I stick to it.'

'Yes, yes, yes. But what,' said Augustine, soothingly, 'are a few orphreys between friends? Reflect! You and our worthy vicar here were at school together. You are bound by the sacred ties of the old Alma Mater. With him you sported on the green. With him you shared a crib and threw inked darts in the hour supposed to be devoted to the study of French. Do these things mean nothing to you? Do these memories touch no chord?' He turned appealingly from one to the other. 'Vicar! Bish!'

The vicar had moved away and was wiping his eyes. The bishop fumbled for a pocket-handkerchief. There was a silence.

'Sorry, Pieface,' said the bishop, in a choking voice.

'Shouldn't have spoken as I did, Boko,' mumbled the vicar.

'If you want to know what I think,' said the bishop, 'you are right in attributing your indisposition at the house supper to something wrong with the turkey. I recollect saying at the time that the bird should never have been served in such a condition.'

'And when you put that white mouse in the French master's desk,' said the vicar, 'you performed one of the noblest services to humanity of which there is any record. They ought to have made you a bishop on the spot.'

'Pieface!'

'Boko!'

The two men clasped hands.

'Splendid!' said Augustine. 'Everything hotsy-totsy now?'

'Quite, quite,' said the vicar.

'As far as I am concerned, completely hotsy-totsy,' said the bishop. He turned to his old friend solicitously. 'You will continue to wear all the orphreys you want – will you not, Pieface?'

'No, no. I see now that I was wrong. From now on, Boko, I abandon orphreys altogether.'

'But, Pieface—'

'It's all right,' the vicar assured him. 'I can take them or leave them alone.'

'Splendid fellow!' The bishop coughed to hide his emotion, and there was another silence. 'I think, perhaps,' he went on, after a pause, 'I should be leaving you now, my dear chap, and going in search of my wife. She is with your daughter, I believe, somewhere in the village.'

'They are coming up the drive now.'

'Ah, yes, I see them. A charming girl, your daughter.'

Augustine clapped him on the shoulder.

'Bish,' he exclaimed, 'you said a mouthful. She is the dearest, sweetest girl in the whole world. And I should be glad, vicar, if you would give your consent to our immediate union. I love Jane with a good man's fervour, and I am happy to inform you that my sentiments are returned. Assure us, therefore, of your approval, and I will go at once and have the banns put up.'

The vicar leaped as though he had been stung. Like so many vicars, he had a poor opinion of curates, and he had always regarded Augustine as rather below than above the general norm or level of the despised class.

'What!' he cried.

'A most excellent idea,' said the bishop, beaming. 'A very happy notion, I call it.'

'My daughter!' The vicar seemed dazed. 'My daughter marry a curate.'

'You were a curate once yourself, Pieface.'

'Yes, but not a curate like that.'

'No!' said the bishop. 'You were not. Nor was I. Better for us both had we been. This young man, I would have you know, is the most outstandingly excellent young man I have ever encountered. Are you aware that scarcely an hour ago he saved me with the most consummate address from a large shaggy dog with black spots and a kink in his tail? I was sorely pressed, Pieface, when this young man came up and, with a readiness of resource and an accuracy of aim which it would be impossible to over-praise, got that dog in the short ribs with a rock and sent him flying.'

The vicar seemed to be struggling with some powerful emotion. His eyes had widened.

'A dog with black spots?'

'Very black spots. But no blacker, I fear, than the heart they hid.'

'And he really plugged him in the short ribs?'

'As far as I could see, squarely in the short ribs.'

The vicar held out his hand.

'Mulliner,' he said, 'I was not aware of this. In the light of the facts which have just been drawn to my attention, I have no hesitation in saying that my objections are removed. I have had it in for that dog since the second Sunday before Septuagesima, when he pinned me by the ankle as I paced beside the river composing a sermon on Certain Alarming Manifestations of the So-called Modern Spirit. Take Jane. I give my consent freely. And may she be as happy as any girl with such a husband ought to be.'

A few more affecting words were exchanged, and then the bishop and Augustine left the house. The bishop was silent and thoughtful.

'I owe you a great deal, Mulliner,' he said at length.

'Oh, I don't know,' said Augustine. 'Would you say that?'

'A very great deal. You saved me from a terrible disaster. Had you not leaped through that window at that precise juncture and intervened, I really believe I should have pasted my dear old friend Brandon in the eye. I was sorely exasperated.'

'Our good vicar can be trying at times,' agreed Augustine.

'My fist was already clenched, and I was just hauling off for the swing when you checked me. What the result would have been, had you not exhibited a tact and discretion beyond your years, I do not like to think. I might have been unfrocked.' He shivered at the thought, though the weather was mild. 'I could never have shown my face at the Athenaeum again. But, tut, tut!' went on the bishop, patting Augustine on the shoulder, 'let us not dwell on what might have been. Speak to me of yourself. The vicar's charming daughter you really love her?'

'I do, indeed.'

The bishop's face had grown grave.

'Think well, Mulliner,' he said. 'Marriage is a serious affair. Do not plunge into it without due reflection. I myself am a husband, and, though singularly blessed in the possession of a devoted helpmeet, cannot but feel sometimes that a man is better off as a bachelor. Women, Mulliner, are odd.'

'True,' said Augustine.

'My own dear wife is the best of women. And, as I never weary of saying, a good woman is a wondrous creature, cleaving to the right and the good under all change; lovely in youthful comeliness, lovely all her life in comeliness of heart. And yet—'

'And yet?' said Augustine.

The bishop mused for a moment. He wriggled a little with an expression of pain, and scratched himself between the shoulder blades.

'Well, I'll tell you,' said the bishop. 'It is a warm and pleasant day today, is it not?'

'Exceptionally clement,' said Augustine.

'A fair, sunny day, made gracious by a temperate westerly breeze. And yet, Mulliner, if you will credit my statement, my wife insisted on my putting on my thick winter woollies this morning. Truly,' sighed the bishop, 'as a jewel of gold in a swine's snout, so is a fair woman which is without discretion. Proverbs xi. 21.'

'Twenty-two,' corrected Augustine.

'I should have said twenty-two. They are made of thick flannel, and I have an exceptionally sensitive skin. Oblige me, my dear fellow, by rubbing me in the small of the back with the ferrule of your stick. I think it will ease the irritation.'

'But, my poor dear old Bish,' said Augustine, sympathetically, 'this must not be.'

The bishop shook his head ruefully.

'You would not speak so hardily, Mulliner, if you knew my wife. There is no appeal from her decrees.'

'Nonsense,' cried Augustine, cheerily. He looked through the trees to where the lady bishopess, escorted by Jane, was examining a lobelia through her lorgnette with just the right blend of cordiality and condescension. 'I'll fix that for you in a second.'

The bishop clutched at his arm.

'My boy! What are you going to do?'

'I'm just going to have a word with your wife and put the matter up to her as a reasonable woman. Thick winter woollies on a day like this! Absurd!' said Augustine. 'Preposterous! I never heard such rot,'

The bishop gazed after him with a laden heart. Already he had come to love this young man like a son: and to see him charging so lightheartedly into the very jaws of destruction afflicted him with a deep and poignant sadness. He knew what his wife was like when even the highest in the land attempted to thwart her; and this brave lad was but a curate. In another moment she would be looking at him through her lorgnette: and England was littered with the shrivelled remains of curates at whom the lady bishopess had looked through her lorgnette. He had seen them wilt like salted slugs at the episcopal breakfast-table.

He held his breath. Augustine had reached the lady bishopess, and the lady bishopess was even now raising her lorgnette.

The bishop shut his eyes and turned away. And then – years afterwards, it seemed to him – a cheery voice hailed him: and, turning, he perceived Augustine bounding back through the trees.

'It's all right, bish,' said Augustine.

'All – all right?' faltered the bishop.

'Yes. She says you can go and change into the thin cashmere.'

The bishop reeled.

'But – but – but what did you say to her? What arguments did you employ?'

'Oh, I just pointed out what a warm day it was and jollied her along a bit

'Jollied her along a bit!'

'And she agreed in the most friendly and cordial manner. She has asked me to call at the Palace one of these days.'

The bishop seized Augustine's hand.

'My boy,' he said in a broken voice, 'you shall do more than call at the Palace. You shall come and live at the Palace. Become my secretary, Mulliner, and name your own salary. If you intend to marry, you will require an increased stipend. Become my secretary, boy, and never leave my side. I have needed somebody like you for years.'

It was late in the afternoon when Augustine returned to his rooms, for he had been invited to lunch at the vicarage and had been the life and soul of the cheery little party.

'A letter for you, sir,' said Mrs Wardle, obsequiously.

Augustine took the letter.

'I am sorry to say I shall be leaving you shortly, Mrs Wardle.'

'Oh, sir! If there's anything I can do—'

'Oh, it's not that. The fact is, the bishop has made me his secretary, and I shall have to shift my toothbrush and spats to the Palace, you see.'

'Well, fancy that, sir! Why, you'll be a bishop yourself one of these days.'

'Possibly,' said Augustine. 'Possibly. And now let me read this.'

He opened the letter. A thoughtful frown appeared on his face as he read.

My dear Augustine,

I am writing in some haste to tell you that the impulsiveness of your aunt has led to a rather serious mistake.

She tells me that she dispatched to you yesterday by parcels post a sample bottle of my new Buck-U-Uppo, which she obtained without my knowledge from my laboratory. Had she mentioned what she was intending to do, I could have prevented a very unfortunate occurrence.

Mulliner's Buck-U-Uppo is of two grades or qualities – the A and the B. The A is a mild, but strengthening, tonic designed for human invalids. The B, on the other hand, is purely for circulation in the animal kingdom, and was invented to fill a long-felt want throughout our Indian possessions.

As you are doubtless aware, the favourite pastime of the Indian Maharajahs is the hunting of the tiger of the jungle from the backs of elephants; and it has happened frequently in the past that hunts have been spoiled by the failure of the elephant to see eye to eye with its owner in the matter of what constitutes sport.

Too often elephants, on sighting the tiger, have turned and galloped home: and it was to correct this tendency on their part that I invented Mulliner's Buck-U-Uppo B. One teaspoonful of the Buck-U-Uppo B administered in its morning bran-mash will cause the most timid elephant to trumpet loudly and charge the fiercest tiger without a qualm.

Abstain, therefore, from taking any of the contents of the bottle you now possess.

And believe me.

Your affectionate uncle,

Wilfred Mulliner.

Augustine remained for some time in deep thought after perusing this communication. Then, rising, he whistled a few bars of the psalm appointed for the twenty-sixth of June and left the room.

Half an hour later a telegraphic message was speeding over the wires.
It ran as follows:

Wilfred Mulliner,
The Gables,
Lesser Lossingham,
Salop.

Letter received. Send immediately, COD, three cases of the B.
'Blessed shall be thy basket and thy store' Deuteronomy xxviii 5.
Augustine.

A DAY WITH THE SWATTESMORE

P.G. Wodehouse

P.G. Wodehouse (1881–1975) was the author of almost a hundred books and the creator of Jeeves, Blandings Castle, Psmith, Ukridge, Uncle Fred and Mr Mulliner. Born in London, he spent two years in banking before becoming a full-time writer, contributing to periodicals including *Punch* and the *Globe*. As well as his novels and short stories, he wrote lyrics for musical comedies with Guy Bolton and Jerome Kern, and at one time had five musicals running simultaneously on Broadway. His time in Hollywood also provided much source material for fiction.

Whit-Monday, which to so many means merely one more opportunity of strewing Beauty Spots with paper bags, has a deeper significance for the hunting man. For, if you look in your diary, you will find the following entry:

May 20 (Whit-Monday) – *Fly Swatting Begins*.

Simple words, but how much they imply. What magic memories of past delights they conjure up, what roseate visions of happy days to come.

English poetry is rich in allusions to this king of sports. Every schoolboy is familiar with those lines of Coleridge:

> *It is the Ancient Mariner,*
> *He swatteth one in three.*

These have been taken by some to suggest a slur on the efficiency of the British Merchant Service, but I do not think that Coleridge had any such interpretation in mind.

Mark the word 'ancient'. 'It is the *ancient* Mariner.' That is to say, he was past his prime, possibly even of an age when he might have been expected to abandon the sport altogether. Yet, such was the accuracy of eye and suppleness of limb resulting from the clean, fresh life of the open sea that he was still bagging one out of every three – a record which many a younger man would be glad to achieve.

It is Chaucer who is responsible for the old saw:

> *When noone is highe.*
> *Then swatte ye flye,*

which has led some to hold that the proper time for a meet is after lunch. Others, of whom I am one, prefer the after breakfast theory. It seems to me that a fly which has just risen from its bed and taken a cold plunge in the milk-jug is in far better fettle for a sporting run than one which has spent the morning gorging jam and bacon and wants nothing more than a quiet nap on the ceiling.

The Swattesmore, the hunt to which I belong, always meets directly after breakfast. And a jovial gathering it is. Tough old Admiral Bludyer has his rolled-up copy of *Country Life,* while young Reggie Bootle carries the lighter and more easily wielded *Daily Mail.*

There is a good deal of genial chaff and laughter because some youngster who is new to the game has armed himself with a patent steel-wire swatter, for it is contrary to all the etiquette of the chase to use these things. Your true sportsman would as soon shoot a sitting bird.

Meanwhile Sigsbee, our host's butler – specially engaged for his round and shiny head, which no fly has ever been known to resist – has opened the window. There is a hush of anticipation, and the talk and laughter are stilled. Presently you hear a little gasp of excitement from some newly joined member, who has not been at the sport long enough to acquire the iron self-control on which we of the Swattesmore pride ourselves. A fine fly is peering in.

This is the crucial moment. Will he be lured in by Sigsbee's bald head, or will he pursue his original intention of going down to the potting-shed to breakfast on the dead rat? Another moment, and he has made his decision. He hurries in and seats himself on the butler's glistening cupola. Instantaneously, Francis, the footman, slams the window. The fly rockets to the ceiling. 'Gone away, sir, thank you, sir,' says Sigsbee respectfully, and with a crashing 'Yoicks!' and 'Tally-ho!' the hunt is up.

Ah me! How many wonderful runs that old library has seen. I remember once a tough old dog fly leading us without a check from ten in the morning till five minutes before lunch.

We found on Sigsbee's head, and a moment later he had made a line across country for the south window. From there he worked round to the bookshelves. Bertie Whistler took a fearful toss over a whatnot, and poor old General Griggs, who is not so keen-sighted as he used to be, came to grief on a sunken art-nouveau footstool.

By the end of a couple of hours only 'Binks' Bodger and myself were on the active list. All the rest were nursing bruised shins in the background. At a quarter to one the fly doubled back from the portrait of our host's grandmother, and in trying to intercept him poor 'Binks' fell foul of the head of a bearskin rug and had to retire.

A few minutes later I had the good luck to come up with the brute as he rested on a magnificent Corot near the fireplace. I was using a bedroom slipper that day, and it unfortunately damaged the Corot beyond recognition. But I have my consolation in the superb brush which hangs over my mantelpiece, and the memory of one of the finest runs a swatter ever had.

There are some who claim that fly-swatting is inferior as a sport to the wasping of the English countryside. As one who has had a wide experience of both, I most emphatically deny this. Wasping is all very well in its way, but to try to compare the two is foolish.

Waspers point to the element of danger in their favourite pursuit, some going so far as to say that it really ought to come under the head of big-game hunting.

But I have always maintained that this danger is more imaginary than real. Wasps are not swift thinkers. They do not connect cause and effect. A wasp rarely has the intelligence to discover that the man in the room is responsible for his troubles, and almost never attacks him. And, even admitting that a wasp has a sting, which gives the novice a thrill, who has ever heard of any one barking his shin on a chair during a wasp hunt?

Wasping is too sedentary for me. You wait till the creature is sitting waist-high in the jam and then shove him under with a teaspoon. Is this sport in the sense that fly-swatting is sport? I do not think so. The excitement of the chase is simply non-existent. Give me a cracking two-hours' run with a fly, with plenty of jumps to take, including a grand piano and a few stiff gate-leg tables. That is the life.

GIRLS TALKING

Victoria Wood

Victoria Wood (1953–2016) was one of the UK's most cherished comedians. A shy child, she later declared, 'stand-up comedy is the ideal place for a shy person because you're completely in control.' She grew up to enjoy a career spanning stand-up, singing, songwriting, script-writing and acting. Appointed CBE in 2008, she won seven Baftas and was profiled twice on the South Bank Show.

Film. A street. Jeanette and Marie in school uniform (ankle socks, track shoes, short skirts, shirts and ties etc) leaning against the mall. A male interviewer is heard in voice over throughout the film.

INTERVIEWER. Jeanette is fifteen, Marie is fourteen and a half. Both are from broken homes and living in an area with a high level of unemployment.

JEANETTE. Not really been to school since I was five. Five or six. I go in, like, if there's something happening, like vaccination, or a nativity play.

[*Cut to Marie in mid-speech.*]

MARIE. Well it's just boring like, isn't it? They don't teach you about anything important – like how to inject yourself, it's all geography and things.

INTERVIEWER. Maybe you think it's not worth being qualified as there are so few jobs in Liverpool…?

JEANETTE. There is lots of jobs. The government wants to keep us unemployed so we won't smoke on the buses.

[*Cut to Jeanette.*]

JEANETTE. I could have been in a film but it was boring…
INTERVIEWER. What film was that?
JEANETTE. Documentary on child prostitution.
INTERVIEWER. You've actually been a prostitute?
JEANETTE. Yeah but it was boring. The sex was all right but they kept wanting you to talk to them.

[*Cut to Marie.*]

MARIE. Music? Kid's stuff really, isn't it?
JEANETTE. The government puts things on the record underneath the music.
INTERVIEWER. Sorry?
JEANETTE. Like, you know, messages that you can only hear with your brain.
INTERVIEWER. What do they say?
JEANETTE. Like telling you what to do.
MARIE. Keep you under.
JEANETTE. Don't say 'tits' in the reference library.
MARIE. Don't gob on each other.
INTERVIEWER. Is there much sleeping around amongst young people?
MARIE. No, it's boring.
JEANETTE. It's like for your Mums and Dads really, isn't it?
MARIE. Like drinking.
INTERVIEWER. Don't you and your, er, mates drink?
JEANETTE. We used to drink battery acid.
MARIE. But it burns holes in your tights.

INTERVIEWER. Do you sniff glue?

JEANETTE. That's for snobs really, isn't it?

MARIE. Grammar school kids sniff glue.

JEANETTE. We sniff burning lino.

MARIE. Cot blankets.

JEANETTE. Estée Lauder Youth Dew.

INTERVIEWER. What effect does it have?

MARIE. Fall over mainly.

INTERVIEWER. Doesn't sniffing heighten your emotions?

JEANETTE. Oh yeah, you get a lot more bored.

MARIE. Things that were a bit boring get really boring, and that's great.

INTERVIEWER. How do you see your future – do you think you'll get married?

JEANETTE. We'd like to, 'cos it's easier to get Valium if you're married.

MARIE. But we can't can we?

INTERVIEWER. Why?

JEANETTE. The government are bringing out this thing – you can't get married unless you've got a going-away outfit. It's got to be—

MARIE. Suit.

JEANETTE. Yeah, suit, and it's got to be in two colours that match.

MARIE. And you have to have a handbag and slingbacks.

JEANETTE. It's just not on.

MARIE. My mother's got enough to do paying off my shoplifting fine.

INTERVIEWER. What happened?

JEANETTE. A duvet fell into my shopping bag.

[*Cut.*]

INTERVIEWER. Have either of you got boyfriends?

JEANETTE. We have, like, one between two.

MARIE. Just to save time really.

INTERVIEWER. And what does your boyfriend do?

MARIE. He gets tattooed a lot.

INTERVIEWER. Yes, what else does he do?

JEANETTE. He has them removed a lot.

[*Cut.*]

INTERVIEWER. Any ambitions?

JEANETTE. I'd like some stretch denims.

INTERVIEWER. I suppose you can't afford any?

JEANETTE. You can apply for a grant.

MARIE. For denims.

JEANETTE. But not stretch denims.

INTERVIEWER. How do you feel about teenage pregnancies?

MARIE. We've got used to them now.

[*They sniff a bottle of perfume. Jeanette
falls over. Marie looks bored.*]

KITTY: ONE

Victoria Wood

Victoria Wood (1953–2016) was one of the UK's most cherished comedians. A shy child, she later declared, 'stand-up comedy is the ideal place for a shy person because you're completely in control.' She grew up to enjoy a career spanning stand-up, singing, songwriting, script-writing and acting. Appointed CBE in 2008, she won seven Baftas and was profiled twice on the South Bank Show.

Kitty is about fifty-three, from Manchester and proud of it. She speaks as she finds and knows what's what. She is sitting in a small bare studio, on a hard chair. She isn't nervous.

KITTY. Good evening. My name's Kitty. I've had a boob off and I can't stomach whelks so that's me for you. I don't know why I've been asked to interrupt your viewing like this, but I'm apparently something of a celebrity since I walked the Pennine Way in slingbacks in an attempt to publicise Mental Health. They've asked me to talk about aspects of life in general, nuclear war, peg-bags…

I wasn't going to come today, actually. I'm not a fan of the modern railway system. I strongly object to paying twenty-seven pounds fifty to walk the length and breadth of the train with a sausage in a plastic box. But they offered me a chopper from Cheadle so here I am.

I'm going to start with the body – you see I don't mince words. Time and again I'm poked in the street by complete acquaintances – Kitty, they say to me, how do you keep so young, do you perhaps inject your-self with a solution deriving from the placenta of female gibbons? Well, no, I say, I don't, as it happens. I'm blessed with a robust constitution, my father's mother ran her own abbatoir, and I've only had the need of hospitalisation once – that's when I was concussed by an electric potato peeler at the Ideal Home Exhibition.

No, the secret of my youthful appearance is simply – mashed swede. As a face-mask, as a night cap, and in an emergency, as a draught-excluder. I do have to be careful about my health, because I have a grumbling ovary which once flared up in the middle of *The Gondoliers*. My three rules for a long life are regular exercise, hobbies and complete avoid-ance of midget gems.

I'm not one for dance classes, feeling if God had wanted us to wear leotards he would have painted us purple. I have a system of elastic loops dangling from the knob of my cistern cupboard. It's just a little thing I knocked up from some old knicker waistbands. I string up before breakfast and I can exert myself to Victor Sylvester till the cows come home.

There's also a rumour going round our block that I play golf. Let me scotch it. I do have what seems to be a golf-bag on my telephone table but it's actually a pyjama-case made by a friend who has trouble with her nerves in Buckinghamshire.

Well, I can't stop chatting, much as I'd like to – my maisonette backs onto a cake factory, so I'm dusting my knick-knacks all the day long.

And I shall wait to see myself before I do any more. Fortunately, I've just had my TV mended. I say mended – a shifty young man in plimsolls waggled my aerial and wolfed my Gipsy Creams, but that's the compre-hensive system for you.

I must go, I'm having tea with the boys in flat five. They're a lovely couple of young men, and what they don't know about Mikhail Barishnikov is nobody's business. So I'd better wrap up this little gift I've got them. It's a gravy boat in the shape of Tony Hancock – they'll be thrilled.

[*She peers round the studio.*]

Now, who had hold of my showerproof? It's irreplaceable, you know, being in tangerine poplin, which apparently there's no call for...

[*She gets up and walks past the camera.*]

There's a mauve pedestal mat of mine, too.

GIVING NOTES

Victoria Wood

Victoria Wood (1953–2016) was one of the UK's most cherished comedians. A shy child, she later declared, 'stand-up comedy is the ideal place for a shy person because you're completely in control.' She grew up to enjoy a career spanning stand-up, singing, songwriting, script-writing and acting. Appointed CBE in 2008, she won seven Baftas and was profiled twice on the South Bank Show.

Alma, a middle-aged sprightly woman, addresses her amateur company after a rehearsal of Hamlet. *She claps her hands.*

ALMA. Right. Bit of hush please. Connie! Thank you. Now that was quite a good rehearsal; I was quite pleased. There were a few raised eyebrows when we let it slip the Piecrust Players were having a bash at Shakespeare but I think we're getting there. But I can't say this too often: it may be *Hamlet* but it's got to be Fun Fun Fun!

[*She consults her notes.*]

Now we're still very loose on lines. Where's Gertrude? I'm not so worried about you – if you 'dry' just give us a bit of business with the shower cap. But Barbara – you will have to buckle down. I mean, Ophelia's mad scene, 'There's rosemary, that's for remembrance' – it's no good just bunging a few herbs about and saying, 'Don't mind me, I'm a loony'. Yes? You see, this is our marvellous bard, Barbara, you cannot paraphrase. It's not like Pinter where you can more or less say what you like as long as you leave enough gaps.

Right, Act One, Scene One, on the ramparts. Now I know the whist table is a bit wobbly, but until Stan works out how to adapt the Beanstalk it'll have to do. What's this? Atmosphere? Yes – now what did we work on, Philip? Yes, it's midnight, it's jolly cold. What do we do when it's cold? We go 'Brrr', and we do this [*slaps hands on arms*]. Right, well don't forget again, please. And cut the hot-water bottle, it's not working.

Where's my ghost of Hamlet's father? Oh yes, what went wrong tonight, Betty? He's on nights still, is he? OK. Well, it's not really on for you to play that particular part, Betty – you're already doing the Player Queen and the back legs of Hamlet's donkey. Well, we don't know he didn't have one, do we? Why waste a good cossy?

Hamlet – drop the Geordie, David, it's not coming over. Your characterisation's reasonably good, David, but it's just far too gloomy. Fair enough, make him a little bit depressed at the beginning, but start lightening it from Scene Two, from the hokey-cokey onwards, I'd say. And perhaps the, er, 'Get thee to a nunnery' with Ophelia – perhaps give a little wink to the audience, or something, because he's really just having her on, isn't he, we decided…

Polonius, try and show the age of the man in your voice and in your bearing, rather than waving the bus-pass. I think you'll find it easier when we get the walking frame. Is that coming, Connie? OK.

The Players' scene: did any of you feel it had stretched a bit too…? Yes. I think we'll go back to the tumbling on the entrance, rather than the extract from *Barnum*. You see, we're running at six hours twenty now, and if we're going to put those soliloquies back in…

Gravediggers? Oh yes, gravediggers. The problem here is that Shakespeare hasn't given us a lot to play with – I feel we're a little short on laughs, so Harold, you do your dribbling, and Arthur, just put in anything you can remember from the Ayckbourn, yes?

The mad scene: apart from lines, much better, Barbara – I can tell you're getting more used to the straitjacket. Oh – any news on the skull, Connie? I'm just thinking, if your little dog pulls through, we'll have to fall back on papier mâché. All right, Connie, as long as it's dead by the dress...

Oh yes, Hamlet, Act Three, Scene One, I think that cut works very well, 'To be or not to be', then Ophelia comes straight in, it moves it on, it's more pacey...

Act Five, Gertrude, late again. What? Well, is there no service wash? I'm sure Dame Edith wasn't forever nipping out to feed the dryer.

That's about it – oh yes, Rosencrantz and Guildenstern, you're not on long, make your mark. I don't think it's too gimmicky, the tandem. And a most important general note – make up! Half of you looked as if you hadn't got any on! And Claudius – no moles again? [*Sighs.*] I bet Margaret Lockwood never left hers in the glove compartment.

That's it for tonight then; thank you. I shall expect you to be word-perfect by the next rehearsal. Have any of you realised what date we're up to? Yes, April the twenty-seventh! And when do we open? August! It's not long!

EXTENDED
COPYRIGHT